A Charming Fellow by Frances Eleanor Trollope

IN THREE VOLUMES

Frances Eleanor Trollope, née Ternan, was born in August 1835 on board a paddle steamer in Delaware Bay in the United States.

After an introduction by Charles Dickens she became the governess to the child of Thomas Adolphus Trollope, the brother to the more famed Anthony. Within months they had married and settled on a new life together in Rome. It was from here that Frances elevated her talents to become a full member of the Trollope writing dynasty

Her fiction is peopled by eccentric cosmopolitan Londoners, Italian and French visitors, and motherless, bright, and educated young women trying to carve out niches for themselves within the boundaries of the middle and upper-middle classes, with varying degrees of success.

Although her work was fashionable at the time it fell into obscurity after her death but is now becoming the subject of growing interest and deservedly so.

Index of Contents

VOLUME III

VOLUME I

CHAPTER I.

"To be frank with you, Mr. Diamond, I don't believe Dr. Bodkin understands my son's genius."

"I beg your pardon, madam, you said your son's—?"

"Genius, sir; the bent of his genius. Algy's is not a mechanical mind."

Mrs. Errington slightly tossed her head as she uttered the word "mechanical."

Mr. Diamond said "Oh!" and then sat silent.

The room was very quiet. The autumn day was fading, and the mingling of twilight and firelight, and the stillness of the scene, were conducive to mute meditation. It was a long, low room, with an uneven floor, a whitewashed ceiling crossed by heavy beams, and one large bow window. It was furnished with the spindle-legged chairs and tables in use in the last century. A crimson drugget covered the floor, and in front of the hearth lay a rug, made of scraps of black and coloured cloth, neatly sewn together in a pattern. Over the high wooden mantelpiece hung, on one side, a faded water-colour sketch of a gentleman, with powdered hair; and on the other, an oval miniature of much later date, which represented a fair, florid young lady, with large languid blue eyes, and a red mouth, somewhat too full-lipped. Notwithstanding the years which had elapsed since the miniature was painted, it was still sufficiently like Mrs. Errington to be recognised for her portrait. There was an old harpsichord in the room, and a few books on hanging shelves. But the only handsome or costly object to be seen were some delicate blue and white china cups and saucers, which glistened from an oaken corner-cupboard; and a large work-box of tortoise-shell, inlaid with mother-of-pearl, lined with amber satin, and fitted with all the implements of needlework, in richly-chased silver. The box, like the china cupboard, stood wide open to display its contents, and was evidently a subject of pride to its possessor. It was entirely incongruous with the rest of the furniture, which, although decent and serviceable, was very plain, and rather scanty.

Nevertheless the room looked snug and homelike. The coal-fire burnt with a deep glowing light; a small copper kettle was singing cheerily on the hob; tea-things were laid on a table in front of the fire; and a fitful, moaning wind, that rattled now and then against the antique casement, enhanced the comfort of the scene by its suggestion of forlorn chilliness without.

But however the influences of the time and place might incline Mr. Diamond to silence, they had no such effect on Mrs. Errington.

After a short pause, during which she seemed to be awaiting some remark from her companion, she observed once more, "No; I do not think the doctor understands Algy's genius. And that is why I was anxious to ask your advice, on this proposition of Mr. Filthorpe's."

"But, madam, why should you suppose me likely to understand Algernon better than Dr. Bodkin does?"

"Oh, because—In the first place, you are younger, nearer Algy's own age."

"Ah! There is a wide gap, though, between his eighteen and my eight-and-twenty—a wider gap than the mere ten years would necessarily make in all cases."

Mrs. Errington glanced at the speaker, and thought, in the maternal pride of her heart, that there was indeed a wide difference between her joyous, handsome Algernon, and Matthew Diamond, second master at the Whitford Grammar School; and she thought, too, that the difference was all to her son's advantage. Mr. Diamond was a grave-looking young man, with a spare, strong figure, and a face which, in repose, was neither handsome nor ugly. His clean-shaven chin and upper lip were firmly cut, and he had a pair of keen grey eyes. But such as it was, it was a face which most persons who saw it often, fell into a habit of watching. It raised an indefinite expectation. You were instinctively aware of something latent beneath its habitual expression of seriousness and reserve.

What the "something" might be, was variously guessed at according to the temperament of the observer.

"Then there is another reason why I wished to consult you," pursued Mrs. Errington. "I have a great opinion of your judgment, from what Algy tells me. I assure you Algy thinks an immense deal of your talents, Mr. Diamond. You must not think I flatter you."

"No," replied Mr. Diamond, very quietly, "I do not think you flatter me."

"And therefore I have told you the state of the case quite openly. And I would not have you hesitate to give your advice, from any fear of disagreeing with my opinion."

Mr. Diamond leaned his elbow on the table, and his face on his hand, which he held so as to hide his mouth—an habitual posture with him—and looked gravely at Mrs. Errington.

"I trust," continued the lady, "that I am superior to the weakness of requiring blind acquiescence from people."

Mrs. Errington spoke in a mellow, measured voice, and had a soft smiling cast of countenance. Both these were frequently contradicted in a startling manner by the words she uttered: for, in truth, the worthy lady's soul and body were no more like each other than a peach-stone is like a peach. Her velvety softness was not affected, but it was merely external, and the real woman was nothing less than tender. Sensitive persons did not fare very well with Mrs. Errington; who, withal, had the reputation of being an exceedingly good-natured woman.

"If you think my advice worth having—" said Mr. Diamond.

"I do really. Now pray don't be shy of speaking out!" interrupted the lady, reassuringly.

"I must tell you that I think your cousin's offer is much too good to be refused, and opens a prospect which many young men would envy."

"You advise us to accept it?"

"Yes."

"Why, then, Mr. Diamond, I don't believe you understand Algy one bit better than the doctor does!" exclaimed Mrs. Errington, leaning back in her chair, and folding her large white hands together in a resigned manner.

"I warned you, you know, that I might not," answered Mr. Diamond, composedly.

"'A prospect which many young men would envy!' Well, perhaps 'many young men,' yes; I daresay. But for Algy! Do but think of it, Mr. Diamond; to sit all day on a high stool in a musty office! You must own that, for a young fellow of my son's spirit, the idea is not alluring."

"Oh, if the question be merely for Algernon to choose some method of passing his time which shall be alluring—"

Mrs. Errington drew herself up a little. "No;" said she, "that is certainly not the question, Mr. Diamond. At the same time, before embracing Mr. Filthorpe's offer, I thought it only reasonable to ask myself, 'May we not do better? Can we not do better?'"

"I begin to perceive," thought Matthew Diamond within himself, "that Mrs. Errington's meaning, when she asks 'advice,' is pretty much like that of most of her neighbours. Having already made up her mind how to act, she would like to be told that her decision is the best and wisest conceivable." He said nothing, however, but bowed his head a little, to show that he was giving attention to the lady's discourse.

"We have an alternative, you must know," said Mrs. Errington, turning her eyes languidly on Mr. Diamond, but not moving her head from its comfortable resting-place against the back of her well-cushioned arm-chair. "We are not bound hand and foot to this Bristol merchant. By the way, you spoke of him as my cousin—"

"I beg your pardon; is he not so?"

"No; not mine. My poor husband's," with a glance at the portrait over the mantelpiece. "None of my family ever had the remotest connection with commerce."

"Ha! The good fortune was all on the side of the Erringtons?"

This time Mrs. Errington turned her head, so as to look full at her interlocutor. There met her view the same calm forehead, the same steady eyes, the same sheltering hand gently stroking the upper lip, which she had looked upon a minute before.

"My good sir!" she answered, in a tone of patient explanation, "my own family, the Ancrams, were people of the very first quality in Warwickshire. My grandfather never stirred out without his coach and four!"

"Ah!"

"Oh, yes, Algy's prospects in life ought to be very, very different from what they are. Of course he ought to go to the university; but I cannot afford to send him there. I make no secret of my circumstances. College is out of the question for him, poor boy, unless he entered himself as a what-do-you-call-it? A sort of pauper, a sizar. And I suppose you would hardly advise him to do that!"

"No; I should by no means advise it. I was a sizar myself."

"Really? Ah well, then you know what it is. And I am quite sure it would never suit Algy's spirits."

"I am quite sure it would not."

Mrs. Errington's good opinion of the tutor's judgment, which had been considerably shaken, began to revive.

"I see you know something of his character," said she, smiling. "Well, then, the case stands thus; Algy is turned eighteen; he has had the best education I could give him—indeed, my chief motive for settling in this obscure little hole, when I was left a widow, was the fact that Dr. Bodkin, who was an old acquaintance of my husband, was head of the Grammar School here, and I knew I could give my boy the education of a gentleman—up to a certain point—at small expense. He has had this offer from the Bristol man, and he has had another offer of a very different sort from my side of the house."

"Indeed!"

"Oh, yes; perhaps if I had began by stating that circumstance, you might have modified your advice, eh, Mr. Diamond?" This was said in a tone of mild raillery.

"Why," answered Mr. Diamond, slowly, "I must own that my advice usually does depend somewhat on my knowledge of the circumstances of the case under consideration."

"Now, that's candid—and I love candour, as I told you. The fact is, Lord Seely married an Ancram."

There was a pause. Mrs. Errington looked inquiringly at her companion. "You have heard of Lord Seely?" she said.

"I have seen his name in the newspapers, in the days when I used to read newspapers."

"He is a most distinguished nobleman."

Another pause.

"Well," continued Mrs. Errington, condescendingly, "I cannot expect all that to interest you, Mr. Diamond. Perhaps there may be a little family partiality, in my estimate of Lord Seely. However, be that as it may, he married an Ancram. She was of the younger branch, my father's second cousin. When Algy first began to turn his thoughts towards a diplomatic career—"

"Eh?"

"A diplomatic—Oh, didn't you know? Yes; he has had serious thoughts of it for some time."

"Algernon?"

"Certainly! And, in confidence, Mr. Diamond, I think it would suit him admirably. I fancy it is what his genius is best adapted for. Well, when I perceived this bent in him, I made—indirectly—application to Lady Seely, and she returned—also indirectly—a most gracious answer. She should be happy to receive Mr. Algernon Ancram Errington, whenever she was in town."

"Is that all?"

"All?"

"All that you have to tell me, to modify—and so on?"

"That would lead to more, don't you see? Lord Seely has enormous influence, and I don't know anyone better able to push the fortunes of a young man like Algy."

"But has he promised anything definite?"

"He could hardly do that, seeing that, as yet, he knows nothing of my son whatever! My dear Mr. Diamond, when you know as much of the world as I do, you will see that it does not do to rush at things in a hurry. You must give people time. Especially a man like Lord Seely, who of course cannot be expected to—to—"

"Do you mean that you seriously contemplate dropping the substance of Filthorpe, for this shadow of Seely?"

"Mr. Diamond! What very extraordinary expressions!"

Mr. Diamond took his hand from his mouth, clasped both hands on his knee, and sat looking into the fire as abstractedly as if there had been no other person within sight or sound of him.

Mrs. Errington, apparently taking it for granted that his attitude was one of profound attention to herself, proceeded flowingly to justify her decision, for it evidently was a decision—to decline the Bristol merchant's offer of employment and a home for her son. Besides Algy's "genius," there were other objections. Mr. Filthorpe had a vulgar wife and a vulgar daughter. Of course they must be vulgar. That was clear. And who could say that they might not endeavour to entangle Algy in some promise, or engagement, to marry the daughter? Nay, it was very certain that they would make such an endeavour. Possibly—probably—that was old Filthorpe's real object in inviting his young relative to accept a place in his counting-house. Indeed, they might confidently consider that it was so. Of course Algy would be a bait to these people! And as to Lord Seely, Mr. Diamond did not know (how should he? seeing that he had been little more than a twelvemonth in Whitford, and out of that time had scarcely ever had an hour's converse with her) that she, Mrs. Errington, was a person rather apt to hide and diminish, than unduly blazon forth her family glories. And she was, moreover, scrupulous to a fault in the accuracy of all her statements. Nevertheless, she must say that there was, perhaps, no nobleman in England whose patronage would have more weight than his lordship's; and whether or not the brilliancy of Algy's parts, and the charm of his manners, would be likely to captivate a man of Lord Seely's taste and cultivation; that she left to the sense and candour of any one who knew, and could appreciate her son.

Mr. Diamond uttered an odd, smothered kind of sound.

"Eh?" said Mrs. Errington, mellifluously.

There was no answer.

"Hulloa!" cried a blithe voice, as the door was suddenly thrown open. "Why, you're all in the dark here!"

"Dear me!" exclaimed Mr. Diamond, jumping to his feet, and then sitting down again, "I believe—I'm afraid I was almost asleep!"

CHAPTER II.

Algernon Errington came gaily into the dim room bringing with him a gust of fresh, cold air. His first act was to stir the fire, which sent up a flickering blaze. The light played upon the tea-table and the two persons who sat at it; and also, of course, illuminated the new comer's face and form, which were such as to justify much of his mother's pride in his appearance. He was of middle height, with a singularly elegant figure, and finely-shaped hands and feet. His smooth, blooming face was, perhaps, somewhat too girlish-looking, but there was nothing effeminate in his bearing. All his movements were springy and elastic. His blue eyes—less large, but more bright than his mother's—were full of vivacity, and a smile of mischievous merriment played round his mouth.

"Mr. Diamond!" he exclaimed, as soon as he perceived who was the other occupant of the room besides his mother.

"You're late," said the tutor, pulling from his waistcoat-pocket a large silver watch, and examining the clumsy black figures on its face by the firelight.

"Why," said Algernon, "I had no idea you were here! I thought my mother had sent word to ask you to put off our reading this evening. You promised to write a note, mother. Didn't you send it?"

It appeared that Mrs. Errington had not sent a note, had not even written one, had forgotten all about it. Her mind was so full of other things! And then when Mr. Diamond appeared, she did not explain at once that Algernon would probably not come home in time for his lesson, because she wanted to have a little conversation with Mr. Diamond. And they began to talk, and the time slipped away: besides, she knew that Mr. Diamond had nothing to do of an evening, so it was not of much consequence, was it?

Algernon winced at this speech, and cast a quick, furtive look at his tutor, who, however, might have been deaf, for any sign he gave of having heard it. He rose from his chair, and addressing Mrs. Errington, declared with his usual brevity that, as no work was to be done, he must forthwith wish her "Good evening."

"Now, no nonsense!" said Mrs. Errington. "You'll do nothing of the kind! Stay and have a cup of tea with us for once in a way."

"Thank you, no; I never—it is not my habit—"

"Not your habit to be sociable! I know that; and it is a great pity. What would you be doing at home? Only poring over books until you got a headache! A little cheerful society would do you all the good in the world. You were all but dropping asleep just now: and no wonder! I'm sure, after teaching all day in a close school, full of boys buzzing like so many blue-bottles, one would feel as stupid as an owl oneself!"

"Perhaps I am peculiarly susceptible to stupefying influences," said Mr. Diamond, with a rueful shake of the head. And, as he spoke, there played round his mouth the faint flicker of a smile.

"Now put your hat down, and take your seat!" cried Mrs. Errington, authoritatively.

"I am very sorry to seem ungrateful, but—"

"I had asked little Rhoda to come up after tea and keep me company, thinking I should be alone. But you won't mind Rhoda. She knows her place."

Mr. Diamond paused in the act of buttoning his coat across his breast. "You are very kind," he murmured.

"There, sit down, and I will undertake to give you a cup of excellent tea. I hope you know good tea when you get it? There are some people who couldn't tell my fine Pekoe from sloe-leaves. Algy, bring me the kettle."

And Mrs. Errington betook herself to the business of making tea. To her it seemed perfectly natural—almost a matter of course—that Matthew Diamond should stay, since she was kind enough to press it. But Algernon, who knew his tutor better, could not refrain from expressing a little surprise at his yielding.

"Why, mother," said he, as he poured the boiling water into the tea-pot, "you may consider yourself singled out for high distinction. Mr. Diamond has consented at your request to stay after having said he would go! I don't believe there's another lady in Whitford who has been so honoured."

If Algernon had not been peering through the clouds of steam, to ascertain whether the tea-pot were full or not, he would have perceived an unwonted flush mount in Matthew Diamond's face up to the roots of his hair, and then slowly fade away.

"And how did you find the doctor and all of them?" asked Mrs. Errington of her son, when they were all seated at the tea-table.

"Oh, the doctor's all right. He only came in for a few minutes after morning school."

"What did he say to you, Algy?"

"Oh, I don't know: something about not altogether neglecting my studies now I had left school, whatever path in life I chose. He always says that sort of thing, you know," answered Algernon carelessly.

"And Mrs. Bodkin?"

"Oh, she's all right, too."

"And Minnie?"

"Oh, she's all—no; she was not quite so well as usual, I think. Mrs. Bodkin said she had had a bad attack of pain in the night. But Minnie didn't mention it. She never likes to be condoled with and pitied, you know. So of course I didn't say anything. It's so unpleasant to have to keep noticing people's health!"

"Poor thing!" said Mrs. Errington. "What a misfortune for that girl to be a helpless invalid for the rest of her life!"

"Is her disorder incurable?" asked Mr. Diamond.

"Oh, quite, I believe. Spine, you know. An accident. And they say that when a child she was such an active creature."

"Her brain is active enough now," observed Mr. Diamond musingly, with his eyes fixed on the fire. "I don't know a keener, quicker intellect."

"What, Minnie Bodkin?" exclaimed Algernon, pausing in the demolition of a stout pile of sliced bread and butter. "I should think so! She's as clever as a man! I mean," he added, reading and answering his tutor's satirically-raised eyebrows, as rapidly as though he were replying to an articulate observation, "I mean—of course I know she's a deuced deal cleverer than lots of men. But I mean that Minnie Bodkin is clever after a manly fashion. Not a bit Missish. By Jove! I wish I knew as much Greek as she does!"

"I do not at all approve of blue-stockings in general," said Mrs. Errington; "but in her case, poor thing, one must make allowances."

"I think she's pretty," announced Algernon, condescendingly.

"She would be if she didn't look so sickly. No complexion," said Mrs. Errington, intently observing her own florid face, unnaturally elongated, in the bowl of a spoon.

"Don't you think her pretty, sir?" asked Algernon, turning to Mr. Diamond.

"A great deal more than pretty."

"You don't go there very often, I think?" said Mrs. Errington interrogatively.

"No, madam."

"Well, now, you really ought. I know you would be welcome. The doctor has more than once told me so. And Mrs. Bodkin is so very affable! I'm sure you need not hesitate about going there."

Algernon jumped up to replenish the tea-pot, with an unnecessary amount of bustle, and began to rattle out a volley of lively nonsense, with the view of diverting his mother's attention from the subject of Mr. Diamond's neglect of the Bodkin family. He dreaded some rejoinder on the part of the tutor which should offend his mother beyond forgiveness. He had had experience of some of Matthew Diamond's blunt speeches, of which Dr. Bodkin himself was supposed to be in some awe. It was clearly no business of Mrs. Errington's where Mr. Diamond chose to bestow his visits; neither could she in any degree be aware what reasons he might have for his conduct. "And the worst of it is, he's quite capable of telling my mother so, if she goes too far," reflected Algernon. So he chatted and laughed, as if from overflowing good spirits, until the peril was past. This young gentleman was so quick and flexible, and had so buoyant a temperament, that he was reputed more careless and thoughtless than was altogether the case. His mind moved rapidly, and he had an instinctive habit of uttering the result of its calculations, in the most impulsive way imaginable. You could not tell, by observing Algernon's manner, whether he were giving you his first thought or his second.

When the meal was over, Mrs. Errington rang to have the table cleared. A little prim servant-maid, in a coarse, clean apron and bib, appeared at the sound of the bell, and began to gather the tea-things together. Algernon sat down at the old harpsichord, and, after playing a few chords, commenced singing softly in a pleasant tenor voice some fragments of sentimental ballads in vogue at that day. (Does the reader ask, "and when was 'that day?'" He must content himself with the information that it was within a year or two of the year 1830.) Mr. Diamond walked to the window, and holding aside the blind, stood looking out at the dark sky.

All at once, when the servant opened the door to go out, there came up from the lower part of the house the sound of singing; slow, long-drawn, rather tuneless singing of a few voices, male and female.

"Oh dear, oh dear, oh dear!" exclaimed Mrs. Errington, "Oh dear me, Sarah, how is this?"

Algernon made a comical face of disgust, and put his hands to his ears.

"It be as Mr. Powell's ha' come back, mum," said Sarah, with much gravity.

"Really! Really!" said Mrs. Errington, in the tone of one protesting against an utterly unjustifiable offence.

"Come back! Where has he been?" asked Algernon, carelessly.

"On 'is rounds, please, sir."

"I do wish Mr. Powell would choose some other time for his performances!" cried Mrs. Errington, when the servant had left the room. "Now Thursday—on Thursday, for instance, we are going to a whist party, at the Bodkins', and then he might squall out his psalms, and shout, and rave, without annoying anybody."

"He'd only annoy the neighbours," said Algernon, "and that wouldn't matter!"

He was smiling with a sort of contemptuous amusement, and touching random notes here and there on the harpsichord with one finger.

"There will be no getting Rhoda upstairs to-night," said Mrs. Errington. "Poor little thing! she's in for a whole evening of psalm-singing."

Algernon rose from the instrument with a clouded brow. His face wore the petulant look of a spoiled child, whose will has been unexpectedly crossed.

"Deuce take Mr. Powell, and all Welsh Methodists like him!" said he.

"My dear Algy! No, no; I cannot approve of that, though Mr. Powell is a Dissenter. Besides, such language in my presence is not respectful."

"Beg pardon, ma'am," said Algernon, laughing. And with the laughter, the cloud cleared from his brow. Clouds never rested there long.

"Will you have a game of cribbage with me, Mr. Diamond? This naughty boy will scarcely ever play with me. Or, if you prefer it, dummy whist—?"

"No whist for me," interposed Algernon, decisively. "It is such a botheration. And I play so atrociously that it would be cruel to ask Mr. Diamond to sit down with me."

With that he returned to the harpsichord, and began singing softly to himself in snatches.

"Cribbage then?" said Mrs. Errington in her mellow, measured tones.

Mr. Diamond let fall the blind from his hand so roughly that the wooden roller rattled against the wainscot, and advanced to the table where Mrs. Errington was already setting forth the cards and cribbage-board. He sat down without a word, cut the cards as she directed, shuffled, dealt, and played in a moody sort of silent manner; which, however, did not affect Mrs. Errington's nerves at all.

Meanwhile, there went on beneath Algernon's love-songs and the few utterances of the players which the game necessitated, a kind of accompanying "bourdon" of voices from downstairs. Sometimes one single voice would rise in passionate tones, almost as if in wrath. Then came singing again, which, softened by distance, had a wild, wailing character of ineffable melancholy. Algernon paused in his fitful playing and singing, as though unwilling to be in dissonance with those long-drawn sounds. Mrs. Errington calmly continued to exclaim, "Fifteen six," and "two for his heels," without regard to anything but her game.

When the rubber was at an end, Mr. Diamond rose to take his leave.

He lingered a little in doing so. He lingered in taking up his hat, and in buttoning his coat across his breast.

"Have you not anything warmer to put on?" said Mrs. Errington. "Dear me, it is very wrong to go out of this snug room into the air—and the wind has got up, too!—with no more wrap than you have been sitting in, here by the fire! Algy, lend him your great-coat."

"Thank you, no. Good night," said the tutor, and walked off without further ceremony.

He still lingered, however, in descending the stairs; and yet more in passing the door of a parlour, whence came a murmur of voices. Finally, he let himself out at the street-door, and encountering a bleak gust of wind, set off down the silent street at a round pace.

"What a fool you are, Matthew!" was his mental ejaculation, as he strode along with his head bent down, and his gloveless hands plunged deep into his pockets.

CHAPTER III.

Mrs. Errington had lodged in Mr. Maxfield's house ever since she first came to Whitford. Jonathan Maxfield, commonly called "Old Max," kept a general shop in that town. The shop was underneath Mrs. Errington's sitting-room, and the great bow window, of which mention has been made, jutted out beyond the shop front, and overhung the street. The house was old, and larger than it appeared from the street, running back some distance. There was a private entrance—a point much insisted upon by Mr. Maxfield's sister-in-law and housekeeper in letting the lodgings to Mrs. Errington—and a long passage divided the shop entirely from the dwelling rooms on the ground-floor.

Old Max was reported to be somewhat of a miser (which report he rather encouraged than the reverse, finding that it had its conveniences), and to have amassed a large sum of money for one in his position in life.

"Old Max!" Whitford people would say. "Why, old Max could buy up half the town. Old Max might retire to-morrow. Old Max has no need ever to stand behind a counter again."

Old Max, however, continued to stand behind his counter day after day, as he had done for the last thirty or forty years, and would serve a child with a pennyworth of gingerbread, or a rich man's cook with stores of bacon and flour, in an impartially crabbed manner.

He was a grey man: grey from head to foot. He had grey hair, closely cropped; twinkling grey eyes; and a grey stubble on his shaven chin. He usually wore a suit of coarse grey clothes, with black calico sleeves tied on at the elbow. But even these had an iron-grey hue, from being more or less dusted with flour; as, indeed, were all his garments, and even his face.

When Mrs. Errington first came to live in Whitford, Jonathan Maxfield was a widower for the second time. He had two sons by his first wife; and, by his second, one daughter, whose birth cost her mother's life. The sister of his first wife had kept house for him ever since his second widowhood. This woman, Betty Grimshaw by name, had been servant in a great family; and at her master's death had received a legacy, which, together with her own savings, had sufficed to purchase a small annuity. She had been able to lay by the greater part of her annuity since she had lived in Whitford, and announced her intention of bequeathing her savings to her nephew James, Maxfield's second son. The elder son had married a farmer's daughter with some money, and turned farmer himself within a few miles of Whitford. Thus the family living at home on the autumn night on which our story opens, consisted of Jonathan Maxfield, Betty Grimshaw his sister-in-law, his son James, and his daughter Rhoda.

The sound of the street-door closing violently behind Mr. Diamond, startled this family party assembled in the parlour, together with Mr. David Powell, Methodist preacher.

They were all seated at a table, on which lay hymn-books and a large bible. Old Maxfield sat nearest to the fire, in his grey suit, just as he appeared in his shop, except that the black calico sleeves had been removed from his coat. He had a harsh face, a harsh voice, and a harsh manner. So much could be observed by any who exchanged ten words with him.

Next to him, on his left hand, sat his son James, a tall, sickly-looking young man, of six-and-twenty. He had a stoop in the shoulders, a pale face, with high cheek-bones, eyes deeply set, light eyebrows, which grew in thick irregular tufts, and hair of a reddish flaxen colour. There was a certain family likeness between him and his aunt, Mrs. Grimshaw, as she was called in Whitford, despite her spinsterhood. She too was tall, bony, and hard-featured; with a face which looked as if it had been painted and varnished, and reminded one, in its colour and texture, of those hollow wooden pears, full of tiny playthings, which used to be—and probably still are—sold at country fairs, and in toy-shops of a humble kind.

The preacher sat next to Betty Grimshaw. He seemed to belong to a different order of beings from the three persons already described.

A striking face this—dark, and full of fire. He had sharply-cut, handsome features, and eyes that seemed to blaze with inward light when he spoke earnestly. His raven-black hair was worn long, and fell straight on to his collar. But although this made his aspect strange, it could not render it either vulgar or ludicrous. The black locks set off his pale dark face, as in a frame of ebony. He was young, and seemed vigorous, though rather with nervous energy than muscular strength.

The last person in the group was Rhoda Maxfield—"little Rhoda," as Mrs. Errington had called her. But the epithet had been used to express rather her social insignificance, than her physical proportions. Rhoda was, in fact, rather tall. She was about nineteen years old, but scarcely looked her age. She had a broad and beautiful brow, on which the rich chestnut hair was smoothly parted; a sensitive mouth, not over-small; and bright hazel eyes, which looked out on the world with an open gaze, that was at once timid and confiding. Her skin was of remarkable delicacy, with a faint flush on the cheeks, which came and went frequently.

And yet Rhoda Maxfield was not much admired among her own compeers. There was something in her face which did not please the taste of the vulgar. And although, if you had asked Whitford persons "Is not Rhoda Maxfield wonderfully pretty?" most of those so addressed would have answered, "Yes, Rhoda is a pretty girl;" yet the assent would probably have been cold and uncertain.

Rhoda, at nineteen years old, had never been known to have a sweetheart. And this fact militated against the popular appreciation of her beauty; for a very cursory observation of the world will suffice to show that on the score of good looks, as on most other subjects, public opinion is apt to find nothing successful but success.

"What a wind there must be, to make the door bang like that!" exclaimed Betty Grimshaw, when the loud sound above recorded reached her ears.

"Who went out?" asked James.

"I suppose it would be that Mr. Diamond, the schoolmaster," replied his aunt.

They both spoke in a subdued voice, and cast furtive glances at Mr. Maxfield, as though fearful of being reprehended for interrupting the evening devotions; but, as they spoke, he closed his hymn-book, and drew his chair away from the table towards the fireside. Upon this signal, Betty Grimshaw rose and bustled out of the room, declaring that she must see about getting the supper; for that that little Sarah could never be trusted to see to the roasted potatoes alone. There was a suspicious alacrity in Betty's departure, suggestive that she experienced some sense of relief at the breaking-up of the devotions. James soon sauntered out of the room after his aunt. Mr. Powell rose.

"Good night," said he, holding out his hand to the old man.

"Nay; won't you stay and eat with us, Brother Powell? The supper will be ready directly."

Mr. Powell shook his head. "You know I never eat supper," he said, smiling.

"Well, well; perhaps you're in the right," responded old Max, very readily.

"And I am not clear," continued the preacher, "but that it would be better for you to leave off the habit."

"Me? Oh, no! I need it for my health's sake."

"But would it not suit your health better, to take your supper early? Say at six o'clock or so; so that you should not go to bed with a full stomach."

"No; it wouldn't," answered the old man, crabbedly.

David Powell stood meditating, with his hand to his chin. "I am not clear about it," he murmured. But Maxfield either did not hear, or chose to ignore the words.

"Father, may I go upstairs to Mrs. Errington?" asked Rhoda, softly; "I don't want any supper."

The old man grunted out an inarticulate sound, and seemed to hesitate. "Go upstairs to Mrs. Errington?" he said, answering his daughter, but looking sideways at the preacher. "Let's see; you promised, didn't you?"

"Yes; you gave me leave, and I promised before—before we knew that Mr. Powell would come to-night."

Rhoda was gifted with a sweet voice by nature, and she spoke with a purer accent, and expressed herself with greater propriety, than the other members of her family. Mrs. Errington had amused herself with teaching the motherless girl, who had been a lonely, shy, little child when their acquaintance first began. And Rhoda was a quick and apt scholar.

"Well—a promise—I can't have you break your word. Don't you stay late, mind. Not one minute after ten o'clock; do you mind, Rhoda?"

Rhoda, with a bright smile of pleasure on her face, promised to obey, and left the room with a step which it cost her an effort to make as staid as she knew would be approved by her father and Mr. Powell. When she got outside the door, they heard her run along the passage as light and as swift as a greyhound.

Maxfield turned to Mr. Powell, with a little constrained, apologetic air, and began expatiating on Mrs. Errington's fondness for Rhoda; and how kind she had always been to the girl; and how he thought it a duty almost, to let the good, widowed lady have as much of Rhoda's company as she could give her without neglecting duties.

"Betty Grimshaw is a worthy woman," he observed, drily; "but no companion for my Rhoda. Rhoda features her mother, and has her mother's nature very much."

Mr. Powell still stood in the same meditative attitude, with his hand to his chin.

"This Mrs. Errington is unconverted?" he said, without raising his eyes.

"Oh, Rhoda won't take much harm from that!"

"Much harm?" The dark lustrous eyes were upraised now, and fixed searchingly on the old man.

"Well, it won't do her any harm," the latter answered, testily. "I know Rhoda; and I have her welfare at heart, as, I suppose, you'll believe. I don't know who should have, if it isn't me!"

"Brother Maxfield," said the preacher, earnestly, "are you sure that you have a clear leading in this matter? Have you prayed for one?"

Maxfield shifted in his chair, and made no answer.

"Oh, consider what you do in trusting that tender soul among worldlings! I do not say that these are wicked people in a carnal sense; but are they such as can edify or strengthen a young girl like Rhoda, who is still in a seeking state, and has not yet that blessed assurance which we all supplicate for her?"

"I have laid the matter before the Lord," said Maxfield, almost sullenly.

Powell was silent for a minute, standing with his hands forcibly clasped together, as though to control them from vehement action, and when next he spoke, his voice had a tone in it which told of a strong effort of will to keep it in subdued monotony.

"Then, have you thought of it?" said he; "there is the young man Algernon."

"What of Algernon?" cried Maxfield, turning sharply to face the preacher.

"He is fair to look upon, and specious, and has those graces and talents which the world accounts lovely. May there not be a snare here for Rhoda? She who is so alive to all beauty and graciousness in God's world, and in God's creatures—may it not be very perilous for her to be thrown unguardedly into the society of this youth?"

Maxfield looked into the fire instead of at Powell, as he said, "What has been putting this into your head?"

"I have had a call to say it to you, for some time past. Before I went away this summer it was on my mind. I sinned in resisting the call, for—for reasons which matter to no one but myself. I sinned in putting any human reasons above my Master's service."

"It may be as you would have done better to resist speaking now," said Maxfield, slowly. "It may be as it was rather a temptation, than a leading from Heaven, made you speak at all."

Powell started back as if he had been struck. The blood rushed into his face, and then, suddenly receding, left him paler than before. But he answered after a moment in a low, sweet voice, and without a trace of anger, "You cannot mistrust me more than I mistrusted myself. But I have wrestled and prayed; and I am assured that I have spoken this thing with a single heart."

"Well, well, well, it may be as you say," said Maxfield, a shade less harshly than he had spoken before. "But you have neither wife, nor daughter, nor sister, and you cannot understand these matters as well as I do, who am more than double your years, and have had the guidance of this young maid from a baby upward."

"Nay," answered Powell, humbly; "it is not my own wisdom I am uttering! God forbid that I should set up my carnal judgment against a man of your years."

"That's very well said—very rightly said!" exclaimed Maxfield, nodding twice or thrice.

"Aye, but I must speak when my conscience bids me. I dare not resist that admonition for any human respect."

"Why, to be sure! But do you think yours is the only conscience to be listened to? I tell you I follow mine, young man. And you can ask any of our brethren here in Whitford, who have known me for the last thirty or forty years, whether I have gone far astray!"

Powell sighed wearily. "I have released my soul," he said.

"And just hearken," pursued old Maxfield, in a lowered voice, "don't say a word of this sort to Rhoda—nay, don't interrupt me! I've listened to your say, now let me have mine—because you might be putting something into her thoughts that wouldn't have come there of itself. And keep a discreet tongue before Betty and James. 'Least said, soonest mended.' And I'll tell you something more. If—observe I say 'if'—I saw that Rhoda's heart was strongly set upon anything, anything as wasn't wrong in itself, I should be very loath to thwart her."

David Powell turned a startled, attentive face on the old man, who proceeded with a sort of dogged monotony of voice and manner: "Christian charity teaches us there's good folks in all communions of believers. And there's different ranks and different orders in the world; some has one thing, and some has another. Some has fine family and great connections among the rulers of the land. Others has the goods of this world earned by honesty, and diligence, and frugality; and these three bring a blessing. Some is fitted to be gentlefolks by nature, let 'em be born where they will. Others, like my sister-in-law Betty, is born to serve. We are all the Lord's creatures, and we are in his hand but as clay in the hands of the potter. But there's different kinds of clay, you know. This kind is good for making coarse delf, and that kind is fit for fine porcelain. We'll just keep these words as have passed between you and me, to ourselves, if you please. And now, I think, we may drop the subject."

"May the Lord give you his counsel!" said Powell, in a broken voice.

"Amen! I have had my share of wisdom, and have walked pretty straight for the last half century, thanks be to Him," observed old Max, drily.

"If it were His good pleasure, how gladly would I cease for evermore from speaking to you on this theme! But it matters nothing what I desire or shrink from. I must deliver my Master's message when it is borne in upon me to do so."

And with a solemnly uttered blessing on the household, the preacher departed.

The master of the house sat thinking, alone by his fireside. He began by thinking that he had a little over-encouraged David Powell. Maxfield considered praise from himself to be very encouraging, and calculated to uplift the heart. When Powell had first come among the Whitford Methodists, old Max had taken him by the hand, and had declared him to be the most awakening preacher they had had for many years. He was never tired of vaunting Powell's zeal, and diligence, and eloquence. Backsliders were brought again into the right way, sinners were awakened, believers were refreshed, under his ministry. The fame of Powell's preaching drew many unwonted auditors to the little chapel; and of those who came at first merely from curiosity, many were moved by his words to join the Wesleyan Connection. On all this Jonathan Maxfield looked with great satisfaction. The young man had been truly a burning and a shining light.

But now—might it not be that the preacher's heart had become puffed up with spiritual pride? Was he not unduly exalting himself, when he assumed a tone of censorship towards such a pillar of the community as Jonathan Maxfield? The old man had been for many years accustomed to much deference, alike from preachers and congregation. The exhortations and admonitions which were doubtless needful for his neighbours, were entirely out of place when addressed to himself. His piety and probity were established on a rock. And the Lord had, moreover, seen fit to gift him with so large a share of the wisdom of the serpent, as had enabled him to hold his own, and to thrive in the midst of worldlings. A dull fire of indignation against David Powell began to smoulder in the old man's heart, as he pondered these things.

Other thoughts, too, more or less disquieting, passed through his brain. He thought of Rhoda's mother—of that second wife whom he, a man past middle-life, had married for her fair young face and gentle ways, much to Betty Grimshaw's disgust, and the surprise of most people. He looked back on the long, dusty, dreary road of his life; and, in the whole landscape, the only spot on which the sun seemed to shine was that brief year of his second marriage. Not that he had been, or that he now was, an unhappy man. His life had satisfactions in it of a sober, sombre kind. He did not grow soft or sentimental in reviewing the past. He was accustomed to the chill, grey atmosphere in which he lived. But he had felt warm sunlight once, and remembered it. And he had a notion—inarticulate, indeed, and vague—that Rhoda needed more light and warmth in her life than was necessary for his own existence, or for James's, or Betty Grimshaw's, or, in fact, for most people's. There was no amount of hardness he could not be guilty of to "most people," and, indeed, he was hard enough to himself; but for Rhoda there was a soft place in his heart.

Nevertheless, there were many hopes, fears, speculations, and reflections connected with Rhoda just now, which had anything but a softening effect on Mr. Maxfield's demeanour; insomuch that Betty and James, coming in presently to supper, found the head of the family in so crabbed a temper, that they were glad to hurry through the meal in silence, and slink off to bed.

CHAPTER IV.

Mention has been made of a whist-party at Dr. Bodkin's, to which Mrs. Errington announced her intention of going. It took place on the Thursday after that evening on which Mrs. Errington was first introduced to the reader: that is to say, on the second night following.

Whist-parties were almost the only social entertainment ever given amongst the genteel persons in Whitford. The Rev. Cyrus Bodkin, D.D., liked his rubber; so did Robert Smith, Esq., M.R.C.S., and Mr. Dockett, the attorney, and Miss Chubb, and one or two more cronies, who were frequently seen at the doctor's green card-tables.

The Bodkins lived in a gloomy stone house adjoining the grammar-school, of which, indeed, it formed part. The house was approached by a gravelled courtyard, surrounded by high stone walls. The garden at the back ran sloping down to a broad green meadow, which in turn was bounded by the little river Whit, all overhung with willows, and covered by a floating mass of broad water-lily leaves, just opposite the doctor's garden gate.

In the full summer time, the view from the back of the house was pretty and pastoral enough. But in autumn and winter the meadow was a swamp, whose vivid green looked poisonous—as indeed it was, exhaling ague and rheumatism from its plashy surface—and a white brooding mist trailed itself, morning and evening, along the sluggish Whit, like a fallen cloud, condemned by some angry prince of the air to crawl serpent-like on earth, instead of soaring and sailing in the empyrean.

Such fancies never came into Doctor Bodkin's head, however, nor into his wife's either—good, anxious, unselfish, sad, little woman! Into his daughter Minnie's brain all sorts of wild, fantastic notions would intrude as she lay on her sofa, looking out upon the garden, and the river, and the meadow, and the gnarled old willows, and the flying scud in the sky; but she very seldom spoke of her fancies to any one. She spoke of other matters, though, freely enough. She had many visitors, who came and sat around her couch, or beside the lounging-chair, on which, on her good days, she reclined. She was better acquainted with the news of Whitford than most of the people who could use their limbs to go abroad and see what was passing. She was interested in the progress of the boys at the grammar-school, and knew the names, and a good deal about the characters, of every one of them. She would chat, and laugh, and joke by the hour with the frequenters of her father's house; but of herself—of her own thoughts, feelings, and fancies—Minnie Bodkin said no word to them. Nor did she, in truth, ever speak much on that subject all her life. And there were days—black days in the calendar of her poor anxious little mother—when Minnie would remain shut into her room, refusing to see or speak with anyone, and suffering much pain of body, with a proud stoicism which rejected sympathy like a wall of granite.

There is no suggestion of granite about her now, however, as she lies, propped up by crimson cushions, on a sofa in her father's drawing-room. The room is bright and warm, despite the white kraken of mist that is coiled around the outer walls of the house. Wax-lights shine in tall, old-fashioned silver candlesticks on the mantelpiece, and on the centre table, and on a pianoforte, beside which stands a canterbury full of music-books. A great fire blazes in the grate, and makes its immediate neighbourhood too hot for the comfort of most people. But Minnie is apt to be chilly, and loves the heat. Some delicate ferns and hothouse plants adorn a stand between the windows. They are rather a rare luxury in Whitford; but Minnie loves flowers, and always has some choice ones about her. A still rarer luxury hangs on the wall opposite to her sofa, in the shape of a very fine copy—on a reduced scale—of Raphael's Madonna di San Sisto. Minnie had fallen in love with a print from that famous picture long ago, and the copy was procured for her at considerable pains and expense. The furniture of the room is of crimson and dark oak. Minnie delights in rich colours and picturesque combinations. In a word, there is not an inch of the apartment, from floor to ceiling, in the arrangement of which Minnie's tastes have not been consulted, and in which traces of Minnie's influence are not plainly to be seen by those who know that household.

Minnie has a face, which, if you saw it represented in time-darkened oil colours, and framed on the walls of a picture-gallery, you would pronounce strikingly beautiful. Such faces are sometimes seen in flesh and blood, and, strange to say, do by no means excite the same enthusiasm in ordinary beholders, who, for the most part, like the picturesque in a picture and nowhere else; and who, to paraphrase what was said of Voltaire's intellect, admire chiefly those women who have, more than other young ladies, the prettiness which all young ladies have.

Minnie's face is pale and rather sallow. Her skin is not transparent, but fine in texture, like fine vellum, and it seldom changes its hue from emotion. When it does, it grows dark-red or deadly-white. Pleasing blushes or pallors are never seen on it. She has dark, thick hair, worn short, and brushed away from a high, smooth, rounded forehead, in which shine a pair of bright brown eyes, under finely-arched eyebrows. But the beauty of the face lies in the perfection of its outlines: brow, cheeks, and chin are alike delicately moulded; her mouth—although the lips are too pale—is almost faultless, as are the white, small teeth she shows when she smiles. There is an indefinable air of sickness and suffering over this beautiful face, and dark traces beneath the eyes, and a pathetic, weary look in them sometimes; but, when she speaks or smiles, you forget all that.

There are people in this world whose intellects remind one of lamps too scantily supplied with oil. The little feeble flame in them burns and flickers, certainly, but it is but a dull sort of dead light after all. Now Minnie Bodkin's spirit-lamp, if the phrase may be permitted, illumined everything it shone upon, and there were some persons who found it a great deal too dazzling to be pleasant.

It is not at all too bright at this moment for Algernon Errington, who, seated close beside her couch, is giving her, sotto voce, a humorous imitation of the psalm-singing in old Max's parlour; and describing, with great relish, his mother's cool suggestion that the family prayers should be put off until she should be absent at a whist-party.

"Poor dear mother," says Algernon, smiling, "she can't forget that she is an Ancram; and sometimes comes out with one of her grande dame speeches, as if she were addressing my grandfather's Warwickshire tenantry forty years ago!" At which simple, candid words Minnie shoots out a queer, keen glance at the young fellow from under her eyelids.

"And the Methodist preacher—what is he like?" she asks. "Whitford is, or was, a little inclined to go crazed about him. I don't know whether the enthusiasm is burning itself out, as such fires of straw will do, but a few weeks ago I heard that the little Wesleyan chapel was crowded to overflowing whenever he preached; and that once or twice, when he addressed the people out of doors on Whit Meadow, there was such a multitude as never was seen there before. I was quite curious to see the man who could so move our sluggish Whitfordians."

Algernon had taken up a sheet of note-paper and a pen from Minnie's letter-writing table, whilst she was speaking. "Look here," he says, "here's the preacher!" And he holds out the paper on which he has drawn, with a few rapid strokes, a caricature of David Powell.

Minnie looks at it with raised eyebrows.

"Oh," says she, "is he like that? I am disappointed. This is the common, conventional, long-haired Methodist, that one sees in every comic print."

And in truth Algernon's portrait is not a good likeness, even for a caricature. He had drawn a lank, hook-nosed man, with long, black hair, expressed by two blots of ink falling on either side of his face.

"He wears his hair just like that!" says Algy, contemplating his own work with a good deal of satisfaction.

The card playing has not yet begun. Mrs. Bodkin, small, thin, with a questioning, sharp, little nose, and a chin which narrows off too suddenly, and an odd resemblance altogether to a little melancholy fox, is presiding at a tea-table. Besides tea and coffee, it is furnished with substantial cakes of many various kinds. Whitford people, for the most part, dine early, so that they are ready for solid food again by about eight o'clock; and will, probably, sustain nature once more with sandwiches and mulled wine before they sleep.

It is not a large party. There is Mrs. Errington, majestic in a dyed silk, and a real lace cap, the latter a relic of the "better days" she is fond of reverting to; Miss Chubb, a stout spinster, with a languishing fat face as round as a full moon, and little rings of hair gummed down all over her forehead, and half-way down her plump cheeks; Mr. Smith, the surgeon, black-eyed, red-faced, and smiling; the Rev. Peter Warlock, curate of St. Chad's, a serious, ghoul-like young man, who rends great bits out of his muffin with his teeth, in a way to make you shudder if you happen to be nervous or fanciful; Mr. Dockett, the attorney, and his wife, each dressed in black, each with a huge double chin and smothered voice, and altogether comically like one another.

On the hearth-rug, with his back to the fire, and his coffee-cup in his hand, stands Dr. Bodkin. He is short and thick. He has an air of command. He looks at the world in general as if it were liable to an "imposition" of ever so many hundred lines of Latin poetry, and as if he were ready to enforce the penalty at brief notice. He is not a hard man at heart, but nature has made him conceited, and habit has made him a tyrant. The boys kotoo to him in the school, and his wife bends submissively to his will at home. There is only one person in the world who habitually opposes and sets aside his assumption of infallibility, and that person—his daughter Minnie—he loves and fears. He tramples on most other people, in the firm persuasion that it is for their good. He is bald, large-faced, with a long upper-lip, which he shoots out into a funnel shape when he talks. He is an honest man in his calling, has a fair share of routine learning, and imparts it laboriously to the boys under his tuition.

Presently the people seem to slacken in eating and drinking. "Another cup of tea, Mrs. Errington? Won't you try any of that pound cake, Mr. Warlock?" (N.B. He has eaten three muffins unassisted; but they do not prosper with him. He has a hungry glare.) "Mrs. Dockett? No?" Mrs. Bodkin looks round, and lifts her meek, foxy little nose interrogatively at each member of the circle. No one will eat or drink more. The doctor prepares to make up the tables.

The card-tables are always set out in an inner drawing-room, adjoining that in which our friends are taking tea. Dr. Bodkin hates to hear any noise when he is at his rubber, so there are thick curtains before the door of communication between the two rooms; and the door is shut, and the curtains drawn, whenever Minnie desires to have music on whist evenings.

The sound of the piano penetrates to the card-players, nevertheless. But Mrs. Bodkin declares that she can never hear a note, when she is in the little drawing-room, with the door shut, and the curtains drawn. And although the doctor wears a frown on his bald forehead, and is more than ordinarily severe on his partner whenever the piano begins to sound during a game, yet he never takes any step to have the instrument silenced.

The players file off in the wake of the host. There is a quartet at the doctor's table. At another, Mrs. Dockett, Mrs. Warlock, and Mr. Smith play dummy. Algernon Errington hates cards, and—naturally—doesn't play. The Rev. Peter Warlock also hates cards, but is wanted to make up the rubber, and—naturally—plays. Mrs. Bodkin hovers between the two rooms, and Minnie and Algernon are left almost tête-à-tête.

"And so you really, really think of going to London?" says Minnie gravely.

"To seek my fortune!" answers Algernon, with a smile. "Turn a-gain, Er-ring-ton—I don't know why that shouldn't be rung out on Bow Bells. You see my name has the same number of syllables as Whit-ting-ton! I declare that is a good omen!"

"Whittington made himself useful to the cook, and took care of his kitten. I wonder what you will do, Algy, to deserve fortune?"

"Do you think fortune favours the deserving? They paint her as a woman!" cries Master Algernon, with a saucy grimace.

"Algy, I like you. We are old chums. Have you considered this step? Have you any reasonable prospect of making your way, if you refuse the Bristol man's proposition."

Minnie seldom speaks so earnestly as she is speaking now; still seldomer volunteers any inquiry into other people's affairs. Algernon is sensible of the distinction, and flattered by it. He forthwith proceeds to lay his hopes and plans before her; that is to say, he talks a great deal with astonishing candour and fluency, and says wonderfully little. His mother is so anxious; these Seeleys are her people. It would vex the dear old lady so terribly, if he were to prefer the Bristol side of the house! Though, perhaps, that would be, selfishly speaking, the right policy.

"Ah, I see!" exclaims Minnie, sinking back among her cushions when he has done speaking.

By-and-by, one or two more guests drop in: young Pawkins, of Pudcombe Hall, some six miles from Whitford; Lieutenant-Colonel Whistler, on half-pay, with his two nieces, Rose and Violet McDougall; and with them Alethea Dockett, who is still a day-boarder at a girls' school in Whitford, and has been spending the afternoon with the Misses McDougall. The latter young ladies never play whist. Little Ally Dockett sometimes takes a hand, if need be, and acquits herself not discreditably; but sixteen rushes in where two-and-thirty fears to tread. Rose and Violet are on the doubtful border-land of life, and keep up a brisk skirmishing warfare with their enemy, Time. They would not give that wily old traitor the triumph of putting themselves at a whist-table for—for anything short of a bonâ fide offer of marriage, with a good settlement.

All those guests Minnie receives very graciously, with a sort of royal condescension. She is quite unconscious that the Misses McDougall (of whose intelligence she has, truth to say, a disdainful estimate) are alive to the fact that she thinks them fools, and that they take a good deal of credit to themselves for bearing with her airs, poor thing! But then she is so afflicted!

"Oh, Minnie, what's that? Do let me see! Is it one of your caricatures, you wicked thing?" cries Rose, darting on the portrait of David Powell.

"It's better drawn than Minnie can do," says Violet, with an air of having evidence wrung from her on oath.

"It may be that, and yet not very good," answers Minnie carelessly. "Mr. Errington has been trying to give me an idea of some one I've never seen, and probably never shall see."

"It's the Methodist preacher, by Jove!" says young Pawkins with his glass in his eye. "I heard him and saw him last summer on Whit Meadow."

Colonel Whistler, after holding the paper out at the utmost stretch of his arm, solemnly puts on a pair of gold spectacles and examines it.

"Monstrous good!" he pronounces. "Very well, Errington! That's just the cut of that kind of fellow."

"Have you seen him, colonel?" asks Minnie.

"No—no; I can't say I have seen him. Don't like these irregular practitioners, Miss Minnie. But I know the sort of fellow. That's just the cut of 'em!"

"I wish I could draw, Miss Bodkin," says a voice behind Minnie at the head of the sofa; "I would show you a better likeness of the man than that!"

Minnie puts her thin white hand over her shoulder to the new comer, whom she cannot see. "Mr. Diamond!" she exclaims very softly.

"How can you tell?"

"I know your voice."

CHAPTER V.

The little group round Minnie's sofa dispersed as Mr. Diamond came forward. He was barely known by sight to most of them, and merely bowed gravely and shyly, without speaking.

"Who's that?" asked Colonel Whistler, in a loud whisper, of his eldest niece. "Eh? oh! ah! second master—yes, yes, yes; to be sure!" And the gallant gentleman walked off to the card-room, and joined the party at Mrs. Dockett's table, where there was a vacant place. It must be owned that the colonel's appearance was by no means rapturously hailed there. He was a notoriously bad player. Fate, however, allotted him as a partner to Mr. Warlock. Mrs. Dockett and Mr. Smith exchanged glances of satisfaction, and the gloom on Mr. Warlock's brow perceptibly deepened as the colonel, polite, smiling, and eager for the fray, took his seat opposite to that clerical victim.

"Algy, give Mr. Diamond your chair," said Miss Bodkin. It was in this imperious manner that she occasionally addressed her young friend. In her eyes he was still a school-boy. And then she was four years his senior, and had been a young woman grown when he was still playing marbles and munching toffy.

Algy by no means considered himself a school-boy, but he had excellent tact and temper. He rose directly, shook hands with his tutor, and then standing opposite to Minnie, put his knuckles to his forehead, after the fashion in vogue amongst rustic children by way of salute, and said meekly, "Yes'm, please'm."

Minnie laughed. "You don't mind, do you, Algernon?" she said, looking up at him.

"Not at all, Miss Bodkin. You have merely cast another blight over my young existence. I am growing to look like the reverend Peter, in consequence of your ill-usage. Don't you perceive a ghastly hue upon my brow? No? Ah, well, you would if you had any feeling. Here, let me put this cushion better for you. Will that do?"

"Capitally, thanks. And, look here, Algy; I can't bear any music to-night, so will you get mamma to set the McDougalls down to a round game? And play yourself, there's a good boy!"

"Oh, Minnie, you ought to have been Mrs. Nero. There never was such a tyrant. Well, Pawkins and I must make ourselves agreeable, I suppose. For England, home, and beauty—here goes!" And Algernon speedily had the two Miss McDougalls, and Mr. Pawkins, and Alethea Dockett engaged in a game of vingt-et-un—played in a very infantine manner by the first-named ladies, and with a good deal of business-like gravity by little Alethea, who liked to win.

Mr. Diamond looked at the group with his hand over his mouth, after his habit.

"Isn't he a nice fellow?" asked Minnie, watching Mr. Diamond's face curiously.

"Errington?"

"Of course!"

"Very."

"But now, tell me—do sit down here; I want to talk to you. You come so seldom. I wonder why you came to-night?"

"I chanced to meet Mrs. Bodkin in the street, and she asked me so pressingly—she is so good!"

Minnie's face wore a pained look. "It is a pity mamma should have teased you," she said, in a low voice.

Matthew Diamond took no notice of the words. Perhaps he did not hear them. "I am not fit to go to evening parties," he continued. "The very wax-lights dazzle me. I feel like a bat or an owl."

"Too wise for your company, that means!"

"How can you say so? No: I assure you I was compared to an owl the other evening by a lady, and I felt the justice of the comparison."

"By a lady! What lady?"

Mr. Diamond smiled a little amused smile at the authoritative tone of the question. Minnie did not see it. She was leaning her elbow on a cushion, and had her face turned towards Mr. Diamond; but her eyes, which usually looked out, open and unabashed, were half veiled by their lids.

"The lady was Mrs. Errington," answered the tutor, after a moment's pause.

"She called you an owl? That eagle? Well, she has this aquiline quality; I believe she could stare the sun himself out of countenance!"

"You were asking me to tell you—" said Mr. Diamond.

"To tell me—? Oh, yes; about the Methodist preacher. That caricature is not like him, you say?"

"Not at all. It is a vulgar conception of the man."

"And the man is not vulgar? I am glad of that! Tell me about him."

Matthew Diamond had heard the preacher more than once. The first time had been by chance on Whit Meadow. The other times were in the crowded, close Wesleyan chapel, into which he had penetrated at the cost of a good deal of personal inconvenience, so greatly had Powell's eloquence impressed him.

"The man is like a flame of fire," he said. "It is wonderful! He must be like Garrick, according to the descriptions I have heard. And, then, this fellow is so handsome—wild and oriental-looking. I always long to clap a turban on his head, and a great flowing robe over his shoulders."

Minnie listened eagerly, with parted lips, to all that Diamond would tell her of the preacher.

"That is for his manner," she said, at length. "Now, as to the matter?"

Mr. Diamond paused. "The man is an enthusiast, you know," he answered, gravely.

"But as to his doctrine? Give me some idea of the kind of thing he says."

"Not now."

"Yes; now. This moment."

"Excuse me; I cannot enter into the subject now."

Minnie raises her brown eyes to his steel-grey ones, and then drops her own quickly.

"Will you ever?" she asks, meekly.

"Perhaps. I don't know."

Miss Bodkin is not accustomed to be answered with such unceremonious curtness; but, perhaps on account of its novelty, Mr. Diamond's blunt disregard of her requests (in that house Minnie's requests have the weight of commands) does not ruffle her. She bears it with the most perfect sweetness, and proceeds to discourse of other things.

"Don't you think it a pity," she says, "that Algernon Errington should have refused his cousin's offer?"

"A great pity—for him."

"Ah! you think Mr. Filthorpe of Bristol is not to be condoled with on the occasion?"

Mr. Diamond's firmly closed lips remain immovable.

Minnie looks at him wistfully, and then says suddenly, "Do you know I like Algy very much! There is something so bright and winning and gay about him! I have known him so long—ever since he came here as a small child in a frock. And papa knew his father, Dr. Errington. He was a very clever man, a brilliant talker, and greatly sought after in society. Algy inherits all that. And he has—what they say his father had not—a temper that is almost perfect, thoroughly sound and sweet. I wish you liked him."

"Who tells you that I do not like him? You are mistaken in fancying so. I think Errington one of the most winning fellows I ever knew in my life."

"Y-yes; but you don't think so well of him as I do."

"Perhaps that is hardly to be expected! And pardon me, Miss Bodkin, but you don't know—"

"I know nothing about your thoughts on the subject!" interrupts Minnie quickly, and with a bright, mischievous glance. "Forgive my interrupting you; but when I am to have a cold shower-bath, I like to pull the string myself. Now it's over."

"You think me a terrible bear," says Diamond, looking down on her beautiful, animated face.

"Ah! take care. If I know nothing about your thoughts, how do you pretend to guess mine? Besides, I am not so zoological in my choice of epithets as your friend, Mrs. Errington. Papa nearly quarrelled with that lady on the subject of Algy's going away. But, you know, it is not all Mrs. Errington's fault. Algy chooses to try his fortune under the auspices of Lord Seely—I can see that plainly enough. And what Algy chooses his mother chooses. He has been terribly spoiled."

"It is a great misfortune—"

"To be spoiled?"

"For him to have lost his father when he was a child. Otherwise he might not have been so pampered: though fathers spoil their children sometimes!"

"Mine spoils me, I think. But then there is an excuse, after all, for spoiling me."

"My dear Miss Bodkin, you cannot suppose that I had any such meaning."

"You? Oh, no! You are honest: you never speak in innuendoes. But it is true, you know. My father and mother have spoiled me. Poor father and mother! I am but a miserable, frail little craft for them to have ventured so much love and devotion in!"

It was not in mortal man—not even in mortal man whose heart was filled with a passion for another woman—to refrain from a tender glance and a soft tone, in answer to Minnie's pathetic little plaint. Her beauty and her intellect might be resisted: her helplessness, and acknowledgment of peculiar affliction, could not be.

"Ah!" said Matthew Diamond; "who would not embark all their freight of affection in such a venture as the hope that you would love them again? I think your parents are paid."

It has been said that Mr. Diamond's calm, grave face raised an indefinite expectation in the beholder. When he said those words to Minnie Bodkin, you would have thought, if you had been watching him, that you had found the key of the puzzle, and that an ineffable tenderness was the secret that lay hid beneath that grave mask. The stern mouth smiled, the stern eyes beamed, the straight brows were lifted in a compassionate curve. Minnie had never seen his face with that look on it, and the change in it gave her a curious pang, half of pain, half of pleasure. Strong conflicting feelings battled in her. She was strung to a high pitch of excitement; and her eyes brightened, and her pulse beat quicker—all for a look, a smile, a beam of the eye from this staid, quiet schoolmaster! What do we know of the thought in our neighbour's brain? of the thrill that makes his heart flutter? We do not care for this air-bubble. How can he? It is yonder beautiful transparent ball, all radiant with prismatic colours, that we expend our breath upon. Up it goes—up, up, up—look! No; our stupid neighbour is watching his own airy sphere, which is not nearly so beautiful; and which, we know, will burst presently!

The game of vingt-et-un comes to an end. Almost at the same moment the whist-players break up, and come trooping into the drawing-room; trooping and talking rather noisily, to say the truth, as though to indemnify themselves for the silence which Doctor Bodkin insists upon during the classic game. Mrs. Bodkin bustles up to her daughter; hopes she is not tired; thinks she looks a little fagged; wonders why she did not have any music, as she generally likes Rose McDougall's Scotch ballads; supposes Mr. Diamond preferred not to play, as she sees he has been sitting out, and trusts he has not been bored.

But of all the people present, Mrs. Bodkin alone guesses that Minnie has enjoyed her evening, and why. And, with her mother's and woman's instinct, she knows that Minnie's pleasure would have been spoiled by guessing that it had been guessed. For the rest, this small anxious-faced woman cares but little. She would tear your feelings to mince-meat to feed the fancies of her daughter, as ruthlessly as any maternal vixen would slay a chicken for her cubs; although, for herself, no hare is milder or more timid.

The Misses McDougall are in good spirits. They have won, and they have had the two young men all to themselves, for Ally Dockett in short frocks doesn't count. Also Minnie Bodkin has kept aloof. That bright lamp of hers is not favourable to such twinkling little rushlights as Rose and Violet are able to display. But this evening they have not been quenched by a superior luminary, and are quite radiant and cheerful. Dr. Bodkin, too, is contented in his lofty manner; for there has been no music, and he has enjoyed his rubber in peace. Colonel Whistler has lost, but the stakes are always modest at Dr. Bodkin's table, and he doesn't mind it. Over the feelings of the Rev. Peter Warlock it will, perhaps, be best to draw a veil. The reverend gentleman stalks in, and sits down in a corner, whence he can stare at Minnie unobserved. It is the only comfort he enjoys throughout the evening. And for this he thinks it worth while to submit to the peine forte et dure of playing whist, with Colonel Whistler for his partner.

Mrs. Errington sails towards Minnie's sofa, and suddenly stops short, and opens her eyes very wide.

Mr. Diamond, who is the object of her gaze, rises and bows. "Good evening, madam," he says, unable to repress a smile at her manifest astonishment on beholding him there.

"Why, how do you do, Mr. Diamond? Dear me! I little expected to see you this evening. Dear Minnie, how are you now? Well, this is a surprise!"

Then, as Mr. Diamond moves away, Mrs. Errington takes his chair beside Minnie, and says to her confidentially—"Now, I hope, Minnie, you won't owe me a grudge for it; but I must confess that if it hadn't been for me, you wouldn't have had that gentleman to entertain this evening."

"What on earth do you mean?" cries Minnie, with scant ceremony, and flashes an impatient glance at the lady's soft, smiling, self-satisfied visage.

"My dear, I advised him to come here a little oftener. I think he felt diffident, you know, and all that. Poor man, he is rather dull, although Algy is always crying up his talents. But it really is kind to bring him forward a little. I asked him to tea the other night. You see he must feel it a good deal when people are affable, and so on, for"—here her voice sank to a whisper—"he told me himself that he had been a sizar."

With all which benevolent remarks Miss Bodkin is, of course, highly delighted. She does not forget them either; for after the negus has been drunk, and the sandwiches eaten, and the company has departed, she says to her father, "Papa, was Mr. Diamond a sizar?"

"I don't know, child. Very likely. None the worse for that, if he were."

"The worse! No!" returns Minnie, with a superb smile.

"Who says he was?"

"Mrs. Errington."

"Pooh! Ten to one it isn't true then. She has her good points, poor woman, but the Ancrams are all liars; every one of them! Greatest liars in all the Midland Counties. It runs in the family, like gout."

"It does not seem likely, certainly, that Mr. Diamond should have confided the circumstance to Mrs. Errington," observed Minnie, thoughtfully.

"Confided! No; I never knew a man less likely to confide anything to anybody."

"However, after all, it is a thing which all the world might know, isn't it, papa?"

Dr. Bodkin was not interested in the question. He gave a great loud yawn, and declared it was time for Minnie to go to bed.

"It doesn't follow that I'm sleepy because you yawn, papa!" she said saucily.

"You are tired though, puss! I see it in your face. Go to bed. Mrs. Bodkin, get Minnie off to rest."

He bent to kiss his daughter, and bid her good night.

"Say 'God bless' me, papa," she whispered, drawing his head down and kissing his forehead.

"Don't I always say it? God bless you, my darling!"

There were tears in Minnie's eyes as she turned her head away among her cushions. But nobody saw them. She talked to the maid who undressed her about Mr. Powell, the Methodist preacher, and asked her if she had heard him, and what the folks said about him in the town.

"No, Miss Minnie. I've never heard him, and I know master wouldn't think it right for any of us to be going to a dissenting chapel. But I do think as there's some good to be got there, miss. For my brother Richard, him that lives groom at Pudcombe Hall—he went and got—got 'conversion,' I think they call it, at Mr. Powell's. And since then he's never touched a drop of liquor, nor a bad word never comes out of his mouth. And he says he's quite happy and comfortable in his mind, miss."

"Is he? How I envy him!"

CHAPTER VI.

It is exceedingly disagreeable to find that a scheme you have set your head on, or a prospect which smiles before you, is displeasing to the persons who surround you. It gives a cold shock to the glow of anticipation.

Algernon did not perhaps care to sympathise very keenly with other folks' pleasure, but he certainly desired that they should be pleased with what pleased him, which is not quite the same thing.

His mother informed him—perhaps with a dash of the Ancram colouring; although we have seen how unjustly the worthy lady was suspected of falsehood by Dr. Bodkin on a late occasion—that Mr. Diamond disapproved of his refusing Mr. Filthorpe's offer, and of his resolve to go to London. Dr. Bodkin, Algernon knew, did not approve it; neither did Minnie, although she had never said so in words. How unpleasantly chilly people were, to be sure!

Mrs. Errington did not like Mr. Diamond. She mistrusted him. His silence and gravity, his odd sarcastic smiles, and taciturn politeness, made her uneasy. Despite the patronising way in which she had spoken of him to Minnie Bodkin, in her heart she thought the young man to be horribly presuming.

"I'm sure he doesn't appreciate you at all, Algy," she declared, winding up a list of Mr. Diamond's defects and misdemeanours with this culminating accusation.

Algy had a shrewd notion that Mr. Diamond's appreciation of himself was likely to be a just one, and he was a little vexed and discomfited, that his tutor had given him no word of praise behind his back. Mrs. Errington saw that she had made an impression, and began to heighten and embellish her statements accordingly. "But, my dear boy," said she, "how can we expect him to recognise talents like yours—gentlemanly talents, so to speak? The man himself is a mere plodder. Why, he was a sizar at college!"

Algy felt himself to be a very generous fellow for continuing to "stand up for old Diamond," as he phrased it.

"Well, ma'am, plenty of great men have been poor scholars. Dean Swift was a sizar."

"And Dean Swift died in a madhouse! So you see, Algy!"

Mrs. Errington plumed herself a good deal upon this retort, and returned to the attack upon Mr. Diamond with fresh vigour; being one of those persons whose mode of warfare is elephantine, and who, never content with merely killing their enemy, must ponderously stamp and mash every semblance of humanity out of him.

Algernon did not like all this. His vanity was—at least during this period of his life—a great deal more vulnerable than his mother's. And she, although she doated on him, would say unpleasant things, indignantly repeat mortifying remarks which had been made, and in a hundred ways unconsciously wound the sensitive love of approbation which was one of Algernon's tenderest (not to say weakest) points.

It was all very disagreeable. But it was not the worst he had to look forward to. There was one person who would be so cast down, so despairing, at the news of his going away, that—that—it would be quite painful for a fellow to witness such grief. And yet it could not be expected—it could never have been expected—that he should stay in Whitford all his life! He must point that out to Rhoda.

Poor Rhoda!

For ten years, that is to say for more than half her life, Algernon Errington had been an idol, a hero, to her. From the first day when, peeping from behind the parlour door, she had beheld the strangers enter—Mrs. Errington, majestic, in a huge hat and plume, such as young readers may have seen in obsolete fashion books (the mode was so absurd fifty years ago, and had none of that simple elegance which distinguishes your costume, my dear young lady), and Algy, a lovely fair child, in a black velvet suit and falling collar—from that moment the boy had been a radiant apparition in her imagination. How small, and poor, and shabby she felt, as she peeped out of the parlour at that beautiful, blooming mother and son! Not poor and shabby in a milliner's sense of the word, but literally of no account, or beauty, or value, in the world, little shy motherless thing! She had an intense delight in beauty, this Whitford grocer's daughter. And all her little life the craving for beauty in her had been starved: not wilfully, but because the very conception of such food as would wholesomely have fed it, was wanting in the people with whom she lived.

That was a great day when she first, by chance, attracted Mrs. Errington's notice. She was too timid and too simple to scheme for that end, as many children would have done, although she tremblingly desired it. What a surprisingly splendid sight was the tortoise-shell work-box, full of amber satin and silver! What a delightful revelation the sound of the old harpsichord, touched by Mrs. Errington's plump white fingers! What a perennial source of wonder and admiration were that lady's accomplishments, and condescension, and kind soft voice!

As to Algernon, there never was such a clever and brilliant little boy. At eight years old he could sing little songs to his mother's accompaniment, in the sweetest piping voice. He could recite little verses. He even drew quite so that you could tell—or Rhoda could—his trees, houses, and men from one another.

In all the stories his mother told about the greatness of her family, and in all the descriptions she gave of her ancestral home in Warwickshire, Rhoda's imagination put in the boy as the central figure of the piece. She could see him in the great hall hung round with armour; although she knew that he had never been in the family mansion in his life; in the grand drawing-room, with its purple carpet and gilt furniture; above all, in the long portrait gallery, of which Rhoda was never tired of hearing. Heaven knows how she, innocently, and Mrs. Errington, exercising her hereditary talent, embellished and transformed the old brick house in its deer park; or what enchanted landscapes the child at all events conjured up, among the gentle slopes and tufted woods of Warwickshire!

Even the period of hobbledehoydom, fatal to beauty, to grace, almost to civilised humanity in most schoolboys, Algernon passed through triumphantly. He had a great sense of humour, and fastidious pampered habits of mind and body, which enabled him to look down with more or less disdain—a good-humoured disdain, always, Algy was never bitter—upon the obstreperous youth at the Whitford Grammar School.

One fight he had. He was forced into it by circumstances, against his will. Not that he was a coward, but he had a greater, and more candidly expressed regard for the ease and comfort of his body, than his schoolfellows conceived to be compatible with pluck. However, our young friend, if less stoical, was a great deal cleverer than the majority of his peers; and perceiving that the moment had arrived when he must either fight or lose caste altogether, he frankly accepted the former alternative. He fought a boy bigger and heavier than himself, got beaten (not severely, but fairly well beaten) and bore his defeat—in the dialect of his compeers, "took his licking"—admirably. He was quite as popular afterwards, as if he had thrashed his adversary, who was a loutish boy, the cock of the school, as to strength. Had he bruised his way to the perilous glory of being cock of the school himself, it would have behoved him to maintain it against all comers; which is an anxious and harassing position. Algy had not vanquished the victor, but he had "taken his licking like a trump," and, on the whole, may be said to have achieved his reputation, at the smallest cost possible under the circumstances.

His mother and Rhoda almost shrieked at beholding his bruised cheek, and bleeding lip, when he came home one half-holiday, from the field of battle. Algy laughed as well as his swollen features would let him, and calmed their feminine apprehensions. Nor would he accept his fond parent's enthusiastic praise of his heroism, mingled with denunciations of "that murderous young ruffian, Master Mannit."

"Pooh, ma'am," said the hero, "it's all brutal and low enough. We bumped and thumped each other as awkwardly as possible. I fought because I was obliged. And I didn't like it, and I shan't fight again if I can help it. It is so stupid!"

The young fellow's great charm was to be unaffected. Even his fine-gentlemanism sat quite easily on him, and was displayed with the frankest good humour. Some one reproached him once with being more nice than wise. "We can't all be wise, but we needn't be nasty!" returned Algy, with quaint gravity. His temper was, as Minnie Bodkin had said, nearly perfect. He had a singular knack of disarming anger or hostility. You could not laugh Algernon out of any course he had set his heart upon—a rare kind of strength at his age—but it was ten to one he would laugh you into agreeing with him. Every one of his little gifts and accomplishments was worth twice as much in him as it would have been in clumsier hands.

If you had a heartache, I do not think that you would have found Algy's companionship altogether soothing. Sorrow is apt to feel the very sunshine cruelly bright and cheerful. But if you were merry and wanted society: or bored, and wanted amusement: or dull and wanted exhilarating, no better companion could be desired.

He was genial with his equals, affable to his inferiors, modest towards his superiors—and had not a grain of veneration in his whole composition.

At seventeen years old Algernon left the Grammar School. But he continued to "read" with Mr. Diamond for nearly a twelvemonth. "My son is studying the classics with Mr. Diamond," Mrs. Errington would say; "I can't send my boy to the University, where all his forefathers distinguished themselves. But he has had the education of a gentleman."

It was a very desultory kind of reading at the best, and it was interrupted by the long Midsummer holidays, during which Mr. Diamond went away from Whitford, no one knew exactly whither. And during these same holidays, Mrs. Errington, who said she required change of air, had taken lodgings in a little quiet Welsh village, and obtained Mr. Maxfield's permission to have Rhoda with her.

That was a time of joy for the girl. It did not at all detract from Rhoda's happiness, that she was required to wait hand and foot on Mrs. Errington; to bring her her breakfast in bed; to trim her caps, to mend her stockings; to iron out scraps of fine lace and muslin; to walk with her when she was minded to stroll into the village; to order the dinner; to make the pudding—a culinary operation too delicate for the fingers of the rustic with whom they lodged—to listen to her patroness when it pleased her to talk; and to play interminable games of cribbage with her when she was tired of talking. All these things were a labour of love to Rhoda. And Mrs. Errington was kind to the girl in her own way.

And above all, was not Algy there? Those were happy days in the Welsh village. On the long delicious summer afternoons, when Mrs. Errington was asleep after dinner, Rhoda would sit out of doors with her sewing; on a bench under the parlour window, so as to be within call of her patroness; and Algy would lounge beside her with a book; or make short excursions to get her wild flowers, which he would toss into her lap, laughing at her ecstasy of gratitude. "Oh, Algy!" she would cry, "Oh, how good of you! How lovely they are!" The words written down are not eloquent, but Rhoda's looks and tones made them so.

"They are not half so lovely," Algy would answer, "as properly educated garden flowers; nor so sweet either. But I know you like that sort of herbage."

Rhoda never forgot those days. How should she forget them?—since it was at this period that Algernon first discovered that he was in love with her. Perhaps he might never have made the discovery if they had all stayed at Whitford. There he saw her, as he had seen her since her childhood, surrounded by coarse common people, and living their life, more or less. It is not every one who can be expected to recognise your diamond, if you set it in lead. Rhoda was always sweet, always gentle, always pretty, but she formed part and parcel of old Max's establishment. When the boy and girl were quite small, she used to help him with his lessons (her one year's seniority made a greater difference between them then, than it did later) and had always been used to do him sisterly service in a hundred ways. And all this was by no means favourable to the young gentleman's falling in love with her.

But at Llanryddan, Rhoda appeared under quite a different aspect. She looked prettier than ever before, Algernon thought. And perhaps she really was so; for there is no such cosmetic for the complexion as happiness. Apart from her vulgar relations, and treated as a lady by the few strangers with whom they came in contact, it was surprising to find how good her manners were, and how much natural grace she possessed. Mrs. Errington had taught her what may be termed the technicalities of polite behaviour. From her own heart and native sensibility she had learnt the essentials. The people in the village turned their heads to admire her, as she walked modestly along. Who could help admiring her? Algernon decided that there was not one among the young ladies of Whitford who could compare with Rhoda. "She is ten times as pretty as those raw-boned McDougalls, and twenty times as well bred as Alethea Dockett, and ever so much cleverer than Miss Pawkins," he reflected. Minnie Bodkin never came into his head in the list of damsels with whom Rhoda could be compared. Minnie occupied a place apart, quite removed from any idea of love-making.

Dear Little Rhoda! How fond she was of him!

Altogether Rhoda appeared in a new light, and the new light became her mightily. Yes; Algy was certainly in love with her, he acknowledged to himself. There was no scene, no declaration. It all came to pass very gradually. In Rhoda the sense of this love stole on as subtly as the dawn. Before she had begun to watch the glowing streaks of rose-colour, it was daylight! And then how warm and golden it grew in her little world! How the birds chirped and fluttered, and the flowers breathed sweet breath, and a thousand diamond drops stood on the humblest blades of grass!

If she had been nine years old, instead of nearly nineteen, she could scarcely have given less heed to the worldly aspects of the situation.

Algernon perhaps more consciously set aside considerations of the future. He was but a boy, however; and he always had a great gift of enjoying the present moment, and sending Janus-headed Care, that looks forward and backward, to the deuce. As yet there was no Lord Seely on his horizon; no London society; no diplomatic career. The latter indeed was but an Ancramism of his mother's, when she spoke of it to Mr. Diamond, and Algy at that time had never entertained the idea of it.

So these two young persons sat side by side, on the bench outside the Welsh cottage, and were as happy as the midsummer days were long.

But long as the midsummer days were, they passed. Then came the time for going back to Whitford. The day before their return home Rhoda received a shock of pain—the first, but not the last, which she ever felt from this love of hers—at these words, said carelessly, but in a low voice, by Algy, as he lounged at her side, watching the sunset:

"Rhoda, darling, you must not say a word to any one about—about you and me, you know."

Not say a word! What had she to say? And to whom? "No, Algy," she answered, in a faint little voice, and began to meditate. The idea had been presented to her for the first time that it was her duty, or Algy's duty, to drag their secret from its home in Fairyland, and subject it to the eyes and tongues of mortals. But being once there, the idea stayed in her mind and would not be banished. Her father—Mrs. Errington—what would they say if they knew that—that she had dared to love Algernon? The future began to look terribly hard to her. The glittering mist which had hidden it was drawn away like a gauze curtain. How could she not have seen it all before? Would any one believe for evermore that she had been such a child, such a fool, so selfishly absorbed in her pleasant day-dreams, as not to calculate the cost of it for one moment until now?

"Oh, Algy!" the poor child broke out, lifting a pale face and startled eyes to his; "if we could only go on for ever as we are! If it would be always summer, and we two could stay in this village, and never go back, or see any of the people again—except father," she added hastily. And a pang of remorse smote her as her conscience told her that the father who loved her so well, and was so good to her, whatever he might be to others, was not at all necessary to the happiness of her existence henceforward.

"Don't let's be miserable now, at all events," returned Algernon cheerfully. "Look at that purple bar of cloud on the gold! I wonder if I could paint that. I wish I had my colour-box here. The pencil sketches are so dreary after all that colour."

Rhoda had no doubt that Algernon could paint "that," or anything else he applied his brush to. After a while she said, with her heart beating violently, and the colour coming and going in her cheeks: "Don't you think it would be wrong, deceitful—to—if we—not to tell—" Poor Rhoda could not frame her sentence, and was obliged to leave it unfinished.

"Deceitful! Am I generally deceitful, Rhoda? Oh, I say, don't cry; there's a pet! Don't, my darling! I can't bear to see you sorry. But, look here, Rhoda, dear; I'm so young yet, that it wouldn't do to talk about being in love, or anything of that sort. Though I know I shall never change, they would declare I didn't know my own mind, and would make a joke of it"—this shot told with Rhoda, who shrank from ridicule, as a sensitive plant shrinks from the north wind—"and bother my—our lives out. Can't you see old Grimgriffin's great front teeth grinning at us?"

It was in these terms that Algy was wont to allude to that respectable spinster, Miss Elizabeth Grimshaw.

Rhoda knew that Algy wished and expected her to smile when he said that; and she tried to please him, but the smile would not come. Her lip quivered, and tears began to gather in her eyes again. She would have sobbed outright if she had tried to speak. The more she thought the sadder and more frightened she grew. Ridicule was painful, but that was not the worst. Her father! Mrs. Errington! She lay awake half the night, terrifying herself with imaginations of their wrath.

Algy found an opportunity the next morning to whisper to her a few words. "Don't look so melancholy, Rhoda. They'll wonder at Whitford what's the matter if you go back with such a wan face. And as to what you said about deceit, why we shan't pretend not to love each other! Look here, we must have patience! I shall always love you, darling, and I'm sure to get my own way with my mother in the long run; I always do."

So then there would be obstacles to contend with on Mrs. Errington's part, and Algy acknowledged that there would. Of course she had known before that it must be so. But Algy had declared that he would always love her; that was the one comforting thought to which she clung. Rhoda had grown from a child to a woman since yesterday. Algy was only older by four-and-twenty hours.

After their return to Whitford came Mr. Filthorpe's letter. Then his mother's application to Lady Seely, brought about by an old acquaintance of Mrs. Errington, who lived in London, and kept up an intermittent correspondence with her. Both these events were talked over in Rhoda's presence. Indeed, the girl filled the part towards Mrs. Errington that the confidant enacts towards the prima donna in an Italian opera. Mrs. Errington was always singing scenas to her, which, so far as Rhoda's share in them went, might just as well have been uttered in the shape of a soliloquy. But the lady was used to her confidant, and liked to have her near, to take her hand in the impressive passages, and to walk up the stage with her during the symphony.

So Rhoda heard Algernon's prospects canvassed. In her heart she longed that he should accept Mr. Filthorpe's offer. It would keep him nearer to her in every sense. She had few opportunities of talking with him alone now—far fewer than at dear Llanryddan; but she was able to say a few words privately to him one afternoon (the very afternoon of Dr. Bodkin's whist-party), and she timidly hinted that if Algy went to Bristol, instead of to London amongst all those great folks, she would not feel that she had lost him so completely.

"My dear child!" exclaimed Algy, whose outlook on life had a good deal changed during the last three months, "how can you talk so? Fancy me on Filthorpe's office stool!"

"London is such a long way off, Algy," murmured the girl plaintively. "And then, amongst all those grand people, lords and ladies, you—you may grow different."

"Upon my word, my dear Rhoda, your appreciation of me is highly flattering! For my part it seems to me more likely that I should grow 'different' in the society of Bristol tradesmen than amongst my own kith and kin—people like myself and my parents in education and manners. I am a gentleman, Rhoda. Lord Seely is not more."

Rhoda shrank back abashed before this magnificent young gentleman. Such a flourish was very unusual in Algernon. But the Ancram strain in him had been asserting itself lately. He was sorry when he saw the poor girl's hurt look and downcast eyes, from which the big tears were silently falling one by one. He took her in his arms, and kissed her pale cheeks, and brought a blush on to them, and an April smile to her lips; and called her his own dear pretty Rhoda, whom he could never, never forget.

"Perhaps it would be best to forget me, Algy," she faltered. And although his loving words, and flatteries, and caresses, were inexpressibly sweet to her, the pain remained at her heart.

She never again ventured to say a word to him about his plans. She would listen, meekly and admiringly, to his vivid pictures of all the fine things he was to do in the future: pictures in which her figure appeared—like the donor of a great altarpiece, full of splendid saints and golden-crowned angels—kneeling in one corner. And she would sit in silent anguish whilst Mrs. Errington expatiated on her son's prospects; wherein, of late, a "great alliance" played a large part. But she could not rouse herself to elation or enthusiasm. This mattered little to Mrs. Errington, who only required her confidante to stand tolerably still with her back to the audience. But it worried Algernon to see Rhoda's sad, downcast face, irresponsive to any of his bright anticipations. It must be owned that the young fellow's position was not entirely pleasant. Yet his admirable temper and spirits scarcely flagged. He was never cross, except, now and then, just a very little to his mother. And if no one else in the world less deserved his ill-humour, at least no one else in the world was so absolutely certain to forgive him for it!

CHAPTER VII.

Parliament was to meet early in February. It seemed strange that that fact should have any interest for Rhoda Maxfield; nevertheless, so it was. Algernon was to go to London, but it was no use to be there unless Lord Seely, "our cousin," were there also; and my lord our cousin would not be in town before the meeting of parliament. Thus the assembling of the peers and commons of this realm at Westminster was an event on which poor Rhoda's thoughts were bent pretty often in the course of the twenty-four hours.

Mrs. Errington announced to the whole Maxfield family that Algernon was going away from Whitford, and accompanied the announcement with florid descriptions of the glory that awaited her son, in the highest Ancram style of embellishment.

"Well," said old Max, after listening awhile, "and will this lord get Mr. Algernon a place?"

Mrs. Errington could not answer this question very definitely. The future was vague, though splendid. But of course Algy would distinguish himself. That was a matter of course. Perhaps he might begin as Lord Seely's private secretary.

"A sekketary! Humph! I don't think much o' that!" grunted Mr. Maxfield.

"My dear man, you don't understand these things. How should you? Many noblemen's sons would only be too delighted to get the position of private secretary to Lord Seely. A man of such distinction! Hand and glove with the sovereign!"

Maxfield did not altogether dislike to hear his lodger hold forth in this fashion. He had a certain pleasure in contemplating the future grandeur of Mr. Algernon, whose ears he had boxed years ago, on the occasion of finding him enacting the battle of Waterloo, with a couple of schoolfellows, in the warehouse behind the shop, and attacking a Hougoumont of tea-chests and flour-barrels, so briskly, as to threaten their entire demolition.

Maxfield was weaving speculations in connection with the young man, of so wild and fanciful a nature as would have astonished his most familiar friends, could they have peeped into the brain inside his grizzled old head.

But this rose-coloured condition of things did not last.

One afternoon, Mrs. Errington looked into his little sitting-room, on her way upstairs, and finding him with an account-book, in which he was, not making, but reading entries, she stepped in, and began to chat; if any speech so laboriously condescending as hers to Mr. Maxfield may be thus designated. Her theme, of course, was her son, and her son's prospects.

"That'll be all very fine for Mr. Algernon, to be sure," said old Max, slowly, after some time, "but—it'll cost money."

"Not so much as you think for. Low persons who feel themselves in a false position, no doubt find it necessary to make a show. But a real gentleman can afford to be simple."

"But I take it he'll have to afford other things besides being simple! He'll have to afford clothes, and lodging, and maybe food. You aren't rich."

Mrs. Errington admitted the fact.

"Algernon ought to find a wife with a bit o' money," said the old man, looking straight and hard into the lady's eyes. Those round orbs sustained the gaze as unflinchingly as if they had been made of blue china.

"It is not at all a bad idea," Mrs. Errington said, graciously.

"But then he wouldn't just take the first ugly woman as had a fort'n."

"Oh dear no!"

"No; nor yet an old 'un."

"Good gracious, man! of course not!"

"Young, pretty, good, and a bit o' money. That's about his mark, eh?"

Mrs. Errington shook her head pathetically. "She ought to have birth, too," she said. "But the woman takes her husband's rank; unless," she added, correcting herself, and with much emphasis, "unless she happens to be the better born of the two."

"Oh, she does, eh? The woman takes her husband's rank? Ah! well, that's script'ral. I have never troubled my head about these vain worldly distinctions; but that is script'ral."

Mrs. Errington was not there to discuss her landlord's opinions or to listen to them; but he served as well as another to be the recipient of her talk about Algernon, which accordingly she resumed, and indulged in ever-higher flights of boasting. Her mendacity, like George Wither's muse,

As it made wing, so it made power.

"The fact is, there is more than one young lady on whom my connections in London have cast their eye for Algy. Miss Pickleham, only daughter of the great drysalter, who is such an eminent member of Parliament; Blanche Fitzsnowdon, Judge Whitelamb's lovely niece; one of Major-General Indigo's charming girls, all of them perfect specimens of the Eastern style of beauty—their mother was an Indian princess, and enormously wealthy. But I am in no hurry for my boy to bind himself in an engagement: it hampers a young man's career."

"Career!" broke out old Max, who had listened to all this, and much more, with an increasingly dismayed and lowering expression of countenance. "Why, what's his career to be? He's been brought up to do nothing! It 'ud be his only chance to get hold of a wife with a bit o' money. Then he might act the gentleman at his ease; and maybe his fine friends 'ud help him when they found he didn't want it. But as for career—it's my opinion as he'll never earn his salt!"

And with that the old man marched across the passage into the shop, taking no further notice of his lodger; and she heard him slam the little half-door, giving access to the storehouse, with such force as to set the jingling bell on it tinkling for full five minutes.

Mrs. Errington was so surprised by this sally, that she stood staring after him for some time before she was able to collect herself sufficiently to walk majestically upstairs.

"Maxfield's temper becomes more and more extraordinary," she said to her son, with an air of great solemnity. "The man really forgets himself altogether. Do you suppose that he drinks, Algy? or is he, do you think, a little touched?" She put her finger to her forehead. "Really I should not wonder. There has been a great deal of preaching and screeching lately, since this Powell came; and, you know, they do say that these Ranters and Methodists sometimes go raving mad at their field-meetings and love-feasts. You need not laugh, my dear boy; I have often heard your father say that nothing was more contagious than that sort of hysterical excitement. And your father was a physician; and certainly knew his profession if he didn't know the world, poor man!"

"Was old Max hysterical, ma'am?" asked Algernon, his whole face lighted up with mischievous amusement. And the notion so tickled him, that he burst out laughing at intervals, as it recurred to him, all the rest of the day.

Betty Grimshaw, and Sarah, the servant-maid, and James, helping his father to serve in the shop, and the customers who came to buy, all suffered from the unusual exacerbation of Maxfield's temper for some time after that conversation of his with Mrs. Errington.

It increased, also, the resentful feeling which had been growing in his mind towards David Powell. The young man's tone of rebuke, in speaking of Rhoda's associating with the Erringtons, had taken Maxfield by surprise at the time; and he had not, he afterwards thought, been sufficiently trenchant in his manner of putting down the presumptuous reprover. He blew up his wrath until it burned hot within him; and, the more so, inasmuch as he could give no vent to it in direct terms. To question and admonish was the acknowledged duty of a Methodist preacher. Conference made no exceptions in favour even of so select a vessel as Jonathan Maxfield. But Maxfield thought, nevertheless, that Powell ought to have had modesty and discernment to make the exception himself.

No inquisitor—no priest, sitting like a mysterious Eastern idol in the inviolate shrine of the confessional—ever exercised a more tremendous power over the human conscience than was laid in the hands of the Methodist preacher or leader according to Wesley's original conception of his functions. But besides the essential difference between the Romish and Methodist systems that the latter could bring no physical force to bear on the refractory, there was this important point to be noted: namely, that the inquisitor might be subjected to inquisition by his flock. The priest might be made to come forth from the confessional-box, and answer to a pressing catechism before all the congregation. In the band-meetings and select societies each individual bound himself to answer the most searching questions "concerning his state, sins, and temptations." It was a mutual inquisition, to which, of course, those who took part in it voluntarily submitted themselves.

But the spiritual power wielded by the chiefs was very great, as their own subordination to the conference was very complete. Its pernicious effects were, however, greatly kept in check by the system of itinerancy, which required the preachers to move frequently from place to place.

There are few human virtues or weaknesses to which, on one side or the other, Methodism in its primitive manifestations did not appeal. Benevolence, self-sacrifice, fervent piety, temperance, charity, were all called into play by its teachings. But so also were spiritual pride, narrow-mindedness, fanaticism, gloom, and pharisaical self-righteousness. Only to the slothful, and such as loved their ease above all things, early Methodism had no seductions to offer.

Jonathan Maxfield's father and grandfather had been disciples of John Wesley. The grandfather was born in 1710, seven years before Wesley, and had been among the great preacher's earliest adherents in Bristol.

Traditions of John Wesley's sayings and doings were cherished and handed down in the family. They claimed kindred with Thomas Maxfield, Wesley's first preacher, and conveniently forgot or ignored—as greater families have done—those parts of their kinsman's career which ran counter to the present course of their creed and conduct. For Thomas Maxfield seceded from Wesley, but the grandfather and father of Jonathan continued true to Methodism all their lives. They married within the "society" (as was strictly enjoined at the first conference), and assisted the spread of its tenets throughout their part of the West of England.

In the third generation, however, the original fire of Methodism had nearly burnt itself out, and a few charred sticks remained to attest the brightness that had been. Never, perhaps, in the case of the Maxfields—a cramp-natured, harsh breed—had the fire become a hearth-glow to warm their homes with. It had rather been like the crackling of thorns under a pot. The dryest and sharpest will flare for a while.

Old Max, nevertheless, looked upon himself as an exemplary Methodist. He made no mental analyses of himself or of his neighbours. He merely took cognisance of facts as they appeared to him through the distorting medium of his prejudices, temper, ignorance, and the habits of a lifetime. When he did or said disagreeable things, he prided himself on doing his duty. And his self-approval was never troubled by the reflection that he did not altogether dislike a little bitter flavour in his daily life, as some persons prefer their wine rough.

But to do and say disagreeable things because it is your duty is a very different matter from accepting, or listening to, disagreeable things, because it is somebody else's duty to do and say them! It was not to be expected that Jonathan Maxfield should meekly endure rebuke from a young man like David Powell.

And now crept in the exasperating suspicion that the young man might have been right in his warning! Maxfield watched his daughter with more anxiety than he had ever felt about her in his life, looking to see symptoms of dejection at Algernon's approaching departure. He did not know that she had been aware of it before it was announced to himself.

One day her father said to her abruptly, "Rhoda, you're looking very pale and out o' sorts. Your eyes are heavy" (they were swollen with crying), "and your face is the colour of a turnip. I think I shall send you off to Duckwell for a bit of a change."

Duckwell Farm was owned by Seth, Maxfield's eldest son.

"I don't want a change, indeed, father," said the girl, looking up quickly and eagerly. "I had a headache this morning, but it is quite gone now. That's what made me look so pale."

From that time forward she exerted herself to appear cheerful, and to shake off the dull pain at the heart which weighed her down, until her father began to persuade himself that he had been mistaken, and over-anxious. She always declared herself to be quite well and free from care. "And I know she would not tell me a lie," thought the old man.

Alas, she had learned to lie in her words and her manner. She had, for the first time in her life, a motive for concealment, and she used the natural armour of the weak—duplicity.

Rhoda had been "good" hitherto, because her nature was gentle, and her impulses affectionate. She had no strong religious fervour, but she lived blamelessly, and prayed reverently, and was docile and humble-minded. She had never professed to have attained that sudden and complete regeneration of spirit which is the prime glory of Methodism. But then many good persons lived and died without attaining "assurance." Whenever Rhoda thought on the subject—which, to say the truth, was not often, for her nature, though sweet and pure, was not capable of much spiritual aspiration, and was altogether incapable of fervent self-searching and fiery enthusiasm—she hoped with simple faith that she should be saved if she did nothing wicked.

Her father and David Powell would have pointed out to her, that her "doing," or leaving undone, could have no influence on the matter. But their words bore small fruit in her mind. Her father's religious teaching had the dryness of an accustomed formality to her ears. It had been poured into them before she had sense to comprehend it, and had grown to be nearly meaningless, like the everyday salutation we exchange a hundred times, without expecting or thinking of the answer.

David Powell was certainly neither dry nor formal, but he frightened her. She shut her understanding against the disturbing influence of his words, as she would have pressed her fingers into her pretty ears to keep out the thunder. And then her dream of love had come and filled her life.

In most of us it wonderfully alters the focus of the mind's eye with its glamour, that dream. To Rhoda it seemed the one thing beautiful and desirable. And—to say all the truth—the pain of mind which she felt, other than that connected with her lover's going away, and which she attributed to remorse for the little deceptions and concealments she practised, was occasioned almost entirely by the latent dread, lest the time should come when she should sit lonely, looking at the cold ashes of Algy's burnt-out love. For she did mistrust his constancy, although no power would have forced the confession from her. This blind, obstinate clinging to the beloved was, perhaps, the only form in which self-esteem ever strongly manifested itself in that soft, timid nature.

There was one person who watched Rhoda more understandingly than her father did, and who had more serious apprehensions on her account. David Powell knew, as did nearly all Whitford by this time, that young Errington was going away; and he clearly saw that the change in Rhoda was connected with that departure. He marked her pallor, her absence of mind, her fits of silence, broken by forced bursts of assumed cheerfulness. Her feigning did not deceive him.

Albeit of almost equally narrow education with Jonathan Maxfield, Powell had gained, in his frequent changes of place and contact with many strange people, a wider knowledge of the world than the Whitford tradesman possessed. He perceived how unlikely it was, that people like the Erringtons should seriously contemplate allying themselves by marriage with "old Max;" but that was not the worst. To the preacher's mind, the girl's position was, in the highest degree, perilous; for he conceived that what would be accounted by the world the happiest possible solution to such a love as Rhoda's, would involve nothing less than the putting in jeopardy her eternal welfare. He could not look forward with any hope to a union between Rhoda and such a one as Algernon Errington.

"The son is a shallow-hearted, fickle youth, with the vanity of a boy and the selfishness of a man; the mother, a mere worldling, living in decent godlessness."

Such was David Powell's judgment. He reflected long and earnestly. What was his calling—his business in life? To save souls. He had no concern with anything else. He must seek out and help, not only those who needed him, but those who most needed him.

All conventional rules of conduct, all restraining considerations of a merely social or worldly kind, were as threads of gossamer to this man whensoever they opposed the higher commands which he believed to have been laid upon him.

Jonathan Maxfield was falling away from godliness. He, too evidently, was willing to give up his daughter into the tents of the heathen. The pomps and vanities of this wicked world had taken hold of the old man. Satan had ensnared and bribed him with the bait of worldly ambition. From Jonathan there was no real help to be expected.

In the little garret-chamber, where he lodged in the house of a widow—one of the most devout of the Methodist congregation—the preacher rose from his knees one midnight, and took from his breast the little, worn pocket-Bible, which he always carried. A bright cold moon shone in at the uncurtained window, but its beams did not suffice to enable him to read the small print of his Bible. He had no candle; but he struck a light with a match, and, by its brief flare, read these words, on which his finger had fallen as he opened the book:

"How hast thou counselled him that hath no wisdom? And how hast thou plentifully declared the thing as it is?

"To whom hast thou uttered words? and whose spirit came from thee?"

He had drawn a lot, and this was the answer. The leading was clear. He would speak openly with Rhoda himself. He would pray and wrestle; he would argue and exhort. He would awaken her spirit, lulled to sleep by the sweet voice of the tempter.

It would truly be little less than a miracle, should he succeed by the mere force of his earnest eloquence, in persuading a young girl like Rhoda to renounce her first love.

But, then, David Powell believed in miracles.

CHAPTER VIII.

All that she had heard of the Methodist preacher had taken strong hold of Minnie Bodkin's imagination. Mr. Diamond's description of him especially delighted her. It was in piquant contrast with her previous notions about Methodists, who were associated in her mind with ludicrous images. This man must be something entirely different—picturesque and interesting.

But there was a deeper feeling in her mind than the mere curiosity to see a remarkable person. Minnie was not happy; and her unhappiness was not solely due to the fact of her bodily infirmities. She often felt a yearning for a higher spiritual support and comfort than she had ever derived from her father's teachings. She passed in review the congregation of the parish church, most of whom were known to her, and she asked herself what good result in their lives or characters was produced by their weekly church-going. Was Mrs. Errington more truthful; Miss Chubb less vain; Mr. Warlock less gloomy; her father (for Minnie, in the pride of her keen intellect, spared no one) less arrogant and overbearing; she herself more patient, gentle, hopeful, and happy, than if the old bell of St. Chad's were silent, and the worm-eaten old doors shut, and the dusty old pulpit voiceless, for evermore? Yet there were said to be people on whom religion had a vital influence. She wished she could know such. She could judge, she thought, by seeing and conversing with them, whether or not there were any reality in their professions. Minnie seldom doubted the sufficiency of her own acumen and penetration.

No; she was not happy. And might it not be that this Methodist man had the secret of peace of mind? Was there in truth a physician who could minister to a suffering spirit? She thought of Powell with the feeling half of shame, half of credulity, with which an invalid hankers after a quack medicine.

Minnie had been taught to look upon Dissenters in general as quacks, and upon Methodists as arch-quacks. Dr. Bodkin professed himself a staunch Churchman and a hater of "cant." He considered that Protestantism, and the right of private judgment, had justly reached their extreme limits in the Church of England as by law established. He detested enthusiasm as a dangerous and disturbing element in human affairs, and he viewed with especial indignation the pretensions of unlearned persons to preach and proselytise. Although he had no leaning to Romanism, he would rather have admitted a Jesuit into his house than a Methodist. Indeed, he sometimes defined the latter to be the Jesuit of dissent—only, as he would take care to point out, a Jesuit without learning, culture, or authority.

"I can listen to a gentleman, although I may not agree with him," the Doctor would say (albeit, in truth, he had no great gift of listening to anyone who opposed his opinions), "but am I to be hectored and lectured by the cobbler and the tinker?"

Minnie had no taste for being hectored or lectured; but it seemed to her that what the cobbler and tinker said, was more important than the fact that it was they who said it. She thought, and pondered, and wondered about the Methodist preacher, and about her chance of ever seeing or hearing more of him, until a thought darted into her mind like an arrow. Little Rhoda! She was a Methodist born and bred, and knew this preacher, and—Minnie would send for little Rhoda.

When she announced this resolution to her mother, Mrs. Bodkin found several difficulties in the way of its fulfilment.

"What do you want with her, Minnie?"

"I want to see her. Mrs. Errington talks so much of her. I remember her coming here with a message once, when she was a child. I recollect only a little fair face and shy eyes, under a coal-scuttle straw bonnet. Don't you, mamma? And I want to talk to her about several things," added Minnie, with resolute truthfulness.

"Oh, dear me! What will your papa say?"

"I don't see how papa can object to my asking this nice little thing to come to me for an afternoon, when he doesn't mind your boring yourself to death with Goody Barton, whose snuff-taking would try the nerves of a rhinoceros, nor forbid my inviting the little Jobsons, who are unpleasant to look upon, and stupid beyond the wildest flights of imagination. He lets me have any one I like."

"Yes; but you teach the little Jobsons the alphabet, my dear. And that is a charitable work."

"And Rhoda will amuse me, and I'm sure that is a charitable work!"

Minnie would get her own way, of course. She always did.

That same evening Minnie said to her father, with her frank, bright smile, "Papa, may I not ask Rhoda Maxfield to take tea with me some afternoon?"

"Rhoda what?"

"Little Maxfield, the grocer's daughter, papa," said Minnie, boldly.

Mrs. Bodkin bent nervously over her knitting.

"What on earth for? Why do you want to associate with such folks? Have you not plenty of friends without—?"

"No, papa. But I don't ask her because I'm in want of friends."

"Oh, Minnie," said Mrs. Bodkin in the quick, low tones she habitually spoke in, "I'm sure nobody has more friends than you have! Everybody is so glad to come to you, always."

"You're my friend, mamma. And papa is my friend. Never mind the rest. I want to have little Maxfield to tea." Minnie laughed at herself, the moment after she had said the words, in the tone of a spoiled child.

Dr. Bodkin crossed and uncrossed his legs, kicked a footstool out of the way, and then got up and stood before the fire.

"If you want amusement, isn't there Miss Chubb or the McDougalls, or—or plenty more?" said he, shooting out his upper lip, and frowning uneasily.

"Now, papa, can you say in conscience that you find Miss Chubb and the McDougalls perennially amusing?" Then, with a sudden change of tone, "Besides, you know, the other people are playing their parts in life, and strutting about hither and thither on the stage, and they find it all more or less interesting. But I—I am like a child at a peep-show. I can but look on, and I sometimes long for a change in the scene and the puppets!"

The doctor began to poke the fire violently. "Laura," said he, addressing his wife, "that last tea you got is good for nothing. They brought me a cup just now in the study that was absolutely undrinkable. Is it Smith's tea? Well, try Maxfield's. You can have some ordered when the message is sent for the girl to come here."

In this way the doctor gave his permission.

The next day Minnie despatched her maid, Jane, with the following note to Mr. Maxfield:—

"Will Mr. Maxfield allow his daughter Rhoda to spend the afternoon with Miss Bodkin? Miss Bodkin is an invalid, and cannot often leave her room, and it would give her great pleasure to see Rhoda. The maid shall wait and accompany Rhoda if Mr. Maxfield permits, and Miss Bodkin undertakes to have her sent safely home again in the evening."

Old Max was scarcely more surprised than gratified on reading this invitation. He stood behind his counter holding the pink perfumed note between his floury finger and thumb, and turning over the contents of it in his mind, whilst his son James served the maid with some tea.

Miss Minnie was a much-looked-up-to personage in Whitford. And here was Miss Minnie inviting Rhoda just as though she had been a lady, and sending her own maid for her. This would be Algy's doing, the old man decided. Algy had more sense than his mother. Algy knew that Rhoda was fit to go anywhere, and could hold her own with the best. The young fellow was very thick with Dr. Bodkin's family, and had, no doubt, talked to Miss Minnie about Rhoda. All sorts of ideas thronged into old Max's head, which, nevertheless, looked as obstinately idealess a one as could well be imagined, as he stood conning the pink note, with his grey eyebrows knotted together, and his heavy under-lip pursed up. Perhaps not the feeblest element in his feeling of exultation was the sense of triumph over David Powell. Powell might approve or disapprove, but anyway, he would see that he was wrong in supposing the Erringtons did not think Rhoda good enough for them! If they introduced her about among their friends, that meant a good deal, eh, brother David? And that the invitation came by means of the Erringtons, Maxfield felt more and more convinced, the more he thought of it. So many years had passed, and Miss Minnie had taken no notice of Rhoda. Why should she now? Maxfield was at no loss to find the answer. Maybe old Mrs. Errington had talked for talk's sake more than she meant. Maybe her boasting was in order to drive a hard bargain, when Algy should come forward and offer to make Rhoda a lady.

The Erringtons' friends were going little by little to make acquaintance with Rhoda, in view of the promotion that awaited her. Well, Rhoda could stand the test. Rhoda was quite different from the likes of him.

He called his sister-in-law out of the kitchen, and in a few hurried words told her of the invitation, and bade her tell Rhoda to get ready without delay. He cut Betty Grimshaw short in her exclamations and inquiries. "I've no time to talk to you now," he said. "The maid is waiting. Bid Rhoda clothe herself in her best garments."

"What! her Sunday frock, Jonathan?" exclaimed Betty in shrill surprise.

"'Sh! woman!" answered Maxfield, and gripped her wrist fiercely. He did not want that family detail to come to the ears of Miss Bodkin's maid.

Rhoda was completely bewildered by the invitation, and by the breathless haste with which Betty announced it to her, and hurried her preparations. "But I don't want to go!" murmured Rhoda plaintively. At the same time she suffered her clothes to be huddled on to her in Aunt Betty's rough fashion.

"Ah! tell that to your parent, my dear. I have the mark of his fingers on my wrist at this moment; he was in such a taking, and so—so uncumboundable." This latter was a word of Betty's own invention, and she frequently employed it with an air of great relish.

The idea of going amongst strangers was more terrible to Rhoda than can easily be conceived by those who have never lived so secluded a life as hers had been. Had she been able to say a word to Algernon, she thought she should have derived a little comfort and support from him. But he and his mother were both from home.

All the way from her own house to Dr. Bodkin's, Rhoda uttered no word, except to ask Jane timidly if she were sure Miss Minnie would be alone—quite alone?

The gloomy courtyard, and the stone entrance hall of the house struck her with awe. The old man-servant who opened the door seemed to look severely on her. She followed Jane with a beating heart up the wide staircase, whose thick carpet muffled her footsteps mysteriously, and then through a drawing-room full of furniture all covered with grey holland. There was the glitter of gilt picture-frames on the walls, and the shining of a great mirror, and of a large, dark, polished pianoforte at one end of the room. And there was a mingled smell of flowers and cedar-wood, and altogether the impression made upon Rhoda's senses, as she passed through the apartment, was one of perfume, and silence, and vague splendour. She had no time, even if she had had self-possession, to examine the details of what seemed to her so grand, for she was led across a passage and into a room opposite to the drawing-room, and found herself in Miss Bodkin's presence.

The room was Minnie's bedroom, but it did not look like a sleeping chamber, Rhoda thought. To be sure a little white-curtained bed stood in one corner, but all the toilet apparatus was hidden by a curtain which hung across a recess, and there were bookshelves full of books, and flowers on a stand, and a writing-table. On one side of the fireplace, in which a bright fire blazed, there was a curious sort of long chair, and in it, dressed in a loose crimson robe of soft woollen stuff, reclined Minnie Bodkin.

Rhoda was, as has been said, extremely sensitive to beauty, and Minnie's whole aspect struck her with admiration. The picturesque rich-coloured robe, the delicate white hands relieved upon it, the graceful languor of Minnie's attitude, and the air of refinement in the young lady and her surroundings, were all intensely appreciated by poor little Rhoda, who stood dumb and blushing before her hostess.

Minnie, on her part, was a good deal taken by surprise. She welcomed Rhoda with her sweetest smile, and thanked her for coming, and made her sit down by the fire opposite to herself; and when they were alone together, she talked on for some time with a sort of careless good-nature, which, little by little, succeeded in setting Rhoda somewhat at her ease. But careless as Minnie's manner was, she was scrutinising the other girl's looks and ways very keenly.

"She is absolutely lovely!" thought Minnie, "And so graceful, and—and—lady-like! Yes; positively that is the word. She is as shy as a fawn, but no more awkward than one. It is not what I expected."

Perhaps Minnie could scarcely have said what it was that she had expected. Probably a quiet, pretty-looking, well-behaved young person, like her maid Jane. Rhoda was something very different, and the young lady was charmed with her new protégée. Only she was obliged to admit, before the afternoon was over, that she had failed in the main object for which she had invited Rhoda to visit her. There was no clear and vivid account of Powell, his teaching, or his preaching, to be got from Rhoda.

Rhoda could not remember exactly what Mr. Powell said. Rhoda could not say what it was which made all the people cry and grow so excited at his preaching. Rhoda cried herself sometimes, but that was when he talked very pitifully about poor people, and little children, and things like that. Sometimes, too, she felt frightened at his preaching, but she supposed she was frightened because she had not got assurance. Many of the congregation had assurance. Yes; oh yes, the people said Mr. Powell was a wonderful man, and the most awakening preacher who had been in Whitford for fifty years.

Minnie looked at the simple, serious face, and marked the childlike demureness of manner with which Rhoda declared Mr. Powell to be "an awakening preacher." "I don't think he has awakened you to any very startling extent!" thought Minnie. "This girl seems to have received no strong influence from him."

That was in a great measure the fact; but also, Rhoda was held back from speaking freely, by the conviction that her Methodist phraseology would sound strange, and perhaps absurd, in the young lady's ears. Moreover, it did not help to put her at her ease, that she felt sundry uneasy pricks of conscience for not "bearing testimony" with more fervour. She knew that David Powell would have had her improve the occasion to the uttermost. But how could she run the risk of being disagreeable to Miss Minnie, who was so kind to her?

That was the form in which Rhoda mentally put the case. The truth was, hers was not one of those natures to which the invisible ever becomes more real and important than the visible. It was incomparably more necessary to her happiness to be in agreeable and smooth relations with the people around her, than to feel herself in higher spiritual communion with unseen powers.

When Minnie at length reluctantly desisted from questioning her on the subject of Powell, and her chapel-going, and her religious feelings, she was surprised to find how the girl's frigid, constrained manner thawed, and how her tongue was loosened.

She chatted freely enough about her visit to Llanryddan in the summer, and about Duckwell Farm, where her half-brother Seth lived, and, above all, about Mrs. Errington. Mrs. Errington had been so good to her, and had taught her, and talked to her; and did Miss Minnie know what a change it was for a lady like Mrs. Errington to live in such a poor place as theirs? For, although she had the best rooms, of course it was very poor, compared with the castle she was brought up in. About Algernon she said very little; but it slipped out that she was in the habit of being present when Mr. Diamond came to read with the young gentleman; and then Miss Minnie was very much interested in hearing what Mr. Diamond said to his pupil, and how Rhoda liked Mr. Diamond, and what she thought of him. And when it appeared that Rhoda had thought very little about him at all, but considered him a very clever, learned gentleman—perhaps a little stiff and grave, but not at all unkind—Miss Minnie smiled to herself and said, "He is a little stiff and grave, Rhoda. Not the kind of person to attract one very much, eh!"

And then tea was brought, and Rhoda sipped hers out of a delicate porcelain cup, like those which Mrs. Errington had in her corner cupboard. And there were some delicious cakes, which Rhoda was quite natural enough to own she liked very much. And then Mrs. Bodkin came in, and sat down beside her daughter; and finally, at Minnie's request, she took Rhoda into the drawing-room, and played to her on the grand piano.

"Rhoda likes music, she says, mamma. But she has never heard a good instrument. Do play her a bit of Mozart!"

"I am no great performer, my dear," said Mrs. Bodkin, opening the piano; "but I keep up my playing on my daughter's account. She is not strong enough to play for herself."

Minnie had her chair wheeled into the drawing-room, in order, as she whispered to her mother, to enjoy Rhoda's face when she should hear the music.

Rhoda sat by and listened, in a trance of delight, while Mrs. Bodkin made the keys of the instrument delicately sound a minuet of Mozart, and then give forth more volume of tone in "The Heavens are telling." This was different, indeed, from the tinkling old harpsichord at home! The music transported her. When it ceased she was breathing quickly, and her eyes were full of tears. "Oh, how beautiful!" she faltered out.

"Why, child, you are a capital audience!" said Mrs. Bodkin, smiling kindly.

Then it was time to go home. She was made to promise that she would come again and see Minnie whenever her father would let her. She left Dr. Bodkin's house in a very different frame of mind from that in which she had entered it. Yet she was as silent on her way home as she had been in the afternoon.

How happy gentlefolks must be, who always can have music, and flowers, and talk in such soft voices, and are so polite in their manners, and so dainty in their persons! She could not help contrasting the coarse, rough ways at home with the smoothness and softness of the life she had had a glimpse of at Dr. Bodkin's. She tried to hold fast in her memory the pleasant sights and sounds of the day.

In this mood, half-enjoying, half-regretful, she arrived at her father's house to find the little parlour full of people—besides her own family and Powell there were two or three neighbours who joined in the exercises—and a prayer-meeting just culminating in a long-drawn hymn, bawled out with more zeal than sweetness by the little assembly.

CHAPTER IX.

Rhoda stood with her hand on the parlour-door for a minute or so. Little Sarah, the servant-maid, who had admitted her into the house, and had left the parlour in order to do so—for all the Maxfield household was held bound to join in these weekly prayer-meetings—told her that the hymn would be over directly. Rhoda felt shy of entering into the midst of the people assembled, and of encountering the questions and expressions of surprise which her unprecedented absence from the evening's devotions would certainly occasion.

Presently the singing ceased. Rhoda ran as quickly and noiselessly as she could along the passage, and half-way up the stairs. From her post there she heard the neighbours go away, and the street-door close heavily behind them. Now she might venture to slip down. Everyone was gone. The house was quite still. She ran into the parlour, and found herself face to face with David Powell.

Her Aunt Betty was piling the hymn-books in their place on the little table where they stood. There was no one else in the room.

"Where's father?" asked Rhoda, hastily. Then she recollected herself, and bade Mr. Powell "Good evening." He returned her salutation with his usual gentleness, but with more than his usual gravity.

"Oh!" exclaimed Betty Grimshaw, looking round from the books. "It's you, is it, Rhoda? Your father is gone with Mr. Gladwish to his house for a bit. They have some business together. He'll be back by supper."

It very seldom happened that Maxfield left his house after dark. Still such a thing had occurred once or twice. Mr. Gladwish, the shoemaker, was a steward of the Methodist society, and Maxfield not unfrequently had occasion to confer with him. Their business this evening was not so pressing but that it might have been deferred. But Maxfield did not choose to give Powell an opportunity of private conversation with himself at that time; he wanted to see his way clearer before he took the decided step of openly putting himself into opposition with the practice of his brethren, and the advice of the preacher; and he knew Powell well enough to be sure that evasions would not avail with him. Therefore he had gone out as soon as the prayers were at an end.

"I must see to the supper," said Betty, and bustled off without another word. Nothing would have kept her in Mr. Powell's society but the masterful influence of her brother-in-law. She escaped to her haven of refuge, the kitchen, where the moral atmosphere was not too rarefied for the comfortable breathing of ordinary folks.

David Powell and Rhoda were left alone together. Rhoda made a little half-timid, half-impatient movement of her shoulders. She wished Powell gone, more heartily than she had ever done before in the course of her acquaintance with him.

Powell stood, with his hands clasped and his eyes cast down, in deep meditation.

At length Rhoda took courage to murmur a word or two about going to take her cloak off. Aunt Betty would be back presently. If Mr. Powell didn't mind for a minute or two—She was gliding towards the door, when his voice stopped her.

"Tarry a little, Rhoda," said the preacher, looking up at her with his lustrous, earnest eyes. "I have something on my soul to say to you."

Rhoda's eyes fell before his, as they habitually did now. She felt as though he could read her heart; and she had something to hide in it. She did not seat herself, but stood, with one hand on the wooden mantelshelf, looking into the fire. In her other hand she held her straw bonnet by its violet ribbon, and her waving brown hair shone in the firelight.

"What is it, Mr. Powell?" she asked.

She spoke sharply, and her tones smote painfully on her hearer. He did not understand that the sharpness in it was born of fear.

"Rhoda," he began, "my spirit has been much exercised on your behalf."

He paused; but she did not speak, only bent her head a little lower, as she stood leaning in the same attitude.

"Rhoda, I fear your soul is unawakened. You are sweet and gentle, as a dove or a lamb is gentle; but you have not the root of the matter as a Christian hath it. The fabric is built on sand. Fair as it is, a breath may overthrow it. There is but one sure foundation whereon to lay our lives, and yours is not set upon it."

"I—I—try to be good," stammered Rhoda, in whom the consciousness of much truth in what Powell was saying, struggled with something like indignation at being thus reproved, with the sense of a painful shock from this jarring discord coming to close the harmonious impressions of her pleasant day, and with an inarticulate dread of what was yet in store for her. "I say my prayers, and—and I don't think I'm so very wicked, Mr. Powell. No one else thinks I am, but you."

"Oh, Rhoda! Oh, my child!" His voice grew tender as sad music, and, as he went on speaking, all trace of diffidence and hesitation fell away, and only the sincere purpose of the man shone in him clear as sunlight. "My heart yearns with compassion over you. Are those the words of a believing and repentant sinner? You 'try!' You 'say your prayers!' You are 'not so wicked!' Rhoda, behold, I have an urgent message for you, which you must hear!"

She started and looked round at him. He read her thought. "No earthly message, Rhoda, and from no earthly being. Ah, child, the eager look dies out of your eyes! Rhoda, do you ever think how much God loveth us? How much he loveth you, poor perishing little bird, fluttering blindly in the outer darkness of the world!—that darkness which comprehended not the light from the beginning."

Rhoda's tears were now dropping fast. Her lip trembled as she repeated once more, "I try—I do try to be good," with an almost peevish emphasis.

"Nay, Rhoda, I must speak. In His hand all instruments are alike good and serviceable. He has chosen me, even me, to call you to Him. However much you may despise the Messenger, the message is sure, and of unspeakable comfort."

"Oh, Mr. Powell, I don't despise you. Indeed I don't! I know you mean—I know you are good. But I don't think there's any such great harm in going to see a—a young lady who is too ill to go out. I'm sure she is a very good young lady. I'm sure I do try to be good."

That was the sum of Rhoda's eloquence. She held fast by those few words in a helpless way, which was at once piteous and irritating.

"Are you speaking in sincerity from the very bottom of your heart?" asked Powell, with the invincible, patient gentleness which is born of a strong will. "No, Rhoda; you know you are not. There is harm in following our own inclinations, rather than the voice of the spirit within us. There is harm in clinging to works—to anything we can do. There is harm in neglecting the service of our Master to pleasure any human being."

"I did forget that it was prayer-meeting night," admitted Rhoda, more humbly than before. Her natural sweetness of temper was regaining the ascendant, in proportion as her dread of what might be the subject of Powell's reproving admonition decreased. She could bear to be told that it was wrong to visit Minnie Bodkin. She should not like to be told so, and she should refuse to believe it, but she could bear it; and she began to believe that this visit was held to be the head and front of her offending. Powell's next words undeceived her, and startled her back into a paroxysm of mistrust and agitation.

"But it is not of your absence from prayer to-night that I would speak now. You are entangling yourself in a snare. You are laying up stores of sorrow for yourself and others. You are listening to the sweet voice of temptation, and giving your conscience into the hand of the ungodly to ruin and deface!" He made a little gesture towards the room overhead with his hand, as he said that Rhoda was giving her conscience into the hands of the ungodly.

"I don't know what you mean, Mr. Powell. And I—I don't think it's charitable to speak so of a person—of persons that you know nothing of."

She was entirely taken off her guard. Her head felt as if it were whirling round, and the words she uttered seemed to come out of her mouth without her will. Between fear and anger she trembled like a leaf in the wind. She would have fled out of the room, but her strength failed her. Her heart was beating so fast that she could scarcely breathe. Her distress pained Powell to the heart; pained him so much, as to dismay him with a vivid glimpse of the temptation that continually lay in wait for him, to spare her, and soothe her, and cease from his painful probing of her conscience. "Oh, there is a bone of the old man in me yet!" he thought remorsefully. "Lord, Lord, strengthen me, or I fall!"

"How hast thou counselled him that hath no wisdom? And how hast thou plentifully declared the thing as it is?"

The remembrance of the lot he had drawn came into his mind, as an answer to his mental prayer. It was natural that the words should recur to him vividly at that moment, but he accepted their recurrence as an undoubted inspiration from Heaven. The belief in such direct and immediate communications was a vital part of his faith; and to have destroyed it would, in great part, have paralysed the impetuous energy, and quenched the burning enthusiasm, which carried away his hearers, and communicated something of his own exaltation to the most torpid spirits.

He murmured a few words of fervent thanksgiving for the clear leading which had been vouchsafed to him, and without an instant's hesitation addressed the tearful, trembling girl beside him. "Listen to me, Rhoda. If it be good for your soul's sake that I lay bare my heart before you, and suffer sore in the doing of it, shall I shrink? God forbid! By His help I will plentifully declare the thing as it is. I have watched you, and your feelings have not been hid from me. No; nor your fears, and sorrows, and hopes, and struggles. I have read them all so plainly, that I must believe the Lord has given me a special insight in your case, that I may call you unto Him with power. You are suffering, Rhoda, and sorry; but you have not thrown your burden upon the Lord. You have set up His creature as an idol in your soul, and have bowed down and worshipped it. And you fancy, poor unwary lamb, that such love as yours was never before felt by mortal, and that never did mortal so entirely deserve it! And you say in your heart, 'Lo, this man talks of what he knows not! It is easy for him!' Well—I tell you, Rhoda, that I too have a heart for human love. I have eyes to see what is fair and lovely; and fancies and desires, and passions. I love—there is a maiden whom I love above all God's creatures. But, by His grace, I have overcome that love, in so far as it perilled the higher love and the higher duty, which I owe to my father in Heaven. I have wrestled sore, God knoweth. And He hath helped me, as He always will help those who rely, not on their own strength, but on His!"

Rhoda was hurried out of herself, carried away by the rush of his eloquence, in whose powerful spell the mere words bore but a small part. Eyes, voice, and gesture expressed the most absolute, self-forgetting enthusiasm. The contagion of his burning sincerity drew a sincere utterance from his hearer.

"But you talk as if it were a crime! Does anyone call you wicked and godless, because you have human feelings? I never should call you so. And, I believe, we were meant to love."

"To love? Ah, yes, Rhoda! To love for evermore, and in a measure we can but faintly conceive here below. The young maiden I love is still dearer to me than any other human being—it may be that even the angels in Heaven know what it is to love one blessed spirit above the rest—but her soul is more precious to me than her beauty, or her sweet ways, or her happiness on earth. Oh, Rhoda, look upward! Yet a little while and the wicked cease from troubling, and the weary are at rest, and there cometh peace unspeakable. This earthly love is but a fleeting show. Can you say that you connect it with your hope of Heaven and your faith in God? Does he whom you love reverence the things you have been taught to hold sacred? Is he awakened to a sense of sin? No! no! A thousand times, no! Rhoda, for his sake—for the sake of that darkened soul, if not for your own—yield not to the temptation which makes you untrue in word and deed, and chills your worship, and weighs down the wings of your spirit! Tell this beloved one that, although he were the very life-blood of your heart, yet, if he seek not salvation, you will cast him from you."

Rhoda had sunk down, half-crouching, half-kneeling, with her arms upon a chair, and her face bowed down upon her hands. She was crying bitterly, but silently; but, at the preacher's last words, she moved her shoulders, like one in pain, and uttered a little inarticulate sound.

Powell bent forward, listening eagerly. "I speak not as one without understanding," he said, after an instant's pause. "I plentifully declare the thing as it is, and as I know it. Your love—! Rhoda, your little twinkling flame, compared to the passionate nature in me, is as the faint light of a taper to a raging fire—as a trickling water-brook to the deep, dreadful sea! Child, child, you know not the power of the Lord. His voice has said to my unquiet soul, 'Be still,' and it obeys Him. Shall He not speak peace to your purer, clearer spirit also? Shall He not carry you, as a lamb, in His bosom? Now—it may be even now, as I speak to you, that His angels are about you, moving your heart towards Him. Rhoda, Rhoda, will you grieve those messengers of mercy? Will you turn away from that unspeakable love?"

The girl suddenly lifted her face. It was a tear-stained, wistfully imploring face, and yet it wore a singular expression of timid obstinacy. She was struggling to ward off the impression his words were making on her. She was unwilling, and afraid to yield to it.

But when she looked up and saw his countenance so pale, so earnest, without one trace of anger or impatience, or any feeling save profoundest pity, and sweetness, and sorrow, her heart melted. The right chord was touched. She could not be moved by compassion for herself, but she was penetrated by sorrow for him.

In an impulse of pitying sympathy she exclaimed, "Oh, don't be so sorry for me, Mr. Powell! I will try! I will do what you say, if—"

The door opened, and her father stood in the room. Rhoda sprang from her knees, rushed past him, and out at the open door.

"Man, man, what have you done?" cried Powell, wringing his hands. Then he sat down and hid his face.

Jonathan Maxfield stood looking at him with a heavy frown. "We must have no more o' this," he said harshly.

CHAPTER X.

The time which elapsed between Rhoda's first visit to Minnie Bodkin and the beginning of February—February, which was to carry Algernon Errington away to the great metropolis—was a vexed and stormy one for the Maxfield household.

Jonathan Maxfield had come to a downright quarrel with the preacher—or to something as near to a quarrel as can be attained, where the violence and vituperation are all on one side—and had ordered Powell out of his house. This was a serious step, and was sure to be searchingly canvassed. Maxfield absented himself from the next class-meeting on the plea of ill-health. There was a general knowledge in the class and throughout the Society that there had been a breach, and many members began to take sides rather warmly.

Maxfield was not a personally popular man, but he had considerable influence amongst his fellow Wesleyans; the influence of wealth, and a strong will, and the long habit of being a leading personage. David Powell, on the other hand, was not heartily liked by many of the congregation.

The Whitford Methodists had slid into a sleepy, comfortable state of mind in their obscure little corner. They acquired no new members, and lost no old ones. Even the well-devised machinery of Methodism, so calculated to enforce movement and quicken attention, had grown somewhat rusty in Whitford. Frequent change of preachers is a powerful spur to sluggish hearers; but even this—among the fundamental peculiarities of Methodism—was very seldom applied to the Whitfordians. Circumstances, and their own apathy, had brought it to pass that two elderly preachers—steady, jog-trot old roadsters—had alternately succeeded each other in exhorting and preaching to this quiet flock for several years. There was, besides, Nick Green, foreman to Mr. Gladwish, the shoemaker, who enjoyed the rank of local preacher for a time, but who finally seceded from the main body, and drew with him half-a-dozen or so of the more zealous or excitable worshippers, who subscribed to hire a room over a corn-dealer's storehouse in Lady Lane, and by the stentorian vehemence of this Sunday devotion there speedily acquired the title of Ranters.

Into this sleepy, comfortable Whitford society David Powell had burst with his startling energy and fiery eloquence, and it was impossible to be sleepy and comfortable any longer. No one likes to be suddenly roused from a doze, and Powell had awakened Whitford as with the sound of a trumpet. Yet, after the effects of the first start and shock had subsided, the Methodists began to take pride in the attention which their preacher attracted. Their little chapel was crowded. His field-preaching drew throngs of people from all the country side. Instead of being merely an obscure little knot of Dissenters, about whom no outsider troubled himself, they felt themselves to be objects of general observation. Old men, who had heard Wesley preach half a century ago, declared that this Welshman had inherited the mantle of their founder.

But then came, by no slow or doubtful degrees, the discovery that David Powell had inherited more than the traditional eloquence of John Wesley; and that, like that wonderful man, he spared neither himself nor others in the service of his Master.

He set up a standard of conduct which dismayed many, even of the leading Methodists, who did not share that exaltation of spirit which supported Powell in his disdain of earthly comforts. And the awful sincerity of his character was found by many to be absolutely intolerable.

He made a strong effort to revive the early morning services, which had quite fallen into desuetude at Whitford. What! Go to pray in the cold little meeting-house at five o'clock on a winter's morning? There was scarcely one of the congregation whose health would allow of such a proceeding.

Then his matter-of-fact interpretations of much of the Gospel teaching was excessively startling. He would coolly expect you to deprive yourself not only of superfluities, but of necessaries—such, for instance, as three meals of flesh-meat a day, which are clearly indispensable for health—in order to give to the poor.

It must be owned that he practised his own precepts in this respect; and that he literally gave away all he had, beyond the trifling sum which was needful to clothe him with decency, and to feed him in a manner which the Whitfordians considered reprehensibly inadequate. Such asceticism savoured almost of monkery. It was really wrong. At least it was to be hoped that it was wrong; otherwise—!

So the awakening preacher by no means had all his flock on his side, when they suspected him to be in opposition to old Max.

Jonathan's mind had been, as he expressed it, greatly exercised respecting his daughter. He was drawn different ways by contending impulses.

To speak to Rhoda openly; to send her to Duckwell, out of Algernon's way; to let things go on as they were going; (for was not Rhoda's reception by the Bodkins manifestly a preliminary step to her permanent rise in the social scale?) to talk openly to Algernon, and demand his intentions: all these plans presented themselves to his mind in turn, and each in turn appeared the most desirable.

Jonathan was not an irresolute man in general, because he never doubted his own perfect competency to deal with circumstances as they arose in his life. But now he felt his ignorance. He did not understand the ways of gentlefolks. He might injure his daughter by his attempt to serve her. And although he had fits of self-assertion (during which he made much of the value of his own money and of Rhoda's merits), all did not avail to free his spirit from the subjection it was in to "gentlefolks."

Again, he was urged not to seem to distrust the Erringtons by a strong feeling of opposition to Powell. Powell had warned him against letting Rhoda associate with them. Powell had even gone so far as to reprehend him for having done so. To prove Powell wholly wrong and presumptuous, and himself wholly right and sagacious, was a very powerful motive with Maxfield.

Then, too, the one soft place in his heart contributed, no less than the above-mentioned feelings, to make him pause before coming to a decisive explanation with the Erringtons, which might—yes, he could not help seeing that it might—result in a total breach between his family and them, and this increased his hesitation as to the line of conduct he should pursue. For the conviction had been growing on him daily that Rhoda's happiness was seriously involved; and Rhoda's happiness was a tremendously high stake to play.

The discussion between himself and Powell did not trouble Maxfield so much. The world—his little world, as important to him as other little worlds are to the titled, or the rich, or the fashionable, or the famous—supposed him to be greatly chagrined and exercised in spirit on this account. And people sympathised with him, or blamed him, according to their prejudices, their passions, or—sometimes—their convictions. But the truth was, old Max cared little about being at odds with the preacher, or with the congregation, or with both.

He had been an important personage among the Whitford Methodists, all through the old comfortable days of sleepy concord. And was he now to become a less important personage in these new times of "awakening?" Better war than an ignominious peace!

Nay, there came at last to be a talk of expelling him from the Methodist Society, unless he would confess his fault towards the preacher, and amend it. Maxfield had no lack of partisans in Whitford, as has been stated; but then there was the superintendent! In those days the superintendent (or, as some old-fashioned Methodists continued to call him, in the original Wesleyan phrase, the assistant) of the circuit in which Whitford was situated, was a man of great zeal and sincere enthusiasm.

For those unacquainted with the mechanism of Methodism, it may be well briefly to state what were this person's functions.

Long before John Wesley's death, the whole country was divided into circuits, in which the itinerant preachers made their rounds; and of each circuit the whole spiritual and temporal business—so far as they were connected with the aims and interests of Methodism—was under the regulation of the assistant (afterwards styled the superintendent), whose office it was to admit or expel members, take lists of the society at Easter, hold quarterly meetings, visit the classes quarterly, preside at the love-feasts, and so forth.

The period for the superintendent's next visit to Whitford was rapidly approaching. Maxfield weighed the matter, and tried to forecast the result of a formal reference of the disagreement between himself and Powell to this man's judgment. Had this superintendent, Mr. John Bateson by name, been a Whitford man, one of the old, comfortable, narrow-minded tradesmen over whom "old Max" had exercised supremacy in things Methodistical for years, Maxfield would have felt no doubt but that the matter would have ended in an unctuous admonition to Powell to moderate his unseemly excess of zeal, and in the establishment of himself, more firmly than ever, in his place as leader of the congregation.

But Mr. Bateson could not be relied on to take this sensible view. He was one of the new-fangled, upsetting, meddling sort, and would doubtless declare David Powell to have been performing his bounden duty, in being instant in season and out of season.

"So that," thought Jonathan, "I should not be master in my own house!"

And if he included in the notion of being master in his own house the power of shutting out his fellow Methodists—preacher and all—from the knowledge of his most private family affairs, the conclusion was a pretty just one. Moreover, it was one to which the very constitution of Methodism pointed à priori. But old Maxfield had never in his life been brought into collision with any one who carried out his principles to their legitimate and logical results, as did David Powell.

Maxfield's creed was a thing to take out and air, and acknowledge at chapel, and prayer-meetings, and field-preachings, and such like occasions; whilst his practice was—well, it certainly was not "too bright or good for human nature's daily food."

David Powell's uncompromising interpretation of certain precepts was intolerable to many besides Maxfield. But the majority of the Whitford Methodists looked forward to Powell's removal to another sphere of action. His stay among them had already been longer than was usual with the itinerant preachers; but it was understood to have been specially prolonged, in consequence of the abundant fruits brought forth by his ministration in Whitford. Still he would go, sooner or later, and then there would be a relaxation of the strong tension in which men's minds and consciences had been strained by the strange influence of this preacher.

But old Maxfield thought it very probable that, before leaving Whitford, the preacher might compass his (Maxfield's) expulsion from the Methodist body.

Then he took a great resolution.

One Sunday, Jonathan, James, and Rhoda Maxfield, together with Elizabeth Grimshaw, were seen at the morning service in the abbey church of St. Chad's, and again in the afternoon.

Dr. Bodkin himself stared down from his pulpit at the Methodist family. Those of the congregation to whom they were known by sight—and these were the great majority—found their devotions quite disturbed by this unexpected addition to their number.

The Maxfields kept their eyes on their prayer-books, and, outwardly, took no heed of the attention they excited. Old Jonathan and his son James looked pretty much as usual; Rhoda trembled, and blushed, and looked painfully shy whenever the forms of the service required her to rise, so as to bring her face above the pew (those were the days of pews) and within easy range of the curious eyes of the congregation.

But Betty Grimshaw held her head aloft, and uttered the responses in a loud voice, and without glancing at her book, as one to whom the Church of England service was entirely familiar. Betty was heartily delighted with the family conversion from the errors of Methodism, and supported her brother-in-law in it with great warmth. Her Methodism had, in truth, been a mere piece of conformity, for "peace and quietness' sake," as she avowed with much candour. And she was fond of saying that she had been "bred up to the Church;" by which phrase it must not be understood that Betty intended to convey to her hearers that she had entered on an ecclesiastical career.

If the sensation created in the abbey church by the Maxfields' appearance there was great, the surprise and excitement caused by their absence from the Methodist chapel was still greater. By the afternoon of that same Sunday it was known to all the Wesleyans that old Max, with his family, had been seen at St. Chad's. No one deemed it strange that the whole family should have seceded in a body from their own place of worship. It appeared quite natural to all his old acquaintances that, whither Jonathan Maxfield went, his son, and his daughter, and his sister-in-law should follow him. It is probable that, had he turned Jew or Mohammedan, they would equally have taken it for granted that his conversion involved that of the rest of his family, which opinion was certainly complimentary to old Max's force of character.

And such force of character as consists in pursuing one's own way single-mindedly, old Max undoubtedly possessed. A good, solid belief in oneself, tempered by an inability to see more than one side of a question, will cleave its way through the world like a wedge. We have seen, however, that into Maxfield's mind a doubt of himself on one subject had entered. And, as doubt will do, it weakened his action very considerably as regarded that subject; but on all other matters he was himself, and perhaps infused an extra amount of obstinacy and self-assertion into his behaviour, as though to counterbalance the one weak point.

Towards his old co-religionists he showed himself inflexible. Mr. Bateson, the superintendent, duly arrived, but Jonathan refused to see him, and walked out of his shop when the superintendent walked into it. Maxfield was grimly triumphant, and kept out of the reach of any expression of displeasure from Mr. Bateson, if displeasure he felt.

His defection was undoubtedly a blow to the Methodist community in Whitford. And much indignation, not loud but deep, was aroused in consequence against Powell, who was looked upon as the prime cause of it. What if the preacher did possess awakening eloquence and burning zeal to save sinners? Here was Jonathan Maxfield, a warm man, a respectable and a thriving man, an ancient pillar of the Society, lost to it beyond recall by Powell's means!

And by whom did Powell seek to replace such a man as old Max? By Richard Gibbs, the groom—brother of Minnie Bodkin's maid—who had hitherto enjoyed a reputation for unmitigated blackguardism; by Sam Smith, the cobbler, once drunken, now drunken no longer; by stray vagrants who were converted at his field-preaching, and by the poorest poor, and wretchedest wretched, generally!

And the worst of it was, that one could not openly find fault with all this. David Powell would, with mild yet fervent earnestness, quote some New Testament text, which stopped one's mouth, if it didn't change one's opinion. As if the words ought to be interpreted in that literal way! Well, he would go away before long; that was some comfort.

The period during which this rift in the Methodist community was widening, was a time of peculiar pleasantness to some of our Whitford acquaintance. Of these was Minnie Bodkin. By degrees the habit had established itself among a few of her friends, of meeting every Saturday afternoon in Dr. Bodkin's drawing-room.

Mr. Diamond usually made one at these meetings. Saturday was a half-holiday at the Grammar School, and he was thus at leisure. He had grown more sociable of late, and Mrs. Errington was convinced that this change was entirely owing to her advice. There was Algernon, whose sparkling spirits made him invaluable. There was Mrs. Errington, who was made welcome, as other mothers sometimes are, in right of the merits of her offspring. There was Miss Chubb very often. There was the Reverend Peter Warlock, nearly always. And of all people in the world there would often be seen Rhoda Maxfield, modestly ensconced behind Minnie's couch, or half hidden by the voluminous folds of Mrs. Errington's gown.

No sooner had Mrs. Errington heard of Rhoda's first visit to Dr. Bodkin's house, than she took all the credit of the invitation to herself. She decided that it must certainly be due to her report of Rhoda. And—partly because she really wished to be kind to the girl, partly because it seemed pretty clear that Minnie was resolved to have her own way about seeing more of her new protégée, and Mrs. Errington was minded that this should come to pass with her co-operation, so as to retain her post of first patroness—the good lady fostered the intimacy by all means in her power. The Italians have a proverb, to the effect that there are persons who will take credit to themselves for the sunshine in July. Mrs. Errington would complacently have assumed the merit of the whole solar system.

Now, at these Saturdays, there grew and strengthened themselves many conflicting feelings, and hopes, and illusions. It was a game at cross purposes, to which none of the players held the key except Algernon.

That young gentleman's perceptions, unclouded and uncoloured by strong feeling, were pretty clear and accurate. However, the period of his departure was fast approaching, and, "after me, the deluge," might be taken to epitomise his sentiments in view of possible complications which threatened to arise among his own intimate circle of friends. To whatever degree the time might seem to be out of joint, Algy would never torment himself with the fancy that he was born to set it right. "If there is to be a mess, I am better out of it," was his ingenuous reflection.

Meanwhile, whatever thoughts might be flitting about under his bright curls, nothing, save the most winning good-humour, the most insouciant hilarity, ever peeped for an instant out of his frank, shining eyes. And the weeks went by, and February was at hand.

CHAPTER XI.

In how few cases would the power to "see oursel's as ithers see us" be other than a very malevolent and wicked fairy-like gift! And, perhaps, the discovery of the real reasons why our friends like us, would not be the least mortifying part of the revelation.

Now, the Bodkins liked Miss Chubb. But they did not like her for her manners, her knowledge of the usages of polite society, her highly respectable clerical connections, or the little gummed-down curls on her forehead; on all of which Miss Chubb prided herself.

Dr. Bodkin liked her principally because she was an old acquaintance. It pleased him to see various people, and to do and say various things daily, often for no better reason than that he had seen the same people, and done and said the same things yesterday, and throughout a long, backward-reaching chain of yesterdays. Mrs. Bodkin liked her because she was good-natured, and neither strong-minded nor strong-willed enough to domineer over her. Minnie liked her because she found her peculiarities very amusing.

"Miss Chubb has the veriest rag-bag of a mind," said Minnie, "and pulls out of it, every now and then, unexpected scraps of ignorance as other folks display bits of knowledge, in the oddest way!" She could often endure to listen to Miss Chubb's chatter, when the talk of wiser people irritated her nerves. And Minnie would speak with Miss Chubb on many subjects more unreservedly than she did with any other of her acquaintances.

"What Minnie Bodkin can find in that affected old maid, to have her so much with her when she is so reserved and stand-offish to—to quite superior persons, and nearer her own age, I am at a loss to understand!" Violet McDougall would say, tossing her thin spiral ringlets. And Rose, the bitterer of the two, would make answer, raspingly: "Why, Miss Chubb toadies her, my dear. That's the secret. Poor Minnie! Of course one wishes to make every allowance for her afflicted state; but there are limits. Miss Chubb is almost a fool, and that suits poor dear Minnie's domineering spirit."

Unconscious of these and similar comments, Minnie and Miss Chubb continued to be very good friends.

There sat Miss Chubb in Dr. Bodkin's drawing-room one Saturday about noon; her round face beaming, and her fat fingers covered with huge old-fashioned rings, busily engaged in some bright-coloured worsted work. She had come early, and was to have luncheon with Mrs. Bodkin and Minnie, and was a good deal elated by the privilege, although she did her best to repress any ebullition of her good spirits, and to assume the languishing air which she chose to consider peculiarly genteel.

Minnie and Miss Chubb were alone. Mrs. Bodkin was "busy." Mrs. Bodkin was nearly always "busy." She superintended the machinery of her household very effectively. But she was one of those persons whose labours meet with scant recognition. Dr. Bodkin had a vague idea that his wife liked to be fussing about in kitchen and storeroom, and that she did a great deal more than was necessary, but, "then, you see, it amused her." He very much liked order, punctuality, economy, and good cookery; and since it "amused" Laura to supply him with these, the combination was at once fortunate and satisfactory.

"My dear Minnie," said Miss Chubb, raising her eyes to the ceiling with a languishing glance, which would have been more effective had it not been invariably accompanied by an odd wrinkling up of the nose, "did you ever, in all your days hear of anything so extraordinary as the appearance of those Methodist people at church on Sunday?"

"It was strange."

"Strange! My dear love, it was amazing. But it ought to be a matter of congratulation to us all, to see Dissenters embracing the canons of the Church! And the Methodists, especially, are such dreadful people. I believe they think nothing of foaming at the mouth, and going into convulsions, in the open chapel. I wonder if those Maxfields felt anything of the kind on Sunday? It would have been a terrible thing, my dear, if they had had to be carried out on stretchers, or anything of that sort. What would Mr. Bodkin have said?"

"I don't think there's any fear of papa's sermons throwing anybody into convulsions."

"Of course not, my dear child. Pray don't imagine that I hinted at such a thing. No, no; Mr. Bodkin is ever gentleman-like, ever soothing and composing, in the pulpit. But people, you know, who have been used to convulsions—they really might not be able to leave them off all at once. You may smile, my dear Minnie; but I assure you that such things have been known to become quite chronic. And, once a thing gets to be chronic—"

Miss Chubb left her sentence unfinished, as she often did; but remained with an expressive countenance, which suggested horrible results from "things getting to be chronic."

"It seems an odd caprice of Fate," said Minnie, who had been pursuing her own reflections, "that, no sooner do I make Rhoda Maxfield's acquaintance, for the sole reason that she is a Methodist, than she and her family turn into orthodox church people."

"People will say you converted her, my dear."

"I daresay they will, as it isn't true."

"Now, I wonder who did convert them."

"If you care to know, I think I can tell you that the real reason why Maxfield left the Wesleyans, was a quarrel he had with their preacher. My maid Jane has a brother who belongs to the Society; and he gave her an account of the matter."

"Dear, dear! You don't say so! Of course the preacher is furious? Those kind of Ranters are very violent sometimes. I remember, when I was quite a girl, a man on a tub, who used to scream and use the most dreadful language. So much so, that poor papa forbade our going within earshot of him."

"No; David Powell is not furious. I am told that he astonished some of the more bigoted of his flock, by reminding them that they ought to have charity enough to believe that a man may worship acceptably in any Christian community."

"Did he really? Now, that positively was very proper of the man, and very right. Quite right, indeed."

"So that I think we may assume that he is on the road to Heaven, Methodist though he be."

"Oh, Minnie!"

"Does that shock you, Miss Chubb?"

"Well, my dear, yes; it does, rather. My family has been connected with the Church for generations. And—one doesn't like to hear Dr. Bodkin's daughter talk of being sure that a Dissenter is on the road to Heaven."

Minnie lay back on her sofa, and looked at Miss Chubb complacently bending over her knitting. Gradually the look of amused scorn on Minnie's face softened into melancholy thoughtfulness. She wondered how David Powell would have met such an observation as Miss Chubb's. He had to deal with even narrower and more ignorant minds than hers. What method did he take to touch them? To Minnie it all seemed very hopeless, so long as men and women continued to be such as those she saw around her. And yet this preacher did move them very powerfully. If she could but meet him face to face, and have speech with him!

There was one person to whom she was strongly impelled to detail her perplexities, and to express her fluctuating feelings and opinions on more momentous subjects than she had ever yet spoken with him upon. But there were a hundred little counter impulses pulling against this strong one, and holding it in check.

Miss Chubb's voice broke in upon her meditations by uttering loudly the name that was in Minnie's mind.

"My dear, I think it's quite a case with Mr. Diamond."

Minnie's heart gave a great bound; and the deep, burning blush which was so rare and meant so much with her, covered her face from brow to chin. Miss Chubb's eyes were fixed on her knitting.

When, after a short pause, she raised them to seek some response, Minnie was quite pale again. She met Miss Chubb's gaze with bright, steady eyes, a thought more wide open than usual.

"How do you mean 'a case'?" she asked carelessly.

"I mean, my dear, a case of falling, or having fallen, in love."

The white lids drooped a little over the beautiful eyes, and a look, partly of pleasure, partly of fluttered surprise, swept over Minnie's face, as the breeze sweeps over a corn-field, touching it with shifting lights and shadows.

"What nonsense!" she said, in a little uncertain voice, unlike her usual clear tones.

"Now, my dear Minnie, I must beg to differ. I might give up my judgment to you on a point of—of—" (Miss Chubb hesitated a long time here, for she found it extremely difficult to think of any subject on which she didn't know best)—"on a point of the dead languages, for instance. But on this point I maintain that I have a certain penetration and coo-doyl. And I say that it is a case with Mr. Diamond and little Rhoda—at least on his side. And of course she would be ready to jump out of her skin for joy, only I don't think the idea has entered into her head as yet. How should it, in her station? Of course—. But as to him—! If I ever read a human countenance in my life, he admires her—oh, over head and ears! To see him staring at her from behind your sofa when she sits by Mrs. Errington—! No, no, my dear; depend upon it, I am correct. And I don't know but what it might do very well, because, although educated, Mr. Diamond is a man of no birth. And the girl is pretty, and will have all old Max's savings. So that really—"

Thus, and much more in the same disjointed fashion, Miss Chubb.

Minnie felt like one who is conscious of having swallowed a deadly but slow poison. For the present there is no pain; only a horrible watchful apprehension of the moment when the pain shall begin.

Some faculties of her mind seemed curiously numb. But the active part of it accepted the truth of what had been said, unhesitatingly.

Miss Chubb paused at last breathless.

"You look fagged, Minnie," she said. "Have I tired you? Mrs. Bodkin will scold me if I have."

"No; you have not tired me. But I think I will go and be quiet in my own room. Tell mamma I don't want any lunch. Please ring for Jane."

Mrs. Bodkin came into the room in her quick, noiseless way. She had heard the bell. Minnie reiterated her wish to be wheeled into her own room, and left quiet. She spoke briefly and peremptorily, and her desire was promptly complied with.

"I never cross her, or talk to her much when she is not feeling well," whispered Mrs. Bodkin to Miss Chubb; thereby checking a lively stream of suggestions, regrets, and inquiries which the spinster was beginning to pour forth in her most girlish manner.

"There, my darling," said her mother, preparing to close the door of Minnie's room softly. "If any of the Saturday people come I shall say you are not well enough to see them to-day."

"No!" cried Minnie, with sharp decisiveness. "I wish to come into the drawing-room by-and-by. Don't send them away. It will be Algy's last Saturday. I mean to come into the drawing-room."

Minnie, during the hour's quiet solitude which was hers before the Saturday guests began to arrive, got her thoughts into some clear order, and began to look things in the face. She did not look far ahead; merely kept her attention fixed on that which the next few hours might hold for her. She pictured to herself what she would say, and even how she would look. Cost what it might, no trace of her real feelings should appear. Her heart might bleed, but none should see the wound. She could not yet tell herself how deep the hurt was. She would not look at it, would not probe it. Not yet! That should be afterwards; perhaps in the long dim hours of her sleepless night. Not yet!

She put on her panoply of pride, and braced up her nerves to a pitch of strained excitement. And then, after all, the effort seemed to have been wasted! There was no fight to be fought, no struggle to be made. The social atmosphere among her visitors that Saturday afternoon was as mildly relaxing as the breath of a misty woodland landscape in autumn, and Minnie felt her Spartan mood melting beneath it.

Whether it were due to the influence of Dr. Bodkin's presence (the doctor usually spent the Saturday half-holiday in his study, preparing the morrow's sermon; or, it may be, occasionally reading the newspaper, or even taking a nap)—or whether it were the shadow of Algernon's approaching departure, the fact was that the little company appeared depressed, and attuned to melancholy.

Rhoda Maxfield was not there. She had privately told Algy that she could not bear to be present among his friends on that last Saturday. "They will be saying 'Good-bye' to you, and—and all that," said the girl, with quivering lips. "And I know I should burst out crying before them all." Whereupon Algy had eagerly commended her prudent resolution to stay at home.

No other of the accustomed frequenters of the Bodkins' drawing-room was absent. The doctor's was the only unusual presence in the little assembly. He stood in his favourite attitude on the hearth, and surveyed the company as if they had been a class called up for examination. Mr. Diamond sat beside Miss Bodkin's sofa, and was, perhaps, a thought more grave and silent than usual.

Minnie lay with half-closed eyes on her sofa, and felt almost ashamed of the proud resolutions she had been making. It seemed very natural to be silently miserable. No one appeared to expect her to be anything else. If she had even begun to cry, as Miss Chubb did when Algernon went to the piano and sang "Auld Lang Syne," it would have excited no wondering remark.

Pathos was not Algy's forte in general, but circumstances gave a resistless effect to his song. The tears ran down Miss Chubb's cheeks, so copiously, as to imperil the little gummed curls that adorned her face. Even the Reverend Peter Warlock, who was a little jealous of Algy's high place in Miss Bodkin's good graces, exhibited considerable feeling on this occasion, and joined in the chorus "For au—auld la—ang syne, my friends," with his deep bass voice, which had a hollow tone like the sound of the wind in the belfry of St. Chad's.

Here Mrs. Errington's massive placidity became useful. She broke the painful pause which ensued upon the last note of the song, by asking Dr. Bodkin, in a sonorous voice, if he happened to be acquainted with Lord Seely's remarkably brilliant pamphlet on the dog-tax.

"No," replied the doctor, shaking his head slowly and emphatically, as who should say that he challenged society to convict him of any such acquaintance.

It did not at all matter to Mrs. Errington whether he had or had not read the pamphlet in question, the existence of which, indeed, had only come to her own knowledge that morning, by the chance inspection of an old newspaper that had been hunted out to wrap some of Algy's belongings in. What the good lady had at heart was the introduction of Lord Seely's name, in whose praise she forthwith began a flowing discourse.

This brought Miss Chubb, figuratively speaking, to her legs. She always a little resented Mrs. Errington's aristocratic pretensions, and was accustomed to oppose to them the fashionable reminiscences of her sole London season, which had been passed in an outwardly smoke-blackened and inwardly time-tarnished house in Manchester Square, whereof the upper floors had been hired furnished for a term by the Right Reverend the Bishop of Plumbunn. And the bishop's lady had "chaperoned" Miss Chubb to such gaieties as seemed not objectionable to the episcopal mind. As the rose-scent of youth still clung to the dry and faded memories of that time, Miss Chubb always recurred to them with pleasure.

Having first carefully wiped away her tears by the method of pressing her handkerchief to her eyes and cheeks as one presses blotting-paper to wet ink, so as not to disturb the curls, Miss Chubb plunged, with happy flexibility of mood, into the midst of a rout at Lady Tubville's, nor paused until she had minutely described five of the dresses worn on that occasion, including her own and the bishopess's, from shoe to head-dress.

Mrs. Errington came in ponderously. "Tubville? I don't know the name. It isn't in Debrett?"

"And the supper!" pursued Miss Chubb, ignoring Debrett. "Such refinement, together with such luxury—! It was a banquet for Lucretius."

"What, what?" exclaimed the doctor in his sharp, scholastic key. He had been conversing in a low voice with Mr. Warlock, but the Latin name caught his ear.

"I am speaking of a supper, Dr. Bodkin, at the house of a leader of tong. I never shall forget it. Although I didn't eat much of it, to be sure. Just a sip of champagne, and a taste of—of—What do you call that delightful thing, with the French name, that they give at ball suppers? Vo—vo—What is it?"

"Vol-au-vent?" suggested Algy, at a venture.

"Ah! vol-o-voo. Yes; you will excuse my correcting you, Algernon, but that is the French pronunciation. Just one taste of vol-o-voo was all that I partook of; but the elegance—the plate, the exotic bouquets, and the absolute paraphernalia of wax-lights! It was a scene for young Romance to gloat on!"

"But what had Lucretius to do with it?" persisted the doctor.

Miss Chubb looked up, and shook her forefinger archly.

"Now, Dr. Bodkin, I will not be catechised; you can't give me an imposition, you know. And as to Lucretius, beyond the fact that he was a Roman emperor, who ate and drank a great deal, I honestly own that I know very little about him."

This time the doctor was effectually silenced. He stood with his eyes rolling from Mr. Diamond to the curate, and from the curate to Algy, as though mutely protesting against the utterance of such things under the very roof of the grammar school. But he said not a syllable.

Mr. Diamond had looked at Minnie with an amused smile, expecting to meet an answering glance of amusement at Miss Chubb's speech. But the fringed eyelids hung heavily over the beautiful dark eyes, which were wont to meet his own with such quick sympathy. Mr. Diamond felt a little shock of disappointment. Without giving himself much account of the matter, he had come to consider Miss Bodkin and himself as the only two persons in the little coterie who had an intellectual point of view in common on many topics. The circumstance that Miss Bodkin was a very beautiful and interesting woman, certainly added a flattering charm to this communion of minds. He had almost grown to look upon her attention and sympathy as peculiarly his own—things to which he had a right. And the unsmiling, listless face which now met his gaze, gave him the same blank feeling that we experience on finding a well-known window, accustomed to present gay flowers to the passers-by, all at once grown death-like with a down-drawn ghastly blind.

Mr. Diamond looked at Minnie again, and was struck with the expression of suffering on her face. He knew she disliked being condoled with about her health; so he said gently, "I think Errington's departure is depressing us all. Even Miss Bodkin looks dull."

Minnie lifted her eyelids now, and her wan look of suffering was rather enhanced by the view of those bright, wistful eyes.

"I think Errington is an enviable fellow," continued Mr. Diamond.

"So do I. He is going away."

"That's a hard saying for us, who are to remain behind, Miss Bodkin! But I meant—and I think you know that I meant—he is enviable because he will be so much regretted."

"I don't know that he will be 'so much regretted.'"

"Surely—Why, one fair lady has even been shedding tears!"

"Oh, Miss Chubb? Yes; but that proves very little. The good soul is always overstocked with sentiment, and will use any friend as a waste-pipe to get rid of her superfluous emotion."

"Well, I should have made no doubt that you would be sorry, Miss Bodkin."

"Sorry! Yes; I am sorry. That is to say, I shall miss Algernon. He is so clever, and bright, and gay, and—different from all our Whitford mortals. But for himself, I think one ought to be glad. Papa says, and you say, and I say myself, that his journey to London on such slender encouragement is a wild-goose chase. But, after all, why not? Wild geese must be better to chase than tame ones."

"Not so easy to catch, nor so well worth the catching, though," said Mr. Diamond, smiling.

"I said nothing about catching. The hunting is the sport. If a good fat goose had been all that was wanted, Mr. Filthorpe, of Bristol, offered him that; and even, I believe, ready roasted. But—if I were a man, I think I would rather hunt down my wild goose for myself."

"You had better not let Errington hear your theory about the pleasures of wild-goose hunting."

"Because he is apt enough for the sport already?"

"N—not precisely. But he would take advantage of your phrase to characterise any hunting which it suited him to undertake, and thus give an air of impulse and romance to, perhaps, a very prosaic ambition, very deliberately pursued."

"I wonder why—," said Minnie, and then stopped suddenly.

"Yes! You wonder why?"

"No, I wonder no longer. I think I understand."

"Miss Bodkin is pleased to be oracular," said Mr. Diamond, with a careless smile; and then he moved away towards the piano, where Mrs. Bodkin was playing a quaint sonata of Clementi, and stood listening with a composed, attentive face. Nevertheless, he felt some curiosity about the scope of Minnie's unfinished sentence.

The sentence, if finished, would have run thus: "I wonder why you are so hard on Algernon!" But with the utterance of the first words an explanation of Diamond's severe judgment darted into her mind. Might he not have some feeling of jealousy towards Algernon? (Miss Chubb's words were lighting up many things. Probably the good little woman had never in her life before said anything of such illuminating power.) Yes, Diamond must be jealous. Algernon had unrivalled opportunities of attracting pretty Rhoda's attention. Nay, had he not attracted it already? Minnie recalled little words, little looks, little blushes, which seemed to point to the real nature of Rhoda's feelings for Algernon. Rhoda did not—no; she surely did not—care for Matthew Diamond. Minnie had a momentary elation of heart as she thus assured herself, and at the same time she felt an impulse of scorn for the girl who could disregard the love of such a man, as though it were a valueless trifle. But, then, did Rhoda know? did Rhoda guess? And then Minnie, suddenly checking her eager mental questioning in mid-career, turned her fiery scorn against herself for her pitiful weakness.

As she lay there so graceful and outwardly tranquil, whilst the studied, passionless turns and phrases of old Clementi trickled from the keys, she had hot fits of raging wounded pride, and cold shudders of deadly depression. The numb listlessness which had shielded her at the beginning of the afternoon had disappeared during her short conversation with Diamond. She was sensitive now to a thousand stinging thoughts.

What a fool she had been! What a poor, blind fool! She tried to remember all the details of the past days. Did others see what Miss Chubb had seen in Diamond's face? And had she—Minnie Bodkin, who prided herself on her keen observation, her cleverness, and her power of reading motives—had she been the only one to miss this obvious fact? She had been deluding herself with the thought that Matthew Diamond came and sat beside her couch, and talked, and smiled for her sake! Poor fool! Why, did not his frequent visits date from the time when Rhoda's visits had begun, too? It was all clear enough now; so clear, that the self-delusion which had blinded her seemed to have been little short of madness. "As if it were possible that a man should waste his love on me!" she thought bitterly.

At that moment she caught Mr. Warlock's eyes mournfully fixed upon her. His gaze irritated her unendurably. "Am I so pitiable a spectacle?" she asked herself. "Is my folly written on my face, that that idiot stares at me in wonder and compassion?"

Minnie gave him one of her haughtiest and coldest glances, and then turned away her head.

Poor Mr. Warlock! It must be owned that there are strange, cruel pangs unjustly inflicted and suffered in this world by the most civilised persons.

The little party broke up sooner than usual. The dispirited tone with which it had begun continued to the end. Algernon made his farewells to Miss Chubb, Mr. Warlock, Mr. Diamond, and Dr. Bodkin. But to Minnie he whispered, "I will run in once more on Monday to say 'Good-bye' to your mother and to you, if I may."

The rest departed almost simultaneously. Matthew Diamond lingered an instant at the door of the drawing-room, to say to Mrs. Bodkin, "I hope this is not to be the last of our pleasant Saturdays, although we are losing Errington?"

It was an unusual sort of speech from the reserved, shy tutor, who carried his proud dread of being thought officious or intrusive to such a point, that Minnie was wont to say, laughingly, that Mr. Diamond's diffidence was haughtier than anyone else's disdain.

Mrs. Bodkin smiled, well pleased. "Oh, I hope not, indeed!" she said in her quick, low accents. "Minnie! Do you hear what Mr. Diamond is saying?"

Minnie did not answer. She thought how happy this wish of his to keep up "our pleasant Saturdays" would have made her yesterday!

CHAPTER XIII.

The manifestations of maternal vanity are apt to appear monotonous to the indifferent spectator; but, in Mrs. Errington such manifestations were, at least, not open to that reproach. Beethoven himself never surpassed her in the power of producing variations on one simple theme. And this surprising fertility of hers prevented her from being a mere commonplace bore. She never told a story twice alike. There was always an element of unexpectedness in her conversation, albeit the groundwork and foundation of it varied but little. In the overflowing gratification of her heart at Algernon's prospects, and under the excitement of his imminent departure, she would fain have bestowed some of her eloquence even on old Max, with whom her relations had been decidedly cool, since the outbreak of rude temper on his part which has been recorded. But old Max continued to be surly and taciturn for a while; he had been bitterly mortified by Mrs. Errington's talk about the marriage her son would be able to make, whenever it should please him to select a wife.

But then, after that, had come Miss Bodkin's frequent invitations to Rhoda, which had greatly mollified the old man. And presently it appeared as if Mrs. Errington had forgotten all about General Indigo's daughters, and the heiress of the eminent drysalter. At all events, she said no more on the subject of those ladies. And old Max gradually, and not slowly, recurred to his former persuasion that the Erringtons would be very glad to secure Rhoda's hand for Algernon, being well aware that her money would balance her birth and connections. True, the young man had, as yet, said nothing explicit. But, of course, he would feel it necessary to have some settled prospect before asking permission to engage himself formally to Rhoda.

"He is connected with the great ones of the earth, to be sure!" reflected Mr. Maxfield, with some exultation. "And he is a comely young chap to look upon, and full of all kinds of book-learning and accomplishments—talks foreign tongues, and sings, and plays upon instruments, and draws pictures!"

An uneasy thought crossed his mind at this point, that David Powell would consider these things as leading to reprehensible frivolity and worldliness; and that, moreover, most of his (Maxfield's) old friends would agree with the preacher in so deeming. It was not to be expected that the thoughts and habits of a lifetime could be so eradicated from old Max's mind by the mere fact of going to worship at St. Chad's, as to leave his conscience absolutely free on these and similar points. But the ultimate effect of such inward feelings was always to embitter the old man against Powell, and to make him clutch eagerly at any circumstance which should tend to prove that Powell had been wrong and himself right in their differing views of the Erringtons' intentions. He was inexpressibly loath to consider himself mistaken. Indeed, for him to be mistaken seemed to argue a general dislocation and turning topsy-turvy of things, and a terrible unchaining of the powers of darkness. If, after walking all his life in the paths of wisdom and prosperity, he were to find himself suddenly astray, and blundering on a point which nearly concerned the only tender feelings of his nature, such a phenomenon must clearly be due to the direct interposition of Satan. However, as he stood one evening in his storehouse, tying up a great parcel of sugar in blue paper, Jonathan Maxfield was feeling neither discontented nor self-distrustful. Mrs. Errington had just been speaking to Rhoda in his presence, and had said:

"Well, little one, you have quite made a conquest of Mrs. Bodkin, as well as Miss Minnie. She was praising you up to me the other day. She particularly remarked your nice manners, and attributed them to my influence—"

"I'm sure, ma'am, if there is anything nice in my manners, it was you who taught it to me," Rhoda had said simply. Upon which Mrs. Errington had been very gracious, and, without at all disclaiming the credit of Rhoda's nice manners, had mellifluously assured Mr. Maxfield that his little girl was wonderfully teachable, and had become a general favourite amongst her (Mrs. Errington's) friends.

Now all this had seemed to Maxfield to be of good augury, and an additional testimony—if any such were needed—to his own sagacity and prudent behaviour.

"It'll come right, as I foresaw," thought he triumphantly. "Another man might have been over hasty, and spoiled matters like a fool. But not me!"

Some one pushed the half-door between the shop and the storehouse, and set the bell jingling. Maxfield looked up and saw Algernon Errington, bright, smiling, and debonair, as usual.

The ordinary expression of old Max's face was not winning; and now, as he looked up with his grey eyebrows drawn into a shaggy frown, and his jaws clenched so as to hold the end of a string which he had just drawn into a knot round the parcel of sugar, he presented a countenance ill-calculated to reassure a stranger or invite his confidence. But Algy was not a stranger, and did not intend to bestow any confidence, so he came forward with the graceful self-possession which sat so well on him, and said, "How are you, Mr. Maxfield? I have not seen you for ever so long!"

"It doesn't seem very long ago to me, since we spoke together," returned old Max, tugging at the string of his parcel.

"You know I'm off to-morrow, Mr. Maxfield?"

The old man shot a hard keen glance at him from beneath the shaggy eyebrows, and nodded.

"I go by the early coach in the morning, so I must say all my farewells to-day."

Maxfield gave a sound like a grunt, and nodded again.

"It's a wonderful piece of luck, Lord Seely's taking me up so, isn't it?"

"Ah! if he means to do anything for you in earnest. So far as I can learn, his taking you up hasn't cost him much yet."

Algernon laughed frankly. "Not a bit of it, Mr. Maxfield!" he cried. "And, after all, why should he do anything that would cost him much, for a poor devil like me? No; the beauty of it is, that he can do great things for me which shall cost him nothing! He is hand and glove with the present ministry, and a regular big-wig at court, and all that sort of thing. The fact of my having good blood in my veins, and being called Ancram Errington, is no merit of mine, of course—just an accident; but it's a deuced lucky accident. I daresay Lord Seely is a stupid old hunks, but then he is Lord Seely, you see. I don't mind saying all this to you, Mr. Maxfield, because you know the world, and you and I are old friends."

It was certainly rather hard on Lord Seely to be spoken of as a stupid old hunks by this lively young gentleman, who knew little more of him than of his great-grandfather, deceased a century ago. But his lordship did not hear the artless little speech, so it did not annoy him; whereas old Max did hear it, and it gratified him considerably for several reasons. It gratified him to be addressed confidentially as one who knew the world; it gratified him to be called an old friend by this relation of the great Lord Seely. And, oddly enough, whilst he was mentally bowing down before the aristocratic magnificence of that nobleman, it gratified him to be told that the bowing down was being performed to a "stupid old hunks," altogether devoid of that wisdom which had been so largely bestowed on himself, the Whitford grocer.

Pleasant and unaffected as was the young fellow's manner to his landlord, there was a nonchalance about it which conveyed that he was quite aware of the social distance between them. And this assumption of superiority—never coarse or ponderous, like his mother's, but worn with the airiest lightness—was far from displeasing to old Max. The more of a gentleman born and bred Algernon Errington showed himself to be, the higher would Rhoda's position be, if—but old Max had almost discarded that form of presenting the future to his own mind; and was apt to say to himself, "when Rhoda marries young Errington." And then the solid advantages of the position were, so far at least, on old Max's side. Wealth and wisdom made a powerful combination, he reflected. And he was not at all afraid of being borne down or overwhelmed by any amount of gentility. Nevertheless, his spirit was in some subjection to this patrician youth, who sat opposite to him on a tea-chest, swinging his legs so affably.

There was a pause. At length Maxfield said, "And how long do you think o' being away? Or are you going to say good-bye to Whitford for evermore?"

"Indeed I hope not!"

"Oh! Then there is some folks here as you would care to see again?" said Maxfield slowly, beginning to tie up another parcel with sedulous care, and not raising his eyes from it.

"Of course there are! I—I should think you must know that, Mr. Maxfield! But I want to put myself in a better position with the world before I can—before I come back to the people I most care for."

"Very good. But it's like to be some time first, I'm afraid."

"As to seeing dear old Whitford again, you know I mean to run down here in the summer; or at least early in the autumn, when Parliament rises."

"Oh, you do?"

"To be sure! And then I hope to—to settle several things."

"Ah!"

"To a man of your experience, Mr. Maxfield, I needn't say how important it is for me to go to Lord Seely, ready and willing to undertake any employment he may offer me."

"Ah!"

"I mean, of course, that I should be absolutely free and unfettered, and ready to—to—to avail myself of opportunities. You see that, of course?"

Maxfield looked sage, and nodded. But he also looked a little glum. The conversation had not taken the turn he expected.

"Once let me get something definite—a Government post, you know, such as my cousin could get for me as easily as you could take an apprentice—and then I may please myself. I may consider myself on the first round of the ladder. And there won't be the same necessity for deferring to this person and that person. But I don't know why I'm saying all this to you, Mr. Maxfield. You understand the whole matter better than I do. By Jove, I wish I'd some of your ballast in my noddle. I'm such a feather-headed fellow!"

"You are young, Algernon, you are young," returned old Max, from whose brow the frown had cleared away entirely. "I have had a special gift of wisdom vouchsafed to me for many years past. It has been, I believe, a peculiar grace, and it is the Lord's doing, thanks be! I am not easy deceived."

"I shouldn't like to try it on, that's all I know!" exclaimed Algernon, pleasantly smiling and nodding his head.

"Albeit there is some as mistrust my judgment; young and raw men without much gift of clear-headedness, and puffed up with spiritual pride."

"Are there, really?" said Algernon, feeling somewhat at a loss what to say.

"Yes, there are. I should like such to be convinced of error. It would be a wholesome lesson."

"Not a doubt of it."

"I should like such to know—for their own soul's sake, and to teach 'em Christian humility—as you and I quite understand each other, my young friend; and as all is clear between us."

Algernon had a constitutional dislike to "clear understandings," except such as were limited to his clear understanding of other people. So he broke in at this point with one of his impulsive speeches about his prospects, and his conviction of Mr. Maxfield's wisdom, and his regrets at leaving Whitford, and his settled purpose to come back at the end of the summer and have a look at the dear old place, and the one or two persons in it who were still dearer to him. And he contrived—"contrived," indeed, is too cold-blooded and Machiavelian a word to express Algy's rapid mental process—to convey to old Max the idea that he was on the high road to fortune; that he had a warm and constant attachment to a certain person whom it was needless to name, seeing that the certain person could be no other than his playmate, pretty Rhoda; and that Mr. Jonathan Maxfield was so sagacious and keen-sighted a personage as to require no wordy explanations such as might have been needful for feebler intelligences. And then Algy said, with a rueful sort of candour, and arching those fair childlike eyebrows of his: "I say, Mr. Maxfield, I shall be awfully short of cash just at first!"

The two hands of Jonathan Maxfield, which had been laid open, and palm downwards, on the counter before him, as he listened, instinctively doubled themselves into fists. He put them one on the top of the other, and rested his chin on them.

"I don't bother my mother about it, poor dear soul, because I know she has done all she can already. Of course, if I were to hint anything to my cousin—to Lord Seely, you know—I might get helped directly. But I don't want to begin with that, exactly."

"H'm! It 'ud be a test of how much he really does mean, though!"

"Yes; but you know what you said about Lord Seely's doing great things for me which shall cost him nothing. And I felt how true your view was, directly. By George, if I want any advice between now and next August, I shall be tempted to write and ask you for it!"

Maxfield gave a little rasping cough.

"Of course I know the manners and customs of high-bred people well enough. A fellow who comes of an old family like mine seems to suck all that in with his mother's milk, somehow. But that's a mere surface knowledge, after all. And some circumstance might turn up in which I should want a more solid judgment to help my own."

Maxfield coughed again, a little less raspingly. One of his doubled-up hands unclasped itself, and he began to pass it across his stubbly chin.

"By-the-by—what an ass I was not to think of that before—would you mind lending me twenty pounds till August, Mr. Maxfield?"

"I—I'm not given to lending, Algernon; nor to borrowing either, I thank the Lord."

"Borrowing! No; you're one of the lucky folks of this world, who can grant favours instead of asking them. But it really is of small consequence, after all; I'll manage somehow, if you have any objection. I believe I have a nabob of a godfather, General Indigo, as yellow as a guinea and as rich as a Jew. My mother was talking of him the other day, and, perhaps, it would be better to ask such a little favour of one's own people. I'll look up the nabob, Mr. Maxfield."

It must not be supposed that Algy, in bringing out the name of General Indigo, had any thought of the three lovely Miss Indigos in his mind. He was quite unconscious of the existence of those young ladies; if, indeed, they were not entirely the figments of Mrs. Errington's fertile fancy. Algy had laid no deep plans. He was simply quick at seizing opportunity. The opportunity had presented itself, of dazzling old Max with his nabob godfather, and of—perhaps—inducing the stingy old fellow to lend him what he wanted, by dint of conveying that he did not want it particularly. Algy had availed himself of the opportunity, and the shot had told very effectually.

Old Max never swore. Had he been one of the common and profane crowd of worldlings, it may be that some imprecation on General Indigo would have issued from his lips; for the mention of that name made him very angry. But old Max had a settled conviction of the probable consignment to perdition of the rich nabob—who was doubtless a purse-proud, tyrannous, godless old fellow—which far surpassed, in its comforting power, the ephemeral satisfaction of an oath. He struck his clenched hand on the counter, and said, testily, "You have not heard what I had it in my mind to say! You are too rash, young man, and broke in on my discourse before it was finished!"

"I beg pardon. Did I?"

"I say that I am not given to lending nor to borrowing; and it is most true. But I have not said that I will refuse to assist you. This is a special case, and must be judged of specially as between you and me."

"Why, of course, I would rather be obliged to you than to the general, who is a stranger to me, in fact, though he is my godfather."

"There's nearer ties than godfathers, Algernon."

Algernon burst into a peal of genuine laughter. "Why, yes," said he, wiping his eyes, "I hope so!"

Old Max did not move a muscle of his face. "What was the sum you named?" he asked, solemnly.

"Oh, I don't know—twenty or thirty pounds would do. Something just to keep me going until my mother's next quarter's money comes in."

"I will lend you twenty pounds, Algernon, for which you will write me an acknowledgment."

"Certainly!"

"Being under age, your receipt is valueless in law. But I wish to have it as between you and me."

"Of course; as between you and me."

Maxfield unlocked a strong-box let into the wall. Algernon—who had often gazed at the outside of it rather wistfully—peeped into it with some eagerness when it was opened; but its contents were chiefly papers and a huge ledger. There was, however, in one corner a well-stuffed black leather pocket-book, from which old Max slowly extracted a crisp, fresh Bank of England note for twenty pounds.

"I'm sure I'm ever so much obliged to you, Mr. Maxfield," said Algernon, taking the note. He spoke without any over-eagerness, but the gleam of boyish delight in his eyes would not be suppressed.

"And now come into the parlour with me, and write the acknowledgment."

"I say, Mr. Maxfield," said Algernon, when the receipt had been duly written and signed, "you won't say anything to my mother about this?"

"Do you mean to keep it a secret?" asked the old man, sharply.

"Oh, of course I don't mind all the world knowing, as far as I'm concerned. But the dear old lady might worry herself at not being able to do more for me. Let it be just simply as between you and me," said Algernon, repeating Maxfield's words, but, truth to say, without attaching any very definite meaning to them. The old man pursed up his mouth and nodded.

"Aye, aye," he said, "as between you and me, Algernon; as between you and me."

"Upon my word, that formula of old Max's seems to be a kind of open sesame to purses and strong-boxes and cheque-books! 'As between you and me.' I wonder if it would answer with Lord Seely? Who'd have thought of old Max doing the handsome thing? Well, it's all right enough. I do mean to stick to little Rhoda, especially since her father seems to hint his approbation so very plainly. But it wouldn't do to bind myself just now—for her sake, poor little pet! 'As between you and me!' What a character the old fellow is! I wish he'd made it fifty while he was about it!"

Such was Algernon's mental soliloquy as he walked jauntily down the street, with his hand in his pocket, and the crisp bank-note between his finger and thumb.

CHAPTER XIV.

David Powell sat in his garret chamber. The fast waning light of a February afternoon fell on him as he sat close to the lattice in the sloping roof. He had placed himself there to be able to read the small print of his pocket-bible. But the light was already too dim for that. It was dusk in the garret. The strip of grey cloud, visible from the window, was beginning to turn red at its lower edge as the sun sank. It was the angry flaring red, which is often seen at the close of a cold and cloudy day, and had no suggestion of genial warmth in its deep flush. Such a snow-laden, crimson-bordered wrack of fleecy cloud, as Powell's eyes rested on, might have hung over a Lapland waste. There was no fire in the room, nor any means of making one. It was bitterly cold. The preacher's face looked white and bloodless, as if it were frozen. But he sat still, staring out at the red sunset light on the strip of sky within his view. From his seat on an old chest, which he had drawn close under the window, he could see nothing but the sky. Not one of the roofs or chimneys of Whitford was visible to him. A black wavering line moved slowly across his field of vision. It was a flight of rooks on their way home to the tall leafless elm-trees in Pudcombe Park. Nothing else moved, except the red flare creeping upward by slow and imperceptible degrees.

Suddenly the little Bible fell from Powell's numbed right hand on to the carpetless floor, and, with a start, he turned his head and looked around him. By contrast with the wintry light without, the garret appeared quite dark to him, and it was not until after a few seconds that his eye became sufficiently accustomed to its gloom, to perceive the book lying almost at his feet. He picked it up, and began to chafe his numbed fingers, rising at the same time, and walking up and down the room.

His thoughts had been straying idly as he sat at the window, with his eyes fixed on the sky. They had gone back to the days of his boyhood, and in memory he had seen the wild Welsh valley where he was born, and heard the bleat of sheep from the hills, as he had listened to it many a summer morning, sitting ragged and barefoot on the turf. And with these recollections the image of Rhoda Maxfield was strangely mingled, appearing and disappearing, like a face in a dream. Indeed, he had been dreaming open-eyed in his solitude, unconscious of the cold and the gathering dusk.

Now, such aimless, vagrant wanderings of the fancy were considered reprehensible by earnest Methodists; and by none were they more strongly disapproved of than by David Powell himself. His life was guided, as nearly as might be, in conformity with the rules laid down by John Wesley himself for the helpers, as his first lay-preachers were called. And among these rules, diligence—unflagging, unfaltering—diligence and the strenuous employment of every minute, so that no fragment of time should be wasted, were emphatically insisted upon. Powell had ceased to read when the daylight waned, and remained in his place by the window, intending to devote a few minutes of the twilight to the rigid self-examination which was his daily habit. And instead, behold! his mind had strayed and wandered in idle recollections and unsanctified imaginings.

Presently he began to mutter to himself, as he paced up and down the chill bare room.

"What have I to do with these things," he said aloud, "when I should be about my Master's business? Where is the comfortable assurance of old days—the bright light which used to shine within my soul, turning its darkness to noon-day? I have lost my first love;[1] I have fallen from grace; and the enemy finds a ready entrance for any idle thoughts he wills to put into my mind. And yet—have I not striven? Have I not searched my own heart with sincerity?"

[Footnote 1: A common expression among the early Methodists, to indicate the first fervour of religious zeal.]

All at once, stopping short in his walk across the garret floor, he threw himself on his knees beside the bed, and, burying his face in his hands, began to pray aloud. The sound of his own voice rising ever higher, as his supplications grew more fervent, hid from his ears the noise of a tap at the door, which was repeated twice or thrice. At length, the person who had knocked pushed the door gently open a little way, and called him by his name, "Mr. Powell! Mr. Powell!"

"Who calls me?" asked the preacher, lifting his head, but not rising at once from his knees.

"It's me, sir; Mrs. Thimbleby. I have made you a cup of herb tea accordin' to the directions in the Primitive Physic,[2] and there is a handful of fire in the kitchen grate, whilst here it is downright freezing. Dear, dear Mr. Powell, I can't think it right for you to set for hours up here by yourself in the cold!"

[Footnote 2: A collection of receipts, published by John Wesley, under the title of "Primitive Physic; or, An Easy and Natural Method of Curing most Diseases."]

The good widow—a gentle, loquacious woman, with mild eyes and a humble manner—had advanced into the room by this time, and stood holding up a lighted candle in one hand, whilst with the other she drew her scanty black shawl closer round her shoulders.

"I will come, Mrs. Thimbleby," answered Powell. "Do you go downstairs, and I will follow you forthwith."

"Well, it is a miracle of the Lord if he don't catch his death of cold," muttered the widow as she redescended the steep, narrow staircase. "But there! he is a select vessel, if ever there was one; and a burning and a shining light. And I suppose the Lord will take care of His own, in His own way."

Mrs. Thimbleby sat down by her own clean-swept hearth, in which a small fire was burning brightly. The little kitchen was wonderfully clean. Not a speck of rust marked the bright pewter and tin vessels that hung over the dresser. Not an atom of dust lay on any visible object in the place. There was no sound to be heard save the ticking of the old eight-day clock, and, now and then, the dropping of a coal on to the hearth. As soon as she heard her lodger's step on the stairs, Mrs. Thimbleby bestirred herself to pour out the herb tea of which she had spoken.

"I wish it was China tea, Mr. Powell," she said, when he entered the kitchen. "But you won't take that, so I know it's no good to offer it to you. Else I have a cup here as is really good, and came out of my new lodger's pot."

"You do not surely take of what is not your own!" cried Powell, looking quickly round at her.

"Lord forbid, sir! No, but the gentleman drinks a sight of tea. And last evening he would have some fresh made, and I say to him"—Mrs. Thimbleby's narrative style was chiefly remarkable for its simplification of the English syntax, by means of omitting all past tenses, and thus getting rid of any difficulty attendant on the conjugation of irregular verbs—"I say, 'Won't you have none of that last as was made for breakfast, as is beautiful tea, and only wants warming up again?' But he refuse; and then I ask him if I may use it myself, seeing I look on it as a sin to waste anything; and he only just look up from his book and nod his head, and say, 'Do what you like with it, ma'am,' and wave his hand as much as to say I may go. He is not much of a one to talk, but he paid the first week punctual, and is as quiet as quiet, and—there he is! I hear his key in the door."

A quick, firm step came along the passage, and Matthew Diamond appeared at the door of the kitchen. "Will you be good enough to give me a light?" he said, addressing the landlady. Then he saw David Powell standing near the fire, and looked at him curiously. Powell did not turn, nor seem to observe the new comer. His head was bent down, and the firelight partially illumined his profile, which was presented to anyone standing at the door. Mr. Diamond silently formed the word "Preacher?" with his lips, at the same time nodding towards Powell, and raising his eyebrows interrogatively. Mrs. Thimbleby answered aloud with alacrity, well pleased to begin a conversation with her taciturn lodger.

"Yes, sir; it is our preacher, Mr. Powell, as is one of our shiningest lights, and an awakening caller of sinners to repentance. You've maybe heard him preach, sir? A many of the unconverted—ahem!—a many as does not belong to the connexion has come to hear him in Whitford Wesleyan Chapel, and on Whit Meadow. And we have had seasons of abundant blessing and refreshment."

Powell had turned round at the beginning of Mrs. Thimbleby's speech, and was looking earnestly at Mr. Diamond. The latter, who had seen the preacher only in the full tide of his eloquence and the excitement of addressing a crowded audience, was struck by the change in the face now before him. It was much thinner, haggard, and deadly pale. There were lines round the mouth, which expressed anxiety and suffering; and the eyes were sunk in their orbits, and startlingly bright. Diamond was, in fact, startled out of his usual silent reserve by the glance which met his own, and exclaimed, impulsively, "I'm afraid you are ill, Mr. Powell!"

"No," returned the other at once, and without hesitation. "I have no bodily ailment. I have seen you at the house of Jonathan Maxfield, have I not?"

"Yes; I have been in the habit of going there to read with a young gentleman. My name is Diamond—Matthew Diamond."

"I know it," answered Powell. "I should like, if you are willing, to say a few words to you privately."

Diamond was a good deal surprised, and a little displeased, at this proposition. He had been interested in the Methodist preacher, and the thought had more than once crossed his mind that he should like to see more of the man, whose whole personality was so striking and uncommon. But Mr. Diamond had felt his wish just as he might have wished to have Paganini with his violin all to himself for an evening; or to learn vivâ voce from Edmund Kean how he produced his great effects. To be the object and subject of a private sermon from this Methodist enthusiast (for Diamond could conceive no other reason for the preacher's desiring an interview with him than zeal for converting) was, however, a different matter; and Diamond had half a mind to decline the private communication. He was a man peculiarly averse to outspokenness about his own feelings. Nor was he given to be frank and diffusive on topics of mere intellectual speculation; although, occasionally, he could exchange thoughts on such matters with a congenial mind. But he knew well enough that, with the Methodists in general, an excited state of feeling, which might do duty for conviction, was the aim and end of their teaching and preaching.

"This man is ignorant and enthusiastic, and will make himself absurd and me uncomfortable, and I shall have to offend him, which I don't wish to do," thought Mr. Diamond, standing stiff and grave with the candle in his hand. But once more the sight of Powell's haggard, suffering face and bright wistful eyes touched him; and once more the resolute Matthew Diamond suffered himself to be swayed by an impulse of sympathy with this man.

"Oh," said he, "well, you can come into my sitting-room."

The invitation was not very graciously given, but Powell did not seem to heed that at all. Mrs. Thimbleby stood in admiring astonishment as her two lodgers left the kitchen together.

The two young men, so strangely contrasted in all outward circumstances, entered the small parlour, which served as dining-room, sitting-room, and study to Matthew Diamond, and seated themselves at a table almost covered with books, one corner of which had been cleared to admit of a little tea-tray being placed upon it.

"Will you share my tea, Mr. Powell?" asked Diamond, as he filled a cup with the strong brown liquid.

"No; I thank you for proffering it to me, but I do not drink tea."

"I am sorry for that, for I am afraid I have no other refreshment to offer you. I don't indulge in wine or spirits."

Diamond threw into his manner a certain determined commonplaceness, as though to quench any tendency to excitement or exaltation which might show itself in the preacher. Although he would have expressed it in different terms, Matthew Diamond had at the bottom of his mind a feeling akin to that in Miss Chubb's, when she declared her dread of the Maxfield family "going into convulsions" in the parish church of St. Chad.

"I will take a cup of tea myself, if you have no objection," said Diamond, suiting the action to the word, and stretching out his legs, so as to bring them within reach of the warmth from the fire. "Won't you draw nearer to the hearth, Mr. Powell?"

Powell sat looking fixedly into the fire with an abstracted air. His hands were joined loosely, and rested on his knees. The firelight shone on his wan, clearly-cut face, but seemed to be absorbed and quenched in the blackness of his hair, which hung down in two straight, thick locks behind his ears. He did not accept Mr. Diamond's invitation to draw nearer to the warm hearth, but, after a pause, turned his face to his companion, and said, "It is on behalf of the young maiden, Rhoda Maxfield, that I would speak with you, sir."

He could scarcely have said anything more thoroughly unexpected and disconcerting to Matthew Diamond. The latter did not start or stare, or make any strong demonstration of surprise, but he could not help a sudden flush mounting to his face, much to his annoyance.

"About Miss Rhoda Maxfield?" he returned coldly; "I do not understand what concern either you or I can have with any private conversation about that young lady."

"My concern with Rhoda is that of one who has had it laid upon him to lead a tender soul out of the darkness into the light, and who suddenly finds himself divided from that precious charge, even at the moment when he hoped the goal was reached. Her father has left our Society, and has thus carried Rhoda away from the reach of my exhortations."

"By Jove!" thought Diamond to himself, as he turned his keen grey eyes on the preacher, "this is a specimen of spiritual conceit on a colossal scale!" Then he said aloud, "You must console yourself with the hope that the exhortations she will hear in the parish church will differ from your own rather in manner than matter, Mr. Powell. There really are some very decent people among the congregation of St. Chad's."

"Nay," answered Powell, with simple gentleness, "do you think I doubt it? It has been the boast of Methodism that it receives into its bosom all denominations of Christians, without distinction. The Churchman and the Dissenter, the Presbyterian and the Independent, are alike welcome to us, and are free alike to follow their own method of worship. In the words of John Wesley himself, 'one condition, and one only, is required—a real desire to save their souls. Where this is, it is enough; they desire no more. They lay stress upon nothing else. They ask only, Is thy heart herein as my heart? If it be, give me thy hand.'"

"Methodism has changed somewhat since the days of John Wesley," said Diamond, drily.

"Not Methodism, but perhaps—Methodists. But it was not of Methodism that I had it on my mind to speak to you now."

Diamond controlled his face and his attitude to express civil indifference; but—his pulse was quickened, and he hid his mouth with his hand. Powell went on: "I have turned the matter in my mind, many ways. And I have sought for guidance on it with much wrestling of the spirit. But I had not received a clear leading until this evening. When I saw you standing in the doorway, it was borne in upon me that you could be an instrument of help in this matter. And the leading was the more assured to me, because that to-day, having opened my Bible after due supplication, mine eyes fell at once on the words, 'I have heard of thee by the hearing of the ear; but now mine eyes seeth thee.'

Now these words were dark to me until just now, when you seemed to appear as the explanation and interpretation thereof."

Diamond could not but acknowledge to himself that all the scriptural phraseology, and the technicalities of sectarianism, which he found merely grotesque or disgusting in men of common, vulgar natures, came from this man's lips with as much ease and propriety as if he had been a Hebrew of old time uttering his native idiom. Indeed, the impression of there being something oriental about David Powell, which Diamond had received on first seeing him, was deepened on further acquaintance. This black-haired Welshman was picturesque and poetic, despite his threadbare cloth suit, made in the ungraceful mode of the day; and impressive, despite his equally threadbare phrases. It is possible to make a wonderful difference in the effect both of clothes and words, by putting something earnest and unaffected inside them.

"What is the help you seek? And how can I help you?" asked Diamond, with grave directness.

"You are acquainted with the daughter of the principal of the grammar school here—"

"Miss Bodkin?"

"Yes. Do you think that, if you carried to her a request that I might be permitted to see and speak with her, she would admit me?"

"I—I don't know," answered Diamond, greatly taken aback.

There was a pause. Each man was busy with his own thoughts. "Rhoda is beyond my reach now," said Powell at length. "I can neither see nor speak with her. Nor do I know of any of those who see her familiarly who would be likely to influence her for good, except Miss Bodkin. I am told that she is a lady of much ability and power of mind; and I hear, moreover, of her doing many acts of charity and kindness. You know her well, do you not?"

"I know her. Yes."

"Would you consent to carry such a request from me?"

Diamond hesitated. "Why not prefer the request yourself?" he said. "If you have any good reason for desiring an interview with Miss Bodkin, I believe she would grant it."

"I had thought of doing so. I had thought, even, of writing all that I have to say. But, for many reasons, I believe it would be more profitable for me to see her face to face. I am no penman. I am indeed, as you perceive, a man very ignorant in the world's learning and the world's ways."

Diamond suspected a covert boast under this humble speech, and answered in his coolest tones, "The first is a disadvantage—or an advantage, as you choose to consider it—which you share with a good many of your brethren, Mr. Powell. As to the latter kind of ignorance—Methodists are generally thought to have worldly wisdom enough for their needs."

Powell bent his head. "I would fain have more learning," he said in a low voice, "but only as a means, not as an end—not as an end."

"But," said Diamond, in a constrained voice, "it seems to me hardly worth while to trouble Miss Bodkin, by asking for an interview on any such grounds. Since you are charitable enough to believe that Miss Maxfield's spiritual welfare is not imperilled by going to St. Chad's, I don't see what need there is for you to be uneasy about her!"

"I am uneasy; but not for the reasons you suppose. Rhoda is very guileless, and I would shield her from peril."

Diamond looked at the preacher sternly. "I don't understand you," he said. "And to say the truth, Mr. Powell, I disapprove of meddling in other people's affairs. Miss Maxfield is a young lady for whom I have the very highest respect."

For the first time a flame of quick anger flashed from Powell's dark eyes, as he answered, "Your high respect would teach you to stand aside and let the innocent maiden pine under a delusion which might spoil her life and peril her soul; mine prompts me to step forward and awaken her to the truth, never heeding what figure I make in the matter."

The sudden passion in the man's face and figure was like a material illumination. Diamond had grown pale, and looked at him attentively, and in silence.

"Do you think," proceeded Powell, his thin hands working nervously, and his eyes blazing, "that I do not understand how pure a creature she is—how innocent, confiding, and devoid of all suspicion of guile? Yea, and even, therefore, the more in need of warning! But because I am a man still young in years, and neither the maiden's brother, nor any kin to her, I must stand silent and withhold my help, lest the world should say I am transgressing its rules, and bid me mind my own affairs, or deride me for a fanatical fool! Do you think I do not foresee all this? or do you think that, foreseeing it, I heed it? I have broken harder bonds than that; I have fought with strong impulses, to which such motives are as cobwebs—" Then, with a sudden check and change of tone which a grain of affectation would have sufficed to render ludicrous, but which, in its simplicity, was almost touching, he added, in a low voice, "I ask pardon for my vehemence; I speak too much of myself. I have had some suffering in this matter, and am not always able to control my words. I have had strange visitings of the old Adam of late. It is only by much striving after grace, and by strong wrestling in prayer, that I have not wandered utterly from the right way."

He had risen from his chair at the beginning of his speech, and now sank down again on it wearily, with drooping head.

Matthew Diamond sat and looked at him still with the same earnest attention; but blended, now, with a look of compassion. He was thinking to himself what must be the force of enthusiastic faith, which could so subdue the fiery nature of this man, and how he must suffer in the conflict. Presently, he said aloud, "I am ready to admit, Mr. Powell, that you are actuated by conscientious motives; I am sure that you are. But your conscience cannot be a rule for all the rest of the world. Mine may counsel me differently, you know."

"Oh, sir, we are neither of us left to our own guidance, thanks be to God! There is a sure counsellor that can never fail us. I have searched diligently, and I have received a clear leading which I cannot mistrust. I do not feel free to tell you more particularly the grounds of my anxiety respecting Rhoda Maxfield. But I do assure you, with all sincerity and solemnity, that I have her welfare wholly at heart, and that I would not injure her by the least shadow of blame in the opinion of any human being."

There was silence for some minutes. Diamond leant his head on his hand, and reflected. Then at length he said, "Look here, Mr. Powell; I believe, if you had pitched on anyone else in all Whitford to speak to about Miss Rhoda Maxfield, I should have declined to assist you. But Miss Bodkin is so superior in sense and goodness to most other folks here, that I am sure whatever you may say to her confidentially will be sacred. And then, she may be able to set you right, if you are wrong. She has the woman's tact and insight which we lack. And, besides, she is fond of Rhoda." He coloured a little as he said the name, and dropped his voice.

"You confirm all that I have heard of this lady. She is abundantly blessed with good gifts."

"Well, then, Mr. Powell, I will write to Miss Bodkin to-morrow, telling her merely that you desire to speak with her, and entreat her good offices on behalf of one who needs them."

Powell sprang up from his seat eagerly. "I thank you, sir, from a full heart," he said. "You are doing a good action. Farewell."

Diamond held out his hand, which the preacher grasped in his own. The two hands were as strongly contrasted as the owners of them. Diamond's was broad, muscular, and yet smooth—a strong young hand, full of latent power. Powell's was slender, nervous, showing the corded veins, and with long emaciated fingers. It, too, indicated force; but force of a different kind. The one hand might have driven a plough, or written out a mathematical problem; the other might have wielded a scimitar in the service of the Prophet, or held up a crucifix in the midst of persecuting savages. As they stood for a second thus hand in hand, Powell's mouth broke into a wonderfully sweet and radiant smile, and he said, "You see, sir, I was right to have faith in my counsellor. You have helped me."

Diamond sat musing late that night, and was roused by the cold to find his fire gone out and his watch marking half-past twelve o'clock. "I wonder," he thought to himself, "if Powell has any foundation for his hints, and if any scoundrel is playing false with her. If there be, I should like to shoot him like a dog!"

CHAPTER XV.

Minnie and her father had been having a discussion about David Powell, and the discussion had heated Dr. Bodkin, and spoiled his half hour after dinner, which was wont to be the pleasantest half hour of his day. For Dr. Bodkin did not sit over his wine alone. When there were no guests, his wife and Minnie remained at the black shining board—in those days the table-cloth was removed for the dessert, and the polish of the mahogany beneath it was a matter of pride with notable housekeepers like Mrs. Bodkin—and his wife poured out his allowance of port and peeled his walnuts for him, and his daughter chatted with him, and coaxed him, and sometimes contradicted him a little, and there would be no more school until to-morrow morning, and altogether the doctor was accustomed to enjoy himself. But on this occasion the poor gentleman was vexed and disturbed.

"It's a parcel of stuff and nonsense!" said the doctor, jerking his legs under the table.

"That remains to be proved, papa. If the man has anything of consequence to say, I shall soon discover it."

"Anything of consequence to say? Fudge! He is coming begging, perhaps—"

"I don't believe that, papa. Nor, I think, do you in your heart," returned Minnie, with a little smile at one side of her mouth.

But the doctor was too much disturbed to smile. "Why shouldn't he come begging? It won't be his modesty that will stand in his way, I daresay. Or perhaps he wants to 'convert' you, as these fellows are pleased to call it!"

"Nobody seems to be afraid of our wanting to convert him!" said Minnie.

"I don't like the sort of thing. I don't like that people should have it to say that my daughter is honoured with the confidences of a parcel of ranting, canting cobblers."

"But, papa, would it not—I am speaking in sober sincerity, and because I really do want your serious answer—don't you think it would be wrong to be deterred from helping anyone with a kind word or a kind deed, by the fear of people saying this or that?"

"Helping a fiddlestick!" cried Dr. Bodkin magisterially, but incoherently.

Minnie's face fell. It had been paler than usual of late, and she had been suffering and feeble. She never lamented aloud, nor was importunate, nor even showed weakness of temper; but her father, who loved her very tenderly, understood the chill look of disappointment well enough, and it was more than he had strength to bear.

"Of course the man can come and say his say," he added, jerking his legs again impatiently under the sheltering mahogany, "especially as you say he is going away from Whitford directly."

"Yes; but there is no guarantee that he will not come back again. I cannot promise you that, on his behalf."

This unflinching straightforwardness of Minnie's was a fertile source of trouble between her father and herself.

It was certainly rather hard on the doctor to be forced to surrender absolutely, without any of those pleasant pretences which are equivalent to the honours of war. Fortunately—we are limiting ourselves to the doctor's point of view—fortunately at this moment his eye fell on Mrs. Bodkin, who, made exquisitely nervous by any collision between the two great forces that ruled her life, was pushing the decanter of port backwards and forwards on the slippery table, quite unconscious of that mechanical movement.

"Laura, what the—mischief are you about? Do you think I want my wine shaken up like a dose of physic?"

This kind of diversion of the vials of the doctor's wrath on to his wife's devoted head was no uncommon finale to any altercation in which the reverend gentleman happened not to be getting altogether the best of it.

"I think," said Mrs. Bodkin, speaking very quickly, and in a low tone, as was her wont, "that very likely Mr. Powell wants to interest Minnie on behalf of Richard Gibbs."

"And who, pray, if I may venture to inquire, is Richard Gibbs?" asked the doctor, in his most awful grammar-school manner, and with a sarcastic severity in his eye, as he uttered the name 'Gibbs,' and looked at Mrs. Bodkin as though he expected her to be very much ashamed of herself.

"Brother of Jane, our maid. He is a groom at Pudcombe Hall, and a Wesleyan. Mr. Powell may want to recommend him, or get him a place."

"What, is the fellow going to leave Pudcombe Hall, then?"

"Not that I know of exactly. But it struck me it might be about Richard Gibbs that he wanted to speak, because Gibbs is a Wesleyan, you know."

"I suppose he wants to meddle and make himself of consequence in some way. Egotism and conceit—rampant conceit—are the mainsprings that move such fellows as this Powell."

The doctor rose majestically from the table and walked towards the door. There he paused, and turning round said to his wife, "May I request, Laura, that somebody shall take care that I get a cup of hot tea sent to me in the study? I don't think it is much to request that my tea shall not be brought to me in a tepid state!"

Mrs. Bodkin had a great gift of holding her tongue on occasions. She held it now, and the doctor left the room with dignity.

That evening Minnie wrote the following note:—

"MY DEAR MR. DIAMOND,—I shall be able to see Mr. Powell at one o'clock to-morrow. Should that hour not suit his convenience, perhaps he will do me the favour to let me know.

"Yours very truly,

"M. BODKIN."

It was the first time she had ever written to Mr. Diamond. The temptation to make her letter longer than was absolutely needful had been resisted. But the consciousness that the temptation had existed, and been overcome, was present to Minnie's mind; and she curled her lip in self-scorn as she thought, "If I wrote him whole pages it would only bore him. He would prefer one line written in Rhoda's school-girl hand, out of Rhoda's school-girl head, to the best wit I could give him; aye, or to the best wit of a wittier woman than I." Then suddenly she tore the note she had just written across, threw it into the fire, and watched it blaze and smoulder into blackness. "I will ask you to write a line for me, mamma," she said, when Mrs. Bodkin re-entered the drawing-room, after having sent in the doctor's cup of tea to the study.

"To whom, Minnie?"

"To Mr. Diamond. Please say that I will receive Mr. Powell at one o'clock to-morrow, if that suits him."

"I daresay it is really about Richard Gibbs," said Mrs. Bodkin, as she sealed her note.

It was not without a slight feeling of nervousness that Minnie Bodkin, the next day, heard Jane's announcement, "Mr. Powell is below, Miss. Mistress wishes to know if you would see him in your own room?"

Minnie gave orders that the preacher should be shown upstairs, and Jane ushered him in very respectfully. Dr. Bodkin's old man-servant took no pains to hide his disgust at the reception of such a guest; and declared in the servants' hall that the sight of one of them long-haired, canting Methodys fairly turned his stomach. But Jane, remembering her brother Richard's reformation, was less militant in her orthodoxy, and expressed the opinion that "Mr. Powell was a very good man for all his long hair"—a revolutionary sentiment which was naturally received with incredulity and contempt.

Minnie looked up eagerly when the preacher entered the room, and scanned him with a rapid glance as she asked him to be seated. "I am a poor feeble creature, Mr. Powell," she said, "who cannot move about at my own will. So you will forgive my bringing you up here, will you not?"

Powell, on his part, looked at the young lady with a steady, searching gaze. Minnie was accustomed to be looked at admiringly, affectionately, deferentially, curiously, pityingly (which she liked least of all)—sometimes spitefully. But she had never been looked at as David Powell was looking at her now; that is, as if his spirit were scrutinising her spirit, altogether regardless of the form which housed it.

"I thank you gratefully for letting me have speech of you," he said; and his voice, as he said it, charmed Minnie's sensitive and fastidious ear.

"Do you know, Mr. Powell, that for some time past I have had the wish to make your acquaintance? But circumstances seemed to make it unlikely that I ever should do so."

"Yes; it was very unlikely, humanly speaking. But I have no doubt that our meeting has been brought about in direct answer to prayer."

Minnie was at a loss what to say. It was almost as startling to hear a man profess such a belief on a week-day, and in a quiet, matter-of-fact tone, as it would have been to find Madame Malibran conducting all her conversation in recitative, or to hear Mr. Dockett begin his sentences with a "whereas."

"You wish to speak to me on behalf of some one, Mr. Diamond tells me?" said Minnie, after a slight hesitation.

"Yes; you have been kind and gracious to a young girl beneath you in worldly station, named Rhoda Maxfield."

"Rhoda! Is it of her you wish to speak?" cried Minnie, in great surprise. She felt a strange sick pang of jealousy. It was for Rhoda's sake, then, that Mr. Diamond had begged her to receive Powell!

"You are kindly disposed towards the maiden?" said Powell, anxiously; for Minnie's change of countenance had not escaped him. For her life, Minnie could not cordially have said "yes" at that moment.

"I—Rhoda is a very good girl, I believe; what would you have me do for her?"

"I would have you dissuade her from resting her hopes—I speak now merely of earthly hopes and earthly prudence—on the attachment of one who is unstable, vain, and worldly-minded."

"What do you mean? I—I do not understand," stammered Minnie, with fast-beating heart.

"May I speak to you in full confidence? If you tell me I may do so, I shall trust you utterly."

"What is this matter to me? Why do you come to me about it?"

"Because I have been told by those whose words I believe, that you are gifted with a clear and strong judgment, as well as with all qualities that win love."

"You are mistaken. I am not gifted with the qualities that win love," said Minnie, bitterly. Then she asked, abruptly, "Did Mr. Diamond advise you to speak to me about Rhoda?"

"Nay; it was I who had recourse to his intercession to get speech of you."

"But he knows your errand?"

"In part he knows it. But I was not free to say to him all that I would fain say to you."

Minnie's face had a hard set look. "Well," she said, after a short silence, "I cannot refuse to hear you. But I warn you that I do not believe I can do any good in the matter."

"That will be overruled as the Lord wills."

Then David Powell proceeded to set forth his fears and anxieties about Rhoda, more fully and clearly than he had done to Diamond. He declared his conviction that the girl was deceived by false hopes, and was fretting and pining because every now and then misgivings assailed her which she could not confess to any one, and because that her conscience was uneasy. "The maiden is very guileless and tender-natured," said Powell, softly.

"Don't you think you a little exaggerate her tenderness, Mr. Powell? Persons capable of strong feelings themselves are apt to attribute all sorts of sentiments to very wooden-hearted creatures."

He looked at her earnestly, and shook his head.

"Rhoda always seems to me to be rather phlegmatic; very gentle and pretty, of course. But, do you know, I should not be afraid of her breaking her heart."

There was a hard tone in Minnie's voice, and a hard expression about her mouth, which hurt and disappointed the preacher. He had expected some warmth of sympathy, some word of affection for Rhoda.

"You do not know her," he said sadly.

"And then, Mr. Powell, Algernon Errington—you know, I suppose, that Mr. Errington is a great friend of mine?"

"I will not willingly say aught to offend you, nor to offend against Christian courtesy. But there are higher duties—more solemn promptings—that must not be resisted."

"Oh, I am not offended. But, let me ask you, what right have we to assume that Mr. Errington has ever deceived Rhoda, or has ever thought of her otherwise than as the friend and playmate of his childhood?"

"I am convinced that he has led her to believe he means, some day, to marry her. I cannot resist that conviction."

"Marry her! Why, Mr. Powell, the thing is absurd on the face of it. A boy of nineteen, and in Algernon's position!—why, any person of common sense would understand that such an idea could not be looked at seriously."

Powell made himself some silent reproaches for his want of faith. This lady might not be soft and sweet; but she had evidently the clear judgment which he sought for to help Rhoda. And yet he had been discouraged, and had almost distrusted his "leading," because of a little coldness of manner. He answered Minnie eagerly:

"It is true! I well know that what you say is true; but will you tell Rhoda this? Will you plentifully declare to her the thing as it is?"

"Rhoda has her father to advise her, if she needs advice."

"Nay; her father is no adviser for her in this matter. He is an ignorant man. He does not understand the ways of the world—at least, not of that world in which the Erringtons hold a place—and he is prejudiced and stiff-necked."

There was a short silence. Then Minnie said:

"I do not see how I can interfere. I should, in fact, be taking an unjustifiable liberty, and—Mr. Errington is going away. They will both forget all about this boy-and-girl nonsense, if people have the wisdom to let it alone."

"Rhoda will not forget; she will brood silently over her secret feelings, and her thoughts will be diverted from higher things. She will fall away into outer darkness. Oh think, a word in season, how good it is! Consider that you may save a perishing soul by speaking that word. I have prayed that I might leave behind me in this place the assurance that this lamb should not be utterly lost out of the fold."

Powell had risen to his feet in his excitement, and walked away from Minnie towards the window, with his head bent, and his hands clasping his forehead. Minnie felt something like repulsion, and the sort of shame which an honest and proud nature feels at any suspicion of histrionism in one whom it has hitherto respected. Surely the man was exaggerating—consciously exaggerating—his feeling on this matter! But, then, Powell turned, and came back towards her; and she saw his face clearly in the full sunlight, and instantly her suspicion vanished. That face was wan and haggard with suffering, and there was a strange brilliancy in the eyes, almost like the brightness of latent tears. The tears sprang sympathetically to her own eyes as she looked at him. It was impossible to resist the pathos of that face. There was a strange appealing expression in it, as of a suffering of which the sufferer was only half-conscious, that went straight to Minnie's heart.

"Mr. Powell, I am so truly sorry to see you distressed! I wish—I really do wish—that I could do anything for you!"

"For me! Oh not for me! But stretch out your hands to this poor maiden, and say words of counsel to her, and of kindness, as one woman may say them to another. I have borne the burden of that young soul; I have had it laid upon me to wrestle strongly for her in prayer; I have—have been assailed with manifold troubles and temptations concerning her. But I am clear now. I speak with a single mind, and as desiring her higher welfare from the depths of my heart."

"Good Heaven!" thought Minnie, "what a tragic thing it is to see men pouring out all the treasures of their love on a thing like this girl!" For something in Powell's face and voice had pierced her mind with a lightning-swift conviction that he loved Rhoda Maxfield. Minnie would have died rather than utter such a speech aloud. The ridicule which, among sophisticated persons, slinks on the heels of all strongly-expressed emotion, was too present to her mind, and too disgusting to her pride, for her to have risked the utterance of such a speech even to her mother. But there in her mind the words were, "Good Heaven; how tragic it is!" And she acknowledged to herself, at the same time, that Powell's lack of sophistication and intensity of fervour raised him into a sphere wherein ridicule had no place.

"I will do what I can, Mr. Powell," said Minnie, after a pause, looking with unspeakable pity at his thin, pallid face. "But do not trust too much to my influence."

"I do trust to it, because it will be strengthened and supported by my prayers."

Then, when he had said farewell, and was about to go away, she was suddenly moved by a mixture of feelings, and, as it were, almost against her will, to say to him, "How good it would be for you to see Rhoda as she is! A shallow, sweet, poor little nature, as incapable of appreciating your love as a wren or a ladybird! I like Rhoda, and I am a poor, shallow creature in many ways myself. But I do recognise things higher than myself when I see them."

David Powell's face grew crimson with a hot, dark flush, and for an instant he grasped the back of a chair near him, like a man who reels in drunkenness. Then he said, "You are very keen to see the truth. You have seen it. Rhoda is dear to me, as no woman ever has been dear, or will be again. Once I thought this love was a snare to me. Now—unless in moments of temptation by the enemy—I know that it is an instrument in God's hands. It has given me strength to pray, courage to ask you for your help."

"But you suffer!" cried Minnie, looking at him with knit, earnest brows. "Why should you suffer for one who does not care for you? It is not just."

"Who dare ask for justice? I have received mercy—abundant, overflowing mercy—and shall I not render mercy in my poor degree? But in truth," he added, in a low voice, and with a smile which Minnie thought the most strangely sweet she had ever seen—"in truth, I cannot claim that merit. I can no more help desiring to do good to Rhoda than I can help drawing my breath. Of others I may say, 'It is my duty to assist this man, to counsel that one, to endure some hard treatment for the sake of this other, in order that I may lead them to Christ.' But with Rhoda there is no sense of sacrifice. I believe that the Lord has appointed me to bring her to Him. If my feet be cut and bleeding by the way, I cannot heed it."

"Would you be glad to see Rhoda married to Algernon Errington if he were to become a religious, earnest man—such a man as your conscientious judgment must approve?" asked Minnie.

And the minute the words had passed her lips she repented having said them; they seemed so needlessly cruel; such a ruthless probing of a tender, quivering soul. "It was as if the devil had put the words into my mouth," said she afterwards to herself.

But Powell answered very quietly, "I have thought of that often. But I ask myself such questions no longer. I hold my Father's hand even as a little child, and whither that hand leads me I shall go safely. It is not for me to tempt the wrath of the Lord by vain surmises and putting a case. 'Yea, though He slay me, yet will I trust Him.'"

"You will come back to Whitford, will you not?" asked Minnie.

"If I may. But I know not when. That is not given me to decide. At present, I feel my conscience in bonds of obedience to the Society."

"Perhaps we may never meet again in this world!" Minnie, as she said the words, was conscious of a strong fellow-feeling for this man, so far removed from her in external circumstances.

"May God bless you!" he said, almost in a whisper.

Minnie held out her hand. As he took it lightly in his own for an instant, he pointed upward with the other hand, and then turned and went away in silence.

When Dr. Bodkin said a word or two to Minnie that evening, as to her interview with the "ranting, canting cobbler," she was very reticent and brief in her answers. But on her father shrugging his shoulders disparagingly and observing, "It is a good thing that this firebrand is taking his departure from Whitford. I've been hearing all sorts of things about him to-day. It seems the fellow even set the Methodists by the ears among themselves," she exclaimed hotly, "I do declare most solemnly that this man gives me a more vivid idea of a saint upon earth—a stumbling, striving, suffering saint—than anything I ever saw or read."

CHAPTER XVI.

Arrived in London, with an influential patron ready to receive him, and twenty pounds in his pocket, over and above the sum his mother had contrived to spare out of her quarter's income, Algernon Errington considered himself to be a very lucky fellow. He had good health, good spirits, good looks, and a disposition to make the most of them, untrammelled by shyness or scruples.

He did feel a little nervous as he drove, the day after his arrival in town, to Lord Seely's house, but by no means painfully so. He was undeniably anxious to make a good impression. But his experience, so far, led him to assume, almost with certainty, that he should succeed in doing so.

The hackney-coach stopped at the door of a grimy-looking mansion in Mayfair, but it was a stately mansion withal. In reply to Algernon's inquiry whether Lord Seely was at home, a solemn servant said that his lordship was at home, but was usually engaged at that hour. "Will you carry in my card to him?" said Algernon. "Mr. Ancram Errington."

Algy felt that he had made a false move in coming without any previous announcement, and in dismissing his cab, when he was shown into a little closet off the hall, lined with dingy books, and containing only two hard horsehair chairs, to await the servant's return. There was something a little flat and ignominious in this his first appearance in the Seely house, waiting like a dun or an errand-boy, with the possibility of having to walk out again, without having been admitted to the light of my lord's countenance. However, within a reasonable time, the solemn footman returned, and asked him to walk upstairs, as my lady would receive him, although my lord was for the present engaged.

Algernon followed the man up a softly-carpeted staircase, and through one or two handsome drawing-rooms—a little dim from the narrowness of the street and the heaviness of the curtains—into a small cosy boudoir. There was a good fire on the hearth, and in an easy-chair on one side of it sat a fat lady, with a fat lap-dog on her knees. The lady, as soon as she saw Algernon, waved a jewelled hand to keep him off, and said, in a mellow, pleasant voice, which reminded him of his mother's, "How d'ye do? Don't shake hands, nor come too near, because Fido don't like it, and he bites strangers if he sees them touch me. Sit down."

Algernon had made a very agile backward movement on the announcement of Fido's infirmity of temper; but he bowed, smiled, and seated himself at a respectful distance opposite to my lady. Lady Seely's appearance certainly justified Mrs. Errington's frequent assertion that there was a strong family likeness throughout all branches of the Ancram stock, for she bore a considerable resemblance to Mrs. Errington herself, and a still stronger resemblance to a miniature of Mrs. Errington's grandfather, which Algy had often seen. My lady was some ten years older than Mrs. Errington. She wore a blonde wig, and was rouged. But her wig and her rouge belonged to the candid and ingenuous species of embellishment. Each proclaimed aloud, as it were, "I am wig!" "I am paint!" with scarcely an attempt at deception.

"So you've come to town," said my lady, fumbling for her eye-glass with one hand, while with the other she patted and soothed the growling Fido. Having found the eye-glass, she looked steadily through it at Algernon, who bore the scrutiny with a good-humoured smile and a little blush, which became him very well.

"You're very nice-looking, indeed," said my lady.

Algy could not find a suitable reply to this speech, so he only smiled still more, and made a half-jesting little bow.

"Let me see," pursued Lady Seely, still holding her glass to her eyes, "what is our exact relationship? You are a relation of mine, you know."

"I am glad to say I have that honour."

"I don't suppose you know much of the family genealogy," said my lady, who prided herself on her own accurate knowledge of such matters. "My grandfather and your mother's grandfather were brothers. Your mother's grandfather was the elder brother. He had a very pretty estate in Warwickshire, and squandered it all in less than twelve years. I don't suppose your mother's father had a penny to bless himself with when he came of age."

"I daresay not, ma'am."

"My grandfather did better. He went to India when he was seventeen, and came back when he was seventy, with a pot of money. Ah, if my father hadn't been the youngest of five brothers, I should have been a rich woman!"

"Your ladyship's grandfather was General Cloudesley Ancram, who distinguished himself at the siege of Khallaka," said Algernon.

Lady Seely nodded approvingly. "Ah, your mother has taught you that, has she?" she said. "And what was your father? Wasn't he an apothecary?"

Algernon's face showed no trace of annoyance, except a little increase of colour in his blooming young cheeks, as he answered, "The fact is, Lady Seely, that my poor father was an enthusiast about science. He would study medicine, instead of going into the Church, and availing himself of the family interest. The consequence was, that he died a poor M.D. instead of a rich D.D.—or even, who knows? a bishop!"

"La!" said my lady, shortly. Then, after a minute's pause, she added, "Then, I suppose, you're not very rich, hey?"

"I am as poor, ma'am, as my grandfather, Montagu Ancram, of whom your ladyship was saying just now that he had not a penny to bless himself with when he came of age," returned Algernon, laughing.

"Well, you seem to take it very easy," said my lady. And once more she looked at him through her eye-glass. "And what made you come to town, all the way from what-d'ye-call-it? Have you got anything to do?"

"N—nothing definite, exactly," said Algernon.

"H'm! Quiet, Fido!"

"I ventured to hope that Lord Seely—that perhaps my lord—might—"

"Oh, dear, you mustn't run away with that idea!" exclaimed her ladyship. "There ain't the least chance of my lord being able to do anything for you. He's torn to pieces by people wanting places, and all sorts of things."

"I was about to say that I ventured to hope that my lord would kindly give me some advice," said Algernon. As he said it his heart was like lead. He had not, of course, expected to be at once made Secretary of State, or even to pop immediately into a clerkship at the Foreign Office. He had put the matter very soberly and moderately before his own mind, as he thought. He had told himself that a word of encouragement from his high and mighty cousin should be thankfully received, and that he would neither be pushing nor impatient, accepting a very small beginning cheerfully. But it had never occurred to him to prepare himself for an absolute flat refusal of all assistance. My lady's tone was one of complete decision. And it was in vain he reflected that my lady might be speaking more harshly and decisively than she had any warrant for doing, being led to that course by the necessity of protecting herself and her husband against importunity. None the less was his heart very heavy within him. And he really deserved some credit for gallantry in bearing up against the blow.

"Advice!" said my lady, echoing his word. "Oh, well, that ain't so difficult. What are you fit for?"

"Perhaps I am scarcely the best judge of that, am I?" returned Algernon, with that childlike raising of the eyebrows which gave so winning an expression to his face.

"Perhaps not; but what do you think?"

"Well, I—I believe I could fill the post of secretary, or—What I should like," he went on, in a sudden burst of candour, and looking deprecatingly at Lady Seely, like a child asking for sugar-plums, "would be to get attached to one of our foreign legations."

"I daresay! But that's easier said than done. And as to being a secretary, it's precious hard work, I can tell you, if you're paid for it; and, of course, no post would suit you that didn't pay."

"I shouldn't mind hard work."

"You wouldn't be much of an Ancram if you liked it; I can tell you I know that much! Well, and how long do you mean to stay in town?"

"That is quite uncertain."

"You must come and see me again before you go, and be introduced to Lord Seely."

"Oh, indeed, I hope so."

Come and see her again before he went! What would his mother say, what would his Whitford friends say, if they could hear that speech? Nevertheless, he answered very cheerfully:

"Oh, indeed, I hope so!" And interpreting my lady's words as a dismissal, rose to go.

"You're really uncommonly nice-looking," said Lady Seely, observing his straight, slight figure, and his neatly-shod feet as he stood before her. "Oh, you needn't look shame-faced about it. It's no merit of yours; but it's a great thing, let me tell you, for a young fellow without a penny to have an agreeable appearance. How old are you?"

"Twenty," said Algernon, anticipating his birthday by two months.

"Do you know, I think Fido will like you!" said my lady, who observed the fact that her favourite had neither barked nor growled when Algernon rose from his chair. "I'm sure I hope he will; he is so unpleasant when he takes a dislike to people."

Algernon thought so too; but he merely said, "Oh, we shall be great friends, I daresay; I always get on with dogs."

"Ah, but Fido is peculiar. You can't coax him and he gets so much to eat that you can't bribe him. If he likes you, he likes you—voilà tout! By-the-way, do you understand French?"

"Yes; pretty fairly. I like it."

"Do you? But, as to your accent—I'm afraid that cannot be much to boast of. English provincial French is always so very dreadful."

"Well, I don't know," said Algernon, with perfect good humour, for he believed himself to be on safe ground here; "but the old Duc de Villegagnon, an émigré, who was my master, used to say that I did not pronounce the words of my little French songs so badly."

"Bless the boy! Can you sing French songs? Do sit down, then, at the piano, and let me hear one! Never mind Fido." (Her ladyship had set her favourite on the floor, and he was sniffing at Algernon's legs.) "He don't dislike music, except a brass band. Sit down, now!"

Algernon obeyed, seated himself at the pianoforte, and began to run his fingers over the keys. He found the instrument a good deal out of tune; but began, after a minute's pause, a forgotten chansonette, from "Le Petit Chaperon Rouge." He sang with taste and spirit, though little voice; and his French accent proved to be so surprisingly good, as to elicit unqualified approbation from Lady Seely.

"Why, I declare that's charming!" she cried, clapping her hands. "How on earth did you pick up all that in—what's-its-name? Do look here, my lord, here's young Ancram come up from that place in the West of England, and he can play the piano and sing French songs delightfully!"

Algernon jumped up in a little flurry, and, turning round, found himself face to face with his magnificent relative, Lord Seely.

Now it must be owned that "magnificent" was not quite the epithet that could justly be applied to Lord Seely's personal appearance. He was a small, delicately-made man, with a small, delicately-featured face, and sharp, restless dark eyes. His grey hair stood up in two tufts, one above each ear, and the top of his head was bald, shining, and yellowish, like old ivory. "Eh?" said he. "Oh! Mr.—a—a, how d'ye do?" Then he shook hands with Algernon, and courteously motioning him to resume his seat, threw himself into a chair by the hearth, opposite to his wife. He stretched out his short legs to their utmost possible length before him, and leant his head back wearily.

"Tired, my lord?" asked his wife.

"Why, yes, a little. Dictating letters is a fatiguing business, Mr.—a—a—"

"Errington, my lord; Ancram Errington."

"Oh, to be sure! I'm very glad to see you; very glad indeed. Yes, yes; Mr. Errington. You are a cousin of my lady's? Of course. Very glad."

And Lord Seely got up and shook hands once more with Algernon, whose identity he had evidently only just recognised. But, although tardy, the peer's greeting was more than civil, it was kind; and Algernon's gratitude was in direct proportion to the chill disappointment he had felt at Lady Seely's discouraging words.

"Thank you, sir," he said, pressing the small thin white hand that was proffered to him. And Algy's way of saying "Thank you, sir," was admirable, and would have made the fortune of a young actor on the stage; for, in saying it, he had sufficient real emotion to make the simulated emotion quite touching—as an actor should have.

My lord sat down again, wearily. "Bush has been with me again about that emigration scheme of his," he said to his wife. "Upon my honour, I don't know a more trying person than Bush." When he had thus spoken, he cast his eyes once more upon Algernon, who said, in the most artless, impulsive way in the world, "It's a poor-spirited kind of thing, no doubt; but, really, when one sees what a hard time of it statesmen have, one can't help feeling sometimes that it is pleasant to be nobody."

Now the word "statesman" applied to Lord Seely was scarcely more correct than the word "magnificent" applied to his outer man. The fact was, that Lord Seely had been, from his youth upward, ambitious of political distinction, and had, indeed, filled a subordinate post in the Cabinet some twenty years previous to the day on which Algernon first made his acquaintance. But he had been a mere cypher there; and the worst of it was, that he had been conscious of being a cypher. He had not strength of character or ability to dominate other men, and he had too much intelligence to flatter himself that he succeeded, where success had eluded his pursuit. Stupider men had done better for themselves in the world than Valentine Sackville Strong, Lord Seely, and had gained more solid slices of success than he. Perhaps there is nothing more detrimental to the achievement of ascendancy over others than that intermittent kind of intellect, which is easily blown into a flame by vanity, but is as easily cooled down again by the chilly suggestions of common sense. The vanity which should be able to maintain itself always at white heat would be a triumphant thing. The common sense which never flared up to an enthusiastic temperature would be a safe thing. But the alternation of the two was felt to be uncomfortable and disconcerting by all who had much to do with Lord Seely. He continued, however, to keep up a semblance of political life. He had many personal friends in the present ministry, and there were one or two men who were rather specially hostile to him among the Opposition; of which latter he was very proud, liking to speak of his "enemies" in the House. He spoke pretty frequently from his place among the peers, but nobody paid him any particular attention. And he wrote and printed, at his own expense, a considerable number of political pamphlets; but nobody read them. That, however, may have been due to the combination against his lordship which existed among the writers for the public press, who never, he complained, reported his speeches in extenso, and, with few exceptions, ignored his pamphlets altogether.

Howbeit, the word "statesman" struck pleasantly upon the little nobleman's ear, and he bestowed a more attentive glance on Algernon than he had hitherto honoured him with, and asked, in his abrupt tones, like a series of muffled barks, "Going to be long in town, Mr. Ancram?"

"I've just been asking him," interposed my lady. "He don't know for certain. But—" And here she whispered in her husband's ear.

"Oh, I hope so," said the latter aloud. "My lady and I hope that you will do us the favour to dine with us to-morrow—eh? Oh, I beg your pardon, Belinda, I thought you said to-morrow!—on Thursday next. We shall probably be alone, but I hope you will not mind that?"

"I shall take it as a great favour, my lord," said Algernon, whose spirits had been steadily rising, ever since the successful performance of his French song.

"You know, Mr. Ancram—I mean Mr. Errington—is a cousin of mine, my lord; so he won't expect to be treated with ceremony."

Algernon felt as if he could have flown downstairs when, after this most gracious speech, he took leave of his august relatives. But he walked very soberly instead, down the staircase and past the solemn servants in the hall, with as much nonchalance as if he had been accustomed to the service of powdered lackeys from his babyhood.

"He seems an intelligent, gentleman-like young fellow," said my lord to my lady.

"Oh, he's as sharp as a weasel, and uncommonly nice-looking. And he sings French songs ever so much better than that theatre man that the Duchess made such a fuss about. He has the trick of drawing the long bow, which all the Warwickshire Ancrams were famous for. Oh, there's no doubt about his belonging to the real breed! He told me a cock-and-a-bull story about his father's devotion to science. I believe his father was a little apothecary in Birmingham. But I don't know that that much matters," said my lady to my lord.

CHAPTER XVII.

Algernon was elated by the success of his song, and by Lady Seely's full acknowledgment of his cousinship, and he left the mansion in Mayfair in very good spirits, as has been said. But when he got back to his inn—a private hotel in a dingy street behind Oxford Street—he began to feel a recurrence of the disappointment which had oppressed him, when Lady Seely had declared so emphatically that my lord could do nothing for him, in the way of getting him a place. What was to be done? It was all very well for his mother to say that, with his talents and appearance, he must and would make his way to a high position; but, just and reasonable as it would be that his talents and appearance should give him success, he began to fear that they might not altogether avail to do so. He thought of Mr. Filthorpe—that substance, which Mr. Diamond had said they were deserting for the shadow of Seely—and of the thousands of pounds which the Bristol merchant possessed. Truly a stool in a counting-house was not the post which Algernon coveted. And he candidly told himself that he should not be able to fill it effectively. But, still, there would have been at least as good a chance of fascinating Mr. Filthorpe as of fascinating Lord Seely, and the looked-for result of the fascination in either case was to be absolution from the necessity of doing any disagreeable work whatever. And, moreover, Mr. Filthorpe, at all events, would have supplied board and lodging and a small salary, whilst he was undergoing the progress of being fascinated.

Algernon looked thoughtful and anxious, for full a quarter of an hour, as he pondered these things. But then he fell into a fit of laughter at the recollection of Lady Seely and Fido. "There is something very absurd about that old woman," said he to himself. "She is so impudent! And why wear a wig at all, if a wig is to be such a one as hers? A turban or a skull-cap would do just as well to cover her head with. But then they wouldn't be half so funny. Fido is something like his mistress—nearly as fat, and with the same style of profile."

Then he set himself to draw a caricature representing Fido, attired after the fashion of Lady Seely, and became quite cheerful and buoyant over it.

In the interval between the day of his visit to the Seelys and the Thursday on which he was to dine with them, Algernon made one or two calls, and delivered a couple of letters of introduction, with which his Whitford friends had furnished him. One was from Dr. Bodkin to an old-fashioned solicitor, who was reputed to be rich, but who lived in a very quiet way, in a very quiet square, and gave very quiet little dinners to a select few who could appreciate a really fine glass of port. The other letter was to a sister of young Mr. Pawkins, of Pudcombe Hall, married to the chief clerk of the Admiralty, who lived in a fashionable neighbourhood, and gave parties as fashionable as her visiting-list permitted, and by no means desired any special connoisseurship in wine on the part of her guests.

On the occasion of his first calls, Algernon found neither Mr. Leadbeater, the solicitor, nor Mrs. Machyn-Stubbs (that was the name of young Pawkins's sister) at home. So he left his letters and cards, and wandered about the streets in a rather forlorn way; for although it was his first visit to London, it was not possible for him to get much enjoyment out of the metropolis, all alone. To him every place, even London, appeared in the light of a stage or background, whereon that supremely interesting personage, himself, might figure to more or less advantage. Now London is a big theatre. And although a big theatre full of spectators may be very exhilarating to the object of public attention who performs in it, a big theatre, practically barren of spectators—for, of course, the only real spectators are the spectators who look at us—is apt to oppress the mind with a sense of desertion. So he was very glad when Thursday evening came, and he found himself once more within the hall door of Lord Seely's house.

My lord was in the drawing-room alone, standing on the hearth-rug. He shook hands very kindly with Algernon, and bade him come near to the fire and warm himself, for the evening was cold.

"And what have you been doing with yourself, Mr. Errington?" asked Lord Seely.

"I have been chiefly employed to-day in losing myself and asking my way," answered Algernon, laughing. And then he began an account of his adventures, and absolutely surprised himself by the amount of fun and sparkle he contrived to elicit from the narration of circumstances which had been in fact dull and commonplace enough.

My lord was greatly amused, and once even laughed out loud at Algernon's imitation of an Irish apple-woman, who had misdirected him with the best intentions, and much calling down of blessings on his handsome face, in return for a silver sixpence.

"Capital!" said my lord, nodding his head up and down.

"The sixpence was badly invested, though," observed Algernon, "for she sent me about three miles out of my way."

"Ah, but the blarney! You forget the blessing and the blarney. Surely they were worth the money, eh?"

"No, my lord; not to me. I can't afford expensive luxuries."

Lady Seely, when she entered the room, gorgeous in pea-green satin, which singularly set off the somewhat pronounced tone of her rouge, found Algy and my lord laughing together very merrily, and, as she gave her hand to her young relative, demanded to be informed what the joke was.

Now it has been said that Algernon was possessed of wonderfully rapid powers of perception, and by sundry signs, so slight that they would have entirely escaped most observers, this clever young gentleman perceived that my lady was not altogether delighted at finding her husband and himself on such easy and pleasant terms together. In fact, my lady, with all her blunt careless jollity of manner and pleasant mellow voice, was apt to be both jealous and suspicious. She was jealous of her ascendancy over Lord Seely, who was said by the ill-natured to be completely under his wife's thumb, and she was suspicious of most strangers—especially of strangers who might be expected to want anything of his lordship. And she usually assumed that such persons would endeavour to "come over" that nobleman, when he was apart from his wife's protecting influence. She had a general theory that "men might be humbugged into anything;" and a particular experience that Lord Seely, despite his stiff carriage and abrupt manner, was in truth far softer-natured than she was herself.

"That young scamp has been coming over Valentine with his jokes and his flummery," said my lady to herself. "He's an Ancram, every inch of him."

At that very moment Algernon was mentally declaring that the conquest of my lady would, after all, be a more difficult matter than that of my lord; but that, by some means or other, the conquest must be made, if any good was to come to him from the Seely connection. And a stream of easy chat flowed over these underlying intentions and hid them, except that here and there, perhaps, a bubble or an eddy told of rough places out of sight.

After some ten minutes of desultory talk, my lady was obliged to own to herself that the "young scamp" had a wonderfully good manner. Without a trace of servility, he was respectful; conveying, with perfect tact, exactly the sort of homage that was graceful and becoming from a youth like himself to persons of the Seelys' age and position. Neither did he commit the error of becoming familiar, in response to Lady Seely's tone of familiarity, a pitfall which had before now entrapped the unwary. For my lady, whom Nature had created vulgar—having possibly, in the hurry of business, mistaken one kind of clay for another, and put some low person's mind into the fine porcelain of an undoubted Ancram—was fond of asserting her position in the world by a rough unceremoniousness in the first place, and a very wide-eyed arrogance in the second place, if such unceremoniousness chanced to be reciprocated by unauthorised persons.

"Do we wait for any one, Belinda?" asked Lord Seely.

"The Dormers are coming. They're such great musicians, you know. And I want Lady Harriet to hear this boy sing. And then there may be Jack Price, very likely."

"Very likely?" said my lord, raising his eyebrows and stiffening his back. "Doesn't Mr. Price do us the honour of saying positively whether he will come or not?"

"Oh, you know what Jack Price is. He says he'll come, and nine times out of ten he don't come; and then the tenth time he comes, and people have to put up with him."

My lord cleared his throat significantly, as who should say that he, at all events, did not feel inclined to put up with this system of tithes in the fulfilment of Mr. Jack Price's promises.

"If he comes," said Lady Seely, addressing Algernon, "you'll have to walk into dinner by yourself. I've only got one young lady; and, if Jack comes, he must have her."

"Where is Castalia?" asked my lord.

"Oh, I suppose she's dressing. Castalia is always the slowest creature at her toilet I ever knew."

Algernon had read up the family genealogy in the "Peerage," under his mother's instructions, sufficiently to be aware that Lord and Lady Seely were childless, having lost their only son in a boating accident years ago. "Castalia," then, could not be a daughter of the house. Who was she? A young lady who was evidently at present living with the Seelys, whom they called by her Christian name, and who was habitually a long time at her toilet! Algernon felt a little agreeable excitement and curiosity on the subject of the tardy Castalia.

The door was thrown open. "Here she comes!" thought Algernon, settling his cravat as he threw a quick side glance at a mirror.

"General and Lady Harriet Dormer," announced the servant.

There entered a tall, elegant woman, leaning on the arm of a short, stout, benevolent-looking man in spectacles. To these personages Algernon was duly presented, being introduced, much to his gratification, by Lady Seely, as "A young cousin of mine, Mr. Ancram Errington, who has just come to town." Then, having made his bow to General Dormer, who smiled and shook hands with him, Algernon stood opposite to the graceful Lady Harriet, and was talked to very kindly and pleasantly, and felt extremely content with himself and his surroundings. Nevertheless he watched with some impatience for the appearance of "Castalia;" and forgot his usual self-possession so far as to turn his head, and break off in the middle of a sentence he was uttering to Lady Harriet, when he heard the door open again. But once more he was disappointed; for, this time, dinner was announced, and Lord Seely offered his arm to Lady Harriet and led the way out of the room.

"No Jack," said Lady Seely, as she passed out before Algernon. "And no Castalia!" said my lord over his shoulder, in a tone of vexation.

Algernon followed his seniors alone; but just as he got out on to the staircase there appeared a lady, leisurely descending from an upper floor, at whom Lord Seely looked up reproachfully.

"Late, late, Castalia!" said he, and shook his head solemnly.

"Oh no, Uncle Valentine; just in time," replied the lady.

"Castalia, take Ancram's arm, and do let us get to dinner before the soup is cold," said Lady Seely. "Give your arm to Miss Kilfinane, and come along." And her ladyship's pea-green satin swept downstairs after Lady Harriet's sober purple draperies. Algernon bowed, and offered his arm to the lady beside him; she placed her hand on it almost without looking at him, and they entered the dining-room without having exchanged a word.

The dining-room was better lighted than the staircase, and Algernon took an early opportunity of looking at his companion. She was not very young, being, in fact, nearly thirty, but looking older. Neither was she handsome. She was very thin, sallow, and sickly-looking, with a small round face, not wrinkled, but crumpled, as it were, into queer, fretful lines. Her eyes were bright and well-shaped, but deeply sunken, and she had a great deal of thick, pale-brown hair, worn in huge bows and festoons on the top of her head, according to the extreme of the mode of that day. Her dress displayed more than it was judicious to display, in an æsthetic point of view, of very lean shoulders, and was of a bright, soft, pink hue, that would have been trying to the most blooming complexion. Altogether, the Honourable Castalia Kilfinane's appearance was disappointing, and her manner was not so attractive as to make up for lack of beauty. Her face expressed a mixture of querulousness and hauteur, and she spoke in a languid drawl, with strange peevish inflections.

"You and I ought to be some sort of relations to each other, oughtn't we?" said Algernon, having taken in all the above particulars in a series of rapid observations.

"Why?" returned the lady, without raising her eyes from her soup-plate.

"Because you are Lady Seely's niece and I am her cousin."

"Who says that I am Lady Seely's niece?"

"I thought," stammered Algernon—"I fancied—you called Lord Seely 'Uncle Valentine?'"

Even his equanimity, and a certain glow of complacency he felt at finding himself where he was, were a little disturbed by Miss Castalia's freezing manner.

"I am Lord Seely's niece," returned she.

Then, after a little pause, having finished her soup, she leaned back in her chair and stared at Algernon, who pretended—not quite successfully—to be unconscious of her scrutiny. Apparently, the result of it was favourable to Algernon; for the lady's manner thawed perceptibly, and she began to talk to him. She had evidently heard of him from Lady Seely, and understood the exact degree of his relationship to that great lady.

"Did you ever meet the Dormers before?" asked Miss Kilfinane.

"Never. How should I? You know I am the merest country mouse. I never was in London in my life, until last Friday."

"Oh, but the Dormers don't live in town. Indeed, they are here very seldom. You might have met them; their place is in the West of England."

Algernon, after a rapid balancing of pros and cons, resolved to be absolutely candid. With his brightest smile and most arched eyebrows, he began to give Miss Kilfinane an almost unvarnished description of his life at Whitford. Almost unvarnished; but it is no more easy to tell the simple truth only occasionally, than it is to stand quite upright only occasionally. Mind and muscles will fall back to their habitual posture. So that it may be doubted whether Miss Kilfinane received an accurate notion of the precise degree of poverty and obscurity in which the young man who was speaking to her had hitherto lived.

"And so," said she, "you have come to London to—"

"To seek my fortune," said Algernon merrily. "It is the proper and correct beginning to a story. And I think I have had a piece of good luck at the very outset by way of a good omen."

Miss Kilfinane opened her eyes interrogatively, but said nothing.

"I think it was a piece of luck for me," continued Algernon, emboldened by having secured the scornful lady's attention, and perhaps a little also by the wine he had drunk, "a great piece of good luck that Mr. Jack Price, whoever he may be, did not turn up this evening."

"Why?"

"Because, if he had, I should not have been allowed the honour of bringing you in to dinner."

"Oh yes! I should have had to go in with Jack, I suppose," answered the lady with a little smile.

"Please, Miss Kilfinane, who is Jack Price? I do so want to know!"

"Jack Price is Lord Mullingar's son."

"But what is he? And why do people want to have him so much, that they put up with his disappointing them nine times out of ten?"

"As to what he is—well, he was in the Guards, and he gave that up. Then they got him a place somewhere—in Africa, or South America, or somewhere—and he gave that up. Then he got the notion that he would be a farmer in Canada, and went out with an axe to cut down the trees, and a plough to plough the ground afterwards, and he gave that up. Now he does nothing particular."

"And has he found his vocation at last?"

"I don't know, I'm sure," said Miss Kilfinane, languidly. Her power of perceiving a joke was very limited.

"Thanks. Now I know all about Mr. Price; except—except why everybody wants to invite him."

"That I really cannot tell you."

"Then you don't share the general enthusiasm about him?"

"I don't know that there is any general enthusiasm. Only, of course—don't you know how it is?—people have got into the way of putting up with him, and letting him do as he likes."

"He's a very fortunate young man, I should say."

"Young man!" Miss Kilfinane laughed a hard little laugh. "Why Jack Price is ever so old!"

"Ever so old, is he?" echoed Algernon, genuinely surprised.

"He must be turned forty," said the fair Castalia, rising in obedience to a look from Lady Seely. And if she had been but fifteen herself, she could not have said it with a more infantine air.

After the ladies had withdrawn, Algernon had to sit for about twenty minutes in the shade, as it were, silent, and listening with modesty and discretion to the conversation of his seniors. Had they talked politics, Algernon would have been able to throw in a word or two; but Lord Seely and his guest talked, not of principles or party, but of persons. The persons talked of were such as Lord Seely conceived to be useful or hostile to his party, and he discussed their conduct, and criticised the tactics of ministers in regard to them, with much warmth. But, unfortunately, Algernon neither knew, nor could pretend to know, anything about these individuals, so he sipped his wine, and looked at the family portraits which hung round the room, in silence.

My lord made a kind of apology to him, as they were going upstairs to the drawing-room.

"I'm afraid you were bored, Mr. Errington. I am sorry, for your sake, that Mr. Price did not honour us with his company. You would have found him much more amusing than us old fogies."

Algernon knew, when Lord Seely talked of Mr. Price not having honoured them with his company, that my lord was indignant against that gentleman. "I have no doubt Mr. Price is a very agreeable person," said he, "but I did not regret him, my lord. I thought it a great privilege to be allowed to listen to you."

Later in the evening Algy overheard Lord Seely say to General Dormer, "He's a remarkably intelligent young fellow, I assure you."

"He has a capital manner," returned the general. "There is something very taking about him, indeed."

"Oh yes, manner; yes; a very good manner—but there's more judgment, more solidity about him than appears on the surface."

Meanwhile, Algernon went on flourishingly, and ingratiated himself with every one. He steered his way, with admirable tact, past various perils, such as must inevitably threaten one who aims at universal popularity. Lady Harriet was delighted with his singing, and Lady Harriet's expressed approbation pleased Lady Seely; for the Dormers were considered to be great musical connoisseurs, and their judgment had considerable weight among their own set. Their own set further supposed that the verdict of the Dormers was important to professional artists: a delusion which the givers of second-rate concerts, who depended on Lady Harriet to get rid of many seven-and-sixpenny tickets during the season, were at no pains to disturb. Then, Algernon took the precaution to keep away from Lord Seely, and to devote himself to my lady, during the remainder of the evening. This behaviour had so good an effect, that she called him "Ancram," and bade him go and talk to Castalia, who was sitting alone on a distant ottoman, with a distinctly sour expression of countenance.

"How did you get on with Castalia at dinner?" asked my lady.

"Miss Kilfinane was very kind to me, ma'am."

"Was she? Well, she don't make herself agreeable to everybody, so consider yourself honoured. Castalia's a very clever girl. She can draw, make wax flowers, and play the piano beautifully."

"Can she really? Will she play to-night?"

"I'm sure I don't know. Go and ask her."

"May I?"

"Yes; be off."

Miss Kilfinane did not move or raise her eyes when Algernon went and stood before her.

"I have come with a petition," he said, after a little pause.

"Have you?"

"Yes; will you play to-night?"

"No."

"Oh, that's very cruel! I wish you would!"

"I don't like playing before the Dormers. They set up for being such connoisseurs, and I hate that kind of thing."

"I am sure you can have no reason to fear their criticism."

"I don't want to have my performance picked to pieces in that knowing sort of way. I play for my own amusement, and I don't want to be criticised, and applauded, and patronised."

"But how can people help applauding when you play? Lady Seely says you play exquisitely."

"Did she tell you to ask me to play?"

"Not exactly. But she said I might ask you."

At this moment General Dormer came up, and said, with his most benevolent smile, "Won't you give us a little music, Miss Kilfinane? Some Beethoven, now! I see a volume of his sonatas on the piano."

"I hate Beethoven," returned Miss Kilfinane.

"Hate Beethoven! No, no, you don't. It's quite impossible! A pianist like you! Oh no, Miss Kilfinane, it is out of the question."

"Yes, I do. I hate all classical music, and the sort of stuff that people talk about it."

The general smiled again, shook his head, shrugged his shoulders, and walked away.

"Miss Kilfinane, you are ferociously cruel!" said Algernon under his breath as General Dormer turned his back on them. The little fear he had had of Castalia's chilly manner and ungracious tongue had quite vanished. Algernon was not apt to be in awe of anyone; and he certainly was not in awe of Castalia Kilfinane. "Why did you tell the general that you hated Beethoven?" he went on saucily. "I'm quite sure you don't hate Beethoven!"

"I hate all the kind of professional jargon which the Dormers affect about music. Music is all very well, but it isn't our business, any more than tailoring or millinery is our business. To hear the Dormers talk, you would think it the most important matter in the world to decide whether this fiddler is better than that fiddler, or what is the right time to play a fugue of Bach's in."

"I'm such an ignoramus that I'm afraid I don't even know with any precision what a fugue of Bach's is!" said Algernon, ingenuously. He thought he had learned to understand Miss Castalia. Nevertheless, when, later in the evening, Lady Harriet asked him in her pretty silver tones, "And do you, too, hate classical music, Mr. Errington?" he professed the most unbounded love and reverence for the great masters. "I have had few opportunities of hearing fine music, Lady Harriet," said he; "but it is the thing I have longed for all my life." Whereupon Lady Harriet, much pleased at the prospect of such a disciple, invited him to go to her house every Saturday morning, when he would hear some of the best performers in London execute some of the best music. "I only ask real listeners," said Lady Harriet. "We are just a few music-lovers who take the thing very much au sérieux."

On the whole, when Algernon thought over his evening, sitting over the fire in his bedroom at the inn, he acknowledged to himself that he had been successful. "Lady Seely is the toughest customer, though! What a fish-wife she looks beside that elegant Lady Harriet! But she can put on airs of a great lady too, when she likes. It's a very fine line that divides dignity from impudence. Take her wig off, wash her face, and clothe her in a short cotton gown with a white apron, and how many people would know that Belinda, Lady Seely, had ever been anything but a cook, or the landlady of a public-house? Well, I think I am cleverer than any of 'em. And, after all, that's a great point." With which comfortable reflection Algernon Ancram Errington went to bed, and to sleep.

CHAPTER XVIII.

On the day following the dinner at Lord Seely's, Algernon received a card, importing that Mrs. Machyn-Stubbs would be at home that evening.

Of the lady he knew nothing, except that she was an elder sister of young Pawkins, of Pudcombe Hall; and that her family, who were people of consideration in Whitford and its neighbourhood, thought Jemima to have made a good match in marrying Mr. Machyn-Stubbs. In giving him the letter of introduction, Orlando Pawkins had let fall a word or two as to the position his sister held in London society.

"I can't send anybody and everybody to the Machyn-Stubbses," said young Pawkins. "In their position, it wouldn't be fair to inflict our bucolic magnates on them. But I'm sure Jemima will be very glad to make your acquaintance, old fellow."

Algernon was quite free from arrogance. He would have been well enough contented to dine with Mr. Machyn-Stubbs, had that gentleman been a grocer or a cheesemonger. And, in that case, he would probably have derived a good deal of amusement from any little vulgarities which might have marked the manners of his host, and would have entertained his genteeler friends by a humorous imitation of the same. But he was not in the least overawed by the prospect of meeting Mrs. Machyn-Stubbs, and was quite aware that he probably owed his introduction to her, to young Pawkins's knowledge of the fact that he was Lady Seely's relation.

Algernon betook himself to the house of Mrs. Machyn-Stubbs, in the fashionable neighbourhood before mentioned, about half-past ten o'clock, and found the small reception-rooms already fuller than was agreeable. Mrs. Machyn-Stubbs received him very graciously. She was a pretty woman, with a smooth fair face and light hair, and she was dressed with as much good taste as was compatible with the extreme of the prevailing fashion. She smiled a good deal, and was quite destitute of any sense of humour.

"So glad to see you, Mr. Errington," said she, when Algernon had made his bow. "You and Orlando are great friends, are you not? You must let me make you acquainted with my husband." Then she handed Algernon over to a stout, red-faced, white-haired gentleman, much older than herself, who shook hands with him, said, "How d'ye do?" and "How long have you been in town?" and then appeared to consider that he had done all that could be expected of him in the way of conversation.

"I suppose you don't know many people here, Mr. Errington?" said Mrs. Machyn-Stubbs, seeing that Algernon was standing silent in the shadow of her husband.

"Not any. You know I have never been in London before."

"Haven't you, really? But perhaps we may have some mutual acquaintances notwithstanding. Let me see who is here!" said the lady, looking round her rooms.

"Are you acquainted with the Dormers, Mrs. Machyn-Stubbs?"

"The Dormers? Let me see—"

"General and Lady Harriet Dormer."

"Oh! no; I don't think I am. Of course I must have met them. In the course of the season, sooner or later, one meets everybody."

"Do you know Miss Kilfinane?"

"Miss Kilfinane? I—I can't recall at this moment—"

"She is a sort of connection of mine; not a relation, for she is Lord Seely's niece, not my lady's."

"Oh, to be sure! You are a cousin of Lady Seely. Yes, yes; I had forgotten. But Orlando did mention it."

In truth, the fact of Algernon's relationship to Lady Seely was the only one concerning him which had dwelt in Mrs. Machyn-Stubbs's memory. Presently she resumed:

"I should like to introduce you to a great friend of ours—the most delightful creature! I hope he will come to-night, but he is very difficult to catch. He is a son of Lord Mullingar."

"What, Jack Price?"

"Oh, you know him, do you?"

"Only by reputation. He was to have dined at Lord Seely's last night, when I was there. But he didn't show."

"Oh, I know he's dreadfully uncertain. But I must say, however, that he is generally very good about coming to me. It's quite wonderful. I'm sure I don't know why I am so favoured!"

Then Algernon was presented to a rather awful dowager, with two stiff daughters, to whom he talked as well as he could; and the nicest looking of whom he took into the tea-room, where there was a great crush, and where people trod on each other's toes, and poked their elbows into each other's ribs, to procure a cup of hay-coloured tea and a biscuit that had seen better days.

"Upon my word," thought Algernon, "if this is London society, I think Whitford society better fun." But then he reflected that Mrs. Machyn-Stubbs was not a real leader of fashionable society. She was not quite a rose herself, although she lived near enough to the roses for their scent to cling, more or less faintly, about her garments. He was not bored, for his quick powers of perception, and lively appreciation of the ludicrous, enabled him to gather considerable amusement from the scene. Especially did he feel amused and in his element when, on an allusion to his cousinship to Lady Seely, thrown out in the airiest, most haphazard way, the awful dowager and the stiff daughters unbent, and became as gracious as temperament in the one case, and painfully tight stays in the other, permitted.

"He's a very agreeable person, your young friend, Mr. Ancram Errington," said the dowager, later on in the evening, to Mrs. Machyn-Stubbs.

"Oh yes; he's very nice indeed. He is a great favourite with my people. He half lives at our place, I believe, when Orlando is at home."

"Indeed! He is—a—a—connected with the Seelys, I believe, in some way?"

"Second cousin. Lady Seely was an Ancram—Warwickshire Ancrams, you know," returned Mrs. Machyn-Stubbs, who knew her "Peerage" nearly by heart. Whereupon the dowager went back to her daughter, by whose side, having nothing else to do, Algernon was still sitting, and told him that she should be happy to see him at her house in Portland Place any Friday afternoon, between four and six o'clock during the season.

Presently, when the company was giving forth a greater amount and louder degree of talk than had hitherto been the case—for Herr Doppeldaun had just sat down to the grand piano—Algernon's quick eyes perceived a movement near the door of the principal drawing-room, and saw Mrs. Machyn-Stubbs advance with extended hand, and more eagerness than she had thrown into her reception of most of the company, to greet a gentleman who entered with a kind of plunge, tripping over a bearskin rug that lay before the door, and dropping his hat.

He was a short, broad-chested man, with a bald forehead and a fringe of curly chestnut hair round his head. He was evidently extremely near-sighted, and wore a glass in one eye, the effort of keeping which in its place occasioned an odd contortion of his facial muscles. He was rubicund, and looked like a man who might grow to be very stout later in life. At present he was only rather stout, and was braced, and strapped, and tightened, so as to make the best of his figure. His dress was the dress of a dandy of that day, and he wore a fragrant hothouse flower in his button-hole.

"That must be Jack Price!" thought Algernon, he scarcely knew why; and the next moment he got away from the dowager and her daughters, and sauntered towards the door.

"Oh, here is Mr. Errington," said Mrs. Machyn-Stubbs, looking round at him as he made his way through the crowd. "Do let me introduce you to Mr. Price. This is Mr. Ancram Errington, a great friend of my brother Orlando. You have met Orlando, I think?"

"Oh, indeed, I have!" said Mr. Jack Price, in a rich sweet voice, and with a very decidedly marked brogue. "Orlando is one of my dearest friends. Delightful fellow, what? Orlando's friend must be my friend, if he will, what?"

The little interrogation at the end of the sentence meant nothing, but was a mere trick. The use of it, with a soft rising inflection of Mr. Jack Price's very musical voice, had once upon a time been pronounced to be "captivating" by an enthusiastic Irish lady. But he had not fallen into the habit of using it from any idea that it was captivating, nor had he desisted from it since all projects of captivation had departed from his mind.

"I was to have met you at dinner, last night, Mr. Price," said Algernon, shaking his proffered hand.

"Last night? I was—where is it I was last night? Oh, at the Blazonvilles! Yes, of course, what? Why didn't you come, then, Mr. Errington? The Duke would have been delighted—perfectly charmed to see you!"

"Well, that may be doubtful, seeing that I cannot flatter myself that his Grace is even aware of my existence," said Algernon, looking at Mr. Price with twinkling eyes, and his mouth twitching with the effort to avoid a broad grin.

Jack Price looked back at him, puzzled and smiling. "Eh? How was it then, what? Was it—it wasn't me, was it?"

Algernon laughed outright.

"Ah now, Mr.—Mr.—my dear fellow, where was it that you were to have met me?"

"My cousin, Lady Seely, was hoping for the pleasure of your company, Mr. Price. She was under the impression that you had promised to dine with her."

Jack Price fell back a step and gave himself a sounding slap on the forehead. "Good gracious goodness!" he exclaimed. "You don't mean to say that?"

"I do, indeed."

"Ah, now, upon my honour, I am the most unfortunate fellow under the sun! I don't know how the deuce it is that these kind of misfortunes are always happening to me. What will I say to Lady Seely? She'll never speak to me any more, I suppose, what?"

"You should keep a little book and note down your engagements, Mr. Price," said Mrs. Machyn-Stubbs, as she walked away to some other guest.

Mr. Price gave Algernon a comical look, half-rueful, half-amused. "I don't quite see myself with the little book, entering all my engagements," said he. "I daresay you've heard already from Lady Seely of my sins and shortcomings?"

"At all events, I have heard this: that whatever may be your sins and shortcomings, they are always forgiven."

"I am afraid I bear an awfully bad character, my dear Mr.—"

"Errington; Ancram Errington."

"To be sure! Ah, I know your name well enough. But names are among the things that slip my memory. It is a serious misfortune, what?"

Then the two began to chat together. And when the crowd began to diminish, and the rattle of carriages grew more frequent down in the street beneath the drawing-room windows, Jack Price proposed to Algernon to go and sup with him at his club. They walked away together, arm-in-arm, and, as they left Mrs. Machyn-Stubbs's doorstep, Mr. Price assured his new acquaintance that that lady was the nicest creature in the world, and one of his dearest friends; and that he could take upon himself to assert that Mrs. Machyn-Stubbs would be only too delighted to receive him (Algernon) at any time and as often as he liked. "It will give her real pleasure, now, what?" said Jack Price, with quite a glow of hospitality on behalf of Mrs. Machyn-Stubbs. Then they went to Mr. Price's club. It was neither a political club, nor a fashionable club, nor a grand club; but a club that was widely miscellaneous, and decidedly jolly. Algernon, before he returned to his lodging that night, had come to the opinion that London was, after all, a great deal better fun than Whitford. And Jack Price, when he called upon Lady Seely the next day, to make his peace with her, declared that young Errington was, really now, the most delightful and dearest boy in the world, and that he was quite certain that the young fellow was most warmly attached to Lord and Lady Seely.

All this was agreeable enough, and Algernon would have been content to go on in the same way to the end of the London season had it been possible. But careless as he was about money, he was not careless about the luxuries which money supplies. Certainly, if tradesmen and landlords could only be induced to give unlimited credit, Algernon would have had none the less pleasure in availing himself of their wares, because he had not paid for them in coin of the realm. But as to doing without, or even limiting himself to an inferior quality and restricted quantity, that was a matter about which he was not at all indifferent. He was received on a familiar footing in the Seelys' house; and his reception there opened to him many other houses, in which it was more or less agreeable and flattering to be received. Among the Machyn-Stubbses of London society he was looked upon as quite a desirable guest, and received a good deal of petting, which he took with the best grace in the world. And all this was, as has been said, pleasant enough. But, as weeks went on, Algernon's money began to run short; and he soon beheld the dismal prospect ahead—and not very far ahead—of his last sovereign. And he was in debt.

As to being in debt, that had nothing in it appalling to our young man's imagination. What frightened him was the conviction that he should not be permitted to go on being in debt. Other people owed money, and seemed to enjoy life none the less. Mr. Jack Price, for instance, had an allowance from his father, on which no one pretended to expect him to live. And he appeared very comfortable and contented in the midst of a rolling sea of debt, which sometimes ebbed a little, and sometimes flowed alarmingly high; but which, during the last ten years or so, he had managed to keep pretty fairly at the same level. But then Mr. Price was the Honourable John Patrick Price, the Earl of Mullingar's son—a younger son, it was true; and neither Lord Mullingar, nor Lord Mullingar's heir, was likely to have the means, or the inclination, to fish him out of the rolling sea aforesaid. At the most, they would throw him a plank now and then just to keep him afloat. Still there was something to be got out of Jack Price by a West-end tradesman who knew his business. Something was to be got in the way of money, and, perhaps, something more in the way of connection. Upon the whole, it may be supposed that the West-end tradesmen understood what they were about, when they went on supplying the Honourable John Patrick Price with all sorts of comforts and luxuries, season after season.

But with Algernon the case was widely different, and he knew it. He had ventured to speak to Lord Seely about his prospects, and to ask that nobleman's "advice." But Lord Seely had not seemed able to offer any advice which it was practicable to follow. Indeed, how should he have done so, seeing that he was ignorant of most of the material facts of the case? He knew in a general way that young Ancram (Algernon had come to be called so in the Seely household) was poor; but between Lord Seely's conception of the sort of poverty which might pinch a well-born young gentleman, who always appeared in the neatest-fitting shoes and freshest of gloves, and the reality of Algernon's finances, there was a wide discrepancy. Algernon had indeed talked freely, and with much appearance of frankness, about his life in Whitford; but it may be doubted whether Lord Seely, or his wife either—although she, doubtless, came nearer to the truth in her imaginings on the subject—at all realised such facts as that Mrs. Errington had no maid to attend on her; that her lodgings cost her eighteen shillings a week; and that the smell of cheese from the shop below was occasionally a source of discomfort in her only sitting-room.

With Lord Seely Algernon had made himself a great favourite, and the proof of it was, that my lord actually thought about him when he was absent; and one day said to his wife, "I wish, Belinda, that we could do something for Ancram."

"Do something for him! I think we do a great deal for him. He has the run of the house, and I introduce him right and left. And he is always asked to sing when we have people."

"That latter looks rather like his doing something for us, I think."

"Not at all. It's a great advantage for a young fellow in his position to be brought forward, and allowed to show off his little gifts in that way."

"He is wasting his time. I wish we could get him something to do."

"I am sure you have plenty of claims on you that come before him."

"I—I did speak to the Duke of Blazonville about him the other day," said my lord, with the slightest hesitation in the world.

The Duke of Blazonville was in the cabinet, and had been a colleague of Lord Seely's years ago.

"What on earth made you do that, Valentine? You know very well that the next thing the duke has to give I particularly want for Reginald."

"Oh, but what I should ask for young Ancram would be something at which your nephew Reginald would probably—"

"Turn up his nose?"

"Something which Reginald would not care about taking."

"Reginald wouldn't go abroad, except to Italy. Nor, indeed, anywhere in Italy but to Naples."

"Exactly. Whether the duke would consider that he was particularly serving the interests of diplomacy by sending Reginald to Naples, I don't know. But, at all events, Ancram could not interfere with that project."

"Serving—? Nonsense! The duke would do it to oblige me. As to Ancram, I have latterly had a kind of plan in my head about Ancram."

"About a place for him?"

"Well, yes; a place, if you like to call it so. What do you say to his coming abroad with us in the autumn?"

"Eh! Coming abroad with us?"

"Of course we should have to pay all his expenses. But I think he would be amusing, and perhaps useful. He talks French very well, and is lively and good-tempered."

"I have no doubt he would be a most charming travelling companion—"

"I don't know about that. But I should take him out of kindness, and to do him a service."

"But I don't see of what use such a plan would be to him, Belinda."

"Well, I've an idea in my head, I tell you. I have kept my eyes open, and I fancy I see a chance for Ancram."

"You are very mysterious, my dear!" said Lord Seely, with a little shrug.

"Well, least said, soonest mended. I shall be mysterious a little longer. And, meanwhile, I think we might make him the offer to take him to Switzerland with us, since you have no objection."

"I have no objection, certainly."

"I think I shall mention it to him, then. And, if I were you, I wouldn't bother the duke about him just yet."

"But what is this notion of yours, Belinda?"

The exclamation rose to my lady's lips, "How inquisitive men are!" but she suppressed it. It was the kind of speech which particularly angered Lord Seely, who much disliked being lumped in with his fellow-creatures on the ground of common qualities. Even a compliment, so framed that my lord was supposed to share it with a number of other persons, would have displeased him. So my lady said, "Well, now, Valentine, you'll begin to laugh at me, very likely, but I believe I'm right. I think Castalia is very well inclined to like this young fellow. And she might do worse."

"Castalia! Like him? Why, you don't mean—?"

"Yes, I do," returned my lady, nodding her head. "That's just what I do mean. I'm sure, the other evening, she became quite sentimental about him."

"Good heavens, Belinda! But the idea is preposterous."

"Yes; I knew you'd say so at first. That's why I didn't want to say anything about it just yet awhile."

"But allow me to say that, if you had any such idea in your head, it was only proper that it should be mentioned to me."

"Well, I have mentioned it."

Lord Seely clasped his hands behind his back, and walked up and down the room in a stiff, abrupt kind of march. At length he stopped opposite to her ladyship, who was assiduously soothing Fido; Fido having, for some occult reason, become violently exasperated by his master's walking about the room.

"Why, in the first place—do send that brute away," said his lordship, sharply.

"There! he's quiet now. Good Fido! Good boy! Mustn't bark and growl at master. Yes; you were saying—?"

"I was saying that, in the first place, Castalia must be ten years older than this boy."

"About that, I should say. But if they don't mind that, I don't see what it matters to us."

"And he has not any means, nor any prospect of earning any, that I can see."

"Why, for that matter, Castalia hasn't a shilling in the world, you know. We have to find her in everything, and so has your sister Julia, when Castalia goes to stay with her. And if these two could set their horses together—could, in a word, make a match of it—why, you might do something to provide for the two together, don't you see? Killing two birds with one stone!"

"Very much like killing two birds, indeed! What are they to live on?"

"If Ancram makes up to Castalia, you must get him a place. Something modest, of course. I don't see that they can either of them expect a grand thing."

"Putting all other considerations aside," said my lord, drawing himself up, "it would be a very odd sort of match for Castalia Kilfinane."

"Come! his birth is as good as hers, any way. If his father was an apothecary, her mother was a poor curate's daughter."

"Rector's daughter, Belinda. Dr. Vyse was a learned man, and the rector of his parish."

"Oh, well, it all comes to the same thing. And as to an odd sort of match, why, perhaps, an odd match is better than none at all. You know Castalia's no beauty. She don't grow younger; and she'll be unbearable in her temper, if once she thinks she's booked for an old maid."

Poor Lord Seely was much disquieted. He had a kindly feeling for his orphan niece, which would have ripened into affection if Miss Castalia's character had been a little less repellent. And he really liked Algernon Errington so much that the notion of his marrying Castalia appeared to him in the light of a sacrifice, even although he held his own opinion as to the comparative goodness of the Ancram and Kilfinane blood. But, nevertheless, such was Lady Seely's force of character, that many days had not elapsed before his lordship was silenced, if not convinced, on the subject. And the invitation to go to Switzerland was given to Algernon, and accepted.

CHAPTER XIX.

As the spring advanced, letters from Algernon Errington arrived rather frequently at Whitford. His mother had ample scope for the exercise of her peculiar talent, in boasting about the reception Algy had met with from her great relations in town, the fine society he frequented, and the prospect of still greater distinctions in store for him. One or two troublesome persons, to be sure, would ask for details, and inquire whether Lord Seely meant to get Algy a place, and what tangible benefits he had it in contemplation to bestow on him. But to all such prosy, plodding individuals, Mrs. Errington presented a perspective of vague magnificence, which sometimes awed and generally silenced them.

The big square letters on Bath post paper, directed in Algernon's clear, graceful handwriting, and bearing my Lord Seely's frank, in the form of a blotchy sprawling autograph in one corner, were, however, palpable facts; and Mrs. Errington made the most of them. It was seldom that she had not one of them in her pocket. She would pull them out, sometimes as though in mere absence of mind, sometimes avowedly of set purpose, but in either case she failed not to make them the occasion for an almost endless variety of prospective and retrospective boasting.

It must be owned that Algernon's letters were delightful. They were written with such a freshness of observation, such a sense of enjoyment, such a keen appreciation of fun—tempered always by a wonderful knack of keeping his own figure in a favourable light—that passages from them were read aloud, and quoted at Whitford tea-parties with a most enlivening effect.

"Those letters are written pro bono publico," Minnie Bodkin observed confidentially to her mother. "No human being would address such communications to Mrs. Errington for her sole perusal."

"Well, I don't know, Minnie! Surely it is natural enough that he should write long letters to his mother, even without expecting her to read them aloud to people."

"Very natural; but not just such letters as he does write, I think."

Minnie suppressed any further expression of her own shrewdness. Her confidence in herself had been rudely shaken; and she made keen, motive-probing speeches much seldomer than formerly. And she could not but agree in the general verdict, that Algernon's letters were very amusing. Miss Chubb was delighted with them; although they were the occasion of one or two tough struggles for supremacy in the knowledge of fashionable life between herself and Mrs. Errington. But Miss Chubb was really good-natured, and Mrs. Errington was unshakeably self-satisfied; so that no serious breach resulted from these combats.

"Dormer—Lady Harriet Dormer!" Miss Chubb would say, musingly. "I think I must have met her when I was staying with Mrs. Figgins and the Bishop of Plumbunn. And the Dormers' place is not so very far from Whitford, you know. I believe I have heard papa speak of his acquaintance with some of the family."

"Oh no," Mrs. Errington would reply; "not likely you should have ever met Lady Harriet at Mrs. Figgins's. She is the Earl of Grandcourt's daughter; and Lord Grandcourt had the reputation of being the proudest nobleman in England."

"Well, my dear Mrs. Errington," the spinster would retort, bridling and tossing her head sideways, "that could be no reason why his daughter should not have visited the bishop! A dignitary of the Church, you know! And as to family—I can assure you the Figginses were most aristocratically connected."

"Besides, Miss Chubb, Lady Harriet must have been in the nursery in those days. She's only six-and-thirty. You can see her age in the 'Peerage.'"

This was a kind of blow that usually silenced poor Miss Chubb, who was sensitive on the score of her age. But, on the whole, she was not displeased at the opportunity of airing her reminiscences of London; and she did not always get the worst of it in her encounters with Mrs. Errington.

Mrs. Errington had one listener who, at all events, was never tired of hearing Algy's letters read and re-read, and whose interest in all they contained was vivid and inexhaustible. Rhoda bestowed an amount of eager attention on the brilliant epistles bearing Lord Seely's frank, which even Mrs. Errington considered adequate to their merits.

Often—not quite always—there would be a little message. "How are all the good Maxfields? Say I asked." Or sometimes, "Give my love to Rhoda." Mrs. Errington took Algernon's sending his love to Rhoda much as she would have taken his bidding her stroke the kitten for him. She did not guess how it set the poor girl's heart beating. It was only natural that Rhoda's face should flush with pleasure at being so kindly and condescendingly remembered. Still less could the worthy lady understand the effect of her careless words on Mr. Maxfield. Once she said in his presence, "Have you any message for Mr. Algernon, Rhoda?" (She had recently taken to speaking of her son as "Mr." Algernon; a circumstance which had not escaped Rhoda's sensitive observation.) "You know he always sends you his love."

"Oh, my young gentleman has not forgotten Rhoda, then?" said old Maxfield, without raising his eyes from the ledger he was examining.

"Algernon never forgets. Indeed, none of the Ancrams ever forget. An almost royal memory has always been a characteristic of our race." With which magnificent speech Mrs. Errington made an impressive exit from the back shop.

Old Max knew enough to be aware that the tenacity even of a royal memory had not always been found equal to retaining such trifles as a debt of twenty pounds. But so long as Algy remembered his Rhoda, he was welcome to let the money slip. Indeed, if Algy behaved properly to Rhoda, there should be no question of repayment. Twenty pounds, or two hundred, would be well bestowed in securing Rhoda's happiness, and making a lady of her. Nevertheless, old Max kept the acknowledgment of the debt safely locked up, and looked at it now and then, with some inward satisfaction. Algernon was coming back to revisit Whitford in the summer, and then something definite should be settled.

Meanwhile, Maxfield took some pains to have Rhoda treated with more consideration than had hitherto been bestowed on her. He astonished Betty Grimshaw by sharply reproving her for sending Rhoda into the shop on some errand. "Rice!" he exclaimed testily, in answer to his sister-in-law's explanation. "If you want rice, you must fetch it for yourself. The shop is no place for Rhoda, and I will not have her come there." Then he began to display a quite unprecedented liberality in providing Rhoda's clothes. The girl, whose ideas about her own dress were of the humblest, and who had thought a dove-coloured merino gown as good a garment as she was ever likely to possess, was told to buy herself a silk gown. "A good 'un. Nothing flimsy and poor," said old Max. "A good, solid silk gown, that will wear and last. And—you had better ask Mrs. Errington to go with you to buy it. She will understand what is fitting better than your aunt Betty. I wish you to have proper and becoming raiment, Rhoda. You are not a child now. And you go amongst gentlefolks at Dr. Bodkin's house. And I would not have you seem out of place there, by reason of unsuitable attire."

Rhoda was delighted to be allowed to gratify her natural taste for colour and adornment; and she shortly afterwards appeared in so elegant a dress, that Betty Grimshaw was moved to say to her brother-in-law, "Why, Jonathan, I'll declare if our Rhoda don't look as genteel as 'ere a one o' the young ladies I see! Why you're making quite a lady of her, Jonathan!"

"Me make a lady of her?" growled old Max. "It isn't me, nor you, nor yet a smart gown, as can do that. But the Lord has done it. The Lord has given Rhoda the natur' of a lady, if ever I see a lady in my life; and I mean her to be treated like one. Rhoda's none o' your sort of clay, Betty Grimshaw. She's fine porcelain, is Rhoda. I suppose you've nothing to say against the child's silk gown?"

"Nay, not I, Jonathan! She's welcome to wear silk or satin either, if you like to pay for it. And, indeed, I'm uncommon pleased to see a bit of bright colour, and be let to put a flower in my bonnet. I'm sure we've had enough of them Methodist ways. Dismal and dull enough they were, Jonathan. But you can't say as I ever grumbled, or went agin' you. Anything for peace and quietness' sake is my way. But I do like church best, having been bred to it. And I always did, in my heart, even when you and David Powell would be preaching up the Wesleyans. I never said anything, as you know, Jonathan. But I kept my own way of thinking all the same. And I'm only glad you've come round to it yourself, at last."

This was bitter to Jonathan Maxfield. But he had had once or twice to endure similar speeches from his sister-in-law, since his defection from Methodism. His autocratic power in his own family was wielded as strictly as ever, but his assumption of infallibility had been fatally damaged. To get his own way was still within his power, but it would be vain henceforward to expect those around him to acknowledge—even with their lips—that his way must of necessity be the best way.

At the beginning of April there came to Whitford the announcement that Algernon had received and accepted an invitation to accompany the Seelys abroad in the late summer; and that, therefore, his visit to "dear old Whitford" was indefinitely postponed. This announcement would have angered and disquieted old Max beyond measure, had it not been that Algernon took the precaution to write him a letter, which arrived in Whitford by the same post as that which brought to Mrs. Errington the news of his projected journey to the Continent. It was a very neat letter. Some persons might have called it a cunning letter. At any rate, it soothed old Max's anxious suspicions, if it did not absolutely destroy them. "I believe, my good friend," wrote Algernon, "that you will quite approve the step I am taking, in accompanying Lord and Lady Seely to Switzerland. They have no son, and I think I may say that they have come to look upon me almost as a child of the house. I remember all the good advice you gave me before I left Whitford. And when I was hesitating about accepting my lord's invitation, I thought of what you would have said, and made up my mind to resist the strong temptation of coming back to dear old Whitford this summer." Then in a postscript he added: "As to that little private transaction between us, I must ask you kindly to have patience with me yet awhile. I try to be careful, but living here is expensive, and I am put to it to pay my way. You will not mention the matter to my mother, I know. And, perhaps, it would be well to say nothing to her about this letter. May I send my love to Rhoda?"

In justification of this last sentence, it must be said that Algernon was quite innocent of Lady Seely's project regarding himself and Castalia; and that there were times when he thought with some warmth of feeling of the summer days in Llanryddan, and told himself that there was not one of the girls whom he met in society who surpassed Rhoda Maxfield in the delicate freshness of her beauty, or equalled her in natural grace and sweetness.

Algernon had really excellent taste.

VOUME II.

CHAPTER I.

"So you are to come to Switzerland with us next month, Ancram," said Miss Kilfinane. She was seated at the piano in Lady Seely's drawing-room, and Algernon was leaning on the instrument, and idly turning over a portfolio of music.

"Yes; I hope your serene highness has no objection to that arrangement?"

"It would be of no use my objecting, I suppose!"

"Of none whatever. But it would be unpleasant."

"Oh, you would still go then, whether I liked it or not?"

"I'm afraid the temptation to travel about Europe in your company would be too strong for me!"

"How silly you are, Ancram!" said Miss Kilfinane, looking up half shyly, half tenderly. But she met no answering look from Algernon. He had just come upon a song that he wanted to try, and was drawing it out from under a heap of others in the portfolio.

"Look here, Castalia," he said, "I wish you would play through this accompaniment for me. I can't manage it."

It will be seen that Algernon had become familiar enough with Miss Kilfinane to call her by her Christian-name. And, moreover, he addressed her in a little tone of authority, as being quite sure she would do what he asked her.

"This?" she said, taking the song from his hand. "Why do you want to sing this dull thing? I think Glück is so dreary! And, besides, it isn't your style at all."

"Isn't it? What is my style, I wonder?"

"Oh light, lively things are your style."

At the bottom of his mind, perhaps, Algernon thought so too. But it is often very unpleasant to hear our own secret convictions uttered by other people; and he did not like to be told that he could not sing anything more solid than a French chansonette.

"Lady Harriet particularly wishes me to try this thing of Glück's at her house next Saturday," he said.

Miss Kilfinane threw down the song pettishly. "Oh, Lady Harriet," she exclaimed. "I might have known it was her suggestion! She is so full of nonsense about her classical composers. I think she makes a fool of you, Ancram. I know it will be a failure if you attempt that song."

"Thank you very much, Miss Kilfinane! And now, having spoken your mind on the subject, will you kindly play the accompaniment?"

Algernon picked up the piece of music, smoothed it with his hand, placed it on the desk of the piano, and made a little mocking bow to Castalia. His serenity and good humour seemed to irritate her. "I'm sick of Lady Harriet!" she said, querulously, and with a shrug of the shoulders. The action and the words were so plainly indicative of ill temper, that Lady Seely, who waddled into the drawing-room at that moment, asked loudly, "What are you two quarrelling about, eh?"

"Oh, what a shocking idea, my lady! We're not quarrelling at all," answered Algernon, raising his eyebrows, and smiling with closed lips. He rarely showed his teeth when he smiled, which circumstance gave his mouth an expression of finesse and delicate irony that was peculiar, and—coupled with the candidly-arched brows—attractive.

"Well, it takes two to make a quarrel, certainly," returned my lady. "But Castalia was scolding you, at all events. Weren't you now, Castalia?"

Castalia deigned not to reply, but tossed her head, and began to run her fingers over the keys of the piano.

"The fact is, Lady Seely," said Algernon, "that Castalia is so convinced that I shall make a mess of this aria—which Lady Harriet Dormer has asked me to sing for her next Saturday—that she declines to play the accompaniment of it for me."

"Well, you ought to be immensely flattered, young jackanapes! She wouldn't care a straw about some people's failures, would you, Castalia? Would you mind, now, if Jack Price were to sing a song and make an awful mess of it, eh?"

"As to that, it seems to me that Jack Price makes an awful mess of most things he does," replied Castalia.

"Ah, exactly! So one mess more or less don't matter. But in the case of our Admirable Crichton here, it is different."

"I think he is getting awfully spoiled," said Castalia, a little less crossly. And there was absolutely a blush upon her sallow cheek.

"And that's the reason you snub him, is it? You see, Ancram, it's all for your good, if Castalia is a little hard on you!"

Miss Kilfinane rose and left the room, saying that she must dress for her drive.

"I think Castalia is harder on Lady Harriet than on me," said Algernon, when Castalia was gone.

"Ah! H'm! Castalia has lots of good points, but—I daresay you have noticed it—she is given to being a little bit jealous when she cares about people. Now you show a decided liking for Lady Harriet's society, and you crack up her grace, and her elegance, and her taste, and all that. And sometimes I think poor Cassy don't quite like it, don't you know?"

"What on earth can it matter to her?" cried Algernon. He knew that Castalia was no favourite with my lady, and he flattered himself that he was becoming a favourite with her. So he spoke with a little half-contemptuous smile, and a shrug of impatience, when he asked, "What on earth can it matter to her?"

But my lady did not smile. She threw her head back, and looked at Algernon from under her half-closed eyelids.

"It's my opinion, young man, that it matters a good deal to Castalia," she said; "more than it would have mattered to me when I was a young lady, I can tell you. But there's no accounting for tastes."

Then Lady Seely also left the room, having first bidden Algernon to come and dine with her the next day.

Algernon was dumfoundered.

Not that he had not perceived the scornful Castalia's partiality for his charming self; not that her submission to his wishes, or even his whims, and her jealous anxiety to keep him by her side whenever there appeared to be danger of his leaving it for the company of a younger or more attractive woman, had escaped his observation. But Algernon was not fatuous enough to consider himself a lady-killer. His native good taste would alone have prevented him from having any such pretension. It was ridiculous; and it involved, almost of necessity, some affectation. And Algernon never was affected. He accepted Castalia's marked preference as the most natural thing in the world. He had been used to be petted and preferred all his life. But it truly had not entered into his head that the preference meant anything more than that Castalia found him amusing, and clever, and good-looking, and that she liked to keep so attractive a personage to herself as much as possible. For Algernon had noted the Honourable Castalia's little grudging jealousies, and he knew as well as anybody that she did not like to hear him praise Lady Harriet, for whom, indeed, she had long entertained a smouldering sort of dislike. But that she should have anything like a tender sentiment for himself, and, still more, that Lady Seely should see and approve it—for my lady's words and manner implied no less—was a very astonishing idea indeed.

So astonishing was it, that after a while he came to the conclusion that the idea was erroneous. He turned Lady Seely's words in his mind, this way and that, and tried to look at them from all points of view, and—as words will do when too curiously scrutinised—they gradually seemed to take another and a different meaning, from the first obvious one which had struck him.

"The old woman was only giving me a hint not to annoy Miss Kilfinane; not to excite her peevish temper, or exasperate her envy."

But this solution would not quite do, either. "Lady Seely is not too fond of Castalia," he said to himself. "Besides, I never knew her particularly anxious to spare anyone's feelings. What the deuce did she mean, I wonder?"

Algernon continued to wonder at intervals all the rest of the afternoon. His mind was still busy with the same subject when he came upon Jack Price, seated in the reading-room of the club, to which he had introduced Algernon at the beginning of his London career, and of which Algernon had since become a member. It was now full summer time. The window was wide open, and the Honourable John Patrick was lounging in a chair near it, with a newspaper spread out on his knees, and his eyes fixed on a water-cart that was be-sprinkling the dusty street outside. He looked very idle, and a little melancholy, as he sat there by himself, and he welcomed Algernon with even more than his usual effusion, asking him what he was going to do with himself, and offering to walk part of the way towards his lodgings with him, when he was told that Algernon must betake himself homeward. The offer was a measure of Mr. Price's previous weariness of spirit; for, in general, he professed to dislike walking.

"And how long is it since you saw our friend, Mrs. Machyn-Stubbs?" asked Jack Price of Algernon, as they strolled along, arm-in-arm, on the shady side of the way.

"Oh—I'm afraid it's rather a long time," said Algernon, carelessly.

"Ah, now that's bad, my dear boy. You shouldn't neglect people, you know. And our dear Mrs. Machyn-Stubbs is exceedingly pleasant."

"As to neglecting her—I don't know that I have neglected her—particularly. What more could I do than call and leave my card?"

"Call again. You wouldn't leave off going to Lady Seely's because you happened not to find her at home once in a way."

"Lady Seely is my relation."

"H'm! Well, would you cut Lady Harriet Dormer for the same reason?"

"Cut her? But, my dear Mr. Price, you mustn't suppose that I have cut Mrs. Machyn-Stubbs!"

"Come, now, my dear fellow, I'm a great deal older than you are, and I'll take the liberty of giving you a bit of advice. Never offend people, who mean to be civil, merely because they don't happen to amuse you. What, the deuce, we can't live for amusement in this life!"

The moralising might be good, but the moralist was, Algernon thought, badly fitted with his part. He was tempted to retort on his new mentor, but he did not retort. He merely said, quietly:

"Has Mrs. Machyn-Stubbs been complaining of me, then?"

"Well, the truth is, she has—in an indirect kind of way; you know—what?"

"I'll go and see her this evening. To-day is Thursday, isn't it? She has one of her 'At home's' this evening."

Jack Price looked at the young man admiringly. "You're an uncommonly sensible fellow!" said he. "I give you my honour I never knew a fellow of your years take advice so well. By Jove! I wish I had had your common sense when I was your age. It's too late for me to do any good now, you know, what? And, in fact," (with a solemn lowering of his musical Irish voice) "I split myself on the very rock I'm now warning you off. I never was polite. And if any one told me to go to the right, sure it was a thousand to one that I'd instantly bolt to the left!" And shaking his head with a sad, regretful gesture, Jack Price parted from Algernon at the corner of the street.

Mrs. Machyn-Stubbs received the truant very graciously that evening. She knew that, during his absence from her parties, he had been admitted into society, to which even her fashionable self could not hope to penetrate. But, though this might be a reason for a little genteel sneering at him behind his back, it was none whatever, Mrs. Machyn-Stubbs considered, for giving him a cool reception when he did grace her house with his presence. She said to several of her guests, one after the other: "We have young Ancram Errington here to-night. He's so glad to come to us, poor fellow, for my people's place is his second home, down in the West of England. And, then, the Seelys think it nice of us to take notice of him, don't you know? He is a relation of Lady Seely's, and is quite in that set—the Dormers, and all those people. Ah! you don't know them? They say he is to marry Castalia Kilfinane. But we haven't spoken about it yet out of our own little circle. Her father was Viscount Kauldkail, and married Lord Seely's youngest sister," and so on, and so on with a set smile, and no expression whatever on her smooth, fair face.

To Algernon himself she showed herself politely inquisitive on the subject of his engagement to Castalia, and startled him considerably by saying, when she found herself close to him for a few minutes near a doorway:

"And are we really to congratulate you, Mr. Errington?"

"If you please, madam," answered Algernon, with a bright, amused smile and an easy bow, "but I should like to know—if it be not indiscreet—on what special subject? I am, indeed, to be congratulated on finding myself here. But, then, you are hardly likely to be the person to do it."

At that moment Algernon was wedged into a corner behind a fat old gentleman, who was vainly struggling to extricate himself from the crowd in front, by making a series of short plunges forward, the rebound of which sent him back on to Algernon's toes with some violence. It was very hot, and a young lady was singing out of tune in the adjoining room; her voice floating over the murmur of conversation occasionally, in a wailing long-drawn note. Altogether, it might have been suspected by some persons that Mr. Ancram Errington was laughing at his hostess, when he spoke of his position at that time as being one which called for congratulation. But Mrs. Machyn-Stubbs was the sort of woman who completely baffled irony by a serene incapability of perceiving it. And she would sooner suspect you of maligning her, hating her, or insulting her, than of laughing at her. To this immunity from all sense of the ridiculous she owed her chief social successes; for there are occasions when some obtuseness of the faculties is useful. Mrs. Machyn-Stubbs tapped Algernon's arm lightly with her fan, as she answered, "Now Mr. Errington, that's all very well with the outside world, but you shouldn't make mysteries with us! I look upon you almost as a brother of Orlando's, I do indeed."

"You're very kind, indeed, and I'm immensely obliged to you; but, upon my word, I don't know what you mean by my making mysteries!"

"Oh, well, if you choose to keep your own counsel, of course you can do so. I will say no more." Upon which Mrs. Machyn-Stubbs proceeded to say a great deal more, and ended by plainly giving Algernon to understand that the rumour of his engagement to Miss Castalia Kilfinane had been pretty widely circulated during the last four or five weeks.

"Oh, Mrs. Machyn-Stubbs," said Algernon, laughing, "you surely never believe more than a hundredth part of what you hear? There's Mr. Price looking for me. I promised to walk home with him, it is such a lovely night. Thank you, no; not any tea! Are you ever at home about four o'clock? I shall take my chance of finding you. Good night."

Algernon was greatly puzzled. How and whence had the report of his engagement to Castalia originated? He would have been less puzzled, if not less surprised, had he known that the report had come in the first place from Lady Seely herself, who had let fall little words and hints, well understanding how they would grow and spread. He had not committed himself in his answer to Mrs. Machyn-Stubbs. He had replied to her in such a manner as to leave the truth or falsehood of the report she had mentioned an open question. He felt the consciousness of this to be a satisfaction. Some persons might say, "Well, but since the report was false, why not say so?" But Algernon always, and, as it were, instinctively, took refuge in the vague. A clear statement to which he should appear to be bound would have irked him like a tight shoe; and naturally so, since he was conscious that he should flexibly conform himself to circumstances as they might arise, and not stick with stubborn stupidity to any predetermined course of conduct, which might prove to be inconvenient.

After saying "Good night" to his hostess he elbowed his way out of the crowded rooms, and went downstairs side by side with Jack Price. The latter knew everybody present, or thought he did. And as, when he did happen to make a mistake and to greet enthusiastically some total stranger whom he had never seen in his life before, he never acknowledged it, but persisted in declaring that he remembered the individual in question perfectly, although "the name, the name, my dear sir, or madam, has quite escaped my wretched memory!" his progress towards Mrs. Machyn-Stubbs's hall door was considerably impeded by the nods, smiles, and shakes of the hand, which he scattered broadcast.

"There's Deepville," said he to Algernon, as they passed a tall, dark, thin-faced man, with a stern jaw and a haughty carriage of the head. "Don't you know Deepville? Ah, then you should! You should really. The most delightful, lovable, charming fellow! He'd be enchanted to make your acquaintance, Errington, quite enchanted. I can answer for him. There's nothing in the world would give him greater pleasure, what?"

Algernon was by this time pretty well accustomed to Jack Price's habit of answering for the ready ecstasies of all his acquaintances with regard to each other, and merely replied that he dared to say Sir Lancelot Deepville was a very agreeable person.

"And how's the fair Castalia?" asked Jack, when they were out in the street.

"I believe she is quite well. I saw her this morning."

"Oh, I suppose you did," exclaimed Jack Price with a little smile, which Algernon thought was to be interpreted by Mrs. Machyn-Stubbs's recent revelations. But the next minute Jack added, very unexpectedly, "I had some idea, at one time, that Deepville was making up to her. But it came to nothing. She's a nice creature, is Castalia Kilfinane; a very nice creature."

Algernon could not help smiling at this disinterested praise.

"I'm afraid she does not always behave quite nicely to you, Mr. Price," he said. And he said it with a little air of apology and proprietorship which he would not have assumed yesterday.

"Oh, you're quite mistaken, my dear boy; she's as nice as possible with me. I like Castalia Kilfinane. There's a great deal of good about her, and she's well educated and clever in her way—not showy, you know, what?—but—oh, a nice creature! There's a sort of bitter twang about her, you know, that I like immensely."

"Oh, well," cried Algernon, laughing outright, "if you have a liking for bitters, indeed—"

"Ah, but she doesn't mean it. It's just a little flavour—a little soupçon. Oh, upon my word, I think Miss Kilfinane a thoroughly nice creature. It was a pity about Deepville now, eh, what?"

"I wonder that you never thought of trying your fortune in that quarter yourself, Mr. Price!" said Algernon, looking at him curiously, as they passed within the glare of a street-lamp.

"Is it me? Ah, now, I thought everybody knew that I wasn't a marrying man. Besides, there never was the least probability that Miss Kilfinane would have had me—none in the world. Sure, she'd never think of looking at a bald old bachelor like myself, what?"

Algernon did not feel called on to pursue the subject. But he had a conviction that Jack Price would not, under any circumstances, have given Miss Kilfinane the chance of accepting him.

The allusion, however, seemed to have touched some long-silent chord of feeling in Jack, and set it vibrating. As they sat at supper together, Jack reverted to the sage, mentor-like tone he had assumed that morning, giving Algernon much sound advice of a worldly nature, and holding up his own case as a warning to all young men who liked to "bolt to the left when they were told to go to the right," and presenting himself in the unusual light of a gloomy and disappointed person; and when a couple of tumblers of hot punch smoked on the table, Jack grew tender and sentimental.

"Ah, my dear Errington," he said, "I wish ye may never know what it is to be a lonely old bachelor!"

"Lonely? Why you're the most popular man in London, out-and-out!"

"Popular! And what good does that do me? If I were dead to-morrow, who'd care, do you think? Although that doesn't seem to me to be such a hard case as people say. Sure, I don't want anyone to cry when I'm dead; but I'd like 'em to care for me a little while I'm living. If I'd been my own elder brother, now; or if I'd taken advantage of my opportunities, and made a good fortune, as I might have done—But 'twas one scrape after another I put my foot into. I did and said whatever came uppermost. And you'll find, my dear boy, that it's the foolish things that mostly do come uppermost."

"It's lucky that, amongst other foolish things, an imprudent marriage never rose to the surface," said Algernon.

"Oh, but it did! Oh, devil a doubt about it!" The combined influence of memory and hot punch brought out Jack's musical brogue with unusual emphasis. "Only, there I couldn't carry out my foolish intentions. It wasn't the will that was wanting, my dear boy."

"Providence looked after you on that occasion?"

"Providence or—or the other thing. Oh, I could tell you a love-story, only you'd be laughing at me."

"Indeed, I would not laugh!"

"On my honour, I don't know why you shouldn't! I often enough have laughed at myself. She was the sweetest, gentlest, most delicate little creature!—Snowdrop I used to call her. And as for goodness, she was steeped in it. You felt goodness in the air wherever she was, just as you smell perfume all about when the hawthorns blossom in May. Ah! now to think of me talking in that way, and my head as smooth as a billiard-ball!"

"And—and how was it? Did your people interfere to prevent the match?"

"My people! Faith, they'd have screeched to be heard from here to there if I'd made her the Honourable Mrs. Jack Price, and contaminated the blood of the Prices of Mullingar. Did ye ever hear that my great-grandfather was a whisky distiller? Bedad, he was then! And I believe he manufactured good liquor, rest his soul! But I shouldn't have cared for that, as ye may believe. But they got hold of her, and told her that I was a roving, unsteady sort of fellow; and that was true enough. And—and she married somebody else. The man she took wasn't as good-looking as I was in those days. However, there's no accounting for these things, you know. It's fate, what? destiny! And she told me, in the pretty silver voice of hers, like a robin on a bough, that I had better forget her, and marry a lady in my own station, and live happy ever after. 'Mary,' said I, 'if I don't marry you I'll marry no woman, gentle or simple.' She didn't believe me. And I don't know that I quite believed myself. But so it turned out, you see, what? And so I was saved from a mésalliance, and from having, maybe, to bring up a numerous family on nothing a year; and the blood of the Prices of Mullingar is in a fine state of preservation, and Mary never became the Honourable Mrs. Jack Price. Honourable—bedad it's the Honourable Jack Price she'd have made of me if she'd taken me; an honourabler Jack than I've been without her, I'm afraid! D'ye know, Errington, I believe on my soul that, if I had married Mary, and gone off with her to Canada, and built a log-house, and looked after my pigs and my ploughs, I'd have been a happy man. But there it is, a man never knows what is really best for him until it's too late. We'll hope there are compensations to come, what? Of all the dreary, cut-throat, blue-devilish syllables in the English language, I believe those words 'too late' are the ugliest. They make a fellow feel as if he was being strangled. So mind your p's and q's, my boy, and don't throw away your chances whilst you've got 'em!"

And thus ended Jack Price's sermon on worldly wisdom.

CHAPTER II.

Minnie Bodkin had loyally tried to keep the promise she had given to the Methodist preacher respecting Rhoda Maxfield, but in so trying she had encountered many obstacles. In the first place, Rhoda, with all her gentleness, was not frank, and she opposed a passive resistance to all Minnie's efforts to win her confidence on the subject of Algernon.

"It is like poking a little frightened animal out of its hole, trying to get anything from her!" said Minnie, impatiently.

Not that Rhoda's reticence was wholly due to timidity. She knew instinctively that she was to be warned against giving her heart to Algernon Errington; that she should hear him blamed; or, at least, that the unreasonableness of trusting in his promises, or taking his boyish love-making in serious earnest, would be safely set forth by Miss Bodkin. Rhoda had not perceived any of the wise things which might be said against her attachment to Algernon in the beginning, but now she thought she perceived them all. And she was resolved, with a sort of timid obstinacy, not to listen to them.

"I'm sure Algy's fond of me. And even if he has changed"—the supposition brought tears into her eyes as the words framed themselves in her mind—"I don't want to have him spoken unkindly of."

But, in truth, latterly her hopes had been out-weighing her fears. In most of his letters to his mother Algernon had spoken of her, and had sent her his love. He was making friends, and looking forward hopefully to getting some definite position. Even her father spoke well of Algernon now;—said how clever he was, and what grand acquaintance he was making, and how sure he would be to succeed. And once or twice her father had dropped a word which had set Rhoda's heart beating, and made the colour rush into her face, for it seemed as if the old man had some idea of her love for Algy, and approved it! All these circumstances together made Minnie's task of mentor a rather hopeless one.

And then Minnie herself, although, as has been said, loyally anxious to fulfil her promise to David Powell, began to think that he had overrated the importance of interfering with Rhoda's love-story if love-story it were. Powell lived in a state of exalted and, perhaps, overstrained feeling, and attributed his own earnestness to slighter natures. Of course, on the side of worldly wisdom there was much to be said against Rhoda's fancying herself engaged to Algernon Errington. There was much to be said; and yet Minnie did not feel quite sure that the idea was so preposterous as Powell had appeared to think it. True, Mrs. Errington was vain, and worldly, and ambitious for her son. True, Algernon was volatile, selfish, and little more than twenty years of age. But still there was one solid fact to be taken into account, which, Minnie thought, might be made to outweigh all the obstacles to a marriage between the two young people—the solid fact, namely, of old Maxfield's money.

"If Algernon married a wife with a good dower, and if the wife were as pretty, as graceful, and as well-mannered as Rhoda, I do not suppose that anybody would concern himself particularly with her pedigree," thought Minnie. "And even if any one did, that difficulty would not be insuperable, for I have no knowledge of Mrs. Errington, if within three months of the wedding she had not invented a genealogy, only second to her own, for her son's wife, and persuaded herself of its genuineness into the bargain!"

As to those other convictions which would have made such a marriage horrible to David Powell, even had it been made with the hearty approval of all the godless world, Minnie did not share them. She did not believe that Rhoda's character had any spiritual depth; and she thought it likely enough that she would be able to make Algernon happy, and to be happy as his wife. "Algy is not base, or cruel, or vicious," she said to herself. "He has merely the faults of a spoiled child. A woman with more earnestness than Rhoda has would weary him; and a wiser woman might, in the long run, be wearied by him. She is pretty, and sufficiently intelligent to make a good audience, and so humble-minded that she would never be exacting, but would gratefully accept any scraps of kindness and affection which Algy might feel inclined to bestow on her. And that would react upon him, and make him bestow bigger scraps for the pleasure of being adored for his generosity."

And there were times when she felt very angry with Rhoda;—Rhoda, who turned away from the better to choose the worse, and who was coldly insensible to the fact that Matthew Diamond was in love with her. Nay, had she been cognisant of the fact, she would, Minnie felt sure, have shrank away from the grave, clever gentleman who, as it was, could win nothing warmer from her than a sort of submissive endurance of his presence, and a humble acknowledgment that he was very kind to take notice of an ignorant little thing like her.

It was with strangely mingled feelings that Minnie, watching day by day from her sofa or easy-chair, perceived the girl's utter indifference to Diamond. How much would Minnie have given for one of those rare sweet smiles to beam upon her, which were wasted on Rhoda's pretty, shy, downcast face! How happy it would have made her to hear those clear, incisive tones lowered into soft indistinctness for her ears, as they so often were for Rhoda's, who would look timid and tired, and answer, "Yes, sir," and "No, sir," until Minnie's nervous sympathy with Diamond's disappointment, and irritation against him for being disappointed, grew almost beyond her own control.

One May evening, when the cuckoo was sending his voice across the purling Whit from distant Pudcombe Woods, and the hyacinths in Minnie's special flower-stand were pouring out their silent even-song in waves of perfume, five persons were sitting in Mrs. Bodkin's drawing-room, the windows of which looked towards the west. They were listening to the cuckoo, and smelling the sweet breath of the hyacinths, and gazing at the rosy sky, and dropping now and then a soft word, which seemed to enhance the sweetness and the silence of the room. The five persons were Minnie Bodkin, Rhoda Maxfield, Matthew Diamond, Mr. Warlock (the curate of St. Chad's), and Miss Chubb. The latter was embroidering something in Berlin wools, as usual; but the peace of the place, and of the hour, seemed to have fallen on her, as on the rest, and she sat with her work in her lap, looking across the stand of hyacinths, very still and quiet.

The Reverend Peter also sat looking silently across the hyacinths, but it was at the owner. Minnie's cheek rested on her thin white hand, and her lustrous eyes had a far-away look in them, as they gazed out towards Pudcombe Woods, where the cuckoo was calling his poet-loved syllables with a sweet, clear tone, that seemed to have gathered all the spirit of the spring into one woodland voice.

Rhoda sat beside the window, and was sewing very gently and noiselessly, but seemingly intent upon her work, and unconscious that the eyes of Mr. Diamond—who was seated close to Minnie's chair—were fixed upon her, and that in some vague way he was attributing to her the perfume of the flowers, and the melancholy-sweet note of the bird, and the melted rubies of the western sky.

"What a sunset!" said Miss Chubb, breaking the silence. But she spoke almost in a whisper, and her voice did not startle any ear. Mr. Warlock, habituated to suppress his feelings and adapt his words to those of his company, answered, after a little pause, "Lovely indeed! It is an evening to awaken the sensibilities of a feeling heart."

"It makes me think of Manchester Square. We had some hyacinths in pots, too, I remember, when I was staying with the Bishop of Plumbunn."

Miss Chubb's odd association of ideas was merely due to the fact that her thoughts were flying back to the rose-garden of youth.

"Do you not like to hear the cuckoo, Miss Bodkin?" said Diamond, softly, speaking almost in her ear. She started, and turned her head towards him.

"Yes; no. I like it, although it makes me sad. I like it because it makes me sad perhaps."

"All sights, and sounds, and scents seem to me to be combined this evening into something sweeter than words can say."

"It is a fine evening, and the cuckoo is calling from Pudcombe Woods, and my hyacinths are of a very good sort. It seems to me that words can manage to say that much with distinctness!"

"What a pity," thought Diamond, "that head overshadows heart in this attractive woman! She is too keen, too cool, too critical. A woman without softness and sentiment is an unpleasant phenomenon. And I think she has grown harder in her manner than she used to be." Then the reflection crossed his mind that her health had been more frail and uncertain than usual of late, and that she bore much physical suffering with high courage; and the little prick of resentment he had begun to feel was at once mollified. He answered aloud, with a slow smile, "Why, yes, words may manage to say all that. I wonder if I may ask you a question? It is one I have long wished to ask."

"You may, certainly."

"There are questions that should not be asked."

"I will trust you not to ask any such."

"Now when she looks and speaks like that, she is adorable!" thought Diamond, meeting the soft light of Minnie's lovely, pathetic eyes, which fell immediately before his own. "I wish I might have you for a friend, Miss Bodkin," he said.

"I think you have your wish. I thought you knew you had it."

"Ah, yes; you are always good, and kind, and—and—but you—I will make a clean breast of it, and pay you the compliment of telling you the truth. I have thought latterly that you were hardly so cordial, so frank in your kindness to me as you once were. It would matter nothing to me in another person, but in you, a little shade of manner matters a great deal. I don't believe there is another human being to whom I would say so much. For I am—as perhaps you know—a man little given to thrust myself where I am not welcome."

"You are about the proudest and most distant person I ever knew, and require to be very obviously implored before you condescend to easy friendship with anyone."

Minnie laughed, as she spoke, a little low rippling laugh, which she ended with a forced cough, to hide the sob in her throat.

"No; not proud. You misjudge me; but it is true that I dread, almost more than anything else, being deemed intrusive."

"If that fear has prevented you from putting the question to which you have so long desired an answer, pray ask it forthwith."

"I think it has almost answered itself," said Diamond, bending over her, and turning his chair so as to cut her and himself off still more from the others. "I was going to ask you if I had unwittingly offended you in any way, or if my frequent presence here were, for any reason, irksome to you? It might well be so. And if you would say so candidly, believe me, I should feel not the smallest resentment. Sorrow I should feel. I can't deny it; but I should not cease to regard you as I have always regarded you from the beginning of our acquaintance. How highly that is, I have not the gift to tell; nor do you love the direct, broadly-spoken praise that sounds like flattery, be it ever so sincere."

"No; please don't praise me," said Minnie, huskily. She was shadowed by his figure as he sat beside her, and so he did not see the tears that quivered in her eyes. After a second or two, during which she had passed her handkerchief quickly, almost stealthily, across her face, she said, "But your question, you say, has answered itself."

"I hope so; I hope I may believe that there is nothing wrong between us."

"Nothing."

"I have not offended you in any way!"

"No."

"Nor unwittingly hurt you? I daresay I am awkward and abrupt sometimes."

"Pray believe that I have nothing in the world to blame you for."

"Thank you. I know you speak sincerely. Your friendship is very precious to me."

She answered nothing, but hesitatingly put out her hand, which he grasped for an instant, and would have raised to his lips, but that she drew it suddenly away, murmuring something about her cushions being awry, and trying tremblingly to rearrange them.

He moved the cushions that supported her shoulders with a tender, careful touch, and placed them so that her posture in the lounging-chair might be easier. She clasped her hands together and laid her head back wearily.

"You don't know how precious your friendship is to me," he went on lowering his voice still more. "I never had a sister. But I have often thought how sweet the companionship of a sister must be. I am very much alone in the world; and, if I dared, I would speak to you with fraternal confidence."

"Pray speak so," answered Minnie, almost in a whisper. "I should like—to be—of some comfort to you."

There was a silence. It was scarcely broken by Miss Chubb's murmured remark to Mr. Warlock, that the moon was beginning to make a ring of light behind the poplar trees on the other side of the Whit, like the halo round the head of a saint. The twilight deepened, Rhoda's fingers ceased to ply the needle, but she remained at the window looking over at the moonlit poplars, while Miss Chubb's voice softly droned out some rambling speech, which jarred no more on the quietude of the hour than did the ripple of the river.

"You have been so good to her!" said Diamond suddenly, under cover of this murmur; and then paused for a moment as if awaiting a reply. Minnie did not speak. Presently he went on. "You know her and understand her better than any of the people here."

"I think every one likes Rhoda," said Minnie at length.

"Yes," Diamond answered eagerly. "Yes; do they not? But it requires the delicate tact of a refined woman to overcome her shyness. I never saw so timid a creature. Has it not struck you as strange that she should have come out from that vulgar home so entirely free from vulgarity?"

"Rhoda has great natural refinement."

"You appreciate her thoroughly. And, then, the repulsive and ludicrous side of Methodism has not touched her at all. It is marvellous to me to see her so perfect in grace and sweetness."

"I do not think that Methodism has ever taken deep hold on Rhoda."

"And yet it is strange that it should be so. She was exposed to the influence of David Powell. And, although he has fine qualities, he is ignorant and fanatical."

"His ignorance and fanaticism are mere spots on the sun!" cried Minnie. And now, as she spoke, her voice was stronger, and she raised her head from the cushion. "In his presence the Scripture phrase, 'A burning and a shining light,' kept recurring to me. How poor and dark one's little selfish self seems beside him!"

Diamond slightly raised his eyebrows as he answered, "Powell has undoubtedly very genuine enthusiasm and fervour. But he might be a dangerous guide to undisciplined minds."

"He would sacrifice himself, he does sacrifice himself, for undisciplined and ungrateful minds, with whom, I own, my egotism could not bear so patiently."

But it was not of Powell that Matthew Diamond wished to speak now. Under the softening influences of the twilight, and the unaccustomed charm of pouring out the fulness of his heart to such a confidante as Minnie, he could talk of nothing but Rhoda.

"Perhaps I am a fool to keep singeing my wings," he said. "It may be all in vain. But don't you believe that a strong and genuine love is almost sure to win a woman's heart, provided the woman's heart is free to be won?"

"Perhaps—provided—"

"And you do not think hers is free?"

"How can I answer you?"

"I know that Powell thought there was some one trifling with her affections. It was on that subject that he begged for the interview with you. I have never asked any questions about that interview, but I have guessed since, from many little signs and tokens, that the person he had in his mind was young Errington."

"Yes."

"Then the matter cannot be serious. He was little more than a boy when he left Whitford."

"But Rhoda was turned nineteen when Algernon went away."

Diamond started eagerly forward, with his hand on the arm of the chair, and fixing his eyes anxiously on her face, said:

"Minnie, tell me the truth! Do you think she cares for him?"

It was the first time he had ever addressed Minnie by her Christian-name; and she marked the fact with a chilly feeling at the heart. "You ask for the truth?" she said, sadly. "Yes; I do think so."

Diamond leant his head on his hand for a minute in silence. Then he raised his face again and answered, "Thank you for answering with sincerity. But I knew you would do no otherwise. This feeling for Algernon must be half made up of childish memories. I cannot believe it is an earnest sentiment that will endure."

"Nothing endures."

"If I know myself at all, my love will endure. I am a resolute man, and do not much regard external obstacles. The only essential point is, can she ever be brought to care for me?"

There was a pause.

"Do you think she might—some day?"

"Is that the only essential point?"

"Yes; to me it is so. I do believe that it would be for her happiness to care for me, rather than for that selfish young fellow."

"And—for your happiness—?"

"Oh, of that I am not doubtful at all!"

"There's the moon above the poplar trees!" cried Miss Chubb. And as she spoke a silver beam stole into the room and lighted one or two faces, leaving the others in shadow. Amongst the faces so illuminated was Minnie Bodkin's. "Did you ever see anything so beautiful as Minnie's countenance in the moonlight?" whispered Miss Chubb to the curate. "She looks like a spirit!"

Poor Mr. Warlock sighed. He had been envying Diamond his long confidential conversation with the doctor's daughter. "She is always beautiful," he replied. "But I think she looks unusually sad to-night."

"That's the moon, my dear sir! Bless you, it always gives a pensive expression to the eyes; always!" And Miss Chubb cast her own eyes upwards towards the sky as she spoke.

"Dear me, you have no lamp here!" said a voice, which, though mellow and musical in quality, was too loud and out of harmony with the twilight mood of the occupants of the drawing-room to be pleasant.

"Is not that silver lamp aloft there sufficient, Mrs. Errington?" asked Diamond.

"Oh, good evening, Mr. Diamond," returned Mrs. Errington, with perhaps an extra tone of condescension, for she thought in her heart that the tutor was a little spoiled in Whitford society. "I can hardly make out who's who. Oh, there's Miss Chubb and Mr. Warlock, and—oh, is that you, Rhoda? Well, Minnie, I left your mamma giving the doctor his tea in the study, and she sent me upstairs. And, if you have no objection, I should like the lamp lit, for I am going to read you a letter from Algy."

CHAPTER III.

"Now isn't that charming?" said Mrs. Errington, finishing a paragraph descriptive of some brilliant evening party at which Algernon had been present, and looking round triumphantly at her audience.

"Very, indeed," said Minnie, who had been specially appealed to.

"Quite a graphic picture of the bow mong," said Miss Chubb. "I know all about that sort of society, so I can answer for the correctness of Algy's description."

Miss Chubb had the discretion to lower her voice as she made the latter remark, so that no one heard it save Mr. Warlock, and thus Mrs. Errington was not challenged to contradiction.

"How well Algernon writes," observed Mr. Diamond. "He has the trick of the thing so neatly, and puts out what he has to say so effectively! I wonder he has never thought of turning his pen to profit."

"My son, sir, has other views," returned Mrs. Errington loftily. "But as to what you are pleased to call 'the trick of the thing,' I can assure you that literary talent is hereditary in our family. I don't know, my dear Minnie, whether you have happened to hear me mention it, but my great uncle by the mother's side was a most distinguished author."

"Really?"

"What did he write?" asked Miss Chubb, with much distinctness. But Mrs. Errington took no heed of the question. "And my own father's letters were considered models of style," she continued. "A large number of them are, I believe, still preserved in the family archives at Ancram Park."

"How did they come there?" asked Miss Chubb. "Unless he wrote letters to himself, they must have been scattered about here and there."

"They were collected after his death, Miss Chubb. You may not be aware, perhaps, that it is not an unfrequent custom to collect the correspondence of eminent men. It was done in the case of Walpole. And—Mr. Diamond will correct me if I am wrong—in that of the celebrated Persian gentleman, whose letters are so well known. Mirza was the name, I think?"

Miss Chubb felt herself on unsafe ground here, and did not venture farther.

"Well, at all events, Algernon appears to be getting on admirably in London," said the Reverend Peter, pacifically.

Minnie threw him an approving glance, for his good-natured words dispelled a little cloud on Miss Chubb's brow, and brought down Mrs. Errington from her high horse to the level of friendly sympathies. "Oh, he is getting on wonderfully, dear fellow!" said she.

"I'm sure we are all glad to hear of Algy's doing well, and being happy. He is such a nice, genial, unaffected creature! And never gave himself any airs!" said Miss Chubb, with a sidelong toss of her head and a little unnecessary emphasis.

"Oh no, my dear. That sort of vulgar pretension is not found among folks who come of a real good ancient stock," replied Mrs. Errington, with superb complacency.

"And we are not to have the pleasure of seeing Algernon back among us this summer?" said Mr. Warlock. In general he shrank from much conversation with Mrs. Errington, whom he found somewhat overwhelming; but he would have nerved himself to greater efforts than talking to that thick-skinned lady for the sake of a kind look from Minnie Bodkin.

"Oh, impossible! Quite out of the question. He is sorry, of course. And I am sorry. But it would be cruel in him to desert poor dear Seely, when he is so anxious to have him with him all the summer!"

"Is there anything the matter with Lord Seely?" asked Minnie.

"N—no, my dear. Nothing but a little overwork. The mental strain of a man in his position is very severe, and he depends so on Algy! And so does dear Lady Seely. I ought almost to feel jealous. They say openly that they look on him quite as a son."

"It's a pity they haven't a daughter, isn't it?" said Miss Chubb.

Mrs. Errington did not catch the force of the hint. She answered placidly, "They have an adopted daughter; a niece of my lord's, who is almost always with them."

"Oh, indeed," said Diamond, quickly. "I had not heard that!"

Mrs. Errington bestowed a stolid, china-blue stare on him before replying, "I daresay not, sir."

The fact was that Mrs. Errington had not known it herself until quite recently; for Algernon, either mistrusting his mother's prudence—or for some other reason—had passed lightly over Castalia's name in his letters, and for some time had not even mentioned that she was an inmate of Lord Seely's house. In his latter letters he had spoken of Miss Kilfinane, but in terms purposely chosen to check, as far as possible, any match-making flights of fancy, which his mother might indulge in with reference to that lady.

"I am not sure, my dear," proceeded Mrs. Errington, turning to Minnie, "whether I have happened to mention it to you, but Castalia—the Honourable Castalia Kilfinane, only daughter of Lord Kauldkail—is staying with the dear Seelys. But as she is rather sickly, and not very young, she cannot, of course, be to them what Algy is."

"Oh! Not very young?" said Miss Chubb, in a tone of disappointment.

"Well, not very young, comparatively speaking, Miss Chubb. She might be considered young compared with you and me, I daresay."

Fortunately, perhaps, for the preservation of peace, much imperilled by this last speech of Mrs. Errington's, Dr. Bodkin and his wife here entered the drawing-room. Although it was May, and the temperature was mild for the season, a good fire blazed in the grate; and on the rug in front of it Dr.

Bodkin, after saluting the assembled company, took up his accustomed station. Diamond rose, and stood leaning on the mantel-shelf near to his chief (an action which Mrs. Errington viewed with disfavour, as indicating on the part of the second master at the Grammar School a too great ease, and absence of due subjection in the presence of his superiors), and the Reverend Peter and Miss Chubb drew their chairs nearer to the fireplace, thus bringing the scattered members of the party into a more sociable circle. The doctor was understood to object to his society being broken up into groups of two or three, and to prefer general conversation; which, indeed, afforded better opportunities for haranguing, and for looking at the company as a class brought up for examination, and, if needful, correction, according to the doctor's habit of mind. Only Rhoda remained at her window, apart from the others, and Dr. Bodkin, seeing her there, called to her to come nearer.

"What, little Primrose!" said the doctor, kindly. "Don't stay there looking at the moon. She is chillier and not so cosy as the coal fire. Draw the curtain, and shut her out, and come nearer to us all."

Rhoda obeyed, blushing deeply as she advanced within the range of the lamp-light, and looking so pretty and timid that the doctor began smilingly to murmur into Diamond's ear something about "Hinnuleo similis, non sine vano burarum et siluæ metu."

The doctor's prejudice against Rhoda had long been overcome, and she had grown to be a pet of his, in so far as so awful a personage as the doctor was capable of petting any one. To this result the conversion to orthodoxy of the Maxfield family may have contributed. But, possibly, Rhoda's regular attendance at St. Chad's might have been inefficacious to win the doctor's favour, good churchman though he was, without some assistance from her blooming complexion, soft hazel eyes, and graceful, winning manners.

The girl came forward bashfully into the circle around the fire, and nestled herself down on a low seat between Mrs. Errington and Mrs. Bodkin. A month ago her place in that drawing-room would have been beside Minnie's chair. But lately, by some subtle instinct, Rhoda had a little shrunk from her former intimacy with the young lady. She was sensitive enough to feel the existence of some unexpressed disapproval of herself in Minnie's mind.

"We have been hearing a letter of Algernon's, papa," said Minnie.

"Have you? have you?"

"Mrs. Errington has been kind enough to read it to us."

The doctor left his post of vantage on the hearth-rug for an instant, went to his daughter, and, bending down, kissed her on the forehead. "Pretty well this evening, my darling?" said he. Minnie caught her father's hand as he was moving away again and pressed it to her lips. "Thank God for you and mother," she whispered. Minnie was not given to demonstrations of tenderness, having been rather accustomed, like most idolised children, to accept her parents' anxious affection as she accepted her daily bread—that is to say, as a matter of course. But there was something in her heart now which made her keenly alive to the preciousness of that abounding and unselfish devotion.

"I think it is quite touching to see that father and daughter together," said Miss Chubb confidentially to her neighbour the curate. "So severe a man as the doctor is in general! Quite the churchman! Combined with the scholastic dignitary, you know. And yet, with Minnie, as gentle as a woman."

As to Mr. Warlock, the tears were in his eyes, and he unaffectedly wiped them away, answering Miss Chubb only by a nod.

"And what," said the doctor, when he had resumed his usual place, and his usual manner, "what is the news from our young friend, Algernon?"

Mrs. Errington began to recapitulate some of the items in her son's last letter—the "lords and ladies gay" whose society he frequented; the brilliant compliments that were paid him by word and deed; and the immense success which his talents and attractions met with everywhere.

"Yes; and Algernon is kindly received by other sorts and conditions of men besides the aristocracy of this realm," said Minnie, with a little ironical smile. "He has shone in evening receptions at Mrs. Machyn-Stubbs's, and sipped lawyer Leadbeater's port-wine with appreciative gusto."

"He has to be civil to people, you know, my dear," said Mrs. Errington, smoothly. "It wouldn't do to neglect—a—a—persons who mean to be attentive, merely because they are not quite in our own set."

"I trust not, indeed, madam!" exclaimed the doctor, with protruding lips and frowning brow. "It would be exceedingly impolitic in Algernon to turn away from proffered kindness. But I will not put the matter on that ground. I should be sorry to think that a youth who has been—I may say—formed and brought up under my tuition, could be capable of ignoble and ungentlemanlike behaviour."

Mrs. Bodkin glanced a little apprehensively at Mrs. Errington after this explosion of the doctor's. But that descendant of all the Ancrams had not the slightest idea of being offended. She was smiling with much complacency, and answered mellifluously to the doctor's thunder, "Thank you, Dr. Bodkin. Now that is so nice in you to appreciate Algy as you do! He is, and ever was, like his ancestors before him, the soul of gentlemanliness."

"Algernon was always most popular, I'm sure," said Miss Chubb. "He was a favourite with everybody. Such lively manners! And at home with all classes!"

"Yes," said Diamond in a low voice. "Superis Deorum gratus, et imis."

"Now what may that mean?" asked Miss Chubb, who had quick ears.

"The words were applied to a mythological personage of very flexible talents, madam," replied Diamond.

"Oh, mythological? Well, I never went very far into mythology. Now, it's a singular circumstance, which has often struck me, and perhaps some of you learned gentlemen may be able to explain it, that none of the studies in 'ology' ever seemed to have much attraction for me; whereas the 'ographies' always interested me very much. There was geography, now. I used to know the names of all the European rivers when I was quite a child. And orthography and biography. We had a translation of Pluto's Lives at the rectory, and I was uncommonly fond of them. But, as to the 'ologies,' I frankly own that I know nothing about them."

The effect of this speech of Miss Chubb's was much heightened by the mute commentary of Dr. Bodkin's face during its utterance. When she came to Pluto's Lives, the scholastic eyes rolled round on Mr. Diamond and the curate with an expression of such helpless indignation, that the former was driven to blow his nose with violence, in order to smother an explosion of laughter. And even Mr. Warlock's sombre brow relaxed, and he ventured to steal a smiling glance at Minnie.

But Minnie did not return the glance. She had shaded her eyes with her hand, and was leaning back in her chair, unheeding the conversation that was going on around her.

"But now, really, you know, there must be some reason for these things, if philosophers could only find it out," pursued Miss Chubb, cheerfully. "Mustn't there, Minnie?"

"Eh? I beg your pardon!"

"Oh you naughty, absent girl! You have not heard a word I've been saying. I was merely remarking that—"

But at this point Dr. Bodkin's patience suddenly snapped. He found himself unable silently to endure a recapitulation of Miss Chubb's views as to the comparative attractions of the "ologies" and the "ographies;" and he abruptly demanded of his wife, in the magisterial tones which had often struck awe into the hearts of the lowest form, "Laura, are we not to have our rubber before midnight? Pray make up the table in the next room. There are—let me see!—Mrs. Errington, Miss Chubb, you will take a hand, Laura? We are just a quartet." And the doctor, giving his arm to Mrs. Errington, marched off to the whist-table.

On this occasion Mr. Warlock escaped being obliged to play. Indeed, the curate's assistance at whist was only called into requisition when a second table besides the doctor's had to be made up; for, although Dr. Bodkin co-operated very comfortably with his curate in all church matters, he found himself not altogether able to do so at the green table, the Reverend Peter's notions of whist being confused and elementary. To be sure, Mrs. Bodkin was not a much better player than the curate; but then she offered the compensating advantage of enduring an unlimited amount of scolding—whether as partner or adversary—without resenting it.

So Diamond, and Warlock, and Minnie, and Rhoda remained in the big drawing-room when their elders had left it. Minnie had the lamp shaded, and the curtains opened, so that the full clear light of the climbing moon poured freely into the room. Warlock timidly drew near to Miss Bodkin's chair, and ventured to say a word or two now and then, to which he received answers so kind and gracious, that the poor fellow's heart swelled with gratitude, and perhaps with hope, for hope is very cunning and stealthy, and hides herself under all sorts of unlikely feelings.

Minnie had grown much more gentle and patient with the awkward, plain, rather dull curate of late. She listened to his talk and replied to it. And all the while she was taking eager cognisance, with eye and ear, of the two who sat side by side near the window, Diamond bending down to speak softly to Rhoda, and the girl's delicate face, white and sprite-like in the moonlight, turning now and then towards her companion with a pretty, languid gesture. Once or twice Rhoda laughed at something Diamond said to her. Her laugh was perhaps a little suggestive of silliness, but it was low, and musical, and rippling; and it was not too frequent.

Minnie sat with her hands clasped in her lap; and when she was carried to her own room that night, Jane exclaimed, as she removed her young mistress's ornaments, "Goodness, Miss Minnie, what have you done to yourself? Why that diamond ring you wear has made a desperate mark in your finger. It looks as if it had been driven right into the flesh, as hard as could be!"

Minnie held up her thin white hand to the light, and looked at it strangely.

"Ah!" said she, "I must have pressed and twisted the ring about, unconsciously. I was thinking of something else."

Time passed, or seemed to pass, with unusual gentleness over Whitford. If some of our acquaintances there had suddenly been called upon to mention the changes that had taken place within two years, they would perhaps have said at first that there had been none. But changes there had been, nevertheless; and by a few dwellers in the little town they had been keenly felt.

The second summer vacation after that happy holiday time which Rhoda had passed with the Erringtons at Llanryddan arrived. A hot July, winged with thunder-clouds, brooded over the meadows by the Whit. The shadow of Pudcombe Woods was pleasant in the sultry afternoons, and the cattle stood for hours knee-deep in dark pools, overhung by drooping boughs. The great school-room at the Grammar School resounded no more with the tread of young feet, or the murmur of young voices. It was empty, and silent, and dusty; and an overgrown spider had thrown his grey tapestry right across the oriel window, so that it was painted, warp and woof, with brave purple and ruby blazonries from the old stained glass.

Dr. Bodkin and his family were away at a seaside place in the South of England. Mr. Diamond had gone on a solitary excursion afoot. Even Pudcombe Hall was deserted; although young Pawkins was expected to return thither, later in the season, for the shooting. Rhoda Maxfield had been sent to her half-brother Seth, at Duckwell Farm, to get strong and sunburned; and as she was allowed to be by herself almost as much as she wished—Mrs. Seth Maxfield being a bustling, active woman, who would not have thought of suspending or modifying her daily avocations for the sake of entertaining any visitor whatever—Rhoda spent her time, not unhappily, in a sort of continuous day-dream, sitting with a book of poetry under a hedge in the hayfield, or wandering with her little nephew, Seth Maxfield the younger, in Pudcombe Woods, which were near her brother's farm. She liked looking back better than looking forward, perhaps; and enacted in her imagination many a scene that had occurred at dear Llanryddan over and over again. But still there were many times when she indulged in hopeful anticipations as to Algy's return. He had come back to London after his foreign travel, and had spent another brilliant season under the patronage of his great relations. And then a rumour had reached Whitford that Lord Seely had at length obtained the promise of a good post for him, and that he might be expected to revisit Whitford in the autumn at latest. Mrs. Errington had been invited to a country house of Lord Seely's, in Westmoreland, to meet her son, and had set out on her visit in high spirits. Rhoda was thus cut off from hearing frequently of Algernon, through his mother, but she looked forward to seeing them together in September. Rhoda missed her friend and patroness; but she missed her less at Duckwell than she would have done in the dull house in the High Street.

On the whole, she was not unhappy during those sultry summer weeks. Modest and humble-minded as she was, she had come to understand that she was considered pretty and pleasing by the ladies and gentlemen whose acquaintance she had made. No caressing words, no flattering epithets, no pet names, had been bestowed upon her by her father's old friends and companions. She was just simply Rhoda Maxfield to them; never "Primrose," or "Pretty one," or "Rhoda dear;" and the Methodists, however blind to her attractive qualities, had displayed considerable vigilance in pointing out her backsliding, and exhorting her to make every effort to become convinced of sin. Certainly the society of ladies and gentlemen was infinitely more agreeable.

Then, too, there had dawned on her some idea that Mr. Diamond felt a warm admiration for her—perhaps something even warmer than admiration. Miss Chubb (who delighted to foster any amatory sentiments which she might observe in the young persons around her, and was fond of saying, with a languishing droop of her plump, rubicund, good-humoured countenance, that she would not for the world see other young hearts blighted by early disappointment, as hers had been) had dropped several hints to that effect sufficiently broad to be understood even by the bashful Rhoda. And, a little to her own surprise, Rhoda had felt something like gratification, in consequence; Mr. Diamond was such a very clever gentleman. Although he wasn't rich, yet everybody thought a great deal of him. Even Dr. Bodkin (decidedly the most awful embodiment of authority whom Rhoda had ever yet known) treated Mr. Diamond with consideration. And Miss Minnie was his intimate friend. Rhoda had not the least idea of ever reciprocating Mr. Diamond's sentiments. But she could not help feeling that the existence of those sentiments increased her own importance in the world. And she had a lurking idea that it might, if known to Algy, increase her importance in his eyes also.

As to Mr. Diamond's part in the matter, Rhoda, to say truth, concerned herself very little with that. Partly from a humble estimate of herself, and partly from that maiden incapacity for conceiving the fire and force of a masculine passion, which often makes girls pass for cruel who are only childish, she never had thought of Mr. Diamond as seriously suffering for her sake. But yet she was less cold and repellent to him than she had once been. It is difficult not to thaw somewhat in the presence of one whose words and looks make a genial atmosphere for that sensitive plant—youthful vanity.

Rhoda's wardrobe, which by this time had become considerable in quantity and tasteful in quality, was a great source of amusement to her. She delighted to trim, and stitch, and alter, and busy her fingers with the manufacture of bright-coloured bows of ribbon and dainty muslin frills. Mrs. Seth looked contemptuous at what she called "Rhoda's finery," and told her she would never do for a farmer's wife if she spent so much time over a parcel of frippery. Seth Maxfield shook his head gravely, and hoped that Rhoda was not given up utterly to worldliness and vanity; but feared that she had learnt no good at St. Chad's church, but had greatly backslided since the days of her attendance at chapel.

For the Seth Maxfields still belonged to the Wesleyan connexion, and disapproved of the change that had taken place among the family at Whitford. Not that Seth was a deeply religious man. But his father's desertion of the Wesleyans appeared to him in the light of a party defection. It was "ratting;" and ratting, as Seth thought, without the excuse of a bribe.

"Look how well father has prospered!" he would say to his wife. "He's as warm a man, is father, as 'ere a one in Whitford. And the Church folks bought their tea and sugar of him all the same when he belonged to the Society. But I don't believe the Society will spend their money with him now as they did. So that's so much clean lost. I'm not so strict as some, myself; nor I don't see the use of it. But I do think a man ought to stick to what he's been brought up to. 'Specially when it's had the manifest blessing of Providence! If the Lord was so well satisfied with father being a Wesleyan, I think father might ha' been satisfied too."

Still there had been no quarrel between the Whitford Maxfields and those of Duckwell. They came together so seldom that opportunities for quarrelling were rare. And Seth had too great a respect for such manifestations of Providential approbation as had been vouchsafed to his father, to be willing to break entirely with the old man. So, when old Max proposed to send Rhoda to the farm for a few weeks, he paying a weekly stipend for her board, his son and his son's wife had at once agreed to the proposition. And as they were not persons who brought their religious theories into the practical service of daily life, Rhoda's conscience was not disturbed by having a high and stern standard of duty held up for her attainment at every moment.

The Wesleyan preacher at that time in the district was a frequent guest at Duckwell Farm. And in the long summer evenings one or two neighbours would occasionally drop in to the cool stone-flagged parlour, where brother Jackson would read a chapter and offer up a prayer. And afterwards there would be smoking of pipes and drinking of home-brewed by the men; while Mrs. Seth and Rhoda would sit on a bench in the apple-orchard, near to the open window of the parlour, and sew, and talk, or listen to the conversation from within, as they pleased.

Rhoda perceived quickly enough that the Duckwell Farm species of Methodism was very different from the Methodism of David Powell. Mr. Jackson never said anything to frighten her. He talked, indeed, of sin, and of the dangers that beset sinners; but he never spoke as if they were real to him—as if he heard and saw all the terrible things he discoursed of so glibly. Then Mr. Jackson was, Rhoda thought, a somewhat greedy eater. He did not smoke, it was true; but he took a good share of Seth's strong ale, and was not above indulging in gossip—perhaps to please himself, perhaps to please Mrs. Seth Maxfield.

Rhoda drew a comparison in her own mind between brother Jackson and the stately rector of St. Chad's, and felt much satisfaction at the contrast between them. How much nicer it was to be a member of a Church of England congregation; where one heard Dr. Bodkin or Mr. Warlock speak a not too long discourse in correct English, and with that refined accent which Rhoda's ear had learned to prize, and where the mellow old organ made a quivering atmosphere of music that seemed to mingle with the light from the painted windows; than to sit on a deal bench in a white-washed chapel, and painfully keep oneself broad awake whilst brother Jackson or brother Hinks bawled out a series of disjointed sentences, beginning with "Oh!" and displaying a plentiful lack of aspirates!

On the whole, perhaps, her stay at Duckwell Farm was a potent agent in confirming Rhoda in orthodox views of religion.

Generally, as she sat beside Mrs. Seth in the parlour, or on the bench outside the window, Rhoda withdrew her attention from the talk of brother Jackson and the others. She could think her own thoughts, and dream her own dreams, whilst she was knitting a stocking or hemming a pinafore for little Seth. But sometimes a name was mentioned at these meetings that she could not hear with indifference. It was the name of David Powell.

The tone in which he was spoken of now was very opposite to the chorus of praise which had accompanied every mention of him among the Whitford Methodists, two years ago. There were rumours that he had defied the authority of Conference, and intended to secede from the Society. He was said to have been preaching strange doctrine in the remote parts of Wales, and to have caused and encouraged extravagant manifestations, such as were known to have prevailed at the preachings of Berridge and Hickes, seventy or eighty years ago; and earlier still, at the first open-air sermons of John Wesley himself, at Bristol. Brother Jackson shook his head, and pursed up his lips at the rumours. He had never much approved of Powell; and Seth Maxfield had distinctly disapproved of him. Seth had been brought up in the old sleepy days, when members of the Society in Whitford were comfortably undisturbed by the voice of an "awakening" preacher. He had resented the fuss that had been made about David Powell. He had been still more annoyed by his father's secession, which he attributed to Powell's over zeal and presumption. And he, by his own example, encouraged a hostile and critical tone in speaking of the preacher.

There was, indeed, but one voice raised in his defence in the parlour at Duckwell Farm. This was the voice of Richard Gibbs, the head groom at Pudcombe Hall, who sometimes came over to Duckwell to join in the prayer-meetings there. Although Richard Gibbs was but a servant, he was a trusted and valued one; and he was received by the farmer and his wife with considerable civility. Richard "knew his place," as Mrs. Seth said, and was not "one of them as if you give 'em an inch they'll take an ell." And then he had a considerable knowledge of farriery, and had more than once given good advice to Farmer Maxfield respecting the treatment of sick horses and cattle. Seth was fond of repeating that he himself was "not so strict as some," finding, indeed, that a reputation for strictness, in a Methodistical sense, put him at a disadvantage with his fellow farmers on market-days. But whenever Richard Gibbs was spoken of, he would add to this general disclaimer of peculiar piety on his own part, "Not, mind you, but what there's some as conversion does a wonderful deal for, to this day, thanks be! Why, there's Dicky Gibbs, head-groom at Pudcombe Hall. Talk of blasphemers—well Dicky was a blasphemer! And now his lips are as pure from evil speaking as my little maid's there. And he's the only man I ever knew as had to do with horses that wouldn't tell you a lie. At first, I believe, there was some at the Hall—I name no names—didn't like Dicky's plain truths. There was a carriage-horse to be sold, and Dicky spoke out and told this and that, and young master couldn't get his price. But in the long run it answers. Oh! I'm not against a fervent conversion, nor yet against conviction of sin—for some."

So Richard Gibbs sat many a summer evening in the flagged parlour at Duckwell Farm, and his melancholy, clean-shaven, lantern-jawed face was a familiar spectacle at prayer-meetings there.

"I have been much grieved and exercised in spirit on behalf of brother Powell,"' said Mr. Jackson, in his thick voice.

The expounding and the prayers were over. Seth had lighted his pipe; so had Roger Heath, the baker, from Pudcombe village. A great cool jug of ale stood on the table, and the setting sun sent his rays into the room, tempered by a screen of jessamine and vine leaves that hung down outside the window.

"Ah! And reason too!" said Seth gruffly. "He's been getting further and further out of the right furrow this many a day."

"They do say," observed sour-faced Roger Heath, "that there's dreadful scenes with them poor Welsh at his field-preachings. Men and women stricken down like bullocks, and screechings and convulsions, like as if they was all possessed with the devil."

"Lauk!" cried Mrs. Seth eagerly. "Why, how is that, then?"

Rhoda, listening outside, behind the screen of vine leaves at the open window, could not repress a shudder at the thought that, had David Powell shown this new power of his a year or two ago, she herself might have been among the convulsed who bore testimony to his terrible influence.

"How is that, Mrs. Maxfield?" returned Richard Gibbs. "Why, how can it be, except by abounding grace!"

"Nay, Mr. Gibbs, but how dreadful it seems, don't it? Just think of falling down in a fit in the open field!"

"Just think of living and dying unawakened to sin! Is not that a hundred thousand times more dreadful?"

"I hope it don't need to roll about like Bedlamites to be awakened to a sense of sin, Mr. Gibbs!" cried Seth Maxfield.

"The Lord forbid!" ejaculated brother Jackson.

"A likely tale!" added Mrs. Seth, cheerfully.

"I'm against all such doings," said Roger Heath, shaking his head.

"But if it be the Lord's doing, sir?" remonstrated Richard Gibbs, speaking slowly, and with an anxious lack-lustre gaze at the white-washed ceiling, as though counsel might be read there. "And I've heard tell that John Wesley did the same at his field-preachings."

Brother Jackson hastily wiped his mouth, after a deep draught of ale, before replying, "That was in the beginning, when such things may have been needful. But now, I fear, they only bring scandal upon us, and strengthen scoffers."

"I tell you what it is," said Seth, taking the pipe from his mouth, and waving it up and down to emphasise his words, "it's my opinion as David Powell's not quite—not quite right in his head."

"'Taint the first time that thought has crossed my mind," said the baker, who had once upon a time been uneasy under the yoke of Powell's stern views as to weights and measures.

"Of course," pursued Seth, argumentatively, "we've got to draw a line. Religion is one thing and rampaging is another. From the first, when Powell began rampaging, I mistrusted what it would come to."

"The human brain is a very delicate and mysterious organ," said brother Jackson.

"Ah!" ejaculated Heath, with an air of profundity, as of one the extent of whose acquaintance with the human brain was not easily to be set forth in words, "you may well say so, sir. There you're right, indeed, brother Jackson."

"Why, there it is!" cried Seth. "And Powell, he overtaxed the human brain. It's like flying in the face of Providence almost, to want to go so much beyond your neighbours. Why, he'd fast till he well-nigh starved himself."

"But he gave all he spared from his own stomach to the poor," put in Gibbs, looking sad and perplexed.

"I call all that rampaging," returned Seth, with a touch of his father's obstinacy.

"Dr. Evans read out an account of these doings in Wales from a newspaper in Mr. Barker the chemist's shop in Whitford last Saturday," said Heath. "I heard it. And Dr. Evans said it was catching, and that such-like excitement was dangerous, for you never know where it might end. And Dr. Evans is of a Welsh family himself," he added, bringing out this clause, as though it strikingly illustrated or elucidated the topic under discussion.

Mrs. Seth drew her little boy close to her, and covered his curly poll with her large maternal hand, as though to protect the little "human brain" within from all danger. "Mercy me!" she said, "I hope Powell won't come into these parts any more! I should be frightened to go to chapel, or to let the children go either."

"Oh, you need not be alarmed, Mrs. Maxfield," said brother Jackson, with a superior smile.

"Nay, but if it is catching, Mr. Jackson!" persisted the anxious mother.

"Tut, lass! It isn't like measles!" said her husband.

The ale being by this time exhausted and the pipes smoked out, brother Jackson rose to depart, and the baker went away with him. Seth Maxfield detained Gibbs for a few minutes to ask his advice about a favourite cart-horse.

"Well, Mr. Gibbs," said the housewife, when, the conference being over, he bade her "Good evening," "and when are your folks coming back to the Hall?"

"Not just yet, ma'am. Young master is gone to Westmoreland, I hear, to a wedding at some nobleman's house there. He'll be back at Pudcombe for the shooting."

"A wedding, eh?" said Mrs. Seth, with eager feminine interest in the topic. "Not his own wedding, I suppose?"

"Oh no, ma'am. 'Tis some friend of his, I believe, that he knew at Whitford; Erringham, I think the name is—a young gentleman that's going to marry the nobleman's niece. The housekeeper at the Hall was telling some of my fellow-servants about it the other day. But I'm ill at remembering the chat I hear. And 'tis unprofitable work too. Good evening, ma'am. Farewell, Seth," stooping down to pat the little one's curly head. "May the Lord bless and keep you!"

Mrs. Seth stood out in the apple-orchard, with two of her children clinging to her skirts, and held up her hand to shade her eyes as she watched the departing figure of Richard Gibbs moving across the meadow, in the rosy evening light. Then she turned to the wooden bench where Rhoda was sitting, huddled together, with her work lying in her lap. "You didn't come in to prayers, Rhoda," said her sister-in-law. "But, however, you can hear it all just as well outside, as in. If it wasn't for civility to Mr. Jackson, I'd liefer stay out here these fine summer evenings, myself. And I was thinking—why, child, what a white face you've got! Like a sheet of white paper, for all the world! And your hands are quite cold, though it's been downright sultry! Mercy me, don't go and get sick on our hands, Rhoda! What will your father say? Come, you'd best get to bed, and I'll make you a hot posset myself."

Rhoda passively followed her sister-in-law to the fresh lavender-scented chamber which she occupied; and she consented to go to bed at once. Her head ached, she said, but she declined the hot posset, and only asked to be left quiet.

"There's always some bother with girls of that delicate sort," said Mrs. Seth to her husband, when she went downstairs again. "Rhoda's mother was just such another; looked as if you might blow her away. I can't think whatever made your father marry her! Not but Rhoda's a nice-tempered girl enough, and very patient with the children. But, do you know, Seth, I'm afraid she's got a chill or something, sitting out in the orchard so late."

"What makes you think so?"

"Well, she had a queer, scared kind of look on her face."

"Nonsense! Catching cold don't make people look scared."

"Something makes her look scared, I tell you. It's either she's sickening for some fever, or else she's seen a ghost!"

CHAPTER V

(From Mrs. Errington to Mrs. Bodkin.)

"Long Fells, Westmoreland, July 26th, 18—.

"DEAR MRS. BODKIN,—Amid the tumult of feelings which have recently agitated me, I yet cannot neglect to write to my good friends in Whitford, and participate my emotions with those who have ever valued and appreciated my darling boy, at this most important moment of his life. It may perhaps surprise, but will, I am sure, gratify you to learn that Algernon is to be married on this day week to the Honourable Castalia Caroline Kilfinane, only daughter of the late Baron Kauldkail, of Kauldkail, who is, though not a relation, yet a connection of our own, being the niece of our dear cousin-in-law, Lord Seely. To say that all my proudest maternal aspirations are gratified by such a match is feebly to express what I feel. Birth (with me the first consideration, dear Mrs. Bodkin, for I make no pretences with you, and confess that I should have deplored Algernon's mating below himself in that respect), elegance, accomplishments, and a devoted attachment to my son—these are Castalia's merits in my eyes. You will forgive me for having said nothing of this projected alliance until the last moment. The young people did not wish it to be talked about. They had a romantic fancy to have the wedding as quiet as possible, amid the rural beauties of this most lovely scenery, and thus escape the necessity for inviting the crowds of distinguished friends and connections on both sides of the house, who would have had to be present had the marriage taken place in London. That would have made it too pompous an affair to satisfy the taste of our Castalia, who is sensitive refinement itself. The dear Seelys are only too indulgent to the least wish of Algernon's, and they at once agreed to keep the secret. What poor Lord and Lady Seely will do when Algy leaves them I assure you I cannot imagine. It really grieves me to contemplate how they will miss him. But, of course, I cannot but rejoice selfishly to know that I shall have my dear children so near me. For (you may, perhaps, have heard the news) Lord Seely has, by his immense influence in the highest quarters, procured dear Algy an appointment. And, as good fortune will have it, the appointment brings him back to Whitford, among his dear and early friends. He is to be appointed to the very arduous and responsible position of postmaster there. But, important as this situation is, it is yet only to be considered a stepping-stone to further advancement. Lord Seely wants Algy in town, which is indeed his proper sphere. And the result of some new ministerial combinations which are expected in certain quarters will, there is no doubt, put him in the very foremost rank of rising young diplomatists. But I must not say more even to you, dear Mrs. Bodkin, for these are State secrets, which should be sacredly respected.

"This is a most lovely spot, and the house combines the simple elegance of a cottage ornée with the luxurious refinement that befits the residence of a peer like Lord Seely. It is not, of course, fitted up with the same magnificence as his town mansion, or even as his ancestral place in Rutlandshire, but it is full of charms to the cultivated spirit, and our dear young people are revelling in its romantic quietude. There are very few guests in the house. By a kind thought of Algy's, which I am sure you will appreciate, Orlando Pawkins is to be best man at the wedding. The young man is naturally gratified by the distinction, and our noble relatives have received him with that affability which marks the truly high bred. There is also an Irish gentleman, the Honourable John Patrick Price, who arrived last evening in order to be present at the ceremony. He is one of the most celebrated wits in town, and belongs to an Irish family of immense antiquity. Castalia will have none of her own intimate young friends for bridesmaids. To make a choice of one or two might have seemed invidious, and to have eight or ten bridesmaids would have made the wedding too ostentatious for her taste. Therefore she will be attended at the altar by the two daughters of the village clergyman—simple, modest girls, who adore her. The bride and bridegroom will leave us after the breakfast to pass their honeymoon at the Lakes. I shall return forthwith to Whitford, in order to make preparations for their reception. Lady Seely presses me to remain with her for a time after the wedding, but I am impatient to return to my dear Whitford friends, and share my happiness with them.

"Farewell, dear Mrs. Bodkin. Give my love to Minnie, who, I hope, has benefited by the sea-breezes; and best regards to the doctor. Believe me your very attached friend,

"SOPHIA AUGUSTA ERRINGTON.

"P.S. Do you happen to know whether Barker, the chemist, has that cottage in the Bristol Road still to let? It might suit my dear children, at least for a while."

(From Miss Kilfinane to her cousin, Lady Louisa Marston.)

"Long Fells, 29th July.

"MY DEAR LOUISA,—I answer your last letter at once, for if I delay writing, I may not have time to do so at all. There are still a thousand things to be thought of, and my maid and I have to do it all, for you know what Aunt Seely is. She won't stir a finger to help anybody. Uncle Seely is very kind, but he has no say in the matter, nor, as far as that goes, in any matter in his own house.

"You ask about the wedding. It will be very scrubby, thanks to my lady's stinginess. She would have it take place in this out-of-the-way country house, which they scarcely ever come to, in order to save the expense of a handsome breakfast. There will be nobody invited but the parson and the apothecary, I suppose. I hate Long Fells. It is the most inconvenient house in the world, I do believe; and so out of repair that my maid declares the rain comes through the roof on to her bed.

"Ancram's mother arrived last week. She was half inclined to be huffy at first, when we told her our news, because she had been kept in the dark till the last moment. But she has got over her sulks now, and makes the best of it. I can see now that Ancram was right in keeping our engagement secret from her as long as possible. She would have been a dreadful worry, and told everybody. She is wonderfully like Lady Seely in the face, only much better looking, and has a fine natural colour that makes my lady's cheeks look as if they had been done by a house painter.

"Ancram has invited an old Whitford acquaintance of his to be his best man at the wedding. He says that as we are going to live there for a time at least, it would never do to offend all the people of the place by taking no notice of them. It would be like going into a hornet's nest. And the young man in question has been civil to Ancram in his school-boy days. He is a certain Mr. Pawkins, who lives at a place with the delightful name of Pudcombe Hall. He is not so bad as I expected, and is quiet and good-natured. If all the Whitfordians turn out as well as he, I shall be agreeably surprised. But I fear they are a strange set of provincial bumpkins. However, we shall not have to remain amongst them long, for Uncle Val. has privately promised to move heaven and earth to get Ancram a better position. You know he is to be postmaster at Whitford. Only think of it! It would be absurd, if it were not such a downright shame. And I more than suspect my lady of having hurried Uncle Val. into accepting it for Ancram. I suppose she thinks anything is good enough for us.

"I wish you could see Ancram! He is very handsome, and even more elegant than handsome. And his manners are admitted on all hands to be charming. It is monstrous to think of burying his talents in a poky little hole like Whitford. But there is this to be said; if he hadn't got this postmastership we could not have been married at all. For he is poor. And you know what my great fortune is! I do think it is too bad that people of our condition should ever be allowed to be so horribly poor. The Government ought to do something for us.

"Uncle Val. has made me a handsome present of money to help to furnish our house. I'm sure this is quite unknown to my lady. So don't say anything about it among your people at home, or it may come round to Lady S.'s ears, and poor Uncle Val. would get scolded. Give my love to Aunt Julia and my cousins. I hope to see you all next season in town, for Ancram and I have quite made up our minds not to stick in that nasty little provincial hole all the year round. Mrs. Errington is to go back there directly after the wedding, to see about a house for us, and get things ready. Of course, if there's anything that I don't like, I can alter it myself when I arrive.

"Good-bye, dear Louisa. Don't forget your affectionate cousin, who signs herself (perhaps for the last time),

"C. C. KILFINANE."

(From Orlando Pawkins to his sister, Mrs. Machyn-Stubbs.)

"Long Fells, Westmoreland. Monday evening.

"My DEAR JEMIMA,—I am sorry that you and Humphrey should have felt hurt and thought I was making mysteries. But I assure you I was quite taken by surprise when I got Errington's letter, telling me about his wedding, and inclosing Lord Seely's invitation to me to come here. I knew nothing about it before, I give you my word.

"You ask me to write you full details of the affair, and I am sure I would if I could. But I don't know any more than the rest of the world. I don't think much of Long Fells. The land is poor, and the house almost tumbling to pieces. Lord Seely is uncommonly polite, but I don't much like my lady. And she has a beast of a lap-dog that snaps at everybody. Errington is the same as ever, only he looks so much older in these two years. Any one would take him to be five or six and twenty, at least. As to the bride, she don't take much notice of me, so I haven't got very well acquainted with her. I ride about the country nearly all day long. Lord Seely has provided me with a pretty decent mount. I shall be glad when the wedding is over, and I can get away, for it's precious dull here. Even your friend Jack Price seems moped and out of sorts, and goes about singing, 'The heart that once truly loves never forgets,' or something like that, enough to give a fellow the blue devils.

"I asked about what you wanted to know about the wedding dresses, but I couldn't make out much from the answers I got. Miss Kilfinane is to wear a white silk gown, trimmed with something or other that has a French name. Perhaps you can guess what it is. The bridesmaids are fat, freckled girls, the daughters of the parson. I think I have now given you all the particulars I can.

"I wish you and Humphrey would come down to Pudcombe in September. Tell him I can give him some fairish shooting, and will do all I can to make you both comfortable. Believe me,

"Your affectionate brother, O. P."

It was the evening before the wedding. In a low long room that was dark with black oak panelling, and gloomy, moreover, by reason of the smallness of the ivy-framed casement at one end, which alone admitted the daylight into it, Lord Seely sat before the hearth.

Although it was August there was a fire. There were few evenings of the year when a fire was not agreeable at Long Fells; and one was certainly agreeable on this especial evening. The day had been rainy. The whole house seemed dark and damp. A few logs that had been laid on the top of the coal fire sputtered and smoked drearily. My lord sat in a large high-backed chair, which nearly hid his diminutive figure from view, except on the side of the fireplace. His head was sunk on his breast; his hands were plunged deep into his pockets; his legs were stretched out towards the hearth; his whole attitude was undignified. It was such, an attitude as few of his friends or acquaintants had ever seen him in, for it was nearly impossible for Lord Seely to be unconscious or careless of the effect he was producing in the presence of an observer.

He was now absorbed in thought, and was allowing his outer man to express the nature of his musings. They were not pleasant musings, as any spectator would at once have pronounced who should have seen his posture, and his pursed mouth, and his eyebrows knitted anxiously under the bald yellow forehead. The entrance even of a footman into the room would have produced an instant change in Lord Seely's demeanour. But no footman was there to see his lordship sunk in a brown study.

At length he raised his head and glanced out of the window. It had ceased to rain, but the drops were still trickling down the window-panes from the points of the ivy leaves; and it was already so dark that the firelight began to throw fantastic shadows from the quaint old furniture, and to shine with a dull red glow on the polished oak panels. Lord Seely rang the bell.

"Has Mr. Errington returned?" he asked of the servant who appeared in answer to the summons.

"Not yet, my lord."

"Tell them to beg Mr. Errington, with my compliments, to do me the favour to step here before he dresses for dinner."

"Yes, my lord."

"Don't light that lamp! or, stay; yes, you may light it. Put the shade over it, and place it behind me. Draw the curtains across the window. Take care that my message is given to Mr. Errington directly he comes home."

The servant withdrew. And Lord Seely, when he was left alone, began to walk up and down the room with his hands behind him. Thus Algernon found him when, in about ten minutes, he appeared, rosy and fresh from his ride.

"I must apologise for my muddy condition," he cried gaily. "Pawkins and I rode over to Applethwaite to get something for Castalia that was found wanting at the last moment. And I am splashed to the eyebrows. But I thought it best to come just as I was, as your lordship's message was pressing."

"Thank you. I am much obliged to you, Ancram. It is not, in truth, that there is any such immediate hurry for what I have to say, that it might not have waited an hour or so; but I thought it likely that we might not have so good an opportunity of speaking alone together."

Lord Seely seated himself once more in the high-backed chair, but in a very different attitude from his former one. He was upright, majestic, with one hand in his breast, and the other reclining on the arm of his chair. But on his face might be read, by one who knew it well, traces of trouble and of being ill at ease. Algernon read my lord's countenance well enough. He stood leaning easily on the mantel-shelf, tapping his splashed boot with his riding-whip, and looking down on Lord Seely with an air of quiet expectation.

"I have been having a serious conversation with Castalia," said my lord, after a preliminary clearing of his throat.

Algernon said, smilingly, "I hope you have not found it necessary to scold her, my lord? The phrase, 'Having a serious conversation' with any one, always suggests to my mind the administering of a reprimand."

"No, Ancram. No; I have not found it necessary to scold Castalia. I am very much attached to her, and very anxious for her happiness. She is the child of my favourite sister."

The old man's voice was not so firm as usual when he said this; and he looked up at Algernon with an appealing look.

Algernon could be pleasant, genial, even affectionate in his manner—but never tender. That was more than he could compass by any movement of imitative sympathy. He had never even been able so to simulate tenderness as to succeed in singing a pathetic song. Perhaps he had learned that it was useless to make the attempt. At all events, he did not now attempt to exhibit any answering tenderness to Lord Seely's look and tone of unwonted feeling, in speaking of his dead sister's child. His reply was hard, clear, and cheerful, as the chirp of a canary bird.

"I know you have always been extremely good to Castalia, my lord. We are both of us very sensible of your kindness, and very much obliged by it."

"No, no," said my lord, waving his hand. "No, no, no. Castalia owes me nothing. She has been to me almost as my own daughter. There can be no talk of obligations between her and me."

Then he paused, for what appeared to be a long time. In the silence of the room the damp logs hissed like whispering voices.

"Ancram," Lord Seely said at length, "Castalia is very much attached to you."

"I assure you, my lord, I am very grateful to her."

"Ahem! Castalia's is not an expansive nature. She was, perhaps, too much repressed and chilled in childhood, by living with uncongenial persons. But she is responsive to kindness, and it develops her best qualities. I will frankly own, that I am very anxious about her future. You will not owe me a grudge for saying that much, Ancram?"

"I never owe grudges, my lord. But I trust you have no doubt of my behaving with kindness to Castalia?"

"No, Ancram. No; I hope not. I believe not."

"I am glad of that; because—the doubt would come rather too late to be of much use, would it not?"

Algernon spoke with his old bright smile; but two things were observable throughout this interview. Firstly, that Algernon, though still perfectly respectful, no longer addressed his senior with the winning, cordial deference of manner which had so captivated Lord Seely in the beginning of their acquaintance. Secondly, that Lord Seely appeared conscious of some reason in the young man's mind for dissatisfaction, and to be desirous of deprecating that dissatisfaction.

At the same time, there seemed to be in Lord Seely an undercurrent of feeling struggling for expression. He had the air of a man who, knowing himself to have right and reason on his side in the main, yet is aware of a tender point in his case which an unscrupulous adversary will not hesitate to touch, and which he nervously shrinks from having touched. He winced at Algernon's last words, and answered rather hotly, "It would be too late. Your insinuation is a just one. If I had any misgivings I ought to have expressed them, and acted on them before. But the fact is that this—the final arrangement of this marriage—took me in a great measure by surprise."

"So it did me, my lord!"

Lord Seely had been gazing moodily at the fire. He now suddenly raised his eyes and looked searchingly at Algernon. The young man's face wore an expression of candid amusement. His arched eyebrows were lifted, and he was smiling as unconcernedly as if the subject in hand touched himself no jot.

"I give you my word," he continued lightly, "that when Lady Seely first spoke to me about it, I was—oh, 'astonished' is no word to express what I felt!"

A dark red flush came into Lord Seely's withered cheeks, and mounted to his forehead. He dropped his eyes, and moved uneasily on his chair, passing one hand through the tuft of grey hair that stood up above his ear. Algernon went on, with an almost boyish frankness of manner:

"Of course, you know, I should hardly have ventured to aspire to such an idea quite unassisted. And I believe I said something or other to my lady—very stumblingly, I have no doubt, for I remember feeling very much bewildered. I said some word about my being a poor devil with nothing in the world to offer to a lady in Miss Kilfinane's position—except, of course, my undying devotion. Only one cannot live altogether on that. But Lady Seely was very sanguine, and saw no difficulties. She said it could be managed. And she was right, you see. Where there's a will, there's a way. And I am really to be married to Castalia to-morrow. It seems too good to be true!"

Lord Seely rose and faced the young man; and as he did so, his lordship looked really dignified; for the sincere feeling within him had for once obliterated his habitual uneasy self-consciousness.

"Ancram," he said, "I am afraid, from what Castalia tells me, that you are greatly dissatisfied with the position I have been able to procure for you."

"Oh, my lord, Castalia ought not to have said so! If she can content herself in it for a time, how can I venture to complain?"

"I am sorry to find," continued Lord Seely, "that your circumstances are more seriously embarrassed than I thought."

"Are they, my lord? I profess I don't know how to disembarrass them!"

"You are in debt—"

"I had the honour of avowing as much to your lordship when my marriage was first discussed; as you, doubtless, remember?"

"Yes; and you named a sum which I—"

"Which your lordship was kind enough to pay. Certainly."

"But it now appears that that sum did not cover the whole of your liabilities, Ancram. Castalia tells me that you have been annoyed by applications for money quite recently."

Algernon smiled, and put his head on one side, as if trying to recall a half-forgotten fact. "Well," said he at length, "upon my word I have forgotten the exact sum which I did name to your lordship, but I have no doubt it was correct at the time. The worst of it is, that my debts have this unfortunate peculiarity—they won't stay paid!"

"It is a great pity, Ancram, for a young man to get into the habit of thinking lightly of debt. It is, in fact," continued his lordship, growing graver and graver as he spoke, "a fatal habit of mind."

"My dear lord, I don't think lightly of it by any means! But, really—is it not best to accept the inevitable with some cheerfulness?"

"'The inevitable,' Ancram?"

"Yes, my lord; in my position, debt was inevitable. I could not be a member of your family circle, a frequent inmate of your house, doing the things you did, going where you went, without incurring some expense."

It was no want of tact which made Algernon speak thus plainly and coarsely. He did not fail (as his mother might have done) to perceive that his words pained and mortified his hearer. He would by no means have aimed such a shaft at Lady Seely, knowing that nature had protected her feelings with a hide of some toughness; and knowing, moreover, that my lady would unhesitatingly have flung back some verbal missile, at least equally rough and heavy. But my lord was at once more vulnerable and more scrupulous. And although Algernon was the last person in the world to be guilty of gratuitous cruelty, yet, if one is to fight, one had best use the most effective weapons, and take advantage of any chink in the enemy's armour to drive one's javelin home!

"I regret," said Lord Seely, with a little catching of the breath, like a man who has received a cold douche, "I deplore that your intimacy with my family should have led you into a false position."

"Not at all, my lord! My position in your family has been a very pleasant one."

"I ought, perhaps—it was my duty—to have inquired more particularly into your means, and to have ascertained whether they sufficed for the life you were leading in London. You were very young, and without experience. I—I reproach myself, Ancram."

"Don't do that, my lord! There is really no need. I'm sure nobody is the worse for the few pounds I owe at this moment: not even my tailor, who has cheated me handsomely, doing me the honour to treat me as one of your lordship's own class!"

Lord Seely bent down his grey head and meditated with a pained and anxious face. Then he looked up, and said:

"You know, Ancram, that I am not a rich man for one in my station."

Algernon bowed gracefully.

"Had I been so, I should have made a settlement upon Castalia; but, although I have no daughters of my own to provide for," (with a little sigh) "yet my property is very strictly tied up. There are claims on it, too, of various sorts—" ("Lady Seely screws all she can out of him for that nephew of hers," was Algy's mental comment.) "And, in brief, I am not in a position to command any large sums of ready money. I believe I said as much to you before?"

Algernon bowed again and smiled.

"Well, I repeat it now, in order to impress on you the fact, that neither you nor Castalia must look to me for pecuniary help in the future."

"Oh, my lord—"

"I do not say that Castalia might not have a right to ask such help of me; but I merely assure you that it will be out of my power to grant it. You, perhaps, scarcely realise how poor a man may be who has a fairly large rent-roll?"

"I think I have begun to realise it, my lord."

Lord Seely looked quickly into the young man's face, but it was smiling and inscrutable.

"Well," he resumed, "I will only add, that for this once, and presuming your present debts are not heavy—"

"Oh dear no! A trifle."

"I will discharge them if you will let me have the amount accurately. I have a great repugnance to the thought of Castalia—and you—beginning your married life in debt."

"A thousand thanks. It will be better for us to start fair."

"I hope, Ancram, that you will use every endeavour to live clearly within your means, and to make the best of your circumstances. The fact is, this marriage has been hurried on—"

Algernon did not answer in words; but he gave an expressive shrug and smile, which said, as plainly as possible, "I have not hurried it on!"

Lord Seely coloured deeply, and seemed to shrink bodily, as if he had received a blow. He went on hastily, and with less than his usual self-possession: "I—I have felt, rather than perceived, a—a little touch of bitterness in your manner lately. There, there, we will not quibble about the word! If not bitter, you have not been, at all events, in the frame of mind I wished and hoped to find you in. You are young; and youth is apt to be a little unreasonable in its expectations. I own—I admit—that your worldly position will not be—a—exactly brilliant. But I assure you that in these days there are many gentlemen of good abilities, and industry, who would be glad of it."

"Oh, I am fully aware of my good fortune, my lord! Besides, you know, this is only a stepping-stone."

"Yes; we—we hope so. But, Ancram—and this is what I had in my mind to say to you frankly—don't neglect or despise the present employment, in looking forward to something better."

"By no means!"

"For your own sake—your own sake, I earnestly advise you not to give way to a feeling of discontent."

"Do I look discontented? Upon my word, your lordship is doing me singular injustice!"

"There is a smiling discontent, as well as a frowning discontent: and I don't know but that it is the worst of the two."

Algernon laughed outright.

"Well," said he, "you must own that it is a little difficult to give satisfaction!"

His light smooth tone jarred disagreeably on Lord Seely. If the latter had thought to make any impression on the young man, to draw from him any outburst of feeling, he had signally failed. Algernon's words could not be objected to, but the tone in which they were uttered was completely nonchalant. His nonchalance increased in proportion to Lord Seely's earnestness. A year ago Algernon would have brought his manner into harmony with my lord's mood. He would have been grave, attentive, eager to show his appreciation of my lord's kindness, and his value for my lord's advice. But now there was some malice in his smiling good-humour; a little cruelty in the brightness of his unruffled serenity. He was genuinely tickled at seeing the pompous little nobleman embarrassed in speaking to him, Algernon Errington, and he enjoyed what comedy there might be in the situation none the less because his patron suffered.

In truth, Algernon was discontented. His was not a gnawing, black sort of discontent. He neither grew lean, nor yellow, nor morose; but his irony was sometimes flavoured with acidity; and instead of being easily tolerant of such follies as zeal, enthusiasm, or fervent reverence, he was now apt to speak of them with a disdainful superiority. And he had, too, an air of having washed his hands of any concern with his own career; of laying the responsibility on Destiny, or whomsoever it might concern; of awaiting, with sarcastic patience, the next turn of the wheel—as if life were neither a battle nor a march, but a gigantic game of rouge-et-noir, with terrible odds in favour of the bank.

Lord Seely was no match for this youth of two-and-twenty. Lord Seely had intended to impress him deeply; to read him a lecture, in which Olympian severity should be tempered by mercy; to convince him, by dignified and condescending methods, of his great good fortune in having secured the hand of Castalia Kilfinane of Kauldkail; and of his great unreasonableness (not to say presumption) in not accepting that boon on bended knee, instead of grumbling at being made postmaster of Whitford. But in order to make an impression, it does not suffice to have tools only; the surface to be impressed must also exist, and be adapted to the operation. How impress the bright, cool, shining liquid bosom of a lake, for instance? Oar and keel, pebble and arrow, wind and current, are alike powerless to make a furrow that shall last.

Lord Seely laboured under the disadvantage, in this crisis, of feeling for other persons with some keenness; a circumstance which frittered away his power considerably, and made him vacillating. Algernon's capacities for feeling were, on this occasion, steadily concentrated on himself, and this gave his behaviour a solid consistency, which was felt even beneath the surface-lightness of his manner.

"I hope," said Lord Seely, rather sadly than solemnly—"I do most earnestly hope, Ancram, that you will be happy in this marriage!"

"Your lordship is very good. I assure you, I feel your goodness."

He said it as if he had been accepting an invitation to dinner.

"And—and that you will do your best to make Castalia happy?"

"You may rely on my doing my best."

"There are discrepancies, perhaps—disparities—but but those marriages are not always the happiest in which the external circumstances on both sides seem to be best matched. You are young. You are untrammelled. You have no irrevocable past behind you to regret. I do not see—no, I do not see why, with mutual regard and respect, you should not make a good life of it."

"These are the most lugubrious nuptial felicitations that ever were offered to a bridegroom, I should fancy!" thought Algernon. And he had some difficulty in keeping his countenance, so vividly did he feel the ludicrous aspect of his lordship's well-meant effort at "impressing" him.

"I should feel some sense of responsibility if—if things were not to turn out as brightly as we hope—and believe—and believe they will turn out."

"Oh, don't distress yourself about that, my lord!" cried Algernon. (He had very nearly said "don't apologise!") "There is the dressing-bell," he added, with alacrity, taking his hat up from the table. "If your lordship has no further commands, I think I—"

"Yes; go, Ancram. I will not detain you longer. Remember," said Lord Seely, taking the young man's hand between both his own, and speaking in a tremulous voice, "remember, Ancram, that I wish to serve you. My intention all along has been to do my best for you. You have been a very pleasant inmate in my home. Ancram, be good to Castalia. For good or for evil, you are her fate now. No one can come between you. Be good to her."

"My dear lord, I beg you to believe that I will make Castalia's happiness the study of my life. And—oh, I have no doubt we shall get on capitally. With your interest, it can't be long before we get into a better berth. I know you'll do your best for us, for Castalia's sake; oh, and mine, too, I am happy to believe. Yes, certainly. I really am in such a state of mud that I believe my very hair is splashed. It will take me all the time there remains for dressing to get myself presentably clean, positively. Au revoir, my lord. And thank you very, very much."

With his jauntiest step, and brightest smile, Algernon left the room.

Lord Seely returned to his chair before the hearth, resumed his moody, musing attitude, and sat there, alone, with his head sunk on his breast until they called him to dinner.

In the first week of August Mrs. Errington returned to Whitford. She had got over her annoyance at not having been intrusted sooner with the news of Algernon's engagement to Miss Kilfinane. By dint of telling her friends so, she had at last persuaded herself that she had been in the secret all along; and, if she felt any other mortifications and disappointments connected with her son's marriage, she kept them to herself. But it is probable that she did not keenly feel any such. She was not sensitive; and she did believe that, by connecting himself so nearly with Lord Seely's family, Algernon was advancing his prospects of success in the world. These sources of comfort, combined with an excellent digestion, and the perennial gratification of contemplating her own claims to distinction as contrasted with those of her neighbours, kept the worthy lady in good spirits, and she returned to Whitford in a kind of full blow of cheerfulness and importance.

Her reception there, at the outset, was, however, far from being what she had looked forward to. She had written to Rhoda announcing the day and hour of her arrival, and requesting that James Maxfield should meet her at the "Blue Bell" inn, where the coach stopped, with a fly for the conveyance of herself and her luggage to her old quarters. Mrs. Errington had not previously written to Rhoda from Westmoreland, but she had forwarded to her at different times two copies of the Applethwaite Advertiser. In one of these journals a preliminary announcement of Algernon's marriage had appeared under the heading of "Alliance in High Life." In the second there was an account of the wedding, and the breakfast, and the rejoicings in the village of Long Fells, which did much credit to the imaginative powers of the writer. According to the Applethwaite Advertiser, the ceremony had been imposing, the breakfast sumptuous, and the village demonstrations enthusiastic.

Mrs. Errington had bought twenty copies of the newspaper for distribution among her friends; and she pleased herself with thinking how grateful the Maxfields would be to her for sending them the papers with the interesting paragraphs marked in red ink. She also looked forward with much complacency to having Rhoda for a listener to all her narrations about the wedding and life at Long Fells, and the great people whom she had met there. Rhoda was such a capital listener! And then, besides and beyond all that, Mrs. Errington was fond of Rhoda, and had more motherly warmth of feeling for her than she had as yet attained to for her new daughter-in-law.

Mrs. Errington's head was stretched out of the coach-window as the vehicle clattered up the archway of the "Blue Bell" inn. It was about seven o'clock on a fine August evening, and there was ample light enough for the traveller to distinguish all the familiar features of the streets through which she passed. "James will be standing in the inn-yard ready to receive me," she thought; "and I suppose the fly will be waiting at the corner by the booking-office. I wonder whether the driver will be the lame old man or young Simmons?" She was still debating this question when the coach turned sharply round under the archway, and stopped in the great rambling yard of the old-fashioned "Blue Bell" inn.

Mrs. Errington got down unassisted; James Maxfield was not there. She looked round in bewilderment, standing hot, dusty, and tired in the yard, where, after a bustling waiter had tripped up to her to ask if she wanted a room, and tripped away again, no one took any heed of her.

A fly was not to be had in Whitford at a moment's notice. After waiting for some ten minutes, Mrs. Errington found there was nothing for it but to walk to her lodgings. She left her luggage in the coach-office to be called for, and set out carrying a rather heavy hand-bag, and hurrying through the streets at a pace much quicker than her usual dignified rate of moving. She wished not to be seen and recognised by any passing acquaintance under circumstances so unfavourable to an impressive or triumphant demeanour.

Arrived at Jonathan Maxfield's house, the aspect of things was not much improved. Betty Grimshaw opened the door, and stared in surprise on seeing Mrs. Errington. She had not been expected. Mr. Maxfield was over at Duckwell at his son's farm. James was busy in the store-house. And as for Rhoda, she was away on a visit to Miss Bodkin at the seaside, and had been for some weeks. A letter? Oh, if a letter had come for Rhoda, her father would have sent it on to her. It was a two days' post from where she was to Whitford. And the newspapers? Betty did not know. She had not seen them. Her brother-in-law had had them, she supposed. Yes; she had heard that Mr. Algernon was married, or going to be married. The servants from Pudcombe Hall had spoken of it when they came into the shop. Jonathan had not said anything on the subject as far as she knew. Mrs. Errington knew what Jonathan was. He never was given to much conversation. And it was Betty's opinion, delivered very frankly, that Jonathan grew crustier and closer as he got older. But wouldn't Mrs. Errington like a cup of tea? Betty would have the kettle boiling in a few minutes.

Mrs. Errington felt rather forlorn, as she entered her old sitting-room and looked around her. It was trim and neat, indeed, and spotlessly clean; but it had the chill, repellent look of an uninhabited apartment. The corner cupboard was locked, and its treasure of old china hidden from view. Algernon's books were gone from the shelf above the piano. A white cloth was spread over the sofa, and the hearth-rug was turned upside down, displaying a grey lining, instead of the gay-coloured scraps of cloth.

She missed Rhoda. She had become accustomed to Algernon's absence from the familiar room; but Rhoda's absence made a blank in it, that was depressing. And perhaps Mrs. Errington herself was surprised to find how dreary the place looked, without the girl's gentle face and modest figure. She gladly accepted Betty Grimshaw's invitation to take her tea downstairs in the comfortable, bright kitchen, instead of alone in the melancholy gentility of her own sitting-room. Betty was as wooden-faced, and grim, and rigid in her aspect as ever. But she was not unfriendly towards her old lodger. And, moreover, she was entirely respectful in her manner, holding it as a fixed article of her faith that "gentlefolks born" were intended by Providence to be treated with deference, and desiring to show that she herself had been trained to becoming behaviour under the roof of a person of quality.

It was little more than nine o'clock when Mrs. Errington rose to go to bed, being tired with her journey. As she did so, she said, "Mrs. Grimshaw, will you get James to send a hand-cart for my luggage in good time to-morrow?"

"Oh, your luggage?" returned Betty. "Well, do you think it is worth while to send for it, if you're not going to stay?"

Mrs. Errington was so much astonished by this speech, that she sat down again on the chair she had just quitted. Then, after a minute's pause, her mind, which did not move very rapidly, arrived at what she supposed to be the explanation of Betty's words. "Oh, I see," she said; "you took it for granted that, on my son's marriage, I should leave you and join him. But it is not so, my good soul. My daughter-in-law has implored me to live with them, but I have refused. It is better for the young people to be by themselves; and I prefer my own independence also. No, my good Mrs. Grimshaw, I shall remain in my old quarters until Mr. Algernon leaves Whitford for good. And perhaps, even then, I may not give you up altogether, who knows?"

Betty hesitated for an instant before replying. "Then Jonathan has not said anything to you about giving up the rooms?"

"Good gracious, no! I have not heard from Mr. Maxfield at all!"

"I suppose he didn't expect you back quite so soon. And—there, I'm sure I won't take upon myself to speak for him. I shouldn't have got on with my brother-in-law all these years if I hadn't made it a rule to try for peace and quietness, and never interfere."

But Mrs. Errington persisting in her demand that Betty should explain herself more fully, the latter at length confessed that, during the past two or three weeks, Jonathan Maxfield had declared his intention of getting rid of his lodger, and of not letting the first floor of his house again. "Your sitting-room is to be kept as a kind of a drawing-room for Rhoda, as I understand Jonathan," said she.

A drawing-room for Rhoda! Mrs. Errington could not believe her senses. "Why, what is Mr. Maxfield thinking of?" she exclaimed.

"Oh, you don't know what a fuss Jonathan has been making lately about Rhoda! Before you went away, you know, ma'am, as he had begun to spend a deal of money on her clothes. And since then, more and more; it's been all his talk as Rhoda was to be a lady. The notion has got stuck fast in his head, and wild horses wouldn't drag it out."

Mrs. Errington rose very majestically. "I much fear," she said, "I much fear that I am responsible for this delusion of your brother-in-law. I have a little spoiled the girl, and taken too much notice of her. I regret it now. But, really, Rhoda is such a sweet creature that I don't know that I have been so very much to blame, either. It is true I have introduced her to my friends, and brought her forward a little beyond her station; but I little thought a man of Mr. Maxfield's common sense would have been so utterly led away by kindly-meant patronage."

"Well, I don't know as it's so much that, ma'am," returned Betty, in a matter-of-fact tone, "as it is that Jonathan has latterly been thinking a deal about his money. And he knows money will do great things—"

"Money can never confer gentle birth, my good creature!"

"No, for sure, ma'am. That's what I say myself. I know my catechism, and I was brought up to respect my superiors. But, you see, Jonathan's heart is greatly set on his riches. He's a well-off man, is my brother-in-law; more so than many folks think. He's been a close man all his life. And, for that matter, he's close enough now in some things, and screws me down in the housekeeping pretty tight. But for Rhoda he seems to grudge nothing, and wants her to make a show and a splash almost—if you can fancy such a thing of Jonathan! But there's no saying how men will turn out; not even the old ones. I'm sure I often and often thank my stars I've kept single—no offence to you, ma'am."

Mrs. Errington went to bed in a bewildered frame of mind. Tired as she was, the news she had heard kept her awake for some time. Leave her lodgings! Leave old Max's house, which had been her home for so many years! It was incredible. And, indeed, before long she had made up her mind to resist old Max's intention of turning her out. "I shall give him a good talking to, to-morrow," she said to herself. "Stupid old man! He really must not be allowed to make himself so absurd." And then Mrs. Errington fell asleep.

But the next day old Max did not return to be talked to; nor the day after that. James Maxfield went over to Duckwell, and came back bringing a formal notice to Mrs. Errington to quit the lodgings, signed by his father.

"What does this mean, James?" asked Mrs. Errington, with much emphasis, and wide-open eyes. James did not know what it meant. He did not apparently much care, either. He had never been on very friendly terms with the Erringtons (having, indeed, come but seldom in contact with them during all the time they had lived under the same roof with him), and had, perhaps, been a little jealous in his sullen, silent way, of their petting of Rhoda. At all events, on the present occasion, he was not communicative nor very civil. He had performed his father's behests, and he knew nothing more. His father was not coming back home just yet. And James volunteered the opinion that he didn't mean to come back until Mrs. Errington should be gone.

All this was strange and disagreeable. But Mrs. Errington was not of an irritable or anxious temperament. And her self-complacency was of too solid a kind to be much affected even by ruder rubs than any which could be given by James Maxfield's uncouth bluntness. "I shall take no notice whatever of this," she said, with serene dignity. "When your father comes back, I shall talk to him. Meanwhile, I have a great many important things to do."

The good lady did in truth begin at once to busy herself in seeking a house for Algernon, and getting it furnished. There was but a month to make all arrangements in, and all Mrs. Errington's friends who could by any possibility be pressed into the service were required to assist her. The Docketts; Rose and Violet McDougall; Mrs. Smith, the surgeon's wife; and even Miss Chubb, were sent hither and thither, asked to write notes, to make inquiries, to have interviews with landlords, and to take as much trouble, and make as much fuss as possible, in the task of getting ready an abode for Mr. and the Honourable Mrs. Algernon Errington.

A house was found without much difficulty. It was a small isolated cottage on the outskirts of the town, with a garden behind it which ran down to the meadows bordering the Whit; and was the very house, belonging to Barker the chemist, of which Mrs. Errington had written to her friend Mrs. Bodkin.

It was really a very humble dwelling. But the rent of it was quite as large as Algernon would be able to afford. Mrs. Errington said, "I prefer a small place for them. If they took a more pretentious house, they would be expected to entertain. And you know, my dear sir," (or "madam," as the case might be) "that there is a great mixture in Whitford society; and that would not suit my daughter-in-law, of course. You perceive that, don't you?" And then the person so addressed might flatter him or herself with the idea of belonging to the unmixed portion of society.

Indeed, this terrible accusation of being "mixed" was one which Mrs. Errington was rather fond of bringing against the social gatherings in Whitford. And she had once been greatly offended, and a good deal puzzled, by Mr. Diamond's asking her what objection there could be to that; and challenging her to point out any good thing on earth, from a bowl of punch upwards, which was not "mixed!" But however this might be, no one believed at all that the mixture in Whitford society was the real reason for young Errington's inhabiting so small a house. They knew perfectly well that if Algernon's means had been larger, his house would have been larger also.

And yet, Mrs. Errington's flourish was not without its effect on some persons. They in their turn repeated her lamentations on the "mixture" to such of their acquaintances as did not happen to be also her acquaintances. And as there were very few individuals in Whitford either so eccentric, or so courageous, as Mr. Diamond, this mysterious mixture was generally acknowledged, with shrugs and head-shakings, to be a very great evil indeed.

At the end of about a fortnight, old Max one day reappeared in his own house, and marched upstairs to Mrs. Errington's sitting-room.

"Well, ma'am," said he, without any preliminary greeting whatsoever, "I suppose you understood the written notice to quit, that I sent you? But as my son James informs me that you don't seem to be taking any steps in consequence of it, I've come to say that you will have to remove out of my abode on the twenty-seventh of this month, and not a day later. So you can act according to your judgment in finding another place to dwell in."

Mrs. Errington was inspecting the contents of a packing-case which had been sent from London by Lady Seely. It contained, as her ladyship said, "some odds and ends that would be useful to the young couple." The only article of any value in the whole collection was a porcelain vase, which had long stood in obscurity on a side-table in Lord Seely's study, and would not be missed thence. Lady Seely, at all events, would not miss it, as she seldom entered the room; and therefore she had generously added it to the odds and ends!

Mrs. Errington looked up, a little flushed with the exertion of stooping over the packing-case, and confronted Mr. Maxfield. Her round, red full-moon face contrasted in a lively manner with the old man's grey, lank, harsh visage. The years, as they passed, did not improve old Max's appearance. And as soon as she beheld him, Mrs. Errington was convinced of the justice of Betty Grimshaw's remark, that her brother-in-law seemed to have grown closer and crustier than ever of late.

"Why, Mr. Maxfield," said the lady, condescendingly, "how do you do? I have been wanting to see you. Come, sit down, and let us talk matters over."

Old Max stood in the doorway glaring at her. "I don't know, ma'am, as there's any matters I want to talk over with you," he returned. "You had better understand that I mean what I say. You'll find it more convenient to believe me at once, and to act accordin'."

"Do you mean to say that you intend to turn me out, Mr. Maxfield?"

"I have given you a legal notice to quit, ma'am. You needn't call it turning you out, unless you like."

He had begun to move away, when Mrs. Errington exclaimed, "But I really don't comprehend this at all! What will Rhoda think of it?"

Maxfield stopped, hesitatingly, with his hand on the banisters at the top of the landing. "Rhoda?" said he gruffly. "Oh, Rhoda has nothing to say to it, one way or t'other."

"But I want to have something to say to her! I assure you it was a great disappointment to me not to find Rhoda here on my return. I'm very fond of her; and shall continue to be so, as long as she merits it. It is not her fault, poor girl, if—other people forget themselves."

Maxfield took his hand off the banisters and turned round. "Since you're so fond of Rhoda," he said, with a queer expression on his sour old face, "you'll be glad to know where she is, and the company she's in."

"I know that she is at the seaside with my friends, Mrs. and Miss Bodkin."

"She is at the seaside with her friends, Mrs. and Miss Bodkin. Miss Minnie is a real lady, and she understands how to treat Rhoda, and knows that the Lord has made a lady of Rhoda by natur'."

Mrs. Errington stared in utter astonishment. The suspicion began to form and strengthen itself in her mind that the old man was positively out of his senses. If so, his insanity had taken an extremely unpleasant turn for her.

"I really was not prepared for being turned out of my lodgings after all these years," she said, reverting to the point that most nearly touched herself.

"I've not been prepared for a many things as have happened after all these years. But I'm ready to meet 'em when they come."

"Well, but now, Mr. Maxfield, let us see if we cannot make an arrangement. If you have any different views about the rent, I—"

"The rent! What do you think your bit of a rent matters to me? I want the rooms for the use of my daughter, Miss Maxfield, and there's an end of it."

"Oh, he certainly cannot be in his right senses to address me in this manner!" thought Mrs. Errington.

Maxfield went on, "I see you've got a box of rubbish there, littering about the place. I give you warning not to unpack any more here, for out everything 'll have to go on the twenty-seventh of this month, as sure as my name's Jonathan Maxfield!"

"Mr. Maxfield! You are certainly forgetting yourself. Rubbish, indeed! These are a few—a very few—of the valuable wedding presents sent to my son and daughter by Lady Seely."

Old Max made a grating sound which was intended for a laugh, although his bushy grey eyebrows were drawn together in a heavy frown the while. Then he suddenly burst out in a kind of cold fury. "Pooh!" he cried. "Presents! Valuable presents! You don't deceive anybody by that! Look here—if the old carpet or any of the furniture in this room would be of any assistance to you, you can take it! I'll give it to you—a free gift! The place is going to be done up and new furnished for Miss Maxfield. Furnished handsome, fit for a young lady of property. Fit for a young lady that will have a sum o' money on the day she marries—if I'm pleased with her choice—as 'll make some folks' mouths water. It won't be reckoned by twenties, nor yet by hundreds, won't Miss Maxfield's fortin'! You can take the old carpet, and mahogany table, and the high-backed chairs, and put 'em among your valuable presents. They're too old-fashioned for Miss Maxfield's drawing-room!" And with a repetition of the grating laugh, old Max tramped heavily downstairs, and was heard to bang the door of his own parlour.

Mrs. Errington sat motionless for nearly a quarter of an hour, staring at the open door. "Mad!" she exclaimed at length, drawing a long breath. "Quite mad! But I wonder if there is any truth in what he says about Rhoda's money? Dear me, why she'll be quite a catch!"

CHAPTER VIII.

Meanwhile Rhoda, at Duckwell Farm, supposed herself to be too unhappy to care much for anything. She did not have a fever, nor fall into a consumption, nor waste away visibly; but she passed hours crying alone in her own room, or sitting idle-handed, whilst her thoughts languidly retraced the past, or strove to picture what sort of a lady Algernon's wife might be. Headaches, pallid cheeks, and red eyes resulted from these solitary hours. Mrs. Seth Maxfield wondered what had come to the girl, having no suspicion that young Errington's marriage could be more to Rhoda than an interesting subject for gossip.

Old Jonathan went over to Duckwell immediately after receiving the first newspaper, sent by Mrs. Errington from Westmoreland.

The announcement of the intended wedding had taken him wholly by surprise. It would be hard to say whether wrath or amazement predominated in his mind, on first reading the paragraph which Mrs. Errington had so complacently marked with red ink. But it is not at all hard to say which feeling predominated within an hour after having read it.

According to old Max's judgment, there was not one extenuating circumstance in Algernon's behaviour; not one plea to be urged on his behalf. Utter vindictive anger filled the old man's soul as he read. He had been deceived, played upon, laughed at by this boy! That was the first, and, perhaps, the most venomous of his mortifications. But many other stinging thoughts rankled in his mind. David Powell had been right! That was almost unendurable. As to Rhoda, old Max could not, in the mood he was then in, contemplate her being bowed down by grief and disappointment. He would have her raise her head, and revenge herself on her faithless lover. He would have her successful, admired, and prosperous. He would have her trample on Algernon's pride and poverty with all the insolence of wealth. Even his beloved money, so hardly earned, so eagerly hoarded, seemed to him, for the first time in his life, to be of small account in comparison with a sentiment.

He took his Bible, and gloated over menaces of vengeance and threats of destruction. Future condemnation was, no doubt, in store for Algernon Errington. But that was too vague and too distant a prospect to appease old Max's stomach for revenge. He wanted to see his enemy in the dust, and that his enemy should be seen there by others. In the midst of his reading, he suddenly recollected the acknowledgment he held of Algernon's debt to him, and jumped up and ran to his strong-box to feast his eyes on it. It seemed almost like a clear leading from on High that the I.O.U. should come into his head just then, old Max thought. He was not the first, nor the worst man who has wrested Scripture into the service of his own angry passions.

Then he sent to order a gig from the "Blue Bell," and set out for Duckwell Farm.

"I hope your father isn't sickening for any disease, or going to get a stroke, or something," said Betty Grimshaw to her nephew James. "But I never see anybody's face such a colour out of their coffin. It's a greeny grey, that's what it is. And he was frowning like thunder."

But Jonathan Maxfield's disorder was not of the body. He arrived at Duckwell unexpectedly, but his arrival did not cause any particular surprise. He had business transactions to discuss with his son Seth, to whom he had advanced money on mortgage. And then there was Rhoda staying at the farm, and, of course, her father would like to see Rhoda.

Rhoda was called from her own room, and came down, pale and nervous. She dreaded meeting her father. Did he, or did he not, know the news from Westmoreland? It had only come to Duckwell Farm by means of Mr. Pawkins's servants. It might possibly not yet have reached Whitford.

On his side, old Max took care to say nothing about the Applethwaite Advertiser. He had destroyed that journal before leaving home, placing it in the heart of the kitchen fire, and holding it there with the poker, until the remains of it fluttered up the chimney in black, impalpable fragments.

But old Max had brought another document in his pocket, which had been placed in his hand just as he was starting in the gig. It was a letter directed to Miss Rhoda Maxfield, High Street, Whitford. And this he pulled out almost immediately on seeing Rhoda. A glance at her face sufficed to show him that she was unhappy and dispirited. "She has heard it!" he thought. And something like an anathema upon Algernon followed the thought in his mind.

The old man's countenance was not so clearly read by his daughter; indeed, she hardly raised her eyes to his, but received his kiss in silence.

"I'm afraid, father, you'll not find Rhoda's looks doing us credit," said Mrs. Seth. "Why or wherefore I don't know, but these last days she has been as peaky as can be."

"It's the heat, maybe," said old Max shortly and withdrew his own and Mrs. Seth's attention from the girl, as she read the letter he handed to her. Rhoda was grateful for this forbearance on her father's part, although it fluttered her, too, a little, as proving that he was aware of the cause of her dejection, and anxious to shield it from observation.

The letter was from Minnie Bodkin. She had written it almost immediately on hearing of Algernon's intended marriage. It invited Rhoda, if her father would consent, to visit the Bodkins during the remainder of their stay at the seaside. There was no word of allusion to the Erringtons in the letter. Minnie only said, "Mamma and I remember that your cheeks had lost their roses, somewhat, when we left Whitford. And we think that a breath of sea-breeze may blow them back again. It is some time since you had complete change of air. Tell Mr. Maxfield we will take good care of you." And in a postscript Mrs. Bodkin had added, in her small running hand, "Do come, my dear. We shall be very glad to have you. Dr. Bodkin bids me send you his love."

It had been no slight effort of self-conquest which had made Minnie Bodkin send for Rhoda, to stay with her at the seaside, and had enabled her to endure the girl's daily presence, and to stand her friend in word and deed, throughout the weeks which succeeded the announcement of Algernon's marriage.

To be kind to Rhoda at a distance would have been pleasant enough. Minnie would willingly, nay, gladly, have served the girl in any way which should not have necessitated frequent personal communion with her. But she told herself unflinchingly that if she really meant to keep her promise to David Powell, she must do so at some cost of self-sacrifice. The only efficacious thing she could do for Rhoda was to take her away from Whitford scenes and Whitford people for a time; to take her out of the reach of gossiping tongues and unsympathising eyes, and to give her the support of a friendly presence when she should be obliged to face Whitford once more. This would be efficacious help to Rhoda; and Minnie resolved to give it to her. But it was a task to which she felt considerable repugnance. There was an invisible barrier between herself and pretty, gentle, winning Rhoda Maxfield.

It is curious to consider of how small importance to most of us actions are, as compared with motives. And perhaps nothing contributes more to hasty accusations of ingratitude than forgetfulness of this truth. We are more affected by what people mean than by what they say, and by what they feel than by what they do. Only when meaning and feeling harmoniously inform the dry husk of words and deeds, can we bring our hearts to receive the latter thankfully, however kind they may sound or seem to uninterested spectators. The egotism of most of us is too exacting to permit of our judging our friends' behaviour from any abstract point of view; and to be done good to for somebody else's sake, or even for the sake of a lofty principle, seldom excites very lively satisfaction.

Thus Rhoda reproached herself for the unaccountable coldness with which she received Miss Bodkin's kindness; having only a dim consciousness that Miss Bodkin's kindness was prompted by motives excellent indeed, but which had little to do with personal sympathy with herself.

She silently handed the letter to her father, and turned away to the window. Mrs. Seth bustled out of the room, saying that she must get ready "a snack of something" for Mr. Maxfield after his drive, and the father and daughter were left alone together.

Jonathan Maxfield's face brightened wonderfully as he read Minnie's gracious words. A glow of pleasure came over his hard features. But it was not a very agreeable sort of pleasure to behold, being considerably mingled with malicious triumph. Here was a well-timed circumstance indeed! What could Powell, or such as Powell, say now? Let the Erringtons behave as they might, it was clear henceforward that Rhoda had not been received amongst gentlefolks solely on their account. His girl was liked and made much of for her own sake.

"Well," said he, "this is a very pretty letter of Miss Minnie's; very pretty indeed." He did not allow his voice to express his exultation, but spoke in his usual harsh, grumbling tones.

"Yes," answered Rhoda, tremulously, "it is very kind of Miss Minnie, and of dear Mrs. Bodkin; wonderfully kind! But I—I don't think I want to go, father."

"Not want to go? Nonsense! That's mere idle nonsense. Of course you will go. I shall take you down by the coach myself."

"Oh thank you, father, but—I really don't want change. I don't care about going to the seaside."

The old man turned upon her almost savagely. "I say you shall go. You must go. Are you to creep into a hole like a sick beast of the field, and hide yourself from all eyes? There, there," he added in a gentler tone, drawing her towards him, as he saw the tears begin to gather in her eyes, "I am not chiding you, Rhoda. But it will be good for you to accept this call from your kind friends. It will be good for mind and body. You will be quiet there, among fresh scenes and fresh faces. And you will return to Whitford in the company of these gentlefolks, who, it is clear, are minded to stand your friends under all circumstances. Seth's wife is a worthy woman, but she is not a companion for you, Rhoda."

One phrase of this speech did seem to offer a glimpse of consolation to Rhoda; the promise, namely, of quiet and fresh scenes, where she and her belongings were utterly unknown. But her father did not know that Minnie Bodkin understood her little love-story from first to last; and that Minnie Bodkin's presence and companionship might not be calculated to pour the waters of oblivion into her heart. Still she reflected, a day must come when she would have to face Miss Minnie, and all the other Whitford people who knew her. There was no chance of her dying at once and being taken away from it all! And Rhoda's teaching had made her shrink from the thought of desiring death, as from something vaguely wicked. On the whole, it might be the best thing for her to go to the Bodkins. She would better have liked to continue her solitary rambles in Pudcombe Woods or the meadows at Duckwell; only that now the pain awaited her, every evening, at the farm, of hearing Algernon's marriage discussed and speculated on. She could not shut out the topic. On the whole, then, it might be the best thing she could do, to get away from Whitford gossip for a time.

These considerations Rhoda brought before her own mind, not with any idea that they could avail to decide her line of conduct, but by way of reconciling herself to the line of conduct she should be compelled to take. It never entered her head that any resistance would be possible when once her father had said, "You must go."

"Very well, father," she answered meekly, after a short pause.

The Bodkins' invitation was duly communicated to Seth and his wife. And it was arranged that Rhoda should start from the farm without returning to Whitford at all, as a cross road could be reached from Duckwell, where the coach would stop to pick up passengers. "If there's any garments you require, beyond those you have here, your aunt Betty shall send them over by the carrier, to-morrow," said Mr. Maxfield.

Mrs. Seth protested (not without a spice of malice) that Rhoda could not possibly want any more clothes, for that she was rigged out already fit for a princess. Nevertheless there did arrive from Whitford several fresh additions to Rhoda's wardrobe, inclosed in a brand-new black trunk studded with brass-headed nails, and with the initials R. M. traced out in the same shining materials on the lid.

"Your father's well-nigh soft-headed about that girl," said Mrs. Seth to her husband, as they stood watching the father and daughter drive away together.

"H'm!" grunted Seth.

His wife went on, "We may make up our minds as our little ones will never be a penny the better for your father's money. I'm as sure as sure, it'll all go to Rhoda."

"As to his will, you may be right," returned Seth. "But I have good hopes that father will cancel that mortgage he holds on the home farm. If he does that, we mustn't growl too much. 'Tis a good lump o' money. And it would come a deal handier to me if I could have the land free now, than if I waited for father's death. He's tough, is father. And the Lord knows I don't wish him dead neither."

In this way Rhoda Maxfield went down to the seaside place where the Bodkins were staying, spent about three weeks with them there, and returned in their company to Whitford, to find Mrs. Errington no longer an inmate of her father's house, the old sitting-room decorated and re-furnished very smartly, and all the circle with whom she had become acquainted at Dr. Bodkin's on the tiptoe of expectation to behold the Honourable Mrs. Algernon Errington, whose arrival was looked forward to with an amount of interest only understood by those who have ever lived an unoccupied life in a remote provincial town.

We have already been present at more than one social gathering at Dr. Bodkin's house. But these entertainments have been of an informal character, and the guests at them all persons in the habit of meeting each other very frequently. On Mr. and Mrs. Algernon Errington's arrival in Whitford, after their marriage, Dr. and Mrs. Bodkin issued cards for an evening party, and invited the leading personages of their acquaintance to meet the bride and bridegroom.

Mrs. Errington was in high delight. She appreciated this attention from her old friends very highly. Castalia, it was true, looked discontented and disdainful about the whole affair; and demanded to know why she must be dragged out to these people's stupid parties before she had had time to turn round in her own house. But then, as Mrs. Errington reflected, Castalia did not understand Whitford society. "The fact is, my dear," said her mother-in-law with suavity, "it may be all a very trumpery business in your eyes, and after the circles you have moved in, but I assure you it is considered a very desirable thing here to have the entrée to Dr. Bodkin's. And then they scarcely ever entertain on a showy scale; nothing but a few friends, tea and cake, your rubber, and a tray afterwards. But, for this occasion, I hear there are great preparations going on. They won't dance, because Minnie can't stand the vibration. But there will be quite a large gathering. Of course, my dear, it is not what I was accustomed to at Ancram Park. But they are most kind, well-meaning people. And Minnie is highly accomplished; even learned, I believe."

"I hate blue-stockings," returned Mrs. Algernon with a shrug.

"Oh! but Minnie is not the least blue in her manners! Indeed, her knowing Greek has ever been a mystery to me; for I assure you she is extremely handsome, and has, I think, the finest pair of eyes I ever saw in my life. But I suppose it is accounted for by her affliction, poor thing!"

Castalia had darted a quick, suspicious glance at her husband on hearing of Minnie's beauty, but relapsed into languid indifference when she was told that Miss Bodkin was a confirmed invalid, suffering from disease of the spine.

In other circles Mrs. Errington was by no means so cool and condescending in speaking of the doctor's projected party. The check administered to her exultation by Castalia's chilly indifference only caused a fuller ebullition of it in other directions. She overwhelmed her new landlady by the magnitude and magnificence of her "Ancramisms"—I have already asked permission to use the phrase in these pages—and was looked up to by that simple soul as a very exalted personage; for the new landlady was no other than the widow Thimbleby.

Mrs. Errington occupied the two rooms on the first-floor above Mr. Diamond's parlours. The place was smaller and poorer altogether than Maxfield's house, although it did not yield to it in cleanliness. Here was Mrs. Errington's old blue china set forth on a side-table in the little oblong drawing-room; and her work-box with its amber satin and silver implements; and the faded miniatures hung over the mantelpiece. Also there was a square of substantial, if somewhat faded, carpet in the middle of Mrs. Thimbleby's threadbare drugget, a mahogany table, and a roomy, comfortable easy-chair, all of which we have seen before.

In a word, Mrs. Errington had taken advantage of old Max's somewhat rash offer, and had carried away with her such articles of furniture out of her old quarters as she fancied might be useful.

Mrs. Errington took some credit to herself for her magnanimity in so doing. "I could not refuse the poor man," she said to Mrs. Thimbleby. "I have lived many years in his house, and although he was led away by mistaken ambition to want his drawing-room for his own use, and certainly did cause me great inconvenience at a moment when I was up to my eyes in important business, yet I could not refuse to accept his little peace-offering. A lady does not quarrel with that sort of person, you know. And, poor old man, I believe he was dreadfully cut up at my going away when it came to the point, and would have given anything to keep me. But I said, 'No, Mr. Maxfield, that is impossible. I have made other arrangements; and, in short, I cannot be troubled any more about this matter. But to show that I bear no malice, and that I shall not withdraw my countenance from your daughter, I am willing to accept the trifles you press upon me.' He was a good deal touched by my taking the things; poor, foolish, misguided old man!"

"Well, it was real Christian of you, ma'am," said simple Mrs. Thimbleby.

The day of the party at Dr. Bodkin's arrived; and there was as intense an excitement connected with its advent as if it were to bring a county ball, or even a royal drawing-room. Whether a satin train, lappets and feathers, be intrinsically more important and worthy objects of anxiety than a white muslin frock and artificial roses, I do not presume to decide. Only I can unhesitatingly assert that the Misses Rose and Violet McDougall could not have given their female attendant more trouble about the preparation and putting on of the latter adornments—which formed their simple and elegant attire on this occasion—if they had been duchesses, and their gowns cloth of gold.

Miss Chubb, too, contemplated her new dress of a light blue colour, laid out upon her bed, with great interest and satisfaction. And when her toilet for the evening was completed, she had more little gummed rings of hair on her cheeks and forehead than had ever before been beheld there at one time.

The company began to assemble in Dr. Bodkin's drawing-rooms about half-past eight o'clock. There were all our old acquaintances—Mr. Smith, the surgeon, and his wife; Mr. and Mrs. Dockett, with Miss Alethea, now promoted to long dresses and "grown-up" young-ladyhood. There was Orlando Pawkins; Mr. Warlock, the curate; and Colonel Whistler, with his charming nieces. Miss Chubb had dined with the Bodkins in the middle of the day, and, after being of great assistance to the mistress of the house in the preparation of her supper-table, had returned to her own home to dress, and consequently arrived upon the festive scene rather later than would otherwise have been the case. But she was not the last guest to arrive. Mr. Diamond came in after her; and so did one or two families from the neighbourhood of Whitford. ("County people," Miss Chubb said in a loud whisper to Rose McDougall, who replied snappishly, "Of course! We know them very well. Have visited them for years.")

"This is a brilliant scene," said good-natured Miss Chubb, turning to Mr. Warlock, whom Fate had thrown into her neighbourhood. Mr. Warlock agreed with her that it was very brilliant; and, indeed, Dr. Bodkin's drawing-rooms, well lighted with wax candles, and with abundance of hot-house flowers tastefully arranged, and relieved against the rich crimson and oak furniture, were exceedingly cheerful, pleasant, and picturesque. There was an air of comfort and good taste about the rooms—a habitable, home-like air—not always to be found in more splendid dwellings.

On her crimson lounging-chair reclined Minnie Bodkin. Her dress was of heavy cream-white silk, with gold ornaments. She wore nothing in her abundant dark hair, and her pale face seemed to many who looked upon it that evening to be more lovely than ever. Her lips had a tinge of red in them, and her eyes were full of lustre. There was a suppressed excitement about her looks and manner, which lighted up her perfectly-moulded features with a strange beauty that struck all observers. Even the

McDougalls could not but admit that Minnie looked very striking, but added that she was a little too theatrically got up, didn't you think so? That was poor Minnie's failing. All for effect! "And," added Rose, "she has a good foil in that little pink and white creature who sits in the corner beside her chair, and never moves. I suppose she is told to do it. But the idea of dressing that chit up in a violet silk gown fit for a married woman! And she has no figure to carry it off. I really think it rather a strong measure on the Bodkins' part to ask us all to meet a girl of such very low origin on equal terms. But there it is, you see! Poor dear Minnie delights in doing startling things, unlike other people. And, of course, her parents refuse her nothing."

Miss Rose's opinion of Rhoda Maxfield's insignificant appearance was not, however, shared by many persons present. Several young gentlemen, and more than one old gentleman, vied with each other in offering her cups of tea, and paying her various little attentions according to their opportunities. Even old Colonel Whistler, when he thought himself unobserved by his nieces, sidled up to pretty Rhoda Maxfield, and was heard to say to one of the "county" gentlemen, "She's the prettiest girl I've seen this many a day, by George! And I know a pretty girl when I see one, sir; or used to, once upon a time!"

To Rhoda, all the strangers who spoke and looked so kindly were merely troublesome. Her colour went and came, her heart beat with anxiety. She started nervously every time the door opened. She could think only of Algernon and Algernon's wife. She made a silent and very earnest prayer that she might be strengthened to sit still and quiet when they should appear, for she had had serious apprehensions lest she should be irresistibly impelled to start up and run away, as soon as she saw them.

It was in vain that young Mr. Pawkins hovered near her, inviting her to accept his arm into the tea-room; it was in vain that old Colonel Whistler softened his martinet voice to ask her, with paternal tenderness, how she had enjoyed her stay at the seaside, and to say that, if one might judge by her looks, she had derived great benefit from the change of air. In the words of the song, "All men else seemed to her like shadows." She was in a dream, with the consciousness of an impending awakening, which she half longed for, half dreaded.

Two persons watched over her, and covered the mistakes she made in her nervous trepidation. Matthew Diamond and Minnie Bodkin exerted themselves to shield her from importunate observation, and to give her time to recover her self-possession, if that might be possible. Diamond was in good spirits. He could wait, he could be patient, he could be silent now, with a good heart. Algernon's marriage had opened a bright vista of hope before him; and perhaps he had never felt so disposed to condone and excuse his old pupil's faults and failings as at the present moment. "Minnie is a good creature," he thought, with a momentary, grateful diversion of his attention from Rhoda, "to keep my timid birdie so carefully under her wing! She might do it with a little more softness of manner. But we cannot change people's natures."

Meanwhile Minnie reclined in her chair, watching his tender lingering looks at Rhoda, and his complete indifference to everyone else, with a heartache which might have excused even less "softness of manner" than Diamond thought she displayed towards the girl beside her.

At length a little commotion, and movement among the persons standing near the door, announced a new arrival. Rhoda felt sick, and grasped the back of Minnie's chair so hard that her little glove was split by the force of the pressure. But that horrible sensation passed away in a few seconds. And then, looking up with renewed powers of seeing and hearing, she perceived that Mrs. Errington had made her entrance alone, and was holding forth in her mellow voice to Dr. and Mrs. Bodkin, and a knot of other persons in the centre of the room.

Mrs. Errington was radiant. She nodded and smiled to one and another with an almost royal suavity and condescension. She was attired in a rich dove-coloured silk gown (Lord Seely's gift to her at her son's wedding), and wore rose-coloured ribbons in her lace cap, and looked altogether as handsome and happy a matron of her years as you would easily find in a long summer's day.

"I have sent back the carriage for them, dear Mrs. Bodkin," she was saying, when Rhoda gained self-possession enough to take account of her words. "Naughty Castalia was not ready. So I said, 'My dear children, I shall go on without you, and put in an appearance for one member of the family at least!' So here I am. And my boy and girl will be here directly. And how is dear Minnie?—How d'ye do, Colonel?—Good evening, Miss Chubb.—Ah, Alethea! Papa and mamma quite well?—Oh, there she is! How are you, my dear Minnie? But I need not ask, for I never saw you looking so well?"

By this time Mrs. Errington had arrived at Minnie's chair, and stooped to kiss her. Almost at the same moment she caught sight of Rhoda, who shrank back a little, flushed and trembling. Mrs. Errington thought she very well understood the cause of this, and thought to herself, "Poor child, she is ashamed of her father's behaviour!"

"What, my pretty Rhoda!" she said aloud. And, drawing the girl to her, kissed her warmly. "I'm very glad to see you again, child," continued Mrs. Errington; "I began to fancy we were not to meet any more. You must come and see me, and spend a long day. I suppose that won't be against the laws of the Medes and Persians, eh?"

The familiar voice, the familiar looks, the kind manner of her old friend, helped to put Rhoda at her ease. The fact, too, that Mrs. Errington had no suspicion of her feelings was calming. Mrs. Errington was not apt to suspect people of any feeling but gratification, when she was talking to them.

In the full glow of her satisfaction Mrs. Errington even condescended to be gracious to Matthew Diamond, who came forward to offer his congratulations. "Why, yes, Mr. Diamond," said the good lady, "it is indeed a marriage after my own heart. And I do not think I am blinded by the partiality of a mother, when I say the bride's family are quite as gratified at the alliance as I am. Do you know that one of Mrs. Algernon's relatives is the Duke of Mackelpie and Brose? A distant relative, it is true. But these Scotch clans, you know, call cousins to the twentieth degree! His Grace sent Castalia a beautiful wedding present: a cairn-gorm, set in solid silver. So characteristic, you know! and so distinguished! No vulgar finery. Oh, the Broses and the Kauldkails have been connected from time immemorial."

Then Colonel Whistler came up, and joined the circle round Mrs. Errington's chair; and Miss Chubb, whose curiosity generally got the better of her dignity when it came to a struggle between the two. To them sauntered up Alethea Dockett on the arm of Mr. Pawkins. The latter, finding it impossible to draw Rhoda into conversation, had philosophically transferred his attentions to the smiling, black-eyed Miss Alethea, much to the disgust and scorn of the McDougalls.

Mrs. Errington soon had a numerous audience around her chair, and she improved the occasion by indulging in such flourishes as fairly staggered her hearers. Her account of the bride's trousseau was almost oriental in the splendour and boldness of its imagery. And Matthew Diamond began to believe that, with very small encouragement, she might be led on to endow her daughter-in-law with the roc's egg, which even Aladdin could not compass the possession of, when a diversion took place.

Algernon Errington appeared close behind Miss Chubb, and said, almost in her ear, and in his old jaunty way, "Well, is this the way you cut an old friend? Oh, Miss Chubb, I couldn't have believed it of you!"

The little spinster turned round quite fluttered, with both her fat little hands extended. "Algy!" she cried. "But I beg pardon; I ought not to call you by that familiar name now, I suppose!"

"By what name, then? I hope you don't mean to cut me in earnest!"

Then there was a general hand-shaking and exchange of greetings among the group. Rhoda was still in her old place behind Minnie's chair, and was invisible at first to one coming to the circle from the other end of the room, as Algernon had done. But in a minute he saw her, and for once his self-possession temporarily forsook him.

If he had walked into the sitting-room at old Max's, and seen Rhoda there, in her accustomed place by his mother's knee, with the accustomed needlework in her hand, and dressed in the accustomed grey stuff frock, he might have accosted her with tolerable coolness and aplomb. The old associations, which might have unnerved some soft-hearted persons, would have strengthened Algernon by vividly recalling his own habitual ascendancy and superiority over his former love. But instead of the Rhoda he had been used to see, here was a lovely young lady, elegantly, even richly, dressed, received among the chief personages of her little world evidently on equal terms, and looking as gracefully in her right place there as the best of them.

Algernon stood for a second, staring point-blank at her, unable to move or to speak. His embarrassment gave her courage. Not less to her own surprise than to that of the two who were watching her so keenly, she rose from her chair, and held out her hand with the little torn glove on it, saying in a soft voice, that was scarcely at all unsteady, "How do you do, Mr. Errington?"

Algernon shook her proffered hand, and murmured something about having scarcely recognised her. Then someone else began to speak to him, and he turned away, as Rhoda resumed her seat, trembling from head to foot.

So the dreaded meeting was over! Let her see him again as often as she might, no second interview could be looked forward to with the same anxious apprehension as the first. She had seen Algernon once more! She had spoken to him, and touched his hand!

It seemed very strange that no outward thing should have changed, when such a moving drama had been going on within her heart! But not one of the faces around her showed any consciousness that they had witnessed a scene from the old, old story; that the clasp of those two young hands had meant at once, "Hail!" and "Farewell!"—farewell to the sweet, foolish dream, to the innocent tenderness of youth and maiden, to the soft thrilling sense of love's presence, that was wont to fill so many hours of life with a diffused sweetness, like the perfume of hidden flowers!

No; the world seemed to go on much as usual. The McDougalls came flouncing up close beside her, to tell Minnie that they had just been introduced to "the Honourable Mrs. Errington;" and a very young gentleman (one of Dr. Bodkin's senior scholars) asked Rhoda if she had had any tea yet, and begged to recommend the pound-cake, from his own personal experience.

"Go with Mr. Ingleby," said Minnie, authoritatively. "I put Miss Maxfield under your charge, Ingleby, and shall hold you responsible for her being properly attended to in the tea-room."

The lad, colouring with pleasure, led off the unresisting Rhoda. All her force of will, all her courage, seemed to have been expended in the effort of greeting Algernon. She simply obeyed Miss Bodkin with listless docility. But, on reaching the tea-room, she was conscious that her friend had done wisely and kindly in sending her away, for there were but two persons there. One was Mr. Dockett, who was as inveterate a tea-drinker as Doctor Johnson; and the other was the Reverend Peter Warlock, hovering hungrily near the cake-basket. Neither of these gentlemen took any special notice of her, and she was able to sit quiet and unobserved. Her cavalier conscientiously endeavoured to fulfil Miss Minnie's injunctions, but was greatly disappointed by the indifference which Rhoda manifested to the pound-cake. However, he endeavoured to make up for her shortcomings by devouring such a quantity of that confection himself as startled even Dr. Bodkin's old footman, accustomed to the appetites of many a generation of school-boys.

But all this time where was the bride? The party was given especially in her honour, and to omit her from any description of it would be an unpardonable solecism.

The Honourable Mrs. Algernon Ancram Errington sat on a sofa in the principal drawing-room, with a discontented expression of countenance, superciliously surveying the company through her eye-glass, and asking where Algernon was, if he were absent from her side for five minutes. Castalia was looking in better health than when we first had the honour of making her acquaintance. She had grown a trifle stouter—or less lean. Her sojourn in Westmoreland had been more favourable to her looks than the fatigues of a London season, which, under other circumstances, she would have been undergoing. Happiness is said to be a great beautifier. And it was to be supposed that Castalia, having married the man of her heart, was happy. But yet the fretful creases had not vanished from her face; and there was even a more suspicious watchfulness in her bright, deeply-set eyes than formerly.

Perhaps it may be well to record a few of the various verdicts passed on the bride's manners and appearance by our Whitford friends after that first evening. Possibly an impartial judgment may be formed from them; but it will be seen that opinions were strongly conflicting.

Said Dr. Bodkin to his wife, "What can the boy have been thinking of to marry that woman? A sickly, faded, fretful-looking person, nearly ten years his senior! I can forgive a generous mistake, but not a mean one. If he had run away with Ally Dockett from her boarding-school, it would, no doubt, have been a misfortune, but—I don't know that one would have loved him much the less!"

"Oh, doctor!"

"I am not counselling young gentlemen to run away with young ladies from boarding-schools, my dear. But—I'm afraid this has been a marriage wholly of interest and ambition on his side. Ah! I hoped better things of Errington." And the doctor went on shaking his head for full a minute.

Said Mrs. Smith to Mrs. Dockett, "What do you think of the bride?" Said Mrs. Dockett to Mrs. Smith, "A stuck-up, unpleasant little thing! And I do wish somebody would tell her to keep her gown on her shoulders. I assure you, if I were to see my Ally half undressed in that fashion, I should box her ears. And Ally has a very pretty pair of shoulders, though I say it. She is not a bag of bones, like Mrs. Algernon, at all events."

Said Miss Chubb to her old woman servant, "Well, the Honourable Mrs. Algernon Errington is very distangy looking, Martha. That's a French word that means—means out of the common, aristocratic, you know. Very distangy, certainly! But she lacks sentiment, in my opinion. And her outline is very sharp, Martha. I prefer a rounder contour, both of face and figure. Some of the ladies found fault with her because of her low dress. But that—as I happen to know—is quite the custom with our upper classes in town. Mrs. Figgins's—wife of the Bishop of Plumbunn, you know, Martha—Mrs. Figgins's sister, who married Sir William Wick, of the Honourable Company of Tallow Chandlers, I believe—that's a kind of City society for dining sumptuously, Martha; you mustn't suppose it has anything to do with selling tallow candles! Well, Lady Wick sat down to dinner in low, every day of her life!"

Mr. Diamond and young Pawkins walked a little way together from the doctor's house to the "Blue Bell" inn. The master of Pudcombe Hall, on attempting to resume his acquaintance with the bride, had been received with scant courtesy. But this was not so much because Castalia intended to be specially uncivil to him, as because at that moment it happened, unfortunately, that she saw her husband in a distant part of the room talking to Minnie Bodkin with an air of animation.

"By Jove!" cried the ingenuous Pawkins, "I don't envy Errington. His wife looks so uncommon ill-tempered, and turns up her honourable nose at everybody."

"She does not turn up her nose at him," returned Diamond. "And Errington will not be over sensitive on behalf of his friends."

"Oh, well! But she's so crabbed, somehow. One expects a bride to have some kind of softness in her manners, and—hang it all, there's not a particle of romance about her."

"My dear fellow, if there is in the United Kingdom a young man of three-and-twenty who can comfortably dispense with romance in his wife, our friend Errington is that young man."

"Oh, well! I know Errington's a very clever fellow, and all that, and perhaps I'm a fool. But I—I shouldn't like my wife to be quite so cool and cutting in her manners, that's all!"

"Neither should I. And perhaps I'm a fool!"

"Shouldn't you, now?" Orlando was encouraged by this admission on Diamond's part, further, to express his opinion that it was all very fine to stick "Honourable" before your name; but that, for his part, he considered little Miss Maxfield to look fifty times more like a lady than Mrs. Algernon. And as for good looks, there was, of course, no comparison. And though Miss Maxfield was too shy and quiet, yet if you offered her any little civility, she thanked you in such a sweet way that a fellow felt as if he could do anything for her; whereas, some women stare at a fellow enough to turn a fellow into stone.

But the Misses McDougall were enthusiastic in their praises of Algernon's wife. They performed a sort of Carmen Amoeboeum after this fashion:

Rose. "That sweet creature, the Honourable Mrs. Algernon! I can't get her out of my head."

Violet. "Dear thing! What high-bred manners! And did she tell you that we are positively related? The Mackelpies, you know, call cousins with us. There was the branch that went off from the elder line of Brose"—&c. &c. &c.

Rose. "Oh yes; one feels at home directly with people of one's own class. How lucky Algernon has been to get such a wife, instead of some chit of a girl who would have had no weight in society!"

Violet. "Yes; but she's quite young enough, Rose?"

Rose. "Oh, dear me, of course! But I meant that Algernon has shown his sense in not selecting a bread-and-butter Miss. I own I detest school-girls."

Violet. "She asked us to go and see her. Do you know I think we were the only girls in the room she seemed to take to at all! Even Minnie Bodkin, now—she was very cool, I thought, to Minnie."

Rose. "My dear child, how often have I told you that the people here have quite a mistaken estimate of Minnie Bodkin? They have just spoiled her. Her airs are really ludicrous. But directly a person of superior birth comes to the place you see how it is! Perhaps you'll believe me another time. I do think you were half inclined to fall down and worship Minnie yourself!"

Violet. "Oh no; not that! But she is very clever, you know. And, in spite of her affliction, I thought she looked wonderfully handsome to-night."

Rose. (Sharply.) "Pshaw! She was dressed up like an actress. I saw the look Mrs. Algernon gave her. How beautifully Mrs. Algernon had her hair done!"

Violet. "And did you notice that little flounce at the bottom of her dress?"—&c. &c.

Both. (Almost together.) "Isn't she charming, uncle?"

"Very," answered Colonel Whistler, twirling his moustaches. Then the gallant gentleman, as he took his bed-candle, was heard to mutter something which sounded like "d—d skinny!"

CHAPTER X.

"Love in a cottage" is a time-honoured phrase, which changes its significance considerably, according to the lips that utter it. To some persons, Love in a cottage would be suggestive of dreary obscurity, privation, cold mutton, and one maid-of-all-work. To others, it might mean a villa with its lawn running down to the Thames, a basket-phaeton and pair of ponies, and the modest simplicity of footmen without powder. To another class of minds, again, Love in a cottage might stand for a comprehensive hieroglyph of honest affection, sufficiently robust to live and thrive even on a diet of cold mutton, and warm-blooded enough to defy the nip of poverty's east winds.

Lady Seely had joked, in her cheerful, candid way, with her niece-in-law about her establishment in life, and had said, "Well, Castalia, you'll have love in a cottage, at all events! Some people are worse off. And at your age, you know (quite between ourselves), you must think yourself lucky to get a husband at all."

Miss Kilfinane had made some retort to the effect that she did not intend to remain all her life in a cottage, with or without love; and that if Lord Seely could do nothing for Ancram, she (Castalia) had other connections who might be more influential.

But, in truth, Castalia did think that she could be quite content to live with Algernon Errington under a thatched roof; having only a conventional and artificial conception of such a dwelling, derived chiefly from lithographed drawing-copies. It was not, of course, that Castalia Kilfinane did not know that thatched hovels are frequently comfortless, ill-ventilated, "the noted haunt of" earwigs, and limited in the accommodation necessary for a genteel family. But such knowledge was packed away in some quite different department of her mind from that which habitually contemplated her own personal existence, present and future. Wiser folks than Castalia are apt to anticipate exceptions to general laws in their own favour.

Castalia was undoubtedly in love with Algernon. That is to say, she would have liked better to be his wife in poverty and obscurity, than to accept a title and a handsome settlement from any other man whom she had ever seen; although she would probably have taken the latter had the chance been offered to her.

Nor is that bringing so hard an accusation against her as may at first sight appear. She would have liked best to be Algernon's wife; but for penniless Castalia Kilfinane to marry a poor man when she might have had a rich one, would have required her to disregard some of the strongest and most vital convictions of the persons among whom she lived. Let their words be what they might, their deeds irrefragably proved that they held poverty to be the one fatal, unforgiven sin, which so covered any multitude of virtues as utterly to hide and overwhelm them. You could no more expect Castalia to be impervious to this creed, than you could expect a sapling to draw its nourishment from a distant soil, rather than from the earth immediately around its roots. To be sure there have been vigorous young trees that would strike out tough branching fibres to an incredible distance, in search of the food that was best for them. Such human plants are rare; and poor narrow-minded, ill-educated Castalia was not of them.

Had she been much beloved, it is possible that she might have ripened into sweetness under that celestial sunshine. But it was not destined to be hers.

In some natures the giving even of unrequited love is beautifying to the character. But I think that in such cases the beauty is due to that pathetic compassion which blends with all love of a high nature for a lower one. Do you think that all the Griseldas believe in their lords' wisdom and justice? Do you fancy that the fathers of prodigal sons do not oftentimes perceive the young vagabonds' sins and shortcomings with a terrible perspicuity that pierces the poor fond heart like sharp steel? Do you not know that Cordelia saw more quickly and certainly than the sneering, sycophant courtiers, every weakness and vanity of the rash, choleric old king? But there are hearts in which such knowledge is transmuted not into bitter resentment, but into a yearning, angelic pity. Only, in order to feel this pity, we must rise to some point above the erring one. Now poor Castalia had been so repressed by "low ambition," and the petty influences of a poverty ever at odds with appearances, that the naturally weak wings of her spirit seemed to have lost all power of soaring.

The earliest days Mrs. Algernon Errington spent in her new home were passed in making a series of disagreeable discoveries. The first discovery was that a six-roomed brick cottage is, practically, a far less commodious dwelling than any she had hitherto lived in. The walls of Ivy Lodge (that was the name of the little house, which had not a twig of greenery to soften its bare red face) appeared so slight that she fancied her conversation could be overheard by the passersby in the road. The rooms were so small that her dress seemed to fill them to overflowing, although those were not the days of crinolines and long trains. The little staircase was narrow and steep. The kitchen was so close to the living rooms that, at dinner-time, the whole house seemed to exhale a smell of roast mutton. The stowing away of her wardrobe taxed to the utmost the ingenuity of her maid. And the few articles of furniture which Lady Seely had raked out from disused sitting-rooms, appeared almost as Brobdingnagian in Ivy Lodge as real tables and chairs would seem beside the furniture of a doll's house.

A second discovery—made very quickly after her arrival in Whitford—was still more unpleasant. It was this: that a fine London-bred lady's-maid is an inconvenient and unmanageable servant to introduce into a small humble household. Poor Castalia "couldn't think what had come to Slater!" And Slater went about with a thunderous brow and sulky mouth, conveying by her manner a sort of contemptuous compassion for her mistress, and a contempt by no means compassionate for everybody else in the house.

The stout Whitford servant-of-all-work offended her beyond forgiveness, on the very first day of their acquaintance, by bluntly remarking that well-cooked bacon and cabbage was a good-enough dinner for anybody; and that if Mrs. Slater had see'd as many hungry folks as she (Polly) had, she would say her grace and fall-to with a thankful heart instead of turning up her nose, and picking at good wholesome victuals with a fork! Moreover, Polly was not in the least awe-stricken by Mrs. Slater's black silk gown, or the gold watch she wore at her belt. She observed, cheerfully, that such-like fine toggery was all very well at church or chapel; and, for her part, she always had, and always would, put a bit of a flower in her bonnet on Sundays, and them mississes as didn't like it must get some one else to serve 'em. But, when she was about her work, she liked to be dressed in working clothes. And a servant as wanted to bring second-hand parlour manners into the kitchen seemed to her a poor cretur'—neither fish, flesh, fowl, nor good red-herring.

All which indignities Slater visited on her mistress, finding it impossible to disconcert or repress Polly, who only laughed heartily at her genteelest flights.

But these things were not the worst. The worst was that Algernon showed very plainly a disinclination to sympathise with his wife's annoyance, and his intention of withdrawing himself from all domestic troubles, as if he considered them to be clearly no concern of his. Mrs. Errington, indeed, would have come to the rescue of her daughter-in-law, but neither of Mrs. Algernon's servants were disposed to submit to Mrs. Errington's authority. And the good lady was no more inclined than her son to take trouble and expose herself to unpleasantness for any one else's sake.

Castalia and her mother-in-law did not grow more attached to each other the more intimate their acquaintance became. They had one sentiment in common—namely, love for Algernon. But this sentiment did not tend to unite them. Indeed—putting the rivalry of lovers out of the question, of course—it would be a mistake to conclude that because A and B both love C, therefore A and B must love each other. Mrs. Errington thought that Castalia worried Algernon by complaints. Castalia thought that Mrs. Errington was often a thorn in her son's side by reason of her indulgence in the opposite feelings; that is to say, over-sanguine and boastful prognostications.

"My dear Algy," his mother would say, "there is not the least doubt that you have a brilliant career before you. Your talents were appreciated by the highest in the land, directly you became known to them. It is impossible that you should be left here in the shade. No, no; Whitford won't hold you long. Of that I am certain!"

To which Castalia would reply that Whitford ought never to have held him at all; that the post he filled there was absurdly beneath his standing and abilities, and that Lord Seely would never have dreamt of offering Ancram such a position if it had not been for my lady, who is the most selfish, domineering woman in the world.

"I'm sorry to have to say it, Mrs. Errington, since she is your relation. And you needn't suppose that she cares any the more for Ancram because he's her far-away cousin. At most, she only looks upon him as a kind of poor relation that ought to put up with anything. And she's always abusing her own family. She said to Uncle Val, in my presence, that the Ancrams could never be satisfied, do what you would for them; so he might as well make up his mind to that, first as last. She told me to my face, the week before I was married, that Ancram and I ought to go down on our knees in thankfulness to her, for having got us a decent living. That was pretty impudent from her to a Kilfinane, I think!"

Algernon laughed with impartial good-humour at his mother's rose-coloured visions and his wife's gloomier views; but the good humour was a little cynical, and his eyes had lost their old sparkle of enjoyment; or, at least, it shone there far less frequently than formerly.

As to his business—his superintendence of the correspondence, by letter, between Whitford and the rest of the civilised world—that, it must be owned, seemed to sit lightly on the new postmaster. There was an elderly clerk in the office, named Gibbs. He was uncle to Miss Bodkin's maid Jane and her brother the converted groom, and was himself a member of the Wesleyan Society. Mr. Gibbs had been employed many years in the Whitford Post-office, and understood the routine of its business very well. Algernon relied on Mr. Gibbs, he said, and made himself very pleasant in his dealings with that functionary. What was the use, he asked, of disturbing and harassing a tried servant by a too restless supervision? He thought it best, if you trusted your subordinates at all, to trust them thoroughly.

And, certainly, Mr. Gibbs was very thoroughly trusted; so much so, indeed, that all the trouble and responsibility of the office-work appeared to be shifted on to his shoulders. Yet Mr. Gibbs seemed not to be discontented with this state of things. Possibly he looked forward to promotion. Algernon's wife and mother freely gave it to be understood in the town that Whitford was not destined long to have the honour of retaining Mr. Ancram Errington. Mr. Gibbs did the work; and, perhaps, he hoped eventually to receive the pay. Why should he not step into the vacant place of postmaster, when his chief should be translated to a higher sphere?

I daresay that, in these times of general reform, of competitive examinations and official purity, no such state of things could be possible as existed in the Whitford Post-office forty odd years ago. I have only faithfully to record the events of my story, and to express my humble willingness to believe that, nowadays, "nous avons changé tout cela." I must, however, be allowed distinctly to assert, and unflinchingly to maintain, that Algernon took no pains to acquire any knowledge of his business; and that, nevertheless, the postal communications between Whitford and the rest of the world appeared to go on much as they had gone on during the reign of his predecessor.

Mr. Gibbs was a close, quiet man, grave and sparing of speech. He had known something of the Erringtons for many years, having been a crony of old Maxfield's once upon a time. Mr. Gibbs remembered seeing Algernon's smiling, rosy face and light figure flitting through the long passage at old Max's in his school-boy days. He remembered having once or twice met the majestic Mrs. Errington in the doorway; and could recollect quite well how the tinkling sound of the harpsichord and Algy's fresh young voice used to penetrate into the back parlour on prayer-meeting nights, and fill the pauses between Brother Jackson's nasal dronings or Brother Powell's passionate supplications. Mr. Gibbs had not then conceived a favourable idea of the Erringtons, looking on them as worldly and unconverted persons, of whom Jonathan Maxfield would do well to purge his house. But Mr. Gibbs kept his official life and his private life very perfectly asunder, and he allowed no sectarian prejudices to make him rusty and unmanageable in his relations with the new postmaster.

Then, Mr. Gibbs was not altogether proof against the charm of Algy's manner. Once upon a time Algy had been pleasant to all the world, for the sheer pleasure of pleasing. Years, in their natural course, had a little hardened the ductility of his compliant manners—a little roughened the smoothness of his once almost flawless temper. But disappointment, and the—to Algernon—almost unendurable sense that he stood lower in his friends' admiration (I do not say estimation) than formerly, had changed him more rapidly than the mere course of time would have done. Still, when

Mr. Ancram Errington strongly desired to attract, persuade, or fascinate, there were few persons who could resist him. He found it worth while to fascinate Mr. Gibbs, desiring not only that his clerk should carry his burden for him, but should carry it so cheerfully and smilingly as to make him feel comfortable and complacent at having made the transfer.

I have said that disappointment had changed Algernon. He was disappointed in his marriage. It was not that he had been a victim to any romantic illusions as regarded his wife. He had had his little love-romance some time ago; had it, and tasted it, and enjoyed it as a child enjoys a fairy tale, feeling that it belongs to quite another realm from the everyday world of nursery dinners, Latin grammars, and torn pinafores, and not in the least expecting to see Fanfreluche fly down the chimney into the school-room, or to find Cinderella's glass slipper on the stairs as he goes up to bed. Romances that touch the fancy only, and in which the heart has no share, are easily put off and on. Algernon had wilfully laid his romance aside, and did not regret it. Castalia's lack of charm, and sweetness, and sympathy would not greatly have troubled him—did he not know it all beforehand?—had she been able to help him into a brilliant position, and to cause him to be received and caressed by her noble relatives and the delightful world of fashionable society. It was not that she failed to put any sunlight into his days, and to fill his home with a sweet atmosphere of love and trust. Algy would willingly enough have dispensed with that sort of sunshine if he could but have had plenty of wax candles and fine crystal lustres for them to sparkle in. Give him a handsome suite of drawing-rooms, filled with the rich odours of pastille and pot-pourri, and Algy would make no sickly lamentations over the absence of any "sweet atmosphere" such as I have written of above. Only put his attractive figure into a suitable frame, and he would be sure to receive praise and sympathy enough, and to have a pleasant life of it.

No; he could not accuse himself of having been the victim of any sentimental illusion in marrying Castalia. And yet he had been cheated! He had bestowed himself without receiving the due quid pro quo. In a word, he began to fear that it had not been worth his while to marry the Honourable Miss Kilfinane. And sometimes the thought darted like a twinge of pain through the young man's mind—might it not have been worth his while to marry someone else?

"Someone else" was talked of as an heiress. "Someone else" was said by the gossips to be so good a match that she might have her pick of the town—aye, and a good chance among the county people! But Algernon smothered down all vain and harassing speculations founded on an "if it had been!" Neither did he by any means hopelessly resign himself to his present position, nor despair of obtaining a better one. He persisted in looking on his employment as merely provisional and temporary; so that, in fact, the worse things became in his Whitford life, the less he would do to mend them, taking every fresh disgust and annoyance as a new reason why—according to any rationally conceivable theory of events—he must speedily be removed to a region in which a gentleman of his capacities for refined enjoyment might be free to exercise them, untrammelled by vulgar cares.

CHAPTER XI.

It was true that Mrs. Algernon Errington had distinguished the Misses McDougall, by her notice, above all the other ladies whom she met at Dr. Bodkin's. The rest had by no means found favour in her eyes. Minnie Bodkin she decidedly disapproved of. Ally Dockett was "a little black-eyed, fat, flirting thing." The elder ladies were frumps, or frights, or bores. Rhoda Maxfield she had scarcely seen. On the evening of the Bodkins' party, Rhoda, as we know, had kept herself studiously in the background.

Mrs. Errington intended to present Rhoda to her daughter-in-law as her own especial pet and protégée, but a favourable moment for fulfilling this intention did not offer itself. Rhoda had not distinctly expressed any unwillingness to be taken to Ivy Lodge, and it could never enter into Mrs. Errington's head to guess that she felt such unwillingness. But in some way the project seemed to be eluded; so that Castalia had been some weeks in Whitford without making the acquaintance of Miss Maxfield, as she began to be called, even by some of those to whom she had been "Old Max's little Rhoda" all her life.

Castalia, indeed, troubled her head very little about Rhoda, under whatever style or title she might be mentioned. We may be sure that Algernon never spoke to his wife of the old days at the Maxfields; indeed, he eschewed all allusion to that name as much as possible. Castalia knew from Mrs. Errington that there had been a young girl in the house where she had lodged, the daughter of the grocer, who was her landlord; but, being pretty well accustomed to Mrs. Errington's highly-coloured descriptions of things and people, she had paid no attention to that lady's praises of Rhoda's intelligence, good looks, and pretty manners.

No; Castalia troubled not her head about Rhoda. But she was troubled about Minnie Bodkin, of whom she became bitterly jealous. She did not suppose, to be sure, that her husband had ever made love to Miss Bodkin; but she was constantly tormented by the suspicion that Algernon was admiring Minnie, and comparing her beauty, wit, and accomplishments with those of his wife, to the disadvantage of the latter. Not that she (Castalia) admired her. Far from it! But—she was just the sort of person to be taking with men. She had such a forward, confident, showy way with her!

Some speech of this sort being uttered in the presence of the Misses McDougall, was seized upon, and echoed, and re-echoed, and made much of by those young ladies, who pounced on poor Minnie, and tore her to pieces with great skill and gusto. Violet, indeed, made a feeble protest now and then on behalf of her friend; but how was she to oppose her sister and that sweet Mrs. Algernon? And then, in conscience and candour, she could not but admit that poor dear Minnie had many and glaring faults.

In fact, Rose and Violet McDougall were installed as toadies in ordinary to Castalia. They were her dearest friends; they called her by her Christian-name; they flattered her weaknesses, and encouraged her worst traits; not, we may charitably believe, with the full consciousness of what they were doing. For her part, Castalia soon got into the habit of liking to have these ladies about her. They performed many little offices which saved her trouble; they were devoted to her interests, and brought her news of the doings of the opposite faction. For there was an opposite faction; or Castalia persuaded herself that there was. The Bodkins were ranged in it, in her jealous fancy; and so were the Docketts, and one or two more of Algernon's old friends. Miss Chubb she considered to hover as yet on neutral ground. As to the unmarried men—young Pawkins, Mr. Diamond, and the curate of St. Chad's—they were not much taken into account in this species of subterranean warfare, carried on with an arsenal of sneers, stares, slights, hints, coolnesses, bridlings, envy, hatred, malice, and all uncharitableness.

I have said that the warfare was subterranean; occult, as it were. Had the enemy been actuated by similar feelings to those of Castalia and her party, hostilities must have blazed up openly. But most of them did not even know that they were being assailed. Among these unconscious ones were Dr. and Mrs. Bodkin. Minnie had at times a suspicion that Algy's wife disliked her. But then the manners of Algy's wife were not genial or gracious to anyone, and Minnie could not but feel a certain compassion for her, which extinguished resentment at her sour words and ways.

With the rest of the Whitford society, the bride did not enter into intimate, or even amicable, relations. She offended most of the worthy matrons who called on her by merely returning her card, and not even asking to be admitted to see them. As to offering any entertainment in return for the hospitalities that were offered to her during the first weeks that she dwelt in Whitford, that, Castalia said, was out of the question. How could more than two persons sit at table in her little dining-room? And how was it possible to receive company in Ivy Lodge?

But Whitford was not quite of her opinion in this matter. It was true her rooms were small; but were they smaller than Mrs. Jones's, who gave three tea-parties every year, and received her friends in detachments? Why was Ivy Lodge less adapted for festive purposes than Dr. Smith's house in the High Street?—a queer, ancient, crooked nook of a dwelling, squeezed in between two larger neighbours, with a number of tiny dark rooms like closets; in which, nevertheless, some of the best crumpets and tea-cakes known to that community, not to mention little lobster suppers in the season, had been consumed by the Smiths' friends with much satisfaction. As Mrs. Dockett observed, it was not so much what you gave as the spirit you gave it in that mattered! And she was not ashamed, not she, to recall the time, in the beginning of Mr. Dockett's career, when she had with her own hands prepared a welsh rabbit and a jorum of spiced ale for a little party of friends, having nothing better to offer them for supper. In a word, it was Whitford's creed that even the most indigestible food, freely bestowed, might bless him that gave and him that received; and that if the Algernon Erringtons did not offer anyone so much as a cup of tea in their house, the real reason was to be sought in the lady's proud reserve and a general state of feeling which Mrs. Dockett described as "stuck-upishness."

Castalia was unaccustomed to walking, and disliked that exercise. Riding was out of her power, no saddle-horse that would carry a lady being kept for hire in Whitford, and the jingling old fly from the "Blue Bell" inn was employed to carry her to such houses as she deigned to visit at. Her mother-in-law's lodging was not very frequently honoured by her presence. The stairs frightened her, she said; they were like a ladder. Mrs. Thimbleby's oblong drawing-room was a horrible little den. She had had no idea that ladies and gentlemen ever lived in such places. In truth, Castalia's anticipations of the Erringtons' domestic life at Whitford had by no means prepared her for the reality. Ancram had told her he was poor, certainly. Poor! Yes, but Jack Price was poor also. And Jack Price's valet was far better lodged than her mother-in-law. However, occasionally the jingling fly did draw up before the widow Thimbleby's door, and Castalia was seen to alight from it with a discontented expression of countenance, and to pick her way with raised skirts over the cleanly sanded doorstep.

One day, when she entered the oblong drawing-room, Castalia perceived that Mrs. Errington was not there; but, instead of her, there was a young lady, sitting at work by the window, who lifted a lovely, blushing face as Castalia entered the room, and stammered out, in evident embarrassment, that Mrs. Errington would be there in a few minutes, and, meanwhile, would not the lady take a seat?

"I am Mrs. Ancram Errington," said Castalia, looking curiously at the girl.

"Yes; I know. I—I saw you at Dr. Bodkin's. I am spending the day with Mrs. Errington. She is very kind to me."

Algernon's wife seated herself in the easy-chair, and leisurely surveyed the young woman before her. Her first thought was, "How well she's dressed!" her second, "She seems very bashful and timid; quite afraid of me!" And this second thought was not displeasing to Mrs. Algernon; for, in general, she had not been treated by the "provincial bumpkins," as she called them, with all the deference and submission due to her rank.

The girl's hands were nervously occupied with some needlework. The flush had faded from her face, and left it delicately pale, except a faint rose-tint in the cheeks. Her shining brown hair waved in soft curls on to her neck. Mrs. Algernon sat looking at her, and critically observing the becoming hue of her green silk gown, the taste and richness of a gold brooch at her throat, the whiteness of the shapely hand that was tremulously plying the needle. All at once a guess came into her mind, and she asked, suddenly:

"Is your name Maxfield?"

"Yes; Rhoda Maxfield," returned the girl, blushing more deeply and painfully than before.

"Why, I have heard of you!" exclaimed Mrs. Algernon. "You must come and see me."

Rhoda was so alarmed at the pitch of agitation to which she was brought by this speech, that she made a violent effort to control it, and answered with, more calmness than she had hitherto displayed:

"Mrs. Errington has spoken once or twice of bringing me to your house; but—I did not like to intrude. And, besides—"

"Oh, Mrs. Errington brings all sorts of tiresome people to see me; she may as well bring a nice person for once in a way."

Castalia was meaning to be very gracious.

"Yes; I mean—but then—my father might not like me to come and see you," blurted out Rhoda, with a sort of quiet desperation.

Mrs. Algernon opened her eyes very wide.

"Why, for goodness' sake? Oh, he had some quarrel or other with Mrs. Errington, hadn't he? Never mind, that must be all forgotten, or he wouldn't let you come here. I believe the truth is, that Mrs. Errington meant slyly to keep you to herself, and I shan't stand that."

Indeed, Castalia more than half believed this to be the case. And, partly from a sheer spirit of opposition to her mother-in-law—partly from the suspicious jealousy of her nature, that led her to do those things which she fancied others cunningly wished to prevent her from doing—she began to think she would patronise Rhoda and enlist her into her own faction. Besides, Rhoda was sweet-voiced, submissive, humble. Certainly, she would be a pleasanter sort of pet and tame animal to encourage about the house than Rose McDougall, who, with all her devotion, claimed a quid pro quo for her services, and dwelt on her kinship with the daughter of Lord Kauldkail, and talked of their "mutual ancestry" to an extent that Castalia had begun to consider a bore.

At this moment Mrs. Errington bustled into the room, holding a small roll of yellow lace in her hand. "I have found it, Rhoda," she cried. "This little bit is nearly the same pattern as the trimming on the cap, and, if we join the frilling—" Here she perceived Mrs. Algernon's presence, and stopped her speech with an exclamation of surprise: "Good gracious! is that you, Castalia? How long have you been here? This is an unexpected pleasure. Now you can give us your advice about the trimming of my cap, which Rhoda has undertaken for me."

Castalia did not rise from the easy-chair, but turned her cheek to receive the elder lady's kiss. Rhoda gathered up her work, and moved to go away.

"Don't run away, Rhoda!" cried Mrs. Errington. "We have no secrets to talk, have we, Castalia? You know my little friend Rhoda, do you not? She is a great pet of mine?"

"Oh, I will go and sit in your bedroom, if I may," muttered Rhoda, hurriedly. "I—I don't like to be in your way." And with a little confused courtesy to Mrs. Algernon, she slipped out of the room and closed the door behind her.

"She is such a shy little thing!" exclaimed Mrs. Errington.

"Well," returned Castalia, "it is a comfort to meet with any Whitford person that knows her place! They are the most presumptuous set of creatures, in general, that I ever came across."

"Oh, Rhoda Maxfield's manners are never at fault, I assure you; I formed her myself, with considerable care and pains."

"She seems to make herself useful, too!" observed Castalia with a languid sneer.

"That she does, indeed, my dear! Most useful. Her taste and skill in any little matter of needlework are quite extraordinary. Poor child! she is so delighted to do anything for me. She is devotedly attached to me, and very grateful. Her father really did behave abominably, and she feels it very much, and wishes to make up for it. No doubt the old man repents of his folly and ill-humour now; but, of course, I can have nothing more to say to him. However, I willingly allow the girl to do any little thing she can. She has just been trimming this cap for me most exquisitely!"

Castalia thought, more and more, that it would be worth her while to patronise Rhoda.

"I shall go to old Maxfield myself, and get him to let her come to my house," said she, as she took leave of her mother-in-law, and slowly made her way down Mrs. Thimbleby's ladder-like staircase, holding fast to the banisters with one hand, and not lifting one of her feet from a step until the other was firmly planted beside it.

On returning home that evening, Rhoda was greatly startled by her father's words, "Well, Miss Maxfield, here's a honourable missis been begging for the pleasure of your company!"

Rhoda turned pale and red, and said something in too low a tone to meet her father's ear.

"Oh yes," the old man went on; "the Honourable Mrs. Algernon Ancram Errington has been here, if you please! Well, I wish that young man joy of his bargain! Our little Sally is ten times as well-favoured. Your Aunt Betty saw her first; and, says she, 'Is Mr. Maxfield at home?'"

"I answered that your father was engaged in business," said Betty Grimshaw, taking up the narration.

"You should ha' said I was serving in the shop," observed old Max, doggedly, "and would sell her fine ladyship a penn'orth of gingerbread if she'd a mind, and could find the penny!"

"Nay, Jonathan, how could I have said that to the lady? Says she, 'I wish to say a word to him.' So I showed her into your drawing-room, Rhoda, and called your father, and—"

"And there she sat," interrupted the old man, with unwonted eagerness in his face and his voice, "in a far better place than any she has of her own, if all accounts are true, looking about her as curious as a ferret. I walked in, in my calico sleeves and my apron—"

("He wouldn't take them off," put in Betty, parenthetically.)

"No; I wouldn't. And she told me she was come to ask my leave to have my daughter Rhoda at her house. 'Of course you'll let her come,' she says, 'for you let her go to Mrs. Errington's and to Mrs. Bodkin's?' 'Why, as to that,' says I, 'I'm rather partic'lar where Miss Maxfield visits.' You should have seen her stare. She looked fairly astounded."

"Oh, father!"

"Did I not speak the truth? I am partic'lar where you visit. I told her plainly that you was in a very different position from the rest of the family. 'I am a plain tradesman,' said I. 'I have my own place and my own influence, and I have been marvellously upholden in my walk of light. But my daughter Rhoda is a lady of the Lord's own making, and must be treated as such. And she has plenty of this world's gear, for my endeavours have been abundantly blessed.'"

"Oh, father!"

"'Oh, father!'" repeated the old man, impatiently. "What did I say amiss? I tell you the woman was cowed by me. I am in subjection to none of their principalities and powers. The upshot was that I promised you should go and take tea with her to-morrow evening."

Rhoda was greatly surprised by this announcement, which was totally unexpected. "Oh, father!" she exclaimed in a trembling voice, "why did you say I should go?"

"Why? For various sufficient reasons. Let that be enough for you."

The truth was, that Castalia had more than hinted her suspicion that her mother-in-law selfishly endeavoured to keep Rhoda under her own influence, and to prevent her visiting elsewhere. And to thwart Mrs. Errington would alone have been a powerful incentive with old Max. But a far stronger motive with him was that he longed, with keen malice, that Algernon should be forced painfully to contrast the love he had been false to with the wife he had gained. He would have Algernon see Rhoda rich, and well-dressed, and courted. If Rhoda would but have flaunted her prosperity in Algernon's face, there was scarcely any sum of money her father would have grudged for the pleasure of witnessing that spectacle. But, although it was hopeless to expect Rhoda to display any spirit of vengeance on her own behalf, yet she might be made the half-unconscious instrument of a retribution that should gall and mortify Algernon to the quick. That Rhoda herself might suffer in the process was an idea to which (if it occurred to him) he would give no harbourage.

Rhoda sat silent until her aunt had left the room to prepare the supper according to her habit. Then she rose, and, going close up to her father, took his hand, and looked imploringly into his face. "Father," she said, "don't make me go there. I—I can't bear it."

"You can't bear it!" burst out old Maxfield. He scowled with a frown of terrible malignity. But Rhoda well knew that his wrath was not directed against her. She stood trembling and pale before him, whilst he spoke more harsh and bitter words against all the family of the Erringtons than she had ever heard him utter on that score. He dropped, too, for the first time in her hearing, a hint that he had some power over Algernon, and would use it to his detriment. Rhoda mustered courage to ask him for an explanation of those words. But he merely answered, "No matter. It is no matter. It is not the money. I shall not get it, nor do I greatly heed it. But I can put him to shame publicly, if I am so minded."

The poor child began to perceive that any display of wounded feeling on her part, of reluctance to meet Algernon and his wife, of being in any degree crushed and dispirited, would inflame her father's wrath against that family. And, although she had only the vaguest notions as to what he could or could not do to spite them, she had a hundred reasons for wishing to mitigate his animosity.

So, with the gentle cunning that belonged to her nature, at once timid and persistent, she began to unsay what she had said, and to try to efface the impression which her first refusal had made upon her father.

"I—I have been thinking that you are right, father, in saying it will be best for me to go to Ivy Lodge. You know Mrs. Errington has always been good to me, and it would please her, perhaps. And—and, after all, why should I be afraid of going there?"

"Afraid of going there!" echoed old Max, with sternly-set jaw and puckered brow. "Why, indeed, should you be afraid? There's some as have reason to be afraid, but not my daughter—not Miss Maxfield. Afraid!"

"Perhaps people might think it strange if I did not go?"

"People! What people?"

"Well, no matter for that. But if you, father, think it well that I should go—"

"You shall go in a carriage from the 'Blue Bell' inn. And Sally shall accompany you and bring you back. And see that you are properly attired. I would have you wear your best garments. You shall not be shamed before that yellow-faced woman. I don't believe she has a better gown to her back than the one I bought you to wear at Dr. Bodkin's."

Rhoda waived the point for the moment; but, after a while, she was able to persuade her father that her grey merino gown, with a lace frill at her throat, was a more suitable garment in which to spend the evening at Ivy Lodge than the rich violet silk he recommended for the purpose. Real ladies, she urged timidly, did not wear their smartest clothes on such occasions. And old Max reluctantly accepted her dictum on this point. But nothing could shake him from his resolve that Rhoda should be conveyed to Mrs. Algernon Errington's door in a hired carriage. So, with a sigh, she yielded; devoutly wishing that a pelting shower of rain, or even a thunderstorm, might arrive the next evening, to serve as an excuse for her appearing at Ivy Lodge in such unwonted state.

CHAPTER XII.

No Jupiter, rainy or thunderous, lent his assistance to account for the extraordinary phenomenon of Rhoda Maxfield's driving up to the garden-gate of Ivy Lodge instead of arriving there on foot. On the contrary, it was a fine autumn evening, with a serene sky where the sunset tints still lingered.

Rhoda alighted hurriedly from the carriage, and walked up the few feet of gravel path, between the garden fence and the house, with a beating heart. "You can go away now, Sally," she said, being very anxious to dismiss the "Blue Bell" equipage before the door should be opened. But Sally was not in such a hurry. Her master had told her that she was to wait and see Miss Rhoda safe into the house, and then she might come back in the carriage as far as the "Blue Bell." And Sally was not averse to have her new promotion to the dignity of "riding in a coach" witnessed by Mrs. Algernon Errington's Polly, with whom she had a slight acquaintance. So Miss Maxfield's equipage was seen by the servant who opened the door, and stared at from the front parlour window by two pairs of eyes, belonging respectively to Miss Chubb and Mrs. Errington.

"You can go into the parlour, miss," said Polly. "Master and missis are still at dinner. But the old lady's in there and Miss Chubb."

That they should be still at dinner, at half-past six o'clock in the evening, seemed a strange circumstance to Rhoda, and was one that she had not reckoned on. But she supposed it was according to the customs of the high folks Mrs. Algernon had been used to live among. The innovation was not accepted so meekly by most of the Whitfordians, whom, indeed, it seemed to irritate in a greater degree than more serious offences. But it is true of most of us, that we are never more angry than when we are unable to explain the reasons for our anger.

"I am afraid I'm too early," said Rhoda, when she had entered the parlour and greeted her old friends, "but father said he thought it was the right time to come."

"Mr. and Mrs. Ancram Errington dine late, my dear. Castalia has not yet got broken of the habits of her own class, as I have had to be. Indeed, she will probably never need to relinquish them. But it is no matter, Rhoda. You can make yourself comfortable here with us for half an hour or so. Miss Chubb called in to see me at my place, and I brought her down here with me. I knew Mrs. Ancram Errington would be happy to see her if she dropped in in an informal way."

"I never can get used to the name of Ancram instead of Algernon," said the spinster, raising her round red face from her woolwork. "It isn't half so pretty. Nine times out of ten I call your son 'Algy' plump and plain. I'm very sorry if it's improper, but I can't help it."

Mrs. Errington smiled with an air of lofty toleration. "Not at all improper," she said. "Algernon is the last creature in the world to be distant towards an old friend. But as to the name of Ancram, why it was, from the first, his appellation among the Seelys. And Castalia always calls him so. You see 'Ancram' was a familiar name in the circles she lived in; like Howard, or Seymour, or any of the great old family names, you know. It came naturally to her."

"Well, I should think that one's husband's Christian-name would come natural to one, even if it were only plain Tom, Dick, or Harry."

"He didn't begin by being her husband, my dear!"

Rhoda had nestled herself down in a corner behind a small table, and was turning over an album and one or two illustrated annuals. She hoped that the discussion as to Algernon's name would effectually divert the attention of the two elder ladies from the unprecedented fact that she had been brought to Ivy Lodge in a carriage. But she was not to be let off altogether. Miss Chubb, folding up her work, declared that it was growing too dark to distinguish the colours, and observed, "I was standing by the window to catch the last daylight, when you drove up, Rhoda. I couldn't think who it was arriving in such style."

"That was the 'Blue Bell' fly you were in, Rhoda," said Mrs. Errington. "I believe it to be the same vehicle that my daughter-in-law uses occasionally. She complains of it sadly. But I tell her she cannot expect to find her Aunt Seely's luxurious, well-hung carriages in a little provincial place like this."

Miss Chubb was about to make what she considered a severe retort, but she stifled it down. Mrs. Errington's airs were very provoking, to be sure; but there were reasons why Miss Chubb was more inclined to bear with her now than formerly. If it pleased this widowed mother to soften her disappointments about Algy's career and Algy's wife (it began to be considered in Whitford that both would prove to be failures!) by an extra flourish or two, why should any one put her—"No!" said Miss Chubb to herself, as the question was half-framed in her mind, "that is not the right word, certainly. I defy the world to put Mrs. Errington out of conceit with herself! But why should one snub and snap at the poor woman?"

Indeed, Miss Chubb never snapped, and rarely attempted to snub. She had a fund of benevolence hidden under a heap of frothy vanities and absurdities, like the solid cake at the bottom of a trifle.

"Well," said she, smiling good-temperedly, "I'm sure Rhoda doesn't quarrel with the 'Blue Bell' fly, do you, Rhoda?"

"I shouldn't have wished to use it, myself, but father said, 'It is rather a long way,' and father thought—"

"Oh, my dear, there is no need to excuse yourself, or to look shy on the subject. We should all of us be glad enough of a coach to ride in, now and then, if we could afford it. I'm sure I should, and I don't mind saying so."

Mrs. Errington did not approve of the coach quite so unreservedly. She observed, with some solemnity, that she was no friend to extravagance; and that, above all things, persons ought to guard against ostentation, or a thrusting of themselves into positions unsuited to that station in life to which it had pleased Providence to call them. And, in conclusion, she announced her intention of availing herself of the circumstance that Rhoda had a carriage at her disposal for the evening, to drive back with her as far as Mrs. Thimbleby's door—"which," said she, "is only a street and a half away from your house, Rhoda; and it will not make any difference to your father in point of expense."

Castalia found her three guests chatting in the twilight; or rather she found Mrs. Errington holding forth in her rich pleasant voice, whilst the others listened, and threw in a word or two now and then, just sufficient to show that they were attending to the good lady's harangue. In Rhoda's case, indeed, this appearance of attention was fallacious, for, although she said "Yes," and "No," and "Indeed!" at due intervals, her thoughts were wandering back to old days, which seemed suddenly to have receded into a far-distant past.

Castalia shook hands languidly with Miss Chubb and condescendingly with Rhoda. "I'm very glad you've come," she said to the latter, which was a speech of unusual warmth for her. And it had the merit, moreover, of being true. Castalia was not given to falsehood in her speech. She was too supercilious to care much what impression she made on people in general; and if they bored her, she took no pains to conceal the fact. Weariness of spirit and discontent had begun to assail her once more. They were old enemies. Her marriage had banished them for a time; but they gathered again, like clouds which a transient gleam of wintry sunshine has temporarily dispersed, and shadowed her life with an increasing gloom. This young Rhoda Maxfield offered some chance of brightness and novelty. She was certainly different from the rest of the Whitford world, and the pursuit of her society had been beset with some little difficulties that gave it zest.

A lamp was brought into the room, and then Castalia sat down beside Rhoda, unceremoniously leaving the other ladies to entertain each other as best they might. She examined her guest's dress; the quality of the lace frill at her throat; the arrangement of her chestnut curls; the delicate little gold chain that shone upon the pearl-grey gown; the neatly-embroidered letters R. M. worked on a corner of the handkerchief that lay in her lap, with as much unreserve and coolness as though Rhoda had been some daintily-furred rabbit, or any other pet animal. On her part, Rhoda took cognisance of every detail in Castalia's appearance, attire, and manner; she marked every inflection of her voice, and every turn of her haughty, languid head. And, perhaps, her scrutiny was the keener and more complete of the two, notwithstanding that it was made with timidly-veiled eyes and downcast head.

"What an odd man your father is!" said the Honourable Mrs. Ancram Errington, by way of opening the conversation.

Rhoda found it impossible to reply to this observation. She coloured, and twisted her gold chain round her fingers, and was silent. But it did not seem that Mrs. Ancram Errington expected, or wished for a reply. She went on with scarcely a pause: "I thought at first he would refuse to let you come here. But he gave his consent at last. I was quite amused with his odd way of doing it, though. He must be quite a 'character.' He's very rich, isn't he?"

"I don't know, ma'am," stammered Rhoda.

"Well, he says so himself; or, at least, he informed me that you were, or would be, which comes to the same thing. And don't call me 'ma'am.' It makes me feel a hundred years old. You and I must be great friends."

"Where is Algernon?" asked Mrs. Errington from the other side of the room.

"He will come presently, when he has finished his wine. Do you know we found that stuff from the 'Blue Bell,' that you recommended us to try, quite undrinkable! Ancram was obliged to get Jack Price to send him down a case of claret, from his own wine-merchant in town."

"Most extraordinary!" exclaimed Mrs. Errington, and began to recapitulate all the occasions on which the wine supplied to her from the "Blue Bell" inn had been pronounced excellent by the first connoisseurs. But Castalia made small pretence of listening to or believing her statements. Indeed, I am sorry to say that obstinate incredulity was this young woman's habitual tone of mind with regard to almost every word that her mother-in-law uttered; whereby the Honourable Mrs. Castalia occasionally fell into mistakes.

"Could you not try Dr. Bodkin's wine-merchant?" suggested Miss Chubb. "I am no judge myself, but I feel sure that the doctor would not put bad wine on his table."

"Oh, I don't know. I don't suppose there is any first-rate wine to be got in this place. Ancram prefers dealing with the London man."

And then Castalia dismissed the subject with an expressive shrug. "Who are your chief friends here?" she asked of Rhoda, who had sat with her eyes fixed on a smart illustrated volume, scarcely seeing it, and feeling a confused sort of pain and mortification, at the tone in which the younger Mrs. Errington treated the elder.

"My chief friends?"

"Yes; you must know a great many people. You have lived here all your life, have you not?"

"Yes; but—father never cared that I should make many acquaintances out of doors."

"You were Methodists, were you not? I remember Ancram telling me of the psalm-singing that used to go on downstairs. He can imitate it wonderfully. Do tell me about how you lived, and what you did! I never knew any Methodists, nor any people who kept a shop."

The naïve curiosity with which this was said might have moved some minds to mirth, and others to indignation. In Rhoda it produced only confusion and distress, and such an access of shyness as made her for a few moments literally dumb. She murmured at length some unintelligible sentences, of which "I'm sure I don't know" were the only words that Castalia could make out. She did not on this account desist from her inquiries, but threw them into the more particular form of a catechism, as, "Were you let to read anything except the Bible on Sundays?" "I suppose you never went to a ball in your life?" "How did you learn to do your own hair?" "Do the Methodist preachers really rant and shriek as much as people say?"

Algernon, coming quietly into the room, beheld his wife and Rhoda seated side by side on a sofa behind the little Pembroke table, and engaged, apparently, in confidential conversation. They were so near together, and Castalia was bending down so low to hear Rhoda's faintly-uttered answers, as to give an air of intimacy to the group.

He lingered in the doorway looking at them, until Miss Chubb crying, "Oh, there you are, sir!" called the attention of the others to him, when he advanced and shook hands with Rhoda, whose fingers were icy cold as he touched them with his warm, white, exquisitely-cared-for hand. Then he bent to kiss his mother, and seated himself between her and his old friend Miss Chubb, in a low chair, stretching out his legs, and leaning back his head, as he contemplated the neatly-shod feet that were carelessly crossed in front of him.

"You did not expect to see Rhoda, did you, my dear boy?" said Mrs. Errington.

"Yes; I believe Castalia said something about having asked her. It is a new freak of Castalia's. I think she had better have left it alone. The old man is highly impracticable, and is just one of those persons whom it is prudent to keep at arm's length."

"I think so, too!" assented Mrs. Errington, emphatically. "Indeed, I almost wonder at his letting his daughter come here."

Algernon quite wondered at it. But he said nothing.

"Of course," pursued Mrs. Errington, "letting her come to me is a very different matter."

"Why?" asked Miss Chubb, bluntly.

"Because, my dear, the girl herself is so devotedly attached to me that I believe she would fret herself into an illness if she were forbidden to see me occasionally. And I believe old Maxfield is fond of his child, in his way, and would not wish to grieve her. But, of course, Rhoda can have no particular desire to visit Castalia. Indeed, I have offered to bring her more than once, and she has not availed herself of the opportunity."

"Old Max is ambitious for his daughter, they say," observed Miss Chubb, "and likes to get her into genteel company. Perhaps he thinks she will find a husband out of her own sphere. I'm told that old Max is quite rich, and that she will have all his money. But I think Rhoda is pretty enough to get well married, even without a fortune."

Then, when Mrs. Errington moved away to speak to her daughter-in-law, Miss Chubb whispered slily to Algernon, "You were a little bit smitten with our pretty Rhoda, once upon a time, sir, weren't you? Oh, it's no use your protesting and looking so unconscious! La, dear me; well, it was very natural! Calf-love, of course. But I'll tell you, between you and me, who is smitten with her, and pretty seriously too—and that's Mr. Diamond!"

"Diamond!"

"Well, you needn't look so astonished. He's a young man, for all his grave ways, and she is a pretty girl. And, upon my word, I think it might do capitally."

"You look tired, Algernon," said Mrs. Errington to her son a little later in the evening. It must have been a very marked expression of fatigue which could have attracted the good lady's attention in any other human being.

"Oh, I've been bored and worried at that confounded post-office."

"What a shame!" cried Mrs. Errington. "Positively some representation ought to be made to Government about it."

"Oh, it's disgusting!" said Castalia, with a shrug of her lean shoulders, and in the fretful drawl, which conveyed the idea that she would be actively angry if any sublunary matters could be important enough to overcome her habitual languor.

"I don't remember hearing that Mr. Cooper found the work so hard," said Miss Chubb, innocently. Mr. Cooper had been the Whitford postmaster next before Algernon.

"It isn't the work, Miss Chubb," said Algernon, a little ashamed of the amount of sympathy and compassion his words had evoked. "That is to say, it is not the quantity of the work, but the kind of it, that bores one. Cooper, I believe, was a steady, jog-trot old fellow, who did his daily task like a horse in a mill. But I can't take to it so comfortably. It is as if you, with your taste for elegant needlework, were set to hem dusters all day long!" Algernon laughed, in his old, frank way, as he made the comparison.

"Well, I shouldn't like that, certainly. But, after all, dusters are very useful things. And then, you see, I do the fancy work to amuse myself; but I should be paid for the dusters, and that makes a difference!"

"Paid!" screamed Castalia. "Why, you don't imagine that Ancram's twopenny salary can pay him! Good gracious, it seems to me scarcely enough to buy food with. It's quite horrible to think how poor we are!"

"Come," said Algernon, "I don't think this conversation is particularly lively or entertaining. Suppose we change the subject. There is Rho—Miss Maxfield looking as if she expected to see us all expire of inanition on the spot!"

And, in truth, Rhoda was gazing from one to the other with a pale, distressed face, and a look of surprise and compassion in her soft brown eyes.

Mrs. Errington did not approve of her daughter-in-law's unscrupulous confession of poverty. Castalia lacked the Ancram gift of embellishing disadvantageous circumstances. And the elder lady took occasion to remark to Miss Chubb that everything was comparative; and that means which might appear ample to persons of inferior rank were very trivial and inadequate in the eyes of the Honourable Mrs. Ancram Errington. "She has been her uncle's pet for many years. My lord denied her nothing. And I needn't tell you, my dear Miss Chubb, that the emoluments of Algernon's official post are by no means the whole and sole income of our young couple here. There are private resources"—here Mrs. Errington waved her hands majestically, as though to indicate the ample nature of the resources—"which, to many persons, would seem positive affluence. But Castalia's measure is a high one. I scold her sometimes, I assure you. 'My dear child,' I say to her, 'look at me! Bred amidst the feudal splendours of Ancram Park, I have accommodated myself to very different scenes and very different associates;' for, of course, my dear soul, although I have a great regard for my Whitford friends, and am very sensible of their kind feelings for me, yet, as a mere matter of fact, it would be absurd to pretend that the society I now move in is equal, in point of rank, to that which surrounded my girlish years. And then Castalia's perhaps partial estimate of her husband's talents (you know she has witnessed the impression they made in the most brilliant circles of the Metropolis) makes her impatient of his present position. For myself, feeling sure, as I do, that this post-office business is merely temporary, I can look at matters with more philosophy."

"Ouf!" panted Miss Chubb, and began to fan herself with her pocket-handkerchief.

"Anything the matter, Miss Chubb?" asked Algernon, raising his eyebrows and looking at her with a smile.

"Nothing particular, Algy. I find it a little oppressive, that's all."

"This little room is so stuffy with more than two or three people in it!" said Castalia.

"I'll do my part towards making it less stuffy," said Miss Chubb, jumping up, and beginning to shake hands all round. "I daresay my old Martha is there. I told her to come for me at nine o'clock. Oh, never mind, thank you," in answer to Castalia's suggestion that she should stay and have a cup of coffee, which would be brought in presently. "Never mind the coffee. I have no doubt I shall find a bit of supper ready at home." And with that she departed.

"I hope it wasn't too severe, that hit about the supper," said the good little woman to herself as she trotted homeward, accompanied by the faithful Martha. "But really—offering one a cup of coffee at nine o'clock at night! And as to Mrs. Errington, I am sorry for her, and can make allowances for her: but she did so go beyond all bounds to-night that, if I had not come away when I did, I think I should have choked."

"Is the little woman affronted at anything?" asked Algernon of his wife, when Miss Chubb's footsteps had ceased to be heard pattering down the gravel path outside the house.

"Eh? What little woman? Oh, the Chubb? No; I don't know. I suppose not."

"No, no; not at all," said Mrs. Errington, decisively. "But you know her ways of old. She has no savoir faire. A good little creature, poor soul! Oh, by-the-way, Castalia, you know the patterns for autumn mantles you asked me to look at? Well, I went into Ravell and Sarsnet's yesterday, and they told me—" And then the worthy matron and her daughter-in-law entered into an earnest discussion in an undertone; the common interest in autumn mantles supplying that "touch of nature" which made them kin more effectually than the matrimonial alliance that united their families.

"I'm afraid you must have had a very dull evening," said the master of the house, looking down on Rhoda as he stood near her, leaning with his back against the tiny mantel-shelf.

"No, thank you."

"I'm afraid you must! There was no amusement for you at all."

"My evenings are not generally very amusing. I daresay you, who have been accustomed to such different things, would find them very dull."

This was not the humble, simple, childlike Rhoda whom he had parted from two years ago. It was not that she had now no humility or simplicity, but the humility was mingled with dignity, the simplicity with an easier grace. Rhoda was more self-possessed at this moment than she had been all the evening before. The weakest creatures are not without some means of self-defence; and, if she be but pure-hearted, the most inexperienced girl in the world can put on an armour of maiden pride over her hurt feelings that has been known to puzzle even very intelligent individuals of the opposite sex; and has perhaps given rise to one or two of the numerous impassioned complaints that have been uttered from time to time as to the inscrutable duplicity of women. In like manner if a man scalds his finger, or gets a bullet in his flesh, he endeavours to bear the pain without screaming.

So little Rhoda Maxfield sat there with a placid face, talking to her old love, turning over the leaves of a picture-book, and scarcely looking at him as she talked.

Now, if Algernon had been consulted beforehand as to what line of conduct he would wish Rhoda to adopt when they should meet, he would, doubtless, have said, "Let us meet pleasantly and frankly as old friends, and behave as if all our old love-making had been the mere amusement of our childhood!" And yet, somehow, it a little disconcerted him to see her so calm.

"You—don't you—don't you go out much in the evening?" he said, feeling (to his own surprise) considerably at a loss what to say.

"Go out much in the evening? No, indeed; where should I go to?" Rhoda actually gave a little laugh as she answered him.

"Oh, I thought my mother mentioned that you were a good deal at the Bodkins."

"Yes; I go to see Miss Minnie sometimes. They are all very good to me."

"And my mother says, too, that you are growing quite a blue-stocking! You have lessons in French, and music, and I don't know what besides."

"Father can afford to have me taught now, and so I have begun to learn a few of the things that girls are taught when they are little children, if they happen to be the children of gentlefolks," answered Rhoda, with considerable spirit.

"I'm sure there is no reason why you should not learn them."

"I hope not. But, of course, I am clumsy, and shall never succeed so well as if I had begun earlier. I am getting very old, you know!"

"Oh, very old, indeed! Your birthday, I remember, falls—" he checked himself with a sudden recollection of the last birthday he had spent with Rhoda, and of the bunch of late roses he had been at the pains to procure for her on that occasion from the gardener at Pudcombe Hall. And, on the whole, he felt positively relieved when Slater came to announce, with her chronic air of resentful gentility, that "Miss Maxfield's young woman was waiting for her in the hall."

"And are you off too, mother?" he asked.

"Yes, my dear Algernon. I am going to drive home with Rhoda."

"Drive! Oh, so you are indulging in the extravagance of a fly, madam! I am glad of it, though you did give me a lecture on the subject of economy only last week!"

"You know that I always do, and always did, disapprove of extravagance, Algernon. A genteel economy is compatible with the highest breeding. But—the fact is, that Rhoda has a coach to go home in, and I'm about to take advantage of it."

There was something in the situation which Algernon felt to be embarrassing, as he gave his arm to his mother to lead her to the carriage. But Mrs. Errington had at least one quality of a great lady—she was not easily disconcerted. She marched majestically down the garden path, entered the vehicle which old Max's money was to pay for, with an air of proprietorship, and invited Rhoda to take her place beside her with a most condescending wave of the hand.

"You must come again soon," Castalia had said to her new acquaintance when they bade each other "Good night."

But Algernon did not support his wife's invitation by a single word, though he smiled very persistently as he stood bare-headed in the moonlight, watching his mother and Rhoda drive away.

CHAPTER XIII.

The accounts which had reached Whitford from Wales, of the wonderful effects produced by David Powell's preaching there, sufficed to cause a good deal of excitement among the lower classes in the little town, when it was reported that Powell would revisit it, and would preach on Whit Meadow, and also in the room used by the "Ranters," in Lady Lane.

The Wesleyan Methodists in Whitford now felt themselves at liberty to allow their smouldering animosity against Powell to break forth openly, for he had seceded from the Society. Some said he had been expelled from it, but this was not true, although there was little doubt that, at the next Conference, his conduct and doctrine would have been severely reprehended; and, probably, he would have been required publicly to recant them on pain of expulsion. Should this be the case, those who knew David Powell had little difficulty in prophesying the issue. However, all speculations as to his probable behaviour under the reproof of Conference were rendered vain by the preacher's voluntarily withdrawing himself from the "bonds of the Society," as he phrased it.

Then broke forth the hostile sentiments of the Whitford Wesleyans against this rash and innovating preacher. Unfavourable opinions of him, which had been concealed, or only dimly expressed, were now declared openly. He was an Antinomian; he had fallen away from the doctrines of Assurance and Christian Perfection; he had brought scandal on large bodies of sober, serious persons, by encouraging wild and extravagant manifestations among his hearers; his exhortations were calculated to do harm, inasmuch as he preached a doctrine of asceticism and self-renunciation, which, if followed, would have the most inconvenient consequences. That some of these accusations—as, for example, that of Antinomianism, and that of too extreme self-mortification—were somewhat incompatible with each other, was no impediment to their being heaped simultaneously on David Powell. The strongest disapprobation of his sayings and doings was expressed by that select body of citizens who attended at the little Wesleyan chapel. And yet there was, perhaps, less bitterness in this open opposition to him than had been felt towards him during the last days of his ministration in Whitford. So long as David Powell was their preacher, approved—or, at least, not disapproved—by Conference, a struggle went on in some minds to reconcile his teaching with their practice, which was an irritating and unsatisfactory state of things, since the struggle in most cases was not so much to modify their practice, in order to bring it into harmony with his precepts, as ingeniously to interpret his precepts so that they should not too flagrantly accuse their practice. But now that it was competent to the stanchest Methodist to reject Powell's authority altogether, these unprofitable efforts ceased, and with them a good deal of resentment.

The chorus of openly-expressed hostility to the preacher, which, I have said, made itself heard in Whitford, arose, in a great measure, from the common delight in declaring, where some circumstances unforeseen by the world in general comes to pass, that we perceived all along how matters would go, and knew our neighbour to be a very different fellow from what you took him to be.

Here old Max was triumphant; and, it must be owned, with more reason than many of his acquaintances. He had openly quarrelled with this fanatical Welshman, long before the main body of the Whitford Wesleyans had ventured to repudiate him.

One humble friend was faithful to the preacher. The widow Thimbleby maintained, in the teeth of all opposition, that, though Mr. Powell might be a little mistaken here and there on points of doctrine—she was an ignorant woman, and couldn't judge of these things—yet his practice came very near perfection; and that the only human being to whom he ever showed severity, intolerance, and lack of love was himself. Mrs. Thimbleby was not strong in controversy. It was not difficult to push her to her last resort—namely, crying silently behind her apron. But there was some tough fibre of loyalty in the meek creature which made it impossible for her to belie her conscience by deserting David Powell. The cold attic at the top of her little house was prepared for his reception as soon as it was known that he was about to revisit Whitford; and Mrs. Thimbleby went to the loft over the corn-dealer's store-house in Lady Lane one Sunday evening to beg that Nick Green would let Mr. Powell know, whenever he should arrive, that his old quarters were waiting for him, and that she would take it as a personal unkindness if he did not consent to occupy them. She could not help talking of the preacher to her grand lodger Mrs. Errington, of whom she was considerably in awe. The poor woman's heart was full at the thought of seeing him again. And not even Mrs. Errington's lofty severity regarding all dissenters and "ignorant persons who flew in the face of Providence and attempted to teach their betters," could entirely stifle her expressions of anxiety as to Mr. Powell's health, her hopes that he took a little more care of himself than he formerly did, and her anecdotes of his angelic charity and goodness towards the poor, and needy, and suffering.

"I should advise you on no account to go and hear this man preach," said Mrs. Errington to her landlady. "Terrible scenes have taken place in Wales; and very likely something of the kind may happen here. You are very weak, my poor soul. You have no force of character. You would be sure to catch any excitement that was going. And how should you like, pray, to be brought home from Lady Lane on a stretcher?"

But even this alarming suggestion did not deter Mrs. Thimbleby from haunting the "Ranters'" meeting-room, and leaving message after message with Nick Green to be sure and tell Mr. Powell to come up to her house, the very minute he arrived. Nick Green knew no more than the widow the day and hour of the preacher's arrival. All he could say was, that Powell had applied to him and to his co-religionists for leave to preach in the room—little more than a loft—which they rented of the corn-dealer in Lady Lane. Powell had been refused permission to speak in the Wesleyan chapel to which his eloquence had formerly attracted such crowds of listeners. Whit Meadow would, indeed, be probably open to him; but the year was drawing on apace, autumn would soon give place to winter, and, at all events in the evening, it would be vain to hope for a large number of listeners in the open air.

"Open air!" echoed Mrs. Thimbleby, raising her hands and eyes; "why, Mr. Green, he ought never to think of preaching in the open air at this season, and him so delicate!"

"Nay, sister Thimbleby," responded Nick Green, a powerful, black-muzzled fellow with a pair of lungs like a blacksmith's bellows, "we may not put our hand to the plough and turn back. We are all of us called upon to give ourselves body and soul in the Lord's service. And many's the night, after my day's work was over, that I've exhorted here in this very room and poured out the Word for two and three hours at a stretch, until the sweat ran down my face like water, and the brethren were fairly worn out. But yet I have been marvellously strengthened. I doubt not that Brother Powell will be so too, especially now that he has given up dead words, and the errors of the Society, and thrown off the yoke of the law."

"Dear, I hope so," answered Mrs. Thimbleby, tremulously; "but I do wish he would try a hot posset of a night, just before going to bed."

The good woman was beginning to walk away up Lady Lane, somewhat disconsolately, for she reflected that if Nick Green measured Mr. Powell's strength by his own, he would surely not spare it, and that the preacher needed rather a curb than a spur to his self-forgetting exertions, when she almost ran against a man who was coming in the opposite direction. They were not twenty paces from the door of the corn-dealer's store-house, and a lamp that burnt above it shed sufficient light for her to recognise the face of the very person who was in her thoughts.

"Mr. Powell!" she exclaimed in a joyful tone. "Thanks be to the Lord that I have met you! Was you going to look for Mr. Green? He is just putting the lights out and coming away. I left a message with him for you, sir; but now I can give it you myself. You will come up with me to my house, now, won't you? Everything is ready, and has been these three days. You wouldn't think of going anywhere else in Whitford but to my house, would you, Mr. Powell?"

She ran on thus eagerly, because she saw, or fancied she saw, symptoms of opposition to her plan in Powell's face. He hesitated. "My good friend," said he, "your Christian kindness is very precious to me, but I am not clear that I should do right in becoming an inmate of your house."

"Oh, but I am, Mr. Powell, quite clear! Why it would be a real unkindness to refuse me."

"It is not a matter to be settled thus lightly," answered Powell, although at the same time he turned and walked a few paces by the widow's side. "I had thought that I might sleep for to-night at least in our friends' meeting-room."

"What! in the loft there? Lord ha' mercy, Mr. Powell! 'Tis cold and draughty, and there's nothing in it but a few wooden benches, and the rats run about as bold as can be, directly the lights is put out. Why 't would be a tempting of Providence, Mr. Powell."

"I am not dainty about my accommodation, as you know; and I could sleep there without payment."

"Without payment! Why, you might pay pretty dear for it in health, if not in money. And, for that matter, I shouldn't think of asking a penny of rent for my attic, as long as ever you choose to stay in it." Then, with an instinctive knowledge of the sort of plea that might be likely to prevail with him, she added, "As for being dainty about your accommodation, why I know you never were so, and I hope you haven't altered, for, indeed, the attic is sadly uncomfortable. I think there's worse draughts from the window than ever. And it would be a benefit to me to get the room aired and occkypied; for only last week I had a most respectable young man, a journeyman painter, to look at it, and he say, 'Mrs. Thimbleby, we shan't disagree about the rent,' he say; 'but I do wish the room had been slept in latterly; for I've a fear as it's damp,' he say, 'and that that's the reason you don't use it yourself, nor haven't let it.' But I tell him the only reason why I didn't use the room was as you might be expected back any day, and I couldn't let you find your place taken. And he say if he could be satisfied of that, he may take it after next month, when you would likely be gone again. So you see as you would be doing me a service, Mr. Powell, not to say a pleasure."

Whether David Powell implicitly believed the good creature's argument to be derived from fact, may be doubtful; but he suffered himself to be persuaded to accompany her to his old lodgings; and they begged Nick Green, who presently overtook them, to send one of his lads to the coach-office, to bring to Mrs. Thimbleby's the small battered valise which constituted all Powell's luggage.

"I would have gone to fetch it myself," said the preacher, apologetically, "but, in truth, I am so exceedingly weary, that I doubt whether my strength would avail to carry even that slender burden the distance from the coach-office to your house."

When he was seated beside Mrs. Thimbleby's clean kitchen hearth, on which burned a fire of unwontedly generous proportions—the widow declared that, as she grew older, she found it necessary to her health to have a glow of warmth in her kitchen these chilly autumn nights—when the preacher was thus seated, I say, and when the red and yellow firelight illuminated his face fully, it was very evident that he was indeed "exceeding weary;" weary, and worn, and wan, with hollow temples, eyes that blazed feverishly, and a hue of startling pallor overspreading his whole countenance. For a few minutes, whilst his good hostess moved about hither and thither in the little kitchen, preparing some tea, and slicing some bacon, to be presently fried for his refection, Powell sat looking straight before him, with a curious expression in his widely-opened eyes, something like that of a sleep-walker. They were evidently seeing nothing of the physical realities around them, and yet they unmistakably expressed the attentive recognition by the mind of some image painted on their wondrous spheres. The true round mirror of the wizard is that magic ball of sight; for on its sensitive surface live and move a thousand airy phantoms, besides the reflection of all that peoples this tangible earth we dwell on. Powell's lips began to move rapidly, although no sound came from them. He seemed to be addressing a creature visible to him alone, on which his straining gaze was fixed. But suddenly his face changed, and was troubled as a still pool is troubled by a ripple that breaks its clearly glazed reflection into fantastic fragments. In another moment he passed his thin hand several times with a strong pressure over his brows, shut and opened his eyes like a dreamer awakened, drew his pocket Bible from his breast, and began to read with an air of resolute attention.

"Will you ask a blessing, Mr. Powell?" said the widow timidly.

He looked up. A comfortable meal was spread on the white deal table before him. Mrs. Thimbleby sat opposite to him in her old chair with the patch-work cushions; the fire shone; the household cat purred drowsily; the old clock clicked off the moments as they flowed past—tick tack, tick tack. Then there came a jar, a burr of wheels and springs, and the tinkle of silver-toned metal striking nine. In a few moments the ancient belfry of St. Chad's began to send forth its mellow chimes. Far and wide they sounded—over the town and the flat-meadow country—through the darkness. Powell sat still and silent, listening to the bells until they had done chiming.

"How well I know those voices!" he said. "I used to lie awake and listen to them here, in the old attic, when my soul was wrestling with a mighty temptation; when my heart was smitten and withered like grass, so that I forgot to eat my bread. The sound of them is sweet to the fleshly ears of the body; but to the ears of the spirit they can say marvellous things. They have been the instruments to bring me many a message of counsel as they came singing and buzzing in my brain."

The widow Thimbleby sat looking at the preacher, as he spoke, with an expression of puzzled admiration, blended with anxiety.

"Oh, for certain the Lord has set a sign on you!" she exclaimed. "He would have us to know that you are a chosen vessel, and He has given you the gifts of the spirit in marvellous abundance. But, dear Mr. Powell, I doubt He does not mean you to neglect the fleshly tabernacle neither; for, as I say to myself, He could ha' made us all soul and no body, if such had been His blessed will."

"We thank Thee, O Father, most merciful. Amen!" said Powell, bending over the table.

"Amen!" repeated Mrs. Thimbleby. "And now pray do fall to, and eat something, for I'm sure you need it."

"It is strange; but, though I have fasted since five o'clock this morning, I feel no hunger."

"Mercy me! fasting since five o'clock this morning? Why, for sure, that's the very reason you can't eat! Your stomach is too weak. Dear, dear, dear; but you must make an effort to swallow something, sir. Drink a sup of tea."

Powell complied with her entreaty, although he expressed some misgiving as to the righteousness of his partaking of so luxurious a beverage. And then he ate a few mouthfuls of food, but evidently without appetite. But seeing his good friend's uneasiness on his behalf, he said, with the rare smile which so brightened his countenance:

"Do not be so concerned for me. There is no need. Although I have not much replenished the carnal man to-day, yet have I been abundantly refreshed and comforted. I tarried in a small town on the borders of this county at midday, and I found that my ministrations there in the spring season had borne fruit. Many who had been reclaimed from evil courses came about me, and we gave thanks with much uplifting of the heart. And, although I had suffered somewhat from faintness before arriving at that place, yet, no sooner were these chosen persons got about me, and I began to pray and praise, than I felt stronger and more able for exertion than I have many a time felt after a long night's rest and an abundant meal."

Poor Mrs. Thimbleby's mind was divided and "exercised," as she herself would have said, between her reverent faith in Powell's being supported by the supernal powers and her rooted conviction regarding the virtues of a hot posset. Was it for her, a poor, ignorant woman, presumptuously to supplement, as it were, the protection of Providence, and to insist on the saintly preacher's drinking her posset? Yet, on the other hand, arose her own powerful argument, that the Lord might have dispensed with our bodies altogether had it so pleased him; and that therefore, mankind being provided with those appendages, it was but reasonable to conclude they were meant to be taken some care of. At length the widow's mental debatings resulted in a resolution to make the hot posset, and carry it up to the preacher's bedside without consulting him on the subject—"For," said she to herself, "if I persuade him to swallow it out of kindness to me, there'll be no sin in the matter. Or, at least, if there is, it will be my sin, and not his; and that is not of so much consequence."

In this spirit of true feminine devotion she acted, and having coaxed Powell to swallow the cordial mixture—as a mother might coax a sick child—she had the satisfaction of seeing him fall into a deep slumber, he being, in truth, exhausted by fatigue, excitement, and lack of nourishment.

CHAPTER XIV.

Among the first persons to hear of David Powell's return to Whitford, and his intention of preaching there, was Miss Bodkin. As the spectators see more of the play than the actors, so Minnie, from her couch or her lounging-chair, witnessed many a scene in its entirety, which those who performed it were only conscious of in a fragmentary manner. The news of the little town was brought to her through many various channels. Her infirmity seemed to set her in a place apart, and many a one was willing to play the part of Chorus for her behoof, and interpret the drama after his or her own fashion.

Minnie's maid, Jane Gibbs; Mrs. Errington; and Mr. Diamond, had all given her the news about Mr. Powell; and all in different keys, and with such variations of detail as universally attend contemporaneous vivâ voce transmissions.

Jane Gibbs had a strong feeling of respect and gratitude towards the preacher for his having "converted" her brother. And, being herself a member of the Church of England, she looked upon his secession from the main body of the Methodists with great leniency. She dared to say that Mr. Powell would do as much good in Lady Lane as he had done in the Wesleyan Chapel. And seeing that whether you called 'em Wesleyans, or Ranters, or Baptists, or Quakers, or Calvinists, they were all Dissenters, it could not so much matter whether they disagreed among each other or not.

Mrs. Errington, without entering into that question, considered herself peculiarly aggrieved by the circumstance that Powell had come to lodge in the same house with her. "I am doomed, it seems, to be a victim to that man!" said she to Minnie Bodkin. "At Maxfield's house I was frequently disturbed by his hymns and his preachments; and even now, it appears, I am not to escape from him. He absorbs Mrs. Thimbleby's attention to a ludicrous extent. If you will credit the fact, my dear Minnie, only yesterday morning my egg was sent up at breakfast greatly over-boiled; and when I remonstrated with Mrs. Thimbleby on this piece of negligence, what excuse do you suppose she made? She answered that she was very sorry, but she had been getting ready a 'little snack'—that was her expression—for Mr. Powell after his early preaching, and it had slipped her memory that my breakfast-egg was still in the saucepan! I have no doubt the man stuffs and crams himself at her cost. All these dissenting preachers do, my dear."

Whereunto Minnie answered gravely, that it was a great comfort to Church people to reflect that moderation in eating and drinking was entirely confined to the orthodox clergy.

Mr. Diamond, again, took a different and more sympathising view of the poor preacher. But even he was very far from entertaining the same exalted admiration for Powell's character as was felt by Minnie. Matthew Diamond had an Englishman's ingrained antipathy to the uncontrolled display of feeling, from which Powell's Welsh blood by no means revolted. Diamond could never divest himself of a lurking notion that no man would publicly exhibit deep emotion if he could help it; and consequently he looked on all such exhibitions as rather pitiable manifestations of infirmity, or else as mere clap-trap and play-acting. Of the latter it was impossible to suspect Powell. Diamond had the touchstone of truthfulness within himself; and it sufficed to convince him that the preacher, however wild and mistaken, was sincere. "Yes," he said to Miss Bodkin, "there can be no doubt that the man's soul is as clear from guile as an infant's. But it is a pity he cannot suppress the outbursts of enthusiasm which exhaust him so much."

"He does not wish to suppress them," answered Minnie. "He looks on them as a means specially vouchsafed to him for moving others, and—to use his own words—saving souls. Some sober, sensible persons remind me, when they speak of David Powell, of a covey of barn-door fowls, complacently staring up at a lark, and exclaiming, 'Poor creature, how unpleasant it must be for it to have to soar and gyrate in that giddy fashion; and making that shrill noise all the time, too! How it must envy us our constitutions!'"

"I suppose I am one of the barn-door fowls, Miss Bodkin?"

"Well—perhaps! Or, rather, you have lived among them until it seems to you that higher-flying creatures have something a little ridiculous about them. And you forcibly restrain any upward tendencies of wing—at least in the presence of your mates of the barn-door."

"I am flattered to be credited with some upward tendencies, at any rate! But, Miss Bodkin, to drop metaphor, in which I cannot attempt to compete with you, I must be allowed to maintain that Powell's outbursts of excitement are neither good for himself nor others. They are morbid, and not the healthy expression of a healthy nature, like the lark's singing and soaring."

"You have seen Powell since his return. How does he seem to be in health?"

"In bodily health not, perhaps, so much amiss, although he is greatly emaciated and startlingly pale. But his mind is in a strange state."

"He was always enthusiastic."

"He is enthusiastic for others, but as regards himself his mind is a prey to overwhelming gloom. I see a great change for the worse in him in that respect."

Minnie felt a strong desire to see the preacher again. She compassionated him from her heart, and thought she might be able to administer some comfort to him, as regarded Rhoda Maxfield. There were days when Minnie was able to walk from one room to another with the assistance of a crutched stick; and it occurred to her that if Mrs. Thimbleby would allow her house to be made the place of meeting, she might see and speak with Powell there more privately, and with less danger of exciting gossiping remark, than elsewhere. Minnie had once or twice latterly driven to the widow Thimbleby's house to see Mrs. Errington, or leave a message for her, although she had never mounted to her sitting-room. For the ladder-like staircase, which was an imaginary difficulty in the way of Castalia's visits to her mother-in-law, was a very real obstacle to Minnie Bodkin.

The project of seeing Powell in this way took possession of her mind. She sent a note to Mrs. Thimbleby, by her maid Jane, asking at what hour Mr. Powell was most likely to be in the house; and saying that she should like to come there and say a few words to him about a person in whose welfare he was interested.

The widow saw nothing very singular in this. She knew that Powell had been to see Miss Bodkin before he left Whitford. And it was quite in accordance with the known characters of the Methodist preacher and the rector's daughter that they should meet and combine on the common ground of charity. "For sure Mr. Powell have recommended some poor afflicted person to the young lady, and she have assisted 'em, whosoever they may be!" thought Mrs. Thimbleby. "And she begs me not to mention her coming to anybody. For sure and certain she's not one o' them as boasts of their good deeds. No, no; like our blessed Mr. Powell, she don't let her left hand know what her right hand doeth. I wonder if she's under conviction! Such a good, charitable lady, it seems as if she must belong to the elect. But, there, all our good works are filthy rags, I s'pose, the best on us. But I can't help thinking as Miss Bodkin's works must be more pleasing to the Lord than Brother Jackson's, as lives among the Wesleyans on the fat of the land, and don't do much in return, except condemning all those folks as isn't Wesleyans. Lord forgive me if I'm wrong!"

Mrs. Thimbleby returned a verbal message to Miss Bodkin, as the latter had desired her to do: Mrs. Thimbleby's duty, and the most likely time would be between four and five o'clock in the afternoon; and she would be sure to obey Miss Bodkin's instructions. "And I'm ever so much obliged to her for excusing me writing, my dear," said the widow to Jane; "for my hands is so stiff and rough with hard work, as holding a pen seems to be a great difficulty. I'd far rather mop out my back yard any day than write the receipt for the lodgers' rent. And 'tis but a smudgy business when all's done."

On the following day Dr. Bodkin's sober green carriage, drawn by a stout, sober-paced horse, was seen standing at Mrs. Thimbleby's door. It was a few minutes after four o'clock in the afternoon. The street was very quiet. There was scarcely a passer-by to be seen from one end of it to the other, when Jane and the old man-servant assisted Miss Bodkin to alight from the carriage, and supported her into the clean, flagged room on the ground floor, which served Mrs. Thimbleby for parlour, kitchen, and dining-hall, all in one. The coachman had orders to return and fetch his young mistress at six o'clock. "Will you give me house-room so long, Mrs. Thimbleby?" asked Minnie with a sweet smile, which so captivated the good woman that she stood staring at her visitor in a kind of rapture, unable to reply for a minute or two.

Minnie was placed in Mrs. Thimbleby's own high-backed chair, with the clean patchwork-covered cushions piled behind her. A horsehair footstool, borrowed for the purpose from Mr. Diamond's parlour, was under her feet. And she declared that she found herself as comfortable as in her own lounging-chair at home.

"You see, miss, I couldn't say to the minute when Mr. Powell would be back, but between four and five he generally do come in, and I make him swallow a cup of herb tea, or something. And I will not deny that I sometimes puts a pinch of China tea in. But he don't know. This is but a poor place, miss," added the widow, glancing round, "but so long as you can make yourself content to stay in it, so long you will be welcome as the flowers in May, if 'twas to be for a twelvemonth?"

Then Minnie praised the brilliant cleanliness of the little kitchen, took notice of the cat that rubbed its velvet head confidingly against her hand, and asked Mrs. Thimbleby how she prospered in her lodging-letting.

The widow was loquacious in her mild slow way; and she was pleased at this opportunity for a little harmless gossip. It was a propensity which received frequent checks from those around her. Mr. Diamond was too taciturn, too grave, too much absorbed in his books, to give any heed to his landlady's conversation, beyond listening to the few particulars of his weekly expenses, which she insisted on explaining to him. Mrs. Errington, on the other hand, was not at all taciturn, but she desired to have the talk chiefly to herself. She loved to harangue Mrs. Thimbleby on a variety of subjects, and to place, in vivid colours before her, the inadequacy of all her domestic arrangements to satisfy a lady of Mrs. Errington's quality. As to gossiping with David Powell, Mrs. Thimbleby would as soon have thought of attempting to gossip with the sculptured figure of a saint, which stood in a niche at one side of the portal of St. Chad's! So the good woman, finding Miss Bodkin more compliant and affable than the two first-named of her lodgers, and nearer to the level of common humanity than the last, indulged herself with an outpouring of chat, as the two sat waiting for Powell's return.

Minnie listened to her at first with but a drowsy kind of attention. Her own thoughts were wandering away from the present time and place. And, for a while, the quiet of the room, where the gathering twilight seemed to bring a deeper hush, was only broken by the monotonous murmur of the widow's voice. But by-and-by Mrs. Thimbleby spoke words which effectually aroused Minnie's attention.

There was, she said, a deal of talk in Whitford about young Mr. Errington. He was such a very nice-spoken gentleman, and most people seemed to like him so much! But yet he had enemies in the town. Folks said he was extravagant. And his wife gave herself such airs as there was no bearing with 'em; she not paying ready money, but almost expecting tradespeople to be satisfied with the honour of serving her. Poor lady, she wasn't used to be pinched for money herself, and knew no better, most likely! But many Whitford shopkeepers grumbled as Mr. Errington got goods on credit from them, and yet sent orders to London with ready money for expensive articles, and it didn't seem fair. There was no use saying anything to old Mrs. Errington about the matter, because, though she was, no doubt, a very good-hearted lady, she was rather "high." And if you mentioned to her, as Mr. Gladwish, the shoemaker, said, unpleasant things about her son's bill, why she would tell you that her grandfather drove four horses to his coach, and that Mr. Algernon's wife's uncle was a great nobleman up in London, as paid his butler a bigger salary than all Gladwish could earn in a year. And if such sayings got abroad, they would not be soothing to the feelings of a respectable shoemaker, would they now? Not to say that they wouldn't help to pay Gladwish's bill; nor yet the fly bill at the "Blue Bell;" nor yet the bill for young madam at Ravell and Sarsnet's; nor yet the bill at the fishmonger and poulterer's; as she (Mrs. Thimbleby) was credibly informed that Ivy Lodge consumed the best of everything, and at a great rate. In the beginning, tradespeople believed all that was said about young Mr. and Mrs. Errington's fine friends and fine prospects, and seemed inclined to trust 'em to any amount. But latterly there had growed up a feeling against 'em. And—if Miss Bodkin wouldn't think it a liberty in her to ask her not to mention it again, seeing it was but a guess on her part—she would go so far as to say that she believed an enemy was at work, and that enemy old

Jonathan Maxfield. Why or wherefore old Max should be so set against young Mr. Algernon, as he had known him from a little child, she could not say. But there was rumours about that young Errington owed old Max money. And old Max was that near and fond of his pelf, as nothing was so likely to make him mad against any one as losing money by 'em; and old Max was a harsh man and a bitter where he took a dislike. Only see how he had persecuted Mr. Powell! And though he let his daughter go to Ivy Lodge—and they did say young Mrs. Errington had taken quite a fancy to the girl—yet that didn't prevent old Max sneering and snarling, and saying all manner of sharp words against the Erringtons. And old Max was a man of substance, and his words had weight in the town. "And you see, miss," said Mrs. Thimbleby, in conclusion, "young Mr. and Mrs. Errington are gentlefolks, and they don't hear what's said in Whitford, and they may think things are all right when they're all wrong. Of course, I daresay they have great friends and good prospects, miss. And very likely they could settle everything to-morrow if they thought fit. Only the tale here is, that not a tradesman in the place has seen the colour of their money, and they deny theirselves nothing, and the lady so high in her manners, and altogether there is a feeling against 'em, miss. And as I know you're a old friend, and a kind friend, I'm sure, and not one as takes pleasure in the troubles of their neighbours, I thought I would mention it to you, in case you should like to say a word to the young lady and gentleman private-like. A word from you would have a deal of weight. And I do assure you, miss, 'tis of no use trying to speak to old Mrs. Errington, for she'll only go on about her grandfather's coach-and-four; and, between you and me, miss, there is some as takes it amiss."

All this pained and surprised Minnie. She understood at once how Castalia's ungracious manner was resented in the little town; and set down a great deal of the hostility which the widow had described to the score of the Honourable Mrs. Algernon's personal unpopularity.

Still there must be something seriously wrong at Ivy Lodge. Debt was a Slough of Despond into which such a one as Algernon Errington would easily put his foot, from sheer thoughtlessness and the habit of refusing himself no gratification within his reach. But he might not find it so easy to extricate himself. A word of warning might possibly do good. At least it could do no harm, beyond drawing forth some languid impertinence from Castalia. And Minnie would not for an instant weigh that chance against the hope of doing some good to her old friend Algy.

Besides, in truth, she had, as has been said, an undefined feeling of compassion for Castalia herself, which rendered her singularly forbearing towards the latter's manifestations of fretful jealousy or haughty dislike. In the first days of his return to Whitford Algernon had many a time shot one of his quick, questioning glances at Minnie, when his wife uttered some coolly insolent speech, directed at, rather than to, the rector's daughter. But instead of the keen sarcasm, or scornful irony, which he had expected, Minnie had, nine times out of ten, replied with a quiet matter-of-fact observation calculated to extinguish anything like a war of words. At first Algernon had attributed such forbearance on the part of the brilliant, high-spirited Minnie entirely to her strong regard for himself. But this flattering illusion did not last long. He soon perceived that Minnie regarded his wife with pity, and that she refrained from using the keen weapons of her wit against Castalia, much as a nurse might refrain from scolding or arguing with a sick child.

Now this discovery was not pleasant to Algernon. If any sympathy were to be expended on the inmates of Ivy Lodge, he was persuaded that much the larger share of it ought to be given to himself. If there were troubles; if there were mortifications; if there was disappointment—who suffered from them as he did? And by whom were they so unmerited? He was not far, sometimes, from resenting any show of compassion for Castalia as a direct injury to himself. After having sacrificed himself, by making a marriage so inadequate to his deserts, it was a little too much to hear his wife pitied for the contrast between her past and present position?

And yet, by a queer strain of inconsistency running through the warp and woof of his character, he would often boast of Castalia's aristocratic antecedents, and ask, with a smile and a shrug, how the deuce his wife could be expected to stand the petty privations and discomforts of Whitford, after having lived all her life in a sphere as remote from such things as the planet Saturn from the earth?

Minnie partly saw, partly guessed, these movements of Algernon's mind. But she judged him with leniency, and put a kind interpretation on his words and ways, whenever such an interpretation was possible. At all events, if a word in season could be useful to him, she would not refrain from speaking that word.

This young woman had latterly passed into regions of thought and feeling, from which much of her old life, with its old pains, and pleasures, and aims, seemed shrunken into insignificance. One solid good she was able to grasp and to enjoy; the satisfaction of serving her fellow-creatures. All else grew poor and paltry as the years rolled by.

Not that Minnie had attained to any saint-like heights of self-abnegation; not that she did not still "desire and admire" many sublunary things. But she had got a hurt that had stricken down her pride. She bore an ache in her heart for which "self-culture," and all the activities and aspirations of her bright intellect, afforded no balm.

But she did not grow sour and selfish in her grief. The example of the poor, unlettered Methodist preacher (whom in former days she would have thought the unlikeliest of human beings to teach her any profitable lesson) had roused the noblest part of her nature to emulation. David Powell had started from a lofty theory to a life of beautiful deeds. Minnie Bodkin, vaguely groping after a theory, had seized on practical benevolence as a means to climb to some higher ideal.

In morals, as in thought, the Deductive and Inductive stand, like the ladders of Jacob's dream, reaching from heaven to earth, from earth to heaven; and the angels of the Lord descend and ascend them continually.

Minnie was roused from a reverie by the entrance of the preacher's tall figure into the kitchen, where the fire was now beginning to throw ruddy lights and fantastic shadows on to the white-washed walls.

"Don't be startled, Mr. Powell," she said, in her clear, sweet tones. "It is I—Minnie Bodkin. I thought I should like to see you, and to say a few words to you, quietly."

Powell advanced, and took her outstretched hand reverently in his hand. "The blessing of our Father in Heaven be on you, lady," he said. "Your kind face is very welcome to me."

CHAPTER XV.

Mrs. Thimbleby set a cup full of hot tea and a slice of bread on the table, and glided out of the kitchen in a humble, noiseless way, as if she feared lest the mere sound of her footsteps should be deemed importunate.

"You have something to say to me?" asked Powell, still standing opposite to Minnie's chair.

"Yes; but first you must take some food. Please to sit down there at the table."

Powell shook his head. "Food disgusts me," he said. "I do not need it."

"That will pain your kind landlady," said Minnie, gently. "She has been so careful to get this refreshment ready for you."

Powell sat down. "I would not pain the good soul for any earthly consideration," he answered. "But if the burthen be laid on me, I must pain her."

"Come, Mr. Powell, no injunction can be laid on you to starve yourself, and grow ill, and be unable to fulfil your duties!"

After an instant's hesitation he swallowed some tea, and began to break off small fragments of the bread, which he soaked in the liquid, and ate slowly.

Minnie watched him attentively. The widow had lighted a candle, which, standing on the high mantel-shelf, shed down its pale rays on the preacher's head and face, the rest of his person being in shadow. Now and again, as he lifted a morsel of bread to his lips, one thin long hand, yellow-white as old ivory, came within the circle of light. His whole countenance appeared to Minnie to have undergone a change since she had seen him last. The features were sharper, the skin more sallow, the lines around the mouth deeper. But the greatest change was in the expression of the eyes. They were wonderfully lustrous, but not with the soft mild lustre which formerly shone in them. They looked startlingly large and prominent; and at times seemed literally to blaze with an inward fire.

"He is ill and feverish," thought Minnie. And then, as she continued to watch him, there came over his face an expression so infinitely piteous, that the sympathetic tears sprang into her eyes when she saw it. It was a pathetic, questioning, bewildered look, like that of a little child that has lost its way, and is frightened.

When he had eaten a few mouthfuls, he asked, "Who told you that you would find me here?"

"Oh, it was not difficult to discover your whereabouts in Whitford, Mr. Powell," answered Minnie, smiling with an effort to seem cheerful and at ease. "Your coming has been spoken of in our little town for weeks past."

"Has it so? Has it so? That is a good hearing. There must be souls ripe for conviction—anxious, inquiring souls."

There was a pause. Minnie had expected him to speak of their last interview. But as he made no allusion to it, she opened the subject herself.

"You remember, Mr. Powell, before you went away from Whitford, giving me a charge—a trust to fulfil for you?"

He looked at her inquiringly, but did not answer.

"There was a young member of your flock whose welfare you had greatly at heart. And you thought that I might be able to help her and show her some kindness. I—I have honestly tried to keep the promise I then made to you," persisted Minnie, on whom Powell's strange silence was producing an unpleasant impression. She could not understand it. "I fancied that you might still feel some anxiety about Rhoda's welfare—"

At the sound of that name, Powell seemed moved as if by an electric shock. The change in his face was as distinct, although as momentary, as the change made in a dark bank of cloud by a flicker of summer lightning.

"You know, of course," continued Minnie, "that the person whose influence you feared is married. And I assure you that, so far as my attentive judgment goes, Rhoda's peace of mind has not been fatally troubled. She fretted for a while, but is now rapidly regaining her cheerfulness. She even visits rather frequently at Mr. Errington's house, having, it seems, become a favourite with his wife."

David Powell's head had sunk down on to his breast. He held one hand across his eyes, resting his elbow on the table, and neither moving nor looking up. But it was evident that he was listening. Minnie went on to speak of Rhoda's improvement. She had always been pretty, but her beauty was now very striking. She had profited by the opportunities of instruction which her father afforded her. She was caressed by the worthiest people in her little world.

Minnie went bravely on—nerved by the sight of that bowed figure and emaciated hand, hiding the eyes—speaking the praises of the girl who had sent many a pang of jealousy into her heart—a jealousy none the less torturing because she knew it to be unreasonable. "He could never have thought of wretched, crippled me, if there had been no Rhoda Maxfield in the world!" she had told herself a hundred times. But she tried to fancy that the withering up of the secret romance of her life would have been less hard to bear, had the sacrifice been made in favour of a higher, nobler woman than simple, shallow, slight-hearted Rhoda Maxfield.

Nevertheless, she spoke Rhoda's praises now ungrudgingly. Nay, more; she believed Powell to be capable of the highest self-sacrifice; she believed that he would welcome a prospect of happiness and security for Rhoda, even though it should shut the door for ever on any lingering hopes he might retain of winning her. So, bracing herself to a strong effort—which seemed to strain not only the nerves, but the very muscles, of her fragile frame as she sat almost upright, grasping the arms of her chair with both hands—she added, "And, as I know you have that rare gift of love which can rejoice in looking at a happiness it may never share, I will say to you in confidence that I believe Rhoda is honourably sought in marriage by a good man—a man who—it is not needful to speak at length of him"—indeed, her throat was dry, and her courage desperately at bay—"but he is a good, high-minded man; one who will value and respect his wife; one who admires and loves Rhoda very fervently."

It was magnanimously said. The words, as she uttered them, sounded the knell of her own youth and hope in her ears.

We believe that a beloved one is dead. We have kissed the cold lips. We have kissed the unresponsive hand. Yes; the beloved one is dead. We surely believe it.

But, no! The death-bell sounds, beating with chill, heavy fingers on our very heart-strings, and then we awake to a sudden confirmation of our grief. The bell sings its loud monotone, over roof-tree and grave-stone, piercing through the murmur of busy life in streets and homes, and then we know that we had not hitherto believed; that in some nook and secret fold of heart or brain a wild, formless hope had been lurking that all was not really over. Only the implacable mental clang carries conviction with its vibrations into the broad daylight and the common air, and the tears gush out as if our sorrow were born anew.

Even so felt Minnie Bodkin when she had put her secret thought into words. The speaking of the words could not hasten their fulfilment. But yet it seemed to her as if, in saying them, she had signed some bond—had formally renounced even the solace of a passing fancy that might flit, fairy-bright, into the dimness of her life; had given up the object of her silent passion by a covenant that was none the less stringent because its utterance was simple and commonplace. She was silent, breathing quickly, and lying back against the cushions after the short speech that had cost her so much.

Powell remained quite still for a few seconds. Then suddenly removing the screening hand, the almost intolerable lustre of his eyes broke upon the startled woman opposite to him, as he said, with a strange smile, "She is safe. She is happy for Time and Eternity. She has been ransomed with a price."

"I knew that you would allow no selfish feeling to sway you," returned Minnie, after an instant's pause. "I was right in feeling sure that you would generously consider her happiness before your own."

But yet she was not satisfied with the result of her well-meant attempt to free Powell's mind from the anxiety concerning Rhoda, which she believed to have been preying on it. There was something strangely unexpected in his manner of receiving it. Presently Powell looked at her again with a sad, sweet smile. The wild blaze had gone out of his eyes. They were soft and steady as they rested on her now.

"You are a just and benevolent woman," he said. "You have been faithful. You came hither with the charitable wish to comfort me. I am not ungrateful. But the old trouble has long been dead. I did wrestle with a mighty temptation on her account. My heart burnt very hot within me; the fleshy heart, full of deceit and desperately wicked. But that human passion fell away like a garment, shrivelled and consumed by the great fire of the wrath of God, that put it out as the sun puts out the flame of a taper at noonday. Neither," he went on, speaking rather to himself than to Minnie, "am I concerned for that young soul. No; it is safe. It has been ransomed. I have had answer to prayer, and heard voices that brought me sure tidings in the dimness of the early morning; but these things are hard to be understood. Sometimes, even yet, the old, foolish yearning of the heart seems to awake and stir blindly within me. When you named that name—no lips had uttered it to my ears for many months—there seemed to run a swift echo of it through all the secret places of my soul! But I heard as though one dead should hear the beat of a familiar footfall above his grave."

The dusk of evening, the low thrilling tones of the preacher's voice, the terrible pallor of his face, with its great glittering eyes shining in the feeble rays of the candle, contributed, not less than the strangeness of his words, to oppress Minnie with a sensation of nervous dread. She was not afraid of David Powell, nor of anything that she could see or touch. But vague terrors seemed to be floating in the air.

She started as her eye was caught by a deep, mysterious shadow on the wall. The fire had burnt low, and shed only a dull red glow upon the hearth. The ticking of the old clock appeared to grow louder with every beat, and to utter some ominous warning in an unknown tongue.

All at once a sound of voices and footsteps in the passage broke the spell. The fire cast only commonplace and comprehensible shadows. The clock ticked with its ordinary indifferent tone. The preacher's pale face ceased to float in a mystical light against the dark background of the curtainless window. The everyday world entered in at the kitchen door in the shape of Mr. Diamond and Rhoda Maxfield.

Of the four persons thus unexpectedly assembled, Minnie was the first to speak.

"What, Rhoda!" she cried, in a quiet voice, which revealed much less surprise than she felt. "What brought you here at this hour?"

As she spoke she glanced anxiously at Powell, uneasy as to the effect on him of Rhoda's sudden appearance. But he remained curiously impassible, looking at those present as if they were objects dimly seen afar off.

"I was coming to drink tea with Mrs. Errington. Mr. Diamond overtook me and Sally in the street. I saw your carriage at the door, and looked in here, hoping that I should find both you and Mrs. Errington in this room, because I know you do not go upstairs."

Thus spoke Rhoda, in a soft, tremulous little voice, and with downcast eyes. Diamond came and shook hands with Minnie. He pressed the hand she gave him with unusual warmth and emphasis. His eyes were bright, and there was a glow of pleasure on his face. He believed that his suit was prospering, and he wished to convey some hint of his hopeful anticipations to his sympathising friend Miss Bodkin. Then he turned to Powell, and touched him on the shoulder. "How are you to-night?" he asked, in a friendly tone, not without a kind of superior pity. "I am glad to see that you have been refreshing the inner man. Our friend is too careless of his health, Miss Bodkin. He fasts too long, and too often."

Powell smiled slightly, but neither looked at him nor answered him. Going straight to Rhoda he laid his hand on her bright chestnut hair, from which the bonnet she wore had fallen backwards, and looked at her solemnly. Rhoda turned pale and gazed back at him, as if fascinated. Neither of the others spoke or moved.

"It is true, then," said Powell, after a pause, and the low tones of his voice sounded like soft music. "I have passed through the Valley of the Shadow of Death, and between me and the dwellers under the light of the sun there is a great gulf fixed!"

He released the bright young head on which his hand had rested, and made as if he would move away. Then, pausing, he said, "I frightened you long ago—in the other life. Fear no more, Rhoda Maxfield. Be no more disquieted by night or by day. Many are called, but few are chosen, yet you are among the chosen." He smiled upon her very sadly and calmly, and went slowly away without looking round.

As soon as he was gone, Rhoda burst into tears. Diamond made an eager step forward as if to take her hand; then stopped irresolutely, and looked anxiously at Minnie. "She is so sensitive," he said half aloud. Minnie was as white as the preacher, and her eyes were full of tears, which, however, she checked from falling by a strong effort of her will. "I must go," she said. "Rhoda tells me my carriage is here. Will you kindly call my servants?" He obeyed her, first making his formal little bow; a sign, under the circumstances, that he was not quite in sympathy with his friend, who showed so little sympathy herself for that "sensitiveness" which so moved him. However, when, assisted by Jane, Miss Bodkin had made her way to the door, Mr. Diamond stood there bare-headed to help her into the carriage. She put her hand for an instant on his proffered arm as she got into the vehicle. Rhoda came running out after her. "Good night, Miss Minnie!" she cried.

Minnie leant back, and seemed neither to see nor hear her. But in an instant she was moved by a generous impulse to put her head out of the window, and say kindly, "Good night, Rhoda. Come and see me soon."

As the carriage began to move away, she saw Diamond tenderly drawing Rhoda's shawl round her shoulders, and trying to lead her in from the chill of the evening air.

CHAPTER XVI.

"Well, you may say as you please, Mr. Jackson, but 'twas a sight I shall never forget; and one I don't expect to see the like of on this side of eternity," said Richard Gibbs.

"No, nor don't wish to, I should think," put in Seth Maxfield.

"Anyway, it was a wonderful manifestation," remarked Mr. Gladwish, musingly.

There was a little knot of Wesleyans assembled in the house of Mr. Gladwish, the shoemaker. Since Jonathan Maxfield's defection, he might be considered the leading member of the Methodist congregation. And a weekly prayer-meeting was held at his house on Monday evenings, as it had formerly been held in old Max's back parlour.

On the present occasion the assembly was more numerous than usual. Besides the accustomed cronies and Mr. Jackson the preacher, there were also Seth Maxfield, who had come into Whitford on some farm business on the previous Saturday, Richard Gibbs, and the widow Thimbleby. The latter was an old acquaintance of Mrs. Gladwish, and much patronised by that matron; although, of late, Mrs. Thimbleby had been under some cloud of displeasure among the stricter Methodists, on account of her fidelity to David Powell.

There had not been, to say the truth, any very fervent or lengthy religious exercises that evening. After a brief discourse by Brother Jackson, and the singing of a hymn, the company had, by mutual agreement, understood but not expressed, fallen into a discussion of the topic which was at that time in the minds and mouths of most Whitford persons high and low—namely, David Powell's preachings, and the phenomena attendant thereon.

"Anyhow," repeated Mr. Gladwish, after a short silence, "it was a wonderful manifestation."

"You may well say so, sir," assented Richard Gibbs, emphatically.

"Humph," grunted out Brother Jackson, pursing up his thick lips and folding his fat hands before him; "I misdoubt whether the enemy be not mixed up somehow or other with these manifestations. I don't say they are wholly his doing. But—my brethren, Satan is very wily; and is continually 'going to and fro in the earth,' and 'walking up and down in it,' even as in the days of Job."

"That's very true," said Mrs. Gladwish, with an air of responsible corroboration. She was a light-haired, pale-faced woman, with a slatternly figure and a sharp, inquisitive nose; and her quiet persistency in cross-questioning made her a little formidable to some of her neighbours.

"When I see a thorn-tree bring forth figs, or a thistle grapes, I will believe that such things as I witnessed yesterday on Whit Meadow are the work of Satan—not before!" rejoined Gibbs.

"Amen!" said Mrs. Thimbleby, tremulously. "Oh! indeed, sir—I hope you don't consider it presumption in me—but I must say I do think Mr. Gibbs is right. It was the working of the Lord's spirit, and no other."

"What was the working of the Lord's spirit?" asked a harsh voice that made the women start, and caused every head in the room to be turned towards the door. There stood Jonathan Maxfield, rather more bowed in the shoulders than when we first made his acquaintance, but otherwise little changed.

He was welcomed by Gladwish with a marked show of respect. The breach made between old Max and his former associates by his departure from the Methodist Society had been soon healed in many instances. Gladwish had condoned it long ago; and, owing to various circumstances—among them the fact that Seth Maxfield and his wife remained among the Wesleyans—the intercourse between the two families had been almost uninterrupted. There was truly no cordial interchange of hospitalities, nor much that could be called companionship; but the strong bond of habit on both sides, and, on Gladwish's, the sense of his neighbour's growing wealth and importance, served to keep the two men as close together as they ever had been.

"I've come to say a word to Seth, if it may be without putting you out," said old Maxfield, with a sidelong nod of the head, that was intended as a general salute to the company.

Mr. and Mrs. Gladwish protested that no one would be in the least put out by Mr. Maxfield's presence, but that they were all, on the contrary, pleased to see him. Then, while the father and son said a few words to each other in a low tone, the others conversed among themselves rather loudly, by way of politely expressing that they did not wish to overhear any private conversation.

"That's all, then, Seth," said old Max, turning away from his son. "I knew I should find you here, and I thought I would mention about them freeholds before it slipped my memory. And—life is uncertain—I have put a clause in my will about 'em this very evening. Putting off has never been my plan, neither with the affairs of this world or the next."

There was something in the mention of a clause in old Max's will which had a powerful attraction for the imagination of most persons present. Brother Jackson made a motion with his mouth, as though he were tasting some pleasant savour. Mrs. Gladwish thought of her tribe of growing children, and their rapid consumption of food, clothing, and doctor's stuff, and she sighed. Two or three of the regular attendants at the prayer-meeting fixed their eyes with lively interest on Jonathan Maxfield; and one whispered to another that Seth had gotten a good bit o' cash with his wife, and would have more from his father. 'Twas always the way: money makes money. Though, rightly considered, it was but dross and dust, and riches were an awful snare. And then they obsequiously made way for the rich grocer to take a seat in their circle, moved, perhaps, by compassion for the imminent peril to his soul which he was incurring from the possession of freehold property.

"Well, I'll sit down for half an hour," said Jonathan, in his dry way, and took a chair near the table accordingly. In fact, he was well pleased enough to find himself once more among his old associates; and if any embarrassment belonged to the relations between himself and Brother Jackson, his former pastor, it was certain that old Max did not feel it. When a man has a profound conviction of his own wisdom, supported on a firm basis of banker's books and solid investments, such intangible sentimentalities have no power to constrain them. Mr. Jackson, perhaps, felt some little difficulty in becomingly adjusting his manner to the situation, being troubled between the desire of asserting his dignity in the eyes of his flock and his natural reluctance to affront a man of Jonathan Maxfield's weight in the world. But he speedily hit on the assumption of an unctuous charity and toleration, as being the kind of demeanour best calculated for the circumstances. And perhaps he did not judge amiss. "I'm sure," said he, with a pious smile, "it is a real joy to the hearts of the faithful, and a good example to the unregenerate, to see believers dwelling together in unity, however much they may be compelled to differ on some points for conscience' sake."

"What was it as some one was saying just now about the working of the Lord's spirit?" asked Maxfield, cutting short Brother Jackson's verbal flow of milk and honey.

There was a little hesitation among those present as to who should answer this question. To answer it involved the utterance of a name which was known to be unpleasing in Mr. Maxfield's ears. Mrs. Thimbleby shrank into the background; she had a special dread of old Jonathan's stern hard face and manner. Richard Gibbs at length answered, simply, "We were speaking, Mr. Maxfield, of David Powell's preaching in Lady Lane and on Whit Meadow."

Maxfield pressed his lips together, and made an inarticulate sound, which might be taken to express contempt or disapprobation, or merely an acknowledgment of Gibbs's information.

"My! I should like to have been there!" exclaimed Mrs. Gladwish.

"Well, now," said Seth Maxfield, "my wife would walk twenty mile to keep out of the way of it. She was quite scared at all the accounts we heard."

"But what did you hear! And what did happen, after all?" asked Mrs. Gladwish. "I wish you would give us an account of it, Mr. Gibbs."

"It is hard to give an account of such thing to them as wasn't present, ma'am. But there was a great outpouring of grace."

Brother Jackson groaned slightly, then coughed, and shook his head.

"I never saw such a beautiful evening for the time of year," put in one of Gladwish's apprentices, a consumptive-looking lad with bright, dreamy eyes. "And all the folks standing in the sunset, and the river shining, and the leaves red and yellow on the branches—it was a wonderful sight."

"It was a wonderful sight!" ejaculated Gibbs. "There was the biggest multitude I ever saw assembled in Whit Meadow. There must have been thousands of people. There were among them scoffers, and ungodly men, and seekers after the truth, and some that were already awakened. Then, women and children; they came gathering together more and more, from the north, and the south, and the east, and the west. And there, in the midst, raised up on a high bench, so that he might be seen of all, stood David Powell. His face was as white as snow, and his black hair hung down on either side of it."

"I thought of John the Baptist preaching in the wilderness," said the apprentice softly.

"I couldn't get to stand very near to him," continued Gibbs, "and I thought I should catch but little of his discourse. But when he began to speak, though his voice was low at first, after a while it rose, and grew every moment fuller and stronger."

"Yes," said the bright-eyed apprentice, "it was like listening to the organ-pipes of St. Chad's; just that kind of tremble in it that seems to run all through your body."

"The man always had a goodish voice," said Brother Jackson. "But that is a carnal gift. 'Tis the use we put our voices to that is all-important, my dear friends."

"He began by prayer," said Gibbs, speaking slowly, and with the abstracted air of a man who is not so much endeavouring to give others a vivid narration, as to recall accurately to his own mind the things of which he is speaking. "Yes, he began with prayer. He prayed for us all there present with wonderful fervour."

"What did he say?" asked Mrs. Gladwish.

"Nay, I cannot repeat the exact words."

"Can't you remember, Joel?" persisted his mistress, addressing the young apprentice.

The lad blushed up, but more, apparently, from eagerness and excitement than bashfulness, as he answered, "Not the very words, ma'am, I can't remember. But it was a prayer that had wings like, and it lifted you up right away into the heavens. When he left off I felt as if I had been dropped straight down on to Whit Meadow out of a cloud of glory."

"Well, there's no harm in all that, Brother Jackson?" said Gladwish, looking round.

"Harm!" echoed Gibbs. "Why, Mr. Gladwish, if you could but have seen the faces of the people! And then presently he began to call sinners to repentance with such power as I never witnessed—no, not when he was preaching in our chapel two years ago. He spoke of wrath and judgment until the whole field was full of the sound of crying and groaning. But he seemed continually strengthened, and went on, until first one fell, and then another. They dropped down just like dead when the arrows of conviction entered their souls. And the cries of some of them were awful to hear. Then there was weeping, and a kind of hard breathing and panting from breasts oppressed with the weight of sin; and then, mixed with those sounds, the rejoicing aloud of believers and those who received assurance. But through all the preacher's voice rose above the tumult, and it seemed to me almost a manifest miracle that he should be able to make himself heard so clearly."

"Aye," said Joel, "it was like a ship on the top of the stormy waves; now high, now low, but always above the raging waters."

There was a short silence. Those present looked first at each other and then at old Max, who sat motionless and grim, with his elbow on the table, and his chin resting on his clenched hand.

"And did you really see any of the poor creeturs as was took?" asked Mrs. Gladwish of the widow Thimbleby.

"Took, ma'am?"

"Took with fits, or whatever it was."

"Oh! yes; I see several. There was a fine fresh-coloured young man, which is a butcher out Duckwell way—Mr. Seth'll likely know him—and he dropped down just like a bullock. And then he stamped, and struggled, and grew an awful dark red colour in the face, and tore up the grass with his hands; such was the power of conviction. And at last he lay like a log, and 'twas an hour, or more, before he come to. But when he did, he had got peace and his burthen was taken away, thanks be!"

"And there was a girl, too, very poor and sickly-looking," said Joel. "And when the power of the Lord came upon her she went into a kind of trance. Her eyes were open, but she saw nothing. Tears were falling down her cheeks, but they were tears of joy; for she kept on saying, 'How Thou hast loved sinners!' over and over again. And there was such a smile on her face! When we go to Heaven, I expect we shall see the angels smile like that!"

"And the man himself—the preacher—did he seem filled with joy and peace?" asked Jackson, covertly malicious.

"Why, that is the strange thing!" returned Richard Gibbs, with frank simplicity. "Although he was doing this great work, and witnessing the mercies of the Lord descend on the people like manna, yet Mr. Powell had such a look of deep sorrow on his face as I never saw. It was a kind of a fixed, hopeless look. He said, 'I speak to you out of a dark dungeon, but you are in the light. Give thanks and rejoice, and hasten to make your calling and election sure. Those who dwell in the blackness of the shadow could tell you terrible things.'"

Mrs. Thimbleby wiped away a tear with the corner of her shabby black shawl. "Ah!" she sighed, "it do seem a hard dispensation and a strange one, as him who brings glad tidings to so many shouldn't get peace himself. And a more angelic creetur' in his kindness to the afflicted never walked this earth. Yet he's a'most always bowed down with heaviness of spirit. It do seem strange!"

Jonathan Maxfield struck the table with his fist so hard that the candlesticks standing on it rocked. "Strange!" he cried, "it would be strange indeed to see anything else! Why this is the work of the enemy as plain as possible. Don't tell me! Look at all the years I've been a member of Christian congregations in Whitford—whether in chapel or church, it is no matter—and tell me if ever there was known such ravings, and fits, and Bedlam doings? And yet I suppose there were souls saved in my time too! I say that Satan is busy among you, puffing up one and another with sperritual pride."

"Lord forgive you!" ejaculated Richard Gibbs, in a tone of such genuine pity and conviction as startled the rest.

"Lord forgive me, sir!" echoed old Max, turning slowly round upon the speaker, and glaring at him from under his grey eyebrows.

There was an awe-stricken silence.

"Our good friend, Richard Gibbs, meant no offence, Mr. Maxfield," said Jackson, looking everywhere except into Gibbs's face.

"I say," cried Maxfield, addressing the rest of the company, and entirely ignoring the rash delinquent Gibbs, "that these things are a snare and a delusion, and the work of the devil. And when them of more wisdom and experience than me comes forward to speak on the matter, I shall be glad to show forth my reasons."

"Why, but, Brother Maxfield, I don't know now. I don't feel so sure," said Gladwish, on whom the accounts of Powell's preaching had produced a considerable effect. "There have been cases, you know, in the early times of Methodism; and John Wesley himself, you know, was ready to believe in the workings of grace, as manifested in similar ways."

"Don't tell me of your David Powells!" returned old Max, declining to discuss the subject on wide or general grounds, but doggedly confining himself to the particulars immediately before him. "Don't tell me of a man as is blown out with pride and vain glory like a balloon. Did I, or did I not, say more'n two years ago, that David Powell was getting puffed up with presumptuousness?"

There was a low murmur of assent. Brother Jackson closed his eyes and uttered a deep, long-drawn "A-a-ah!" like a man reluctantly admitting a painful truth.

"Did I, or did I not, say to many members of the Society, 'This man is dangerous. He has fallen from grace. He is hankering after new-fangled doctrine, and is ramping with red-hot over-bearingness?'"

"Yon did, sir," answered a stout, broad-faced man named Blogg, who looked like a farmer, but was a linendraper in a small way of business. "You said so frequently; I remember your very words, and can testify to 'em."

(This speech appeared to produce a considerable effect. Mrs. Thimbleby began to cry; and, not having an apron at hand, threw the corner of her shawl over her face.)

"Did I, or did I not, say that if things went on at this kind of rate, I should withdraw from the Society? And did I, or did I not, withdraw from it accordin'?"

"Sir," said Mr. Blogg, "I saw you with my own eyes a-coming out of the parish church of St. Chad's, at ten minutes to one o'clock in the afternoon of the Sunday next following your utterance of them identical expressions; and cannot deny or evade the truth, but must declare it to the best of my ability, with no regard to any human respects, but for the ease and liberation of my conscience as a sincere though humble professor."

There was a general feeling that, in some conclusive though mysterious way, the linendraper had brought a crushing weight of evidence to bear against David Powell; and even the preacher's best friends would find it difficult to defend him after that!

Old Max looked round triumphantly, and proceeded to follow up the impression thus made. "And then I'm to be told," said he, "that the lunatic doings on Whit Meadow are the work of Heavenly powers, eh? Come, Gladwish—you're a man as has read theologies and controversies, and are acquainted with the history of Wesleyan Methodism as well as most members in Whitford—I should like to know what arguments you have to advance against plain facts—facts known to us all, and testified to by Robert Blogg, linendraper, now present, and for many years a respected class-leader in this town?"

"Well, but we have plain facts to bring forward too," said Richard Gibbs, with anxious earnestness.

"I ask you, Gladwish, what arguments you have to bring forward," repeated Maxfield, determinedly repressing any outward sign of having heard the presumptuous Gibbs.

"If this be not Satan's doing, I have no knowledge of the words of the devil, and I suppose I shall hardly be told that, after regular attendance in a congregation of Wesleyan Methodists for fifty odd years, man and boy! But," continued the old man, after a short silence, which none of those present ventured to break, "there's no knowing, truly. These are new-fangled days. I cannot say but what I may live to hear it declared that I know nothing of Satan, nor cannot discern his works when I see them!"

"Nay, father," said Seth Maxfield, speaking now for the first time, in deprecation of so serious a charge against the "new-fangled days," on which Whitford had fallen. "Nay, no man will say that, nor yet think it. But my notion is, that it may neither be Heaven nor t'other place that has much to do with these kind of fits and screechings. I believe it to be just as Dr. Evans said—and he a Welshman himself, you'll remember—when he first heard of these doings of David Powell in Wales. Says he, 'It's a epidemic,' says the doctor. 'A catching kind of nervous disease, neither more nor less. And you may any of you get it if you go to hear and see the others. Though forewarned is forearmed in such cases,' says the doctor. 'And the better you understand the real natur' of the disorder, the safer you'll be from it.'"

Seth was of a materialistic and practical turn of mind, and he offered this hypothesis as an explanation which had approved itself to his own judgment (not because he thoroughly comprehended Dr. Evans's statements, but rather because of the inherent repugnance of his mind to accept a supernatural theory about any phenomenon, when a natural theory might be substituted for it), and also as a neutral ground of conciliation, whereon the opposing celestial and diabolic partisans might meet half way. But it speedily appeared that he had miscalculated in so doing. Neither the friends nor the opponents of David Powell would for an instant admit any such rationalistic suggestion. It was scouted on all hands. And Seth, who had no gift of controversy, speedily found himself reduced to silence.

"Well," said he, quietly, when he and his father rose to go away, "think what you please, but I know that if one of my reapers was to fall down in the field that way, let him be praying or cursing, I should consider it a hospital case."

"Good night, Gladwish," said old Max. "Good night, Mrs. Gladwish. I am glad, for the sake of all the decent, sober, godly members of the Society, as this firebrand had left it before things came to this pass. And I only wish you'd all had the gift of clear-sightedness to see through him long ago, and cut yourselves off from him as I did."

Richard Gibbs advanced towards the old man with outstretched hand. "I hope, Mr. Maxfield," he said, humbly, "that you'll not think I meant any offence to you just now. But I was so full of conviction, and you know we can but speak the truth to the best of our power. I hope you, nor any other Christian man, will be in wrath with me, because we don't see things just alike. I know Mr. Powell is always for making peace, for he says we many a time fancy we're fighting the Lord's battles, when, in truth, we are only desiring victory for our own pride. Anyway, I know he would bid me ask pardon for a hasty word, if any offence had come by it. And so I hope you'll shake hands."

Jonathan Maxfield took no notice of the proffered hand, neither did he make any answer directly. But as he reached the door he turned round and said, "Well, Mr. Jackson, you have your work cut out for you with some of your flock, I doubt. Like to like. I expect that ranting Welshman will draw some away from decent chapel-going. But them as admires such doings are best got rid of, and that speedily." With that he walked off.

"I think Maxfield was rather hard on poor Dicky Gibbs," said Mr. Gladwish to his spouse when they were alone together. "He might ha' shook hands. Dicky came forward in a real Christian spirit. Maxfield was very hard in his wrath."

"Well," returned the virtuous matron, "I can't so much wonder. Having the Lord's forgiveness called down on his head in that way! And I don't know, Gladwish, as we should like it ourselves!"

CHAPTER XVII.

Minnie Bodkin had not dismissed from her mind the rumours about Algernon Errington, which she had heard from the widow Thimbleby. After some consideration she resolved to speak to him directly on the subject, and decided on the manner of doing so.

"I will not try to speak to him in the presence of other people," she thought. "He would wriggle off and slip through my fingers if he found the conversation had any tendency to become disagreeable. And then, too, it might be difficult to speak to him without interruption."

This latter consideration had reference to Minnie's observation of Mrs. Algernon, who never saw her husband engaged in conversation with Miss Bodkin without unceremoniously thrusting herself between them.

The result of Minnie's deliberations was the sending of the following note to the Whitford Post-office:—

"MY DEAR ALGERNON,—I want to say a word to you quietly. Can you come to me on your way home this afternoon? I will be ready to receive you at any hour between four and six. Don't disappoint your old friend,

"M. B."

At a few minutes before five that evening Mr. Ancram Errington presented himself at Dr. Bodkin's house, and was shown up to Minnie's room.

It was one of Minnie's good days. She was seated in her lounging-chair by the fire, but she was not altogether reclining in it—merely leaning a little back against the cushions. A small writing-table stood in front of her. It was covered with papers—amongst them a copy of the local newspaper—and she had evidently been busily occupied. When Algernon entered she held out her hand with a smile of welcome. "This is very good!" she exclaimed. "I was not sure that I should succeed in tearing your postmastership away from the multifarious duties—"

Algernon winced, and held up his hand. "Don't, Minnie!" he cried. "For mercy's sake, let me forget all that for half an hour!"

"Oh, reassure yourself, most overworked of public servants! It is not about the conveyance of his Majesty's mails that I am going to talk to you."

"Upon my word, I am infinitely relieved to hear it."

And, indeed, his countenance brightened at once, and he took a chair opposite to Minnie with all his old nonchalant gaiety.

"How you hate your office!" said Minnie, looking at him curiously. "More, even, than your native laziness—which I know to be considerable—would seem to account for."

"Not at all! There is no difficulty in accounting for my distaste for the whole business. There can be no difficulty. It is the simplest, most obvious thing in the world!"

"Don't things go smoothly? Have you any special troubles or difficulties in the office, Algernon?"

"Special troubles! My dear Minnie, what on earth are you driving at?"

"I am 'driving' at nothing more than the simple sense of my words implies," she answered, with a marked shade of surprise in her countenance. "I mean just what I say. Is your work going pretty smoothly? Have you any complaints? Does your clerk do well?"

"Oh, Gibbs? Capitally, capitally! Old Obadiah is a first-rate fellow. Did you know his name was Obadiah? Absurd name, isn't it? Oh yes; he's all right. I trust him entirely—blindly. He has the whole thing in his hands. He might do anything he liked in the office. I have every confidence in Gibbs. But now, Minnie, let us have done with the subject. If you had as much of it as I have you would understand—Come, dismiss the bugaboo, or I shall think you have entrapped me here to talk to me about the post-office. And I warn you I don't think I should be able to stand that, even from you!"

"How absurdly you are exaggerating, Algy," said Minnie, shaking her head at him, and yet smiling a little at the same time. "But be at peace. I have nothing to say on the subject of the Whitford post-office. My discourse will chiefly concern the Whitford postmaster, and—No! Don't be so ridiculous! not in his official capacity, either!"

"Oh! Well, in his private character, I should think it impossible to find a more delightful topic of conversation than that interesting and accomplished individual," returned Errington, laughing and settling himself comfortably in his chair.

"I hope it may prove so. Tell me, first, how is Mrs. Algernon Ancram Errington?"

"Why, Castalia is not very well, I think, although I don't know what is the matter. She grows thinner and thinner, and sallower and sallower. Entre nous, Minnie, she frets and chafes against our life here. She has not the gift of looking on the bright side of things. She is rather peevish by nature. It's a little trying sometimes, coming on the back of all the other botherations. Ha! There!" (passing his hand quickly across his forehead) "let us say no more on that subject either. And now to return to the interesting topic—the delightful and accomplished—eh? What have you to say to me?"

Minnie seized on the opportunity, which chance had afforded her, to introduce the matter she wished to speak about.

"Do you think your wife is annoyed by the importunities of tradespeople, Algy? That would be enough to fret her and sour her temper."

"Importunities of tradespeople? Good gracious, no! And, besides, I don't think Castalia would allow the importunities of tradespeople to disturb her much. I should fancy that a Bourbon princess could scarcely look on such folks from a more magnificent elevation than poor Castalia does. But, Que voulez-vous? She was brought up in that sort of hauteur."

"I quite believe in your wife's disregard for the feelings of the tradespeople," answered Minnie drily. "But this is a question of her own feelings, you see. Come, Algernon, may I take the privilege of our old friendship, and speak to you quite frankly?"

"Pray do, my dear Minnie. You know I always loved frankness."

He looked the picture of candour as he turned his bright blue eyes on his friend.

"Well, then, to begin with a question. Do you not owe money to several persons in Whitford?"

"My dear Minnie, don't look so solemn, for mercy's sake! 'Owe money!' Why I suppose everybody owes money. A few pounds would cover all my debts. I assure you I am never troubled on the subject."

"I am glad to hear it. But—will you forgive the liberty I am taking for the sake of my motive, and give me carte blanche to be as impertinent as I please."

"With all my heart!" he answered unhesitatingly.

"Thanks, Algy. Then, to proceed without circumlocution: I am afraid that, since neither you nor your wife are accustomed to domestic economy, you may possibly be spending more money than is quite prudent, without being aware of it. You say you are not disturbed by your debts; but, Algy, I hear things on this subject which are never likely to reach your ears; or not until it is too late for the knowledge of them to serve you. And I have reason to think that there is a good deal of unpleasant feeling among the Whitford tradespeople about you and yours."

"You will excuse me for observing that the Whitford tradespeople always have been, within my recollection, a set of pig-headed, prejudicial ignoramuses, and that I see no reason to apprehend any speedy improvement in the intelligence of that highly respectable body."

"Don't laugh, Algernon. The matter is serious. You have not been troubled yet, you say. But the trouble may begin at any moment, and I should wish you to be prepared to meet it. You may have bills sent in which—"

"Bills? Oh, as to that, there's no lack of them already! I must acknowledge the great alacrity and punctuality with which the mercantile classes of this town send in their weekly accounts. Oh dear yes, I have a considerable collection of those interesting documents; so many, in fact, that the other day, when Castalia was complaining of the shabbiness of the paperhangings in our dining-room, I proposed to her to cover the walls with the tradesmen's bills. It would be novel, economical, and moral; a kind of memento mori—a death's head at the feast! Fancy seeing your butcher's bill glaring down above the roast mutton every day, and the greengrocer's 'To account delivered,' restraining the spoon that might otherwise too lavishly dispense the contents of the vegetable dishes!"

"Algy, Algy!"

"Upon my honour, Minnie, I made the suggestion. But Castalia looked as grave as a judge. She didn't see it at all. The fact is, poor Cassy's sense of humour is merely rudimentary."

Minnie joined her hands together on the table, and thus supported, she leant a little forward, and looked searchingly at the young man.

"Algernon," she said with slow deliberation, "I begin to be afraid that the case is worse than I thought."

"What do you mean?" he asked, almost roughly, and with a sudden change of colour.

"I mean that you really are in difficult waters. How has it come to pass that the weekly accounts have accumulated in this way?"

He laughed a little forced laugh, but he looked relieved, too.

"The process is simple. They keep sending 'em in!"

"And then it is said—forgive me if I appear intrusive—that you gave orders for wine and such things out of Whitford. And that does not incline the people of the place to be patient."

"Well, by Jove!" exclaimed Algernon, throwing himself back in his chair and thrusting his hands into his pockets, "that is the most absurd—the most irrational—the most preposterous reason for being angry with me! They grumble when I run up a bill with them, and they are affronted when I don't!"

"Does your wife understand—or—or control the household expenditure?"

"Bless you, no! She has not the very vaguest ideas of anything of the kind. When she had an allowance from her uncle for her dress, my lord used to have to come down every now and then with a supplementary sum of money to get her out of debt."

He spoke with an air of perfectly easy amusement, and without a trace of anxiety; unless, perhaps, an accustomed ear might have detected some constraint in his voice.

"But could she not be made to understand? Why not give her some hints on domestic economy? It should be done kindly, of course. And surely her own good sense—"

Algernon pursed up his mouth and raised his eyebrows.

"She considers herself an unexampled victim as it is. I think 'lessons on domestic economy' would about put the finishing stroke to the internal felicity of Ivy Lodge!"

Minnie looked pained. They were trenching here on ground on which she had no intention of venturing farther. It formed no part of her plan to be drawn into a discussion respecting the defects and shortcomings of Algernon's wife. She was silent.

Algernon got up from his chair, and came and stood before Minnie, taking both her hands in his.

"My dear girl," he said, "I cannot tell you how much I feel your kindness and friendship. But, now, pray don't look so terribly like the tragic muse! I assure you there is no need, as far as we are concerned. Castalia is perhaps a little extravagant; but, after all, what does it amount to? A few pounds would cover all I owe. The whole of our budget is a mere bagatelle. The fact is, you have attached too much importance to the chatter of these thick-headed boobies. They hate us, I suppose, because Castalia's uncle is a peer of the realm, and because we dine late, and because we prefer claret to Double X—or for some equally excellent and conclusive reasons."

"I don't know that they hate you, Algy," returned Minnie, but not with an air of very perfect conviction. "And, after all, it is scarcely a proof of personal malignity to wish to be paid one's bill!"

Algernon laughed quite genuinely. "Oh yes it is!" he cried. "A proof of the direst malignity. What worse can they do?"

"Well, Algernon, I cannot presume to push my sermonisings on you any farther. You will give me credit at least for having ventured to make them from a single-minded wish to be of some service to you."

"My dear Minnie! you are the 'best fellow' in the world! (You remember I used to call you so in my saucy, school-boy days, and when your majesty condescended to permit my impertinences?) And to show you how thoroughly I appreciate your friendship, I don't mind telling you that when I am removed from this d— delightful berth that I now occupy, I shall have to get Uncle Seely to help us out a little. But I feel no scruple about that. Something is due to me. I ought never to have been placed here at all. Well, no matter! It was a mistake. My lord sees it now, and he is setting to work in earnest for me in other quarters. I have every reason to believe that I shall get very pretty promotion before long. It isn't my business to go about proclaiming this to the butchers and bakers, is it? And between you and me, Miss Bodkin, your dear Whitfordians are as great rogues as the tradesmen in town, and vastly less pleasant to deal with. They make us pay an enormous percentage for the trifling credit we take. So let 'em wait and be—paid! Dear Minnie, I assure you I shall not forget your affectionate kindness."

He bent down over her as he said the last words, still holding her hands. A change in Minnie's face made him look round, and when he did so, he saw his wife standing just within the room behind him.

Minnie was inexpressibly vexed with herself to feel a hot flush covering her face. She knew it would be misconstrued, and that made her colour the more. Mrs. Algernon Errington was the first to speak.

"I beg your pardon, Miss Bodkin," she said, "I didn't know that you were so particularly engaged."

"What the deuce brought you here?" asked her husband, with a not altogether successful assumption of thinking the whole trio, including himself, completely at their ease.

"There was no one in the drawing-room nor in the study," continued Castalia, still addressing Minnie, "so I thought I would come direct to your room. I see now that I ought not to have taken that liberty."

"Well, frankly, I don't think you ought, my dear," said her husband, lightly.

Minnie was sorely tempted to say so too. But she felt that any show of anger on her part would but increase the unpleasantness of the situation, and a quarrel with Algernon's wife under such circumstances would have been equally revolting to her pride and her taste; so she held out her hand to Castalia with grave courtesy, and said, "I have to apologise, on my side, for having taken the privilege of old friendship to sermonise your husband a little. He will tell you what I have ventured to speak to him about. I hope you will forgive me."

Castalia appeared not to see the proffered hand. She stood quite still near the door as she answered, "Oh, I daresay it is all quite right. I don't suppose Ancram will tell me anything about it; I am not in his secrets."

"This is no secret, Mrs. Errington; at all events, not from you."

"Oh, I don't know. But I daresay it doesn't matter."

Through all the languid insolence of her manner there was discernible so much real pain of mind, that Minnie once more checked a severe speech, and answered gently, "You will judge of that. Of course Algernon will discuss the subject of our conversation with you."

Mrs. Algernon Errington scarcely condescended to return Minnie's parting salutation, but walked away, saying to her husband over her shoulder, "I am going to drive home. It is nearly dinner-time. I suppose you are coming? But don't let me interfere with your arrangements."

"Interfere with a fiddlestick!" cried Algernon in the quick, testy tone that was the nearest approach to loss of temper Minnie had ever seen in him. Then he added after an instant, with a short laugh, "I don't know why I'm supposed not to include dinner in my 'arrangements' to-day of all days in the year!"

And then the husband and wife went away together, and entered the fly that awaited them before Dr. Bodkin's door.

"How did you know where to find me?" asked Algernon suddenly, after a silent drive of some ten minutes.

"Oh, I knew you had a rendezvous."

"I had no 'rendezvous.' You could not know it!"

"Couldn't I? I tell you I saw that creature's letter. 'Dear Algernon!' What right has she to write to you like that?"

And Castalia burst into angry tears.

Algernon turned upon her eagerly.

"Saw her letter? Where? How?"

"I—they told me—it was at the office."

"You went to the office? And you saw Minnie's letter?"

"I—it's no use scolding me, or pretending to be injured. I know who is injured of us two."

"I suppose I must have left the note lying open on the table of my office," said Algernon, speaking very distinctly, and not looking at his wife.

"Yes; that must be it! I—I—I tore it up. You will find the fragments on the floor if you think them worth preserving."

"What a goose you are, Castalia!" exclaimed her husband, leaning back in the carriage and closing his eyes.

Now, the fact was that Algernon distinctly remembered having placed Minnie's note in a drawer of a little secretaire which he kept habitually locked, and of which the key was at that moment in his waistcoat pocket. And the discovery that his wife had in some way or other obtained access to the said secretaire gave him, for reasons known only to himself, abundant food for conjecture and reflection during the rest of the drive home.

VOLUME III.

CHAPTER I.

There was a "scene" that evening at Ivy Lodge—not the less a "scene" in that it was conducted on genteel methods. Mrs. Algernon Errington inflicted on her husband during dinner a recapitulation of all her wrongs and injuries which could be covertly hinted at. She would not broadly speak out her meaning before "the servants." The phrase shaped itself thus in her mind from old habit. But in truth "the servants" were represented by one plump-faced damsel in a yellow print gown, into which her person seemed to have been inserted in the same way that bran is inserted into the cover of a pincushion. She seemed to have been stuffed into it by means of considerable force, and with less reference to the natural shape of her body than to the arbitrary outlines of the case made for it by a Whitford dressmaker.

This girl ministered to her master and mistress during dinner, pouring water and wine, changing knives and plates, handing vegetables, and not unfrequently dropping a spoon or a sprinkling of hot gravy into the laps of her employers. She had succeeded to Slater, who resigned her post after a trial of some six weeks' duration. Castalia, in despair at this desertion, had written to Lady Seely to send her a maid from London forthwith. But to this application she received a reply to the effect that my lady could not undertake to find any one who would suit her niece, and that her ladyship thought Castalia had much better make up her mind to do without a regular lady's-maid, and take some humbler attendant, who would make herself generally useful.

"I always knew Slater wouldn't stay with you," wrote Lady Seely; "and you won't get any woman of that kind to stay. You can't afford to keep one. Your uncle is fairly well; but poor Fido gives me a great deal of unhappiness. He eats nothing."

Not by any means from conviction or submission to the imperious advice of Lady Seely, but under the yoke of stern necessity, Castalia had consented to try a young woman of the neighbourhood, "highly recommended." And this abigail, in her tight yellow gown, was the cause of Mrs. Algernon's reticence during dinner. The poor lady might, however, have spared herself this restraint, if its object were to keep her servants in the dark as to domestic disagreements; for no sooner had Lydia (that was the abigail's name) reached the kitchen, than she and Polly, the cook, began a discussion of Mr. and Mrs. Algernon Errington's private affairs, which displayed a surprising knowledge of very minute details, and an almost equally surprising power of piecing evidence together.

When Lydia was gone, Algernon lit a cigar and drew up his chair to the fireside, where he sat silent, staring at his elegantly-slippered feet on the fender. Castalia rose, fidgeted about the room, walked to the door, stopped, turned back, and, standing directly opposite to Algernon, said querulously, "Do you mean to remain here?"

"For the present, yes; out of consideration for you. You dislike me to smoke in the drawing-room, do you not?"

"Why should you smoke at all?"

Algernon raised his eyebrows, shrugged his shoulders, crossed one leg over the other, and made no answer. His wife went away, and sitting down alone on a corner of the sofa in her little drawing-room, cried bitterly for a long time.

She was made to raise her tear-stained face by feeling a hand passed gently over her hair. She looked up, and found her husband standing beside her. "What's the matter, little woman?" he asked, in a half-coaxing, half-bantering tone, like one speaking to a naughty child, too young to be seriously reproved or argued with.

Now, although Castalia was haughty by education and insolent by temper, she had very little real pride and no dignity in her character. To be noticed and caressed by Algernon was to her a sufficient compensation for almost any indignity. There was but one passion of her nature which had any chance of resisting his personal influence, and that passion had never yet been fully aroused, although frequently irritated. Her jealousy was like a young tiger that had never yet tasted blood.

"What's the matter, little woman?" repeated Algernon, seating himself beside her, and putting his arm round her waist. She shrugged her shoulders fretfully, but at the same time nestled herself nearer to his side. She loved him, and it put her at an immense disadvantage with him.

"Don't you mean to vouchsafe me an answer, Mrs. Algernon Ancram Errington?"

"Oh, I daresay you're very sorry that I am Mrs. Errington. I have no doubt you repent."

"Really! And is that what you were crying for?"

No reply.

"It looks rather as if you repented, madam!"

"Oh, you know I don't; unless you like other people better than you like me!"

"'Other people' don't cry in my company."

"No; because they don't care for you. And because they're—they're nasty, artful minxes!"

"Hear, hear! A charming definition! Castalia, you are really impayable sometimes. How my lord would enjoy that speech of yours!"

"No, he wouldn't. Uncle Val would never enjoy what vexed me. My lady might; nasty, disagreeable old thing!"

"There, I can agree with you. A vulgar kind of woman—though she is my blood-relation—thoroughly coarse in the grain. But now that we have relieved our feelings, and spoken our minds on that score, suppose we converse rationally?"

"I don't want to converse rationally."

"Why not?"

"Because that means that you are going to scold me."

"Well—that might be highly rational, certainly; only I never do it."

"Well, but you'll manage to make out that I'm in the wrong and you're in the right, somehow or other."

"Cassy, I want you to write a letter."

"A letter? Whom do you want me to write to?"

Her tears were completely dried, and she looked up at him with a faint smile on her countenance, which, however, looked rueful enough, with red nose and swollen eyes.

"You must write to my lord, and get him to help us with a little money."

Her face fell.

"Ask Uncle Val for money again, Ancram? It is such a short time since he sent me some!"

"And to-morrow, at this hour, it will be 'such a short time' since you had your dinner! Nevertheless, I suppose you will want another dinner."

"I—I don't think Uncle Val can afford it, Ancram."

"Leave that to him. Afford it? Pshaw!"

Algernon made the little sharp ejaculation in a tone expressive of the most impatient contempt.

"But do we really—is it absolutely necessary for us to beg of my uncle again?"

"Not at all. Do just as you please," answered her husband, rising and walking away from the sofa to a distant chair.

Castalia's eyes followed him piteously.

"But what can I say?" she asked. "What excuse can I make? I hate to worry Uncle Val. It isn't as if he had more money than he knew what to do with. And if Lady Seely knew about his helping us, she would lead him such a life!"

"Do as you please. It would be a thousand pities to worry your uncle. Let all the worry fall on me."

He took up a book and threw himself back in his chair as if he had dismissed the subject.

"I don't know what to do!" exclaimed Castalia, with fretful helplessness. At length, after sitting silent for some time twisting her handkerchief backwards and forwards in her fingers, she got up and crossed the room to her husband's chair.

"Ancram!" she said softly.

"Eh? I beg your pardon!" looking up with an appearance of great abstraction, as if the perusal of his book had absorbed all his attention.

"I wish to do what will please you. I only care to please you in the world. But—can't you explain to me a little better why I must write to Uncle Val?"

Explain! Of course he would! He desired nothing better. He had brought her to a point at which encouragement was needed, not coldness. And with the singular flexibility that belonged to him, he was able immediately to plunge into an animated statement of his present situation, which sufficed to persuade his hearer that no course of conduct could be so desirable, so prudent—nay, so praiseworthy, as the course he had suggested.

To be sure the details were vague, but the general impression was vivid enough. If Algernon's pictures were a little inaccurate in drawing, they were at least always admirably coloured. And the general impression was this: that there never had been a person of such brilliant abilities and charming qualities as Algernon Ancram Errington so unjustly consigned to obscurity and poverty. And no contributions to his comfort, luxury, or well-being were too much to expect and claim from the world in general, and his wife's relations in particular. Common honesty—common decency almost—would compel Lord Seely to make all the amends in his power for having placed Algernon in the Whitford Post-office. And there was an insinuation very skilfully and delicately mixed with all the seemingly unstudied and spontaneous outpourings of Algy's conjugal confidence—an insinuation which affected the flavour of the whole, as an accomplished cook will contrive to mingle garlic in a ragoût, never coarsely obtrusive, and yet distinctly perceptible—to the effect that the hand of Miss Castalia Kilfinane had been somewhat officiously thrust upon her charming husband; and that the family owed him no little gratitude for having been kind enough to accept it.

Poor Castalia had an uneasy feeling, at the end of his fluent discourse, that Algernon had been a victim to her great relations, and, in some dim way, to herself. But the garlic was so admirably blended with the whole mass, that it was impossible for her to pick it out, or resent it, or do anything but declare her willingness to help her husband by any means in her power.

"Why, my dear girl, it is as much for your sake as for mine! And as to the necessity for it, I must tell you what Minnie Bodkin said to me to-day. Minnie is an excellent creature, full of friendly feeling—a little too conceited and fond of lecturing" (Castalia's face brightened); "but much must be excused to an afflicted invalid, who never meets her fellow-creatures on equal terms."

Castalia looked almost happy. But she said, "As to her affliction, it seems to me that she has been growing much stronger lately."

"Yes; I am glad to think so too. But let the best happen that can be hoped—let the disease, that has kept her helpless on her couch all these years, be overcome—still she must always be so lame as to make her an object of pity."

"Poor thing! I daresay it does warp her mind a good deal. What did she say to you?"

Algernon recapitulated a part of Minnie's warnings, but gave them such a turn as to make it appear that the greatest wrath and impatience of the Whitford tradesmen were directed against his wife. "They have a narrow kind of provincial prejudice against you, Cassy, on account of your being a 'London fine lady.' Me they know; and, in their great condescension, are pleased to approve of."

"Oh, everybody likes you better than me, of course," answered Castalia, simply. "But I don't care for that, if you will only like me better than anybody."

The genuine devotion with which this was said would have touched most men. It might have touched Algernon, had he not been too much engrossed in mentally composing the rough draft of Castalia's letter to her uncle, and putting his not inconsiderable powers of plausible persuasion to the task of making it appear that his wife's personal extravagance was the chief cause of their need for ready money.

"Don't tell him that I even know of your writing. My lord will be more willing to come down handsomely if he thinks it's for you only, Cassy," said Algernon, as he drew up his wife's writing-table for her, placed a chair, opened her inkstand, and performed several little acts of attention with a really charming grace and gallantry.

So Castalia, writing almost literally what her husband dictated—(although he kept saying at every sentence, "My dear child, you ought to know best how to address your uncle;" "Well, I really don't know, but I think you might put it thus;" and so forth)—completed an appeal to Lord Seely to anticipate by nearly a quarter the allowance he continued to make her for her dress out of his private purse, and, if possible, to increase its amount.

One such appeal had already been made and responded to by a gift of money. It had been made immediately after the arrival of the newly-married couple in Whitford, on the ground of the unforeseen expenses attendant on installing themselves in their new habitation. In answering it Lord Seely had written kindly, but with evident disapproval of the step that had been taken. "I cannot, Castalia," he said, "bid you keep anything secret from your husband, and yet I can scarcely help saying that I wish he did not know of the cheque I inclose. I fear he is disposed to be reckless in money matters; and nothing encourages such a disposition more than the idea that aid can be had from friends for the asking. Ancram will recollect a serious conversation I had with him the evening before your marriage, and I can only now reiterate what I then assured him of—that it will be impossible for me to repeat the assistance I gave him on that occasion."

"What assistance was that, Ancram?" asked Castalia, who knew not a word of the matter.

"Oh, I believe my lord made me the munificent present of two pair of breeches, and an old coat and waistcoat, or so."

"Made you a present of an old coat and breeches! What on earth do you mean?"

"I mean that he paid a twopenny outstanding tailor's bill for me. And he writes now as if he had conferred the most overwhelming obligation."

The fact was that Lord Seely had discharged a great number of Algernon's debts; all of them, as his lordship imagined. But there was clearly no need of troubling Castalia with these details.

When the letter was finished and sealed, Castalia still sat musingly tracing unmeaning figures with the point of her pen on the blotting-book. At length she said with some hesitation, "Ancram, how is it that we spend so much money? I don't think I am very extravagant."

"'So much money!' Good Heavens, Castalia—but you really have no conception of these things. Our whole income, and twice our income, is a miserable pittance. The Dormers pay their butler more."

She was again silent for a little while. Then she said, "Isn't there anything we could do without?"

Her husband looked at her in astonishment. It was a quite unexpected suggestion on Castalia's part. "Could you be kind enough to point out anything?" he asked drily. She looked somewhat cast down by his tone, but answered, "There's that last case of wine from town—the Rhine wine. Don't you think we might send it back unopened, and do with a bottle of sherry, now and then, from the 'Blue Bell?' Your mother finds that very good."

"Pshaw!" with the accustomed sharp, impatient contempt. "My mother knows no more about wine than a baby. To drink bad wine is absolutely to poison oneself. I can't do it, and I don't mean to let you do it, either. And when one knows that it is only a question of a few months, more or less, and that directly I get a better berth these greedy rascals will be paid their extortionate bills in full—positively, Castalia, it seems to me childish to talk in that way!"

It was the same with one or two other suggestions of retrenchment she ventured to make. Algernon showed conclusively (conclusively enough to satisfy his hearer, at all events) that it would not do—that it would be absolutely imprudent, on their part, to make any open retrenchment. All these sharks would come round them at once, if they smelt poverty. "I know these gentry better than you do, Castalia," said he. "There is no way of getting on with them except by not being in a hurry to pay them. Nothing spoils tradespeople so much as any over-alacrity of that kind. They immediately conclude that you can't do without them!"

"Oh, they're disgustingly impudent creatures, these Whitford tradespeople! There is no doubt in the world about that," said Castalia, in perfect good faith. "Only I thought you seemed to be made uneasy by what Miss Bodkin said to you on the subject."

"To be sure! But, my dear girl, your method would never answer! I do want money, very badly. And I do hope and expect—as I think I have some right to do—that my lord will assist us without delay, and without making one of his intolerable prosy preachments on the occasion. And we must have a few pounds to go on with, and stop the mouths of these rapacious rascals. But no retrenchment, Castalia! No 'Blue Bell' sherry! Good Heavens, it makes one bilious to think of it! I really cannot sacrifice my digestion to advance the commercial prosperity of Whitford. And when one considers it, why should we destroy our peace of mind by worrying ourselves? Lord Seely has got us into this scrape, and Lord Seely must get us out of it. Voilà tout!"

After that the rest of the evening was spent very harmoniously. Algernon could not repress two or three prodigious yawns, but he politely concealed them. And when Castalia went to her pianoforte, he woke up at the conclusion of an intricate fantasia quite in time to thank her for the performance, and to praise its brilliancy. In a word, so agreeable an evening, Castalia told herself, she had not passed for many weeks, although it had certainly begun in an unpromising way. So softened was she, indeed, by this gleam of happiness, that several times she was on the point of making a confession to her husband, and entreating his forgiveness. But she could not bear to risk bringing a cloud over the light of his countenance, which was the only sunshine in her life. "Ancram would be so angry!" was a thought that checked back words which were on her lips a dozen times. "And since the matter is all over, and he need never know anything about it, I may as well hold my tongue."

It needed, however, no confession on Castalia's part to convince Algernon that she had opened his secretaire, and taken Minnie Bodkin's letter thence, instead of having found it lying open on his table, as she had said. For on the next morning, when he entered his private room at the office, his first action was to try the little secretaire, which was unlocked. He then remembered that, after having secured that repository of his private papers, he had re-opened it, to throw Minnie's note into a drawer of it; and, having been called away at that moment, must have forgotten to re-lock it.

"Damnably provoking!" muttered Algernon to himself as he stood looking at the little cabinet with gloomy, anxious brows. Then, having first bolted the door of his room, he made a thorough search throughout the secretaire. "Nothing disturbed! She probably flew off to Dr. Bodkin's house directly after reading Minnie's note; and that lay in the little empty drawer right in front. It would be the first she opened."

Then he sat down in a mighty comfortable armchair, which was placed in front of an official-looking desk, and meditated so deeply that he forgot to unbolt the door, and was roused by Mr. Gibbs tapping at it, and desiring to speak with him on business.

CHAPTER II.

Mr. Gibbs's errand was not a pleasant one. He came to speak to his chief of complaints that had reached the office as to lost and missing letters. The most serious case was that of a man living in the neighbourhood of Duckwell, who complained that a money letter had never reached him, although it had been posted in Bristol three weeks back. Some inquiries had previously been made, but without result. And now the Duckwell man declared he would make a fine fuss, and bring the matter before the very highest authorities, if his letter were not forthcoming.

"What does the bumpkin mean, Gibbs?" asked Algernon, impatiently tapping with his fingers on the desk before him.

"I'm afraid he'll give us a deal of bother, sir," returned Mr. Gibbs slowly. "And I can't understand what has come of the letter. It's very awkward."

"Very awkward for him, if he really has lost his money. But I should not be surprised to learn that it never was posted at all."

"Humph! I don't know. He swears that the sender at Bristol can prove that it was posted."

"And why the deuce do people go on sending bank-notes by post, without the least care or precaution? One must have been connected with a post-office in order fully to appreciate the imbecility of one's fellow-creatures!"

"I don't know that it was bank-notes, sir. It may have been a cheque."

"Oh, depend upon it, it was whatever was stupidest to send, and most calculated to give trouble; if it was sent, that is to say! If it was sent!"

"I can't call to mind such a thing happening for twenty years back; not in this office. But lately there seems to be no end to things going wrong."

"Well, don't distress yourself about it, Gibbs. I have full reliance on you in every way."

"Oh no, sir! It is unpleasant, but I don't know that I specially need distress myself about it."

"Only because you have had the uncontrolled management of the office, Gibbs. And it is too bad, when one has worked so conscientiously as you have, to be worried by blundering bumpkins. I assure you, Gibbs, I am constantly singing your praises to Lord Seely. I tell him frankly, that if it were not for you, I don't know in the least how I should fulfil my onerous duties here! When I'm removed from this place, the powers that be won't have far to look for my successor."

This was the most explicit word that had yet fallen from Mr. Errington on the subject of his subordinate's promotion. And it decidedly gratified Mr. Obadiah Gibbs. Nevertheless, that steady individual was not so elated by the prospect held out to him as to dismiss from his mind the business he had come to speak about. "It is the most unaccountable thing!" said he. "Three or four cases of the kind within two months! And up to that time no office in the kingdom bore a better character than Whitford. I hope the thing may be cleared up. But it is next to impossible to trace a stolen letter. The Duckwell man—Heath, his name is; Roger Heath—says he is determined to complain to the Postmaster-General. I suppose we shall be having the surveyor coming to look after us. You see, it isn't like a solitary case. That's the worst of it. There's what you may term an accumulation, sir."

Whilst Mr. Gibbs poured forth his troubled mind in these and many more slow sentences, Algernon rose, took his hat, brushed it lightly with his glove, put it on, and was evidently about to depart. Gibbs ventured to lay his hand on his coat-sleeve to detain him. The clerk was not satisfied that the matter should be dismissed so lightly. It might not be possible to do anything, truly; but (in common with a great many other people) Mr. Obadiah Gibbs felt that, where efficacious action was impracticable, it was all the more desirable to mark the gravity of an unpleasant circumstance by copious talking of it. Life would become, in some sort, too frivolous and easy if, when a matter clearly could not be remedied, every one agreed to say no more about it! A vast deal of sage eloquence would thus be choked and dammed up. And Mr. Gibbs, for his special part, was conscious of having some reputation amongst his fellow Wesleyans for a gift of utterance.

"I really don't know, sir, what to say to Roger Heath," he persisted.

"Oh—tell him inquiries will be made in the proper quarters."

"That, sir, has been said already. He has been here twice or thrice."

"Then tell him to go to the devil!" said Algernon, sharply jerking his arm away from the clerk's grasp, and walking off.

The pious and respectable Mr. Gibbs shook his head disapprovingly at this profane speech, and went back to his stool in the outer office with a lowering brow.

Algernon walked along the High Street, and turned down a narrow lane leading towards the river, and past one corner of the Grammar School. The boys were just coming out of school with the usual shrill babble and rush. A party of Dr. Bodkin's private scholars were on their way to Whit Meadow.

"Good day, Ingleby," said Algernon, addressing the eldest of them, the same lad who had been Rhoda's squire in the tea-room on the night of Mrs. Algernon Errington's début in Whitford society. "Where are you off to?"

"We're going to have a row. I've got a boat, and we're going up the river as far as Duckwell Reach. We have leave from the doctor. Deuce of a job to get it, though!"

"Why?"

"Oh, because he's nervous about the river; thinks it dangerous, and all that."

"Well, you know, Ingleby," said a younger boy, with much eagerness, "lots of people have been drowned in that bit of the river between here and Duckwell Reach."

"Lots of people! Gammon!"

"Well, two since I've been here!"

"Oh, I daresay. Well, if you funk it you needn't come. There's plenty without you."

"You know I don't funk it for myself, Ingleby. I can swim."

"Yes, my friend. You wouldn't get into my boat if you couldn't. I'm on honour with the doctor to take none but swimmers," said Ingleby, turning to Algernon; "and of course that settles the matter. But, for my part, I should have thought anybody but the quite small boys might walk out of the Whit if they tumbled into it." "Oh no! You do our noble river injustice. You are not a Whitfordian or you would know better than that. There are some very ugly places between here and Duckwell Reach; places where I wouldn't give much for your chance of getting out if once you fell in, swimmer though you are. Good-bye. A pleasant row to you."

The boys pursued their way to the boat, and Algernon, turning off at right angles when he reached the bottom of the lane, got into Whit Meadow through a turnstile at the foot of the Grammar School playground.

There was a footpath through the meadow, and some fields beyond, which made a pleasant walk enough in fine summer weather, and was then a good deal frequented. But at this season it was damp, muddy, and lonely. The day was fine, but the ground had been saturated by previous rains, and that part of the meadow nearest to the margin of the river was almost a swamp. The path continued to skirt the Whit for some miles, running in the direction of Duckwell, and as Algernon walked along it he saw the windings of the river shining in the sun, and presently there appeared on it the boat full of schoolboys. One of them wore a scarlet cap, and thus made a bright spot of colour in the landscape. The sound of their young voices was carried across the water to Algernon's ears.

He stood for a minute or so at the gate of his own garden, which ran down behind the house to the river path, and watched them. The thought crossed his mind that, if any accident should occur to the boat at that spot, there would be little chance of assistance reaching it quickly. Ivy Lodge was the last house on that side of the river between Whitford and Duckwell Reach. And on the willow-fringed shore opposite not a living creature was to be seen, except some cattle grazing in the plashy fields.

The whole scene—the vivid green of the marsh grass, the grey willows, the boat with its wet oars flashing at regular intervals, the red-capped boy, and the sound of the fresh, shrill laughter of the crew, all fixed themselves on his mind with that vividness of impression which trivial external things so often make upon a brain labouring with some inward trouble.

CHAPTER III.

"What a state your boots are in!" exclaimed Castalia, pausing at the foot of the stairs, which she happened to be descending as her husband entered the house. "And why did you come by the back way?"

"I was worried, and did not wish to meet people and be chattered to. I thought the meadow-path would be quiet, and so it was."

"Quiet! Yes; but how horribly muddy! Do change your wet boots at once, Ancram!"

There was little need for her to insist on this proceeding. Algernon hastened to his room, pulled off his wet boots, and desired that they should be thrown away.

"They can be dried and cleaned, sir," said plump-faced Lydia, aghast at this order.

"My good girl you may do what you please with them. I shall never wear them again. Slight boots of that sort that have once been wet through become shapeless, don't you understand? Take them away."

When the master of the house descended to the drawing-room, he found a paper, squarely folded in the shape of a letter, lying in a conspicuous position on the centre table. It was Mr. Gladwish the shoemaker's bill, accompanied by an urgent request for immediate payment.

"More wall-paper, Cassy," said her husband, flinging himself on the sofa.

"Do you know, Lydia tells me the man was quite insolent!" said Castalia. "What can be done with such people? They don't seem to me to have the least idea who we are!"

"Oh, confound the brutes! Don't let us talk about them!"

But Castalia continued to talk about them in a strain of mingled wonder and disgust. She did not cease until dinner was announced, and Algernon was by that time so thoroughly wearied by his conjugal tête-à-tête, that he even received with something like satisfaction the announcement that Castalia expected the Misses Rose and Violet McDougall to pass the evening at Ivy Lodge.

"I daresay your mother will come too," said Castalia, "and bring Rhoda Maxfield with her. I asked her."

"Rhoda? Why on earth do you invite that little Maxfield?"

"What is your objection to her, Ancram?"

"Oh, I have no objection to her in the world. But I should not have thought she was precisely the sort of person to suit you."

"That's exactly what Miss Bodkin says! Miss Bodkin tried to keep Rhoda apart from me, I am perfectly sure. And I can't fathom her motive. And now you say the same sort of thing. However, I always notice that you echo her words. But I don't intend to be guided by Miss Bodkin's likes and dislikes. I haven't the same opinion of Miss Bodkin's wisdom that the people have here, and I shall choose my friends for myself. It's quite absurd, the fuss that is made in this place about Miss Bodkin; absolutely sickening. Rose McDougall is the only person of the whole set who seems to keep her senses on the subject."

"Rose McDougall will never lose her senses from admiration of another woman," returned Algernon. And then the colloquy was broken up by the arrival of the Misses McDougall, clogged and cloaked, and attended by their maid-servant. After having exchanged greetings with these ladies, Algernon withdrew, murmuring something about going to smoke his cigar.

"You'll not be long, Ancram, shall you?" said his wife, in a complaining tone. But he disappeared from the room without replying to her.

"I'm so dreadfully afraid that I drive your husband away when I come here, my dear," said Rose McDougall with a spiteful glance at Algernon's retreating figure.

"Good gracious, no! He doesn't think of minding you at all."

"Oh, I daresay he does not mind me; does not think me of importance enough to be taken any notice of. But I cannot help observing that he always keeps out of the way as much as possible when I am spending an evening here."

"Nonsense!" said Castalia, tranquilly continuing to string steel beads on to red silk for the manufacture of a purse.

"You might as well say that it is I who drive Mr. Errington away, Rose," put in Violet.

"Not at all!" returned her sister, with sudden sharpness. "That's quite a different matter."

"I don't see why, Rose!"

The true answer to this remark, in the elder Miss McDougall's mind, would have been, "You are so utterly insignificant, compared with me, that you are effaced in my company, and are neither liked nor disliked on your own merits." But she could not quite say that, so she merely repeated with increased sharpness, "That's a very different matter."

Rose McDougall was one of those persons who prefer animosity to indifference. That any one should simply not care about her was a suggestion so intolerable that she was wont to declare of persons who did not show any special desire for her society, that they hated her. She was sure Mr. A. detested the sight of her, and Miss B. was her bitter enemy. But, perhaps, in Algernon's case, she had more reason for declaring he disliked her than in many others. He did in truth object to the sort of influence she exercised over Castalia. He knew that Castalia was insatiably curious about even the most trifling details of his past life in Whitford; and he knew that Miss McDougall was very capable of misrepresenting—even of innocently misrepresenting—many circumstances and persons in such a way as to irritate Castalia's easily-aroused jealousy; and Castalia's easily-aroused jealousy was an element of discomfort in his daily life. In a word, there had arisen since his marriage a smouldering sort of hostility between him and Rose McDougall. But he was far from conceiving the acrid nature of her feelings towards him. For his part, he laughed at her a little in a playful way, and contradicted her, and, above all, he did not permit her to bore him by exacting any attention from him which he was disinclined to pay. But there was no bitterness in all that. None in the world!

Only he did not reckon on the bitterness excited in Miss Rose's breast by being laughed at and neglected. The graceful and charming way in which the laughter and neglect were accomplished by no means mollified the sting of them; a point which graceful and charming persons would do well sometimes to consider, but to which they are often singularly blind.

"And what have you been doing with yourself all day, Castalia dear?" asked Violet with a great display of affection.

"Oh—what can one do with oneself in this horrid hole?"

"To be sure!" responded Violet. But she responded rather uncertainly. To her, Whitford seemed by no means a horrid hole. She had been content enough to live there for many years—ever since her uncle had brought her and her sister from Scotland in their mourning clothes, and received his orphan nieces into his home.

"Don't speak of it, my dear!" exclaimed Rose, on whom the reminiscences of the years spent in Whitford wrought by no means a softening effect. "What possessed Uncle James to stick himself down in this place, of all places, I cannot conjecture. He might as well have buried us girls alive at once."

"Oh, well, I suppose you have had time enough to get used to it," said Castalia, coolly. "Violet, will you ring the bell? It is close to you. Thank you.—Lydia," when the girl appeared, "where is your master?"

"In the dining-room, ma'am."

"What is he doing?"

"Smoking and reading, ma'am."

"Go and ask him to come here, with my love."

"How the woman worrits him! She doesn't leave him a minute's peace," was Lydia's comment to the cook on this embassy.

"She worrits everybody, in her slow, crawley kind o' way; but I'm sorry for her sometimes, too. It's a trying thing to care more for a person's little finger than a person cares for your whole body and soul," returned Polly, who had a kind of broad good-nature and candour. But Lydia felt no sympathy with her mistress, and maintained that it was all her own fault then! What did she be always nagging at him for?—having that pitiless contempt for other women's mistakes in the management of their husbands which is not uncommon with her sex.

Some such thoughts as Lydia's probably passed through the minds of the Misses McDougall, but, of course, that was not the time or place to express them. They exerted themselves to entertain their hostess with a variety of Whitford gossip, while Castalia—her attention divided between the purse she was making and the drawing-room door, at which she hoped to see her husband presently appear—merely threw in a languid interjection now and then as her contribution to the conversation.

At length she rose, and flung the crimson and steel purse down on the table.

"Do you want anything, dear?" asked the obliging Violet with officious alacrity.

"No; I shan't be long gone. Sit still, Violet."

"She's gone to implore her husband to honour us with a little of his society," whispered Rose, when Castalia had shut the door. "I'm certain of it. More fool she!"

The sisters sat silent for a few minutes. Then they heard the door of the dining-room open, as though Castalia were coming back, and the sound of voices. Rose was seated nearest to the door, which was separated from that of the little dining-room opposite by a very narrow passage, and she distinctly heard Algernon say, "Pooh! The old girl doesn't want me." And again, "Says I hate her? Nonsense! I look on her with the veneration due to her years and virtues." And then Castalia said, "Well, she can't help her years. Besides, that's not the question. You ought to come, for my sake. It's very unkind of you, Ancram." After that there was a lower murmur of speech, as though the speakers had changed their places in the room, and Rose was able to distinguish no more.

When Mrs. Algernon Errington returned to the drawing-room, she found Violet in her old seat near the pianoforte; but Rose had shifted her position, and was standing near the window.

"What are you doing there, Rose? Enjoying the prospect?" asked Castalia. The shutters were not closed, but, as the night was very dark, there certainly did not seem to be any inducement to look out of the window.

"Can't you persuade your husband to come, dear? I'm so sorry!" said Rose, turning round; and her sister looked up quickly at the sound of her voice, which, to Violet's accustomed ear, betrayed in its inflections suppressed anger. Her face, too, was crimson, and her little light blue eyes sparkled with unusual brightness.

Castalia, however, noticed none of these things. "Oh, he'll come presently," she said. "He really was finishing a cigar. I told him that you were offended with him, and—"

"I offended with your husband? Oh dear no! Why on earth should I be? You ought not to have said that, Castalia."

"Well, you thought he was offended with you, or something of the sort. It's all the same," returned Castalia, with her air of weary indifference. "And he says it's nonsense."

"My dear, I am only sorry on your account that he won't come. Really, to myself, it matters very little; very little indeed. What a pity that you have not some one to amuse him! We are none of us clever enough, that is clear."

"Oh, you are quite mistaken if you think Ancram cares particularly for clever women!" said Castalia, whose thoughts instantly reverted to Minnie Bodkin. "Even Miss Bodkin, whom everybody declares to be such a wonder of talent, bores him sometimes, I can tell you. Of course he has known her from his childhood, and all that; but he said to me only yesterday that she was conceited, and too fond of preaching. So you see! I daresay, poor thing, she fancies all the time that she is enchanting him by her wisdom."

"Dear me," said Violet timidly, and with a sort of strangled sigh. "I think that, as a rule, gentlemen don't like any kind of women except pretty women! Though, to be sure, Minnie is handsome enough if it wasn't for her affliction."

"Oh, I wasn't thinking of Minnie," said Rose, viciously twitching at her sewing thread. "I meant it was a pity there was no one here who was clever enough, and who thought it worth while, to play off pretty airs and graces for Mr. Errington's amusement. That's the kind of cleverness that attracts men. And your husband, my dear, was always remarkably fond of flirting."

Violet opened her eyes in astonishment, and, from her place a little behind Castalia, made a warning grimace to her sister; but Rose only responded by a defiant toss of the head. Castalia's attention was now effectually aroused, and although she still spoke in the querulous drawl that was natural to her (or had become so from long habit), it was with a countenance earnestly addressed to her interlocutor, instead of, as hitherto, with carelessly averted eyes. "I never heard any one say before that Ancram was fond of flirting," she said.

"I should have thought it was not necessary to hear it. You might see it for yourself; unless, indeed, he is very sly about it in your presence. He, he, he!"

"See it for myself? Why—there's nobody here for him to flirt with!"

This naïve ignoring of any pretensions on the part of her present guests to be eligible for the purposes of flirtation was not lost on Rose.

"Not many who would flirt with a married man. No, I hope and believe not! But there are many kinds of flirtation, you know. There's the soft and sentimental, the shy, sweet sixteen style—little Miss Maxfield's style, for instance."

"Rhoda!"

"Yes; that is her name, I believe. I have never been intimate with the young person myself. Uncle James has always been very particular as to whom we associated with. However, since you have taken her up, my dear, I suppose she may be considered visitable."

"We have met her at Dr. Bodkin's, you know, Rose," put in Violet, who was looking and listening with a distressed expression of face.

"Oh yes; I believe Minnie asked her there at first to please Algernon. Minnie can be good-natured in that sort of way. But I don't know that it was very judicious."

"Why should you suppose it was to please my husband that Rhoda was invited to the Bodkins?" asked Castalia. "I don't see that at all. The girl might have been asked to please Miss Bodkin. I daresay she had heard of her from Mrs. Errington. Mrs. Errington is always raving about her."

Rose smiled with tightly-closed lips, and nodded. "To be sure! Poor dear Mrs. Errington—I mean no disrespect to your mother-in-law, Castalia, who is really a superior woman, only in some things she is as blind as a bat."

Castalia's sallow face was paler than ever. Her nostrils were dilated as if she had been running fast. "You never told me a word of this before," she said.

"My dear creature," said Rose, looking full at Castalia for the first time, "why, what was there to tell? The subject was led to by chance now, and I had not the least idea that you did not know all Algy's old love-stories. Everybody here—except, I suppose, poor dear Mrs. Errington—knew of the boy-and-girl nonsense between him and that little thing. But of course it never was serious. That was out of the question."

"I don't believe it!" said Castalia, suddenly.

"Well, I daresay the thing was exaggerated, as so often happens. For my part, I never could see what there was in the girl to make so many people admire her. A certain freshness, perhaps; and some men do think a great deal of that pink-and-white sort of insipidity."

"At all events, Ancram does not care about her now," said Castalia, speaking in broken sentences, and twisting her watch-chain nervously backwards and forwards in her fingers.

"Oh, of course not! I daresay he never did care about her in earnest. But that sort of philandering is a little dangerous, isn't it?"

"He does not like me to ask her to the house even."

"Doesn't he?"

"No; he has said so more or less plainly several times. He said so this very evening."

"Did he, indeed? Well, I really am glad to hear it. I scarcely gave Algy—Mr. Errington—credit for so much—prudence!"

"Mrs. Errington and Miss Maxfield," announced Lydia at the door of the drawing-room.

CHAPTER IV.

Mrs. Errington advanced towards her daughter-in-law with her habitual serene stateliness, and Rhoda followed her, modestly, looking very pretty in a new dress, the delicate hue of which set off her fair complexion to great advantage. Castalia received them much as usual; that is to say, without displaying any emotion whatever. But when Mrs. Errington took her daughter-in-law's hand, she exclaimed, "Good gracious, Castalia, how cold you are! A perfect frog! And yet this little room of yours is very warm; oppressively warm to one coming from without."

"We find the temperature so comfortable here!" said Violet. "Dear Castalia always has her rooms deliciously warm, we think."

"Perhaps, Violet, you are chilly by nature. Some constitutions are so. For myself, I have a wonderful circulation. But it is hereditary. All my branch of the Ancrams were renowned for it. I don't know, my dear Castalia, whether my cousin, Lady Seely, has the same peculiarity?"

"I don't know, I'm sure."

"With us it was a well-known thing among the Faculty for miles around Ancram Park. Our extremities were never cold, nor had we ever red noses. I believe a red nose was absolutely unknown in our family. No doubt that was part of the same thing; perfect circulation of the blood."

With that Mrs. Errington sat down tolerably near the fire and made herself comfortable. "Where is my dear boy?" she asked after a little while. "Not at that dreadful office I hope and trust!"

"He is at home," replied Castalia, slowly. "I asked him to come into the drawing-room, and he said he would by-and-by."

"Oh, I daresay he will come now, dear," said Rose McDougall, without raising her eyes from her sewing.

"Well, my dear," said Mrs. Errington to her daughter-in-law, "and if he does come 'now' you must not be jealous."

The two sisters glanced at the good lady in quick surprise, and then at Rhoda. Rhoda was looking, for the hundredth time, at a book of prints. It was her usual evening's occupation at Ivy Lodge. Mrs. Errington proceeded, placid, smiling, and condescending as ever: "You must not be jealous, Castalia, if he does come directly he learns that his mother is here. To be sure a wife ranks first. I have always acknowledged that; and, indeed, insisted on it. I am sure it was my own case with poor dear Dr. Errington, who would never have dreamed of putting any human being into competition with me. Still, allowances must be made for the very peculiar and devoted attachment Algy has always felt for me. He is, and ever was, an Ancram to the core. And this kind of—one may say romantic—affection for their mothers has always distinguished the scions of our house from time immemorial. Good evening, my dear Algy. I find our dear Castalia looking a little worn and ill, and I tell her she keeps her rooms too hot. What do you say?"

Algernon had sauntered into the room during his mother's harangue, delivered in the full mellow voice that belonged to her, and now bent to kiss the worthy lady's cheek as he greeted her. It was a cool, firm, rosy cheek. Indeed, Mrs. Errington's freshness and bloom were in singular opposition to Castalia's sallow haggardness, and made the elder lady look doubly buxom and buoyant by the force of contrast.

"You're flourishing, at all events, chère madame," said Algernon, looking at his mother with unfeigned satisfaction. It was a relief to him to see a contented, smiling, comfortable countenance. Nevertheless, although agreeable to look upon, Mrs. Errington was apt to become a little wearisome in point of conversation, and her dutiful son cast his eyes round the circle in search of a pleasant seat wherein to bestow himself. But his glance met no response. Rose McDougall had drawn near his wife, and after very stiffly returning his bow, had ceased to take any notice of him, markedly avoiding his eye, and keeping silence after he had spoken. Violet was divided between listening to the elder Mrs. Errington and watching her sister. Castalia was more lazy, more silent, more indifferent than usual. Algernon was as unaccustomed as a spoiled child to be taken no notice of. He to stand among those women as a person of secondary importance, not greeted, not flattered, not smiled upon!

He looked across the group round the fire to Rhoda, who happened to raise her eyes at that moment, and being taken by surprise at meeting his, dropped them hastily, with a vivid blush. Rhoda's blushes were as unmeaning as the smiles of an infant. The most trivial cause made her change colour, as Algernon very well knew. But at least the soft bright pink hue on pretty Rhoda's cheek showed some emotion, however slight or transient, at the sight of him. And, moved partly by a boyish, pettish resentment against the others, partly by the desire to hear a pleasant voice and pleasant words, and look upon a pretty woman's face with its delicate contour and fine subtle changes of tint, he walked across the room and seated himself beside Rhoda Maxfield.

Castalia pushed her chair back out of the lamplight. "You can't see to do your purse in that dark corner, Castalia," exclaimed Mrs. Errington.

"I don't want to do my purse. I'm sick of it."

"Naughty, fickle girl!" This was said playfully. Then in a loud whisper, addressed to the McDougalls as well as to her daughter-in-law, Mrs. Errington exclaimed, "Doesn't Rhoda look charming to-night? That pale lilac is the very colour for her. Trying to skins that have the least tinge of yellow in them, but she is so wonderfully fair! Dear me, it reminds one of old times to see those two side by side. As children they were always together."

No one responded. Violet McDougall fidgeted nervously on her chair and cast an appealing look at her sister. She would have tried to lead Mrs. Errington to talk of something else had she dared, but in Rose's presence Violet never ventured to take the initiative; and, besides, she was afraid of doing more harm than good, Mrs. Errington not being one of those persons who take a hint easily. The silence of her three listeners was no check to the worthy lady's eloquence. She continued to descant on Rhoda's attractions, and graces, and good manners; she dropped hints of the excellent opportunities Rhoda now had of "settling in life," only that she was a little fastidious from long association with such refined persons as the Erringtons, and had turned the cold shoulder to several well-to-do wooers in her own rank of life; she related anecdotes of Rhoda's early devotion to herself and her son, until Violet McDougall muttered under her breath, in a paroxysm of nervous impatience, "One would think the woman was doing it on purpose!"

Meanwhile Algernon was talking to Rhoda more freely and confidentially than he had spoken to her for a long, long time. He was indulging in the luxury of playing victim before a spectator whose pity would certainly be admiring, not contemptuous. And, as he spoke, the old habit of appealing to Rhoda, and confiding in Rhoda, and taking Rhoda's sympathy for granted, resumed its power over him. There was no strain of tenderness in his words. He said not a syllable that his wife and all the world might not freely have listened to. He talked as a petted boy might talk to an idolising sister—with a mixture of boastfulness and repining, which he would have been ashamed to display to a man.

Rhoda listened with sorrowful interest. How could it be that Algernon should have to endure all these troubles and mortifications? He was so clever, so accomplished, so highly connected, had such great and powerful relations! It appeared natural enough that folks like Mrs. Thimbleby, and the Gladwishes, and even her brother Seth, should sometimes be pressed for money. She herself, although she had never known privation in her father's house, had, until within the last year or so, been accustomed to the most rigid economy—not to say parsimony—and it had never cost her a care. But that Algernon Errington should desire money for various purposes, and not be able to get it, seemed to her a very hard case.

But Algernon's note was not all of complaint. There were occasional intervals in which he spoke of the brightness of his prospects ultimately, when once he should have tided over his present difficulties and had got out of Whitford. And there were a few flourishes about his social successes in town last year. In the indulgence of his all-absorbing egotism, he seemed to forget that the girl beside him had ever been—or had ever had either expectation or right to be—anything more to him than the patient, admiring, sisterly, humble confidante on whom he had relied for praise and sympathy from the time of his earliest recollections, and who supplied him with the most delicious food for his vanity, because unmingled with any doubt of its genuineness. No thought of her feelings (save that they were kindly and admiring towards himself) crossed his mind whilst he talked to her, bending down his head and gesticulating slightly with his white, handsome hands.

But when his mother called to her, "Come, Rhoda, I think, we must be going; I heard the carriage at the gate, child. You and Algy have been having a famous long chat! Reminded you of old times, didn't it?"

When I say Algernon heard these words, a spark of manhood made his cheeks tingle and his tongue stammer as he said, "I—I'm afraid I must have been—boring you dreadfully, Rhoda?"

In truth he was surprised to find that he had spent the whole evening in talking to Rhoda about himself. He glanced quickly at his wife, but she was occupied with the Misses McDougall. So occupied was she that she hardly returned Mrs. Errington's "Good night," which negligence, however, little ruffled that lady's equanimity. But when Rhoda approached to take leave of Castalia, the latter moved aside so suddenly that the movement might almost be called a start, and facing round, came opposite to her own image in the mirror above the chimney-piece, with Rhoda's fair image looking over its shoulder.

For one second, perhaps—it could scarcely have been more—the smooth surface of the glass gave back the two women's faces: one youthful, lily-hued, innocently surprised, with chestnut eyebrows and shining chestnut curls, and tender rosy lips parted like those of a child; the other yellow, worn full of fretful creases, with glittering eager eyes, and a thin mouth set into a straight line, and yet over all the undefinable pathos of a suffering spirit; behind the two, Algernon looking into his wife's dark eyes and recognising something there that he had never seen in them before.

In no longer time than it would take for a breath to dim the mirror all these images were gone, and the cold shiny glass indifferently showed a confusion of cloaks and shoulders and the back of a huge bonnet crowning Mrs. Errington's majestic figure.

From that day forth Castalia gave herself up to a devouring jealousy of Rhoda. She spied her goings and comings; she watched her husband's face when the girl was spoken of; she opened the letters that she found in the pockets of his clothes; she lay in wait to surprise some proof, no matter what, of a tender feeling on his part for his old love. In a word, she pursued her own misery with more eagerness, vigilance, and unflagging singleness of purpose than most people devote to the attainment of any object whatsoever.

CHAPTER V.

The discovery of Minnie Bodkin's note in Algernon's secretaire at the office had incited Castalia to make some other attempts to pry into that depository of her husband's papers. She made excuses to step into the post-office whenever she had any reason for thinking Algernon was absent. Sometimes it was with the pretence of wishing to see him, sometimes on the plea of wanting to rest. She had learned that her husband frequently went into the "Blue Bell," to have luncheon, in the middle of the day; and that, from one cause or another, the Whitford Post-office was not really honoured with so much of his personal superintendence as she had been led to suppose. And this again was a fertile source of self-tormenting. Where was he, when he was not at the office?

It whetted her suspicious curiosity to find the secretaire always carefully locked, ever since her discovery of Miss Bodkin's note there. She now wished that she had searched it thoroughly when she had the opportunity, instead of hastening off to Dr. Bodkin's house, after having read the first letter she came upon. But her feelings at that time had been very different from what they now were. She had been nettled, truly, and jealous of any private consultation between Minnie Bodkin and her husband; hating to think that he could trust, and be confidential with, another woman than herself, but not distinctly suspecting either Minnie or Algernon of any intent to wrong her. Miss Bodkin loved power, and influence, and admiration, and Castalia wished no woman to influence Algernon, or to be admired by him for any qualities whatsoever, except herself; but all her little envious resentments against Minnie had been mere pinpricks compared with the cruel pangs of jealousy that now pierced her heart when she thought of Rhoda Maxfield.

That secretaire! It seemed to have an irresistible attraction for her thoughts. She even dreamt sometimes of trying to open it, and finding fresh fastenings arise more and more complicated, as she succeeded in undoing one lock after the other. It was not Algernon's habit to lock up anything belonging to him. There must be some special reason for his doing so in this case! And to Castalia's jaundiced mind it seemed that the special reason could only be a desire to keep his letters secret from her. She grew day by day more restless. The servants at Ivy Lodge remarked with wonder their mistress's frequent absences from home. She, who had so dreaded and disliked walking, was now constantly to be seen on the road to the town, or on the meadow-path by the river. This kind of exercise, however, merely fatigued without refreshing her, and she became so lean and haggard, and her eyes had such a feverish glitter, that her looks might have alarmed anyone who loved her, and witnessed the change in her.

"There she goes again!" exclaimed Lydia to her fellow servant, as she watched her mistress down the garden-path, behind the house, one afternoon. "She can't bide at home for an hour together now!"

"She wears herself to the bone," said Polly, shaking her head.

"She wears other folks to the bone, and that's worse," returned the pitiless Lydia.

Meanwhile Castalia had passed out of the little wicket-gate of her garden into the fields, and so along the meadow-path towards Whitford. She made her way along the path resolutely, though with a languid step. The ground was hardened by recent frost, and the usually muddy track was dry. At the corner of the Grammar School playground she turned up the lane towards the High Street, keeping close to the wall of the Grammar School, so as to be out of view of any from the side windows. Before she quite reached the High Street she caught sight of Mr. Diamond, walking briskly along in the direction of his lodgings. He did not see Castalia, or did not choose to see her; for, although she had once or twice saluted him in the street, she had on another occasion regarded him with her most unrecognising stare, and Matthew Diamond was not a man to risk enduring that a second time. But Castalia quickened her step so as to intercept him before he crossed the end of Grammar School Lane.

"Mr. Diamond!" she said almost out of breath.

"Madam!"

Diamond raised his hat and stood still, in some surprise.

"Would you be kind enough—do you happen to know whether Mr. Errington has left the post-office? You must have passed the door. You might have seen him coming out."

"I am sorry, madam, that I cannot inform you."

"You—you haven't seen him anywhere in the town?"

"No; I have only just left the Grammar School. Have you any further commands?"

He asked the question after a slight pause, because Castalia remained standing exactly across his path, glancing anxiously up and down the High Street, and apparently oblivious of Diamond's existence.

"Oh no! I beg your pardon," she answered, moving aside. As she did so young Ingleby came up, and was about to pass them when Diamond touched him on the shoulder and said, "Ingleby, have you chanced to see Mr. Errington?"

"Yes, sir; I saw him going down the High Street not two minutes ago, close to old Maxfield's shop. Do you want him, Mrs. Errington? I can easily catch him if I run."

"No, no, no! Don't go! You must not go after him."

She walked away without any word or sign of farewell, leaving Diamond and the boy looking after her in surprise.

"That is the most disagreeable woman I ever came across!" exclaimed Ingleby, with school-boy frankness. "I hate her stuck-up airs. But Errington is such a capital fellow—! I'd do anything for him."

Diamond did not choose to discuss either the husband or the wife with young Ingleby, but he said to himself, as he pursued his homeward way, that Mrs. Errington's manner had been not only disagreeable but very strange.

Castalia reached the office and walked in. She entered the inner part that was screened off from the public, and passed Mr. Gibbs, behind his desk, without any recognition. She was about to enter Algernon's private room at the back, when Gibbs, rising and bowing, said "Did you want anything, ma'am? Mr. Errington is not there."

"Oh! I'll go in and sit down."

Gibbs looked uneasy and doubtful, and presently made an excuse to follow her into the room. Her frequent visits to the office of late by no means pleased Mr. Obadiah Gibbs.

"I didn't know how the fire was," said he, poking at the hot coals, and looking furtively at Mrs. Errington.

She was seated in her husband's chair in front of his desk. The little secretaire stood on a table at one side of it.

"I'm afraid Mr. Errington may not be back very soon," said Gibbs.

"Do you know where he's gone?"

"Not I, ma'am."

"Does he often go away during business hours?"

"Why—I don't know what you would call 'often,' ma'am—I crave pardon. I must attend to the office now; there is some one there." And Mr. Gibbs withdrew, leaving the door half open.

Castalia shut it, and fastened it inside. Then she pulled out a bunch of keys from her pocket, and tried them, one after the other, on the lock of the secretaire. This time it was safely secured, and not one of her keys fitted it. Then she opened the drawer of the table, and examined its contents. They consisted of papers, some printed, some written, a pair of driving gloves, and the cover of a letter directed to Algernon Errington, Esq., in a woman's hand. Castalia pounced on the cover, and thrust it into her pocket. After that, she looked behind the almanac on the chimney-piece, and rummaged amongst a litter of newspapers, and torn scraps of writing that lay in a basket. She was thus engaged when Mr. Gibbs's hand was laid on the handle of the door, and Mr. Gibbs's voice was heard demanding admission.

Castalia opened the door at once, and Mr. Gibbs came in with a look of unconcealed annoyance on his face. He looked round the room sharply.

"What do you want?" asked Castalia.

"I want to see that all's right here, ma'am. I'm responsible."

"What should be wrong? What do you mean?" she demanded with so coldly-haughty an air, that Gibbs was abashed. He felt he had gone too far, and muttered an apology. "I wanted to see to the fire. I'm afraid the coal-box is nearly empty. That old woman is so careless. I beg your pardon, but Mr. Errington is very particular about the room being kept warm."

Castalia deigned not to notice him or his speech. She drew her shawl round her shoulders, and began to move away.

"Can I give any message for you to Mr. Errington, ma'am?"

"No—you need not mention that I came. I shall tell him myself this evening."

As she walked down the High Street, she reflected on Mr. Gibbs's unwonted rudeness of look and manner.

"He is told to watch me; to drive me away if possible; to prevent me making any discoveries. I daresay they are all in a league together. I am the poor dupe of a wife—the stranger who knows nothing, and is to know nothing. We shall see; we shall see. I wonder where Ancram can have gone! That boy spoke of seeing him near Maxfield's house."

At that moment she found herself close to it, and with a sudden impulse she entered the shop, and, walking up to a man who stood behind the counter, said, "Is Mr. Errington here?"

The man was James Maxfield, and he answered sulkily, "I don't know whether he's gone or not. You'd better inquire at the private door."

Castalia's heart gave a great throb. "He has been here, then?" she said.

"You'd better inquire at the private door," was all James's response, delivered still more surlily than before.

Castalia left the shop, and knocked at the door indicated to her by James's thumb jerked over his shoulder. "Is Mr. Errington gone?" she asked of the girl who opened the door.

"Yes, ma'am."

"Did he—did he stay long?"

"About half an hour, I think."

"Is Mr. Maxfield at home?"

"No, ma'am; master is at Duckwell, and has been since Saturday."

"Who is it, Sally?" cried Betty Grimshaw's voice from the parlour, and upon hearing it Castalia walked hastily away.

When she reached her own home again, between fatigue and excitement she could scarcely stand. She threw herself on the sofa in her little drawing-room, unable to mount the stairs.

"Deary me, missus," cried Polly, who happened to admit her, "why you're a'most dead! Where-ever have you been?"

"I've been walking in the fields. I came round by the road. I'm very tired."

"Tired? Nay, and well you may be if you took all that round! I thought you'd happen been into Whitford. Lawk, how you're squashing your bonnet! Let me take it off for you."

"I don't care; leave it alone."

But Polly would not endure to see "good clothes ruinated," as she said, so she removed her mistress's shawl and bonnet—folding, and smoothing, and straightening them as well as she could. "Now you'd better take a drop o' wine," she said. "You're a'most green. I never saw such a colour."

Despite her rustic bluntness, Polly was kind in her way. She made her mistress swallow some wine, and put her slippers on her feet for her, and brought a pillow to place beneath her head. "You see you han't got no strength to spare. You're very weak, missus," she said. Then she muttered as she walked away, "Lord, I wouldn't care to be a lady myself! I think they're mostly poor creeturs."

Left alone, Castalia closed her eyes and tried to review the situation, but at first her brain would do nothing but represent to her over and over again certain scenes and circumstances, with a great gap here and there, like a broken kaleidoscope.

Ancram had been to Maxfield's house, and it could not have been to see the old man, who had been absent for some days. Perhaps Ancram was in the habit of going thither! He had never said a word to her about it. How sly he had been! How sly Rhoda had been! All his pretended unwillingness to have Rhoda invited to Ivy Lodge had been a blind. There was nothing clear or definite in her mind except a bitter, burning, jealous hatred of Rhoda.

"We shall see if Ancram confesses to having been to that house to-day," said Castalia to herself. Then she went upstairs wearily. She was physically tired, being weak and utterly unused to much walking, and called Lydia to dress her and brush her hair. And when her toilet was completed, she sat quite still in the drawing-room, neither playing, reading, nor working—quite still, with her hands folded before her, and awaited her husband.

She would first try to lead him to confess his visit to the Maxfields, and, if that failed, would boldly tax him with it. She even went over the very words she would say to her husband when he should descend from his dressing-room before dinner.

But she could not foresee a circumstance which disturbed the plan she had arranged in her mind. When Algernon returned to Ivy Lodge he did not go into his dressing-room as usual, but marched straight into the drawing-room, where Castalia was sitting.

"That's an agreeable sort of letter!" he said, flinging one down on the table.

He was not in a passion—he had never been known to be in a passion—but he was evidently much vexed. His mouth was curved into a satirical smile; he drew his breath between his teeth with a hissing sound, and nodded his head twice or thrice, after repeating ironically, "That's an uncommonly agreeable sort of letter!" Then he thrust his hands deep into his pockets, threw himself into an easy-chair, stretched his legs straight out before him, and looked at his wife.

Castalia was surprised, and curious, and a little anxious, but she made an effort to carry out her programme despite this unexpected beginning. She remained motionless on the sofa, and said, with elaborate indifference of manner, "Do you wish me to read the letter? I wonder at your allowing me to know anything of your affairs."

"Read it? Of course! Why else did I give it to you? Don't be absurd, Castalia. Pshaw!" And he impatiently changed the position of his feet with a sharp, sudden movement.

Castalia's sympathy with his evident annoyance overcame her resentment for the moment. She could not bear to see him troubled. She opened the letter.

"Why it's from Uncle Val!" she exclaimed.

It was from her uncle, addressed to her husband, and was written in a tone of considerable severity. To Castalia it appeared barbarously cruel. Lord Seely curtly refused any money assistance; and stated that he wrote to Algernon instead of to Castalia, because he perceived that, although the application for money had been written by Castalia's hand, it had not been dictated by her head. Lord Seely further advised his niece's husband, in the strongest and plainest terms, to use every method of economy, to retrench his expenditure, to refrain from superfluous luxuries, and to live on his salary.

"The little allowance I give Castalia for her dress will be continued to her," wrote his lordship. "Beyond that, I am unable to give either her or you one farthing. Understand this, and act on it. And, moreover, I had better tell you at once, as an additional inducement to be prudent, that I see no prospect of procuring advancement for you in any other department of his Majesty's service than the one you are in at present. My advice to you is to endeavour to merit advancement by diligence in the performance of your duties. You have abilities which are sure to serve you if honestly applied. You are so young, that even after ten or fifteen years' work you would be in the prime of all your faculties and powers. And ten or fifteen years' good work might give you an excellent position. As to Castalia, I cannot help feeling a conviction that her discontent is chiefly reflected, and that if she saw you cheerful and active in your daily business, she would not repine at her lot."

Castalia put the letter down on the table in silence. She was astonished, indignant; but yet a little gleam of satisfaction pierced through those feelings—a hope that she and her husband might be drawn closer together by this common trouble. She would show him how well able she was to endure this, and worse, if he would only love her and trust her entirely. Even her jealousy for Rhoda Maxfield was mitigated for the moment. All that fair-weather prettiness and philandering would be put out of sight at the first growl of a storm. The wife would be the nearest to him if troubles came. No pink-and-white coquetry could usurp her right to suffer with him and for him, at all events.

"That's a pleasant sort of thing, isn't it?" said Algernon, who had been watching her face as she read.

"It is too bad of Uncle Val, Ancram."

"Too bad! Yes; to put it mildly, it is too bad, I think. Too bad? By George, I never heard of anything so outrageous!"

"Do you know, I think that my lady is at the bottom of it."

"I wish she was at the bottom of the Thames!"

"Ancram, I do feel sorry for you. It is such a shame to bury your talents, and all that. But still, you know, it is true what he says about your having plenty of time before you. And as to being poor—of course it is horrid to be poor, but we can bear it, I daresay. And, really, I don't think I should mind it so much if once we were acknowledged to be quite, quite poor; because then it wouldn't matter what one wore, and nobody would expect one to have things like other people of one's rank."

Poor Castalia was not eloquent, but had she possessed the most fluent and persuasive tongue in the world, it would not have availed to make Algernon acquiesce in her view of the situation. She was for indignantly breaking off all connection with relatives who could behave as Uncle Val had behaved. It was not his refusing to advance more money (in her conscience Castalia did not believe he could afford much assistance of that kind), but his writing with such cruel coldness to Ancram—his declaring that Ancram's case was not a hard one—his lecturing about duties, and cheerful activity, and so on, just as if Ancram had been an ordinary plodding young man instead of a being exceptionally gifted with all sorts of shining qualities—these were offences not to be forgiven. Castalia, for her part, would have endured any privation, rather than beg more favours of Uncle Val and my lady.

But Algernon's feeling in the matter was by no means the same as Castalia's. He dismissed all her attempts to express her willingness to share his lot for good or ill as matters of no importance. She might find it easy enough. Yes; the chief burthen would not fall on her! And, besides, she did not at all realise what it would be to have to live on the salary of the postmaster of Whitford, and to practise "rigid economy," as my lord phrased it. It was really provoking to see the cool way in which she took it for granted that matters would be mended by their being "acknowledged to be quite, quite poor." "My dear Castalia," he said, with an air of superior tolerance, "you have about as much comprehension of the actual state of the case as a canary-bird."

She paused, silently looking at him for a moment. Then she drew nearer to him, and laid her arm round his shoulder. She wore a dinner-dress with loose hanging sleeves, which were not becoming to her wasted frame. But the poor thin arm clung with a loving touch to her husband, as she said, "I know I am not so clever as you, Ancram, but I can see and understand that if we haven't money enough to pay for things we must do without them." (Castalia advanced this in the tone of one stating a self-evident proposition.) "And I shan't care, Ancram, if you trust me, and—and—don't put any one else before me. I never put any one before you. I was fond of Uncle Val. I think he was the only person I really loved in the world before I saw you. But if he treats you badly I shall give him up."

Algernon shook off the clinging arm from his shoulder, not roughly, but slightingly.

"What on earth are you talking about, Cassy? What do you suppose we are to do? I tell you I must have some money, and you must write to your uncle again without delay."

She drew back with a hurt sense of having been unappreciated. The tears sprang to her eyes, and she put her hand into her pocket to take her handkerchief. The hand fell on something that rustled, and was stiff. It was the letter cover she had found in her husband's office that morning. The touch of the crisp paper recalled not only the events of the afternoon, but her own sensations during them. "Where were you this afternoon?" she asked, suddenly checking her tears, as the dry, burning, jealous feeling awoke again in her heart.

"Where was I? Where must I be? Where am I every afternoon? At the office—confound it!"

"You were not there all the afternoon. I—happened to look in there, and you were gone."

"I suppose you came just at the moment I happened to be absent, then. I had to see one or two men on business. Not pleasant business. I was not amusing myself, I assure you," he added with a short hard laugh.

"What men had you to see?"

"Oh, no one whom you know anything about. Isn't dinner ready? I shan't dress. I have to go out again this evening."

"This evening!"

"Yes; it is a frightful bore, but I have a business appointment. Do ring and tell the cook to make haste."

"You are not going out again this evening, Ancram?"

"I tell you I must. How can you be so childish, Castalia? Whilst I am gone you can employ yourself in making out the draught of a letter to your uncle."

"I will not write to my uncle! I will not. You don't care for me. You—you deceive me," burst out Castalia. And then a storm of sobs choked her voice, and she hurried away, filling the little house with a torrent of incoherent sounds.

Algy looked after her, with his head bent down and his eyebrows raised. Castalia was really very trying to live with. As to her refusal to write to her uncle, she would not of course persist in it. It was out of the question that she should persist in opposing any wish of his. But she was really very trying.

When dinner was announced, Castalia sent word that she had a headache and could not eat. She was lying down in her own room. Her husband murmured a few words of sympathy, but ate his dinner with no sensible diminution of appetite, and, as soon as it was despatched, he lit a cigar, wrapped himself in his great-coat, and went out.

Castalia heard the street-door shut. She rose swiftly from the bed on which she had thrown herself, put on a bonnet and cloak, muffled her face in a veil, and followed her husband.

CHAPTER VI.

The night was dark and cheerless. It was one of those murky November nights when one seems to see and breathe through a dusky gauze. The road from Ivy Lodge to Whitford was not lighted. At a long distance before her, Castalia saw a red, glowing speck, which she knew to be the lamp over the chemist's shop, kept by Mr. Barker, her landlord. After that, a few street lamps glimmered, and the town of Whitford had fairly begun.

It was not late, and yet most of the shops were shut, and the streets very silent and deserted. Castalia strained her eyes onward through the darkness, and presently saw her husband's figure come into the circle of faint light made by a street lamp, traverse it, and disappear again into the shade. She had walked so quickly in her excitement as to have overtaken him sooner than she had expected. Whither was he going?

She slunk along in the shadow of the houses, frightened at the faint sound of her own footfall on the flagstones, starting nervously at every noise, hurrying across the lighted spaces in front of the few shops that remained open with averted face and beating heart, fearing to be noticed by those within. But never once did she falter in her purpose of following her husband. She would have been turned back by no obstacle short of one which defied her physical powers to pass it.

Algernon was now nearing Maxfield's house. The shutters of the shop were closed, but the door was still open, and a light streamed from it on to the pavement. Castalia followed, watching breathlessly. Her husband passed the shop, went on a pace or two, stopped at the private door, and rang the bell. She could see the action of his arm as he raised it. The door was opened without much delay, and Algernon went in.

Castalia stood still, trying to collect her thoughts and determine on her course of action. What should she do? Her husband might be an hour—hours—in that house. She could not stand there in the street. An impulse came upon her to make herself known—to go in and tax Algernon with perfidy and deception then and there. But she checked the impulse. It would have been a desperate step. Algernon might never forgive her. It might be possible for her to reach a pitch of rage and jealousy which would make her deaf to any such considerations—careless as to the consequences of her actions if she could but gratify the imperious passion of the moment. She was dimly conscious that this might be possible; but for the present she had sufficient control over her own actions to pause and deliberate. There she stood, alone at night, in Whitford High Street—stealthily, trembling, and wretched—she, Castalia Kilfinane! Who would believe it? What would her uncle feel if he could see her now, or guess what she was enduring?

The idea came into her mind—floating like a waif on the current of indignant misery that seemed to flood all her spirit—that there might be hundreds of human beings whom she had seen and thought happy smarting with some secret wound like her own, and living lives the half of which was never known to the world. Castalia had never been apt to let her imagination busy itself with the sorrows of others, and at this moment the conception had no softening effect. It only added an extra flavour of bitterness and rebellion to her sufferings. It was too cruel. Why should such things be? And what had she done to merit so much unhappiness? She shivered a little as a breeze from the river came bringing with it the clammy breath of the marsh mists—the white cloud-kraken that Minnie Bodkin had so often watched from her window.

How long Castalia remained standing at her post she could never reckon; she was conscious only of burning pain of mind, and of a determination not to shrink from her purpose because of the pain. A footstep came sounding along the quiet street and startled her. She shrank back as far as she could, pressing her shoulder close against the wall, and uncertain whether to walk on or remain still. It was a man who came towards her, turning from a narrow street opening into the High Street, which

Castalia knew to be Lady Lane. He walked with a very rapid step, hanging his head, and looking neither to the right nor to the left. Castalia was, perhaps, the only dweller in Whitford who would not have recognised the figure as being that of David Powell, the Methodist preacher.

As Powell neared Castalia, he seemed to become aware of her presence by some sixth sense, for to all appearance he had not looked towards her. The truth was, that all his outward perceptions were habitually disregarded by him, except such as carried with them some suggestion of helpfulness and sympathy. A fashionable lady might have stood facing him during a long sermon in chapel, or in the open fields, and (unless she had displayed signs of "grace") he would have taken no heed of her—would not have been able to tell the colour of her garments. But let the same woman be tearful, ragged, sick, or injured, and no observation could be more rapid and comprehensive than David Powell's, to convey all needful particulars of her state and requirements. So this night, as he passed along the quiet Whitford streets, the few persons he had met hitherto were to him as shadows. But when the vague outline of a woman's form made itself a blot of blacker shadow in the darkness, those accustomed sentinels, his senses, gave the spirit notice of a fellow-creature in want, possibly of bread, certainly of sympathy.

He stopped within a few paces of Castalia, and perceived by that time that she was well and warmly clad, and that her trouble, whatever it was, could not be alleviated by alms. In her desire to avoid notice, she shrank away more and more almost crouching down against the wall. It occurred to Powell that she might be ill. "Are you suffering?" he asked, in a low musical voice. "Can I help you?"

Finding that she did not reply, he advanced a step farther, and was stretching out his hand to touch her on the shoulder, when, driven to bay, she raised herself up to her full height, and answered quickly and resentfully, "No; I am not ill. I am waiting for some one."

He stood still, irresolutely. Her voice and accent struck him with surprise, he recognised them as belonging to a person of a different class from any he had expected. How came such a lady to be alone at that hour, standing in the cold street? At length he said, gently, "If I may advise you, it would be well for you to go home. The person who keeps you waiting in the street in such weather, and at this hour, must surely be very thoughtless. Can I not assist you? I am David Powell, a poor preacher of the Word. You need have no fear of me."

"No; please to go away. I am not at all afraid. Go away, go away!" she added with an imperative emphasis, for she began to fear lest her husband should come out of the house, hear the sound of her voice, and find her there. Powell obeyed her, and walked slowly away. There was, in truth, so far as he knew, no reason to fear that any evil could happen to the woman in Whitford High Street, except the evil of standing so long in the cold, raw weather. It had now begun to rain; a fine drizzling rain, that was very chill.

When he had walked some distance along the High Street, and was close to the turning that led to Mrs. Thimbleby's house, he stopped and looked back. Almost at the same moment he saw a man come out of Maxfield's house, and advance along the street towards him. Then, at rather a long interval, the cloaked lady began to move onward also, but without overtaking the man, or apparently trying to do so. It was a strange adventure, and one entirely unparalleled in Powell's experience of the little town; and after he had reached his lodgings he could not, for a long time, divert his thoughts from dwelling on it.

Meanwhile, Algernon, unconscious of the watcher behind him, proceeded straight onward to the post-office. Then he turned up the narrow passage or entry in which was the side door that gave access to his private office. Castalia did not follow him beyond the mouth of the entry. Standing there and listening, she heard the sharp sound of a match being struck, then the turning of a key, and a door softly opened and shut.

It then struck Castalia for the first time that this unexpected visit to the office afforded an opportunity for her to reach home without her husband's discovering her absence. She had not considered before how this was to be accomplished; and, indeed, had Algernon returned directly to Ivy Lodge from Maxfield's house it would have been impossible.

She now saw this, and hastened back along the road, in a tremor at her narrow escape; for, although the impulse had crossed her mind to declare herself, and boldly enter Maxfield's house in quest of her husband, that was a very different matter from being suddenly discovered against her will. In the latter case she would, as she well knew, have been at an immense disadvantage with her husband, who, instead of being accused, would become accuser.

Nothing short, indeed, of the passion of jealousy within her would have given her strength to combat her husband. This was the only way in which her idolatrous admiration, her very love for him, could be turned into a weapon against him.

"I could bear anything else! Anything else!" she said to herself. "But to be fooled and deceived, and put aside for that girl—!" A great hot wave of passion seemed to flow through her whole body as she thought of Rhoda. "Let the servants see me! What do I care?" she said recklessly. At that moment she would not have heeded if the whole town had seen her, and known her errand into Whitford, and its result. She rang loudly at the bell of Ivy Lodge, and walked in past the servant, with a white face and glittering eyes.

"Isn't master coming?" stammered the girl, staring at her mistress.

"I don't know. Go to bed. I don't want you."

There was something in her face which checked further speech on Lydia's part. Lydia was fairly frightened. She crept away to the garret, where Polly was already sleeping soundly, and vainly tried to rouse her fellow-servant, to feel some interest in her account of how missus had stalked into the house by herself like a ghost, and had ordered her off to bed, and to get up a discussion as to missus's strange goings on altogether of late.

Castalia went to her own room, uncertain whether to undress and go to bed or to remain up and confront her husband when he should return. One dominant desire had been growing in her heart for many days past, and had now become a force overwhelming all smaller motives, and drawing them resistlessly into its strong current. This dominant desire was to be revenged—not on her husband, but on Rhoda Maxfield. And it might be that by waiting and watching yet awhile, by concealing from Ancram the discovery she had that night made, she might be enabled more effectually to strike at her rival. If Ancram knew, he would try to shield Rhoda. He would put the thing in such a light before the world as to elicit sympathy for Rhoda and make her (Castalia) appear ridiculous or obnoxious. He had the gift to do such things when it pleased him. But Rhoda should not escape. No; she would keep her own counsel yet awhile longer.

When Algernon came home about midnight, letting himself into the house with a private key which he carried, he found his wife asleep, or seeming to sleep, and congratulating himself on escaping the querulous catechism as to where he had been, and what he had been doing, which he would have to endure had Castalia been awake on his return. As he crossed the bedchamber to his dressing-room, she moved, and put up one hand to screen her eyes from the light.

"Don't let me disturb you, Cassy," he said. "I have been detained very late. I am going downstairs again—there is a spark of fire in the dining-room—to have one cigar before I turn in. Go to sleep again."

He bent down to kiss her, but she kept her face obstinately buried in the pillow. So he took her left hand, which hung down, and lightly touched it with his lips, saying, "Poor sleepy Cassy!" and went away.

And then she raised her thin left hand, on which her wedding-ring hung loosely, and passionately kissed it where her husband's lips had rested, and burst into a storm of crying, until she fairly sobbed herself to sleep.

CHAPTER VII.

"So you had that fine gentleman, Mr. Algernon—What-d'ye-call-it—Errington, here last evening?" said Jonathan Maxfield to his daughter, on his return from Duckwell.

"Yes, father; he had been before in the afternoon. He was very anxious to see you; but Aunt Betty told him you wouldn't be back until to-day."

"Very anxious to see me, was he? I have my own opinion about that. But, no doubt, he wants me to believe that he's anxious."

"He seems in a good deal of distress of mind, father."

"I daresay. And what about the minds of the folks as hold his promises to pay? Just so much waste paper, those are, I take it; I'd as lief have his word of honour myself. And most people in Whitford know what that's worth."

"I think he has been very unfortunate, father."

"H'm! What worldly folks calls misfortin' is generally the Lord's dealing according to deserts. It's set forth in Scripture that the righteous man shall prosper, and the unrighteous be brought to naught."

"But—father, even good people are sometimes chastened by afflictions," said Rhoda timidly.

Old Max knitted his brows.

"There's nothing," said he, "more dangerous than for the young and inexperienced to wrest texts; it leads 'em far astray. When that kind o' chastening is spoken of, it don't mean the sort of trouble as has fallen on young Errington. The Almighty has given every man reason enough to understand that, if he spends thirteenpence out of every shilling, he'll be beggared before the year's end. I don't believe in men being ruined without fault or foolishness of their own."

"He asked me if I—if you—if I thought—he asked me to ask you to have a little patience with him about some bills. I didn't know that he had any bill here; but he said you would understand."

"Aye, aye! I understand. It isn't bills for tea, and flour, and bacon, and such like. It's a different kind o' bills the young gentleman's been meddling with; and a fine hand he's made of it."

"Couldn't you help him, father?"

Rhoda spoke pleadingly, but with the timidity which always attended her requests to her father, whose recent indulgence had never reached a point of weakness, and who clearly showed, in all his dealings with his daughter, that he was not carried away by his affection for her, but acted with the consciousness of a will unfettered by precedents, and perfectly able to choose its course without regard to what other people might expect of him.

For herself, in pleading for Algernon, she was not moved by self-conscious sentimentality, neither did she suppose herself to be doing anything heroic. The peculiar tenderness she still felt for him was made up of pity and memory. The Algy she had loved was gone—had melted into thin air, like a dream under the morning sunlight. Mr. Errington, the postmaster of Whitford, and the husband of the Honourable Castalia Kilfinane, was a very different personage. Still he was inextricably connected in her mind with that bright idol of her childhood and her youth. His marriage had put all possibility of love-making between him and herself as much out of the question, to her mind, as if he had been proved to be her brother. Rhoda had read no romances, and she was neither of an innovating spirit nor a passionate temperament, and it is surprising what power a sincere conviction of the irrevocable and inevitable has to control the "natural feelings" we hear so much of! But she clung tenaciously to a better opinion of Algernon than his actions warranted—as has been the case with many another woman—chiefly to justify herself for ever having loved him.

"Couldn't you help him, father?" she repeated, seeing that her father did not at once reply, but was sitting meditating, with a not altogether ill-pleased expression of face.

"Help him!" cried old Max. "Why should I help him? A reprobate, unregenerate, vain, ungrateful worldling! I did help him once, and earned much gratitude for my pains. And what a sneaking, poor, mean, pitiful fellow he must be to come here and whine to you! A poor, pitiful fellow! Talk of a gentleman! Yah!"

Old Max derived so much grim satisfaction from the contemplation of Algernon's pitiful behaviour that it seemed almost to soften him towards the culprit, in whom any glimpse of nobility would not have been very welcome to his enemy. When you hate a man on excellent private grounds, it is certainly unpleasant to see him displaying qualities in public which win a fallacious admiration. And this aggravation was one which old Max had been suffering for some time at the hands of the popular Algernon. His present money difficulties, combined with his unworthy methods of meeting them, at once gratified and justified Jonathan Maxfield's vindictiveness.

He gave forth the queer grunting noise that served him for a laugh, as he said, "And a lot o' good his fine marriage has done him! And his grand relations! I told him long ago that if he wanted help from such as them, he must ask it with a pocket full of money. Then he might ha' been uplifted into high places. And it wasn't only my own wisdom neither, though that might ha' been enough for such a half-fledged young cockerel as he was in them days, seeing it has been enough for his betters before now. I had the warrant of Scripture; for what says Solomon? 'Wealth maketh many friends; but the poor is separated from his neighbour.'"

Still Rhoda did not altogether despair of inducing her father to do something for Algernon. What that something might be, or how far it was possible for her father to assist young Errington, except by simply giving or lending him money, Rhoda was ignorant. Algernon in talking to her had spoken very glibly, but, to her, very unintelligibly, of bills which were in her father's hands; and had pointed out, with an air of candour and conviction, that it would be imprudent on Mr. Maxfield's part to drive matters to extremity. It had all sounded very convincing, simply from the tone in which it was said. Many of us are astonishingly uncritical as to the coherence and cogency of words if they be but set to a good tune.

Algernon himself was rather hopeful since that interview with Rhoda. It could not be, after all, that Jonathan Maxfield would actually cause him, Algernon Errington, any personal inconvenience for the sake of a sum which was really a mere trifle to Maxfield, and which appeared very trifling to Algernon under every aspect except that of being called upon to pay it.

He had learned not long previously that certain bills he had given, backed by the name of that solid capitalist, the Honourable Jack Price, had found their way into old Max's hands. This startled him considerably, for he had no reason to count on the old man's forbearance. The time was drawing nigh when the bills would become due.

About a month ago some other bills had fallen due, and had been duly honoured. They had been given to a London wine merchant, who would certainly not have scrupled to take any strong measure for getting his money. And even the name of Jack Price was no talisman to charm away this grasping tradesman's determination to be paid for goods delivered; the wine merchant in question doing a large City business, and feeling no anxiety as to the opinion entertained by the Honourable Mr. Price's fashionable connection about himself or his wares. Under the pressure of this disagreeable conviction, the money had been found to honour the bills held by the wine merchant.

For the discharge of the liabilities represented by the bills now in Maxfield's hands, Algernon had reckoned on Castalia's extracting some money from her uncle. Algernon did not abandon the hope that she might yet succeed in doing so. Castalia must be urged to make new and stronger representations of their necessities to Lord Seely. But it could not be denied that my lord's last letter had been a very heavy blow; and that, moreover, a number of slight embarrassments, which Algernon had hitherto looked on as mere gossamer threads, to be broken when he pleased, had recently exhibited a disconcerting toughness and power of constraining his actions and destroying his comfort.

The thought not infrequently occurred to him that, if he were alone in the world, unhampered by a wife who had no flexibility of character, and who had recently displayed a stubborn kind of obtuseness, showing itself in such remarks as that if they had not money to pay for luxuries, they must do without luxuries, and that if they were poor, it would be better to seem poor, and the like dull commonplaces, which were peculiarly distasteful to Algernon's vivacious intelligence—if, he thought, he had no wife, or a different wife, things would undoubtedly go better with him. He was too quick not to perceive that his marriage, far from improving his social position, had been eminently unpopular amongst his friends and acquaintances. To be sure he had never intended to return to Whitford after allying himself with the family of Lord Seely. He had meant to shake the dust of the sleepy little town from his feet for ever. He reckoned up the advantages he had expected to gain by marrying Castalia, and set the real result against each one in his mind.

He had expected to get into the diplomatic service. He was a provincial postmaster!

He had expected to live in some splendid metropolis. He found himself in the obscure town which, of all others, he wished to avoid!

He had expected to be courted and caressed by wealthy, noble, and distinguished persons. He was looked coldly or shyly upon by even the insignificant middle-class society of a county town!

All this seemed peculiarly hard and unjust, because Algernon had always intended to bear his honours gracefully, without stiffness or arrogance. He would cut nobody; he would turn the cold shoulder to nobody. He had pictured himself sometimes making a meteoric reappearance in Whitford some day; flashing with brief brilliancy across the horizon of that remote neighbourhood, affably shaking hands with old acquaintance, occupying the best rooms in the "Blue Bell," and scattering largesse among the servants, rattling through the streets side by side with some county magnate, whose companionship should by no means chill his recognition of such local stars of the second or third magnitude as the Pawkinses of Pudcombe Hall. He was inclined by taste and temperament to be thoroughly "bon prince."

Such fancies may seem childish, but it was a fact that Algernon had indulged in them. With all his tact, he had a considerable strain of his mother's Ancramism in his blood. And the contrast between those former day-dreams and the present reality was so terrible, so mortifying, so ridiculous (direst and most soul-chilling word of all to Algernon!) that he was unable to face it. Some way out must be found. It was impossible, on any tenable theory of society, that he should be permanently consigned to oblivion and the daily round of inglorious duties.

As to what Lord Seely said about meriting advancement by diligence, and working for ten or fifteen years, it seemed to Algernon pretty much like exhorting a convict to step his daily round of treadmill in so painstaking a manner as to win the approbation of the gaol authorities. What would he care for their approbation? It was impossible to take either pride or pleasure in working out one's penal sentence.

Algernon felt very bitter against Lord Seely as he pondered these things, and not a little bitter against Castalia, who had, as it were, bound him to this wheel, and had latterly added the sting of her intolerable temper to his other vexations. Fate had used him despitefully. He seemed to consider that some gratitude was due to him on the part of the supernal powers for his excellent intentions—he would have borne prosperity so well! A feeling grew upon him, which would have been desperation but for his ever-present, instinctive efforts not to hurt himself.

On the morning after the visit to Maxfield's house—of which Castalia had been an unseen witness—Algernon went to the post-office somewhat earlier than usual. As he reached it a man was coming out, who scowled upon him with so sullen and hostile a countenance, that it affected him like a blow.

He was, on the whole, in better spirits on this special morning than he had been for some time past. Not that he was habitually depressed by his troubles, but there was a certain apprehension and anxiety in his daily life which flavoured it all unpleasantly. But on this morning he was, for various reasons, feeling hopeful of at least a reprieve from care, and the man's angry frown not only hurt but startled him.

"Who is that fellow who has just gone out?" he asked of Gibbs, entering the office by the public door instead of his own private one, in order to put the question.

"That is Roger Heath, the man who has lost his money-letter."

"An uncommonly ill-looking rascal, I take leave to think."

"Ahem! He is a decent, God-fearing man, sir, I believe; but at present he is wrath, and not without some excuse, either. He tells me he has written to the head office—"

"And what then?"

"And has been told that due inquiries will be made, of course."

"And what then?"

"Why then—I suppose that's the last he'll hear of it."

Algernon lightly flicked a white handkerchief over his face and bright curling hair, filling the close little office with a delicate perfume as he said, "So there's an end of that!"

"An end of it, I suppose, so far as Heath is concerned. But I doubt we shall hear more of the matter in the office."

Algernon paused with his hand on the lock of the door leading to his private room. He kept his hand there, and scarcely turned his head as he asked, "How so?"

Mr. Gibbs shook his head, and began to expatiate on the singular misfortunes which had been accumulated on the Whitford Post-office, and to hint that when two or three suspicious cases had followed each other in that way, an office was marked by the superior authorities, and means were taken to discover the culprit.

"Means! What means?" said Algernon, carelessly. "You said yourself that it was next to impossible to trace a stolen letter. And, really, if people will be such idiots as to send money by post without precaution, in spite of all the warnings that are given to them, they deserve to lose it."

"That may be, sir. Still, of course, it is no light matter to steal a letter. And as to the means of tracing it, why I have heard of trap-letters being sent, containing marked money."

The handle clicked, the door was opened and sharply shut again, and the Whitford postmaster disappeared into his private room.

It was more than an hour before Algernon reappeared in the outer office. He advanced towards Gibbs, and leaning on his shoulder with great affability, said to him in a low voice, "You've no suspicion of any one about this place, eh? The old woman that cleans the office, that boy Jem, no suspicion of anybody, eh? Oh! well I'm excessively glad of that! One hates to be distrustful of the people about one."

Gibbs shook his head emphatically and decisively. "No one has access to the office unless in my presence, sir; not a creature."

"The fact is," said Algernon, slowly, "that I have missed one or two papers of my own lately; matters of no consequence. God knows why anyone should have thought it worth while to take them! But they're gone."

Gibbs looked up with serious alarm in his face.

"Dear me, sir!" he exclaimed; "dear me, Mr. Errington! I wish you had mentioned this before."

"Oh well, you know, I thought I might be mistaken. I hate being on the watch about trifles. But latterly I am quite sure that papers have disappeared from my secretaire."

"From that little cabinet with drawers in it, that stands in your room?"

"Exactly."

"But—I was under the impression that you kept that carefully locked!"

Algernon laughed outright. "What a fellow you are, Gibbs! Fancy my keeping anything carefully locked! The fact is, it is as often open as shut. Only a few days ago, for instance, Mrs. Errington mentioned to me that she found it unlocked when she was here—" He stopped as if struck by a sudden thought, and turned his eyes away from Gibbs, who was looking up at him with the same uneasy expression on his face. "By-the-way, Mrs. Errington did not stay very long here, did she?" asked Algernon, with a degree of marked embarrassment very unusual in him. It was an embarrassment so ingeniously displayed that one might almost have suspected he wished it to be observed.

"When do you mean, sir? Mrs. Errington comes very often; very often indeed."

"Does she?—I mean—I mean the last time she was here. Did she stay long then?"

"N—no," answered Gibbs, removing his eyes from Algernon's face, and biting the feather of his pen thoughtfully. "At least, I think not, sir. I cannot be sure. She very often does not pass out through my office, but goes away by the private door in the passage."

There was a pause.

"I really am very glad that you don't suspect any of the people about the place, Gibbs," said Algernon at length, rousing himself with some apparent effort from a reverie. "As long as I have any authority here, no innocent person shall be made unhappy for one moment by watchfulness and suspicion."

"That's a very kind feeling, Mr. Errington. But I shouldn't think an innocent person would mind being watched in such a case. For my own part, I hope we shall trace the matter out. It shan't be my fault if we don't."

"You are wonderfully energetic, Gibbs. An invaluable public servant. But, Gibbs, it will not, I think, be any part of your duty to mention to any one at present the losses I have spoken of from my secretaire. There is no reason, as yet, to connect them with the missing letters. I did not duly consider what I was saying. The papers, after all, were only private letters of my own, Gibbs. They concern no one but myself. One was a mere note—an invitation from a lady. They could have had no value for a thief, you know. I—I daresay I mislaid it, and never put it into the secretaire at all."

Algernon went away with downcast eyes and hurried step, and Mr. Gibbs stared after him with a bewildered gaze. Then slowly the expression of his face changed to one of consternation and pity. "Poor young man!" he exclaimed, half aloud. "That woman has been making free with his papers beyond a doubt. And he does his best to shield her. A worldly-minded, vain woman she is, that looks at us as if we were made of a different kind of clay from her. And they say she is furiously jealous of her husband. But this—this is serious! This is very serious, indeed. I am sorry for the young man with all my heart!"

CHAPTER VIII.

It was no more possible to do anything unusual in Whitford without arresting attention, and being subjected to animadversion, than it was possible for atmospheric conditions to change without affecting the barometer.

Who could tell how it got abroad in the town that young Mrs. Errington was in the habit of following her husband about; of watching him, spying on his actions, and examining his private correspondence? Mr. Obadiah Gibbs, who could have told more than any one on the latter head, was not given to talking. Yet the fact oozed out.

It assumed, of course, a great variety of forms and colours, according to the more or less distorting mediums through which it passed. The fact, as uttered by Miss Chubb, for example, was a very different-looking fact from that which was narrated with bated breath, and nods, and winks, by Mrs. Smith, the surgeon's wife. And her version, again, varied considerably from those of Mr. Gladwish, the Methodist shoemaker; Mr. Barker, the Church of England chemist; and the bosom friends of the servants at Ivy Lodge. Still, under one shape and another, Mrs. Algernon Errington's jealousy of her husband, and her consequent behaviour, were within the cognisance of Whitford, and were discussed in all circles there.

The predominant feeling ran strongly against Castalia. There were persons, indeed, who, exercising an exemplary impartiality (on which they much prided themselves), refused to take sides in the matter, but considered it most probable that both parties were to blame. Mrs. Smith was among these. She had, she declared, that rare gift in woman—a judicial mind, although her conception of the judicial functions appeared to be limited to putting on the black cap and passing sentence. But in the main, public sympathy was with Algernon. He had offended many old acquaintances by his aristocratic marriage; but at least he was now making the only amends in his power by being extremely unhappy in it! A great many wiseacres, male and female, were now able to shake their heads, and say they had known all along how it would turn out. This came of flying too high; for, if Mrs. Errington, senior, was an Ancram by birth, her husband had been only a country surgeon—not even M.D., though she called him "doctor." And this justifying of their predictions was, in a vague way, imputed to Algernon as a merit; or, at the least, it softened disapproval. Then, too, in justice to Whitfordians, it must be said that all their knowledge of Castalia showed them an insolent, supercilious, uninteresting woman, who made no secret of her contempt for them and their town, and who, "although but a poor postmaster's wife, when you came to look at it," as Mrs. Smith the judicial truly observed, gave herself more airs than a duchess. What good, or capacities for good, there might be in her, was hidden from Whitford, whilst her unpleasant qualities were abundantly manifested to all beholders.

Poor Castalia, in her quite unaffected nonchalance and disregard of "all those people," was totally ignorant how much resentment and dislike she was creating, and in what a hostile atmosphere she was living. Her husband's popularity, dimmed by his alliance with her, began to revive when it was perceived that she persecuted and harassed him, and (as was shrewdly suspected) involved him in money difficulties by her extravagance. Some of the men thought it served him right; why did he marry such a woman? But the ladies, as a rule, were on Algernon's side.

There were exceptions, of course. Miss McDougall stood up for her friend, as she said, albeit with some admixture of Mrs. Smith's judicial tendency to blame everybody all round, and a personal disposition towards spitefulness. Minnie Bodkin said very little when the subject was mentioned in her presence; but when an opinion was forced from her, she did not deliver it entirely in favour of Algernon. She was sorry for his wife, she said. And nine-tenths of her hearers would retort with raised hands and eyes, that they, for their part, were sorry for the young man, and that they could not understand what dear Minnie found to pity in Mrs. Algernon Errington. "A woman who spies on her husband, my dear! Who condescends to open his letters—how a woman can so degrade herself is a mystery to me! And they say she actually follows him about the street at nights—skulks after him! Oh! it is almost too bad to repeat!"

"I don't know that all that is true. But if it be so, it seems to me that there is great cause for pity," Minnie would reply. And the answer was set down to poor dear Miss Bodkin's eccentricity.

There had been, for some time back, a talk of carelessness and mismanagement at the Whitford Post-office. Then Roger Heath made no secret of his loss, and was not soft-hearted or mild in his manner of speaking of it. He complained aloud, and spared nobody. And there were plenty of voices ready to carry his denunciations through all classes of Whitford society. It was very strange! Such a thing as the loss of a money-letter had been almost unknown during the reign of the late postmaster; and now there was, not one case, but two—three—a dozen! The number increased, as it passed from mouth to mouth, at a wonderful rate. There must be great negligence (to say the least of it) somewhere in the Whitford Post-office. If the present postmaster was too much above his business to look after it properly, it was a pity his high friends didn't remove him to some situation better suited to such a fine gentleman!

To be sure he was worried out of his wits by that woman. It really was true that she haunted the office at all hours. She had been seen slipping out of the private door in the entry. She was even said to have a pass key which enabled her to go in and out at her will. Was it not rumoured on very good authority that she had actually gone to the office alone, in the dead of night? What could she want to be always prowling about there for? It was all very well to say she went to spy on her husband, but if things went wrong in the office in consequence of her spyings, it became a public evil. Anyway, it was most extraordinary and unheard-of behaviour, and somebody ought to take the matter up! This latter somewhat vague suggestion was a favourite climax to gossip on the subject of the Algernon Erringtons.

With respect to their private affairs, things did not mend. Tradesmen dunned, and grumbled, and could not get their money, and some declined to execute further orders from Ivy Lodge until their accounts were settled. Among the angriest had been Mr. Ravell, the principal draper of the town, whom Castalia had honoured with a good deal of her custom. But one day, not long after Algernon's conversation with his clerk, mentioned in the last chapter, he was met in the High Street by Mr. Ravell, who bowed very deferentially, and stopped, hesitatingly. "Could I say a word to you, sir?" said Mr. Ravell.

"Certainly," replied Algernon. They were close to the post-office, and he took the draper into his private room, and bade him be seated.

"I suppose, Mr. Ravell," said Algernon, with a shrug and a smile, "that you have come about your bill! Mrs. Errington mentioned to me a short time ago that you had been rather importunate. Upon my word, Mr. Ravell, I think you need not have been in such a deuce of a hurry! I know Mrs. Errington does not understand making bargains, and I suppose you don't neglect to arrange your prices so as not to lose by giving her a little credit, eh?"

This was said lightly, but either the words or the tone made Mr. Ravell colour and look a little confused. He was seated, and Algernon was standing near him with his back to the fire, expressing a sense of his own superiority to the draper in every turn of his well-built figure and every line of his half-smiling, half-bored countenance.

"Why, you see, Mr. Errington, we are not in the habit of giving long credit, unless to a few old-established customers who deal largely with us. It would not suit our style of doing business. And it was reported that you were not settled permanently here. And—and—one or two unpleasant things had been said. But I hope you will not continue to feel so greatly offended with us for sending in the account. It was merely in the regular way of our transactions, I assure you."

"Oh, I'm not offended at all, Mr. Ravell! And I hope by the end of this month to clear off all scores between us entirely. Mrs. Errington has not furnished me with any details, but—"

Ravell looked up quickly. "Clear off all scores between us, sir?" he said.

"I presume you will have no objection to that, Mr. Ravell?"

"Oh, of course, sir, you will have your joke! I am glad you are not offended. You see ladies don't always understand these matters. Mrs. Errington was a little severe on us when she paid the account yesterday. At least, so my cashier said."

"My wife paid your account yesterday?" cried Algernon, with a blank look.

"Yes, sir, in full. We should have been quite satisfied if settlement had been made up to the end of last quarter. But it was paid in full. Oh, I thought you had been aware of it! Mrs. Errington said—my people understood her to say, that it was by your wish, as you were so greatly annoyed at the bill being sent in so often."

"Oh! Yes. Quite right, Mr. Ravell."

He spoke slowly, and as if he were thinking of something other than the words he uttered. Ravell looked at him curiously. Algernon suddenly caught the man's eye, and broke into a little careless laugh. "The fact is," said he, with a frank toss of his head, "that I did not know Mrs. Errington had paid you. I suppose she had received some remittances, or—but in short," checking himself, and laughing once more, "I daresay you won't trouble yourself as to where the money comes from so long as it comes to you!"

Mr. Ravell laughed back again, but rather in a forced manner. "Not at all, sir! Not at all," he said, bowing and smiling. And, seeing Algernon look significantly at his watch, he bowed and smiled himself out of the office.

Then Mr. Ravell went away to report to his wife the details of his interview with the postmaster, and before noon the next day it was reported throughout Whitford that Mrs. Algernon Errington had the command of mysterious stores of money whereof her husband knew nothing; and that, nevertheless, she ran him into debt right and left, and refused to pay a farthing until she was absolutely forced to do so.

This report was not calculated to make those tradesmen who had not been paid more patient and forbearing. If Mrs. Algernon Errington could find money for one she could for another, they argued, and a shower of bills descended on Ivy Lodge within the next week or two. Algernon said they came like a swarm of locusts, and threatened to devour all before them. He acknowledged to himself that the payment of Ravell's bill had been a fatal precedent. "And, perhaps," he thought, "there was no need for getting rid of the notes after all! However, the thing is done and can't be undone."

The necessity for another appeal to Lord Seely grew more and more imminent. Castalia had displayed an unexpected obstinacy about the matter. She had held to her refusal to ask for more money from her uncle, but Algernon had not yet urged her very strongly to do so. The moment had now come, he thought, when an appeal absolutely must be made, and he doubted not his own power to cause Castalia to make it. Her manner, to be sure, had been very singular of late; alternately sullen and excited, passing from cold silence to passionate tenderness without any intermediate phases. He had surprised her occasionally crying convulsively, and at other times on coming home he had found her sitting absolutely unoccupied, with a blank, fixed face. The few persons who saw Castalia frequently, observed the change in her, and commented on it. Miss Chubb once dropped a word to Algernon indicating a vague suspicion that his wife's intellect was disordered. He did not choose to appear to perceive the drift of her words, but the hint dwelt in his mind.

"You must write to Lord Seely this evening, Cassy," he said one day on returning home to dinner. He had found his wife at her desk, and, on seeing him, she huddled away a confused heap of papers into a drawer, and hastily shut it.

"Must I?" she answered gloomily.

"Well, I don't wish to use an offensive phrase. You will write to oblige me. It has been put off long enough."

"Why should I oblige you?" said Castalia, looking up at him with sunken eyes. She looked so ill and haggard, as to arrest Algernon's attention—not too lavishly bestowed on her in general.

"Cassy," said he, "I am afraid you are not well!"

The tears came into her eyes. She turned her head away. "Do you really care whether I am ill or well?" she asked.

"Do I really care? What a question! Of course I care. Are you suffering?"

"N—no; not now. I believe I should not feel any suffering if you only loved me, Ancram."

"Castalia! How can you be so absurd?"

He rose from his seat beside her, and walked impatiently up and down the room. Nothing irritated him so much as to be called on for sentiment or tenderness.

"There!" she exclaimed, with a little despondent gesture of the head, "you were speaking and looking kindly, and I have driven you away! I wish I was dead."

Algernon stopped in his walk, and cast a singular look at his wife. Then after a moment he said, in his usual light manner, "My dear Cassy, you are low and nervous. It really is not good for you to mope by yourself as you do. Come, rouse yourself to write this letter to my lord, then after dinner you can have the fly to drive to my mother's. She complains that she sees you very seldom."

"Will you come too, Ancram?"

"I—well, yes; if it is possible, I will come too."

"I think," said Castalia, putting her hands on his shoulders, and gazing wistfully into his face, "that if you and I could go away to some quiet strange place—far away from all these odious people—across the seas somewhere—I think we might be happy even now."

"Upon my honour, there's nothing I should like so much as to get away across the seas! And you might as well hint to my lord, in the course of your letter, that I should be very well contented with a berth in the Colonies. A good climate, of course! One wouldn't care to be shipped off to Sierra Leone!"

"I will write that to Uncle Val, willingly. But—don't ask me to beg money of him again."

Algernon made a rapid calculation in his mind, and answered without appreciable pause, "Well, Cassy, it shall be as you will. But as to begging—that, I think, is scarcely the word between us and Lord Seely."

"I'll run upstairs and bathe my eyes, and I shall still have time to write before dinner," said Castalia, and left the room.

When he was alone, Algernon opened the writing-table drawer, and glanced at the papers in it. Castalia's hurried manner of concealing them had suggested to his mind the suspicion that she might have been writing secretly to her uncle. He found no letter addressed to Lord Seely, but he did find an unfinished fragment of writing addressed to himself. It consisted of a few incoherent phrases of despondency and reproach—the expression of confidence betrayed and affection unrequited. There was a word or two in it about the writer's weariness of life and desire to quit it.

Castalia had written many such fragments of late; sometimes as a mere outlet for suppressed feeling, sometimes under the impression that she really could not long support an existence uncheered by sympathy or counsel, embittered by jealousy, and chilled by neglect. She had written such fragments, and then torn them up in many a lonely hour, but she had never thought of complaining of Algernon to Lord Seely. She would complain of him to no human being. But all Algernon's insight into his wife's character did not enable him to feel sure of this. Indeed, he had often said to himself that no rational being could be expected to follow the vagaries of Castalia's sickly fancies and impracticable temper. He would not have been surprised to find her pouring out a long string of lamentations about her lot to Lord Seely. He was not much surprised at what he did find her to have written, although the state of feeling it displayed seemed to him as unreasonable and unaccountable as ever. He gave himself no account of the motive which made him take the fragment of writing, fold it, and place it carefully inside a little pocket-book which he carried.

"I wonder," he thought to himself, "if Castalia is likely to die!"

CHAPTER IX.

The letter to Lord Seely was duly written, and this time in Castalia's own words. Algernon refused to assist her in the composition of it, saying, in answer to her appeals, "No, no, Cassy; I shall make no suggestion whatsoever. I don't choose to expose myself to any more grandiloquence from your uncle about letters being 'written by your hand, but not dictated by your head.' I wonder at my lord talking such high-flown stuff. But pomposity is his master weakness."

Castalia's letter was as follows:

"Whitford, November 23rd.

"DEAR UNCLE VAL,—I am sure you will understand that I was very much surprised and hurt at the tone of your last letter to Ancram. Of course, if you have not the money to help us with, you cannot lend it. And I don't complain of that. But I was vexed at the way you wrote to Ancram. You won't think me ungrateful to you. I know how good you have always been to me, and I am fonder of you than of anybody in the world except Ancram. But nobody can be unkind to him without hurting me, and I shall always resent any slight to him. But I am writing now to ask you something that 'I wish for very much myself;' it is quite my own desire. I am not at all happy in this place. And I want you to get Ancram a berth somewhere in the Colonies, quite away. It is no use changing from one town in England to another. What we want is to get 'far away,' and put the seas between us and all the odious people here. I am sure you might get us something if you would try. I assure you Ancram is perfectly wasted in this hole. Any stupid grocer or tallow-chandler could do what he has to do. Do, dear Uncle Val, try to help us in this. Indeed I shall never be happy in Whitford.—Your affectionate niece,

"C. ERRINGTON.

"Give my love to Aunt Belinda if she cares to have it. But I daresay she won't.—C. E."

"I think my lord will not doubt the genuineness of that epistle!" thought Algernon, after having read it at his wife's request.

Then the fly was announced, and they set off together to pass the evening at the elder Mrs. Errington's lodgings. The "Blue Bell" driver touched his hat in a very respectful manner. His master's long-standing account was unpaid, but he continued to receive, for his part, frequent half-crowns from Algernon, who liked the immediate popularity to be purchased by a gift somewhat out of proportion to his means. Indeed, our young friend enjoyed a better reputation amongst menials and underlings than amongst their employers. The former were apt to speak of him as a pleasant gentleman who was free with his money; and to declare that they felt as if they could do anything for young Mr. Errington, so they could! He had such a way with him! Whereas the mere payment of humdrum debts excites no such agreeable glow of feeling, and is altogether a flat, stale, and unprofitable proceeding.

"What o'clock shall we say, Castalia?" asked her husband, as they alighted at Mrs. Thimbleby's door.

"Tell him to come at half-past ten," returned Castalia.

It chanced that David Powell was re-entering his lodgings at the moment the younger Erringtons reached the door. He stood aside to let the lady pass into the house before him, and thus heard her answer. The sound of her voice made him start and bend forward to look at her face when the light from the open door fell upon it. She turned round at the same instant, and the two looked full at each other. David Powell asked Mrs. Thimbleby if that lady were not the wife of Mr. Algernon Errington.

"Yes, Mr. Powell, she is his wife; and more's the pity, if all tales be true!"

"Judge not uncharitably, sister Thimbleby! Nor let your tongue belie the gentleness of your spirit. It is an unruly member that speaks not always out of the fulness of the heart. The lady seems very sick, and bears the traces of much sorrow on her countenance."

"Oh yes, indeed, poor thing! Sickly enough she looks, and sorry. Nay, I daresay she has her own trials, but I fear me she leads that pleasant young husband of hers a poor life of it. I shouldn't say as much to anyone but you, sir, for I do try to keep my tongue from evil-speaking. But had you never seen her before, Mr. Powell?"

Powell answered musingly, "N—no—scarcely seen her. But I had heard her voice."

Mrs. Errington received her son and daughter-in-law with an effusive welcome. She was so astonished; so delighted. It was so long since she had seen them. And then to see them together! That had latterly become quite a rare treat. The good lady expatiated on this theme until Castalia's brow grew gloomy with the recollection of her wrongs, her solitary hours spent so drearily, and her suspicions as to how her husband employed the hours of his absence from her. And then Mrs. Errington began playfully to reprove her for being dull and silent, instead of enjoying dear Algy's society now that she had it! "I am sure, my dear Castalia," said the elder lady with her usual self-complacent stateliness, "you won't mind my telling you that I consider one of the great secrets of the perfect felicity I enjoyed during my married life to have been the interest and pleasure I always took—and showed that I took—in Dr. Errington's society."

"Perhaps he liked your society," returned Castalia with a languid sneer, followed by a short bitter sigh.

"Preferred it to any in the world, my dear!" said Mrs. Errington, mellifluously. She said it, too, with an aplomb and an air of conviction that mightily tickled Algernon, who, remembering the family rumours which haunted his childhood, thought that his respected father, if he preferred his wife's society to any other, must have put a considerable constraint on his inclinations, not to say sacrificed them altogether to the claims of a convivial circle of friends. "The dear old lady is as good as a play!" thought he. Indeed, he thoroughly relished this bit of domestic comedy.

"But then," proceeded Mrs. Errington, as she rang the bell to order tea, "I have not the vanity to suppose that he would have done so without the exercise of some little care and tact on my part. Tact, my dear Castalia—tact is the most precious gift a wife can bring to the domestic circle. But the Ancrams always had enormous tact—Give us some tea, if you please, Mrs. Thimbleby, and be careful that the water boils—proverbial for it, in fact!"

Algernon thought it time to come to the rescue. He did not choose his comfort to be destroyed by a passage of arms between his mother and his wife, so he deftly turned the conversation to less dangerous topics, and things proceeded peacefully until the tea was served.

"Who was that man that was coming in to the house with us?" asked Castalia, as she sipped her tea from one of Mrs. Errington's antique blue and white china cups.

"Would it be Mr. Diamond—? But no; you know him by sight. Or—oh, I suppose it was that Methodist preacher, Powell!"

"Powell! Yes, that was the name—David Powell."

"Most likely. He is in and out at all hours. Really, Algernon, do you know—you remember the fellow, how he used to annoy us at Maxfield's. Well, do you know, I believe he is quite crazy!"

"You have always entertained that opinion, I believe, ma'am."

"Oh, but, my dear boy, I think he is demented in real downright earnest now. I do indeed. I'm sure the things that poor weak-minded Mrs. Thimbleby tells me about him—! He has delusions of all kinds; hears voices, sees visions. I should say it is a case of what your father would have called 'melancholy madness.' Really, Algy, I frequently think about it. It is quite alarming sometimes in the night if I happen to wake up, to remember that there is a lunatic sleeping overhead. You know he might take it into his head to murder one! Or if he only killed himself—which is perhaps more likely—it would be a highly unpleasant circumstance. I could not possibly remain in the lodgings, you know. Out of the question! And so I told that silly Thimbleby. I said to her, 'Observe, Mrs. Thimbleby, if any dreadful thing happens in this house—a suicide or anything of that sort—I shall leave you at an hour's notice. I wish you well, and I have no desire to withdraw my patronage from you, but you could not expect me to look over a coroner's inquest.'"

Algernon threw his head back and laughed heartily. "That was a fair warning, at any rate!" said he. "And if Mr. David Powell has any consideration for his landlady, he will profit by it—that is to say, supposing Mrs. Thimbleby tells him of it. What did she say?"

"Oh, she merely cried and whimpered, and hid her face in her apron. She is terribly weak-minded, poor creature."

Castalia had been listening in silence. All at once she said, "How many miserable people there are!"

"Very true, Cassy; provincial postmasters and others. And part of my miserable lot is to go down to the office again for an hour to-night."

"My poor boy!" "Go to the office again to-night?" exclaimed his mother and his wife simultaneously.

"Yes; it is now half-past eight. I have an appointment. At least—I shall be back in an hour, I have no doubt."

Algernon walked off with an air of good-humoured resignation, smiling and shrugging his shoulders. The two women, left alone together, took his departure very differently. Mrs. Errington was majestically wrathful with a system of things which involved so much discomfort to a scion of the house of Ancram. She was of opinion that some strong representations should be made to the ministry; that Parliament should be appealed to. And she rather enjoyed her own eloquence, and was led on by it to make some most astounding assertions, and utter some scathing condemnations with an air of comfortable self-satisfaction. Castalia, on the other hand, remained gloomily taciturn, huddled into an easy-chair by the hearth, and staring fixedly at the fire.

It has been recorded in these pages that Mrs. Errington did not much object to silence on the part of her companion for the time being; she only required an assenting or admiring interjection now and then, to enable her to carry on what she supposed to be a very agreeable conversation, but she did like her confidante to do that much towards social intercourse. And she liked, moreover, to see some look of pleasure, interest, or sympathy on the confidante's face. Looking at Castalia's moody and abstracted countenance, she could not but remember the gentle listener in whom she had been wont for so many years to find a sweet response to all her utterances.

"Oddly enough," she said, "I have been disappointed of a visitor this evening, and so should have been quite alone if you and Algy had not come in. I had asked Rhoda to spend the evening with me."

Castalia looked round at the sound of that name. "Why didn't she come?" she asked abruptly.

"Oh, I don't know. She merely said she could not leave home to-night. That old father of hers sometimes takes tyrannical fancies into his head. He has been kinder to dear Rhoda of late, and has treated her more becomingly—chiefly, I believe I may say, owing to my influence, although the old booby chose to quarrel with me—but when he takes a thing into his head he is as obstinate as a mule."

"I don't know about treating her 'becomingly,' but I think she needs some one to look after her and keep her in check."

"Who, Rhoda? My dear Castalia, she is the very sweetest-tempered creature I ever met with in my life; and that is saying a good deal, let me tell you, for the Ancram temper was something quite special. A gift. I don't boast of it, because I believe it was simply constitutional. But such was the fact."

"The girl is dressed up beyond her station. The last time I saw her it was absurd. Scarcely reputable, I should think."

Mrs. Errington by no means liked this attack. Over and above the fact that Rhoda was her pet and her protégée, which would have sufficed to make any animadversions on her appear impertinent, she was genuinely fond of the girl, and answered with some warmth, "I am sure, Castalia, that whatever Rhoda Maxfield might be dressed in, she would look modest and sweet, not to say excessively pretty, for I suppose there cannot be a doubt about that?"

"I thought you were a stickler for people keeping to their own station, and not aping their betters!"

"We must distinguish, Castalia. Birth will ever be with me the first consideration. Coming of the race I do, it could not be otherwise. But it is useless to shut one's eyes to the fact that money nowadays will do much. Look at our best families!—families of lineage as good as my own. What do we see? We see them allying themselves with commercial people right and left. Now, there was Miss Pickleham. The way in which she was thrown at Algy's head would surprise you. She had a hundred thousand pounds of her own on the day she married, and expectations of much more on old Picklekam's decease. But I never encouraged the thing. Perhaps I was wrong. However!—she married Sir Peregrine Puffin last season. And the Puffins were in Cornwall before the Conquest."

Castalia shrugged her shoulders in undisguised scorn. "All that nonsense is nothing to the purpose," said she, throwing her head back against the cushion of the chair she sat on. Mrs. Errington opened her blue eyes to their widest extent. "Really, Castalia! 'All that nonsense!' You are not very polite."

"I'm sick of all the pretences, and shams, and deceptions," returned Castalia, her eyes glittering feverishly, and her thin fingers twining themselves together with nervous restlessness. "I don't know whether you are made a fool of yourself, or are trying to make a fool of me—"

"Castalia!"

"But, in either case, I am not duped. Your 'sweet Rhoda!' Don't you know that she is an artful, false coquette—perhaps worse!"

"Castalia!"

"Yes, worse. Why should she not be as bad as any other low-bred creature who lures on gentlemen to make love to her? Men are such idiots! So false and fickle! But, though I may be injured and insulted, I will not be laughed at for a dupe."

"Good heavens, Castalia! What does this mean?"

"And I will tell you another thing, if you really are so blind to what goes on, and has been going on, for years: I don't believe Ancram has gone to the post-office to-night at all. I believe he has gone to see Rhoda. It would not be the first time he has deceived me on that score!"

Mrs. Errington sat holding the arms of her easy-chair with both hands, and staring at her daughter-in-law. The poor lady felt as if the world were turned upside down. It was not so long since old Maxfield had astonished her by plainly showing that he thought her of no importance, and choosing to turn her out of his house. And now, here was Castalia conducting herself in a still more amazing manner. Whilst she revolved the case in her brain—much confused and bewildered as that organ was—and endeavoured to come to some clear opinion on it, the younger woman got up and walked up and down the room with the restless, aimless, anxious gait of a caged animal.

At length Mrs. Errington slowly nodded her head two or three times, drew a long breath, folded her hands, and, assuming a judicial air, spoke as follows:

"My dear Castalia! I shall overlook the unbecomingness of certain expressions that you have used towards myself, because I can make allowance for an excited state of feeling. But you must permit me to give you a little advice. Endeavour to control yourself; try to look at things with calmness and judgment, and you will soon perceive how wrong and foolish your present conduct is. And, moreover, you need not be startled if I have discovered the real motive at the bottom of all this display of temper. There never was a member of my family yet who had not a wonderful gift of reading motives. I'm sure it is nothing to envy us! I have often, for my own part, wished myself as slow of perception as other people, for the truth is not always pleasant. But I must say that I can see one thing very plainly—and that is, that you are most unfortunately and most unreasonably giving way to jealousy! I can see it, Castalia, as plain as possible."

Mrs. Errington had finished her harangue with much majesty, bringing out the closing sentences as if they were a most unexpected and powerful climax, when the effect of the whole was marred by her giving a violent start and exclaiming, with more naturalness than dignity, "Mercy on us! Castalia, what will you do next? Do shut that window, for pity's sake! I shall get my death of cold!"

Castalia had opened the window, and was leaning out of it, regardless of the sleet which fell in slanting lines and beat against her cheek. "I knew that was his step," she said, speaking, as it seemed, more to herself than to her mother-in-law. "And he has no umbrella, and those light shoes on!" She ran to the fireplace and stirred the fire into a blaze, displaying an activity which was singularly contrasted with her usual languid slowness of movement. "Can't you give him some hot wine and water?" she asked, ringing the bell at the same time. When her husband came in she removed his damp great-coat with her own hands, made him sit down near the fire, and brought him a pair of his mother's slippers, which were quite sufficiently roomy to admit his slender feet. Algernon submitted to be thus cherished and taken care of, declaring, with an amused smile, as he sipped the hot negus, that this fuss was very kind, but entirely unnecessary, as he had not been three minutes in the rain.

As to Mrs. Errington, she was so perplexed by her daughter-in-law's sudden change of mood and manner, that she lost her presence of mind, and remained gazing from Algernon to his wife very blankly. "I never knew such a thing!" thought the good lady. "One moment she's raging and scolding, and abusing her husband for deceiving her, and the next she is petting him up as if he was a baby!"

When the fly was announced, and Castalia left the little drawing-room to put on her cloak and bonnet, Mrs. Errington drew near to her son and whispered to him solemnly, "Algy, there is something very strange about your wife. I never saw such a changed creature within the last few weeks. Don't you think you should have some one to see her?—some professional person I mean? I fear that her brain is affected!"

"Good gracious, mother! Another lunatic? You are getting to have a monomania on that subject yourself!" Algernon laughed as he said it.

"My dear, there may be two persons afflicted in the same way, may there not? But I said nothing about lunatics, Algy. Only—really, I think some temporary disturbance of the brain is going on. I do, indeed."

"Pooh, pooh! Nonsense, ma'am! But it is odd enough that you are the second person who has made that agreeable suggestion to me within a fortnight. Poor Cassy! That's all she gets by her airs and her temper."

"Another person, was there?"

"Yes; it was little Miss Chubb, and—"

"Miss Chubb! Upon my word, I think that Miss Chubb was guilty of taking a considerable liberty in suggesting anything of the kind about the Honourable Mrs. Ancram Errington!"

"Oh, I don't know about liberty; but, of course, I laughed at her; and, of course, you will too, if she says anything of the kind to you."

"I shall undoubtedly check her pretty severely if she attempts anything of the sort with me! Miss Chubb, indeed!"

The consequence was, that Mrs. Errington went about among her Whitford friends elaborately contradicting and denying "the innuendos spread abroad about her daughter-in-law by certain presumptuous and gossiping persons;" and thus brought the suggestion before many who would not otherwise have heard of it. All which, of course, surprised and annoyed Algernon very much, who had, naturally, not expected anything of the sort from his mother's well-known tact and discretion.

CHAPTER X.

One dreary Sunday afternoon, about this time—that is to say, about the end of November—Matthew Diamond rang at the bell of Mr. Maxfield's door. He had a couple of books under his arm, and he asked the servant, who admitted him, if she could give him back the volume he had last lent to Miss Maxfield. Sally looked askance at the books as she took them from his hand, and shook her head doubtfully.

"It's one o' them French books, isn't it, sir? I don't know one from another. Would you please step upstairs yourself? Miss Rhoda's in the drawing-room."

Diamond went upstairs and tapped at the door of the sitting-room.

"Come in," said a soft, sweet voice, that seemed to him the most deliciously musical he had ever heard, and he entered.

The old room looked very different from what it had looked in the days when Matthew Diamond used to come there to read Latin and history with Algernon Errington. There were still the clumsy beams in the low ceiling, and the old-fashioned cushioned seats in the bay-window, but everything else was changed. A rich carpet covered the floor; there were handsome hangings, and a couch, and a French clock on the chimney-piece; there was a small pianoforte in the room, too; and, at one end, a bookcase well filled with gaily-bound books. These things were the products of old Max's money. But there were evidences about the place of taste and refinement, which were due entirely to Rhoda. She had got a stand of hyacinths like those in Miss Bodkin's room. She had softened and hidden the glare of the bright, brand-new upholstery by dainty bits of lacework spread over the couch and the chairs; and she had, with some difficulty, persuaded her father to substitute for two staring coloured French lithographs, which had decked the walls, a couple of good engravings after Italian pictures. There was a fire glowing redly in the grate, and the room was warm and fragrant. Rhoda was curled up on the window-seat, with a book in her hand, and bending down her pretty head over it, until the soft brown curls swept the page.

Diamond stood still for a moment in the doorway, admiring the graceful figure well defined against the light.

"Come in, Sally," said Rhoda. And then she looked up from her book and saw him.

"I'm afraid I disturb you!" said Diamond. "But the maid told me to come up."

"Oh no! I was just reading—"

"Straining your eyes by this twilight! That's very wrong."

"Yes! I'm afraid it is not very wise, but I wanted to finish the chapter; and my eyes are really very strong."

"I thought you might be at church," said Diamond, seating himself on the opposite side of the bay-window, and within its recess, "so I asked the maid to get me the book I wanted. But she sent me upstairs."

"Aunt Betty is at church, and James; but father wouldn't let me go. He said it was so raw and foggy, and I had been to church this morning."

"Yes; I saw you there. But have you not been well, that your father did not wish you to go out?"

"Oh yes; I'm very well, thank you. But I had a little cold last week; and I should have had to walk to St. Chad's and back, you know. Father doesn't think it right to drive on the Lord's day, so he made me stay at home."

"How very right of him! What were you reading?"

He drew a little nearer to her as he asked the question, and looked at the book she held.

"Oh, it's a Sunday book," said Rhoda, simply. "'The Pilgrim's Progress.' I like it very much."

"I wonder whether you will care to hear of some good news I had to-day?"

"Oh yes; I shall be very glad to hear it."

"I think I stand a good chance of getting the head-mastership of Dorrington Proprietary School. Dorrington is in the next county, you know."

"Oh! I'm very glad."

"It would be a very good position. I am not certain of it yet, you know; but Dr. Bodkin has been very friendly, and has promised to canvass the governing committee for me."

"Oh! I'm very glad indeed."

"I don't know yet myself whether I am very glad or not."

"Don't you?"

Rhoda looked up at him in genuine surprise; but her eyes fell before the answering look they encountered, and she blushed from brow to chin.

"No; it all depends on you, Rhoda, whether I am glad of it to the bottom of my heart, or whether I give it all up as a thing not worth striving for."

There was a pause, which Rhoda broke at length, because the silence embarrassed her unendurably.

"Oh, I don't think it can depend upon me, Mr. Diamond," she said, speaking in a little quivering voice that was barely audible; whilst, at the same time, she hurriedly turned over the pages of "The Pilgrim's Progress" with her eyes fixed on them, although she assuredly did not see one letter. Diamond gently drew the book from her hand and took the hand in his own.

"Yes, Rhoda," he said—and, having once called her so, his lips seemed to dwell lovingly on the sound of her name—"I think you do know! You must know that, if I look forward hopefully and happily to anything in my future life, it is only because I have a hope that you may be able to love me a little. I love you so much."

She trembled violently, but did not withdraw her hand from his clasp. She sat quite still with downcast eyes, neither moving nor looking to the right or the left.

"Rhoda! Rhoda! Won't you say one word to me?"

"I'm trying—thinking what I ought to say,'" she answered, almost in a whisper.

"Is it so difficult, Rhoda?"

She made a strong effort to command her voice, but she had not the courage to look full at him as she answered, "Yes; it is very difficult for me. I want to do right, Mr. Diamond. I want not to deceive you."

"I am very sure that you will not deceive me, Rhoda!"

"Not if I can help it. But it is so hard to say just the exact truth."

"I don't find it hard to say the exact truth to you. You may believe me implicitly, Rhoda, when I say that I love you with all my heart, and will do my best to make you happy if you will let me."

"I do believe you. I believe you are really fond of me. Only—of course you are much cleverer and wiser than I am, except in thinking too much of me—and you can say just whatever is in your mind. But I can't; not all at once."

"I will wait, Rhoda. I will have patience, and not distress you."

The tears were falling down her cheeks now, not from sorrow, but from sheer agitation. She thanked him by a gesture of her head, and drew her hand away from his very gently, and wiped her eyes. He could not command himself at sight of her tears, although he had resolved not to speak again until she should be calm and ready to hear him.

"My darling," he said, clasping his hands together and looking at her with eyes full of anxious compassion, "don't cry! Is it my fault? You must have had some knowledge of what was in my heart to say to you! I have not startled you and taken you by surprise?"

"No; that's just it, Mr. Diamond. It's that that makes me feel so afraid of doing wrong and deceiving you. I—I—have thought for some time past that you were getting to like me very much. Some one said so too. But yet I couldn't do anything, could I? I couldn't say, 'Don't get fond of me, Mr. Diamond!'"

"It would have been quite in vain to say, 'Don't get fond of me.' I'm a desperately obstinate man, Rhoda!"

"So then I—I mean to tell you the exact truth, you know, as well as I can. I began to think whether I liked you very much."

"Well, Rhoda?"

There was a rather long silence.

"Well, I thought—yes, I did."

He clasped his arms round her with a sudden impetuous movement, but she held him off with her two hands on his shoulders. "No, but please listen! I did love somebody else once very much. Of course we were very young, and it was nonsense. But I did wrong in being secret, and keeping it from father. And I never want to be secret any more. And—though I do like you very much, and—and—I should be very sorry if you went away—yet it isn't quite the same that I felt before. That is the truth as well as I can say it, and I am very grateful to you for thinking so well of me."

He drew the young head with its soft shining chestnut curls down on to his breast, and pressed his lips to her cheek.

"Now you are mine, my very own—are you not, Rhoda?"

"Yes; if you like, Mr. Diamond."

Matthew Diamond had been successful in his wooing, after feeling very doubtful of success. And he should naturally have been elated in proportion to his previous trepidation. And he was happy, of course; yet scarcely with the fulness of joyful triumph he had promised himself if pretty Rhoda should incline her ear to his suit. There was a subtle flavour of disappointment in it all. Rhoda had behaved very well, very honestly, in making that effort to be quite clear and candid about her feelings. It was a great thing to be able to feel perfect confidence in the woman who was to be his companion for life. And as to her loving him with the same fervour he felt towards her, that was not to be expected. He never had expected that. She was gentle, sweet, modest, thoroughly feminine, and exquisitely pretty. She was willing to give herself to him, and would doubtless be a true and affectionate wife. He held her slight waist in his arm, and her head rested confidingly on his bosom. Of course he was very happy. Only—if only Rhoda were not quite so silent and cold; if she would say one little word of tenderness, or even nestle herself fondly against his shoulder without speaking!

Some such thoughts were vaguely flitting through Diamond's mind when Rhoda raised her head, and, emboldened by the gathering dusk, looked up into his face and said, "You know it cannot be unless father consents."

"I shall speak to him this evening. Do you think he will be stern and hard to persuade, Rhoda?"

"I don't know. He said once that he would like to—to—that he would like to know I had some one to take care of me."

"On that score I am not afraid of falling short. Your father could give his treasure to no man who would take more loving care of her than I!"

"And then you are a gentleman; and father thinks a great deal of that, although he makes no pretence at being anything more than a tradesman himself. And of course I am only a tradesman's daughter. I am greatly below you in station—I know that."

"My Rhoda! As if there could be any question of that between us! God knows I have been poor and obscure enough all my life. But now I shall be able to tell your father that I hope to have a home to offer you that will be at least not sordid, and the position of a lady."

"I hope you won't repent, Mr. Diamond."

"Repent! But, Rhoda, won't you call me by my name? Say Matthew, not Mr. Diamond."

"Yes; I will if you like. But I'm afraid I can't all at once. It seems so strange."

"I wish you liked my name one thousandth part as much as I love the sound of yours! It seems so sweet to be able to call you Rhoda."

"Oh, I like your name very much indeed. But I think, please, that you had better go now. The people are coming out of church, and Aunt Betty may be back at any moment; and I don't wish her to find you here before you have spoken to father."

Rhoda stood up as she said it, and Diamond had no choice but to rise too, and say farewell. He drew her gently towards him and kissed her. "Will you try to love me, Rhoda?" he said, in a tone of almost sad entreaty. "Do you think you shall be able to love me a little?"

"I should not have accepted you if I felt that I could never be fond of you," returned Rhoda, and a little flush spread itself over her face as she spoke. "But you know I have told you the truth. I have told you about—"

He put up his hand to check her. "Yes, yes; you have been quite candid and honourable, and I won't be exacting or unreasonable, or too impatient." He did not think he could endure to hear Rhoda, in her anxiety not to deceive him, recapitulate the confession of her "different feeling" for another man in days past; and yet he had known, or guessed, that it had been so.

Then he took his leave, an accepted lover; and he told himself that he was a very fortunate and happy man. As he passed the door of old Max's little parlour downstairs, he saw a light gleaming under the door into the almost dark passage. He stopped and tapped at the door. "Come in," said Jonathan Maxfield's harsh voice. And Diamond went into the parlour.

CHAPTER XI.

Old Max looked up at his visitor over the great tortoise-shell spectacles on his nose. He had a large Bible open on the table before him. The large Bible was placed there every evening, and on Sunday evenings any other mundane volume which might chance to be lying in the parlour was carefully removed out of sight, to be restored to the light of day on Monday morning. This was the custom of the house, and had been so for years. It had obtained all through the Methodist days, and now lasted under the new orthodox dispensation. Since old Max had his spectacles on, it was to be supposed that he had been reading, and, since there was no other printed document within sight, not even an almanac, it was clear that he could have been reading nothing but his Bible. And yet it was nearly an hour since he had turned the page before him. He had been dozing, sitting up in his chair by the fire. This had latterly become a habit with him whenever he was left alone in the evening. And once, even, he had fallen into a sleep, or a stupor, in the midst of the assembled family, and, on awaking, had been lethargic in his movements, and dazed in his manner for some time.

He was quite awake now, however, as he peered sharply at Diamond over his glasses. The latter found some little difficulty in beginning his communication, not being assisted by a word from old Max, who stared at him silently.

"I have a few words to say to you, Mr. Maxfield, if you are at leisure to hear them," he said at length.

"If it's anything in the natur' of a business communication, I can't attend to it now," returned old Max deliberately. "It has been a rule of mine through life to transact no manner of business on the Lord's day, and I have found it prosper with me."

"No, no; it is not a matter of business, Mr. Maxfield," said Diamond smiling, but not quite at his ease. Then he sat down and told his errand. Maxfield listened in perfect silence. "May I hope, Mr. Maxfield, that you will give us your consent and approbation?" asked Diamond, after a pause.

"You're pretty glib, sir! I must know a little more about this matter before I can give an answer one way or another."

"You shall know all that I can tell you, Mr. Maxfield. Indeed, I do not see what more I have to say. I have explained to you what my prospects in life are. I have told you every particular with the most absolute fulness and candour. As to my feeling for your daughter, I don't think I could fully express that if I talked to you all night."

"What did my daughter say to you?"

"She—she told me that she was willing to be my wife, but that it must depend upon your consent."

"Rhoda has always been a very dutiful daughter. There's not many like Rhoda."

"I appreciate her, Mr. Maxfield. You may believe that I do most heartily appreciate her. I have long known that all my happiness depended on winning Rhoda for my wife. I have loved her long. But, of course, I could not venture to ask her to marry me, or to ask you to give her to me, until I had some prospect of a home to offer her."

"Ah! And this prospect, now—you aren't sure about it?"

"No; I am not quite sure."

"And, supposing you don't get the place—how then?"

"Why, then, Mr. Maxfield, I should look for another. If you will give your consent to my engagement to Rhoda, I am not afraid of not finding a place in the world for her. I have a fair share of resolution; I am industrious and well educated; I am not quite thirty years old. If you will give me a word of encouragement I shall be sure to succeed."

"Head-master of Dorrington Proprietary School, eh? Will that be a place like Dr. Bodkin's?"

"Something of that kind, only not so lucrative."

"Dr. Bodkin is thought a good deal of in Whitford."

"Mr. Maxfield, may I hope for a favourable answer from you before I go?"

Old Max struck his hand sharply on the table as he exclaimed, almost with a snarl, "I will not be hurried, sir! nor made to speak rashly and without duly pondering and meditating my words." Then he added, in a different tone, "You are glib, sir! mighty glib! Do you know what Miss Maxfield will have to her portion—if I choose to give it her?"

"No, Mr. Maxfield, I do not. Nor do I care to know. I would take her to my heart to-morrow if she would come, although she were the poorest beggar in the world!"

"And would you take her without my consent?"

"I would, if you had no reasonable grounds for withholding it."

"You would steal my daughter away without my consent?"

"I said nothing about stealing. I should not think of deceiving you in the matter. I think you must acknowledge that I am speaking to you pretty frankly, at any rate!"

Maxfield could not but acknowledge to himself that the young man was honest and straightforward, and spoke fairly. He was well-looking too, and had the air of a gentleman, although there was not a trace about him of the peculiar airy elegance, the graceful charm of face and figure, which made Algernon Errington so attractive. Neither had he Algernon's gift of flattery, so adroitly conveyed as to appear unconscious; nor—what might, under the present circumstances, have served him equally well with the old tradesman—Algernon's good-humoured way of taking for granted his own incontestable social superiority over the Whitford grocer. Maxfield had his doubts as to whether this young man, ex-usher at the Grammar School, a fellow who went about to people's houses and gave lessons for money, could prove to be a fine enough match for his Rhoda, even though he should become head-master at Dorrington—Maxfield had so set his heart on seeing Rhoda "made a lady of," in the phraseology of his class.

"I shall have some conversation with my daughter, and let you have my answer after that, sir," said he, looking half sullenly, half thoughtfully at the suitor. "And as there will be questions of figures to go into, maybe, I am not willing to consider the subject more at length on the Lord's day."

But I am bound to confess that this was an afterthought on old Max's part.

When Diamond had gone, the old man sent for his daughter to come to him in the parlour. "You can take yourself off, Betty Grimshaw," said he to that respectable spinster, very unceremoniously. "You and James can bide in the kitchen till supper's ready. When it is, come and tell me."

Rhoda came, in answer to her father's summons, very calmly. She had, of course, expected it. She had quite got over the agitation of the interview with her lover, and was her usual sweet, placid self again. Yes; she said Mr. Diamond had asked her to marry him, and she was willing to marry him if her father would consent. She believed Mr. Diamond loved her very much, and she liked him very much. She had been afraid of him once because he was so very learned and clever, and seemed rather proud and stern. But he was really extremely gentle when you came to know him. She was sure he would be kind to her.

"It's not a thing to decide upon all in a moment, Rhoda," said her father.

"No, father; but I have thought of it for some time past," answered Rhoda, simply.

The old man looked at her with a slight feeling of surprise. "Rhoda has a vast deal of common sense," thought he. "She has some of my brains inside that pretty brown head of hers, that is so like her poor mother's!" Then he said aloud, "You see, this Mr. Diamond is nobody after all. A schoolmaster! Well, that's no great shakes."

"Dr. Bodkin is a schoolmaster, father."

"Dr. Bodkin is rector of St. Chad's and D.D., and a man of substance besides."

"Mr. Diamond is a gentleman, father. Everybody allows that."

"Do you think you could be happy to be his wife, Rhoda?" As he asked this question her father's voice was almost tender, and he placed his hand gently on her head.

"Yes, father; I think so. He would take care of me, and be good to me, and guide me right. And he would never put himself between you and me, father. I mean he would wish me always to be dutiful and affectionate to you."

"Well, Rhoda, we must consider. And I hope the Lord will send me wisdom in the matter. I would fain see thee happy before I am called away. God bless thee, child."

Jonathan Maxfield turned the matter in his mind during the watches of the night with much anxious consideration, according to his lights. In social status there was truly not much to complain of, he thought. A man in a position like that of Dr. Bodkin, who should have money of his own (or of his wife's) to render him independent of the profits of his place, might come to be a personage of importance. "And money there will be; more'n they think for," said old Max to himself. "The young man seemed to worship Rhoda; as he ought." She had shown herself to be very dutiful, very honest, very sensible on this occasion. "He's out and away a better man than that t'other one! Lives clear and clean before the world, and is ashamed to look no man in the face."

Thus old Max reflected. And it will be seen that his reflections tended more and more to favour the acceptance of Matthew Diamond as his son-in-law. Yes; he should be glad to see Rhoda safe and happy under a husband's care before he died. And yet—and yet—he felt, as the prosperous wooer had felt, a dim sense of dissatisfaction. Old Max could not be accused of being sentimental, but he had looked forward to Rhoda's marriage as an occasion of triumph and exultation. If she found a husband whom he approved of, he would be large and generous in his dealings with them. He would show the world that Rhoda Maxfield was no tocherless lass, but an heiress, courted, and sought after, and destined to belong to a sphere far above that of Whitford shopkeepers. Now the husband had been found—he had almost made up his mind as to that—but there was no exultation; certainly no triumph. Rhoda was so cool and quiet. Very sensible! Oh, admirably sensible; but—. In a word, the whole affair seemed a little flat and chilly. Of all the three personages chiefly interested, Rhoda was the only one who was conscious of no disappointment.

CHAPTER XII.

Miss Chubb could keep a secret. She was proud of being entrusted with one. She was much gratified when Rhoda Maxfield, on the Monday after Diamond's proposal, called at the maiden lady's modest lodgings, and confided to her the fact that Mr. Diamond had asked her to marry him, and that she had accepted him subject to her father's consent. It may seem strange that Rhoda should have chosen to make this confidence to Miss Chubb, rather than to Mrs. Errington, or to Minnie Bodkin, with both of whom she was more intimate. But she told Miss Chubb that she wanted her help.

"My help, my dear! I'm sure I don't know how I can help you. But if I can I will. And I congratulate you sincerely. I've seen how it would be all along. You know I told you that a certain gentleman was falling over head and ears in love, a long time ago. Didn't I, now?"

Rhoda acknowledged that it was so; and then she said she had come to ask a great favour. Would Miss Chubb mind saying a word or two on Mr. Diamond's behalf to her father? "Father told me this morning, after breakfast, that he should make some inquiries about Mr. Diamond. I am quite sure that nothing will come out that is not honourable to him; I am not the least afraid of that. And I believe Dr. Bodkin will praise him very highly, but he will not perhaps say the sort of things that would please father most. He will tell him what a good scholar he is, and all that, but he will never think of making father understand that Mr. Diamond is looked upon as being as much a gentleman as he is himself. Gentlefolks like Dr. Bodkin take those things for granted. But father would like to be told them. He thinks so very much of my marrying—above my own class, for, of course, I have learnt enough to know that Mr. Diamond belongs to a different sort of people from mine."

"I understand, my dear," returned Miss Chubb, nodding her head shrewdly. "And you may depend on my doing my best, if I have the chance. But I'm afraid it is not likely that Mr. Maxfield will consult me on the subject."

"I told him to come to you. Father knows you are one of the few people with whom Mr. Diamond has associated in Whitford."

"Why don't you send him to Mrs. Errington? Oh, I forgot! Your father and she are two." Miss Chubb laughed to cover a little confusion on her own part, for she guessed that Rhoda might have other reasons for not asking Mrs. Errington's testimony in favour of her suitor. Then she added quickly, "Or Minnie Bodkin, now! Minnie's word would go farther with your father than mine would. And Minnie and Mr. Diamond are such cronies. You had better send him to Minnie."

"No, thank you."

"But why not? Good gracious, she is the very person!"

"No, I think not. We don't wish it known until father has given his decided consent. I have only told you in confidence, Miss Chubb."

"But—if the doctor knows it, Minnie must know it! And if I know it, why shouldn't she?"

"No, thank you. I don't want to ask Miss Minnie about it."

"I wonder why that is, now!" pondered Miss Chubb, when Rhoda was gone. And very probably Rhoda could not have told her why.

Old Maxfield duly paid his visit to Miss Chubb. The good-natured little woman waited at home all day lest she should miss him. And about an hour after her early dinner Mr. Maxfield sent in his respects, and would be glad to have a word with her if she were at leisure.

"I hope you will overlook the intrusion, ma'am," said Maxfield, standing up with his hat in his hand, just inside the door of the little sitting-room, where Miss Chubb asked him to walk in.

"No intrusion at all, Mr. Maxfield! I'm very glad to see you. Please to sit down."

He obeyed, and holding his thick stick upright before him, and his hat on his knees, he thus began:

"I'm not a-going to waste your time and mine with vain and worldly discourse, ma'am. I am a man as knows the value of time, thanks be! And I have a serious matter on my mind. You know my daughter Rhoda?"

"I know Rhoda, and like her, and admire her very much."

"Yes; Rhoda is a girl such as you don't see many like her. There's a young man seeking her in marriage."

"I'm not surprised at that!"

"No; there has been several others too. But she gave 'em no encouragement; nor should I have been willing that she should. Some of them were persons in my own rank of life, and that would not do for Rhoda."

"I think you are quite right there, Mr. Maxfield. Rhoda is naturally very refined, and she has associated a good deal with persons of cultivated manners. I don't think Rhoda would be happy if she were obliged to give up certain little graces of life, which a great many excellent people can do without perfectly well."

Maxfield nodded approvingly. "You speak with a good deal of judgment, ma'am," said he, with the air of a recognised authority on wisdom. "But it isn't only that. Rhoda will have money—a great deal of money—more than some folks that holds their heads very high ever had or will have. Now it is but just and rightful that I should expect her husband to bring some advantages in return."

"Of course. And—ahem!—I'm sure you are too sensible a man not to consider that the best thing a husband could bring in exchange would be an honest, loving heart, and a real esteem and respect for your daughter."

Little Miss Chubb became quite fluttered after making this speech, and coloured as if she had been a girl of eighteen.

"Not at all," returned old Max decisively. "The loving heart and the esteem and respect are due to my Rhoda if she hadn't a penny. In return for her fortin' I expect something over and above."

"Oh!" exclaimed Miss Chubb, a good deal taken aback.

"Now I don't feel sure that the young man in question has that something over and above. It is Mr. Matthew Diamond, tutor at the Grammar School in this town."

"A most excellent young man! And, I'm sure, most devotedly in love with Rhoda."

"But very poor, and not of much account in the world, as far as I can make out."

"Oh, don't say that, Mr. Maxfield! He is proud and shy, and has kept himself aloof from society because he chose to do so. But he would be a welcome guest anywhere in the town or county. Young Mr. Pawkins, of Pudcombe Hall, quite courts him; he is always asking him to go over there."

Thus much and more Miss Chubb valiantly spoke on behalf of Matthew Diamond in his character of Rhoda's wooer. And then she expatiated on the excellent position he would hold as master of Dorrington School. It was such a "select seminary;" and so many of the first county people sent their boys there. "Dear me," said Miss Chubb, "it seems to me to be the very position for Rhoda! Not too far from Whitford, and yet not too near—of course she couldn't keep up all her old acquaintances here, could she?—and altogether so refined, and scholastic, and quiet! And really, Mr. Maxfield, see how everything turns out for the best. I thought at one time that young Errington was very much smitten with Rhoda; but, if she had taken him, you wouldn't have been so satisfied with her position in life now, would you? With all his talent and connection, see what a poor place he has of it. Mr. Diamond has done best, ten to one."

This was a master-stroke, and made a great impression on old Max. Not that the latter even now was at all dazzled by the prospect of having the head-master of Dorrington School for his son-in-law. But Miss Chubb's allusion did suffice to show him that the world would consider Diamond to be a triumphantly successful man in comparison with Errington.

"Oh, him!" said Maxfield in a tone of bitter contempt. "No; such as him was not for Miss Maxfield. And I'll tell you, moreover, that I don't know but what she's throwing herself away more or less if she takes this other. She's a great catch for him; I know the world, and I know that she is a great catch. But I've felt latterly one or two warnings that my end is near—"

"Dear me, Mr. Maxfield! Don't say so! I'm sure you look very hearty!" exclaimed Miss Chubb, much startled by this cool announcement.

"That my end is near," repeated old Max doggedly, "and I wish to set my house in order, and see my daughter provided for, before I go. And she seems to be contented with this young man. Rhoda ain't just easy to please. It might be a long time, if ever, before she found some one to suit her so well."

Miss Chubb was a little shocked at this singularly prosaic and unemotional way of treating the subject of love and marriage, as to which she herself preserved the most romantic freshness of ideas. She would have liked the young couple to be like the lovers in a story-book, and the father to bestow his daughter and his blessing with tears of joy. However, she did her best to encourage Mr. Maxfield in giving his consent after his own fashion, and they parted on excellent terms with each other.

"That dry old chip, Jonathan Maxfield, has been to me to-day," said Dr. Bodkin after dinner to his wife and daughter. "He came to ask me what prospect I thought Diamond had of getting the mastership of Dorrington, explaining to me that Diamond was a suitor for his daughter's hand. It took me quite by surprise. Had you any inkling of the matter, Minnie?"

"Oh yes, papa."

"Dear me! Well, women see these things so quickly! H'm! Well, Master Diamond has shown good taste, I must say. That little Rhoda is the prettiest girl I know. And such a sweet, soft, lovable creature! I think she's too good for him."

"It is a singular thing, but I have remarked very often that men in general are apt to think pretty girls too good for anybody but themselves!"

The doctor frowned, and then smiled. "Have you so, Saucebox?" he said.

"I don't know about her being too good for him," said Mrs. Bodkin, in her quick, low tones; "but I suppose he knows very well what he is about. Old Maxfield has feathered his nest very considerably. It will be a very good match for a poor man like Matthew Diamond."

Mrs. Bodkin had for some time past exhibited symptoms of dislike to Diamond. She never had a good word for him; she even was almost rancorous against him at times, although she seldom allowed the feeling to express itself in words before her daughter. Minnie understood it all very well.

"Poor mother!" she thought to herself, "she cannot forgive him. I wish I could persuade her that there is nothing to forgive. How could he help it if I was a fool?" Yet the mother and daughter had never exchanged a word on the subject. And Minnie comforted herself with the conviction that her mother was the only person in the world who guessed her secret. "Mamma has a sixth sense where I am concerned," said she to herself.

"I hope you said a good word for the lovers to Mr. Maxfield, papa," she said aloud, in a clear, cheerful voice.

"I had not much to say. I told him that I thought Diamond stood a good chance of getting Dorrington School."

"When will it be known positively, papa?"

"About Dorrington? Oh, before Christmas. I should say by the end of the first week in December. Diamond will be a loss to me, but I shall be glad of his promotion. He's a gentleman, and a very good fellow, although his manner is a trifle self-opiniated. And," added the doctor, shaking his head and lowering his voice as one does who is forced to admit a painful truth, "I am sorry to say that his views as to the use of the Digamma are by no means sound."

"Perhaps Rhoda won't find that a drawback to her happiness!" said Minnie, laughing her sweet, musical laugh.

"Probably not, Puss!"

Then the Rev. Peter Warlock and Mr. Dockett dropped in. A whist-table was made up in the drawing-room. The doctor and Mr. Dockett won three rubbers out of four against Mrs. Bodkin and the curate. And the latter—being seated where he could command a full view of Minnie as she reclined near the fire with a book—made two revokes, and drew down upon himself a very severe homily and a practical lecture or short course on the science of whist, illustrated by all the errors he had made during the evening, from Dr. Bodkin. For the doctor, although he liked to win, cared not for inglorious victory, and was almost as indignant with his opponents as with his partner for any symptom of slovenly play. The Reverend Peter's brow grew serious, even to gloom, and it seemed to him as if the doctor's scolding were almost more than human patience could endure. "I don't mind losing my sixpences," thought the curate, "and I could make up my mind to sacrificing an hour or two over those accursed," (I'm afraid he did mentally use that strong expression!) "those thrice-accursed bits of pasteboard. But to be lectured and scolded at into the bargain—!" He arose from the green table with an almost defiant sullenness.

However, when the tray was brought in and the victimised gentleman had comforted his inner man with hot negus, and was at liberty to sip it in close proximity to Miss Bodkin's chair, and had received one or two kind looks from Miss Bodkin's eyes, and several kind words from Miss Bodkin's lips, his heart grew soft within him, and he began to think that even six, ten—a dozen rubbers of whist with the doctor would not be too high a price to pay for these privileges! Then they talked of Diamond's engagement to Rhoda—it had been spoken of all over Whitford hours ago!—and of his prospects. And Mr. Warlock was quite effusive in his rejoicings on both scores. He had been dimly jealous of Minnie's regard for Diamond, and was heartily glad of the prospect of getting rid of him. Mr. Dockett, too, seemed to think the match a desirable one. He pursed up his mouth and looked knowing as he dropped a mysterious hint as to the extent of Rhoda's dowry. "I made old Max's will myself," said he; "and without violating professional secrecy, I may confirm what I hear old Max bruits abroad at every opportunity—namely, that he is a warm man—a very warm man in—deed!

But I'm sure Mr. Diamond is a young man of sound principles, and will make the girl a good husband. And it is decided promotion for her too, you know. A grocer's daughter! Eh? I'm sure I wish them well most sincerely." And shall we blame Mr. Dockett if, in his fatherly anxiety, he rejoiced at the removal of a dangerous rival to his little Ally, on whom young Pawkins had recently bestowed a good deal of attention whenever Rhoda Maxfield was out of his reach?

"I never knew such a popular engagement," said Dr. Bodkin, innocently. "Everybody seems to approve! One might almost fear it could not be a case of true love, it runs so very smooth. There does not appear to be a single objection."

"Except the Digamma, papa!"

"Except the Digamma," echoed the doctor merrily. And when he was alone with his wife that night, he remarked to her that he was immensely thankful to see the great improvement in their beloved child this winter.

"Minnie is certainly stronger," said the mother.

"And in such excellent spirits!" said the father.

CHAPTER XIII.

The days passed by and brought no letter, in answer to Castalia's, from Lord Seely. Dreary were the hours in Ivy Lodge. The wife was devoured by passionate jealousy and a vain yearning for affection; the husband found that even the bright, smooth, hard metal of his own character was not impervious to the corrosive action of daily cares, regrets, and apprehensions. Algernon was not apt to hate. He usually perceived the absurd side of persons who were obnoxious to him with too keen an amusement to detest them; and the inmost feeling of his heart with respect to his fellow-creatures in general approached, perhaps, as nearly to perfect indifference as it is given to a mortal to attain. But it was not possible to preserve a condition of indifference towards Castalia. She was a thorn in his flesh, a mote in his eye, a weariness to his spirit; and he began to dislike the very sight of the sallow, sickly face, red-eyed too often, and haggard with discontent, that met his view whenever he was in his own home. It was the daily "worry" of it, he told himself, that was unendurable. It was the being shut up with her in a box like Ivy Lodge, where there was no room for them to get away from each other. If he could have shared a mansion in Grosvenor Square with Castalia he might have got on with her well enough! But then, that mansion in Grosvenor Square would have made so many things different in his life.

At length one day came a letter to Castalia, with the London post-mark and sealed with the well-known coat of arms, but it did not bear Lord Seely's frank. Another name was scrawled in the corner, and the direction was written in Lady Seely's crooked, cramped little characters.

"I'm afraid Uncle Val must be ill!" exclaimed Castalia, opening the letter with a trembling hand. She was so weak and nervous now that the most trifling agitation made her heart beat painfully. My lady's epistle was not long, and, as a knowledge of its contents is essential to the due comprehension of this story, it is given in full, with her ladyship's own phraseology and orthography:—

"MY DEAR CASTALIA,—I cannot think what on earth you are about to write such letters to your uncle. Go abroad, indeed! I suppose Ancram would like the embassy to St. Petersburg, or to be governor of the Ionian Islands. It's all nonsense, and you had better put such ideas out of your head at once, and for all. I should think you might know that we have other people to think of besides your husband, especially after all we have done for him. Your uncle is very ill in bed with an attack of the gout, and can't write himself. The doctor thinks he won't be about again for weeks. You can guess what trouble this throws on to my shoulders, so I hope you won't worry me by any more such letters as the last. As if there was not anxiety enough, Fido had a fit on Thursday. I hope you are pretty well. What a blessing you've no sign of a family. With only you two to keep, you ought to do very well on Ancram's salary, and you can tell him I say so. Yours affectionately,

"B. SEELY."

"Poor Uncle Val!" exclaimed Castalia, dropping the letter from her hand. "I was afraid he was ill."

"Pshaw! A touch of the gout won't kill him," said Algernon, who had been reading over her shoulder. "But it's deuced unfortunate for me that he should be laid up at this time, and quite helpless in the hands of that old catamaran."

"Poor Uncle Val! Perhaps he never got my letter at all."

"Nothing more likely, if my lady could prevent his getting it."

"Perhaps, when he gets better, I can write to him again, and ask him—"

"When he gets better? Oh yes, certainly. We have plenty of time. There is no hurry, of course!"

"I see that you are speaking satirically, Ancram, but I don't know why."

Her husband shrugged his shoulders and walked out of the room. As he left the house he was met at the garden-gate by a bright-eyed, consumptive-looking lad, in shabby working clothes, who touched his cap, and held out a paper to Algernon. "What do you want?" asked the latter. "Mr. Gladwish, sir. His account, if you please, sir."

"And who the devil is Mr. Gladwish?"

"The shoemaker, sir."

"Oh! Mr. Gladwish, then, is an extremely importunate, impatient, troublesome fellow. This is the third or fourth time within a very few weeks that he has sent in his bill. I'm not accustomed to that sort of thing. I don't understand it. Don't give me the paper, boy. Take it into the house."

"Please, sir," began the lad, and stopped, hesitatingly. Then seeing that Mr. Errington was walking off without taking any further notice of him, he repeated in a louder, firmer tone, "Please, sir, Mr. Gladwish is really in want of the money. He has two of the children bad with fever. And I was to say that even five pounds on account would be acceptable."

"Five pounds! He's too modest. I haven't got five pounds, nor five minutes. I'm busy."

"Then, I'm sorry to say, sir, that Mr. Gladwish will take legal proceedings for the debt at once. He told me to tell you so."

"Nice state of things!" muttered Algernon, as he walked towards the post-office, with his head bent down and his hands deep in his pockets. "But that's nothing. It's those cursed bills in Maxfield's hands that are on my mind like lead."

His spirits were not lightened by that which awaited him at the office. He had to undergo an interview with the district surveyor, who was very grave, not to say severe, in speaking of the irregularities which had been complained of, and were looked on as very serious at the head office. The surveyor ended by plainly hinting his hope that persons having no business at the office would be strictly forbidden from having access to it at abnormal hours. "I—I don't understand you," stammered Algernon.

"Mr. Errington," said the surveyor, "I am speaking to you, not officially, but confidentially, and as man to man. I have been having a little conversation with Mr. Gibbs—who seems to have none but good feeling towards you, but who—in short, I think it is not needful to be more explicit. I advise you in all friendliness to be stern and decisive in keeping every person out of this office except such as have recognised business to be here. If further trouble arises, I shall have to do my duty, and make my report without respect of any persons whatsoever."

"Perhaps," said Algernon, who was white to his lips, but otherwise apparently unmoved, "perhaps it would be best for me to resign my post here at once. If the authorities above me find cause for dissatisfaction—"

"I can give you no advice as to that, Mr. Errington. You must know your own affairs better than I do."

"There are things which a man can scarcely say even to himself; considerations which are painful as they float dimly in one's own mind, but which would be unendurable uttered aloud in words. Anything like a public scandal—or—or—disgrace to me, would involve a large circle of persons—many of them persons of rank and consideration in the world. You are possibly aware that—my wife"—there was a peculiar tone in Algernon's voice as he said these two words—"is a niece of Lord Seely?"

But the official gentleman declined to enter into the question of Mr. Errington's family connections. "Oh," said he, coldly; "we must hope there will be no question of scandal or disgrace." Then he went away, leaving Algernon in a chaos of doubt as to whether he should, or should not, speak further on the subject to Obadiah Gibbs. Obadiah Gibbs, however, decided the question for him. He came into Algernon's room, closing the door carefully behind him, and asked to speak a few words in private. Algernon was sitting in the luxurious easy-chair which he had had carried into the office for his own use. It was about three o'clock in the afternoon of a dull November day. The single window which looked on to a white-washed court threw a ghastly pallid light on Algernon's face as he sat opposite to it, with his head thrown back against the cushions of the high chair. Mr. Gibbs was touched with compassion at seeing how changed the bright young face looked since he had first been acquainted with it. And yet, in truth, the change was not a very deep one: it was more in colouring, and the expression of the moment, than in any lines which care had graven.

"Come in, Gibbs; come in," said Algernon, with his affable air. The clerk seemed the more anxious and disturbed of the two. He sat down on the chair Algernon pointed out to him in a constrained posture, and seemed to have some difficulty in beginning to speak, albeit not a man usually liable to embarrassment of manner. His superior stretched his feet out nearer to the hearth, and slightly moved his white hand to and fro, looking, as a child might have done, at the glitter of a ring he wore in the firelight.

"Mr. Wing did not seem very well pleased, sir," said Gibbs, after clearing his throat.

"Of course he had to appear displeased, whether he was or not, Gibbs. A little hocus-pocus, a little official solemnity, is the thing to assume, I suppose. I think that man's nose is the very longest I ever saw. Remarkable nose, eh, Gibbs?"

"But, sir," continued Gibbs, declining to discuss the surveyor's nose, "he said that from inquiries that had been made, it's pretty certain that the missing letters were—stolen—they must have been stolen—at Whitford."

"Very intelligent on the part of the official, Mr. Wing! Only I think you and I had come to pretty nearly the same conclusion before."

"He made strict inquiries about the people in the office here, and I had to give him what information I could, sir."

"Of course, of course, Gibbs! I quite understand," said Algernon, putting his hand out to shake that of the clerk with so frank a cordiality that the latter felt the tears spring into his eyes as he took the cool white hand into his own. "I have felt very much for you, Mr. Errington," said he. "Your position is a trying one, indeed. I would do almost anything in my power to set your mind more at rest. But I'm sorry to say that I have an unpleasant matter to speak of."

"I wonder," thought Algernon, leaning back in his chair once more, "whether my friend Obadiah conceives our conversation hitherto to have been of an agreeable and entertaining nature, that he now announces something unpleasant by way of a change!"

"You will understand," said Gibbs, "that I am speaking to you in the very strictest confidence. I should be sorry for it to come out that I had meddled in the matter. Nor, sir, would it be well for you to have it known that I gave you any warning."

"I wish the old bore would not be so confoundedly long-winded!" thought Algernon, nodding meanwhile with an air of thoughtful attention.

But Gibbs was prone to long-windedness and to the making of speeches. And he now availed himself of the opportunity of haranguing the postmaster (one of whose chief faults was a vivacious impatience of his clerk's eloquence) to the fullest extent. But the gist of what he had to say was this: Roger Heath, the man whose money-letter had been lost, now declared that his correspondent at Bristol, being interrogated in the hope that he might be able to furnish some clue to the identification of the missing notes, stated that he remembered one was endorsed in blue ink instead of black: and that he, Heath, had reason to know that one of the notes paid by young Mrs. Errington to Ravell, the mercer, had been endorsed in blue ink!

"Now, sir," proceeded Gibbs, "I remember its being a good deal talked of in the town at the time, that young Mrs. Errington had money unknown to you, and Mrs. Ravell spoke of it to many."

"Damn Mrs. Ravell! What does it all mean, Gibbs?"

Algernon got up from his chair, and leant his elbows on the chimney-piece, and hid his face in his hands, but he so stood that he could watch the clerk's countenance between his fingers. That countenance expressed trouble and compassion. Gibbs got up too, and stood looking at Algernon and shaking his head ruefully.

"I thought it well you should know what was being said, Mr. Errington," said he.

"What can I do, Gibbs? How can I stop their cursed tongues?" Algernon still spoke with his face hidden.

"No, sir, you cannot stop their tongues, but—you might possibly put a stop to what sets their tongues going. Of course, the matter may be all explained simply enough. There may be plenty of bank-notes endorsed in blue ink—"

"Of course there may! Chattering idiots!"

"And as to that particular note, Mr. Ravell paid it away, as well as the others Mrs. Errington gave him, to the agent of a Manchester house he deals with, the next day after it came into his hands. I ascertained that from Ravell himself."

"I'll have the note traced!" exclaimed Algernon, looking up for the first time.

"That would be a difficult matter, sir. It has gone far and wide before now."

"I tell you I will have it traced! And I will have that malignant scoundrel, Heath, pulled up pretty sharply, if he dares to make any more insinuations that—it is not difficult to see what he is driving at!"

Gibbs laid his hand on the young man's shoulder.

"I feel for you, Mr. Errington," he said. "If I did not, I shouldn't put myself in the disagreeable position of saying what I have said. I should have attended to my own business, and let matters take their course. I hope you believe that I had only a kind motive in speaking?"

"I do believe it—heartily!"

"Thank you, sir. Then I shall make bold to give you one word of advice. Don't stir in the matter, nor make any threats against any one, until you have ascertained from Mrs. Errington where she got the notes that she paid to Ravell."

Algernon had bent down his head again, and he now answered without looking up:

"No doubt Mrs. Errington can account for them to me, but she is not bound to do so to any one else. Nor can I allow any one to hint that she is so bound. I should be a blackguard if I could listen to a word of that sort."

"I hope it may come right, Mr. Errington. After all, there has been nothing, and, so far as I see, there can be nothing, but talk to hurt you."

"My good fellow," said Algernon, as he once more gave his hand to his clerk, "it's a kind of talk which poisons a man's life. You know that as well as I do."

Then Gibbs took his leave of his superior, and went back into the outer office to watch over the epistolary correspondence of Whitford. As he sat at his desk there his mind was full of sympathy with Algernon Errington. "Poor young man! He took it beautifully. It must be a terrible blow—an awful blow. But, no doubt, he has had his suspicions before now. What a warning against worldly-mindedness! He is a victim to that vain and godless woman; and that's all that comes of the marriage that so uplifted the heart of his mother. But he would be a beautiful character, if he had only got religion, and would leave off profane swearing. He is so guileless and outspoken, like a child, almost. Ah, poor young man! I hope the Lord may bless this trial to him. But—religion or no religion—I don't believe he'll ever be fit to be postmaster of Whitford." Thus ran the reflections of Mr. Obadiah Gibbs.

When Algernon reached home that evening, he bade Lydia put up a few things for him into a little travelling valise; and when he met his wife at the dinner-table, he told her he should go up to London that night by the mail-coach. He explained, in answer to her surprised inquiries, lamentations, and objections, uttered in a querulous drawl, that he must get help from Lord Seely; that it was useless to write to him under the present circumstances, seeing that his wife would probably intercept the letter; and that, therefore, he had resolved to go to town himself and obtain a personal interview with Lord Seely.

"But, Ancram!—what's the use? Why on earth should you fly off in this way? I'm sure it won't do! Do you suppose for an instant that Aunt Belinda will let you get at him?"

"I must try for it. Things have got to that pass now, that—Do you know what happened to me just as I went out after lunch? Gladwish, the shoemaker, sent to threaten me with arrest! I shall be walked off to prison, I suppose, for a few wretched pairs of abominable shoes. The fellow has no more notion of fitting my foot than a farrier."

"To prison! Oh, Ancram! But Gladwish's bill cannot be so very large—"

"Of course it's not 'so very large!'"

"Then, if we paid it, or even part of it—"

"Paid it! Upon my word, Cassy, you are too absurd! 'Paid it!' In the first place, I have only a very few pounds in the house—barely enough to take me to town, I think; and, in the next place, if I paid Gladwish, what would be the result? The butcher, the baker, and the candlestick-maker would be all down on me with summonses, and writs, and executions, and bedevilments of every imaginable kind. But you have no more notion—you take it all so coolly. 'Pay him!' By George! Cassy, it's very hard to stand such nonsense!"

Castalia withdrew from the table, and sat down on the little sofa and cried. Her husband looked at her across a glass of very excellent sherry, which he was just about to hold up to the light. "I think, Castalia," he said, "I really do think, that when a man is in such trouble as I am, reduced to the brink of ruin, not knowing which way to turn for a ten-pound note, struggling, striving, bothering his brains to find a way out of the confounded mess, he might expect something more cheering and encouraging from his wife than perpetual snivelling." With that he cracked a filbert with a sharp jerk of indignation. But Algernon's forte was not the minatory or impressively wrathful style of eloquence. He could hurl a sarcasm, sharp, light, and polished; but when he came to wielding such a ponderous weapon as serious reproof on moral considerations, he was apt to make a poor hand of it. It was excessively disagreeable, too, to see that woman's thin shoulders moving convulsively under her gay-coloured dress, as she sobbed with her head buried in the sofa cushions. That really must be put a stop to. So, as it appeared evident that scolding would not quench the tears, he tried coaxing. The coaxing was not so efficacious as it would have been once. Still, Castalia responded to it to the extent of endeavouring to check the sobs which still shook her frail chest and throat. "When shall you be back, Ancram?" she said, looking beseechingly at him. He answered that he hoped to be in Whitford again on Tuesday night, or Wednesday at the latest (it was then Monday), and he particularly impressed on her the necessity of telling any one who might inquire the cause of his absence, that he had been suddenly called up to town by the illness of Lord Seely. He had, in fact, said a word or two to that effect when, on his way home, he had ordered the fly, which was to carry him and his valise to the coach-office. Castalia insisted on accompanying him to the coach, despite the damp cold of the night, a proceeding which he did not much combat, since he felt it would serve to give colour to his statement to the landlord of the "Blue Bell."

"Keep up your spirits, Cassy," he cried, waving his hand from the coach-window as he stood in the inn yard, muffled in shawls and furs. "I hope I shall bring back good news of your uncle."

Then Castalia was trundled back to Ivy Lodge in the jingling old fly, whilst her husband rolled swiftly behind four fleet horses towards London.

CHAPTER XIV.

Stiff, tired, and cold, Algernon alighted the next morning at the coach-office in London after his night journey. He drove to a fashionable hotel not very far from Lord Seely's house, and refreshed himself with a warm bath and a luxurious breakfast. By the time that was done it was eleven o'clock in the forenoon. He had been considering how best to proceed, in a leisurely way, during his breakfast, and had decided to go to Lord Seely's house without further delay. He knew Lady Seely's habits well enough to feel tolerably sure that she would not be out of her bed before eleven o'clock, nor out of her room before mid-day. He thought he might gain access to his lordship by a coup de main, if he so timed his visit as to avoid encountering my lady. So he had himself driven to within a few yards of the house, and walked up to the well-known door. It was a different arrival from his first appearance on that threshold. Algernon did not fail to think of the contrast, and he told himself that he had been very badly used by the whole Seely family: they had done so infinitely less for him than he had expected! The sense of injury awakened by this reflection was as supporting to him as a cordial.

The servant who opened the door, and who at once recognised Algernon, stared in surprise on seeing him, but was too well trained to express emotion in any other way. After a few inquiries about Lord Seely's health, Algernon asked if he could be allowed to see his lordship. This, however, was a difficult matter. My lord was better, certainly, the footman said, but my lady had given strict orders that he was not to be disturbed. No one was admitted to his room except the doctor, who would not make his visit until late in the afternoon.

"Oh, I shouldn't think of disturbing my lady at this hour," said Algernon, "but I must speak with Lord Seely. It is of the very greatest importance."

"I'll call Mr. Briggs, sir," the footman was beginning, when Algernon stopped him. Mr. Briggs was Lord Seely's own man, and, like all the servants in the house, was certain to obey his mistress's orders rather than his master's, if the two should happen to conflict. Algernon slipped some money into the footman's hand, together with a note which he had written that morning. "There, James," said he; "if you will manage to convey that into his lordship's own hand, I know he will see me. And, moreover, he would be seriously annoyed if I were sent away without having spoken to him on business of very great importance."

James reflected that the worst that could happen to him would be a scolding from my lady. That was certainly no trifling evil; but he decided to risk it, being moved to do so not only by the bribe, but by a real liking for young Errington, who was generally a favourite with other people's servants.

The note which James carried upstairs was as follows:—

"MY LORD,—I write in the driest and most matter-of-fact terms I can find, to ask for an interview with your lordship with the least possible delay, being unwilling to make, or to appear to make, any claim on the regard you once professed for me, or on the connection which unites us, and desiring you to understand that I appeal to you on behalf of another person; and that, were it not for that other person I should ask no more favours of your lordship—nor, perhaps, need any.

"A. ANCRAM ERRINGTON."

In a few moments James came running downstairs and begged Algernon, almost in a whisper, to walk up to his lordship's room.

Lord Seely was not in bed. He was reclining in an easy-chair, with one foot and leg supported on cushions. He seemed ill and worn, but his dark eyes sparkled as he looked eagerly at Algernon, who entered quietly and closed the door behind him. "What is it? I'm afraid you have bad news, Ancram," said Lord Seely, holding out his hand.

Algernon did not take it. He bowed very gravely, and stood opposite to the little nobleman.

"Castalia—!" cried Lord Seely, much dismayed by the young man's manner. "Don't keep me in suspense, for God's sake! Is she ill? Is she dead?"

"No, my lord. Castalia is not dead. Neither, so far as I know, is she ill—in body."

"What is the matter?"

"I must crave a patient hearing, my lord. I regret to have to trouble you whilst you are ill and suffering; but what I have to say must be said without delay. May I ask if there is anyone within hearing?"

"No! No one. You can close the door of that dressing-closet if you choose. But there is no one there."

Algernon adopted the suggestion at once, and then sat down opposite to Lord Seely's chair. His whole manner of proceeding was so unusual and unexpected that it produced a very painful impression on Lord Seely. Algernon rather enjoyed this. He began to speak with only one distinct purpose in his mind: namely, to frighten his wife's uncle into making a strong effort to help him out of Whitford. How much pressure would be necessary to achieve that purpose he could not yet tell. And he began to speak with a sort of reckless abandonment of himself to the guidance of the moment, a mood of mind which had become very frequent with him of late.

"Did your lordship receive a letter from Castalia begging you to obtain a post abroad for me?"

"Certainly. My wife answered it. I—I was unable to write myself. But I intended to reply more at length so soon as I should be better."

"Castalia showed me Lady Seely's reply. That was the first intimation I had of Castalia's having made such an application. I mention this because I know your lordship suspected me of being the prime mover in all her applications to you for assistance."

Lord Seely coloured a little as he replied, "It was natural to suppose that you influenced your wife, Ancram."

"Your lordship must not judge all cases by your own," returned the young man, with a candid raising of his brows; and the colour on Lord Seely's face deepened to a dark red flush, which faded, leaving him paler than before. "As I said," continued Algernon, "I did not know what it was that Castalia had asked you to do for us. But, now that I do know it, I may say at once that I heartily concur with her as to its desirability."

"I cannot agree with you there; but, even if it were so, I assure you it is out of my power—"

"Allow me, my lord! I must tax your patience to listen to what I have to say before you give me any positive answer."

Lord Seely leaned back in his chair, and motioned with his head for Algernon to proceed. The latter went on:

"Exile from England and from all the hopes and ambitions not very unnatural at my age, is not such an alluring prospect that I should be suspected of having incited Castalia to write as she has done? However, I will say no more as to my own private and personal feelings in the matter. I did not mean to allude to them. I beg your pardon." Algernon sat leaning a little forward in his chair. His hands were clasped loosely together, and rested on his knees. He kept his eyes gloomily fixed on the carpet for the most part, and only raised them occasionally to look up at Lord Seely without raising his head at the same time. "I could not write what I had to say to you, my lord. I dared not write it. Perhaps, even, if I had written, the letter might not have reached you at once; and I could not wish its falling into other hands, so I came away from Whitford last night quite suddenly. I have no leave of absence; the clerk at the post-office, even, did not know I was coming away."

"Do you mean to say, Ancram, that you have deliberately risked the loss of your situation?"

"My 'situation' was as good as lost already. Do you know what happened yesterday, Lord Seely? I was subjected to the agreeable ordeal of a visit from the surveyor of the postal district in which Whitford is situated. I was catechised magisterially. The whole office—including my private room—was subjected to a sort of scrutiny. There have been a great many letters missing at Whitford lately; some money-letters. That is to say, letters which should have passed through our office have never reached their destination. Nothing has been traced. Nothing is known with certainty. But the concurrence of various circumstances points to Whitford as the place where the letters have been—stolen. I am told on all hands that such things never happened in Mr. Cooper's time. (Mr. Cooper was my predecessor as postmaster.) I am scowled at, and almost openly insulted in the streets, by a miller, or a baker, or something of the kind, who lives in the neighbourhood. He declares he has lost a considerable sum of money by the post, and plainly considers me responsible. You may guess how pleasant my 'situation' has become in consequence of these things being known and talked about."

"But, good Heavens, Ancram—! I don't comprehend your way of looking at the matter. These irregularities are doubtless very distressing, but surely your rational course would be to use every effort to discover the cause of them and set matters right; not run away as if you were a culprit!"

"Your lordship judges without knowing all the facts."

"Pardon me, Ancram, but no facts can justify such rash behaviour. I have some experience of men and of the world, and I give you my deliberate opinion that you have acted very indiscreetly, to say the least. I am disappointed in you, Ancram. I regret to say it, but I am disappointed in you. You have shown a want of steadiness, and—and—almost of common sense! The more I think of it, the more I disapprove of the step you have taken. It shows a great want of consideration for others; for your wife. If you were alone it might be pardonable—although, excessively ill-judged—to throw up your post at the first experience of the rough side of things. We all have difficulties to contend with. The most exalted position is not secure from them, as, indeed, it would appear almost superfluous to point out! The record of my own—my own—official life might supply you with more than one example of the value of steadfast energy, and an inflexible determination to conquer antagonistic circumstances."

Poor Lord Seely! He had been subdued by sickness more completely under the dominion of his wife than could ever be the case when he was able to move about, to get away from her, and to converse with persons who were not entirely devoid of any semblance of respect for his opinion. Lady Seely, it might be said, respected nobody—a point of resemblance between herself and her young kinsman which had not led to any very great sympathy or harmony between them; for, as it is your professed joker who can least bear to be laughed at, so those persons who most flippantly ignore any sentiment of reverence towards others are by no means prepared to tolerate a want of deference towards themselves. Certainly, my lady had snubbed her husband during his illness almost unmercifully; she wished him to get better, and she took care that the doctor's orders were faithfully carried out. But her course of treatment was anything but soothing to the spirit, and my lord's pet vanities received no consideration whatever from her. His mind being now relieved from the first shock of apprehension which Algernon's sudden visit had occasioned (for, though things were bad, it was a relief to him to find that Castalia was safe and well), he could not resist the temptation to lecture a little, and be pompous, and display his suppressed self-esteem with a little more emphasis than usual.

Poor Lord Seely! By so doing he unconsciously drew down a terrible catastrophe. It seemed a trivial cause to determine Algernon to speak as he next spoke—as trivial as the heedless footfall or too-loudly spoken word which brings the avalanche toppling down from the rock.

"The selfishness and egotism of the man are incredible!" thought Algernon, looking at Lord Seely. "Not one word of sympathy with me! Not a syllable to show that my feelings are worthy of any consideration whatever. Pompous little ass!" Then he said, very gravely and quietly, "I think, my lord, that you have forgotten what I said to you in the hurried note I sent upstairs, about appealing to you on behalf of another person."

Lord Seely had forgotten it.

"Ha!—no, Ancram. I—I remember what you said; but, I—I take leave to think that if you wish to consider that other person—it is your wife of whom you spoke, I presume?"

Algernon bowed his head.

"If you wish to consider that person effectually, you ought not to have flown off at a tangent in the manner you have done. You might—ahem!—you might, at least, have written to me for advice."

"Lord Seely, I am sorry to say that you are under an entire misapprehension as to the state of the case."

Lord Seely was not accustomed to be told that he was under an entire misapprehension on any subject.

"If so, Ancram," he answered, with some hauteur, "the fault must be yours. I believe I should succeed in comprehending any moderately clear and accurate statement."

"I will try to speak plainly. During the last six weeks I have been made seriously unhappy by rumours floating about in Whitford respecting my wife."

"Rumours—! Respecting your wife?"

"They reach my ears through various channels, and appear to be rife in every social circle in the place."

"Rumours! Of what nature?"

There was a little pause; then Algernon said, "The least terrible of them is, that Castalia's reason is affected, and that she is not responsible for her actions."

Lord Seely started into a more upright posture, and then sank back again with a suppressed cry of pain. Algernon went on, without looking up: "Her manner has been very singular of late. She has taken to wandering about alone, and to make her wanderings as secretly as may be; she haunts the post-office in my absence, carefully informing herself beforehand whether I am in my private room or not; and if I am reported absent, she enters it, searches the drawers, and, I have the strongest reason to believe—indeed I may say I know—that she has tampered with a little cabinet in which I keep a few private papers, and taken letters out of it!"

"Ancram!"

"These things, my lord, are commonly reported and spoken of by every gossiping tongue in Whitford. I can't help the people talking. Castalia is not liked there; her manners are unpopular, and even the persons who were inclined to receive her kindly for my sake have been offended and alienated. Still, the things I have told you are facts."

"I am shocked—I am surprised—and, forgive me, Ancram, a little incredulous. You may have listened to malicious tongues; you say that my niece is not liked by the—the class of persons with whom she now associates, and it may be—"

"I am sorry to say, my lord, that Castalia cannot be said to associate with any 'class of persons' in Whitford, for latterly it has become plain to me that all our acquaintances have given her the cold shoulder."

The mingled expression of amazement, incredulity, and offended pride on Lord Seely's face, when Algernon made this announcement, did not operate with the latter as an inducement to spare him. Indeed, he had now gone almost too far to stop short. He held up his hand to deprecate any interruption, and said, "One moment, my lord! I must ask you a question. Have you at any time privately supplied Castalia with money unknown to me?"

"Never! I—"

"Then, Lord Seely, I have only one more circumstance to add: Castalia, the other day, paid a bill of considerable amount to a mercer in Whitford without my knowledge, and without my knowing where she found the money to pay it; and yesterday my clerk, an honest fellow and much attached to me, told me in private and in strict confidence, that it was currently reported in the town that one of the notes paid by my wife to the mercer was endorsed in the same way as a note in one of the missing money-letters I have told you of."

"Good God, Ancram! what do you mean?"

"I told you that the least terrible rumour about Castalia was the rumour that her mind was affected."

Lord Seely's face was almost lead-coloured. He pressed his hands one on each side of his head with a gesture of hopeless bewilderment. "This is the most appalling thing!" he murmured, and his voice was scarcely audible as he said it.

"I had to make my choice without delay, Lord Seely. I regret to inflict this blow on you in your present suffering state of body; but, if I spared you, I could not have spared Castalia. I chose to spare my wife."

"Yes, yes;—quite—quite right. Spare Castalia! I—I thank you, Ancram—for choosing to spare her rather than me." The poor little nobleman's face was convulsed by a kind of spasm for a second or two, and then he burst into tears, sobbing out, with his face hidden in his trembling hands, "What is to be done? Gracious heavens! what is to be done?"

"I talked about choosing to spare Castalia," said Algernon, looking at her uncle with a sort of furtive curiosity and a feeling that was more akin to contempt than pity, "but I don't know how long it may be in my power, or anyone's power, to spare her. The only chance for either of us is to get away out of Whitford as quickly as possible."

"But—but—My head is so confused. I am stunned, Ancram—stunned! But—what was I going to say? Oh! have you interrogated Castalia? What representations does she make as to the money? There is so much to be said—to be asked. It cannot be but that there is some error. It cannot be. My poor Castalia!"

"Interrogating Castalia would be quite useless; worse than useless. You don't know what her behaviour and temper have been lately. She is utterly unreasonable. Ask anyone who knows our house in Whitford; ask my servants what my home has been latterly. I have bought the honour of your lordship's alliance somewhat dear."

Lord Seely sank down in his chair as if he had been struck, and his grey head drooped on his breast. "What can I do, Ancram?" he asked, in a tone so contrasted in its feebleness with his usual self-assured, rather strident voice, that it might have touched some persons with compassion. "What can I do?" Then he seemed to make a strong effort to recover some energy of manner, and added, "If it were not for this unfortunate attack which disables me, I would return with you to Whitford to-night. I would see Castalia myself."

Algernon heartily congratulated himself on the fit of gout which kept Lord Seely a prisoner. There was nothing he less desired than that her uncle should be confronted with Castalia. He represented that the only efficacious help Lord Seely could give under the circumstances would be to furnish them with money to pay their debts and leave Whitford forthwith. He pointed out that Castalia must have felt this herself, when she wrote urging her uncle to get them some post abroad. Algernon became eager and persuasive as he spoke, and offered a glimpse to the man before him, whose pride and whose affections were equally wounded, of a future which should make some amends for the bitter present—a future in which Castalia might have peace and safety at least, and in which her mind might regain its balance. He would be gentle, and patient, and tender with her; and, if they were in a position that offered no such temptations as the post-office at Whitford, the anxiety to all who regarded Castalia would be greatly lessened. Lord Seely was, as he had said, too much stunned by the whole interview to follow Algernon's rapid eloquence step by step. He felt that he must have time for reflection; besides, he was physically exhausted. He bade Algernon leave him for a time, and return later in the day. He would give orders that he should be admitted at once. "You—you have not seen my lady?" said Lord Seely hesitatingly.

"No; I purposely avoided doing so. She would have naturally inquired the cause of my unexpected presence in town, and I could speak of all this trouble to nobody on earth but yourself, my lord."

"Right, right, Ancram. But my lady will not fail to learn that you have been here, and we must give her some reason."

"I can say, if you choose, that I came to London on post-office business."

Lord Seely bowed his head almost humbly, and Algernon left him. He left him with an air of sombre resignation, but inwardly he felt himself to be master of the situation.

CHAPTER XV.

"Rubbish!" cried my lady. "It's a trick. I know the Ancrams, and there isn't one of them, and never was one of them—of the Warwickshire Ancrams, that is—who would stick at a lie!"

Lady Seely was in a towering passion. She had met Algernon Errington on the stairs as he was leaving her husband's room for the second time that afternoon. Algernon had slipped past her with a silent bow, and had refused to return, although she screamed after him at the full pitch of her lungs. Upon this Lady Seely had gone to her husband's room, and in a few minutes had drawn from him the confession that he had promised Algernon to use his utmost endeavours to obtain a post for him on the Continent. And then, on her violent opposition to this scheme, Lord Seely had been led on to tell her pretty nearly what Algernon had told him; dwelling very strongly on the circumstance that Castalia was in a strange, excited state, and might not be deemed responsible for her actions. But neither did this terrible revelation make much impression on my lady.

"Rubbish!" she said again. "And if she is in this queer excited condition, what makes her so?"

"Belinda, you do not realise the full extent. This is a more serious, a more frightful matter than you seem to think."

"Oh no it isn't, my lord! You'll see! A young rascal, to come here with his cock-and-a-bull stories, and try to frighten you into getting a berth for him! Why, there's nothing to be had, if one was willing to try, except the consulate at what's-his-name, on the Mediterranean, that Mr. Buller mentioned when you spoke to him about my nephew."

"I thought that might be got for Ancram, Belinda."

"Got for Ancram! Fiddlestick's end! What next? If the consulate is to be had, Reginald shall have it, that's flat!"

Lord Seely lay back in his chair and groaned.

"Yes," cried his wife, her cheeks flaming with anger until the rouge she wore seemed but a pale pigment on the hot colour beneath, "there it is! He has made you ever so much worse; upset you completely; thrown you back a fortnight, as Dr. Nokes said. He couldn't think what was the matter when he came at one o'clock. No more could I. 'My lord appears to have been agitated!' said he. Agitated! Yes; I'd agitate that young villain with a vengeance if I could get hold of him!"

"But you agitate me—me, Belinda. And, let me tell you, that you are not showing a proper feeling in the case as regards Castalia; my niece Castalia; poor unhappy girl!"

My lady stood up—she had risen to her feet in her wrath against Algernon—big, florid, loud of voice, and vehement of will, and looked down upon her husband in his invalid's chair. And as she looked into his face she perceived, and acknowledged to herself, that it would not do to drive him to extremities; that on this occasion neither indolence, habit, and bodily weakness on the one hand, nor sheer force of tongue and temper on the other, would avail to make him succumb to her. She changed her tone, and began to give her view of the case. She gave it the more effectively in that she spoke the truth, as far as the representation of her genuine opinion went. She did not believe a word about Castalia's having stolen money-letters. (Lord Seely winced when she blurted out the accusation nakedly in so many words.) Not one word! As to the gossip in Whitford, that might be, or might not; they had but Ancram's word for it. If Castalia was in this nervous, miserable state of mind; if she did pry on her husband, and prowl about the post-office, and even open his letters (that might be; nothing more likely!); if all these statements were true, what conclusion did they point to? Not that Castalia was a thief (my lord put his hand up at the word, as if to ward off a stab), but that she was insanely jealous.

The suggestion brought a gleam of comfort to Lord Seely. And it approved itself to his reason. The one explanation was in harmony with all that he knew of his niece's character. The other was not.

"Jealous, eh, Belinda?"

"Of course! Insanely jealous, that always was her character, when she lived in our house. She was jealous of Lady Harriet Dormer; she was jealous of everybody and everything that Ancram looked at."

"Jealous!" repeated my lord musingly. "But to act so strangely—to expose herself to animadversion—to go the length of opening desks and letters!—She must have had some cause, some great provocation."

"Nothing more likely! Ancram is good-looking and young; and Castalia—isn't."

"But where did she procure that money without her husband's knowledge?"

"Don't know, I'm sure."

"And her extravagance, and running him into debt as she has done—it seems to point to some mental aberration, does it not, Belinda?"

"Oh, fiddle-faddle, my lord! Why this, and how that! How do we know what truth there is in the whole story?"

"Belinda?"

"Oh, bless you, I'm too old a bird to be caught by any chaff the Ancrams can offer me."

"But, good heavens, Belinda, it is utterly incredible—"

"Nothing's incredible of an Ancram in the way of lying," returned the great lady of that family with much coolness. "This young jackanapes has got into a scrape down at What-do-ye-call-it. Things have gone wrong in the office—(I'll be bound he don't mind his business a bit)—he and his wife have got into debt between them. He don't like the place; and after bothering your life out for money, he comes off here without 'with your leave' or 'by your leave,' and asks to be sent abroad. That's my notion of the matter. And any way, if I were you, Valentine, I should take no sort of action, nor commit myself in any way, until I'd had Castalia's version of the story."

Lord Seely pressed his hand to his forehead, and writhed on his chair. "I wish to God that I could go to the place and speak with Castalia myself!" he cried. "There are things that cannot be written. But here I am a prisoner. It is a dreadful misfortune."

"I can't undertake to go trapesing down there in this weather," exclaimed my lady. "And, besides, I wouldn't leave you just now."

Lord Seely by no means wished that his wife should interfere personally in the matter. He well knew that nothing but discord was likely to arise from any interview between Castalia and her aunt. "There is no one I could send," he murmured. "No one I could trust."

"No, no! It would never do to send anybody at all. This kind of family wash had better be done in private. I tell you what you do, Valentine—you just dictate a letter to me to be sent to Castalia. Send it off at once. When does Ancram return? To-morrow? Very well, then. Send it off at once, so that it shall reach Whitford before he does."

"Why so, Belinda?" asked my lord anxiously.

"Why so? Dear me, Valentine; how st—unsuspicious you are! If Ancram was there when the letter arrived, do you suppose she would ever get it?"

Lord Seely stared at the florid, fat, unfeeling face before him, with a sensation of oppression and dismay. How was it possible to attribute such actions and motives to persons of one's own family with an air of such matter-of-fact indifference? It was not the first time that his wife's coarseness of feeling had been thrust on his observation to the shocking of his own finer taste and sentiment—for my lord was a gentleman at heart—but this was an amount of phlegmatic cynicism which hurt him to the core. He could not forget that it was his wife who had promoted the marriage of Castalia with this young man. It was his wife who had declared that the Honourable Miss Kilfinane was not likely to make a better match. It was his wife who had urged him to put young Errington into the Whitford

Post-office, declaring that the place was in every way a suitable one for him. And now it was his wife who coolly described Ancram as a wretch, full of the vilest duplicity!

The fact was, that my lady was by no means so indifferent on the subject as her words and manner would seem to imply. She was—not pained as Lord Seely was, but—angered excessively. She foresaw various troubles to herself and her husband—even the distant possibility of having Castalia "returned upon their hands," as she phrased it, and of having, sooner or later, to find money, or make interest, to get Ancram a berth which she would more willingly have bestowed on some of her nearer kith and kin. And her fashion of venting her anger was roundly to declare Ancram Errington capable of anything! And in her heart she believed him capable of a good deal of falsehood.

Lord Seely made no immediate reply to his wife's suggestion. He was ill and grieved, and he felt as if his final exit from this world of troubles might not be altogether undesirable. His interview with Algernon had agitated him terribly. His interview with his wife—although she had opened the door for a ray of hope that things might be not quite so terribly bad as he had feared—had certainly not soothed him. But before the departure of the evening mail that night, he had completed and despatched a letter to Castalia. He had insisted on writing it with his own hand, sitting up in bed to do so, although his fingers were scarcely able to guide the pen.

Meanwhile, Algernon was spending a very pleasant evening. He went to the club to which the Honourable Jack Price had introduced him during the brief butterfly period of his London existence. There he found the genial Jack, friendly, affectionate, expansive, as ever: a trifle balder, maybe, but otherwise unchanged. There, too, he found several of his former acquaintances ("old friends," he called them), who, after having his name recalled to their recollection by Jack Price, said, "Hulloa, Errington, where the dooce have you been hiding yourself?" and shook hands with the utmost cordiality. Then Jack Price insisted on adjourning to a favourite haunt of his, and ordering supper in celebration of Algernon's unexpected visit. And the "old friends" were flatteringly willing to do Algernon the honour of eating it. They were mostly unfledged lads, such as affected very often the society of Jack Price, who was really a kind companion, and gave the boys long lectures on steadiness of purpose and energy, illustrated by warning examples from his own career, and delivered amid such agreeable accompaniments to moral reflection as hot whisky-punch and first-rate Havanas. But there were one or two older men: a newspaper editor from Dublin, who had been at college with Jack; and a grey-whiskered major of cavalry, who had served with Jack during his brief military career; and a middle-aged attaché to His Majesty's legation at the Grand Duchy of Prundenhausen, who had been a contemporary of Jack in the Foreign Office. And all these gentlemen, being warmed by wine and meat, became excessively companionable and entertaining. The Dublin editor, a fat, short, rather humorous-looking individual, sang Irish sentimental ballads with a sweet tenor voice, and, at the whisky-punch stage of the entertainment, brought tears into the eyes of the cavalry major and Jack Price. The middle-aged attaché did not cry; he considered such a manifestation beneath the dignity of the diplomatic service. And although he affected a bitter tone, and secretly considered himself to be a mute inglorious Talleyrand, much injured and unappreciated by the blundering chiefs at the Foreign Office, yet to outsiders he maintained the dignity of the service, at the cost of a good deal of trouble and starch.

Algernon did not cry either. Indeed, the combination of sentimental ballad and stout Dublin editor struck him as being pleasantly comic. But he paid the singer so easy and well-turned a compliment as put to shame the clumsy "Thanks, O'Reilly!" "By Jove, that was delightful!" "What a sweet whistle you have of your own!" and the general shout of "Bravo!" by which the others expressed their approbation. And then he sang himself—one of the French romances for which he had gained a little reputation among a certain society in town. The romance was somewhat thread-bare, and the singer's voice out of practice; still, the performance was favourably received. But Algernon soon changed his ground, and, eschewing music altogether, began to entertain his hearers with stories about the eccentric worthies of Whitford, illustrated by admirable mimicry of their peculiarities of voice, face, and phraseology, so that he soon had the table in a roar of laughter, and achieved a genuine success. Jack Price was enchanted—partly with the consciousness that it was he who had provided his friends with this diverting entertainment, and explained to every one who would listen to him: "Oh, you know, it's great! What? Great, sir! Mathews isn't a patch on him. Inimitable, what? He is the dearest, brightest, most lovable fellow! What a burning shame that a thing of this sort should be hidden under a bushel—I mean, down in what-d'ye-call-it! By George! What?"

Yes; Algernon spent a very agreeable evening, and thoroughly enjoyed himself. He certainly had a wonderful share of what his mother called "the Ancram elasticity!"

CHAPTER XVI.

Mrs. Errington was greatly astonished to hear of Algernon's sudden departure from Whitford. The news came to her through Mrs. Thimbleby, who had learned it from the baker, who had been told by the barman at the "Blue Bell" that young Mr. Errington had gone off to London by the night mail on Monday. At first Mrs. Errington was incredulous. But Mrs. Thimbleby's information was so circumstantial, that at length her lodger resolved to go to Ivy Lodge and ascertain the truth. She found Castalia in a very gloomy humour. Yes; Ancram was gone, she said. Why? Well, he said he went because Lord Seely was ill. She, for her part, made no such statement. And, beyond that, it was not possible to draw much information out of her.

Mrs. Errington, however, returned not altogether ill-pleased to her lodgings, and assumed an air of majestic melancholy. She desired Mrs. Thimbleby to prepare a cup of chocolate for her, and to bring it forthwith to the sitting-room. And when it appeared she began to sip it languidly, and to hold forth, and to enjoy herself.

"Oh, my dear good soul," she said, half closing her eyes and slowly shaking her head, "I've had a great shock—a great shock!"

"Deary me, ma'am!" cried simple Mrs. Thimbleby, with ready sympathy, looking into her lodger's round comely face. "Nothing wrong with Mr. Algernon, I hope?"

"No, thank Heaven! Not that; but perhaps the next greatest trial that could befall me, in the illness of a dear relative."

"Young Mrs.—" Mrs. Thimbleby checked herself, having been reproved for using that distinctive epithet of "young" to Algernon's wife, and substituted the form of words her lodger had taught her. "The Honourable Mrs. Errington ain't ill, ma'am, is she?"

"No, my good creature. We had a despatch last evening announcing the illness of Lord Seely. It was sent to Algy, because dear Lady Seely was so fearful of startling me. And, for the same reason, dear Algy went off without telling me a word about it."

Mrs. Thimbleby had only the haziest notion as to what kinship existed between Mrs. Errington and the nobleman in question. But she knew that her lodger was nearly connected with high folks; but she had often been troubled by doubts and misgivings, as to how far this fact might militate against her lodger's spiritual welfare, as being apt to promote worldliness and vain-glory. But Mrs.

Thimbleby was full of abounding charity, and she was always ready to attribute what appeared to her evil to her own "poor head," rather than to other people's poor heart. So she merely expressed a hope that "the poor gentleman would soon get over it."

"I trust so, Mrs. Thimbleby. His removal from the scene of life would be a terrible loss to this country. From the sovereign downwards, we should all feel it."

"Should we, ma'am?"

"Not, of course, as acutely as the family would feel it. That could not be, of course! But I trust he will recover. I wish I could have accompanied Algy to town, to help to nurse the dear patient, and take some of the care off the shoulders of my poor darling cousin, Belinda. Belinda is Lady Seely's Christian-name, my good Thimbleby. But of course that was impossible. I have not strength for it."

"No, for sure, ma'am; but them high gentle-folks like them—lords, I mean, will be sure to have nurse-tenders, and doctors, and servants, as many as they need!"

"Oh, as to that—! The king's own physician twice daily."

"I hope," said Mrs. Thimbleby, timidly, before leaving the room, "that the Lord will soften your daughter-in-law's heart to you in this trouble."

It must be understood that Mrs. Errington had of late, and especially since Castalia's outburst against Rhoda Maxfield, spoken of her daughter-in-law with a good deal of disapprobation; pitying her son for all he had to endure, and lamenting that he should have thrown himself away as he had done, when so many brilliant matches were, as it might be said, at his feet. "The dear Seelys," she would say, "considered that he was making a sacrifice. That, I happen to know. But she displayed so undisguised an attachment—and Algy—Algy is the soul of chivalry. All the Ancrams ever have been."

It had certainly taken some time for the worthy lady to discover that her son's marriage wasn't quite a satisfactory one. But when the discovery did force itself on her perceptions, she was by no means tender to Castalia. Her moral toughness of hide prevented her from being much hurt by such speeches as, "Dear me! Not happy together! Why, I thought this was such a model marriage, Mrs. Errington!" Or, "Ah! jealous and fretful, is she? Well, I always thought it wouldn't do. But of course I said nothing. You plumed yourself so much on the match, you know, at the time." She could always retreat to illogical strongholds of unreason, whence she sent forth retorts, and arguments, and statements, which were found to be unanswerable by the average intellect of Whitford.

"I wonder the woman isn't ashamed—really now!" exclaimed Miss Chubb once in the exasperation of listening to Mrs. Errington calmly superior to facts, and of being quite unable to touch her self-complacency by any recapitulation of them.

"Do you?" asked Rose McDougall tartly. "How odd! Now, as to me, nothing would surprise me more than to find Mrs. Errington ashamed of anything."

These and similar things had been freely spoken in Whitford, and although the world resented Mrs. Errington's manner of complaint, as being deficient in humility and candour—for it is provoking to find people who ought to lament in sackcloth and ashes, holding up their heads and making a merit of their deserved misfortunes—yet the world admitted that Mrs. Errington had substantial cause for complaint. The Honourable Castalia was really intolerable, and the only possible excuse for her behaviour was—what had been whispered with many nods and becks, and much mystery—that she was not quite of sound mind. And when the news began to circulate in Whitford that young Errington had gone to London suddenly, and almost secretly, the first, and most general, impression was that he had run away from his wife. To this solution the tradesmen to whom he owed money added, "And his debts!" Mrs. Errington's statement as to Lord Seely's illness was not much believed. And if he were ill, was it likely that my lord should cause Algernon Errington to be sent for? Later on in the course of the day, it began to be known that Castalia had accompanied her husband to the coach-office, so that his departure had not been clandestine so far as she was concerned, at all events. But was it not rather odd, the postmaster rushing off in this sudden manner? How did he manage to leave his business? Mr. Cooper never did such things! Not, probably, that it would make much difference whether Algernon Errington were here or not; for everybody knew pretty well that he was a mere cipher in the office, and Mr. Gibbs did everything!

As to Mr. Gibbs, he was inwardly much disquieted at his chief's unwarranted absence. He had received a note which Algernon had left behind him to be delivered on the morning after his departure. But the note was not very satisfactory:—

"MY DEAR GIBBS," it said—"I am off to town by the night mail. My wife's uncle, Lord Seely, is ill, and I must see him. I shall speak to him on your behalf, of course. The inheritance must soon fall to you, without waiting for the demise of the present holder. I shall be back on Wednesday at latest. Meanwhile, I trust implicitly to your discretion.

"Yours always,

"A. A. E."

This was oracular enough. But Mr. Obadiah Gibbs understood very well, as he read it, that by the "inheritance" which must soon fall to him, Algernon meant the place of postmaster. Still there was nothing in the note to commit Algernon in any way whatever. And his going off to London without leave and without notice, was a proceeding which shocked all the old clerk's notions of what was fitting. The thought did cross his mind, "Suppose he should never come back! Suppose he is off to America, as a short cut out of his troubles!" The thing was possible. And the possibility haunted Mr. Obadiah Gibbs persistently, though he tried to argue it away.

In the afternoon of Tuesday, Rhoda Maxfield walked into the post-office, and asked to speak with Mr. Errington. She was on foot and alone, and was looking so pretty and blooming as to arrest the attention of the dry old clerk. When he told her that Mr. Errington was away in London, and would not be back until the next day, she appeared disappointed. "Will you tell him, please, that I came, and wanted to speak to him particularly, and beg him to come to me as soon as ever he gets back to Whitford?" she said, in her soft lady's voice. Mr. Gibbs did not answer her. He stared straight over her shoulder as if Medusa's head had suddenly appeared behind her. Rhoda turned to see what had petrified Mr. Gibbs into silence, and saw Castalia Errington.

Rhoda was startled, but more from sympathy with Gibbs than from any other reason. The quick colour mounted into her cheeks and deepened their blush rose hue to damask. "Oh, Mrs. Errington," she said, and held out her hand. Castalia did not take it; did not speak; did not, after one baleful stare of anger, look at her. "Come into the private office," she said, addressing Gibbs in a dry, husky voice, and with a manner of imperious harshness. As she stood with her hand on the lock of the door leading into the inner room, she looked round over her shoulder and flung these words at Rhoda like a missile; "You have made a mistake. My husband is not here to-day, of all days. He has been remiss in not letting you know of his journey. But men are apt, I have been told, to fail in polite attention to persons of your sort."

"Mrs. Errington!" cried Rhoda, turning pale, less at the words than at the look and tone which interpreted their meaning so that it was impossible altogether to misunderstand it. "I came here to speak to Mr. Errington about something he wished to hear of. And if I may say it to you instead—"

"To ME? How dare you?" Castalia turned full on her with a livid, furious face, lit by a pair of hollow, burning eyes. Poor, artificial, small product of her social surroundings as she usually seemed, the passion in the woman transfigured her now with a tragic fire and force, before which Rhoda's innocent lily nature seemed shrivelled and discoloured, like a flower in the blast of a furnace. It was strange to himself, but Mr. Gibbs, as he looked at the two women, and was fully conscious on which side lay the right in the matter, could not help feeling an inexplicable thrill of sympathy with Castalia as she stood there breathing quickly and hard, with dilated nostrils and suffering, tearless eyes. The truth is that there was some subtle ingredient in Mr. Gibbs's composition which was more cognate with flesh and blood—even erring, passionate flesh and blood—than with the cool fluid that circulates in the petals of a lily. David Powell would have said that it was a manifest stirring of the Old Adam which caused the regenerate Obadiah Gibbs—a professing Christian, a confirmed and tried pillar of Methodism, a man whose precious experiences had been poured forth for the edification of many a band meeting—to be conscious for the first time of some fellow-feeling with Castalia, at the very moment when she was conducting herself in a manner to shock every sentiment of what was just and fitting. But whether it were due to original sin, or to whatever other cause, the fact remained that Obadiah Gibbs for the first time in his life now felt disposed to spare and screen the postmaster's wife.

"I'll give the message when Mr. Errington comes back," said he to Rhoda, almost hustling her out of the office as he spoke. "The poor thing is not very well," he added, in a lower voice. "She has been a good deal cut up, one way and another. You mustn't think anything of her manner, nor bear malice, Miss Maxfield. Good morning."

When Rhoda was gone—feeling almost dizzy with surprise and fright—Gibbs followed Mrs. Errington into the inner office. He found her openly examining the contents of the table-drawer, having tossed all the papers she had found in it pell-mell on to the table. Gibbs entered and closed the door carefully. "Mrs. Errington," he began, intending to remonstrate with her—or, perhaps, utter something stronger than a remonstrance—on her manner of conducting herself in the office, when she interrupted him at once, looking up from the heap of papers. "What message did that creature give you for my husband?" she asked abruptly.

"Now, Mrs. Errington, you really must not go on in this way! I'm responsible to Mr. Errington, you know, for things being right here."

"Did you hear me? What message did that creature give you?"

"Oh now, really, Mrs. Errington, I think you ought not to speak of Rhoda Maxfield in that way. She is a very good girl, and you hurt her terribly by your manner."

Castalia smiled bitterly. "Did I?" she said. "Of course you're in league with her. Why does this good young woman come here in secret to see my husband? What can she want to say to him that cannot be said openly?"

"I cannot hear such things, ma'am; I cannot, indeed. If you would give yourself an instant for reflection, you would remember that Miss Maxfield offered to tell her message to you yourself."

"Offered to tell me! Do you really suppose I am duped by such low tricks? I heard her say, 'Send him to me directly he comes back'—heard it with my own ears. But of course you won't tell me the truth."

"I am obliged to say, Mrs. Errington, that you really must leave the office. I am very sorry, but I am responsible in Mr. Errington's absence, and I cannot allow you to turn everything topsy-turvy here in this way. There has been trouble enough by your coming here already."

"Trouble enough! Who says so? Who is troubled?"

"Mr. Errington is troubled, and I am troubled, and—in short, it's altogether out of rule."

"Then he confesses, does he, that he is afraid of my coming here to make discoveries about him? Why should he be troubled if he had nothing to conceal?"

Castalia spoke with trembling eagerness and excitement. She had thrown all semblance of dignity or reserve to the winds. She would have spoken as she was speaking at that moment in Whitford market-place. Gibbs looked at her, and a doubt came into his mind as to whether his suspicions, and other people's suspicions, about her were quite so well-founded as he had thought. She was terribly violent, jealous, insolent, unconverted, full of the leaven of unrighteousness—but was she a practised hypocrite, a woman experienced in dishonesty? For the life of him, Obadiah Gibbs could not feel so sure of this as he had felt, now that he looked into her poor, haggard face, and met her eyes, and heard her utterly incautious and vehement speeches.

"As to me not telling you the truth, Mrs. Errington," he said, "I suppose you know the truth as to why your visits here bring trouble on everybody?"

"Tell it me, you!"

"Well, I—oh you must be aware of it, I suppose. And if I was to tell you, you would only be more angry and offended with me than ever, though what I have done to excite your displeasure I don't know."

"Tell me this truth that I know so well! Do you think I should seriously care for anything you could say, except as it concerned my husband?"

"Mrs. Errington, I don't know whether you are feigning or not. But, anyway, I think it my duty to answer you with Christian sincerity. It is borne in upon me that I ought to do so."

"Go on, go on, go on!" cried Castalia, drumming with restless fingers on the table and looking up at the clerk with eyes that blazed with excitement and impatience.

"You are aware that there have been unpleasant circumstances at the post-office—letters lost—money-letters lost. Well, your name has been mentioned in connection with those losses. It is known in Whitford that you come haunting the office at all hours when your husband is away. A little while ago you paid a bill with some notes that were endorsed in a peculiar way. People ask where you got those notes. I thought it my duty to mention the subject to Mr. Errington the other day. He was greatly distressed, of course. He said he should interrogate you about the notes. My advice to you is—in all sincerity and charity, as the Lord sees me—to tell your husband the truth, whatever it is."

He ended his speech with a tremor of compassion in his voice, and with a sudden breakdown of his rhetorical manner, for Castalia's face changed so piteously, so terribly, as he spoke, that the man's heart was deeply touched by it. She grew ashy pale. The quick fingers that had been tapping impatiently on the table seemed turned to lead. They lay there heavy and motionless. Her mouth was half open, and her eyes stared straight before her at the blank wall of the yard, as though they saw a spectre.

"Lord have mercy on us, she is guilty!" thought Obadiah Gibbs. And at that moment if he could have hidden her crime from the eyes of all men, I believe he would have done it at the cost of a lie.

"Of course you're not bound to say anything to me, you know, Mrs. Errington," he went on, after a short pause. And as he spoke he bent nearer to her, to rouse her, for she seemed neither to hear nor to see him. "You'd better go home now at once, you don't seem very strong."

Still she did not move.

"Look here, Mrs. Errington, I—you may rely upon my not breaking a word—not one syllable to anybody else, if you—if you will try to make things straight again as far as in your power lies. Go home now, pray do!"

Still she did not move.

"You don't look much able to walk, I fear. Shall I send the boy for a fly? Let me send for a fly?"

He softly touched her shoulder as he spoke, and she immediately turned her head and answered with a composure that startled him, "Yes; get me a fly." Then she sat quite still again, staring at the wall as before.

Gibbs went out into the outer office and sent the boy for a vehicle. There he remained, pen in hand, behind his desk until the jingle of the fly was heard at the door. He went back himself to the private office to call Castalia, and found her sitting in exactly the same place and attitude. She rose mechanically to her feet when he told her the fly was ready, but as she began to walk towards the door she staggered and caught at Gibbs's arm. He supported her with a sort of quiet gravity;—much as if he had been her old servant, and she a cripple whose infirmity was a matter of course,—which showed much delicacy of feeling, and as they neared the door he said in her ear, "Take my advice, ma'am, and tell your husband the truth." She turned her eyes on him with a singular look, but said nothing. "Tell him the truth! and—and look upward. Lift your heart in prayer. There is a fountain of grace and love ready for all who seek it!"

"Not for me," she answered in a very low but distinct voice.

"Oh, my poor soul, don't say so! Don't think so!"

By this time she was in the carriage, having been almost lifted into it by Gibbs. She was perfectly quiet and tearless, and as the vehicle drove away, and Gibbs stood watching it disappear, he said to himself that her face was as the face of a corpse.

CHAPTER XVII.

Castalia was driven home, and walked up the path of the tiny garden in front of Ivy Lodge with a step much like her ordinary one. She went into the drawing-room and looked about her curiously, as if she were a stranger seeing the place for the first time. Then she sat down for a minute, still in her bonnet and shawl. But she got up again quickly from the sofa, holding her hand to her throat as if she were choking, and went out to the garden behind the house, and from thence to the meadows near the river. There was at the bottom of the garden, and outside of it, a miserable, dilapidated wooden shed, euphoniously called a summer-house. There was a worm-eaten wooden bench in it looking towards the Whit, and commanding a view of the wide meadows on the other side of it, of a turn in the river, now lead-coloured beneath a dreary sky, and of the distant spire of Duckwell Church rising beyond the hazy woods of Pudcombe. No one ever entered this summer-house. It was rotting to pieces with damp and decay, and was inhabited by a colony of insects and a toad that squatted in one corner. In this wretched place Castalia sat down, being indeed unable to walk farther, but feeling a sensation of suffocation at the mere thought of returning to the house. She fancied she could not breathe there. A steaming mist was rising from the river and the damp meadows beyond it. The grey clouds seemed to touch the grey horizon. It was cold, and the last brown leaf or two, hanging, as it seemed, by a thread on the boughs of a tree just within sight from the summer-house, twirled, and shook, and shuddered in the slight gusts of wind that arose now and again. There was not a sound to be heard except the mournful lowing of some cattle in a distant field, until all at once a movement of the air brought from Whitford the sound of the old chimes muffled by the heavy atmosphere. There sat Castalia and stared at the river, and the mist, and the brown withered leaves, much as she had stared at the blank yard wall in the office.

"My heart is sore pained within me, and the terrors of death are fallen upon me. Fearfulness and trembling are come upon me, and horror hath overwhelmed me!"

She heard a voice saying these words distinctly. She did not start. She scarcely felt surprise. The direful lamentation was in harmony with all she saw, and heard, and felt.

Again the voice spoke: "Our fathers trusted in thee: they trusted, and thou didst deliver them. They cried unto thee and were delivered; they trusted in thee and were not confounded. But I am a worm, and no man; a reproach of men, and despised of the people!"

Castalia heard, scarcely listening. The words flowed by her like a tune that brings tears to the eyes by mere sympathy with its sad sound.

Presently a man passed before her, walking with an unequal pace—now quick, now slow, now stopping outright. He had his hands clasped at the back of his neck; his head was bent down, and he was talking aloud to himself.

"Aye, there have been such. The lot has fallen upon me. I know it with a sure knowledge. It is borne in upon me with a certainty that pierces through bone and marrow. I am of the number of those that go down to the pit. Why, O Lord—Nay! though he slay me, yet will I trust in Him. For he is not a man, as I am, that I should answer him, and we should come together in judgment."

He stopped in his walk; stood still for a second or two, and then turned to pace back again. In so doing he saw Castalia. She also looked full at him, and recognised the Methodist preacher. David Powell went up to her without hesitation. He remembered her at once; and he remembered, too, in a confused way, something of what Mrs. Thimbleby had been recently telling him about dissensions between this woman and her husband; of unhappiness and quarrels; and—what was that the widow had said of young Mrs. Errington being jealous of Rhoda? Ah, yes! He had it all now.

The time had been when David Powell would have had to wrestle hard with indignation against anyone who should have spoken evil of Rhoda. He would have felt a hot, human flush of anger; and would have combated it as a stirring of the unregenerate man within him. But all such feelings were over with him. No ray from the outside world appeared able to pierce the gloom which had gathered thicker and thicker in his own mind, unless it touched his sense of sympathy with suffering. He was still sensitive to that, as certain chemicals are to the light.

He went close up to Castalia, and said, without any preliminary or usual greeting, "You are in affliction. Have you called upon the Lord? Have you cast your burthen upon him? He is a good shepherd. He will carry the weary and footsore of his flock lest they faint by the way and perish utterly."

It was noticeable when he spoke that his voice, which had been of such full sweetness, was now hoarse, and even harsh here and there, like a fine instrument that has been jarred. This did not seem to be altogether due to physical causes; for there still came out of his mouth every now and then a tone that was exquisitely musical. But the discord seemed to be in the spirit that moved the voice, and could not guide it with complete freedom and mastery.

Castalia shook her head impatiently, and turned her eyes away from him. But she did not do so with any of her old hauteur and intimation of the vast distance which separated her from her humbler fellow-creatures. Pain of mind had familiarised her with the conception that she held her humanity in common with a very heterogeneous multitude. Had Powell been a sleek, smug personage like Brother Jackson, veiling profound self-complacency under the technical announcement of himself as a miserable sinner, she might have turned from him in disgust. As it was, she felt merely the unwillingness to be disturbed, of a creature in whom the numbness of apathy has succeeded to acute anguish. She wanted to be rid of him. He looked at her with the yearning pity which was so fundamental a part of his nature. "Pray!" he said, clasping his hands together. "Go to your Father, which is in Heaven, and He shall give you rest. Oh, God loves you—he loves you!"

"No one loves me," returned Castalia, with white rigid lips. Then she got up from the bench, and went back into her own garden and into the house, with the air of a person walking in sleep.

Powell looked after her sadly. "If she would but pray!" he murmured. "I would pray for her. I would wrestle with the Lord on her behalf. But—of late I have feared more and more that my prayers are not acceptable; that my voice is an abomination to the Lord."

He resumed his walk along the river bank, speaking aloud, and gesticulating to himself as he went.

Meanwhile, Castalia wandered about her own house "like a ghost," as the servants said. She went from the little dining-room to the drawing-room, and then she painfully mounted the steep staircase to her bed-room, opened the door of her husband's little dressing-closet, shut it again, and went downstairs once more. She could not sit still; she could not read; she could not even think. She could only suffer, and move about restlessly, as if with a dim instinctive idea of escaping from her suffering. Presently she began to open the drawers of a little toy cabinet in the drawing-room, and examine their contents, as if she had never seen them before. From that she went to a window-seat, made hollow, and with a cushioned lid, so that it served as a seat and a box, and began to rummage among its contents. These consisted chiefly of valueless scraps, odds and ends, put there to be hidden and out of the way. Among them were some of poor Mrs. Errington's wedding-presents to her son and daughter-in-law. Castalia's maid, Slater, had unceremoniously consigned these to oblivion, together with a few other old-fashioned articles, under the generic name of "rubbish." There was a pair of hand-screens elaborately embroidered in silk, very faded and out of date. Mrs.

Errington declared them to be the work of her grand-aunt, the beautiful Miss Jacintha Ancram, who made such a great match, and became a Marchioness. There was an ancient carved ivory fan, yellow with age, brought by a cadet of the house of Ancram from India, as a present to some forgotten sweetheart. There was a little cardboard box, covered with fragments of raised rice-paper, arranged in a pattern. This was the work of Mrs. Errington's own hands in her school-girl days, and was of the kind called then, if I mistake not, "filagree work." Castalia took these and other things out of the window-seat, and examined them and put them back, one by one, moving exactly like an automaton figure that had been wound up to perform those motions. When she came to the filagree box, she opened that too. There was a Tonquin bean in it, filling the box with its faint sweet odour. There was a pair of gold buckles, that seemed to be attenuated with age; and a garnet-brooch, with one or two stones missing. And then at the bottom of the box was something flat, wrapped in silver paper. She unwrapped it and looked at it.

It was a water-colour drawing done by Algernon immediately on his return from Llanryddan, in the first flush of his love-making, and represented himself and Rhoda standing side by side in front of the little cottage where they had lodged there. Algernon had given himself pinker cheeks, bluer eyes, and more amber-coloured hair than nature had endowed him with. Rhoda was equally over-tinted. There was no merit in the drawing, which was stiff and school-boyish, but the very exaggerations of form and colour emphasised the likeness in a way not to be mistaken.

Castalia trembled from head to foot as she looked on the two rosy simpering faces. A curious ripple or tremor ran over her body, such as may be observed in persons recovering consciousness after a swoon. She tore the drawing into small fragments. Her teeth were set. Her eyes glared. She looked like a murderess. She trod the scattered bits into the carpet with her heel. Then, as if with an afterthought, she swept them contemptuously into the bright steel shovel, and threw them into the fire, and stood and watched them blaze and smoulder. After that she wrapped her shawl more tightly round her—she had forgotten to remove either it or her bonnet on coming in—and went out at the front door, and walked straight into Whitford, and to Jonathan Maxfield's house.

She asked for "the master." The old man was at home, in the little parlour, and Sally showed Mrs. Errington into the room almost without the ceremony of tapping with her knuckles at the door, and then made off to the kitchen to tell Mrs. Grimshaw. The lady's face had scared her.

Old Max was sitting near the dull fire which burned in the grate. The big Bible, his constant companion now, lay open on the table. But he had not been devoting his attention to that solely. He had had a large old-fashioned wooden desk brought down from his own room, and had been fingering the papers in it, reading some, and merely glancing at the outside folds of others. He now looked up at Castalia without recognising her.

"What is your business with me?" he asked, peering at her in perplexity.

"I've come to speak to you—" began Castalia; and at the first sound of her voice, Maxfield recognised her. He remembered the only visit she had paid him previously, when she came to beg that Rhoda might be allowed to visit her. She had taken a great fancy to his pretty Rhoda, this skinny, yellow-faced, fine lady. Ha! Well, she might show what civilities she pleased to Rhoda. No objection to that. Indeed, it was a proceeding to be encouraged, seeing that it probably caused a good deal of discomfort and embarrassment to Algernon! So he gave a little nod, meant to be courteous, and said, "Oh, I didn't just know you at first. Won't you be seated?"

Castalia refused by a gesture, and stood still opposite to him with one hand on the table, apparently in some embarrassment how to begin. Then it flashed on old Max that this "Honourable Missis," as he called her, had probably come to thank him, and found it not altogether easy to do so. But what could Castalia have to thank him for? This; Rhoda had so implored her father to relieve Algernon from his anxiety about the bills, that at length the old man had said with a chuckle, "Tell you what, Rhoda, I'll hand 'em over to Mr. Diamond, and maybe he will give them to you as a wedding present if he gets the school. And then you can do what you like with 'em. My gentleman won't be above taking a present from you or your husband. I've seen what meanness she can do and what dirt he can swallow, and not even make a wry face over it! Aye, dirt as would turn many a poor labouring man's stomach."

Rhoda, upon this, had consulted Matthew Diamond, and had not found it difficult to make him agree with her wish to give up the bills to Algernon. Indeed, although he had almost come to old Max's opinion of his former pupil, he would not for the world have behaved so as to make Rhoda suppose that he bore him a grudge. Rhoda's errand to the post-office that afternoon had been to bring Algernon this comforting news. She had taken care not to tell her father of Mrs. Algernon's behaviour, but had come home and cried a little quietly in her own room, and kept her tears and the cause of them to herself. Therefore it was that Jonathan Maxfield supposed the fine lady to have come to thank him for his magnanimity on behalf of her absent husband, and he was already preparing to give her "a dose," as he phrased it, and to spare her no item of Rhoda's prosperity, and wealth, and good prospects in the world.

Castalia remained leaning with one hand on the table, and did not continue her speech during the second or two in which these thoughts and intentions were passing through old Maxfield's brain. But it was by no means that she hesitated from embarrassment or lack of words: rather the words crowded to her lips too quickly and fiercely for utterance.

"I've come to speak to you about your daughter," she said at length.

"Aye, aye. Miss Maxfield's a bit of a friend o' yours. Miss Maxfield's allus been very kind to all the fam'ly ever since we've known 'em. But you'd best be seated."

"They say you are an honest, decent man," Castalia went on, neither seating herself nor noticing the invitation to do so. "It may be so. I am willing to believe it. But, if so, you are grossly deceived, cheated, and played upon by that vile girl."

Maxfield brought his two clenched fists heavily down on the table, and half raised himself in his chair. "Stop!" said he. "Who are you talking of?"

"You may believe me. I tell you I have watched—I have seen. She was in love with my husband years ago. She used every art to catch him. And now—now that he is married, she receives secret visits from him. Do you know that he came at night—ten o'clock at night—to your house when you were away? She goes to the post-office slily to see him. I caught her there this morning leaving a private message for him with the clerk! Is that decent? Is it what you wish? Do you sanction it? She writes to him. She has turned his heart against me. He schemes to keep me out of the office. I know why now. Oh yes; I am not the blind dupe they think for. She has made him more cruel, more wicked to me than I could have imagined any man could be. My heart is broken. But as true as there is a God in Heaven I'll have amends made to me. She shall beg my pardon on her knees. And you had better look to it, if you don't want her character to be torn to pieces by every foul tongue in this town. I have borne enough. Keep her at home. Keep her from decoying other women's husbands, I warn you—"

Maxfield, who had been struggling to reach the bell, pulled it so violently that the wire was broken. At the peal Betty Grimshaw came running in, terrified. "Mercy, brother-in-law!" she cried. "What is it?"

"Get the police," gasped old Max, as if he were choking. "Send some one for a policeman, to turn that mad quean out of my house. She's not fit for a decent house. She's—she's—Oh, but you shall repent this! I'll sell you up, every stick of trumpery in the place. You audacious Jezebel! Turn her out of doors, I say! Do you hear me?"

Betty and the servant stood white and quivering, looking from the old man unable to rise from his chair without help, and the lady who stood opposite to him, glaring with a Medusa face. Neither of the two frightened women stirred hand or foot to fulfil the master's behest. But Castalia relieved them from any perplexity on that score, at least, by voluntarily turning to leave the room. In the doorway she met Rhoda, who had run downstairs in alarm at the violent pealing of the bell. Castalia drew herself suddenly aside, as though something unspeakably loathsome stood in her path, held her dress away from any passing contact with the amazed girl, and rushed out of the house.

CHAPTER XVIII.

Algernon's state of mind during his return journey to Whitford was very much pleasanter than it had been on his way up to town. To be sure, he had committed himself distinctly to a very grave statement. That was always disagreeable. But then he had made an immense impression on Lord Seely by his statement. He had crushed and overwhelmed that "pompous little ass." He had humiliated that "absurd little upstart." And—best of all; for these others were mere dilettante pleasures, which no man of intelligence would indulge in at the cost of his solid interests—he had terrified him so completely with the spectre of a public scandal and disgrace, that my lord was ready to do anything to help him and Castalia out of England. Of that there could be no doubt.

It must be owned that Algernon had so far justified the quick suspicions of his Whitford creditors and acquaintances as to have conceived for a moment the idea of never more returning to that uninteresting town. It was extremely exhilarating to be in the position of a bachelor at large; to find himself free, for a time, of the dead weight of debt, which seemed to make breathing difficult in Whitford; for, although by plodding characters the relief might not have been felt until the debts were paid, Algernon Errington's spirit was of a sort that rose buoyant as ever, directly the external pressure was removed. It was delightful to be reinstated in the enjoyment of his reputation as a charming fellow—much fallen into oblivion at Whitford. And perhaps it was pleasantest of all to feel strengthened in the assurance that he still was a charming fellow, with capacities for winning admiration and making a brilliant figure, quite uninjured (although they had been temporarily eclipsed) by all the cloud of troubles which had gathered around him.

So he had, for a moment, thought of fairly running away from wife, and duns, and dangers of official severities. But it was but a brief unsubstantial vision that flashed for an instant and was gone. Algernon was too clear-sighted not to perceive that the course was inconvenient—nay, to one of his temperament, impracticable. People who started off to live on their wits in a foreign country ought to be armed with a coarser indifference to material comforts than he was gifted with. Alternations of ortolans and champagne, with bread and onions, would be—even supposing one could be sure of the ortolans, which Algernon knew he could not—entirely repugnant to his temperament. He had no such strain of adventurousness as would have given a pleasant glow of excitement to the endurance of privation under any circumstances whatever. Professed Bohemians might talk as they pleased about kicking over traces, and getting rid of trammels, and so forth; but, for his part, he had never felt his spirit in the least oppressed by velvet hangings, gilded furniture, or French cookery! Whereas to be obliged to wear shabby gloves would have been a kind of "trammel" he would strongly have objected to. In a word, he desired to be luxuriously comfortable always. And he consistently (albeit, perhaps, mistakenly, for the cleverest of us are liable to error) endeavoured to be so.

Therefore he did not ship himself aboard an emigrant vessel for the United States; nor did he even cross the Channel to Calais; but found himself in a corner of the mail-coach on the night after Jack Price's supper party, bowling along, not altogether unpleasantly, towards Whitford. He had not seen Lord Seely again. He had inquired for him at his house, and had been told that his lordship was worse; was confined to bed entirely; and that Dr. Nokes had called in two other physicians in consultation. "Deuce of a job if he dies before I get a berth!" thought Algernon. But before he had gone many yards down the street, he was in a great measure reassured as to that danger, by seeing Lady Seely in her big yellow coach, with Fido on the seat beside her, and her favourite nephew lounging on the cushions opposite. The nephew had been apparently entertaining Lady Seely by some amusing story, for she was laughing (rather to the ear than the eye, as was her custom; for my lady made a great noise, sending out "Ha-ha-ha's!" with a kind of defiant distinctness, whilst all the while eyes and mouth plainly professed themselves disdainful of too cordial a hilarity, and ready to stop short in a second), and stroking Fido very unconcernedly with one fat tightly-gloved hand. Now although Algernon did not give my lady credit for much depth of sentiment, he felt sure that she would, for various reasons, have been greatly disquieted had any danger threatened her husband's life, and would certainly not have left his side to drive in the Park with young Reginald. So he drew the inference that my lord was not so desperately ill as he had been told, and that the servants had had orders to give him that account in order to keep him away—which was pretty nearly the fact.

"The old woman would be in a fury with me when my lord told her he had promised me that post without consulting her," thought Algernon; "and would tell any lie to keep me out of the house. But we shall beat her this time." As he so thought he pulled off his hat and made so distinguished and condescending a bow to my lady, that her nephew, who was near-sighted and did not recognise Errington, pulled off his own hat in a hurry, very awkwardly, and acknowledged the salute with some confused idea that the graceful gentleman was a foreigner of distinction; whilst my lady, turning purple, shook her head at him in anger at the whole incident. All which Algernon saw, understood, and was immensely diverted by.

In summing up the results of his journey to town, he was satisfied. Things were certainly not so pleasant as they might be. But were they not better, on the whole, than when he had left Whitford? He decidedly thought they were; which did not, of course, diminish his sense of being a victim to circumstances and the Seely family. Anyway he had broken with Whitford. My lord must get him out of that baraque! The very thought of leaving the place raised his spirits. And, as he had the coach to himself during nearly all the journey, he was able to stretch his legs and make himself comfortable; and he awoke from a sound and refreshing sleep as the mail-coach rattled into the High Street and rumbled under the archway of the "Blue Bell."

The hour was early, and the morning was raw, and Algernon resolved to refresh himself with a hot bath and breakfast before proceeding to Ivy Lodge. "No use disturbing Mrs. Errington so early," he said to the landlord, who appeared just as Algernon was sipping his tea before a blazing fire. "Very good devilled kidneys, Mr. Rumbold," he added condescendingly. Mr. Rumbold rubbed his hands and stood looking half-sulkily, half-deferentially at his guest. His wife had said to him, "Don't you go chatting with that young Errington, Rumbold; not if you want to get your money. I know what he is, and I know what you are, Rumbold; and he'll talk you over in no time."

But Mr. Rumbold had allowed his own valour to override his wife's discretion, and had declared that he would make the young man understand before he left the "Blue Bell" that it was absolutely necessary to settle his account there without delay. And the result justified Mrs. Rumbold's apprehension; for Algernon Errington drove away from the inn without having paid even for the breakfast he had eaten there that morning, and having added the vehicle which carried him home to the long list beginning "Flys: A. Errington, Esq.," in which he figured as debtor to the landlord of the "Blue Bell." He had flourished Lord Seely in Mr. Rumbold's face with excellent effect, and was feeling quite cheerful when he alighted at the gate of Ivy Lodge.

It was still early according to Castalia's reckoning—little more than ten o'clock. So he was not surprised at not finding her in the drawing-room or the dining-room. Lydia, of whom he inquired at length as to where her mistress was, having first bade her light a fire for him to have a cigar by, before going to the office—Lydia said with a queer, half-scared, half-saucy look, "Laws, sir, missus has been out this hour and a half."

"Out!"

"Yes, sir. She said as how she couldn't rest in her bed, nor yet in the house, sir. Polly made her take a cup of tea, and then she went off to Whit Meadow."

"To Whit Meadow! In this damp raw weather at nine o'clock in the morning!"

"Please, sir, me and Polly thought it wasn't safe for missus, and her so delicate. But she would go."

Algernon shrugged his shoulders and said no more. Before the girl left the room, she said, "Oh, and please, sir, here's some letters as came for you," pointing to a little heap of papers on Castalia's desk.

Left alone, Algernon drew his chair up to the fire and lit a cigar. He did not hasten himself to examine the letters. Bills, of course! What else could they be? He began to smoke and ruminate. He would have liked to see Castalia before going to the office. He would have liked to make his own representation to her of the story he had told Lord Seely. She must be got to corroborate it unknowingly if possible. He reflected with some bitterness that she had lately shown so much power of opposing him, that it might be she would insist on taking a course of conduct which would upset all the combination he—with the help of chance circumstances—had so neatly pieced together. And then he reflected further, knitting his brows a little, that at any cost she must be prevented from spoiling his plans; and that her conduct lately had been so strange that it wouldn't be very difficult to convince the world of her insanity. "'Gad, I'm almost convinced of it myself," said Algernon, half aloud. But it was not true.

The fire was warm, the room was quiet, the cigar was good, the chair was easy. Algernon felt tempted to sit still and put off the moment when he must re-enter the Whitford Post-office. He shuddered as he thought of the place with a kind of physical repulsion. Nevertheless, it must be faced once or twice more. Not much more often, he hoped. He rose up, put on a great-coat, and said to himself lazily as he ran his fingers through his hair in front of the looking-glass, "Where the devil can Castalia have gone mooning to?" Then he turned to leave the room. As he turned his eyes fell on the little heap of letters. He took them up and turned them over with a grimace.

"H'm! Ravell—respectful compliments. Ah! no; your mouth ought to have been stopped, I think! But that's the way. More they get, more they want. Never pay an instalment. Fatal precedent! What's this—a lawyer's letter! Gladwish. Oh! Very well, Mr. Gladwish. Nous verrons. Chemist! What on earth—? Oh, rose-water! Better than his boluses, I daresay, but not very good, and quite humorously dear. Extortionate rascal! And who are you, my illiterate-looking friend?"

He took a square blue envelope between his finger and thumb, and examined the cramped handwriting on it, running in a slanting line from one corner to the other. It was addressed to "Mr. Algernon Errington." "Some very angry creditor, who won't even indulge me with the customary 'Esquire,'" thought Algernon with a contemptuous smile and some genuine amusement. Then he opened it. It was from Jonathan Maxfield!

CHAPTER XIX.

In about a quarter of an hour after reading that letter, Algernon called to the servants to know if their mistress had come back. He did not ring as usual, but went to the door of the kitchen and spoke to both the women, saying that he was uneasy at Mrs. Errington's absence, and did not like to go to the office without seeing her. He said two or three times, how strange it was that his wife should have wandered out in that way; and plainly showed considerable anxiety about her. Both the women remarked how pale and upset their master looked. "Oh, it's enough to wear out anybody the way she goes on," said Lydia. "Poor young man! A nice way to welcome him home!"

"Ah," returned Polly, the cook, shaking her head, "I'm afraid there's going to be awful trouble with missus, poor thing. I believe she's half out of her mind with jealousy. Just think how she's been going on about Miss Maxfield. Why 'tis all over the place. And they say old Max is going to law against her, or something. But I can't but pity her, poor thing."

"Oh! they say worse of her than being out of her mind with jealousy," returned Lydia. "Don't you know what Mrs. Ravell's housemaid told her young man at the grocer's?" Et cetera, et cetera.

The discussion was checked in full career by their master returning to say that he should not go to the office until he had seen Mrs. Errington, and that he was then going to Whit Meadow to look for her. He went out past the kitchen and through the garden at the back of the house.

He looked about him when he got to the garden gate. Nothing to be seen but damp green meadow, leaden sky, and leaden river. Where was Castalia? A thought shot into his mind, swift and keen as an arrow—had she thrown herself into the Whit? And, if she had, what a load of his cares would be drowned with her! He walked a few paces towards the town, then turned and looked in the opposite direction. For as far as he could see, there was not a human being on the meadow-path. His eyes were very good and he used them eagerly, scanning all the space of Whit Meadow within their range of vision. At length he caught sight of something moving among a clump of low bushes—blackberry bushes and dog-roses, a tangle of leafless spikes now, although in the summer they would be fresh and fragrant, and the holiday haunt of little merry children—which grew on a sloping part of the bank between him and the Whit. He walked straight towards it, and as he drew nearer, became satisfied that the moving figure was that of his wife. He recognised a dark tartan shawl which she wore. It was not bright enough to be visible at a long distance; but as he advanced he became sure that he knew it. In a few minutes the husband and wife stood face to face.

"This is a nice reception to give me," said Algernon, in a hard, cold voice, after they had looked at each other for a second, and Castalia had remained silent and still. In truth, she was physically unable to speak to him in that first moment of meeting. Her heart throbbed so that every beat of it seemed like an angry blow threatening her life.

"Why do you wander out alone in this way? Why do you conduct yourself like a mad woman? Though, indeed, perhaps you are not so wrong there; madness might excuse your conduct. Nothing else can."

"I couldn't stay in that house. I should have died there. Everything in every room reminded me of you."

She answered so faintly that he had to strain his ear to hear her, and her colourless lips trembled as the lips tremble of a person trying to keep back tears. But her eyes were quite dry.

Algernon was pale, with the peculiar ghastly pallor of a fresh ruddy complexion. His blue eyes had a glitter in them like ice, not fire; and there was a set, sarcastic, bitter smile on his mouth.

"Look here, Castalia; we had better understand one another at once. I shall begin by telling you what I have resolved upon, and what I have done, and you will then have to obey me implicitly. There must be no sort of discussion or hesitation. Come back to the house with me at once."

She shook her head quickly. "No! no! Tell me here—out here by ourselves, where no one can hear us. I cannot bear to go into that house yet."

"Pshaw! What intolerable fooling! Well, here be it. I have no time to waste. I have seen your uncle. Don't interrupt me! He has promised to get us out of this cursed place, and to find a post for me abroad as consul. I had to exercise a good deal of persistence and ability to bring him to that point, but to that point I have brought him. We must keep him to it, and be active. My lady will move heaven and earth—or t'other place and earth, which is more in her line—to thwart us. Now, when it is necessary to keep things here as smooth as possible, to arouse no suspicion that we may be off at a moment's notice, to hold out hopes of everything being settled by Lord Seely's help, what do I find? I find that you have gone to a man who is a creditor of mine, who is not over fond of me to begin with, and have grossly and outrageously insulted him and his daughter! Just as if you had ingeniously cast about for the most effectual means of doing me a mischief. I found this letter on the table. He threatens to ruin me, and he can do it. If my name is posted, my bills protested, and a public hullabaloo made about them and other matters, your uncle's influence will hardly suffice to get me the berth I want in the face of the opposition newspapers' bellowing on the subject. Your uncle is but small beer in London at best. But that much he might have managed, if you hadn't behaved in this maniacal way."

"And how have you behaved? Oh, Ancram, Ancram, I would not have believed—I could not—" She burst into tears, and sank down on the damp grass, covering her face with her hands, and shaking with sobs.

"Listen! Castalia! Do you hear me?" said her husband, shaking her lightly by the arm.

She did not answer, but continued to cry convulsively, rocking herself to and fro.

Algernon stood looking down upon her with folded arms. "Upon my soul!" he said, after a minute, and with a contemptuous little nod of the head, which expressed an unbounded sense of the hopeless imbecility of the woman at his feet, and of his own long-suffering tolerance towards her, "Upon my life and soul, Castalia, I have never even heard of anyone so outrageously unreasonable as you are. Your jealousy—we may as well speak plainly—your jealousy has passed the bounds of sanity. But, as I told you, I am not going to argue with you. I am going to give directions for your guidance, since it is quite clear you are unable to guide yourself. In the first place—for God's sake stop that noise!" he cried, a sudden fierce irritation piercing through his self-restraint. "In the first place, you must make a full, free, and humble apology to Rhoda Maxfield!"

Castalia started to her feet and confronted him. "Never!" she said. "I will never do it!"

"I told you I was not going to argue with you. I am giving you your orders. A full, free, and humble—very humble—apology to Rhoda Maxfield is our one chance of softening her father. And if you have any sense or conscience left, you must know that Rhoda richly deserves every apology you can make her."

"You think so, do you?"

"Yes; I think so. She is a thoroughly good and charming girl. The only crime she has ever committed against you is being young and pretty. And if you quarrel with every woman who is so, you will find the battle a rather unequal one." He could not resist the sneer. He detested Castalia at that moment. Her whole nature, her violence, her passionate jealousy, her no less passionate love, her piteous grief, her demands on some sentiment in himself, which he knew to be non-existent; every turn of her body, every tone of her voice, were at that moment intensely repulsive to him.

The poor thing was stung into such pain by his taunt that she scarcely knew what she said or what she did.

"Oh, I know," she cried, "that you care more for her than for me! A pink-and-white face, that's all you value! More than wife, or—or—anything in the world. More than the honour of a gentleman. She's a devil; a sly, sleek little devil! She has got your love away from me. She has made you tell lies, and be cruel to me. But I'll expose her to all the world."

"What, in the name of all that's incomprehensible, has put this craze into your head against Rhoda Maxfield? It's the wildest thing!"

"Oh, Ancram! you can't deceive me any longer. I know—I have seen. She came on the sly to see you at the office. You used to go to her when you told me you had to be busy at the office. I watched you, I followed you all down Whitford High Street one night, and found out that you were cheating me."

"Ha! And you also opened my desk at the office, and took out letters and papers! Do you know what people are called who do such things?" said Algernon, now in a white heat of anger.

She drew back and looked at him. "Yes," she said, "I know."

"Have you no shame, then? No common sense? You attack a young lady—yes, a lady! A far better lady than you are!—of whom you take it into your head to be jealous, merely because she is pretty and admired by everybody. By me amongst the everybodies. Why not? I didn't lose my eyesight when I married you. You talk about my not loving you—! Do you think you go the way to make me do anything but detest the sight of you? You disgrace me in the town. You disgrace me before my clerk in the office. You and your relations persecuted me into marrying you, and now you haven't even the decency to behave like a rational being, but make yourself a laughing-stock, and me a butt for contemptuous pity in having tied myself to such a woman. One would have thought you would try to make some amends for the troubles I have been plunged into by my marriage."

She put her hands up one to each side of her head, and held them there tightly pressed. "Ancram," she said, "do you detest the sight of me?"

"You've tried your best to make me."

"Have you no spark of kindness or affection for me in your heart—not one?"

"Come, Castalia, let us have done with this! I thoroughly dislike and object to 'scenes' of any kind. You have a taste for them, unfortunately. What you have to do now is to do as I bid you, and try to make your peace by begging Rhoda's pardon, and so trying to undo a little of the mischief your insane temper has caused."

"Ancram, say one kind word to me!"

"Good God, Castalia! How can you be so exasperatingly childish?"

"One word! Say you love me a little still! Say you did love me when you married me! Don't let me believe that I have been a miserable dupe all along."

She no longer refused point-blank to obey him. She was bending into her old attitude of submission to his wishes. His ascendancy over her was paramount still. But she had made herself thoroughly obnoxious to him, and must be punished. Algernon's resentments were neither quick nor numerous, but they were lasting. His distaste for certain temperaments was profound. Castalia's intensity of emotion, and her ungoverned way of showing it, roused a sense of antagonism in him, which came nearer to passion than anything he had ever felt. With the sure instinct of cruelty, he confronted her wild, eager, supplicating face with a hard, cold, sarcastic smile, and a slight shrug. A blow from his hand would have been tender by comparison. Then he pulled out his watch and said, "How long do you intend this performance to last?" in the quietest voice in the world. And all the while he was in a white heat of anger, as I have said.

"Oh, Ancram! Oh, Ancram!" she cried. Then with a sudden change of tone, she said, "Will you promise me one thing? Will you swear never to see Rhoda Maxfield again? If you will do that, I will—I will—try to forgive you."

"To forgive me! Then you really have lost your senses?"

"No; I wish I had! I would rather be mad than know what I know. But think, Ancram, think well before you refuse me! This one thing is all I ask. Never see or speak to her, or write to her again—not even when I am dead! Swear it. I think if you swore it you would keep to it, wouldn't you? This one poor thing for all I have borne, for all I am willing to bear. I'll take that as a proof that you don't love her best. I'll be content with that. I'll give up everything else in the whole world. Only do this one thing for me, Ancram; I beg it on my knees!"

She did, indeed, fall on her knees as she spoke, and stretched out her clasped hands towards him. For one second their eyes met, then he turned his way and said, as quietly as ever, "I am going to Mr. and Miss Maxfield at once, with the most effectual apology which could be offered to them—namely, that you are a maniac, and in any case not responsible for your actions, nor to be treated like a rational being."

She staggered up to her feet. "Very well," she gasped out, "then I shall not spare you—nor her. I have had a letter from my uncle. He has told me what you accused me of. I went to the office. That man there told me the same. The notes that I paid away to Ravell—you 'wondered'—you were 'uneasy!' Why, you gave me them yourself. Oh, Ancram, how could you have the heart? I wish I was dead!"

"I wish to God you were!"

She was standing close to the edge of the steep, slippery bank; and when he said these words she staggered and, with a little heart-broken moan, put out her hand to clutch at him, groping like a blind person. He shook off her grasp with a sudden rough movement, and the next instant she was deep in the dark ice-cold water.

CHAPTER XX.

It was past mid-day when a loud peal at the bell of Ivy Lodge startled the women in the kitchen. Polly ran to the front door to open it. There stood her master, who pushed quickly into the house past her. "Is your mistress come back?" he asked almost breathlessly.

"No, sir! Oh, mercy me, what's the matter? What has happened?" she cried, for his face showed undisguised terror and agitation. He sat down in the dining-room and asked for a glass of wine. Having drunk it at a gulp, he said, "I cannot understand it. I have been nearly to Whitford along the meadow-path; I didn't try the other way, but then she would not have wandered towards Duckwell, surely! Then I crossed the fields and came back by the road, looking everywhere, and asking every one I met. Nothing to be seen of her. Your mistress's manner has been so strange of late. You must have noticed it. I—I—am afraid—I cannot help being afraid that some terrible thing has happened to her. I have had a dreadful weight and presentiment on my mind all the morning. Where can she be?"

"Oh no, no, sir. Never fear! She'll be all safe somewheres or other. She'll just have gone wandering on into the town. She have been strange in her ways, poor thing! and we couldn't but see it, sir. But she can't have come to no harm. There's nothing to hurt her here-about."

Thus honest Polly, consolingly. But she was infected, too, by the terror in her master's white face.

"You don't know," said he tremulously, "what reason I have for uneasiness." He drew out from his pocket-book a torn scrap of paper with some writing on it. "I found this on the floor by her desk this morning. This is what alarmed me so before I went out, but I wouldn't say anything about it then."

Polly stared at the paper with eager curiosity, but the sharp, slanting writing puzzled her eyes, never quite at their ease with the alphabet in any shape. "Is it missus's writing?" she asked.

"Yes; see, she talks of being so wretched. Why, God knows! Her mind has been quite unhinged. That is the only explanation. And, you see, she says, 'It will not be long before this misery is at an end. I cannot live on as I am living. I will not.'"

"Lord, ha' mercy upon us!" ejaculated the woman, on whom the full force of her master's anxiety and alarm suddenly broke. Her round ruddy cheeks grew almost as white as his, and Lydia, who had been peeping and listening at the door, burst out crying, and began uttering a series of incoherent phrases.

"Hold your noise!" said Polly roughly. "There's troubles enough without you. Now look ye here, sir. I'll put on my bonnet and go right down into Whitford. You take a look along Whit Meadow up Duckwell way. I bet ten pounds she's there somewhere's about. She has taken to going about through the fields, hasn't she, Lydia? Oh, hold your noise, and try and do something to help, you whimpering fool!"

Polly's violent excitement and trepidation took a practical form, whilst the other woman was utterly helpless. She was bidden to stay at home and "receive missus," and tell her that master was come back, and beg her "to bide still in the house, until he should return."

"But I'm afraid she'll never come back!" sobbed Lydia. "I'm so frightened to stop here by myself."

"Ugh, you great silly! Haven't you got no feeling for the poor husband? He looks scared well-nigh to death, poor lad. And as for you, it ain't much you care what's become of missus. You never had a good word for her. You're only crying because you're a coward."

Meanwhile Algernon sat in the little dining-room, with a strange sensation, as if every muscle in his body had been turned into lead. He must get up, and go out as the woman had said. He must! But there he sat with that sensation of marvellous weight holding him down in his chair. The house was absolutely still. Lydia, unable to remain alone in the kitchen, had gone to stand at the front door and stare up and down the road. Thus she heard nothing of footsteps approaching the house at the back, coming hurriedly through the garden, and pausing at the threshold of the door, which was open.

Presently, after some muttered conversation, in which two or three voices took part, a man entered the house and came along the passage, looking, as he went, into the kitchen and finding no one. Just as he reached the door of the dining-room, Algernon came out and confronted him.

"There's been an accident, sir, I'm sorry to say," said the man. "The alarm was given up our way about an hour and a half ago. Somebody's fallen into the Whit. I'm very sorry, sir, but I'm afraid you must prepare for bad news."

Whilst he was still speaking, the house had filled with an ever-gathering crowd. People stood in the passage, peeping over each other's shoulders, and pushing to get a glimpse of Algernon. There were even faces pressed to the windows outside, and the garden was blocked up. Polly had come hurrying back from the town, and now elbowed her way through the crowd to her master. She soon cleared the passage of the throng of idlers who blocked it up, and shut them outside the door by main force. They still swarmed about the house and garden, both on the side of the road and that of Whit Meadow. And their numbers increased every minute. Polly pulled the man who had been spokesman into the dining-room, and bade him say what he had to say without further preamble. "It's no use 'preparing' him," she said, pointing to Algernon, who had sunk into a chair, and was holding his forehead with his hands; "you'll only make it worse. I'm afraid you can't tell him anything dreadfuller than he's got into his head already. Speak out!"

Thus requested, the man, a carpenter of Pudcombe village, told his tale. Some men, working in the fields about a mile above Whitford—half a mile, perhaps, from Ivy Lodge, had heard cries for help from the meadows near the river. He, the carpenter, happened to be passing along a field path from a farmhouse where he had been at work, and ran with the labourers down to the water's edge. There they saw David Powell, the Methodist preacher, wildly shouting for help, and with clothes dripping wet. He had waded waist-deep into the Whit to try to save some one who was drowning there, but in vain. He could not swim, and the current had carried the drowning person out of his reach. "You know," said the carpenter, "there are some ugly swirls and currents in the Whit, for all it looks so sluggish." A boat had been got out and manned, and had made all speed in the direction Powell pointed out. He insisted on accompanying them in his wet clothes. They searched the river for some time in vain. They had got as far as Duckwell Reach when they caught sight of a dark object close in shore. It was the form of a woman. Her clothes had caught in the broken stump of an old willow that grew half in the water; and she was thus held there, swinging to and fro with the current. She was taken out and carried to Duckwell Farm, where every effort had been made to restore her to consciousness. Powell understood the best methods to employ. The Seth Maxfields had done everything in their power, but it was no use. She had never moved, nor breathed, nor quivered an eyelash.

That was the substance of the carpenter's story.

"Is she dead?" asked Algernon with his face hidden. They were the first words he had spoken. And when the man answered with a mournful but positive "Yes; quite, quite dead," he said not a syllable further, but turned away from them, and buried his head in the cushions of the chair.

"He hasn't even asked who the woman was!" whispered the carpenter to Polly. The tears were streaming down the woman's cheeks. Castalia had not made herself beloved in her own house, but Polly had felt the sort of regard for her which grows by acts of kindness, and forbearance and compassion, performed. She shook her head, and answered in an equally low tone, "No need for him to ask, poor young fellow. We've all been fearing something dreadful about missus all morning. And he had his reasons for being afraid as she had gone and done something desperate."

"What—you don't mean that she made away with herself?" said the carpenter, raising his hands.

"Oh, that's more than you and I know. Best say nothing. How can we judge? Poor soul! Well, I always did feel sorry for her, and that I'll say. Though, mind you, I'm sorry for him too. But there's some folks as can't stroke the dog without kicking the cat."

The news spread rapidly through Whitford, and caused the utmost excitement there. Mrs. Algernon Errington had been found drowned in the Whit. How—whether by accident or design—no one knew. But that did not prevent people from hazarding a thousand conjectures. She had wandered out alone, had ventured too near the edge of the slippery bank, and had lost her footing. She had been robbed and thrown into the river. She had committed suicide from ungovernable jealousy. She had committed suicide in a fit of insanity. She had become a hypochondriac. She had gone raving mad. She had committed various frauds at the post-office, and had killed herself in terror at the prospect of their coming to light. This latter hypothesis found much credence. So many circumstances—trifling, perhaps, in themselves, but important when massed together—seemed to corroborate it. And then, if that did not seem an adequate motive for the desperate deed, Castalia's notorious and passionate jealousy was thrown in as a make-weight. There would be a coroner's inquest, of course. And the chief witness at it would probably be David Powell. It appeared he was the last person who had seen the unfortunate woman alive.

Mrs. Thimbleby was in terrible affliction. Mr. Powell was very ill. He had plunged into the ice-cold river, and had then remained for hours in his wet clothes. He had not been able to walk back from Duckwell Farm, and Farmer Maxfield had brought him home himself in his spring-cart, and had bidden widow Thimbleby look after him a little, for he (Maxfield) thought the preacher in a very bad way. He was seized with violent fits of shivering, and the doctor whom Mrs. Thimbleby sent for to see him, on her own responsibility, told them to get him into bed at once, to keep him warm, and to administer certain remedies which he ordered. But no word would Powell speak about his ailments to the doctor, or to anyone else. He waved off all questions with a determined though gentle resolution. He allowed himself to be helped into bed, being absolutely unable to stand or walk without assistance. And he did not refuse the warm clothing which the widow heaped upon him. He lay still and passive, but he would say no word of his symptoms and sensations to the doctor. "The man can in no wise help me," he said to Mrs. Thimbleby. "All the wisdom of this world is foolishness to one whom the Lord has laid his hands on. I am bowed as a reed; yea, I am broken."

His voice was hoarse and feeble, and his eyes blazed with a feverish light. The widow found it vain to importune him to swallow the medicines that had been sent. In her heart she had some misgivings that it might be wrong to interfere in the dealings of Providence with so holy a man, by administering drugs to him. But the misgivings never reached a point of conviction that might have comforted her.

"I'll leave you quiet awhile, Mr. Powell," she said. "Maybe you'll sleep, and that would do you more good than anything. Sleep is God's own cure for a many troubles, isn't it?"

He looked at her with a wild unrecognising stare. "When I say my bed shall comfort me, my couch shall ease my complaint, then thou scarest me with dreams, and terrifiest me through visions," he murmured.

The good woman softly went away, wiping the tears from her eyes. "One thing is a mercy," said the poor soul to herself, "and that is, that Mr. Diamond is so kind and thoughtful. He gives no trouble, and is a help on the contrary. And I'm sure I don't know how we should have managed without his arm to help Mr. Powell upstairs. And another thing is a mercy—I hope it isn't wrong to feel it so!—that Mrs. Errington is out of the house. I do not know how I should have been strengthened to keep up and attend upon her, and she in such a way, poor thing! The Lord has had pity on us for Mr. Powell's sake."

Minnie Bodkin had driven to Mrs. Thimbleby's house early in the afternoon, and taken Mrs. Errington away with her. Mrs. Errington had rushed to Ivy Lodge under the first shock of the terrible news which Mr. Smith, the surgeon, communicated to her. She had seen her son for a few minutes. Her intention had been to remain with him, but this he would not allow. He had insisted on his mother's returning to her own lodgings after a very brief interview with him.

"No wonder he can't bear to have her about, though she is his mother. Tiresome old thing!" exclaimed Lydia, peevishly.

But if Algernon got rid of his mother as quickly as possible, he refused to admit any one else at all, and remained shut up in the dining-room, whither he had had a sofa carried, meaning to sleep there. He had been obliged to receive Seth Maxfield, who came to ask when and how he would wish his wife's body conveyed from Duckwell Farm to Whitford. "Can't she stay there?" he had asked in a dazed sort of manner. Then added quickly, turning away his head, "I'll leave it all to you. You've been very good. You've done everything for the best, I am sure." And he put out his hand to the farmer with his face still turned away. And later on he had had to see some officials about the inquest. But after that was over, he locked his door, and refused to open it except to Polly, when she brought him food. He ate almost ravenously, drank a great deal of wine, and then lay down and dozed away the hours until dawn next day.

CHAPTER XXI.

The inquest was to be held at the "Blue Bell" inn. And after the inquest, the dust of the Honourable Castalia Errington was to be laid beneath the turf of the humble village churchyard, amidst less noble dust, with the daisies growing impartially above all, and spreading their pink-edged petals over the just and the unjust alike.

It was now currently reported that the thefts at the post-office had been Castalia's doing. Mrs. Smith and Mrs. Dockett had been "sure of it all along"—so they said, and so they really imagined now. The story of the mysterious notes paid to Ravell, the draper, was in every mouth. Roger Heath went about saying that Mr. Errington ought to make his loss good out of his own pocket, if he had any feelings of honour. But all the people who had not lost any money in the post-office were disgusted at Roger Heath's hardness and avarice, and asked indignantly if that was the moment to speak of such things? For the tragedy of Castalia's death had produced a strong effect in Whitford. Perhaps there was not one human being in the town who grieved that she was gone; but many were oppressed by the manner of her going. People had an uneasy feeling in remembering how much they had disliked her; almost as if their dislike made them guilty of her death in some vague, far-off, inexplicable way. They told themselves and each other that though "her manners had been repellent, poor thing," yet for their part they had always felt sorry for her, and had long perceived that her mind was astray, and that she was falling into a low melancholy state, that was likely to lead to some terrible catastrophe. By this time scarcely any one in Whitford entertained a doubt as to Castalia's having destroyed herself. And the social verdict, "Temporary insanity," was pronounced in assured anticipation that the legal verdict would be to that effect also.

There were two men who did not mystify themselves by conjuring up any factitious tenderness about Castalia's memory, and who gave way to no superstitious uneasiness of conscience as to their dislike of her when she was alive. One of these men was Jonathan Maxfield; the other was the dead woman's husband.

Maxfield had no retrospective softness on the subject. He, indeed, being accustomed to take certain passages of the Old Testament very seriously and literally, and having fed his mind almost exclusively upon those passages, was of opinion that Castalia's tragic fate had been brought about by a direct interposition of Providence as a judgment on her for her bad behaviour to himself and his daughter. And if this opinion on Maxfield's part should appear incredibly monstrous, let it be remembered that in his own mind "the godly" were typified by the Maxfield family, and "the ungodly" by the enemies of that family.

As to Algernon—harassed, anxious, and doubtful of the future as he might be, he was glad that his wife was dead, and he knew that he was glad. Her death made a way out—apparently the only possible way out—of a labyrinth of troubles, and relieved Algernon from the apprehension of an exposure which it made him sick to think of. He had not meant to kill her, he said to himself. He had certainly laid no deliberate plan to do so. Had he, in truth, been the cause of her death? In the state of mind she was in, would she not have thrown herself into the river, or otherwise put an end to herself, without that touch from him which he had given, he knew not how?

It all seemed unreal to him when he thought of it—the leaden water, the grey sky and meadows, and the slippery bank with its tufts of blackberry bushes. He went over and over again in his mind the words that had passed between himself and Castalia; her violence, and her wild jealousy and suspicions, and her allusion to her uncle's letter, and to what Gibbs had told her, and then her fierce threat that she would not spare him! She had become utterly unmanageable—mad, in fact. She had resolved to die. She had a suicidal mania. That scrap of writing would suffice to prove it. To be sure he had found it and put it in his pocket-book weeks ago, although he told the servant that he had picked it up off the floor that morning of his return from London. But that only indicated that the idea had long been rooted in her mind. And besides, the paper bore no date. There was nothing to show how long it had been written.

No, it was not he who had killed Castalia. She had gone down willingly to death. She had uttered no sound, no cry. He should have heard a cry all across the silent meadows. He had not looked back. He had fled away from the river at his topmost speed after he saw her slip, and stagger, and fall heavily into the black water under the shadow of the bank. Had she risen again to the surface? It was said that drowning persons always rose three times. But she had made no sound. Surely she would have cried out if she had longed for life. Ugh! It was horrible to imagine her white face and staring eyes rising above the strong dragging current and looking for help. That was all very ghastly, very hideous. He would not think of it. It was over. Castalia was dead. And although he would have given much that she should have died in any other way, yet he was glad that she was dead, and he knew that he was glad.

He made no pretence to himself of a factitious tenderness about her. She had been thoroughly antagonistic and distasteful to him of late. She had been the bitter drop flavouring every action, every hope, every minute of his life. He had been the victim of a hard fate, and of the false promises (implied, if not expressed) of Lord Seely. Those paltry sums—those notes that he had taken—he had been driven into committing that action altogether by stress of circumstances. It was strange to himself to think of the light that action would appear in to other people. To his own mind, knowing how it had come to pass in an instant, by the tug of a sudden impulse, it seemed so clear that there was no real ground for blaming him in the matter! He had felt the difficulty of getting money with a severity which the rest of the world probably could not conceive. He was absolutely indifferent to the question of abstract right or wrong, justice or injustice, in the case. But the concrete hardship to himself of being poor he had keenly felt to be undeserved.

And now, if it were not for one thing, he should begin to breathe more freely. The one thing that weighed on him with a gloomy, though formless foreboding, was the inquest. He had been obliged to go to Duckwell Farm. He had been asked to look at Castalia's dead body. He had not dared to refuse to do so; but he had requested to be shown into the room where she lay, alone and without witnesses. The room was that sunny parlour where Rhoda Maxfield had sat on many a summer evening, and where the neighbours had discussed the news of his own marriage less than a year ago. But Algernon's imagination did not wander very far from the present. He walked to the window and looked out through the black trellis-work of leafless vine branches. Then he stared at the prints on the walls, and the gay china vases filled with winter nosegays of trembling grass and chrysanthemums. And then his eyes, which had wandered in every other direction, were compelled to turn towards the broad, old-fashioned sofa covered with fair white linen, under which the outlines of a human shape revealed themselves.

Was that stiff, white, silent thing Castalia? He could not realise it. He would scarcely have started if the door had opened and his wife had walked into the room in her ordinary dress, and with her ordinary gait. He had seen her last full of passionate excitement. That stiff, white, silent thing could not be she. He would not lift the coverlet, though, nor look on that which lay beneath. But he stood and gazed at it until the heap beneath the linen sheet seemed to stir and change its outlines. Then he turned away shuddering to the window, and looked at his watch to see whether he might venture to leave the room yet. Would the people think he had been there too short a time? He came out at length, looking pale and depressed enough to excite a good deal of sympathy in the breast of Mrs. Seth Maxfield. And with his usual quick susceptibility to the impression he produced on others, he was fully aware of this, and gratified by it, despite the chill vision of the still white heap under the coverlet which persistently haunted his memory. He saw looks of pity; he heard whispered exclamations of admiration, and they did more than gratify, they reassured him. It had entered into nobody's mind to conceive that he had been the cause of his wife's death. Into whose head, indeed, should it enter? or how? He remembered the last lightning-quick glance he had cast over the wide meadows, and how it had shown them to him empty and bare of any living thing for as far as his eye could reach. No; he was safe from suspicion. Of course he was safe from suspicion! And yet—he would have given a year of his life to have the inquest over, and the dead woman safely put away beneath the daisies in Duckwell churchyard.

Meanwhile the mortal frame that had so throbbed and suffered for his sake, lay there lonely and neglected. Strangers' hands had composed it decently; a stranger's roof sheltered it. It was to lie in a stranger's grave. Only one woman came and stood beside the couch in the sunny parlour, and looked on the dead shape with eyes full of compassionate tears; and, before going away, laid some sprays of fern and delicate hothouse blossoms on the quiet breast, and fastened there a curl of light hair. The hair had been cut jestingly from Algernon Errington's head when he was a school-boy, and then put away and forgotten for years. It now lay above his dead wife's heart. "She was so fond of him, poor soul!" said the compassionate woman. It was Minnie Bodkin.

CHAPTER XXII.

The big room at the "Blue Bell" was full. It was a room associated in the minds of most of the people present with occasions of festivity or entertainment. The Archery Club balls were held in it. It was used for the exhibitions of any travelling conjurer, lecturer, or musician, whose evil fate brought him to Whitford. Once a strolling company of players had performed there before some fifteen persons and several dozen cane-bottomed chairs. There were the tarnished candelabra stuck in the walls, the little gallery up aloft where the fiddlers sat on ball nights, and the big looking-glass at one end of the room, muffled with yellow muslin, and surmounted by a dusty garland of paper flowers. Now the wintry daylight coming through the uncurtained windows, made all these things look chill, ghastly, and forlorn. People who had thought the "Blue Bell" Assembly Room a cheerful place enough under the bright illumination of wax candles, now shivered, and whispered to each other how dreary it was.

The coroner's jury had been out to Duckwell Farm to view the body, and to look at the exact spot on the bank where it had been landed from the boat, and to stare at the willow stump to which it had been found fastened by the clothes. And they had returned to the "Blue Bell" inn to complete the inquiry into the causes of the death of Castalia Errington. A great many witnesses had already been examined. Their testimony went to show that the deceased lady's behaviour of late had been very strange, capricious, and unreasonable. Almost every one of the witnesses, including the servants at Ivy Lodge, confessed that they had heard rumours of young Mrs. Errington being "not right in her mind." They had observed an increasing depression of spirits in her of late. Obadiah Gibbs's evidence was the strongest of all, and his revelations created a great sensation. He described his last interview with Castalia at the post-office, and left the impression on all his hearers which was honestly his own; namely, that on Castalia, and on her alone, rested the onus of the irregularities and robberies of money-letters at Whitford. He did his best to spare her memory. He sincerely thought her irresponsible for her actions. But the facts, as he saw and represented them, admitted of but one conclusion being come to.

Algernon Errington's appearance in the room elicited a low murmur of sympathy from the spectators. His manner of giving his evidence was perfect, and nothing could have been better in keeping with the circumstances of his painful position, than the subdued, yet quiet tones of his voice, and the white, strained look of his face, which revealed rather the effect of a great shock to the nerves than a deep wound to the heart. Of course he could not be expected to grieve as a husband would grieve who had lost a dearly-loved and loving wife; but their having been on somewhat bad terms, and Castalia's notorious jealousy and bad temper, made the manner of her death all the more terrible. Poor young man! He was dreadfully cut up, one could see that. But he made no pretences, put on no affectations of woe. He was so simple and quiet! In a word, he was credited with feeling precisely what he ought to have felt.

His statement added scarcely any new fact to those already known. He had not seen his wife alive since he parted from her when he started for London to visit Lord Seely, who was ill. He corroborated his servants' testimony to the facts that Castalia had wandered out on to Whit Meadow about nine o'clock in the morning; that he had been made uneasy by her strange absence, and that he had gone himself to seek her, but without success. In reply to some questions by a juryman, as to whether he had gone to London solely because of Lord Seely's illness, he answered, with a look of quiet sadness, that that had not been his sole reason. There were private matters to be spoken of between himself and his wife's uncle—matters which admitted of no delay. Could he not have written them? No; he did not feel at liberty to write them. They concerned his wife. He had mentioned to Lord Seely his fears that her mind was giving way, as Lord Seely would be able to affirm. A letter found in the pocket of the deceased woman's gown was produced and read. It had become partly illegible from immersion in the water, but the greater portion of it could be made out. It was from Lord Seely, and referred to a painful conversation he had had with his niece's husband about herself. It was a kind letter, but written evidently in much agitation and pain of mind. The writer exhorted and even implored his niece to confide fully in him, for her own sake, as well as that of her family; and promised that he would help and support her under all circumstances, if she would but tell him the truth unreservedly.

Nothing could have been better for Algernon's case than that letter. Instead of being the cause of his disgrace and exposure, it was obviously the means of confirming every one of his statements, implied as well as expressed. It showed clearly enough—first, that Algernon had given Lord Seely to understand that his wife laboured under grave suspicions of having stolen money-letters from the Whitford Post-office; secondly, that he (Algernon) believed those suspicions to be well founded; thirdly, that symptoms of mental aberration, which had recently manifested themselves in Castalia, were at once the explanation of, and the excuse for, her conduct. This letter, which, if Castalia were alive to speak for herself, would have been like a brand on her husband's forehead for life, was now a most valuable testimony in his favour.

Algernon's hard and unrelenting mood towards his dead wife grew still harder and more unrelenting as he listened to this letter, and remembered that Castalia had threatened him with exposure, and had resolved not to spare him. Nothing in the world but her death could have saved him from ruin. Even supposing that she could have been cajoled into promising to comply with his directions, she would not have been able to do so. She was so stupidly literal in her statements. A direct lie would have embarrassed her. And then, at the first jealous fit which might have seized her, he would have been at her mercy. Lord Seely's letter showed a strong feeling of irritation—almost of hostility—against Algernon. It might not be recognisable by the audience at the inquest, but Algernon recognised it completely, and felt a distinct sense of triumph in the impotence of Lord Seely to harm him, or to wriggle away from under his heel. Algernon was master of the position. He appeared before the world in the light of a victim to his alliance with the Seelys. There could be no further talk on their part of condescension, or honour conferred. He and his mother had lived their lives as persons of gentle blood and unblemished reputation until the Honourable Castalia Kilfinane brought disgrace and misery into their home. In making these reflections Algernon was not, of course, considering the inward truth of facts, but their outward semblances. It made no difference to his indignation against the "pompous little ass" who had treated him with hauteur, nor to his satisfaction in humbling the "pompous little ass," that if all the secret circumstances hidden and silenced for ever under the cold white shroud that covered his dead wife could be revealed before the eyes of all men, Lord Seely would have the right to detest and despise him. Lord Seely had not treated him as he ought. He was firmly persuaded of that. And as he measured Lord Seely's duty towards him accurately by the extent of all he desired and expected of Lord Seely, it will be seen how far short the latter had fallen of Algernon's standard.

The Seth Maxfields gave their testimony as to how the deceased body had been carried into their house; how they had tried all means to revive her; and how every effort had been in vain, and she had never moved nor breathed again. The two men who had rescued the body from the water, and the carpenter who had brought the news to Ivy Lodge, repeated their story, and corroborated all that the Maxfields had said. There only remained to be heard the important testimony of David Powell. He had been so ill that it was feared at one time that the inquest must be adjourned until he should be able to give his evidence. But he declared that he would come and speak before the jury; that he should be strengthened to do so when the moment arrived; and had opposed a fixed silence to all the representations and remonstrances of the doctor. On the morning of the inquest he arose and dressed himself before Mrs. Thimbleby was up, albeit she was no sluggard in the morning. He had gone out, while it was still dark, into the raw foggy atmosphere of Whit Meadow, and had wandered there for a long time. On returning to the widow Thimbleby's house, he had seated himself opposite to the blazing fire in the kitchen, staring at it, and muttering to himself like a man in a feverish dream.

Nevertheless, when the due time arrived, he entered the room at the "Blue Bell" to give his evidence with a quiet steady gait. His appearance there produced a profound impression.

A stranger contrast than he presented to the Whitford burghers by whom he was surrounded could scarcely be imagined. Not only were his bodily shape and colouring different from theirs, but the expression of his face was almost unearthly. There was some subtle contradiction between the expression of David Powell's sorrow-laden eyes and brow, and that of the mouth, with its tightly-closed lips drawn back at the corners with what on ordinary faces would have been a smile. But on his face, being coupled with a singular pinched look of the nostrils and a strained tightness of the upper lip, it became something which troubled the beholder with a sense of inexplicable pain—almost terror.

As he advanced along the room, there was a hush of attentive expectation, during which Dr. Evans, the coroner, curiously examined the Methodist preacher with grave professional eyes. After a few preliminary questions, to which Powell gave brief, clear answers, he said, "I have been brought hither to testify in this matter. I am an instrument in the hands of the great and terrible God. He works not as men work. In His hand all tools are alike."

"What can you tell us of the death of this unfortunate lady, Mr. Powell?" asked the coroner, quietly. "You were the first to see her struggling in the water, were you not? And you made a gallant effort to save her."

"She struggled but little. She went to her death as a lamb to the slaughter; nay, as a victim who desires to die."

Powell spoke in a low but distinct voice; broken and harsh, indeed, compared with what it once was, but still with a soft tremulous note in it now and then, that seemed to stir deep fibres of feeling in the hearts of those who heard him. In such a tone it was that he uttered the words, "as a victim who desires to die." And tears sprang into the eyes of many from sheer emotional sympathy with the sound of his voice.

"You are of opinion, then, Mr. Powell," said the coroner, "that the deceased wilfully put an end to her own life."

"No."

"You think that she was not in a state of mind to be responsible for her actions?"

"She was murdered," said Powell, in a distinct, grating tone, which was audible in every corner of the crowded room.

CHAPTER XXIII.

There was a momentary rustling, as if every person present had moved slightly, and then a deep hush. The silence seemed to last a long time; but, in fact, only a second or two elapsed before Powell, drawing up his tall, lean figure to its utmost height, and pointing with outstretched hand full at Algernon, exclaimed with a kind of cry, "There is her murderer! Woe to the cruel, woe to the unrighteous man! Ye have ploughed wickedness; ye have reaped iniquity; ye have eaten the fruit of lies!"

There arose a murmur, a movement, a confused sound of ejaculations. Algernon started up, and some one laid a hand on his shoulder and pushed him back into his seat. "Ask what he means," said Algernon; but his voice was so weak and faint that the words were not heard beyond the few persons who immediately surrounded him. He could scarcely grow paler than he had been from the beginning of the inquest, but a ghastly ashen-grey hue showed itself round his mouth. His lips were quite colourless. Terror, agonising terror, was in his heart. What did this preacher know? What had he seen? Had Castalia spoken and accused him before her death?

Anguish for anguish; perhaps he suffered at that moment as much as his victim had suffered when she felt the hand she loved send her to her death.

The movement and the murmur in the crowd were over in an instant. The coroner sternly commanded order. There was silence again, and the very air seemed charged with a horrible apprehension, which weighed upon every one as a coming thunderstorm oppresses the cowering birds.

"You must speak clearly and plainly, Mr. Powell," said the coroner in a severe tone. "State what grounds you have for this very extraordinary accusation. The evidence laid before us to-day goes to show that Mr. Errington did not see his wife since parting from her on the Monday night to go to London, until he was called on to identify her dead body at Duckwell Farm."

"He spoke with her in the meadow by the river's brink. She appealed to him; she implored him; she knelt to him. I saw her gestures. Then he hurled her down the steep bank into the water and fled away, leaving her to perish!"

A most profound sensation was caused by these words throughout the whole assembly. The jury looked at each other like men suddenly aroused from sleep. They seemed not only startled but scared. Indeed, a singular expression of disquietude appeared on every face—almost as if each individual in the crowd had felt himself accused. Before any further questions could be put to Powell, there was a stir and a commotion at the lower end of the room and a murmur of voices. Algernon Errington had swooned dead away. He must have fallen to the ground had he not been caught in the arms of his next neighbour, who happened to be Mr. Ravell, the draper. Some one in the crowd handed a smelling-bottle to be held under his nose, and they cleared a little space around him to give him air, by the directions of Mr. Smith, the surgeon, who was at hand. It was proposed to carry him away out of the heat and the throng; but in less than a couple of minutes he revived, and immediately on recovering consciousness he desired to remain where he was. The terror of listening to what Powell said was not so appalling to his imagination as the terror of fancying what he might be saying when he (Algernon) should not be there to hear it.

Order being restored, the preacher's examination was continued. On being asked where he had been when the circumstances alleged to have taken place happened, he replied that he had been at some distance up the river, in the midst of a thick coppice which grew low down on the bank there. He had been near enough to see, although not to hear, the interview between young Errington and his wife. And to the questions what had brought him to that remote spot at such an hour, and why he did not make his presence known at once on seeing the deceased lady fall into the water, he answered, waving his hands to and fro, "I was prostrate on the earth—not praying, I may not pray, but suffering under the wrath of the powers of the air. The voices were very terrible on that day. They had aroused me from my bed. They had hunted me forth in the early morning. I had wandered for a long time—for hours, after your reckoning, but for years according to the time of the spirits."

"Mr. Powell," said Dr. Evans, sternly, "this will not do. You must speak less wildly. Remember what a tremendous responsibility rests on you after making such an allegation as you have made! Answer the questions put to you clearly and seriously."

But it was in vain that David Powell was catechised and cross-examined in the endeavour to draw from him any more definite account of the events of that last morning of Castalia's life. He reiterated, indeed, his statement that Algernon had wilfully and forcibly thrust his wife down the bank into the river, and had then fled away at his utmost speed. And he added that he (Powell) had not thought of pursuing or calling to the murderer, being absorbed in his attempts to rescue the drowning woman. He persisted, too, in declaring that Castalia had been willing, nay, wishful, to die. She had not struggled. She had not cried out. She had not tried to reach his outstretched hand. She had closed her eyes, and given herself up to the power of the death-cold waters. So far he was coherent and consistent; but when he endeavoured to describe how or why he had found himself on that spot at that hour, he wandered off into the wildest statements, and grew ever more and more excited. His face flushed. His eyes blazed. His voice rose almost to a scream. He broke into a torrent of words, standing up in face of the crowd and emphasising his discourse with strange violent gestures. "I will declare the truth," he exclaimed. "I will cry aloud, and spare not. Now, therefore, be content; look upon me, for it is evident unto you if I lie!" Then with a sudden change of tone, sinking his voice to a hoarse, hollow monotone, and gazing straight before him with wide, horror-stricken eyes, he added, "Let me speak, let me confess the truth, before I go whence I shall not return, even to the land of darkness and the shadow of death. A land of darkness as darkness itself; and of the shadow of death without any order, and where the light is as darkness."

A shudder ran through the audience. The preacher seemed to hold them in a spell. No voice was raised to interrupt him. Many persons turned pale as they listened. But on one face in the crowd the colour faintly dawned again. In one breast the preacher's voice giving utterance to the awful and glowing imagery of the Hebrew of old time, awoke something like a sensation of relief and comfort.

Algernon Errington felt the life-blood pulsing warmly again in his veins. This Methodist man was mad—clearly mad! What was his testimony worth?

Powell went on, speaking still more brokenly and incoherently. "I am a castaway," he said. "I declare it before you all. Some of you have listened to my ministrations in other days. I spoke then of assurance—of Christian perfection. Those words were vain. There are but the elect and the reprobate, and unto the number of those latter am I doomed. I have long known it and struggled against the knowledge, but I declare it to ye now as a testimony. How shall a man be just with God? This is one thing, therefore I said it. He destroyeth the perfect and the wicked."

The coroner recovered his presence of mind. In truth he had been so absorbed in studying David Powell with the professional interest of a doctor and a psychologist, that he had suffered him to ramble on thus far unchecked. But now he broke in upon him abruptly. "We cannot listen to this sort of thing, Mr. Powell," he said. "All this has no bearing on the present inquiry." Then he said a few words as to the desirability of an adjournment. Mr. Errington might wish to call some other witnesses. Powell had acknowledged that he had been too far distant to hear a word of the conversation he alleged to have taken place between the husband and wife. It was possible, therefore, that he had been too distant to see the two persons with sufficient distinctness to swear to their identity. Some more particular testimony might be obtained as to the precise hour at which the deceased lady had been last seen alive, and as to what her husband had been doing at that time. Upon this, Algernon Errington arose in his place and said in a clear, though slightly tremulous voice, "For myself, I desire no adjournment. But I should like to put a few questions to this witness."

There was a sudden hush of profound attention. David Powell still stood up in face of the assembly. He was rocking himself to and fro in a singular, restless way, and muttering under his breath very rapidly. It was observable, too, that his eyes seemed continually attracted to one point in the room just behind Algernon Errington. Every now and then he passed his hands over his eyes, as if to obliterate, or shut out, some painful sight, but he did not turn his head away; and the next instant after making that gesture, he would stare at the same point again, with an expression of intense horror. Algernon waited for an instant before speaking. Then he said in such a tone as one uses to attract the attention of a very young child, "Mr. Powell, will you try to listen to me?"

The preacher immediately looked full at him, but without replying. Algernon did not meet his eye, but turned his face aside towards the coroner and the jury. He looked at them with an appealing glance, and a slight movement of his head in the direction of Powell. Then he resumed:

"The accusation you have brought against me is so overwhelming, so amazing, that it is not very wonderful if I feel almost stunned and dizzy. How such a notion ever entered your brain Heaven only knows! I deny it completely, unequivocally, solemnly. To me it seems that such a denial must be unnecessary. The thing is so monstrous! But will you try to answer one or two questions with some calmness? How long had you been in the copse before you saw my wife walking by the river-side?"

Powell shook his head restlessly, and passed his hand over his forehead with the action of brushing something off. "I was called out before the dawn," he said. "The voices bade me go forth. They sounded like brazen bells in the silence, beating and quivering here," and he pressed his fingers on his temples.

"You hear voices which are unheard by other people, then?"

"Often. Every day. Every hour."

"Tell me—do you not sometimes see forms that other persons cannot see?"

Powell started, trembled violently, and looked at Algernon with an expression of bewildered terror. But it was at the same time manifest that some gleam of reason was struggling against the delusions in his mind. He felt and perceived dimly, as one perceives external circumstances through sleep, that a trap was being laid for him. The pathetic questioning look in his eyes, as he vainly tried to recover the government of his mind, was intensely painful. For a second or two, he remained silent with parted lips and clenched hands, like a man making a violent and supreme effort. It seemed as if in another instant he might succeed in gaining sufficient mastery over himself to reply collectedly. But Algernon did not give time for such a chance to happen. He repeated his question more eagerly and loudly, looking at the preacher almost threateningly as he spoke.

"Tell me, Mr. Powell, and remember what a responsibility you have assumed before God and man in making this accusation—tell me truly whether you do not see visions—figures of men and women, that other people cannot see? Don't forms appear before your eyes and vanish again as suddenly? Have you not told your landlady, Mrs. Thimbleby, as much on many occasions? How can you dare to assert with confidence, that from the distance you say you were at, you could distinguish my face and that of my wife? All your description of her violent gestures, and kneeling on the ground, and clasping her hands—does not that seem more like the delusions of fancy than the information of your sober senses?"

Algernon spoke with indignant heat and rapidity—a calculated heat, a purposed rapidity meant to have a confusing effect on the preacher, and which had that effect; but which also excited a sympathetic indignation in many of the auditors. Powell looked wildly around him, and clasped his hands above his head.

"You must put one question at a time, Mr. Errington," said Dr. Evans.

"Then I put this question: David Powell, do you, or do you not, see visions and faces and figures that the rest of the world is as unconscious of as of the voices that called you out on to Whit Meadow that morning that my poor wife was drowned?"

Powell, with his eyes still fixed on the same point that he had been gazing on so long, suddenly cried out with a loud voice, "As God liveth, who hath taken away my judgment, and the Almighty, who hath vexed my soul, my lips shall not speak wickedness, nor my tongue utter deceit! God forbid that I should justify you! Till I die I will not remove my integrity from me. It is there—there behind his shoulder. It has been holding me with the power of its eyes. Oh, how dreadful are those eyes, and that ashen-grey face! Look, behold! the Lord has brought a witness from the grave to testify to the truth. See, behold! Can you not see her? Look where she stands in her cold wet garments, with the water dripping from her hair! She points at him—oh God most terrible!—the drowned woman points her cold finger at her murderer!" He stretched out his arms towards Algernon, and then with one bound leaped shrieking into the midst of the crowd.

A dozen hands were put forth to hold him. He struggled with the tremendous strength of insanity; but was at length forcibly carried out of the room a raving maniac.

After that there were not many words of an official nature spoken in the room. The inquest was adjourned to the following day, and the assembly dispersed to carry the account of the strange scene that had happened all over Whitford and its neighbourhood.

CHAPTER XXIV

The next day medical evidence was forthcoming as to the insanity of David Powell, who had been removed to the County Asylum. Testimony was, moreover, given by many persons showing that the preacher's mind had long been disordered. Even the widow Thimbleby's evidence, given with many tears, went to prove that. But she tried with all her might to bear witness to his goodness, and clung loyally to her loving admiration for his character. "He may not be quite in his right senses for matters of this world," sobbed the poor woman, "and he has been sorely tormented by taking up with these doctrines of election. But if ever there was an angel sent down to suffer on this earth, and help the sorrowful, and call sinners to repentance, Mr. Powell is that angel. I know what he is. And I have had other lodgers—good, kind gentlemen, too; I don't say to the contrary. But overboil their eggs in the morning, or leave a lump in their feather-bed, and you'd soon get a glimpse of the old Adam. Now with Mr. Powell, nothing put him out except sin; and even that did but make him the more eager to save your soul."

Several witnesses who had testified on the previous day were re-examined. And some new ones were found who swore to having met Mr. Errington going along the road from his own house towards Whitford in great agitation, and asking everyone he met if they had seen his wife. The hour was such that to the best of their belief it was impossible he should have had such an interview as Powell described, with the deceased, between the time at which the cook swore he left his own house and their meeting him in the road. On this point, however, the evidence was somewhat conflicting. But the Whitford clocks were well known to be conflicting also; St. Mary's being always foremost with its jangling bell, the Town Hall clock coming next—except occasionally, when it hastened to be first with apparently quite capricious zeal—and the mellow chimes of St. Chad's, that were heard far over town and meadow, closing the chorus with their sweet cadence.

There certainly appeared to be no cause, no conceivable motive for Algernon Errington to have committed the crime. Many witnesses combined to show with what sweetness and good-humour he bore his wife's jealous tempers. And, besides, it was notorious that he had hoped through her influence to obtain assistance and promotion from her uncle, Lord Seely. Whereas, on the other hand, there did seem to be several motives at work to induce the unfortunate lady to put an end to her own existence. There could be little doubt that she had committed the post-office robberies, and the fear of detection had weighed on her mind. Moreover, that she had for some time past been made unhappy by jealousy and discontent, and had contemplated making away with herself, was proved by several scraps of writing besides that which her husband had found and produced at the inquest the first day. In brief, no one was surprised when the foreman of the coroner's jury delivered a verdict to the effect that the deceased lady had committed suicide while under the influence of temporary insanity; and added a few words stating the opinion of the jury that Mr. Algernon Errington's character was quite unstained by the accusation of a maniac, who had been proved to have been subject to insane delusions for some time past. It was just the sort of verdict that every one had expected, and the general sympathy with Algernon still ran high.

As for him, he got away from the "Blue Bell" as quickly as possible after the inquest was over, slipping away by a back door where a closed fly was waiting for him. When he reached his home he locked himself into the dining-room, and sat down on the sofa with closed eyes and his body leaning listlessly against the cushions, as if all vital force were gone from him. The prevailing—and, for a time, the only sensation he felt was one of utter weariness. He was so completely exhausted that the restful attitude, the silence, and the solitude seemed positive luxuries. He was scarcely conscious of his escape. He felt merely that the strain was over, and that voice, face, and limbs might sink back from the terrible tension he had held them in to a natural lassitude.

But by-and-by he began to realise the danger he had passed, and to exult in his new sense of freedom. Castalia being removed, it seemed as if all troubles must be removed with her!

The funeral of Mrs. Algernon Errington was to take place on the following day, and it was known that Lord Seely would be present at it if it were possible for him to make the journey from London. It was said that he had been very ill, but was now better, and would use his utmost endeavours to pay that mark of respect to his niece's memory. Mrs. Errington, indeed, talked of my lord's coming as a proof of his sympathy with her boy. But the world knew better than that. It knew, by some mysterious means, that Lord Seely had quarrelled with Algernon. And when his lordship did appear in Whitford, and took up his quarters at the "Blue Bell," rumours went about to the effect that he had refused to see young Errington, and had remained shut up in his own room, attended by his physician. This, however, was not true. Lord Seely had seen Algernon and spoken with him. But he had not touched his proffered hand; he had said no word to him of sympathy; he had barely looked at him. The poor old man was overpowered by grief for Castalia, and it was in vain for Algernon to put on a show of grief. About a matter of fact Lord Seely would even now have found it difficult to think that Algernon was telling him a point-blank lie; but on a matter of feeling it was different. Algernon's words and voice rang false and hollow, and the old man shrank from him.

Lord Seely had come down to Whitford on getting the news of Castalia's terrible death, without knowing any particulars about it. Those were not the days when the telegraph brought a budget of intelligence from the most distant parts of the earth every morning. A few hurried and confused lines were all that Lord Seely had received, but they were sufficient to make him insist on performing the journey to Whitford at once. Lady Seely had tried to impress on him the necessity of shaking off young Errington now that Castalia was gone. "Wash your hands of him, Valentine," my lady had said. "If poor Cassy has done this desperate deed, it's he that drove her to it—smooth-faced young villain!" To all this Lord Seely had made no reply. But in his own mind he had almost resolved to help Algernon to a place abroad. It was what his poor niece would have desired.

But, then, after his arrival in Whitford all the painful details of the coroner's inquest were made known to him. He made inquiries in all directions, and learned a great deal about his niece's life in the little town. The prominent feelings in his mind were pity and remorse. Pity for Castalia's unhappy fate, and acute remorse for having been so weak as to let her marriage take place without any attempt to interfere, despite his own secret conviction that it was an ill-assorted and ill-omened one. "You couldn't have helped it, my lord," said the friendly physician, to whom he poured out some of the feelings that oppressed his heart. "Perhaps not; perhaps not. But I ought to have tried. My poor, dear, unhappy girl!"

On the day of the funeral Lord Seely stood side by side with Algernon at Castalia's grave, in Duckwell churchyard. But, when it was over, they parted, and drove back to Whitford in separate carriages. Lord Seely was to return to London early the next morning, but before he went away he determined to pay a visit to the county lunatic asylum and see David Powell.

On the day of the funeral Algernon had spoken a few words to Lord Seely about his wish to get away from the painful associations which must henceforward haunt him in Whitford; and had reminded his lordship of the promise made in London. But Lord Seely had made no definite answer, and, moreover, he had said that, by his doctor's advice, he must decline a visit which Algernon offered to make him that evening. Was the "pompous little ass" going to throw him over after all?

In the course of that afternoon he heard that old Maxfield intended to come down on him pitilessly for the full amount of the bills he held. A reaction had set in in public sentiment. Tradesmen, who could not get paid, and whose hopes of eventual payment were greatly damped by the coolness of Lord Seely's behaviour to his nephew-in-law, began to feel their indignation once more override their compassion. The two servants at Ivy Lodge asked for their wages, and declared that they did not wish to remain there another week. Algernon's position at the post-office was forfeited. He knew that he could not keep it even if he would.

It began to appear that the removal of Castalia had not, after all, removed all troubles from her husband's path!

But the heaviest blow of all was to come.

Lord Seely left Whitford without seeing him again, and sent back unopened a note, which Algernon had written, begging for an interview, with these words written outside the cover in a trembling hand: "Dare not to write to me or importune me more."

Algernon received this late at night; and before noon the next day the fact was known all over Whitford. People began to say that Lord Seely had obtained access to David Powell, had spoken with him, and had gone away convinced of the substantial truth of his testimony; that his lordship had left orders that Powell should lack no comfort or attention which his unhappy state permitted of his enjoying; and that he had strongly expressed his grateful sense of the poor preacher's efforts to save his niece.

From London Lord Seely—who had heard that Miss Bodkin had visited Duckwell Farm while his niece lay dead there, and had placed flowers on her unconscious breast—sent a mourning-ring and a letter, the contents of which Minnie communicated to no one but her parents. Nevertheless, its contents were discussed pretty widely, and were said to be of a nature very damnatory to Algernon Errington's character. However, the painful things that were said in Whitford could not hurt him, for he had gone—disappeared in the night like a thief, as his creditors said—and no one could say whither.

CHAPTER XXV.

CONCLUSION.

Our tale is almost told. The last words that need saying can be briefly said. When some weeks had passed away, Mrs. Errington received a letter from her son demanding a remittance to be sent forthwith Poste Restante to a little seaport town on the Italian Riviera. He had not during the interval left his mother in absolute ignorance as to what had become of him, but had sent her a few brief lines from London, saying that he had been obliged to leave Whitford in order to escape being put in prison for debt; that his present intention was to go abroad; and that she should hear again from him before long.

Algernon had been so quick in his movements that he managed to be in town before the story of Lord Seely's having cast him off had had time to be circulated amongst his acquaintance there. And he was enabled, as the result of his activity, to obtain from Mrs. Machyn-Stubbs and others several letters of introduction calculated to be of use to him abroad. He was described by Mrs. Machyn-Stubbs as a nephew of Lord Seely and her intimate friend, who was travelling on the Continent to recruit his health after the shock of his wife's sudden death.

He had brought away from Whitford such few jewels belonging to his dead wife as were of any value, and he sold them in London. He furnished himself handsomely with such articles as were desirable for a gentleman of fortune travelling for his pleasure; and allowed the West-end tradesmen, to whom the Honourable John Patrick Price had recommended him during his brilliant London season, to write down against him in their books some very extortionate charges for the same. His outfit being accomplished in this inexpensive manner, he was enabled to travel with as much comfort as was compatible in those days with a journey from London to Calais, and he stepped on to the French shore with a considerable sum of money in his pocket.

For a long time the tidings of him that reached Whitford were uncertain and conflicting; then they began to arrive at even wider and wider intervals; and, finally, after Mrs. Errington left the town, they ceased altogether to reach the general world of Whitfordians. The real history of the circumstances which induced Mrs. Errington to leave the home of so many years was known to very few persons. It was this:

About a twelvemonth after Algernon's departure Mrs. Errington made a sudden journey to London; and, on her return, she confided to her old friend, Dr. Bodkin, that she had sold out of the funds nearly the whole sum from which her little income was derived and transmitted it to Algy, who had an absolute need for the money, which she considered paramount. "But, my dear soul, you have ruined yourself!" cried the doctor aghast. "Algernon will repay me, sir," replied the poor old woman, drawing herself up with the ghost of her old Ancram grandeur. The upshot was that Dr. Bodkin, in concert with one or two other old friends of her late husband, made some representations on her behalf to Mr. Filthorpe, the wealthy Bristol merchant, who was, as the reader may remember, a cousin of Dr. Errington; and that Mr. Filthorpe benevolently allowed his cousin's widow a small annuity, which, together with the few pounds that still remained to her of her own, enabled her to live in decent comfort. But she professed herself unable to remain in Whitford, and removed to a cottage in Dorrington, where she had a kind friend in the wife of the head-master of the proprietary school, whom we first presented to the reader as "little Rhoda Maxfield."

Mrs. Diamond (as she was now) lived in a very handsome house, and wore very elegant dresses, and was looked upon as a personage of some importance in Dorrington and its vicinity. Her husband had decidedly opposed a proposition she made to him to receive Mrs. Errington as an inmate of his home. But he put no further constraint on Rhoda's affectionate solicitude about her old friend.

And the two women drove together, and sewed together, and talked together; and their talk was chiefly about that exiled victim of unmerited misfortune, Algernon Errington. Rhoda preserved her faith in the Ancram glories. And although she acknowledged to herself that Algernon had treated her badly, he was invested in her mind with some mysterious immunity from the obligations that bind ordinary mortals.

A visitor, who was often cordially welcomed at Dorrington by Matthew Diamond, was Miss Chubb. And the kind-hearted little spinster endured a vast amount of snubbing and patronage from her old enemy on the battle-ground of polite society—Mrs. Errington—with much charitable sweetness.

Old Max lived to see his daughter's first-born child; but he was unable to move from his bed for many months before his death. Perhaps it was the period of quiet reflection thus obtained, when the things of this world were melting away from his grasp, which occasioned the addition of a codicil to the old man's will, that surprised most of his acquaintance. He had settled the bulk of his property on his daughter at her marriage, and, in his original testament, had bequeathed the whole of the residue to her also. But the codicil set forth that his only and beloved daughter being amply provided for, and his son James inheriting the stock, fixtures, and good-will of his flourishing business, together with the house and furniture, Jonathan Maxfield felt that he was doing injustice to no one by bequeathing the sum of three thousand pounds to Miss Minnie Bodkin as a mark of respect and admiration. And he, moreover, left one hundred pounds, free of duty, to "that God-fearing member of the Wesleyan Society, Richard Gibbs, now living as groom in the service of Orlando Pawkins, Esquire, of Pudcombe Hall;" a bequest which sensibly embittered the flavour of the sermon preached by the un-legacied Brother Jackson on the next Sunday after old Max's funeral.

Dr. Bodkin still lives and rules in Whitford Grammar School. His wife's life is brightened by the sight of her Minnie's increased health and strength. But she has never quite forgiven Matthew Diamond, and has been heard to say that young Mrs. Diamond's children are the most singularly uninteresting she ever saw!

Of Minnie herself, the chronicle hitherto records a life of useful benevolence, undisfigured by ascetic affectation, or the assumption of any pious livery whatever. She keeps her old delight in all the beautiful things of art and nature, and old Max's legacy has enabled her to enjoy some foreign travel. She is still in the first prime of womanhood, and more beautiful than ever. But, at the latest accounts, poor Mr. Warlock has not been tortured by the spectacle of any successful rival. For his part, he goes on worshipping Miss Bodkin with hopeless fidelity.

For a long time Minnie continued to visit David Powell in the lunatic asylum at stated periods. He generally recognised her, and the sight of her seemed to soothe and comfort him. After a while he was pronounced cured, and left the asylum; but his madness returned on him at intervals, and he would voluntarily go and place himself under restraint when he felt the black fit coming. He did not live very long, being assailed by a mortal consumption. But as his body wasted, his mind grew clearer, stronger, and more serene; and before his death Minnie had the satisfaction to hear him profess a humble faith in the Divine Goodness, and a fearless confidence in the mysterious hand that was leading him even as a little child into the shadowy land. There was as large a concourse of people at his burial as had ever thronged to hear his fiery preaching on Whit Meadow. His memory became surrounded by a saintly radiance in the imaginations of the poor. Stories of his goodness and his afflictions, and the final ray of peace which God sent to cheer his last moments, were long retailed amongst the Whitford Methodists. And his grave is still bright with carefully-tended flowers.

Of Algernon Errington the strangest rumours were circulated for a time. Some said he had become croupier at a foreign gambling-table; others declared he had married a West Indian heiress with a million of money, and was living in Florence in unheard-of luxury. Others, again, affirmed that they had the best authority for believing that he had gone to the United States, and had appeared on the stage there with immense success. However, the remembrance of him passed away from men's minds in Whitford within a few years; in London within a few months. But it was a long time before Jack Price left off recounting his final interview with Errington. "That young Ancram, you know. Captivating way of his own. What? On my honour, the rascal borrowed ten pounds of me. Ready money, sir, down on the nail! Bedad, it was a tour de force, for I never have a shilling in my pocket for my own use. But Ancram would coax the little birds off the bushes, as they say in my part of the world. Principle? Oh, devil a rag of principle in his whole composition. What? I wonder what the deuce has become of him! I give ye my word and honour he was really—really now—a CHARMING FELLOW."

Frances Eleanor Trollope, née Ternan, as most probably befits a writer, was born in August 1835 on board a paddle steamer in Delaware Bay. Her parents were on a three year acting tour of North America after their marriage in Edinburgh earlier that year. Frances was to be the eldest of three surviving daughters to Thomas Lawless Ternan and Frances Eleanor Ternan (née Jarman)

On their later return to England her father became the manager of the Theatre Royal in Newcastle upon Tyne where her mother was a leading actress. The three daughters were occasionally included in some of the stage productions to show off their skills.

In adult life Ellen, her younger sister, had become the mistress of England's famed novelist Charles Dickens. Dickens helped to arrange an interview for Frances to become the governess to the child of the widowed writer Thomas Adolphus Trollope. Thomas lived in Florence, often working in collaboration with his mother, the social justice writer, Frances Milton Trollope.

Her relationship with Thomas grew very rapidly and, despite an age difference bordering on a quarter of a century, she married him within five months of becoming his child's governess.

Thomas Adolphus had built a successful and prolific career. The villa he had established with his former wife, Theodosia, was both beautiful and a meeting place for the literary and expatriate circles.

Soon Frances and Thomas decamped from Florence to Rome where they again entertained a wide literary circle of friends as they built a beautiful estate to encompass their lives.

By this marriage she became also the sister-in-law of the world famous Anthony Trollope and daughter-in-law of Frances Milton Trollope, whose biography Frances Trollope: Her Life and Literary Work from George III to Victoria she would later author.

Frances Eleanor also wrote many novels. Her fiction is peopled by eccentric cosmopolitan Londoners, Italian and French visitors, and motherless, bright, and educated young women trying to carve out niches for themselves within the boundaries of the middle and upper-middle classes, with varying degrees of success.

She also contributed pieces to many periodicals, predominantly travel writings which showcase her sustained interest in the art, culture, and history of Italy.

With Thomas Adolphus serving as editor she translated plays and travel books from Italian and German origins.

Their time in Italy endured from their marriage in 1866 until 1890, when they returned to England. Sadly Thomas Adolphus died in 1892.

Frances Eleanor Trollope died on August 14th, 1913 at Southsea, where she had been living with her sister Ellen.

Whilst her works are, of course, overshadowed by Anthony Trollope and other family members they were well regarded at the time and although they fell out of public view they are now coming back into favour and deserved recognition.

Frances Eleanor Trollope – A Concise Bibliography

Novels
Aunt Margaret's Trouble (1866) (as by "A New Writer"; all her other books carried her own name)
Mabel's Progress (1867)
The Sacristan's Household (1869)
Veronica (1870)
Anne Furness (1871)
A Charming Fellow (1876)
Black Spirits and White (1877)
Like Ships Upon the Sea (1883)
That Unfortunate Marriage (1888)
Among Aliens (1890)
Madame Leroux (1890)
That Wild Wheel (1892)
The Fate of Fenella (co-written, 1892)
The Sacristan's Household

Non Fiction
Frances Trollope: Her Life and Literary Work from George III to Victoria (1895)